ASHES IN THE WIND

DEREK KINGSTON

DEDICATION

To my dear Family - each and every one of them.

Copyright © Derek Kingston, 2016

All rights reserved. No part of this publication may be reproduced, stored in a retrieval system, or transmitted, in any form or by any means, electronic, mechanical, photocopying, recording or otherwise, without the prior permission of both the copyright owners and the publisher, nor be otherwise circulated in any form or binding or cover other than that in which it is published and without a similar condition being imposed on the subsequent purchaser.

Derek Kingston has asserted his right to be identified as the author of this work in accordance with the Copyright, Designs and Patents Act 1988.

*

Fart!
8 C
1 A
SC

http://www.] ing.com

info(

ISBN -4

Nc

ASHES IN THE WIND
BERLIN. OCTOBER 1942

24 October was Willie Rosenfeld's birthday; 34 years of age but with no wife or family to celebrate his special day with, Willie decided to give himself a present. 'Today' he decided, 'I will die. Not in some God-forsaken Nazi resettlement camp in the East but here in Berlin, my birthplace and home.'

Having made his decision, Willie laid down the shovel he had been using in a vain attempt to clear frozen ice from an unyielding pavement, straightened up and began his short journey to oblivion. His numbed brain ignored the shouted command to halt nor did he feel the bullet which shattered his skull. Other members of the forced labour gang, their senses deadened with fatigue and hunger, purposely ignored his lifeless body; its red blood slowly congealing as it leached into the grey ice on the frozen pavement. An unremarkable man... born a Jew and for this accident of birth, a man fated to die.

As the capital of a nation subjugating much of Western and Eastern Europe, Berlin was a city enmeshed in the grey drabness of war; its Nazi Government spreading calculated terror throughout Germany and its occupied territories particularly to Jews like Willie Rosenfeld.

The political and economic uncertainties in the decade before Willie's death had provided a unique opportunity for right-wing parties to come to the fore; none more sinister than the National Socialist German Workers Party; later to be renamed the Nazi Party by its leader, an Austrian émigré by the name of Adolf Hitler.

From its violent gestation in the beer halls of Munich, the Nazi Party had systematically undermined the vulnerable democracy of the Weimar Republic until, on 31 January 1933, it finally achieved 'Machtergreifung'... political power through the ballot box.

Appointed to the office of Chancellor by a reluctant President Von Hindenburg, Adolf Hitler began immediately to implement the murderous policies contained within his malevolently hateful 'Mein Kamp' in which he exalted the purity of the Aryan race whilst propounding virulent anti-Semitism and anti-Communism.

Having anointed its Messiah, the Nazi Party now sought a scapegoat to blame for the Fatherland's current woes and who better than the Jews; a secular race of people with a tragic history of persecution throughout much of Eastern Europe

With the Nazi Government controlling both radio and press it was left to Hitler's sycophantic Jew-hater, Joseph Goebbels, a master of the staged propaganda event to convince a demoralised German nation that Germany's defeat in 1918 had been the result of a conspiracy contrived by the Nazi Party's avowed political opponents in incestuous league with international Jewry.

In June 1934, barely a year after gaining power, the newly elected Nazi government destroyed all vestige of political resistance in a night of murderous infamy with numerous political rivals arrested and many executed without any semblance of a trial.

Having brutally removed those opposed to the totalitarianism of its one-party rule, the Nazi regime then turned its focus on the Jews, instituting a reign of terror which in the next decade would respect no boundaries in terms of human suffering.

As the first step on its calculated path towards genocide, the Nazi Government passed the Nuremburg Laws of September 1935 stripping Jews of their German citizenship thereby setting them apart as a stateless people.

Several months later, the Nazi Government implemented the second phase of Hitler's master plan. As stateless persons, there was now to be no place for Jews within a future ethnically cleansed Aryan Germany and a further decree was implemented for their mass transportation and forced resettlement in Eastern Europe.

The defining phase of the plan was agreed in February 1942 at the highly secret Wannsee Conference where the policy of resettlement was changed to that where the Nazi Government determined that Jews should no longer exist as a race and the 'final solution' was approved for immediate implementation.

From being foremost among the cultured nations of the civilised world, a nation which excelled in the sciences and technology, philosophy, music and literature, the Nazi Government of the Third Reich knowingly turned its back on Germany's proud cultural heritage implementing in its stead a tyrannical policy of State sponsored genocide whilst the rest of the civilised world looked on in unknowing ignorance and silence.

No longer would the *Untermenschen...* Jews, gypsies, homosexuals and mentally infirm peoples be allowed to contaminate the purity of the Aryan race and so began the purging of a nation by a government led by a psychologically obsessed orator; in every sense an evil and preposterous heir to the legacies of Frederick the Great and Otto Von Bismarck,

Successive waves of oppressive decrees each enforced by a thuggish army of brown shirted Storm Troopers, themselves to be purged by the even more sinister Schutzstaffel (SS) Gestapo, methodically eradicated all vestiges of democracy and free speech.

Ironically, it was the licentious decadence of Berlin's highly visible nightlife which had provided the fledgling Nazi Party with an opportunity to promise to eliminate all forms of sexual notoriety. In its stead, a receptive population were promised a new moral code enshrined within the Nazi Party's 'Strength through Joy' creed reflecting the purity and ideals of the new 'Master Race'.

To a population experiencing hyperinflation, mass unemployment and looming poverty this was a persuasive message. And now, in the fourth year of the war and the harshest winter in living memory, Berliners could be forgiven for thinking that even the weather was conspiring against them.

The streets of the capital had barely coped with unusually heavy snowfalls and freezing temperatures. Even the occasional glimmer of pale winter sunshine did little to raise the weather gauge above freezing whilst the coming of darkness would once more plunge the mercury to extreme lows of coldness.

Earlier, on the pavement outside the State Opera House on once-luminescent Unter den Linden, gangs of slave labourers, mostly foreigners and Jews had worked throughout the day to clear the impacted snow and ice from the frozen pathways. Even the removal of Willie Rosenfeld's body had afforded these pathetic men only the briefest respite from their thankless task.

And the coming of night was now bringing yet more misery with Allied bombers unleashing their retaliatory cargoes of death from the darkened skies above the city. But Berliners with their historic disregard for Government edicts largely ignored the order to black-out their city. Having been assured by Air Marshall Hermann Goering that no enemy bomber would penetrate the air defences of the capital, these same Berliners were now humorously referring to the raids as 'Herman's hallucinations' whilst other city dwellers were deriving a perverse sense of cynical pleasure from the overnight appearance of graffiti exhorting Berliners to 'enjoy the war... the peace will be worse!'

***

Within the portals of the City's premier opera hall, its gilded interior of red monogrammed seats, golden drapes and lustrous crystal chandeliers reflecting the splendour of its pre-war eminence, the Berlin Philharmonic was approaching the finale of its evening's performance; determined to conclude its programme before the mournful wail of air raid sirens could draw its audience back to the reality of life beyond the façade of this still imposing concert hall.

Inside the magnificent auditorium the audience were being entertained by Germany's premier orchestra, captivated by the eye-catching artistry of its young principle soloist Hannah Bergmann. In her singularly distinctive style of delivery and with the challenging score committed to memory, the young soloist was performing flawlessly, reflecting the sheer vivacity of the music with every syncopated movement of her body. Her black full length strapless evening gown discreetly accentuated her stunning figure, leading the eye to the enigmatic beauty of her face. The high cheekbones, highlighting her dark iridescent eyes, gave a tantalising hint of a lineage more akin to warmer Mediterranean climes than that of Northern Europe as did the soft honey toned hue of her skin. Her face, reflecting the intensity of the music, was framed by the gleaming lustre of her black hair which for tonight's performance had been drawn back from her forehead and gathered in a tight chignon at the nape of her neck.

In Berlin's wartime environment, concerts of such quality were increasingly rare and when they did take place, tickets were always difficult to obtain even for former pre-war patrons of the orchestra. Now it was the new elite... high-ranking Party Members and military personnel, who procured the best seats.

Glancing down at the audience from her vantage point on the platform, Hannah Bergmann recalled her father's oft-stated admonition from childhood; 'rank and privilege will always be inseparable. Perhaps even truer tonight' she thought.

'That was a truly wonderful performance, hardly a misplaced note!'

'Hannah smiled; 'thank you Maestro, at least we managed to finish together!'

Their whispered exchange was lost in the rapturous applause filling the auditorium to its very rafters. Despite the privations of wartime Berlin, the more perceptive members of the orchestra often noticed that wartime audiences were more inclined to respond with greater enthusiasm than in pre-war days; days when the orchestra performed to somewhat more knowledgeable patrons.

As the evening's principle soloist, Hannah Bergman took her final bow before leading the internationally renowned conductor Max Feldman from the concert platform.

Feldman had taken over the role of principle conductor from Wilhelm Furtwangler, an engaging man who had fallen out of favour with the Nazi regime for his refusal to become a member of the Nazi Party or to offer the obligatory Nazi salute even when the Fuhrer himself was present in the audience. Hannah had admired Furtwangler both for his principled stance against Nazism and his excellence as a conductor and had been extremely disappointed when he had voluntarily relinquished the role.

Her relationship with Max Feldman had coincided with her admission to the Berlin Academy of Music at the tender age of 16. As a student violinist it was there that she had first met the man who was to become her mentor and friend. Winning a place in Germany's premier orchestra, she had quickly ascended through the various ranks of violinists and despite being a Jew, she had been appointed as the orchestra's principle violin soloist; an appointment surprisingly ratified by the orchestra's normally staid Trustee board. And tonight in front of a full house she had flawlessly performed Bruch's Violin Concerto No.1 in G minor; a score to challenge even the most gifted of musicians in a style and virtuosity which belied her 26 years of age.

Gaining the sanctuary of her dressing room, she let her tired body sink into the embracing contours of the old leather armchair which looked to be as old as the Opera House itself. The adrenalin which had carried her through the evening's performance was now beginning to diminish; replaced by a feeling of increasing fatigue. With one hand lazily drooped over the side of the armchair, she let her fingers lightly run over the familiar contours of her beautifully toned violin, an instrument crafted by Angelo Bellini in his Venetian workshop at the turn of the 18th century.

Feeling wearier by the minute, her thoughts inevitably turned to the reality of life beyond the concert platform. Even if the Trustee Board were to allow her to continue, she wondered how much longer she would be able to cope with the stark disparity of one moment fronting the Berlin Philharmonic as a lauded solo artiste contrasting with the reality of daily life in war-torn Germany; a comparison made more stark by being a Jew. A Jew trapped in a country hell-bent on the obliteration of her race.

Her childhood thoughts of family life always exuded the same tearful memories; the comfortable family home in fashionable Charlottenburg with its green parks and wide avenues lined with leafy Sycamore trees, their overhanging branches and summer foliage forming tree tunnels along many of the narrower streets. She recalled those special Sundays spent with family and friends picnicking alongside the River Spree but that Berlin, the Berlin of her childhood was now just a pale shadow of those happy days. At the very heart of the Axis war administration, today's Berlin reflected the grimness of a war initially fought far beyond the borders of Germany but now rapidly becoming the epicentre of the Allies determination to exact airborne retribution on the pariah of Europe.

Drawing her thoughts back to the present she wondered whether tonight's audience would have lauded her virtuosity quite so enthusiastically had they been aware they were applauding a Jewish performer. But on the other hand, she wondered whether the orchestra's uplifting performance could perhaps override, if only for a fleeting moment, the grim reality of the war itself. 'Or am I being hopelessly naïve' she wondered.

The increasing chatter from across the corridor thankfully interrupted her chain of thought. She knew that dressing rooms could be odd places after a particularly spirited performance. Some musicians would try to cling on to the adrenalin created by the orchestra's performance for as long as possible but once away from the concert platform daily life in war-torn Berlin became a great leveller; dragging even the most sensitive of musician back to the real world, a world dominated by war and the stultifying effect it was having on each of their daily lives.

As the chatter from the main dressing room gradually lessened she knew it was time for her to go home too. Even in a city still clinging to its sensual and oft-times eccentric night life, it was hardly sensible to venture on to the street wearing the evening gown she had performed in so she quickly changed into the drab blouse and skirt she had worn earlier. As she did so, she thought again about the overlong rehearsal period which had taken up most of the afternoon

Whilst she admired Max Feldman for his single-minded approach to music, there were a number of characteristics in his complex nature she did not care for. No musician deliberately played a wrong note on purpose; it was something which happened to them all including Max Feldman, she recalled. But when such mistakes did occur, Max could be caustically unforgiving with barbed comments intended to not only rebuke the offending musician but intended to cause acute embarrassment in the process.

Humming quietly to herself, she barely heard the gentle tap on the door until it was repeated... this time a touch louder.

'Yes... come in.'

As the door slowly opened, it was Max Feldman's elderly dresser, Edward Richter, who appeared in the doorway, his outmoded sense of modesty preventing him from fully entering the dressing room of the opposite sex.

'Forgive me interrupting you Miss Bergmann but Mr. Feldman would like to speak with you before you leave. Can I tell him if you might be available?'

'Good evening to you, Mr. Richter.' Amused by the formal manner with which he addressed her and other leading members of the orchestra, she often found herself responding in similar vein..

'Did he say what he wanted to speak about? I was just about to leave.'

'He is available now Miss Bergmann.' He gave an involuntary bow of the head before adding, 'but only if this is convenient to yourself of course?'

'M'mmm... just give me a moment and I'll be right across'

'Grateful thanks Miss Bergmann; most kind of you.' The door quietly closed and with that Edward Richter was gone.

'Hannah, my dear talented girl, do come in and take a seat. You were wonderful this evening. You obviously had a good teacher!' The effusive greeting was quintessential Max Feldman following the conclusion of a successful concert.

'Thank you Max; you clearly enjoyed it more than I did.' Finding a chair next to the dressing table, she sat down. 'It's not my favourite piece of music as you know; it's far too turgid for me. I prefer music which is instinctive with less chance of the audience noticing the occasional fluffed note or two which of course you would have instantly detected.'

'Would I?. His eyebrows raised in unison. 'I can't say I noticed anything other than your wonderful virtuosity. And if you did fluff a note or two and I wasn't able to spot them then neither did our audience. Anyway,' he gave an expressive wave of his hand, 'it's now time for both of us to relax.' Pointing towards the old Dutch dresser standing against the far wall of the dressing room she noticed a bottle which from its bulbous top she guessed might be champagne.

Following her gaze, Max's voice took on an air of excitement. 'What you see there, my dear young girl is real champagne, compliments of a General Keitel who, Edward informs me, was our principle guest this evening. He also sent those flowers for you.' Turning towards his assistant, he snapped his fingers. 'Edward, would you be kind enough to bring two glasses, please.'

As Edward Richter glided towards the pine dresser, she spotted the large bouquet of flowers enticingly wrapped in clear cellophane. Impulsively, she felt herself bridle with anger.

'Max, in normal circumstances flowers would be a thoughtful gesture but don't you think everything we do here is becoming more and more bizarre?' She paused, wondering whether to go on.

Clearly surprised, Max wisely chose to make no comment.

'You seem quite able to ignore what's happening in the world outside of your all-consuming concert hall and frankly I don't know how you manage to do it.' She stopped again to give Max a further opportunity to respond but his uncharacteristic silence only encouraged her to continue. 'And even if I did know, I could never be like you.' Lowering her voice, she made eye contact with her mentor. 'Max, we've known each other for many years and I regard you as a very dear friend. But the basis of our relationship has always been our music and the fact that we are both Jews despite your miraculous conversion to agnosticism when you realised that being Jewish would endanger your career.'

Inwardly, Max Feldman winced as the frankness of her words struck home.

'But even you must find it difficult to ignore what is happening outside this sheltered environment we live in where stateless Jews, people just like us, Max, are now being forced from their homes and if rumours are true, being transported in countless numbers to some awful parts of Eastern Europe. And while all this is happening, what are we doing? She let her question hang in the air but again she was greeted by Max's unnerving silence.

'We, by which I mean both you and me, Max, we continue to entertain the very people committing these awful crimes but who are just thoughtful enough to send us champagne and flowers. Doesn't that strike even you as cynically contradictory?'

Stung at last by her words, Max finally broke his silence but his voice was unnaturally subdued.

'Hannah, listen to me.' He drew a deep breath. 'What would you like me to do? Send them back with a caustic note saying 'thanks but no thanks' or perhaps be slightly more pragmatic and accept what they offer. Who knows where we might be tomorrow, next week or next month, whatever our religious leanings may or may not be. Life isn't going to change overnight so why not accept that and for a brief moment enjoy their champagne and remember better times.' Lowering his voice to an almost conspiratorial whisper, he added 'and who knows, if the Allies eventually win this war then maybe we will still be around to live like human beings again.' He paused to inhale deeply. 'Hannah, I hate the Nazis as much as you do but I suppose my survival instincts are somewhat stronger than your own.'

'Is it survival Max... or collaboration?'

Visibly recoiling as the force of Hannah's accusation struck home, it took several seconds before he could bring himself to reply. Taking a deep breath, his voice took on an imposing tone.

'Hannah, I have always admired your direct approach to life but aren't you being a little sanctimonious. Because of your position in this orchestra you are able to lead a moderately privileged life and to do... ' He stopped in mid-sentence, realising he had unwittingly stepped into a trap of his own making.

'Go on Max... to do what precisely? What would you know what being a privileged Jew means?' She waited for Max to respond but looking at him, she could see he was noticeably shaken. 'Yes, I'm spared having to wear a yellow star and so far I haven't been arrested or forced to move to a house packed with other Jewish families but what else am I privileged to have'? And how long do you think this meaningless privilege will last in the present climate?'

Again there was no reply from the man she had known for all of her musical career. Feeling a tinge of sympathy for him, she reached out and touched the arm of his jacket. 'Max, listen to me. Can you bring yourself to think what happened to those two young cello players or your principle trombonist? Or why we cannot play the music of Pavel Haas or Viktor Ullmann or do I need to prick your memory?'

Agitated and in full flow, she stood up and fixed Max with a penetrating stare. 'Those musicians were arrested and probably transported to heaven knows where. And for what reason?' She drew a deep breath. 'Not because they were Communists or enemies of the State but because they were Jews, nothing more than that. An accident of birth for God's sake!'

Inwardly her anger was reaching boiling point. 'Does that resonate even in your private little world, Max?' Now it was her turn to pause.

Seizing the opportunity afforded by her silence, Max attempted to regain a semblance of control. 'Hannah, listen to me... please! Just stop for a moment and for God's sake keep your voice down. I can't dispute what you say but it's about survival for people like you and me. Our priority and focus must be to survive everything that's happening around us. We may not succeed but in God's name don't throw your life away for nothing. Even a whisper of what you have just said would get you and your family arrested regardless of who or what you are. If you can't keep your emotions to yourself at least consider your husband and your baby son.'

The reference to Ephraim and Aaron made Hannah mentally recoil. Suddenly contrite, she dropped her head. 'Forgive me Max. I shouldn't pick on you of all people.' Glancing down at her watch, she feigned surprise. 'Oh lord... is that the time? I must go home, it's late.'

'Yes, you're right.' He gave Hannah an affectionate touch on her cheek. 'Look, I still have the use of a car and driver for this evening, again courtesy of our champagne and flowers General. Let me drop you off at your apartment. And please, no more discussion on this dreadful subject; promise?' His voice lilted upwards as he ended his exhortation..

'OK, Max... I promise. In truth I'm too mortified to say another word.'

Entering the quiet residential area of Charlottenburg, the Opel staff car drew to a halt outside the familiar apartment building. Conversation between her and Max had been stilted in the presence of the driver, a young Army conscript who too had barely uttered a word other than to seek directions in a city he obviously was not familiar with.

'Max, thank you so much for your kindness; I will see you at rehearsal on Tuesday so until then.' Her words trailed off.

'I will look forward to that, air raids permitting. Lowering his voice to a barely audible level he waited until the driver got out of the car before whispering, 'please remember what I said. As with our music, so with our lives. We have to make it through to the finish.'

Still in a state of mild anxiety from Max's reference to Ephraim and Aaron, she did not immediately respond. Instead she offered her cheek for a token kiss before alighting from the car, its door obligingly held open by the driver.

'Thank you and goodnight to you both.' With that, she moved cautiously away from the car towards the entrance to No.48, carefully avoiding the icy patches that still remained from the earlier snowfall.

The comfortable apartment located on the third floor of the building had been home to Ephraim and herself since their marriage. Thankfully undamaged despite the increasing number of air raids, the property had the benefit of a lift recently installed by Siemens but at this time of night the noise of the winding mechanism would resonate throughout the upper floors so she chose to walk up the six flights of stairs to her apartment on the third floor.

The light switches in the foyer and stair-wells allowed sufficient time for tenants to insert keys and open doors before clicking off and tonight was no exception. Stepping into the hall of the familiar apartment she felt an acute sense of relief to be home.

Ephraim, half dozing in the dimly lit lounge gradually became aware of her presence.

'Hannah, you're earlier than I expected; how did the concert go?' Not given to displays of overt warmth, Ephraim came to meet her in the hallway as she took off her coat.

'I played well, not too many errors. In fact I can't recall any' she joked. 'I received a lift home with Max in an Army staff car can you believe. I'd almost forgotten what it's like to travel in a car.'

'How on earth did Max manage to have use of an official car?' Not for the first time in recent days she noticed the tetchiness in Ephraim's voice.

'Well you know Max; he sways with the wind and always takes the line of least resistance.' She decided to change the conversation. 'How was our darling boy tonight? What time did he go to bed?'

'Oh, no problem other than for the watery milk and what might pass as food for a hungry, growing child. Fortunately he still manages to eat my variations on a potato, mouldy or otherwise.' He smiled, remembering Aaron's screwed-up face as he swallowed his supper. 'Tonight it was cordon bleu potato flavoured with a couple of mushrooms which one of my former patients gave me at what used to be my clinic.' The frustration in Ephraim's remark was not lost on Hannah.

Ephraim had enjoyed his vocation as a physician but the Nazi Government's decree prohibiting Aryans from being treated by Jewish doctors now meant that he spent much of his time pleading with former colleagues for illicit medical supplies in order to treat his dwindling number of Jewish patients. But many of these good-will outlets had now virtually dried up due to a fear of punitive punishment which many of them knew would follow if they were caught or informed on as the Government remorselessly tightened the screw on the Jewish population and its sympathisers.

The talk of food caused her to remember the small package she had been given earlier during a break in rehearsal by a younger member of the violin section whom she often mentored when time allowed. Delving into her bag she drew out a small parcel wrapped in brown paper and was touched to discover four eggs cushioned in soft muslin within a cardboard holder together with a sachet of powdered milk.

'Ephraim, look at this; how can people be so thoughtful when they are so short of food themselves?'

'Unlike ourselves Hannah, our fellow Germans still have their food coupons... remember?'

'Yes I know but I'm still touched by such kindness. Speaking of food, have you eaten this evening?'

'What is there to eat other than potatoes? I am heartily sick of potatoes even when they aren't mouldy.' He winced at the thought. 'You've eaten already I suppose?'

'No I haven't. I told you I came home immediately after the concert finished.' She thought it prudent to not mention the champagne offered by Max which she was now pleased she had declined.

'In which case and with thanks to your benevolent fiddle-player, I'll prepare an omelette for us which will mean I will need to use the last of our ersatz coffee. But at least tonight, we won't go to bed feeling hungry.'

'Darling, that sounds very tempting but can you make do with just two eggs please?' Her voice took on a pleading note. 'I'd like to keep the other two to make pancakes for Aaron tomorrow.'

'And pretend they are latkes and it's Hanukkah? Even Aaron will spot the difference.' He gave a quiet chuckle, smiling at his own observation.

She was always amused by Ephraim's interest in cooking which had never interested her in the slightest. She saw the preparation and eating of food as a necessary interruption between other more important things.

From the kitchen she heard Ephraim ask, 'thinking about your friend Max, do you think he may be too close to the Nazi bigshots, Hannah?'

The suddenness of his question took her by surprise.

'I'm not sure. Who can say why anyone does anything these days either just to eat or even to survive. It may be he's trying to make the most of his international status. I really don't know how to answer your question.'

Busying himself with the food preparation, Ephraim let several more seconds elapse before he spoke again.

'Then do you think that perhaps you may be too close to Max?'

The essence of Ephraim's question jolted her from the increasing tiredness beginning to overtake her.

'Of course I'm close to Max. He's been my professional mentor for many years but that isn't your real question is it, Ephraim?' Angered by his probing words, she strode into the kitchen. 'What is it that you really want to ask? How close is our friendship? Am I attracted to him? Are we lovers perhaps? Is that what you really want to know?' Now it was her turn to pause, embarrassed by her outburst.

'Hannah, listen to me. I was alluding to your professional relationship with Max. I am concerned that his closeness to the Nazis could rebound on you and us, if for any reason he falls out of favour with them. That was the only reason for my question... OK?'

'OK... OK; I hear what you say.' She took a deep breath, a habit she had developed when she needed time to think. 'Look, I'm sorry I reacted as I did but I have had an exhausting day and the last thing I need at this precise moment is to be interrogated by my husband. So, can we drop the subject and think about eating... please?'

That night, lying next to Ephraim she tried to imagine the emotional stress he must be going through. Virtually unemployed as a physician and reduced more and more to acting as child-minder to Aaron whilst she, at least for the moment, was still able to perform as a classical musician. Before sleep finally overwhelmed her tired mind, she reflected on the comment made earlier by Max Feldman and his apparent willingness to close his mind to what was happening in their daily lives provided such selective unawareness offered even the slimmest chance of survival in the longer term. For herself, she sleepily wondered what she would be prepared to do to ensure the continuing safety of herself and her precious family.

TWO

The following morning it was the familiar sound of Frieda bustling around the kitchen grumbling about the used plates and omelette pan left from the previous evening's meal that awoke her from her blissful reverie. Some six years earlier, Frieda had been a patient at Ephraim's surgery. With Hannah spending an increasing amount of time travelling with the orchestra on its international engagements, Frieda had willingly responded to Ephraim's plea for help in cleaning the apartment. Her short stocky appearance and habit of dressing in clothes more befitting of her grandmother's generation made it difficult to accurately assess her precise age. Hannah guessed she had never been particularly attractive even as a young girl and now in middle age she looked positively dowdy but a woman redeemed by a down to earth personality which fully reflected her cheerful approach to life.

The arrival of Aaron had emphasised just what a gem of a person Frieda actually was. Before working for them, she had cared for her ailing parents and younger brother. With both parents now dead and her brother serving in the Army, she maintained the family apartment by working as an evening cleaner at a nearby primary school as well as being employed each weekday morning at their apartment.

Throwing off the last vestige of sleep, Hannah forced herself out of the warm bed and made her way to the bathroom where she waited for the warm water to flow through the recently installed shower system before stepping into the cubical. Several minutes later and fully refreshed, she quickly dressed and made her way to the kitchen.

'Good morning Frieda and how are you today?'

'I am well Hannah but what about you?' Staring hard, she added, 'from where I'm sitting you look like shit! Are you sickening for something?' Frieda's earthy language and delivery reminded her of an irreverent old Jewish lady she remembered from her childhood unlike Frieda who was a regular Lutheran church-goer albeit with her own views on matters both temporal and spiritual.

'Frieda! Your language! What on earth would the Nuns at the nursery say if they heard children repeat words like that?'

Impulsively they broke into laughter at the reaction they imagined such a word would cause among the strait-laced child-carers at the kindergarten which Aaron was no longer able to attend.

'Actually Frieda, I'm tired... tired and exhausted. I don't really know how much more of this I can take.' Seeing the look of concern on Frieda's face, her mood brightened. 'But today is a new day so let's make the most of it. I'm not practicing this morning; I simply can't face it at the moment so when you have finished your chores we'll cheer ourselves up and take Aaron to the park. By the way, where is my little darling?'

'Your husband took him out as I was coming in. Didn't say where he was going.'

'In that case let's have a cup of something before we go. I'm afraid we're out of coffee; we finished it last night after I came home.'

A smug look appeared on Frieda's face. 'Well then, you'll be pleased to know I've brought some of my own and perhaps there may even be enough for you, young lady.'

Hannah enjoyed the intimacy of Frieda's repartee which rekindled fond memories of her own dearly missed Mother.

'Victor came home on leave from France yesterday and brought three jars of coffee and would you believe... several bottles of French wine!'

Seeing the look of sisterly pride on Frieda's face recalled memories of her own childhood and her fervent wish for a brother to share it with but a wish which had never materialised. Impulsively, she reached out and gave Frieda a hug. 'How is Victor and how long is he home for?'

Awkwardly embarrassed by Hannah's show of affection, Frieda felt her face redden. 'Just 10 days I think. He's not supposed to know but he's fairly certain his unit is being transferred to the Russian front very soon.'

'Oh dear God, that doesn't sound like good news. Even without the Russian army to contend with, the weather by all accounts can be truly awful.'

Quickly disengaging herself from Hannah's hug, Frieda's face brightened up. 'Actually, he's not too concerned about going. He tells me that the Red Army is at last beginning to fight back especially around Stalingrad and that France is now too quiet for him. Mind you, he'll probably change his mind when he gets there. He thinks we are having a tougher time than he is what with the air raids now becoming more frequent. Speaking of which, do you realise we haven't had a bombing raid for five nights and I heard on the radio this morning that the trains are running on time again.' Her eyebrows raised in mock disbelief: 'can you believe that?'

'Well that's good old Teutonic efficiency for you... at least until the next air raid!' Hannah abruptly became serious. 'I sometimes wonder how the British must feel, being bombed day and night by the Luftwaffe. Can you imagine what that must be like? God in heaven Frieda, when will all this madness end?'

'If we knew the answer to that, young lady, I think we'd be even more depressed?' She paused as she poured hot water into the two coffee cups.

'Suppose we knew this war would last for another five or even ten years, what could we do? Nothing... absolutely nothing! Even if Germany wanted peace I doubt whether the Allies would agree. So the only option our great Leader has would be to surrender and why would he do that when our military forces occupy most of Europe? '

Listening to her forthright views on the politics of the war, Hannah's curiosity was aroused. 'Frieda, where do you get this information from? We aren't allowed to have a radio but I do know the information they do broadcast is strictly controlled.'

But Frieda, now in full flow, drew a clear distinction between herself and those she held responsible. 'My brother Victor tells me. Apparently, soldiers pick up news from soldiers in other units and I believe him more than what I hear on the radio.'

Pausing to sip her coffee, the sudden intake of caffeine appeared to give Frieda renewed impetus. 'You don't need a radio to realise how much misery Germany has brought to this world Hannah. Even if Hitler did want peace, I think the Allies would refuse. My brother thinks they will continue the war until we are not only beaten but utterly crushed.' She stopped for another sip. 'Can you imagine what will happen to us if the Russians should ever get through to Berlin?' She shuddered in mock horror but she hadn't yet finished her diatribe. 'You have to remember Hannah, we couldn't beat the British when they were on their own so what does Hitler do?' Frieda paused for breath, hoping to draw a response from Hannah but none was forthcoming.

'He invades the Soviet Union hoping for a quick victory which hasn't happened and we are also fighting the Americans as well. I tell you Hannah, Germany cannot win this war.' At last running out of steam, she sat down, hands wringing in theatrical despair.

'Hush, Frieda, hush. Look, I said we would go for a stroll in the park so let's do that and stop depressing ourselves. Who knows, with the Americans and the Russians now involved, perhaps the war may be over in months so let's stop thinking about it. Thanks to Victor, we will have our coffee and then we'll test the air in the park assuming of course that Jews are still allowed to walk in it! Let's hurry before Ephraim and Aaron get back so drink up and lets go.'

THREE

Hannah rarely enjoyed rehearsals. The constant stopping and starting taxed her limited patience and once again Max Feldman was exercising his acerbic sarcasm on those members of the orchestra unfortunate enough to incur his displeasure.

'What is it about this passage which gives you such a problem?' The question was directed in the general direction of the cello section. 'Is it the arrangement itself or are you just not familiar with the degree of sensitivity this score deserves?' Fixing his gaze on one hapless individual, Hannah saw the man's face colour up and felt a touch of sympathy for him.

'Everybody... listen to what I am about to say. For those among you who haven't yet woken up this morning, let me introduce you to one of Germany's greatest composers, Felix Mendelssohn; not only a composer but a conductor and gifted piano, organ and viola player. And today we are attempting to play his well-known Violin Concerto.' He let his gaze wander over each section of the orchestra. 'Are you with me so far?' To emphasise the question, Max Feldman raised his left eyebrow and peered at no one person in particular. 'Good, then perhaps we can now continue but this time with a degree of concentration and understanding notably absent so far.'

'Why does he do it' she thought, before focussing on the score before her? Again the music commenced and this time allowed to flow slightly longer before being halted yet again by an irritated gesture from the man on the podium.

'I want more emphasis on the andante passage; moderately slow means just that so stop attempting to gallop through it and watch me for the timing. And when we get to the allegro twelve bars on, please remember it needs to be attacked with gusto if only to wake up those in the audience who may at this stage be drifting off. But it's better... not much, but it's improving. And wind section, when we arrive at the lead-in to the second movement, watch me carefully for the volume. From where I stopped, if you please.'

Once more the baton moved with effortless grace and imperceptibly the orchestra began to meld as a team working together under the direction of this irritating and demanding man.

Such moments normally typified the repetitious nature of rehearsals and her degree of concentration normally allowed her to lose herself in the music; more so because of her demanding role as the orchestra's principle violin soloist... the same orchestra in which she had begun her career. But this morning her mind simply refused to focus and inevitably Max Feldman began to cast enquiring looks in her direction. Stopping the orchestra once more, Max looked at his watch. Casting a furtive sideways look at Hannah, he nodded to the orchestra; we'll take a short break and Hannah, may we have a brief word in my room, please?'

It took a few moments for her to cushion her violin in its leather case and to then locate Max Feldman in what served as his room behind the main changing area.

'You wanted to speak with me Max or should I guess what you want to say?'

'You won't need to guess Hannah. I'm not satisfied with your timing, your emphasis or your focus. Frankly, you're playing well below what I expect and for your sake as much as mine; I'd rather you feigned illness rather than continue like this.'

Stung by his words, she reacted angrily. 'All right Max, but why say I'm unwell, why not tell them I'm sick; sick of music and sick of egoistical conductors like you and sick of life in this country so go ahead and tell them that I'm sick of just about everything. You tell them that from me, OK.' Without waiting for Max to respond, she turned and made for the door... trying to remember where she had left her coat in the outer dressing room. Behind her, she heard his hurrying footsteps.

'Hannah, if you run off now, you needn't bother to come back!' The threat in his voice was unmistakeably real. 'The last thing I need is a major tantrum from you. Do you think you are the only person in that room with problems?' His voice perceptibly softened. 'Come back and let's talk this through. If you then wish to leave at least I won't feel so bad.'

Extending his arm around her shoulder, he gently led her back to his room and closed the door. 'Now tell me... what is this really about? Talk to me... please?'

Looking into Max's eyes she saw a level of concern she had never seen before. Without uttering a word, she moved forward and felt Max's arms enfold her. Unable to contain her pent up feelings any longer, her whole body began to shake, fuelled by the intensity of the conflicting emotions racing through her mind. Sensibly, Max did not attempt to speak. Instead, he tightened his embrace and felt Hannah's warm tears moisten the front of his shirt. For what seemed a timeless interlude they held the embrace until finally her tears stopped and she was able to control the involuntary tremor of her shoulders.

'If I were a psychiatrist you would now owe me a fee far in excess of what you earn as the principle soloist of this orchestra.' His features took on a paternal look. 'My dear sweet girl, I would do anything to make you feel better, you know that, don't you.' Max made to move gently away but sensed Hannah was not yet ready to do so.

'Please Max... just a moment longer.' The plaintive note in Hannah's voice touched him inwardly and he let his arms respond. Nestling against Max's chest, she thought she detected the beat of his racing heart but couldn't be certain whether it was his or her own. Slowly, very slowly, she drew back and looking up into Max's eyes, pulled his head down and kissed him gently on his lips. They held the kiss for several lingering seconds before mutually pulling apart.

'Please don't say a word Max.. Whatever it was that came over me, I wanted to do that. Now I'm ready to pay better attention and what else were you complaining of? Oh yes... I remember now; timing, focus and emphasis on Mr. Mendelssohn's masterpiece.' Still maintaining eye contact, she added 'and by the way, I admire your courage in playing Mendelssohn tonight; the Nazis won't like that and could cause them to react... even against a famous person like you.'

'Whatever.' He shrugged in dismissal. 'War doesn't stop beautiful music being listened to whoever may have composed it.' Looking into Hannah's eyes, his voice became unusually tender. 'But before we go, let me tell you what a beautiful, capricious and sensual lady you have become. But if you ever do that to me again, don't expect me to simply stop because you feel better... OK?'

'Max, if I ever do that again, it could be me that may not want to stop... OK?

Not having to wear the obligatory yellow star on her coat, she decided to risk catching the tram back to her apartment in Charlottenburg. Sitting on the uncomfortable wooden seat she let her thoughts reflect on her brief liaison with Max; an encounter entirely of her own making. 'I was upset and he comforted me,' she reasoned but inwardly she felt disturbed by the realisation that she had physically enjoyed the experience of doing something which had undoubtedly excited her, however briefly, with someone other than Ephraim... a feeling intensified even more by the knowledge that he did not know about it.

On a lighter note she also reflected on the fact that upon their return to the orchestra, her concentration had improved immeasurably with no further reprimands or raised eyebrows from Maestro Feldman. He too had an unusually relaxed air about him and this made for a rare and pleasurable rehearsal session.

FOUR

That evening's performance at the Opera House was again played before a full house with the majority of stall seats and private boxes once more occupied by military personnel and civilian bureaucrats. Looking at the sea of faces before her, she guessed most were probably employed in the burgeoning Government Ministries now being centralised in Berlin

Waiting for her lead-in to the first movement she nervously glanced down at the audience occupying the front row of the stalls and thought she vaguely recognised a number of familiar faces from previous performances. 'How many of these military people' she wondered, 'actually go to the front line?'

In addition to her gifted brilliance as a violinist she was also blessed with an ability to commit the most difficult of scores to memory enabling her to add even greater individuality to her performance. Tonight, wearing a familiar full-length strapless black gown designed to emphasise her slender figure, she felt inwardly confident that her performance would be at its scintillating best. The dress, created for her on a pre-war visit to Zurich by a leading Swiss couturier, fortunately captured in its flowing design the sensuality of current Berlin cabaret fashion with its ruched silk folds artfully shimmering with each movement of her lithe body.

As one of the very few female violin soloists in Europe, she had readily adapted to Max Feldman's wish for her to perform standing alongside the podium rather than sitting down at the head of the violin section. Her demonstrative and engaging delivery allowed the audience, particularly those at the front of the theatre, to appreciate more fully her wondrous sense of timing allied to a fluidity which characterised her prodigious talent and alluring beauty to maximum effect.

Focussed on the score and waiting for her lead-in, she once more nervously glanced at the people sitting immediately in front of the rostrum and found her eyes drawn to a particularly striking individual in Army uniform. Disconcertingly he seemed to lock eyes with her whenever she glanced in his direction. Vaguely intrigued, she noticed the small but distinctive scar just below his left eye, marring his otherwise striking features. She had seen a number of older officers with similar scars which Ephraim had told her were usually the result of duelling contests in their cadet days; a practice now firmly discouraged by the Nazi regime. Nowadays, scars among the younger officers invariably reflected genuine war wounds much like the one she was now looking at.

Under the subtle tutelage of Max Feldman, she had learned to reduce inevitable stage fright by imagining she was playing to a single person in the audience. On some occasions she brought the comforting features of Ephraim to mind but tonight it was the face of this same Army officer which drew her attention, naively unaware that her sensitive interpretation of the score allied to her effusive and sensuous movement was unwittingly creating a level of curiosity in the mind of a man used to military certainty.

From the podium, Max Feldman had begun to feel a growing sense of unease. With the memory of the afternoon still etched in his mind, he believed he was now witnessing his principle soloist making a discreet overture to another man. The end of the third movement allowed him to look into the audience and his eyes too were immediately drawn to the same officer in the front row. More concerning was the fact that he appeared to be unaccompanied. At least with a wife or partner, the chance of him leaving at the end of the concert would be reasonably predictable. But mixed with his concern, Max was also experiencing a faint touch of jealously, heightened by his own earlier encounter with Hannah.

In the nine years since first meeting his young prodigy, Hannah had always been a fully committed person; firstly to her music and then to Ephraim. With the birth of Aaron this commitment had become even more intense. Yet here she now was, appearing to deliberately attract a senior German Army officer. And for what purpose?

Despite his growing concern, Max too was giving a sterling performance as were the orchestra; lifted by the sheer exuberance being generated by its vivacious soloist.

With the climatic finale to the symphony approaching, Hannah appeared to be even more animated. Completing the last stanza, Max brought the music to a finish with an exuberant flourish. Before turning to acknowledge the mounting applause he brought both hands together in a salute to the orchestra. He had rarely heard them perform better. Turning to direct the applause to Hannah Bergmann he gave a deep bow and together they took a number of deserved curtain calls from the audience.

Off stage at last, Max could see that Hannah was still high on the adrenalin created by her performance which he knew wouldn't last.

'Well, well, well... what a performance! I have never heard you play better. It was like watching you flying through space on a magic carpet, completely aloof and never wanting to come down.' Their arrival at the door of Max's dressing room was fortuitous in bringing his fulsome praise to an end. Pushing it open with a flourish, Max made a final attempt to recapture his protégé's attention. 'If you have no other plans, would you care to join me for dinner or do you have to dash home to husband and child?' Max rarely referred to Ephraim or Aaron by name.

'I have no plans Max.' Dropping her hands in a gesture of growing tiredness she considered Max's invitation. 'I know what I should be doing but it would be nice to forget about this war if only for a few hours.' She sighed partly for Max's benefit. 'But I suppose this dutiful woman will go home as she always does.' Giving him one of her warmest smiles to help alleviate his obvious disappointment, she added 'but thanks for the offer Max... always good for a girl's ego.'

Reaching her own dressing room she turned and faced her thwarted mentor. 'And Max... thanks for this afternoon'. Quickly stepping inside before he could react, she closed the door gently, not wishing to hurt his feelings even more.

Once inside, she glanced at herself in the full-length mirror hung behind the door. Since her teenage days, she had become more aware that her looks and personality were increasingly attractive to men but her marriage to Ephraim and the birth of Aaron had closed her mind to being anything other than a good Jewish wife and mother. And tonight, looking at her reflected image closely, she realised that motherhood had if anything, made her even more attractive... especially to a man like Max who had known her since her late teenage years and who until today, had never shown any interest in her other than for their mutual affinity with music.

Turning away from the mirror, she removed her clammy dress with some difficulty and placed it on a hangar ready to be collected for cleaning.

Having played in this venue on numerous occasions, she was familiar with the layout of the magnificent dressing room and was particularly looking forward to its luxurious shower system located at the rear of the dressing area; a shower with an unusually large showerhead dispensing jets of therapeutic hot water designed to ease the tiredness from even the weariest body.

Stepping into the shower, the force of the water was sheer bliss tempting her to stay longer than she normally did. But gradually even the seemingly endless supply of hot water began to noticeably cool. Sliding the glass door open, she watched as the trapped steam billowed out, filling the shower room like an autumn mist. Groping for the large white towel hanging on the rear of the door, she enveloped herself in its warm folds and put a smaller hand towel around her wet shoulders. Stepping back into the dressing area with the steam following in her wake, she laughingly imagined she was a grand dame making a dramatic entrance in a children's pantomime. Smiling at the thought, she felt the towel around her slim waist begin to slip. Humming softly to herself, she quickly readjusted it and stepped gingerly across the damp tiles towards the dressing table. A sudden movement caught her eye and glancing up, she gave an involuntary start. Standing motionless in front of her dressing table was a German officer, his tall form backlit by the soft lights around the mirror. Peering at him through the swirling steam, she thought she recognised him as the same man she had unwittingly locked eyes with at odd moments during the evening's performance. Startled and fearful, she took a step back, instinctively pulling the smaller towel closer around her shoulders.

Staring at her with a look of faint amusement, it was several seconds before the man spoke in a soft yet authoritative voice. 'Miss Bergmann... allow me to introduce myself. I am Colonel Von Hartmannn.'

The fright of seeing not just a stranger but a senior military officer within the confines of her dressing room was total... especially for a Jew.

Clicking his heels together in a manner which reminded her of some long forgotten pre-war Hollywood actor, the scar faced Army officer from the front row of the stalls stood facing her.

Trying frantically to recover her poise, she took a deep breath and pulled the large towel more firmly around her still wet body. 'Can I ask what you are doing in this private dressing room?' She hoped the emphasis she placed on 'private' albeit in a tremulous voice would not betray her growing fear.

The man standing in front of her gave a hint of a smile which only served to increase the feeling of fear and anxiety beginning to well up within her.

Slowly gathering her composure despite the man's intimidating military rank, she took another deep breath. 'How dare you stroll in here as though this was one of your barrack rooms? I want you to leave before I call the management,' realising even as she spoke just how empty her words must have sounded. Moving carefully across the tiled floor in her bare feet to the dressing room door she opened it with a flourish of feigned irritation. As it widened, several members of the orchestra furtively glanced in but the sight of the uniform and rank of its wearer caused them to hurriedly look away.

'Please close the door Miss Bergmann; I want to talk to you.'

'You can speak to me when I'm fully dressed and preferably on the other side of this door. In the meantime I would ask you to leave. If you don't go, I will.'

'Dressed only in a towel?' He laughed gently. 'I don't think it would be appropriate for the orchestra's leading soloist to be seen like that.' His voice hardened. 'Close the door and come and sit down,' adding as an afterthought 'or would you prefer to hear that as an official order!'

Despite her shock, Hannah found herself wanting to smile at the manner in which the man had turned her indignation with humorous effect. For a brief moment, she actually considered obeying his instruction but instead, she forced herself to retain her grip on the handle of the still open door. 'What is it you want to talk about?'

'I want to know why you were being so obviously provocative to me during your performance. And please don't tell me that I was imagining it. You were clearly trying to engage my attention and I want to know why?'

The directness and simplicity of his question made Hannah think he sounded more like a querulous teenager than a senior officer.

Relaxing her grip on the handle she let the door close. 'So you want to know why?' She repeated his question. 'Ok, I'm happy to answer that but it will undoubtedly spoil any illusion you may be harbouring.' Taking time to gather her thoughts, she stepped around him and sat down at the dressing table and made eye contact through the misted mirror. 'It's nothing more than a professional trick of the trade, Colonel. You may have noticed that with the score committed to memory I play without music in front of me so it helps my concentration if I can shut out the audience and avoid distraction. And for me to do that, I sometimes focus on a person in the front stalls and pretend I'm playing just for that individual; nothing more than that. And tonight, you were that person so I'm sorry if you may have thought differently.

The Officer's face showed no emotion. 'If that is the case then I am not only disillusioned but also disappointed... very disappointed.' He moved closer causing her to quickly glance down to reassure herself that both towels were still firmly in place.

'Miss Bergmann, I am not a person with a great understanding of music, particularly your type of music; to me classical music can be extremely boring except for the better known pieces. But tonight you gave me... what shall I say?' He paused, choosing his next words with care, 'a different insight not only to your music but how it can be interpreted by someone like you.'

Unsure whether he was expecting a response, she resisted the urge to reply, leaving an awkward silence. After a brief moment he spoke again.

'I was captivated by your performance whether it was for me or not.' He smiled as he spoke.

'Well thank you for those kind thoughts. Perhaps what you experienced tonight may even make you want to attend more such concerts in future and who knows... you may even get to like my type of music. Life can be full of surprises, Colonel. Or so I'm told.'

Pulling the damp towel even closer around her shoulders, she pretended to shiver. 'So now if you will excuse me, I'm getting very cold and I want to get dressed and go home to my husband and child.' Mentioning her family she hoped would add further disillusionment to whatever he had in mind. 'Also, I have another busy rehearsal period tomorrow so without wishing to appear rude, can I again ask you to leave so that I can get dressed and go home.' She stood up and moved towards the door. 'Thank you again for your kind words; I appreciate them most sincerely but it's now time for me to go home and catch up with the domestic side of my life.'

For a long moment, the Colonel stared at her and for a fleeting moment she thought he might decide not to leave. Heaving his shoulders, he pursed his lips and expelled a deep breath.

'You are right. I trust you will forgive my intrusion. I will leave as you ask but thank you again for this evening's unique but in light of your explanation, a somewhat disillusioning experience. Perhaps we will meet again; in wartime you never know what may happen.' Again, the heels clicked as he drew himself up to his full height. Opening the door, he turned to look at this captivating and sensuous woman, adorned in nothing more than two damp towels, before striding out, leaving the door behind him still open.

Swiftly closing it, she dressed more hurriedly than usual, fearful that at any moment the man might change his mind and return.

Putting on her shoes, she thought about her day. A purely instinctive moment with Max which had clearly provoked something more than just friendship to surface from within her and now unwittingly eliciting the attention of a senior Army officer and for what purpose? 'Perhaps I'm being changed by what is happening around me' she thought... but changed into what?

FIVE

It was the sound of persistent knocking from the ground floor of the building which slowly broke through her dreamless sleep. For a moment she could not think where she was until the heavy sound was repeated. Quickly gathering her senses she reached out for the comforting nearness of Ephraim and felt him sit up and swing out of bed, his bare feet padding across Frieda's newly waxed floor to the window.

'What is it Ephraim? Who on earth is knocking at this time of night?' As Ephraim parted the heavy brocade curtains, she saw the early light of dawn enter the room. 'What time is it? I feel we've only been asleep for an hour or so.' Ephraim's extended silence caused a growing sense of fear to well up in the pit of her stomach.

Turning away from the window but leaving the curtains still parted, she saw a look of anxiety cross her husband's face.

'I think we should get dressed; that looked like the Police at the front door.' But even as he spoke, the sound of approaching footsteps coming from the stairwell only served to add to their rising fears. The footsteps stopped and the same authoritative pattern of knocking was repeated... this time even more intimidating in its loudness at the door of the next apartment.

'Police. Open the door!

From within the apartment across the hallway, Ephraim and Hannah both heard the much quieter response from their elderly neighbour, Shamuel Glickstein, a widower who lived alone in his apartment. The hubbub quietened as the Police entered the apartment and they heard the door close with a slam.

'Ephraim, I'm scared. We must get Aaron dressed and leave here now.'

'And go where, Hannah? We have nowhere to run to. If they had come for us, they would be in this apartment by now. But they haven't so sit down, we need time to think. Let Aaron sleep for the moment while I make some coffee while you get dressed.' With that, he disappeared into the kitchen.

From the stillness of her bedroom, she became aware of raised voices coming from the other side of the adjoining wall. The muffled voices of the Police officers increased in volume followed by a chilling cry of agony which could only be that of their neighbour. Then all went quiet. Terrified, she ran from the bedroom and nearly collided with Ephraim returning with two steaming cups of coffee. Motioning with her finger for him to remain silent they hurried into the lounge, closing the door as if to provide added protection from what was happening in the next apartment.

Listening intently, they heard the apartment door slam shut and the sound of footsteps descending down the stairs and all was silent once more.

Telling Hannah to remain where she was, Ephraim went into the hallway and peered down the stairwell before crossing to Mr. Glikstein's apartment. The latch on his door had failed to engage and it yielded to his tentative push.

'Mr. Glickstein, its Ephraim Fischer. .' There was no response. Walking into the lounge, Ephraim repeated his call. Receiving no reply, he moved towards the bedroom and cautiously pushed the half closed door open. The body of Mr. Glickstein lay on the floor at the foot of his bed, its unnatural posture indicating to Ephraim's trained eye that his elderly neighbour was dead. Checking for a pulse merely confirmed this.

'Oh dear God, what have they done to him.' Not having heard her enter the bedroom, Hannah's fearful exclamation startled him. He felt her trembling hand on his shoulder as she knelt beside him. 'He's dead isn't he? Those men, they've killed him but why?' Her voice trembled with emotion.

Standing up, Ephraim pulled Hannah upright and guided her from the room. 'We must leave here. Believe me, there is nothing you or I can do for him.'

Sobbing, she allowed her husband to lead her back into their apartment. Feeling incapable of speaking she made to go into her bedroom before recoiling at the thought of their neighbour lying dead... murdered... on the other side of the adjoining wall. Inexplicably, she remembered his kindness when they first moved into their apartment some four years ago. Hannah was concerned that her need to practice endless scales before leaving for rehearsal each day would disturb their welcoming neighbour but to their relief, he never complained. It was only later that they realised Mr. Glickstein suffered from acute deafness which became an even greater 'blessing' when Aaron was born. And now this gentle old man was dead; murdered by the very Police who in a normal society were supposed to protect people like him.

Later that morning, still in their apartment but now dressed, they again heard the sound of footsteps on the stairs. This time there was no conversation, only the sound of entry into their neighbour's apartment. Minutes later, they heard heavy footsteps labouring down the stairs which they presumed was the body of Mr. Glickstein being carried from the building. Later still, a locksmith appeared and changed the lock on the front door of the apartment before he too disappeared.

Inside their own apartment, Hannah, still in shock, hugged her baby son and would not allow Ephraim to move from her side.

The next 48 hours passed in a daze with Hannah's thoughts constantly in turmoil as she recounted again and again the violent and needless murder committed in the next apartment. Later that night when she was at last able to sleep, it was fitful, interrupted by nightmarish dreams centred on what had occurred the previous morning. She sensed from his unusual quietness that Ephraim too was struggling to come to terms with the same awful happening. Neither had spoken at any length, just fragmentary snatches of conversation as if any prolonged discussion might somehow tempt fate and cause the same murderous thugs to return but this time for them. In those brief moments when they did manage to overcome their apprehension, the question which came constantly to mind was why the Nazi Government had abetted the murder such an inoffensive old man like Mr. Glickstein. Both knew there could be only one answer to that question. He was a Jew and his murder clearly signalled a further escalation of the terror being waged against people like themselves.

On the third day it was Ephraim who attempted to make sense of their neighbour's murder. 'It can only be to intimidate us even more than they do now. But what do they expect us to do? Do they want to drive us Jews to rise up so they then have a legitimate reason to kill us all?' He paused, needing time to consider his own question before speaking to Hannah. 'Do you think there is one chance in a thousand we can get out of this God-awful country? Does Max have any influence with any of his Nazi friends who might be persuaded to help us?'

Hannah didn't respond immediately. Her first thought was about friends they would be leaving behind even if by some miracle they could get out. 'I think it most unlikely and I'm not sure whether Max has any real influence with these murderers and even if he did then why would he use it for our benefit? If Jews are now being openly murdered by the Nazis then I should think that Max will probably need all the help he can get to save his own skin.' Hesitating for a moment, she thought about Ephraim's question. 'Tell me, why did you think he might help us?'

Ephraim hesitated and the silence became uncomfortably long.

'Because you and Max are close and he appears to know a number of high-ranking officials. He doesn't appear to be in any imminent danger himself so perhaps he could be persuaded to help us.'

'Assuming he has any influence, which I doubt, I think he would retain it for himself, just in case he needed to get out.

Max can always be relied upon to look after himself, believe me.'

Looking at her husband, she saw his shoulders visibly sag as he considered her reply. 'I thought that might be the case.' Sinking both hands deep into his trouser pockets, he turned and stared out of the window. 'Look, Hannah, we need to talk about what is happening out there.' He waved his hand towards the street below. 'We both know that the restrictions are getting worse every month. Unlike other Germans, we're living on rations set at starvation-levels. We're not allowed to use public transport, own a bicycle or radio, buy clothes or shoes and now Jews are being transported to God-knows where in Eastern Europe. And if that isn't bad enough, they are now beginning to murder innocent people in their homes. What happened to Mr. Glickstein is probably happening elsewhere in this city and perhaps in other cities as well. Who knows what's really going on in this country anymore?'

Shocked by his words, Hannah took him by the shoulder. 'Ephraim, look at me; how do you know that other Jews are being murdered here in Berlin? Who told you this?'

Turning to face her, Ephraim lowered his voice hoping to lessen the impact of what he was about to say. 'Because Hannah, the cemeteries are filling up with dead Jews; phoney accidents, suicides and unexplained deaths just like that of Mr. Glickstein. That's how I know.' He turned back towards the window.

Hannah felt an icy chill course through her body and stumbled towards the nearest chair to prevent herself from falling. Ephraim came and knelt before her and took her hands in his and she noticed the tears forming in the corner of his eyes. 'Whatever happens, my dear beautiful wife, we will face it together, the three of us. We can do no more.'

SIX

Two days later the Police called again. Alone in the apartment, it was Frieda who opened the door to them. Three officers, each wearing full-length black leather coats favoured by members of the Gestapo stood at the entrance with armbands confirming their membership of that sinister organisation.

Frieda never saw the blow which knocked her against the rear wall of the hallway. The force of the blow drove several teeth deep into her upper lip and within seconds she felt the warm taste of blood filling her mouth as she sank to the floor. The kick to her unprotected stomach which followed drove the wind from her body, causing an involuntary cry of pain to escape from her damaged mouth. As she gasped for air, she felt acidic bile rise from her stomach and through tear-stained eyes she saw her vomit splatter onto the polished floor in front of her prostrated body.

'Get up... on your feet!'

Dazed and barely able to breath, Frieda managed to struggle to her feet, her cut lip continuing to pump blood, filling her mouth and spotting the front of her white blouse. Staggering back, she fell against the hallway wall for support. The leading thug, rubbing his leather gloves together as though to sanitise them from the contact made with Frieda's face, stepped carefully over the blood and vomit on the floor and made his way into the lounge. The second official followed whilst the third closed the front door and roughly shoved Frieda into the kitchen.

'Put a towel on your face and clean yourself up.' He appeared to be younger than the other two men but his face showed the same expression of malevolence. 'Where are the Jews that live here and when are you expecting them to return?'

Slowly, very slowly, Frieda began to regain her composure despite her head continuing to spin whilst the pain in her solar plexus severely restricted her ability to breathe deeply. 'I don't know when they'll be back. I stay here until they return.' Still groggy, she gulped a shallow lungful of air. 'If they're not back by mid-afternoon then I collect their child from the family that cares for him during the day.' Frieda stopped speaking, her mouth continuing to fill with blood. From the lounge she heard the sound of cupboards being opened and drawers pulled out, their contents tipped onto the floor.

'How long have you worked for these Yids?' The question came from the lounge.

Frieda tried to reply but her damaged mouth and jaw refused to respond. She felt the blood begin to clot in her mouth and she was able to spit the congealing lumps into the towel. Her attempt to speak was seen by her watcher who translated her raised hand with its five fingers extended.

'She can't speak Sergeant but she's indicating five years.'

Her assailant, clearly the senior of the three men, re-appeared in the kitchen. He placed a piece of paper on the table. 'Tell your Jew friends they are required to report to this address,' emphasising the point by stabbing his finger on the paper. 'Gestapo HQ at 8 a.m. tomorrow. If they fail to turn up both they and you will be arrested.' Pointing with his foot to the blood and vomit on the polished floor, he leaned closer to Frieda's ear. 'And let your Jew friends clean this up. Understood?'

Ephraim was first to return home. In the meantime, Frieda had managed to wash the visible signs of blood from her face and had changed into one of Hannah's dresses but there was no hiding the swollen lip and the dark bruising beginning to appear on her left cheek

'I think they took away your medical records and some of Hannah's jewellery has gone too but what else, I can't be sure.

I don't even know if I would recognise them again'. Tears filled her eyes and she wrung her hands in anguish. 'How can I go home looking like this for God's sake.'

Reacting to her despairing words, Ephraim extended his arm and gently placed it around her shoulder and made her sit down. Reaching into his medical bag, he found a small brown bottle containing the last of his remaining pain killing tablets but knew it would be some time for them to take effect.

'Frieda, you have been a dear friend to our family for a very long time but this obviously changes everything. The only reason you were attacked today is because you work for us. And I'm certain it will happen again We can't expose you to this sort of gratuitous violence so I am going to walk you home and Hannah or myself will call by tomorrow to see how you are.'

'Ephraim please, don't fuss me. We need to think about collecting Aaron. He should have been picked up ages ago.'

'No, I'm not forgetting Aaron but the carers will hold on to him and I will pick him up on my way back.' Still holding her around her shoulders, his voice lowered; 'come along my dear woman, let's get you home as quickly as we can.'

'Ephraim, you're a good man but this afternoon you are being a very stupid man.' Even in her distressed state, Frieda did not mince her words. 'I can travel on the tram but you would be arrested immediately. And if you remove your star you risk something even worse. And for what? There's nothing wrong with my legs and my face has never been my strong point! So for my sake I want you to stay here and keep Hannah calm when she returns home.' Frieda stopped speaking, her mouth too painful to continue. 'And no arguing otherwise I will be forced to call the Police!'

SEVEN

Neither Ephraim nor Hannah were able to sleep restfully that night and well before dawn, Ephraim exchanged the comforting warmth of their bed for the distinctly colder temperature of the kitchen from where he emerged minutes later holding two cups of coffee. In her half-sleep, she had been dimly aware of Ephraim getting up but now, fully awake she gratefully took the hot cup in both hands. Its warmth caused a tingling sensation in her fingers just moments before the recollections of the previous day flooded into her mind. She felt her grip on the cup loosen and watched helplessly as the coffee spilled on to the floor.

'Ephraim, I can't think sensibly anymore. What if we are arrested and separated. And what's to become of our baby? Dear God, I wish we had never brought him into this horrible world.'

Reaching out, Ephraim drew Hannah to him and pressed her head gently against his chest but he too was wondering whether they would still be together at the end of this day.

With increasing anxiety, they left the apartment earlier than was necessary and carried a still sleepy Aaron to a friend's apartment, each knowing they might never see him again. Ephraim had to support a tearful Hannah as they took their first hesitant steps towards the once elegant Museum of Decorative Arts on Prinz-Albrechstrasse but now the HQ and security prison of the dreaded Gestapo Secret Police. Arriving at the front of the building, Hannah's legs were barely able to propel her up the dozen or so steps and she held on tightly to Ephraim's arm for assurance.

The interior of the building was purposely intimidating. In the centre of the elegant entrance hall with its high vaulted ceiling was a wide marble staircase leading to a mezzanine floor. Draped from its overhanging balustrade hung four huge red and black flags, each emblazoned with the chilling swastika of the Nazi Party drawing their eyes down to a bronze bust of Adolph Hitler staring sightlessly into the distance.

Two uniformed officials, one wearing his greatcoat and cap and looking as though he had just come on duty, staffed the reception area.

Hannah's eyes focussed on the silver badge in the cap, which even from a distance clearly resembled a skull. It sent an icy chill down her spine and once more she felt her legs begin to tremble.

Without looking up, the greatcoated official checked their names against a typed list in front of him. Incongruously, the number of names on the list had the odd effect of helping to calm her inner turmoil knowing that she and Ephraim were but two of many other Jews due to report that morning.

'Come this way.' His deep stentorian voice reflected the pervading mood of despair they both felt as he led the way to a flight of stairs leading to a basement area. In a poorly lit corridor they were able to make out numerous rooms with cell-like doors on both sides of the passageway.

Partway along the corridor, he kicked open a door leading into an unlit room. 'Wait here... and do not speak to each other.' He slammed the door shut and they heard his heavy footsteps fade along the corridor.

Illumination came through a small panel of diffused glass in the centre of the heavy door and it took a while for their eyes to adjust to the gloom. The cell was sparsely furnished with a single desk and two chairs on either side of it. Ephraim protectively extended his arm around Hannah's shoulder and pulled her closer. 'Whatever may happen to us, my dear sweet girl, I want you to know I love you with all of my being.' Instinctively, she turned into Ephraim's embrace and kissed him, tasting the saltiness of his tears on her lips.

A few minutes later they heard returning footsteps. The door was again roughly shoved open and the light switch activated by the same officer who had escorted them to this room. The second man, dressed in civilian clothes, took a seat behind the desk and both watched with increasing apprehension as the uniformed officer slowly took his time to shed his greatcoat and cap before sitting alongside him.

'Sit down and confirm your names;' it was the accented voice of the civilian who broke the silence.

'Ephraim Fischer and Hannah Bergmann.' It was Ephraim who responded.

'You have different surnames; are you married to each other?'

This time it was Hannah who replied; 'yes we are married. Bergmann is my professional name. I am a professional musician.'

'I didn't ask what you do for a living. I asked why you have different surnames.'

Now it was the turn of the one in uniform. 'Were you both present when my officers called at your home yesterday?'

Unseen by the two inquisitors, Ephraim squeezed Hannah's hand. 'No; we were out when your officers 'interviewed' our child carer. Would you care to know what injuries this Aryan person suffered during the course of this interview?'

The silence instantly became menacingly tangible as though the two officials seemed unable to believe the temerity of Ephraim's reply

Hannah saw the civilian interrogator stiffen and sit back in his chair, his stare exuding pure venom.

'If you open your Jewish gob like that just once more, I will have you taken from this room and shot? Do you understand me?' Ephraim nodded his understanding but this had the effect of appearing to enrage the civilian interrogator even more.

'I said... do you understand me, you piece of Yiddish dog shit.'

'Yes. I fully understand both of you?'

'So you never saw nor met any of the officers who came to your apartment?'

Duly chastened, this time Ephraim responded only to the question. 'You are correct. We never met them either at our apartment or subsequently.'

'Did you speak to anyone about what happened to your Carer yesterday?'

'No. Neither of us left our apartment other than to come here this morning.'

'Did you have any visitors after my officers left yesterday?'

Wondering where this line of questioning was leading, Ephraim again responded with the brevity demanded by the interrogator. 'None.'

'Do you know an Army officer by the name of Colonel Von Hartmannn?'

'No.' Ephraim again fielded the question.

Suddenly, the image of the scar-faced officer who had entered her dressing room several evenings before flashed into Hannah's mind but she remained silent..

As if reading her mind, the civilian interrogator looked up from his notes and locked eyes with Hannah. 'And what about you, the professional musician. Do you know this officer?'

'Was this the Army officer who came to my dressing room last week?' Feeling Ephraim's eyes on her, she realised she had to say more, if only for his sake.

'At the end of that evening's concert I was preparing to leave my dressing room when this man introduced himself to me. That was all there was to our meeting. In fact I barely recognised his name; that's how much impression he made on me.'

'What business would a senior Wehrmacht officer have with you, a Jew, in the privacy of your dressing room and why would he risk breaking Army regulations to just 'introduce himself' to you'. He paraphrased Hannah's words. 'Is that what you expect us to believe?'

Now in full deadly flow, he turned his penetrating gaze on Ephraim. 'Did you know your wife is in the habit of entertaining German officers?' He paused, obviously hoping for a response. 'Or does she conveniently forget to tell you?'

'Look, my wife meets many people in her profession. The fact that one such person was a German officer would not be of interest to me. Why should it be?' Ephraim's response pushed the insidious thrust of the interrogation back to the other side of the desk.

Ignoring his boldness, the civilian pressed on. 'Because doctor, you are both Jews yet your wife has been granted privileged status which you do not share. Doesn't it strike you as odd that she obviously has friends in high places which you appear to know nothing of?'

'My wife enjoys what you term "privileged status" and spared having to wear a yellow star because of her profession as a leading musician with this city's principle orchestra.' Ephraim waited, wondering whether to add more.

'My question was whether she has friends of influence and what she does for these people to obtain such favours for herself. Or do I have to be more graphic?'

Still gripped by Ephraim's unseen hand, Hannah could contain herself no longer. 'I understand perfectly what you are suggesting to my husband but if I did have such influential 'friends' then what am I doing here? If such people actually exist then wouldn't they have intervened on my behalf?' Hannah's pent-up exasperation evaporated as quickly as it had risen and she again felt an icy stab of fear lodge in the pit of her stomach.

The civilian official leaned forward, his rheumy grey eyes staring directly at her. 'Oh but he has; why else would this Colonel Von Hartmannn, express an interest in your case which is the only reason why you will be allowed to leave this building... at least for the time being.' Leaning back, he looked directly at Ephraim. 'But you doctor, you have no such protection which means you will stay for further questioning to enable us to find out what you know about the murder of the officer who came to your home yesterday. The man you claim never to have met.' Reaching across the desk, he grasped Ephraim's lapel and pulled him to within inches of his face. 'And while you remain here, you may care to ponder more fully on the extent of your wife's relationship with her influential friend... a man your wife conveniently forgot to mention to you.'

EIGHT

Escorted from the building through a rear exit, her eyes were temporarily dazzled by the unexpected brightness of the day. After weeks of dark wintry weather, she had expected the day to be grey and gloomy. Instead, looking up at the unseasonably blue sky with small clouds scudding past, it strangely reminded her of sheep moving across a wide fenceless meadow.

She had not been able to say goodbye to Ephraim. Summoned by a hidden alarm button, two burly guards had appeared and roughly pulled her out of the room.

Desperately concerned at Ephraim's continuing detention, she had to force herself to decide what to do next. Thinking it might be too risky to return to the apartment she walked aimlessly for several minutes before realising it was probably the safest place to be as she was unlikely to further warrant the Gestapo's attention so soon after her release.

Still in a sense of panic, she decided to walk back to Goethestrasse rather than risk taking the tram. Increasing her pace to get as far from the building as possible, she tried to become more focussed. With no immediate prospect of Ephraim being released, she knew her first priority must be to collect Aaron from the family they had left him with earlier that morning. After that, she would gather his things from her apartment and make their way to Frieda's apartment.

After the thuggish assault on Frieda just 24 hours earlier, she wondered whether she would even open her front door let alone agree to shelter Aaron for the next few days. If Frieda did refuse then she had no other person she would trust Aaron with. But first she had to collect him and not get ahead of herself. Approaching the detached house where she had left Aaron just hours before, she began to panic even more. Trying to control her growing anxiety she took several deep breaths before pressing the brass bell push on the front door of her friend's house.

It was opened by Inga, a young mother whom she had first met in the maternity hospital before Jews were barred from admission or treatment at German hospitals or clinics. They had shared a small ward and during a long night of seemingly endless labour, Inga, on yet another painful journey to the washroom abruptly went into a spasm and failed to make it, throwing up onto the highly polished linoleum-covered floor. The Charge Nurse, an elderly Nun, had ordered Inga to clean the floor but the sight and smell of the acidy bile was just too much, causing her to heave even more. Despite her own discomfort, it was Hannah who had cleaned the floor for her. Within minutes Inga had delivered a baby girl who seemed able to sleep during every waking second, especially when attempting to feed whilst clasped to her mother's breast. Aaron on the other hand had given her a difficult birth making it necessary for her to stay in the clinic for a further two days. Inga meantime had been discharged and it had been some weeks before they met again, this time at a post-natal clinic. The genuine warmth of Inga's greeting had heartened Hannah and since that meeting they had become good friends. Inga and husband Claus, a Government official in the Defence Ministry, obviously knew she was Jewish but this had not visibly affected their relationship. Whilst this was reassuring, it was also a cause of worry, knowing how punitive the Nazis could be to people known to be consorting with Jews.

Aaron and Carla, each now fourteen months old, were engrossed in building a tower with wooden blocks when Hannah arrived. Over a warming cup of real coffee, Hannah tearfully related what had happened at the interview with the Gestapo. Looking at both children happily playing on the patterned rug, it seemed so much longer than three hours ago since she and Ephraim had brought Aaron here earlier that morning. Despite Inga's tempting invitation to stay for a meal, she politely declined. Looking up from the assorted building blocks Aaron became aware of her for the first time and immediately wanted to know where his daddy was but Hannah knew she couldn't answer without bursting into tears. Instead, she hurriedly scooped him up in her arms, mumbled barely audible thanks to Inga and began another tiring trudge with the weight of Aaron taxing her already tired limbs.

Arriving at Frieda's ground floor apartment with Aaron's sleepy head resting on her shoulder, she hardly dared to ring the front door bell. Instead, she gave a tentative knock with her knuckles and waited. Several uneasy seconds elapsed before the door flew open and there was a tearful Frieda rushing to embrace them both. Hannah saw the purple bruising on Frieda's face and looking beyond her, she caught sight of Victor, her younger brother.

Dressed in an open-necked Army shirt and grey battledress trousers, there was no mistaking their relationship to each other. In facial looks and sturdy build they were remarkably alike.

Finally letting go, Frieda turned and introduced her brother. 'This is Victor; I told you about him last week. He's due to report back to his unit later this week.' The sisterly pride in her voice was very apparent. 'Victor, this is my friend Hannah and her baby son Aaron.' Frieda appeared able to speak more easily than Ephraim had reported yesterday when her damaged mouth had given her words an indistinct lisp.

'I'm pleased to meet you Hannah; my sister has told me much about you.' His precise delivery and refined accent surprised her. She wasn't quite sure why but she had expected Victor to speak in the same colloquial manner as his older sister.

Letting Victor ease her coat from her shoulders, she became aware of the growing sensation of pins and needles in her aching arms now she was no longer carrying Aaron's weight.

'Can I get you a coffee and how about you, my little man. Would you like some warm milk and a biscuit perhaps?' The word biscuit caused an instant reaction. Wriggling free from Hannah's grasp, Aaron clasped hold of Victor's outstretched hand and together they made for the kitchen.

'A coffee would be just fine Victor. Can I help you?'

'No thanks. I think I can handle the cafetere. Why don't you both come in here; it's much warmer.'

The traditional stove, its blue tiles extending from floor to ceiling exuded gratifying warmth which slowly began to dispel the numbing chill which had seeped into her body during the walk to Frieda's home. But with the warmth came an overwhelming sense of tiredness. Feeling her trembling legs might give way at any moment, she quickly sat down.

She felt Frieda's hand on her shoulder and impulsively covered it with her own. As neither Frieda nor her brother had mentioned Ephraim, she realised they were probably waiting for her to tell them what had happened at Gestapo HQ.

She watched as Victor let Aaron finish a small beaker of milk before letting him catch sight of the arrowroot biscuit tantalisingly held just out of reach of his grasping fingers. Spotting it, the milk drink was quickly pushed aside as Victor allowed him to snatch the enticing biscuit, bringing a look of triumph to Aaron's baby-like features as he sank his tiny teeth into his prize.

Hannah knew she couldn't hold back any longer. Taking a deep breath, she looked up at Frieda. 'Ephraim has been detained and God knows when he will be released. It was so awful. One of those men who came to the apartment yesterday was apparently killed last night. They didn't say how but I think they believed we knew something about it.' Still looking at Aaron, she failed to see the almost imperceptible glance Frieda exchanged with her brother.

'Hannah, I want you to listen to me because you are speaking nonsense. Their only reason for coming to your apartment yesterday was to tell you and Ephraim to be at Gestapo headquarters this morning. So whatever happened to this man after that would have nothing to do with you or your husband.' Frieda stopped for breath. 'Besides, you didn't even see the three animals that came to your apartment so how would you know which one to kill?' Despite her inner turmoil, Hannah managed to force a smile as she realised the humorous logic in Frieda's words.

'So what did they question you about?' The enquiry came from Victor.

'They implied that my so-called privileged status was because of an imaginary relationship with a Nazi officer who in fact I had met just once and then for only a few minutes. They obviously wanted to hear from us whether there was any substance to what they were insinuating and I suspect this murder business was added to their investigation. Other than both of us being Jewish... and you don't need me to tell you what that means today, I really have no idea why they wanted to see us.'

'Hannah, I always seem to be talking to you like your dear old mother would. But this time I want you to listen carefully and then think before replying.' Frieda paused, knowing her next words would touch Hannah to her very core. 'I want you to leave Aaron with me, at least until the situation with Ephraim becomes clearer. Because of the bombing and families becoming separated and God knows what else, no one will be surprised or suspicious of a child staying here. You know he will be well looked after with me so will you think about it... if only for Aaron's sake?'

It took Hannah a second or two to absorb the import of what Frieda was suggesting. Having suffered a brutal beating at the hands of Gestapo thugs less than 24 hours earlier for merely associating with her family, this wonderful woman was now offering to shelter her dearest possession. Overwhelmed and unable to speak, she impulsively pulled Frieda towards her and nodded her acceptance through a welter of tears.

NINE

Later that evening, in the unusual quietness of the apartment, she once more went over the events of that awful day. Touring with the orchestra had accustomed her to being away from Ephraim but tonight was so utterly different. Despite knowing that Aaron was now comparatively safe with Frieda, at least for the moment, it was the thought of being separated from Ephraim which troubled her most. The realisation of not ever being able to see, hear or touch him again filled her with unspeakable sadness and terrifying dread.

Resisting the need to sleep, she fitfully reached out to his side of the bed, her probing fingers serving only to emphasise the emptiness of their separation. Peering at the empty space, she imagined she could detect the aroma which Ephraim exuded... a clean, manly tang coming from the linen pillow case on his side of the bed and which tonight seemed to magnify his absence even more.

Lying there, she recalled her first meeting with Ephraim at a dinner party given by the parents of her then boyfriend. She remembered the attractive woman who had accompanied him that night; a woman who despite her blond Aryan features and impressive fluency in German was in fact Swedish. To her surprise the young doctor had contacted her some days later and invited her to join him and some friends to a Schubert concert, which she had declined. He made no mention of the Swedish girl or her own boyfriend and several months passed before they met again; this time at a post-concert gala dinner. Both were without their previous partners. The glamorous Swede, fearful of the gathering war clouds, had apparently returned home to the neutrality of her own country, whilst her own boyfriend, acutely aware of the growing dangers facing Jews and tiring of her long absences on tour with the orchestra had left Germany to join his recently emigrated parents in America. Thinking back, it all seemed so very long ago.

Inevitably sleep finally overcame her until she awoke with a start, realising she was still fully dressed. Glancing at the bedside clock she was surprised to see that nearly four hours had passed. Her overwhelming tiredness had gone and lying in that pleasant state between sleep and wakefulness, her feelings once more inevitably drifted toward Ephraim. She wondered whether she could turn to Max for help but immediately rejected the thought, realising that any influence he might have would surely not extend into the sinister realms of the Gestapo. Even a well-connected Jew, apostate or otherwise, would think twice before risking their own safety at a time when depredations against the Jewish population were plumbing new depths of terror.

The next notion to drift into her still sleepy mind had the effect of dispelling any further thought of sleep. The scar faced colonel referred to by the Gestapo interrogator. Would he be able or even willing to help? She recalled the civilian interrogator's chilling words. 'You have a powerful friend who has expressed an interest in your case'. His spiteful insinuation also came to mind together with the officer's name; Hartmann... Colonel Von Hartmann.

'How would he react if I managed to make contact with him' she wondered; 'and where would I find him? And if by some minor miracle I did find him and even more implausibly, he agreed to actually meet with me, would he feel inclined to assist her and what might he want in return for his intervention? Or would he politely remind her that she was already indebted to him for her own release?'

In her mind the questions ebbed and flowed. Becoming increasingly agitated as to what she should do, she impulsively threw back the sheet and heavy eiderdown but then straightaway regretted her impetuosity as the coldness of the unheated bedroom began to chill her exposed body. No longer able to control her fluctuating thoughts, she reluctantly concluded that nothing could be done before morning but despite this, her overworked brain began to compose an imaginary supplication to the man who just days before she had been so rudely indifferent to. Yet on the basis of that single encounter, she now knew he had expressly intervened on her behalf without any subsequent contact or communication let alone expecting something in return from her.

Slipping off her nightdress she went into the shower but the chilling coldness of the water had the effect of driving any further deliberations from her mind. Visibly shivering but with her senses now fully energised, she decided that in the morning she would do her utmost to contact this Colonel Von Hartmann but before then the thought of her still warm bed offered the most sensible place to spend the rest of her disturbed night

The crump of heavy explosions and the sound of anti-aircraft fire woke her from her shortened sleep and for a few blissful moments she had to think where she was. Having no idea of the time and guessing the explosions meant yet another bombing raid, she sensibly decided to remain where she was. As a Jew she was barred from taking refuge in the emergency shelters now being hastily constructed for the burgeoning population in Berlin but if need be, she knew she could seek shelter in the basement of the building. The residential district of Charlottenburg had initially escaped the attention of Allied bombers strategically targeting the important industrial areas located mainly in the outlying districts of the capital but in recent weeks this had changed to where the entire city of Berlin had now become a target for the Allied bombers.

A staunch member of the Nazi Party and self-appointed warden for the building, had with a remarkable degree of prescience recently written to every tenant in the building with a dire warning that Allied bombers might soon be changing their strategy to that of indiscriminate bombing designed to terrorise the population. Quite how he knew this was a mystery but his injunction for each tenant to store as much water as possible in the event of damage to the water mains was now gaining grudging acceptance as the once sporadic bombing raids significantly increased in frequency.

Lying there, she began to question her decision to first find and then approach Von Hartmannn later that day but with Ephraim's detention foremost in her thoughts, she knew she had to try. Surprisingly, sleep did come again and this time it was the mournful wail of air raid sirens signalling a belated 'all-clear' that finally woke her. Dawn was showing through a gap in the black-out curtains so she guessed it must be after 7.00 am or even later. Even though all windows in the apartment were closed the acrid smell of cordite, burning timber and brick dust had somehow managed to penetrate into the apartment though she had no idea how this was possible. Not able to face another cold shower, she settled instead for a quick splash of water to take the sleep from her eyes. She noticed that the pressure of the tap water was much lower than normal and its colour was decidedly murky against the whiteness of the wash basin. Notwithstanding the ongoing trauma of yesterday and her disturbed night, her face still managed to project a youthful appeal other than for the hint of dark shadows beginning to appear beneath each eye which if anything, actually added to their allure.

Thankfully, Max had agreed to a warm-up session before that evening's concert which dispensed with the need for a full-programme rehearsal so she hoped he would be at home. Having known Max for many years, she was acutely aware that when given a choice, his marked inclination was not to become involved in any matter which did not personally concern him. But on the basis of their long-standing relationship, she hoped he would want to help and know of some means whereby she could contact Von Hartmannn. But now in the cold light of day she began to feel more and more anxious as to whether such a high ranking Nazi officer would even agree to see her let alone risk his own position to help a Jew.

The walk to Max's apartment, located near the old Reichstag building, took longer than expected. A number of roads were blocked by mountains of debris from buildings damaged or destroyed by the overnight bombing raid. Some were still blazing with thick palls of black smoke rising into the early morning sky. Fire crews, their faces lined with fatigue and uniforms covered in layers of dust and grime, were directing limp streams of water at a fractured gas main, its roaring flames seemingly unquenchable.

The bombers had long since disappeared from the sky above the capital but their deadly payloads had left a swathe of death and destruction in their wake. Countless buildings were now no more than piles of rubble whilst others, their outer walls destroyed, exposed what remained of furniture and household belongings clinging to floors which leaned downwards at seemingly impossible angles. In several buildings she was able to see into a number of rooms with photographs and pictures still hanging on walls. On the pavement outside of buildings which only hours before had been family homes, she saw bemused people aimlessly sorting through the rubble, searching for whatever could be salvaged. Further along the road, she saw two elderly women attempting to heat or cook something in a grimy saucepan on a small paraffin stove.

Thankfully Max was at home and from his effusive greeting actually seemed pleased to see her. His agent, an elderly Austrian impresario who had represented Max since he had established an international reputation, was also present but he quickly excused himself when she entered the sumptuous lounge.

'Spiegel wants me to relocate to Switzerland. He thinks our future here is becoming increasingly untenable which I suppose is stating the obvious. He also thinks our stage is no longer truly international which again I can't argue with, and...' he lowered his voice as though in danger of being overheard, 'should Germany lose this altercation with the rest of the world then he believes I could become a musical pariah.' His smirk told Hannah he did not really accept this prognosis.

'I recall you expressed it somewhat differently, Hannah; 'collaborator' was the word you used so it appears that both you and Spiegel are saying much the same thing.'

He stopped, realising that his early morning guest was not engaging in his small talk. 'Hannah, you haven't said a word. Why are you here and why so early?'

'I'm here Max because Ephraim was arrested yesterday and I don't know what to do. You inferred last week that you have some contacts with military people and I need to speak to a German officer by the name of Hartmannn. Would you have any idea where I could begin to look?' A faint note of despair was apparent in her voice. 'I am so utterly, utterly desperate and I don't know who else to turn to.'

The imploring tone of Hannah's voice touched a chord. 'Hartmannn, Hartmannn.' He rolled the name around his tongue. 'I don't know the name; should I?'

'He was the officer you thought I was seducing when he came to my dressing room following our last concert. I'm sure you remember that.'

'Oh, the scar faced army type you dedicated your evening's performance too.' His muted sarcasm was infuriating, 'Yes I do remember him now, albeit vaguely.' Max's face took on a quizzical look as the lines on his forehead drew together. 'Am I missing something here? Didn't you tell me you had given him short shrift when he later followed up on your highly spirited performance?'

'What I told you Max, is exactly what happened, as you well know when you saw him leave my room in double quick time after the concert.'

Remembering she needed a favour from him her voice softened. 'But what you wouldn't be aware of is that both Ephraim and I were interviewed yesterday at Gestapo headquarters. Ephraim has been detained and I was only able to leave that awful building at the behest of this man

Hartmannn. That's why I need to know whether you can help me or at least suggest what I can do.'

The hint of desperation in Hannah's voice seemed to register as Max inwardly digested the thought of his star performer being interviewed by the Gestapo which frankly was of more concern to him than the plight of her husband.

'Tell me Hannah, what was the thrust of the conversation you had with these gentlemen who are now detaining your husband.'

Hearing his measured form of words, Hannah suppressed the urge to scream at him. Instead she silently counted to five before trusting herself to reply.

'Max, it wasn't a discussion. It was an extremely terrifying experience conducted by men who would most certainly not fit your description of gentlemen. They are murderers and thugs. These are the people who murdered our poor old neighbour Mr. Glickstein and since then beaten my cleaner almost senseless when they called at our apartment yesterday.' Hannah realised it was in fact the day before yesterday but didn't bother to correct herself. 'And because Ephraim spoke up for us yesterday, I have no doubt that he too will now have been beaten senseless.' Her voice tailed off as she recalled the deadly threat made by the civilian interrogators to have Ephraim executed for no other reason than his refusal to be intimidated by them.

'Look Hannah, I do not doubt the seriousness of this situation but my question was meant to understand why they were interviewing both of you in the first place. Did the interview have a point to it? Were any direct accusation put to you or was it just an interview because you both happen to be Jewish and this is what is happening in Germany and indeed elsewhere at the moment.'

Maddening as it was to hear Max so mildly summarise the reality of wholesale arrests and State sponsored murder in such a clinical fashion, she decided not to challenge his benign view of life and pressed on with a direct question.

'Max, I need to know... can you help me or not?'

'Personally I'm afraid the answer to that question is 'no' but first let me check with Richter. He occasionally gets requests to supply concert tickets to a junior officer at Army HQ for his superiors so he may be the most appropriate person to speak to or at least to begin with. Richter should be here very soon; in fact I thought that was him when you rang the doorbell. Let me make you a coffee and I don't suppose you've had anything to eat yet, have you?'

'No, I left my apartment as soon as I could safely venture out after the all-clear.' Plainly relieved, she took her coat off. 'Max, let me make the coffee while you tidy up those papers and I'll help myself to these biscuits which your agent appears to have left; including this half-eaten one!'

Although Edward Richter had been his personal assistant for the last seven years, Max Feldman remained in blissful ignorance of just how well connected such a position commanded. As general factotum to an internationally renowned musician and conductor, the constant requests for last minute concert tickets had presented the humble dresser with access to an informal and influential network of contacts. Within minutes of him telephoning his military supplicant at General Staff H.Q at Gatow, an appointment was made for her to meet with a Capt. Karl Heidrick, aide–de-camp to the very officer she was endeavouring to meet. Ironically the address written in Richter's neat hand showed a military unit close to Spandau and less than a kilometre from her apartment in Charlottenburg! Barred from using public transport she had no other option than to retrace her steps along the same streets she had passed through just an hour or so earlier.

The unexpected ease of setting up the meeting had surprised her but trudging back on legs which were becoming wearier by the minute she began to feel twinges of anxiety as her every step drew her closer to the address of the military unit in Spandau. Remembering the earlier diversions caused by the overnight air raid, she was able to make faster progress than earlier that morning and nearing Charlottenburg she realised that she would arrive at Spandau with time to spare.

In spite of the coldness of the weather, she began to sweat profusely as her pace quickened. Stopping to look at her reflection in one of the few undamaged shop windows, she saw an untidy figure peering back at her. 'I wouldn't get past the gate sentry looking like this' she thought, 'let alone this Captain Heidrick whoever he may be.'

Realising she had time to spare and perturbed by her dishevelled appearance, she decided to stop at her apartment to change into something less drab and to consider what she would say if she actually managed to meet with the German officer?

Entering the apartment, everything was exactly as she had left it. Glancing at herself in the mirror behind the bedroom door she was dismayed to see she looked even dowdier in appearance than when looking at herself through the grimy shop window. Pulling off the woollen dress chosen earlier for its warmth, she replaced it with a newly laundered white blouse before choosing a neat grey skirt to wear with it. Reaching further into the wardrobe she drew out an elegant cashmere winter coat she had bought in Vienna to celebrate her debut as a solo artiste. A further sortie found her black lace-up ankle boots, which meant exchanging the warm woollen socks for her last remaining pair of sheer silk stockings. At the bedroom door, she stopped and this time took a longer look at herself. Satisfied at the transformation from dowdiness to the image now staring back at her, she remembered something Ephraim had said soon after their marriage... 'you have no idea of the effect you have on other men.' Perhaps today she thought, that statement would be put to the test; if only to help the man who said it.

TEN

The regimental sign at the entrance to the military complex showed it to be the Command Office of the General Staff. Nervously approaching its guarded entrance, she belatedly hoped it would be staffed by normal Army personnel and not the loathsome Gestapo.

As if in answer to her silent invocation, she was immediately escorted to a small reception area by a smiling young soldier where a tall loose-limbed individual in an immaculately pressed uniform detached himself from a small group of Wehrmacht soldiers and came striding towards her.

'You are?'

'Bergmann. Hannah Bergmann.'

'Miss Bergmann, thank you for being on time, a rare occurrence these days. You will follow me, please.' He turned and headed towards a large internal door, walking at a pace which allowed Hannah to keep up with him.

'I am Capt. Heidrick. I had the pleasure of attending your performance several nights ago. A most enjoyable evening and far removed from all this.'

'Was this the same concert which Colonel Von Hartmannn attended?'

'Yes it was. Clearly you made quite an impression on him. Unfortunately, he doesn't share the same appreciation for classical music as you and I; he's more the cabaret type.'

Smiling to herself, she wondered how Von Hartmann would react to such a remark but thought it prudent not to comment; more so because they were now passing through what was obviously an Operations Centre.

From banks of telephones monitored by shirtsleeved Army personnel and ticker-tape machines spilling streams of information on thin strips of paper, she guessed this to be the nerve centre of the unit. Every metre of wall space was covered with maps of Russia and its Soviet satellites which even to her non-military eye, appeared to show the disposition of both German and Soviet air and ground forces. Not realising she had slowed her pace, she felt Captain Heidrick exert slight pressure on her arm to hurry her through the sensitive area until they reached the comparative quietness of a nearby room which she guessed was the office of her escort.

'You will wait here please Miss Bergmann. I will tell the Colonel you are here.'

Left alone, she couldn't be sure whether it was the sudden realisation that her impetuous request to meet Von Hartmann was about to materialise or the fact she had completely forgotten her carefully rehearsed plea that made her feel physically sick but fortuitously a smiling Capt. Heidrick reappeared at that very moment, stopping any further panic before leading her into the office of Colonel Von Hartmannn.

The office was surprisingly large as was the desk which dominated the centre of the room. Behind it, Von Hartmann looked up from the document before him as she approached, waiting until she stopped before speaking.

'Tell me, why I am not surprised by you wishing to see me.' His tone of voice appeared devoid of recognition or warmth; quite different from the tenor of their previous encounter.

'May I sit down please or would you prefer me to stand?' His apparent coldness had the effect of belaying her stupor but the directness of her question and the firmness in her voice surprised even herself.

'Forgive me; sit down please and you may take your coat off if you wish.' In his precise military manner, it sounded like an order and not an invitation. 'To spare us both time Miss Bergmann, let me tell you what I already know and why I believe you are here.' Leaning back he placed both hands behind his head and stared into Hannah's deeply reflective eyes, coolly appraising her appearance as she sat down on the leather chair he pointed to.

'As you wish Colonel but I think you know that I am capable of speaking for myself.' Again the temerity in her voice overrode the caution she knew she should sensibly be exercising.

'Having already been on the receiving end of a justified rebuke from yourself, I am fully aware of what you are capable of, Miss Bergmann. I am merely trying to save time for both of us.' He reached across his desk and drew a cigarette from a silver box, the top of which bore a regimental crest. 'I suppose you don't touch these things, do you?' Without waiting for a reply, Von Hartmannn lit the cigarette and leaned back in his chair. Savouring the flavour of the tobacco, he inhaled deeply.

'I don't smoke but I have no objection to you doing so. After all, it's your office.'

Fixing Hannah with a penetrating stare it was several long seconds before he spoke. 'Yes, it is my office and you would do well to remember that.' Pausing, he drew again on his cigarette. 'If this is the way you wish to continue this discussion then I would suggest you take a deep breath and think again.'

Removing his arms from behind his head, he sat up in his chair. When he spoke his voice was again devoid of warmth. 'I presume you are here because you hope I can help to get your husband released. Yet your attitude, not only today but when we first met, has been little short of dismissive. You would do well to keep in mind that I am a senior officer serving a government which has decreed that stateless Jews which of course include both you and your husband, are now to be regarded as undesirable aliens and treated accordingly. So let me remind you, Miss Hannah Bergmann... you are not handling this situation as well as you might so I would suggest you give some thought to what you say next.'

Hannah hardly noticed that the Colonel had addressed her by her given name in the same awful realisation that any fleeting hope of obtaining help from this man had probably been dashed by her nervous boldness and pronounced lack of respect. Suitably chastened, she lifted her head and looked directly at the man delivering the reprimand.

'Colonel Hartmannn, my husband and I were born in this country. Our fathers fought for Germany in the Great War and until Kristalnacht we were Germans too. Do you think we are any less a people now than we were then? And if your wife or any member of your family had been arrested, wouldn't you do whatever you could to help them? So am I any different to you? And please allow me to say this too. I am grateful, deeply grateful but puzzled, for your help so far in respect of myself even if I appear not to show it.'

Maintaining his unnerving stare, he leaned back in his chair and it was some moments before he spoke again. 'You ask me what I would do if a member of my family were to be arrested. Let me turn that question back on you. What would you be prepared to do to obtain the release of your husband?'

Unable to decipher where this game of verbal tennis was heading, she decided to respond in similar vein. 'You have reminded me that as a Jew I have no standing in this country so what else can I do? As she spoke, Hannah wondered whether Von Hartmann's question was deliberately intended to be suggestive and if so, how best to respond to it. 'So can you suggest something I might do to obtain his release?'

Again she met the same inscrutable look but this time she thought she detected a note of concern. 'I will make certain enquiries later today but please understand that your husband is detained by the Gestapo and I have no direct authority in that direction.'

'But you obviously had sufficient influence to ensure my release.'

'As much as I would like to take credit for that, I'm afraid it isn't true. I understand it was never the intention to detain you but unfortunately your husband does not enjoy the same status as yourself. I merely expressed an interest in your case due to having met you so recently.'

'Tell me Colonel, did you know I was a Jew when you came to my dressing room?'

'Yes I did. My ADC told me during the course of your performance.'

'Then knowing that, weren't you taking an unnecessary risk in meeting with me?'

'I have already explained it had nothing to do with you being a Jew but everything to do with your performance and the way you appeared to relate to me. Let me be totally frank with you, Miss Bergmann, I don't need to have the same appreciation of classical music as either you or Captain Heidrick, to see you are an extremely beautiful and talented woman. So when I came to your dressing room it had nothing to do with politics or status, just simple curiosity on my part.'

Surprised by Von Hartmann's unexpected frankness, Hannah was temporarily lost for words but recovered quickly. 'I'm extremely flattered by your comments, Colonel; more so because they are somewhat unexpected.' Sensing that their conversation had now edged away from the initial coldness of Von Hartmann's earlier remarks, Hannah determined to try and increase the personal tempo.

'I hope you will not misinterpret this Colonel but suppose that you, a lonely Army officer, away from your wife and home, had come to my room that night and I admitted that I had been attracted by you, what would you have done? You say I'm beautiful and talented but you also knew I was Jewish. If I had encouraged you, how would you have reacted?' She paused, expecting Von Hartmann to respond but he remained silently impassive. So she tried again; 'and if I were to come on to you now, would that get my husband released? Is that what you inferred when you asked me what I would be prepared to do to make this happen?'

Inwardly shocked by her boldness and afraid she had again said too much, she nervously edged back in the leather chair.

Rising purposefully from his seat and maintaining eye contact, Von Hartmann came to the front of his desk and leaned back against it. 'Miss Bergmann, will you stand up please.' The tone of his voice once more reflected a steely edge and his instruction brooked no argument.

Instantly regretting her audacity, she rose and took two steps towards the man who moments earlier had appeared to offer a glimmer of hope but who now, through her own impetuousness, seemed about to close that access. Standing close to this puzzling man, she felt his warm breathe on her face and detected the clean smell of starch which seemed to be synonymous with military uniforms.

'I told you I would make a discreet enquiry about your husband and I will do that but you need to understand that even a Wehrmacht colonel has little influence with the Gestapo. As for sleeping with you, which I believe was the point of your question, it would be a pointless sacrifice on your part however pleasurable an experience it may have been for me. I cannot guarantee I can in any way help your husband but I will do my best.'

Instinctively, as with Max several days earlier, she reached out and grasped Von Hartmann's hand. 'Thank you Colonel... I am truly in your debt.' Although emotionless to her contact, intuitively, she knew a dangerous line had been crossed.

ELEVEN

It was the intense cold which woke Ephraim from his fitful sleep. Lying in the darkness of the basement cell he had no way of knowing whether it was night or day or how long he had slept for. From the pangs of hunger in his stomach he guessed it was probably about six hours since he had forced himself to eat the slop which passed for a meal. The threadbare blanket on the iron bedstead had offered little protection against the near freezing temperature and his body was now beginning to shiver with the intensity of the cold. The dim light which entered the cell each time the guard looked through the spy hole in the door incongruously reminded him of a darkened theatre just before the curtain rose.

Fully awake and with the prospect of further sleep unlikely, Ephraim let his mind turn to Hannah. At no time had he ever questioned her close relationship with Max Feldman but had he been too trusting or perhaps too naïve? The darkened cell seemed only to magnify the insinuations put to him by the Nazi interrogator. If Hannah's encounter with the Army officer had been so innocent then why had she not mentioned it? But on the other hand, he knew she met with any number of people in the course of her profession so wouldn't it be somewhat unrealistic to expect her to mention each one?

But there again he recalled Hannah's despairing words on wanting to get out of Germany on the morning of Sydney Glikstein's murder. Given the opportunity which her career could maybe still allow, could she be planning to escape out of this God-awful country... perhaps even with Max Feldman? Both had internationally acclaimed reputations and could find refuge in any number of non-occupied countries. And why had he been detained when Hannah had been allowed to leave, apparently due to the intervention of this Nazi officer? And why would this person risk his career to openly assist a Jew? Unless the Jew in question was more than just a friend to this man. In her innocent naivety, he knew Hannah had little awareness of the effect she had on men but was she now beginning to capitalise on a growing realisation of this? And if so... with whom?

Like a turning carousel the questions kept spinning round and round in his mind until in sheer frustration, he stood up and felt his way to the centre of the cell. Taking several deep breaths to calm himself, he began to slowly exercise his upper body by gently swinging his arms in a circular motion, slowly at first but increasingly faster as he grew confident that he had sufficient room in the blackness of the cell.

Engrossed in his routine, it was the sudden influx of light which caused him to stop. It took several seconds for his eyes to adjust before he saw the outline of two burly guards appearing to fill every centimetre of the open doorway. Each gripped a heavy truncheon and from their grim, unsmiling expressions, Ephraim sensed their willingness to use them should he give them the slightest reason to do so.

'Step outside... now!' The snarled command came from the taller of the two men who emphasised his command by smacking the truncheon in the palm of his gloved hand,
'This way Jew boy! And no talking.' Sandwiched between the two men, Ephraim was forced to change step to avoid walking into the feet of the guard ahead of him.

Manhandled into the interrogation room he recognised the same two Gestapo officials from the first meeting seated behind an even larger desk than he recalled from their previous encounter.
'Sit down.' This time it was the uniformed official taking the lead while his civilian counterpart fixed Ephraim with a cold, baleful stare. Glancing through the paperwork in front of him, the man let several long seconds elapse before he spoke. 'You

are a doctor of medicine, are you not? Where did you qualify?'

'Leipzig for my doctorate degree and Berlin for my post-graduate qualification.'

'And what is your particular speciality?'

Ephraim hesitated, wondering where these questions might be leading. 'I am, or was, a general practitioner working in the General Hospital here in Berlin until being prevented by Government decree from treating German nationals.

'But none of this happens now.' This time it was the civilian interrogator smugly joining the inquisition.

'You must know the answer to that question without input from me.' Sensibly, he knew it could be perilous to antagonise these men but once more anger overcame caution. 'As a Jew I am allowed to treat only Jewish patients but not allowed or able to obtain medicine for them so there is little I can do as a medical practitioner which in reality means my career as a doctor has come to a stop... at least until the end of this war.'

His provocative remark struck home. 'Doctor... ', the interrogator's voice became coldly menacing. 'Your continuing insolence is straining my patience to its limit so take this as a final warning. You will only answer the questions which are put to you without added comment; understand?' Leaning over, he whispered something to the other official.

From his side of the table, Ephraim felt a renewed stab of fear in the pit of his stomach knowing these men held the power of life and death of not just him but Hannah and Aaron too. Having witnessed the murder of their harmless old neighbour, he knew that threat was tangibly real.

'So you are now unemployed with time on your hands. Is that correct?

'Correct.' Perversely, his short affirmation to the question now seemed to disappoint both men.

'In which case, would you like the opportunity to practice being a doctor again' adding with a sardonic leer, 'with real medicine and who knows, with more practice you may even get to become as proficient as your former Aryan colleagues.'

Taken off-guard, Ephraim thought he must have misheard the question so it took several moments for his brain to understand what was being suggested.

'Of course but how would that be possible and why would you make an exception for me?'

'Doctor, understand this.' The intimidating voice of the civilian official cut across the desk. 'We do not make exceptions for any Jews, especially arrogant pigs like you.'

Hearing this, he knew he was still managing to irritate them even with an innocuous question. A brief smile flitted across his face.

Seeing this, the civilian interrogator sprang to his feet. Leaning across the desk he struck Ephraim a glancing blow to his head. 'I'm pleased you seem amused doctor so perhaps this will spoil your little joke. You are going to be transported to Thereisenstadt where you will serve as the camp Medical Officer.' He glanced up; savouring the look of surprise on Ephraim's face. 'I take it you know where Theresienstadt is?'

Theresienstadt... the name seemed vaguely familiar but nothing more than that. Racking his brain for inspiration he suddenly recalled Frank Lampl, a fellow Jewish medical student from Bohemia. He remembered Frank showing him where Bohemia was on an old map of Czechoslovakia and suddenly he recalled the name of Thereisenstadt. He had no idea why his brain had retained this obscure fact but for whatever reason, it was now about to surface.

'As it happens I do know where Theresienstadt is.' A look of disappointment appeared on the interrogator's face. 'It's in what Germany now euphemistically calls the Protectorate of Bohemia and Moravia but why in God's name would I want to go there? My home and family are here in Berlin so why would I leave them at a time like this to go to some miserable destination in the East... even if it might mean being able to practice medicine again and presumably to Jews I take it?'

From his side of the table he watched with growing nervousness as the two men glanced at each other but surprisingly neither reacted to his comment. Encouraged by their silence, Ephraim pushed even further. 'And just what is it I'm supposed to have done to warrant this so-called opportunity?'

This time his question did provoke an answer. 'Because you are a low-life Jew and the Fuhrer has determined that vermin like you must be expelled from Germany and resettled in the East. And whilst your concern for your wife is touching, I think you may have some difficulty in convincing her to accompany you as she seems to have found'... a mocking tone crept into his voice... 'a new 'friend' here in Berlin.'

'If by 'friend' you mean the Army officer who came to her dressing room recently, then you are wrong. I happen to know my wife far better than either one of you two 'gentlemen'.' The sarcasm was evident but surprisingly ignored by both men, clearly intent on seeing his reaction to their next question.

'So you think I'm wrong, do you?' He leant back, a look of unalloyed triumph on his face. 'Then perhaps you can explain why she spent much of today with this man... in his private quarters?'

Convinced this was meant to unsettle him, Ephraim felt his throat begin to constrict. He visibly gulped, hoping to create a temporary respite. 'May I have some water please?'

'Not before you answer my question.'

'Which is?'

'Why do you think your wife chooses to spend so much time with this Colonel Hartmann whilst you remain here?'

'Not being able to speak to my wife since my arrest, I have no idea why she would want to spend time with an Army person. But if what you say is true, then she was probably seeking help to try and secure my release.'

'From a senior officer she claims to have met just once?' Leaning back in his chair, the civilian emitted a high pitched laugh. 'Are you naïve or just plain stupid, doctor?' He gave a disbelieving laugh. 'Whatever favours your faithful wife may be extending to this man, sexual or otherwise, are quite pointless as this particular officer has no authority within the Gestapo.'

Sensing they expected him to react, instead he kept his temper under control and remained silent.

Clearly disappointed, the interrogator tried again. 'So tell us doctor, why would she expect help from this officer unless she was confident of his assistance and to repeat myself, after just one brief meeting?' He laughed again, this time in obvious derision. 'Come now doctor, not only are you stupid but you appear to be in complete denial.'

Anticipating an angry reaction, both officials leaned back in their chairs, staring at a still silent Ephraim.

After what seemed an interminable silence and clearly disappointed, it was the uniformed interrogator who spoke again.

'We're getting away from the point of this interview.' Shuffling through his handwritten notes before looking up, his voice reflected a growing note of frustration. 'We can arrest your wife to accompany you so that is not an issue but let me tell you this. It will be much easier for you and your family if you go willingly to Theresienstadt.

'And if I refuse?'

If you refuse then you really are an incredibly stupid man... even for a Jew. If that is what you're saying then you make our job very easy. Your wife and child will be sent to one of the newer camps in Poland which your high-living wife would find extremely disagreeable at least for the short time she and your child would remain there.' Staring at Ephraim, his voice took on a mocking edge. 'Do you really need me to spell out the other option available to you?'

'I think I am intelligent enough... even for a Jew... to know what that option is.'

'No need to think, doctor, let me make it perfectly clear so that you fully understand what I'm saying to you. If we decide not to send you to Thereisenstadt then you won't be leaving this building alive. You will be taken to the prison yard where you will be shot in the back of your head.' He gave a sardonic smile. 'Even a stupid Jewish doctor would know that such a procedure is invariably fatal. Does that help with your decision making?'

Despite the chilling coldness in the room, Ephraim felt beads of warm sweat begin to form at the nape of his neck. He took a sharp intake of breath. 'And if I agree, will I be released until being... 'resettled'?'

'We'll think about that and should we decide it appropriate then perhaps we'll let you say a fond farewell to that capricious wife of yours. There are certain formalities to be finalised but in the meantime you will be returned to your cell assuming of course that you agree to your new calling.' Seeing Ephraim frown, he gave a satisfied smile.

The opportunity to resume his medical career as an alternative to ignominious death was starkly obvious. Daring to return the taunting looks of the two Nazi interrogators, he spoke with forced deliberation 'To be able to work as a doctor or face a bullet in my skull is hardly a decision I need think about too much.

'For a belligerent Yid like you, doctor, that could well be a sensible choice.'

'So having made it, can I now meet with my wife?'

'You will meet with her when we say you can; but be assured we will keep you informed of her latest contacts as soon as we know of them. Provided of course you want to know who your wife is consorting with whilst you remain under arrest in this building.'

Behind Ephraim the door swung open and the same two guards appeared, summoned by a hidden alarm button on the other side of the desk. Realising that the interrogation was over, a sense of relief began to course through his whole being. Standing up, he turned towards the door only to be halted by the oily voice of the civilian interrogator. 'Oh, there is one last point. As a doctor we wouldn't want you to worry too much about hygiene standards here. We ensure every cell is thoroughly fumigated between each of our Jewish guests!'

TWELVE

Before the evening concert commenced, Hannah spoke hurriedly with Max Feldman to tell him she wished to remain seated during the programme. Having spoken with Von Hartmann earlier and sensing he may again be in tonight's audience she had no further wish to meet him knowing that he too was under surveillance by the Gestapo. She wanted, indeed needed, to believe that Von Hartmann would make a further enquiry regarding Ephraim's release but in the meantime she did not wish to cause him any conceivable level of embarrassment.

During brief interludes in the programme her thoughts constantly turned to Ephraim. At other moments, she found herself casting furtive glances over the sea of faces in the front stalls of the packed audience but this time hoping not to spot the man whom she had tried so hard to meet earlier that day.

Concentrating on the difficult score in front of her, the interval seemed to come quickly, giving her the opportunity to leave the platform for the welcome solitude of her dressing room. She needed to be alone, if only to be able to think more fully of the mental anguish she knew Ephraim must be experiencing. Sitting in the comfortable old armchair, she felt her body relax and within seconds the physical exertions of the day began to catch up on her. She knew she had nine minutes after the orchestra commenced the second half of its programme before being required to make her final appearance. In normal circumstances, this would be an opportunity to run through any difficult passages but tonight she knew she simply would not be able to focus. She recalled a gifted American musician who had guested with the Berlin Philharmonic before the war and how impressed she had been by his ability to 'wing it' during the actual performance rather than practice during the interval. 'Exactly what I'm about to do' she thought.

Confident that the Stage Manager would call her in time for the second performance, she let her head rest against the high back cushion and within seconds she felt herself drifting into the welcoming arms of Mordor.

It seemed only a matter of seconds before the sound of tapping began to intrude into her private sanctuary; distant at first but progressively louder with each knock. Startled, she had to think where she was and worse, whether she had missed her cue? Reaching quickly for her violin and bow, she drew a deep breath as she hurried to the door. Glancing in the mirror she pushed several loose strands of hair back into place and in mild panic snatched the dressing room door open only to collide with a surprised Von Hartmann... hand poised in mid-knock!

'Miss Bergman. We meet again. May I enter?'

Embarrassed but now more aware of his cultured air of formality, it took her a moment to collect herself.

'I understand you are required back on stage soon and I need to return to my quarters too but I did tell you I would make a further enquiry regarding your husband.

'Please come in. I have about nine minutes before I'm due back..'

'Are you sure about me coming in to your dressing room?' He gave a slight chuckle. 'The last time I did that, you ordered me to leave.'

She gave him a coy smile. 'Unlike that last occasion, tonight I'm fully dressed!'

Closing the door behind him, Von Hartmann positioned his angular frame on the edge of the dressing table. In the unforgiving light from the battery of bulbs around the mirror, she saw all too clearly the weariness in his face.

'As you know, your husband is detained at Gestapo HQ but not being questioned as far as I can tell. You should regard that as good news bearing in mind the beatings or worse, which usually accompany interrogations by these people'.

The candid manner in which Von Hartmann described the feared Gestapo and their methods surprised Hannah.

'Were you able to establish whether he will be released'?

'I understand that will not happen for a while; perhaps several more days but there is something unusual about this case which I find interesting'.

'Interesting?' Alarm bells began to ring in her head. 'What do you mean by that and why do you say it's unusual?' Her initial optimism began to fade as quickly as it had taken root.

'It's difficult to tell at this stage so perhaps I shouldn't say too much. Just accept that your husband is well and not being badly treated and hopefully he will be released within days. If I hear anything further, I will try and get word to you through Captain Heidrick as I will be leaving Berlin very soon.'

Surprised by his announcement, it occurred to her that she might be seeing Von Hartmannn for the last time. 'Colonel, I'm genuinely sorry to hear that; you have been so kind and I truly am grateful. Am I allowed to ask where you will be going?'

'You can ask but I am not able to tell you as I'm sure you will understand.' He gave a hint of a sigh. 'Regrettably it means I will not be able to continue my education in fine music which Berlin and you in particular have endeavoured to introduce me to.'

'Two minutes Miss Bergman'. The voice of the back-of-house manager loudly interrupted their conversation.

Encouraged by Von Hartmann's unexpected informality, Hannah posed the question which had been troubling her since their meeting earlier that day. 'Colonel, when we met earlier you asked me what I would do to get my husband released and as you know I turned that question back on you. But if you were to ask me that same question now what would you hope I would say?

She saw a puzzled expression cross Von Hartmann's handsome features so she quickly carried on before he could reply. 'Look, I know you can't facilitate Ephraim's release but I am deeply touched by your kindness... more so as I am a Jew. I would dearly like to repay you in some small way but I don't know how.'

Hannah wasn't prepared for the long silence which followed. After what seemed an eternity, Von Hartmann slowly eased his body off the corner of the dressing table and regaining his full height, he looked down at Hannah.

'I obtained what little information I could for you because whatever this Nazi Government may decree, we both know that you and your husband are as much German as I am. You also touched a nerve when you asked what I would do if a member of my own family were to find themselves in a similar position as that of your husband. So, however tempting your offer, my answer would still be the same.'

Rising from her chair, she looked directly into his tired eyes. 'Colonel, it may seem little to you but in my husband's present circumstance your words are reassuring and I truly mean that.' Daringly, she reached out and clasped his hands in hers.

Barely audible, she whispered 'please close your eyes. I want to offer you something in return... a Hebrew blessing in one simple word. Shalom my dear man; may you have an inner peace wherever this war may take you. And may you find safety in that place of peace which you will know as Shiloh.'

Moved by her words, Von Hartmann softly squeezed Hannah's hands and brought them level to his face and touched them to his lips. 'And may that peace find you too, Hannah Bergmann'. With that, he turned and in a moment was gone.

THIRTEEN

The report lying on the desk of SS Major Oskar Nagel made fascinating reading; especially when he allowed his imagination to fill in those sections of the report when his surveillance team had not been able to report or record on those happenings which had taken place behind closed doors.

The badly typed report stated that 'The Jew woman named Hannah Bergmann left her apartment located in the unnamed close off Goethestrasse at 18.25 hours and walked to the State Opera House where she was seen to engage in an animated conversation with a person later identified as Max Feldman, conductor of the Berlin Philharmonic Orchestra. When questioned, Feldman, also a Jew, stated that the basis of this discussion was of a professional nature relating to the programme due to be performed that evening.'

The report went on to state 'Bergmann participated in the first half of the concert and left the platform during the interval and went to her dressing room. There she was joined by an Army officer subsequently identified as Colonel Von Hartmann, Officer I/C General Staff Abwehr Intelligence Unit based at Gatow/Spandau.' It had not been possible to record any part of the conversation or report on any activity, which may have occurred.'

'Colonel Von Hartmann spent six minutes in the dressing room before leaving in what was observed to be an emotional state.'

The report concluded by stating that 'Hannah Bergmann exited the dressing room almost immediately following the departure of the above Officer, and returned to the concert platform. The program concluded at 22.56 hours when she left the Opera House at 23.14 hours and walked to her home alone.'

Putting the report to one side, the Major turned to his aide. 'What are we to make of this woman, Hugo? I've seen her perform on stage so I can understand why Hartmann would be attracted to her but what can he thinking of? She is a Jew and we know what they can do to a man... ' a cautionary note entered his voice; 'and his career.'

'I don't understand your puzzlement, Oskar. She's a woman needing a favour and he's a man who has obviously seen an advantage in that situation. He's a soldier for God's sake... not a priest in holy orders! If she had come to you instead of Von Hartman would you have turned her away? Of course she will deny any sexual activity with this man but who can believe the word of a Jew anyway, no matter how attractive she may be. So for me it's not a big mystery.'

There was a long, awkward moment before the Major deigned to reply. When he did finally speak his voice had an unusually hard edge.

'Lieutenant, we have known each other from the day we became soldiers together. The fact that I am senior in rank has rarely presented either of us with a problem when it comes to speaking our minds. But be careful my friend. Don't ever repeat what you have just said in the presence of others. I hate these Jews even more than I hate the Bolsheviks. At least with the Commies we know who the enemy is and why we are fighting this war but the Jews are the enemy within our Fatherland. They should be likened to a malignant disease gnawing at our innards so don't you ever dare think or suggest I would touch a Jew, any Jew, no matter how appealing they may appear to men like you.'

The Major's icy reprimand and his reversion to rank momentarily surprised the Lieutenant. 'Sorry Major, I meant no offence; I feel the same as you about Jews but not all soldiers are the same as you and me.'

'You and me, Hugo?' He repeated the Lieutenant's words back to him. 'Since when have you ever remotely been like me? You're a follower, Hugo, whereas I am a leader so you need to understand the difference if you wish to avoid a conversations like this in the future.'

Duly chastened, the Lieutenant's face showed what he hoped the Major would see as genuine contrition. 'Major, I have already apologised for my error so with your permission, can we move on. What action do you intend to take against this Jew-loving Colonel?

'What do I intend to do?' He gave a knowing smile. 'Nothing, Hugo... absolutely nothing. Whatever our Colonel may have promised this woman amounts to nothing,' emphasising his last word with a vacuous wave of his hand. 'He has no jurisdiction within this unit so we can forget him, more so as he will be returning to the Eastern front where the Ruskies or their winter weather will no doubt take care of him.'

Seeing the look of disappointment on the face of his subordinate, he felt a twinge of conscience for the coldness of his admonishment. 'But the woman we can do something about, Hugo. I want you to pay her a visit and find out what she's been doing to cause this besotted Colonel to risk his career.' Examine her as you see fit. That will make her more pliable for later questioning but whatever method you apply, make sure you don't kill her; that will be my prerogative. And when you think she's ready to speak openly about our lovelorn Colonel, call me immediately and bring her in for further questioning.. You can then watch a master at work.'

FOURTEEN

During every spare moment of that long wintry day, Hannah's thoughts constantly shuttled between Ephraim and Aaron. She drew some comfort in knowing that Aaron was relatively safe in Frieda's maternal care but increasingly frustrated by knowing that to visit him would inevitably be upsetting for them both. But with the darkness of the unlit streets affording a degree of protection from being stopped by the Police, she could resist no longer especially as she knew that tonight could well be the last time she would see him whilst she was still at liberty to do so. Thinking beyond tonight was just too dreadful to even contemplate.

Having made her decision and wrapped in her darkest coat she was about to leave when she heard the sound of approaching footsteps in the stairwell and stop outside her apartment. Stricken with fear she froze, sorely tempted not to open it. Subconsciously, she knew it would be the Police; maybe even the same men who had murdered her neighbour in the adjoining apartment. Two sharp knocks followed.

In her chest she could feel her heart racing and she attempted to control it by breathing deeply and exhaling slowly.

A further heavier knock was followed by a shouted order to open the door. Barely had she lifted the internal latch before the door was forced inwards causing her to step quickly back.

Standing in the open doorway were two uniformed officers whom she was now able to recognise as Gestapo. Pushing the door fully open, both men stepped into the hallway. The severity of their black uniforms contrasted sharply against the silver piping around the epaulettes of their uniform jackets and the silver runes of the SS badges affixed to each lapel. She noticed they were breathing heavily from the exertion of having climbed the stairs the six flights of stairs to the third floor.

'Hannah Bergmann? You are Hannah Bergmann aren't you?' It was a statement of fact; not a question. Without waiting for a response, the leading officer glanced about him and nodded for her to lead into the lounge.

'You shouldn't be too surprised to see us Miss Bergmann. After all, you seem to make a habit of meeting military personnel, particularly senior Army officers whether it be in their units, in your dressing room and who knows where else? Perhaps even in this apartment now that your husband is no longer here.'

Cowed by the suddenness of their entry, she tried quickly to regain her composure. Stopping in the centre of the lounge, she turned and faced them. 'If you are referring to my two meetings with Colonel Von Hartmannn, then you must already know that neither took place here.'

Without warning the man's hand snaked out, roughly grasping the front of her blouse and pulling her to within inches of his face. His tight grip, reinforced by one finger hooking round the front of her bra, prevented her from pulling back. Standing behind her, she felt the second man grab hold of both arms and pull them behind her back and felt the cold metal of handcuffs snapping around her wrists.

'You could be severely punished for resisting arrest. And should you actually be tempted to strike a Gestapo officer... ' he paused, letting the silence add further menace. 'That would warrant a very slow and painful death so maybe you should thank my Sergeant for preventing you from committing an act of extreme stupidity.' He smiled. 'So having saved you from yourself do you have anything you would wish to say on that particular subject?'

Still in shock from the suddenness of the assault, Hannah felt the hold on her blouse and bra savagely tighten as her assailant pulled her even closer.

'Please... take your hands off me... you're hurting me;' her voice betrayed the stark terror within her. 'What is it you want? If it's about the officer who was killed, there's nothing I can tell you; I never even met him.'

'Just close that pretty little bouche for a moment and remember what happened to your neighbour who, unlike you, hardly said a word.' His forehead creased as if he was trying to remember something; 'Ah yes, it's coming back to me now. He was a Jew too wasn't he, name of Glickstein I seem to recall or was he too old for you to even notice unlike your friend Colonel Von Hartmann. Now that is a person you can tell me about.'

In growing dread, Hannah could not get her words out fast enough. 'I can't tell you anything because the Colonel you speak of is not a friend or even an acquaintance. He was just an officer who came to see me after one of my concerts.' She tried to take a deep breath but the tightness of her assailant's grip prevented her from doing so. 'After my husband was arrested, I asked him if he could help to get him released. I swear that was the full extent of our relationship'.

'And why should he help a Jew like you unless of course there's something which you aren't telling me?'

'I've told you everything. There really is nothing more I can say to you.'

Even in her shocked state Hannah wasn't prepared for what happened next. Prevented from looking down by the closeness of her interrogator's face, she felt her skirt roughly jerked up and with his free hand he gripped the soft flesh of her inner thigh, the coldness of his probing fingers stifling the rising scream in her throat.'

'This, my Jewish whore is what our dear colonel was smitten with. Not your music but what you have between these shapely legs. Perhaps you need a little encouragement to help you to remember what you're forgetting to tell me?' Unable to respond, she felt his grip savagely tighten, squeezing the soft, tender flesh even more. The excruciating pain was total, unleashing the pent-up scream stifled in her throat.

'So my little angel, at last we have a reaction which I suppose is progress of sorts but hardly enough to satisfy my Major. You must learn that it pays to be cooperative when I ask you a question so tell me, what happened between you and the Colonel or do I need to jolt your memory again?'

Without giving her time to reply, Hannah felt his hand apply further pressure sending a paralysing pain radiating down her leg, her agonising scream echoing throughout the apartment.

'Stop for God's sake! Stop, stop, stop!' Screaming as she attempted to suck air into her frantically beating chest, she experienced instant relief as the Lieutenant loosened his grip.'

'OK, begin to talk.'

'Can you please take your hands off me and give me some space; I can't think when I'm being held like this.'

'I'm certain your music-loving Colonel would have held you much closer but I do believe you are about to be sensible so sit down and tell us what happened between the two of you.'

Stepping back, she quickly moved to Ephraim's favourite armchair, deliberately avoiding the sofa to ensure that neither of her assailants could sit beside her.

Shaking from the suddenness and pain of the assault and desperate to gain time, Hannah frantically racked her brain for words that would satisfy her tormentor. Looking up at the two men she forced herself to take a deep breath before speaking.

'I assume you are carrying out this Major's orders in coming here to molest and arrest me?

The simultaneous look of amusement which appeared on both men's faces was ominous but she pressed on.

'What will he or your brother officers think if I should report you tried to rape me... a Jewish whore in your book but to the world at large, an internationally famous musician. And you, a pure Aryan Gestapo officer.'

It took several worrying seconds for the significance of Hannah's words to register. With menacing slowness the Lieutenant stood up and advanced towards Hannah, the measured tread of his highly polished boots resonating on the bare floorboards beyond the edge of the large carpet.

'Stand up.' The quietness of the command merely served to accentuate the fear of further violence.

With her hands still restrained by the handcuffs and unable to use her arms to assist in rising, Hannah briefly fell back into the soft cushion of the chair. Regaining her footing at the second attempt, she took an unflinching step towards her tormentor, deliberately engaging his mean stare.

'So, let me understand what you're saying. You threaten to report that we tried to rape you, is that correct?' The prolonged silence which followed only served to magnify her mounting terror. 'Let me tell you something, you arrogant bitch. We could beat the very life out of you right here in this apartment and nobody would give a damn, least of all our commanding officer. So you need to get it into your pretty head that you are a Jew and you have no rights in this country, OK?'

Hannah, unable to maintain eye contact, let her gaze drop.

'I said OK. Did you hear me?'

'I hear you and understand precisely what you are saying. Thank you for reminding me of what it's like to be a Jew in your pure Aryan world.

Heinz's response was instantaneous. Constrained by the handcuffs, she was powerless to stop him taking hold of her blouse and tearing it violently open, forcing the expensive silk material and bra straps down over her shoulders to deliberately expose her breasts. Mortified, she closed her eyes in a throwback to childhood days when she would employ this same tactic to avoid seeing things which scared her. But this was no childhood situation and neither could she avoid it.

'Now, what was it you wished to report to our Commanding Officer?' His lips pursed as though he was considering various options, 'If my memory serves me correctly, I think you said you would report having been raped, did you not?' He gave two disbelieving clicks of his tongue. 'But of course we know that to be a lie, don't we Sergeant.'

Hannah couldn't see whether the soldier standing behind her responded but felt his grip on her pinioned arms tighten even more.

'So that means we have a problem with you, our internationally renowned violinist. We can choose to administer instant punishment here and now for your intention to deliberately lie about two honest soldiers going about their daily business and to do that,' he paused in his menacing deliberation, 'we could start by breaking each of your delicate little fingers, one at a time which I guess would affect your ability to play your violin ever again, whether internationally or even in your local synagogue, would it not?'

Hearing this, the silence became even more suffocating. 'But on the other hand, we could give substance to your wicked lie by actually doing what you report had happened to you. I trust you follow my drift?'

Nodding in sheer terror, Hannah felt as if the very life was being sucked out of her body.

'So, my little siren of the synagogue, what is your choice? And by the way, I wouldn't want you to worry about us despoiling our pure Aryan blood. As soldiers, we are used to taking risks for the Fatherland, aren't we Sergeant?' This time she heard an assenting grunt from his subordinate.

Hannah felt the Lieutenant's hand reach under her chin and with unexpected softness raise her head forcing her to make eye to eye contact.

'I asked you a question Jew girl and I won't ask you again.' His clipped way of speaking and his tone of voice added even more tension. 'You should consider yourself a very fortunate Jew. Normally we don't give you people a choice.'

Despite the imminent threat facing her, she felt an unstoppable surge of anger well up within her but no sound emerged from her throat.

'So, what have you decided? Or would you prefer me to make the decision for you?' As if to guide her thoughts towards his own inclination, Hannah felt the Lieutenant's free hand clamp over her exposed breast and take her nipple between finger and thumb, sending an erogenous sensation begin to course through her trapped body. Gripped firmly from behind and unable to move, Hannah again closed her eyes in a vain attempt to suppress what her body was experiencing by the man now sensuously touching where no man other than Ephraim had touched her before.

'Come my little soloist; let's see how well you perform with real soldiers. Lay on the sofa and if you promise not to resist, I will ask my Sergeant to remove your handcuffs. Do I have your word?'

Before being able to respond, Hannah felt herself forcibly pushed towards the sofa. Daring to open her eyes she bizarrely noticed that the richly embossed fabric was woven with a raised pattern; something she had never noticed before. 'Dear God, I'm going mad' she thought.

'I'm still waiting, Jew girl; cuffs or no cuffs?'

'Please take them off; they're cutting into my wrists'. Inside her fraught brain, another desperate plan was beginning to crystallise.'

'But first, your word;' a hint of impatience was now dangerously evident in his voice.

'Very well... you have my word.'

So Sergeant, we appear to have an acquiescent Jew; wonder of wonders! Remove the bracelets and strip her off. If she struggles you have my permission to break each of her fingers... one at a time but don't hurry.' Hannah saw him give the Sergeant an exaggerated wink. 'Get on with it.'

Feeling her numbed wrists freed from behind, Hannah attempted to pull her torn blouse back over her shoulders to cover her exposed breasts. The stinging blow to the side of her head instantly stopped any further attempt at modesty and briefly dazed, she felt herself being forcibly pushed down on to the soft cushions of the sofa.

'You're not listening Jew-girl. The idea is to take your clothes off, not cover yourself up.' He glanced up at his NCO. 'Sergeant, remind our friend what happens to people who go back on their word.'

This time the blow to the other side of Hannah's face was delivered with the inside of the soldier's open hand. The ceiling seemed to spin like an illuminated orb with flashing lights reaching in to the very core of her brain. Vaguely, she felt her skirt being pulled from under her and eased over her ankles and her legs being lifted on to the sofa. From a distance she heard the voice of the Gestapo officer angrily berating his subordinate.

'I said to remind her, you heavy handed dolt... not knock her senseless!'

'Sorry Lieutenant, just give her a moment to recover; she'll soon come round.' Standing back in mock admiration, the Sergeant pursed his lips and gave a low whistle. 'Would you look at these now... black nylon stockings? Where do these goddamn Jews get things like this in wartime?

'Vienna. They were bought in Vienna.' She recognised her own mumbling voice responding to the distant question. Slowly, painfully, her senses began to re-focus. She became aware of a hand on her shoulder preventing her from sitting up and with her own hands now free to move, she felt her own nakedness.

'Ah, so our little angel re-joins the living world. Are you ready to receive visitors yet or would you like a few minutes more?' She heard the second soldier laugh and for the first time was able to see him clearly; a powerfully built man with short cropped hair, probably in his mid-thirties. As her vision cleared she saw the menacing features of his face... the face of a man clearly enjoying her all too obvious distress.

The hand on her shoulder was that of the Gestapo officer, leaning over her prostrated body, his jacket removed and his white shirt partially undone. More slender in build than his NCO, he had an autocratic demeanour about him which tallied with his arrogance but despite his good looks, his face exuded undoubted malice.

'My comrade is about to leave us for a while but be assured you will be in good hands.'

As if on cue, Hannah heard the front door of the apartment close, its familiar sound serving only to emphasise the imminent danger she faced in being alone with this volatile and dangerous man. With her head becoming clearer, she was able to see him as he stood over her vulnerable body.

'For a Jew you have a good body which I suspect you would like me to believe you have shared only with your husband.' He gave a disbelieving laugh. As he spoke he lowered himself to a kneeling position so that he was now able to look directly into her eyes. Unbuttoning the last shirt button she saw that his chest was devoid of hair.

Barely recognising her own voice as the constriction in her throat eased, she sighed in apparent submission and muttered 'of course it isn't true.'

'You fascinate me, Jew girl; are you about to admit that your colonel friend also drew solace and comfort from your body perhaps?' She felt his cold hands dwell once more on her breasts which seemed to have a fascination for him before moving slowly downwards.

'No he didn't and neither does my husband and d'you want to know why?' Her delivery was slurred. 'Because both knew I have syphilis which I picked up from an American musician in Vienna 8 months ago. My husband was treating me for it until he was unable to get the appropriate medication. So whilst I can't stop you from having me, don't say you haven't been warned'. Seeing no reaction to her lie, she attempted to sit up to retrieve her skirt from the floor.

Galvanised by her movement, the Lieutenant awoke from his inertia. 'Pushing her roughly down again, his voice reflected a terrifying level of anger and frustration. 'Lay down. If you move again I will kill you!' For the first time since entering the apartment his self-control slipped to a dangerous level; instantly replaced by an icy coldness which in its intensity was even more frightening. She saw his face redden with suppressed anger, the veins in his forehead standing out in small rivulets. Slowly regaining his feet, he began to button up his shirt in a unhurried manner, all the time staring down at her naked body.

'You will get dressed and when Sergeant Koestler returns, he will take you to Gestapo HQ, you disgusting whore. The sooner we clear filth like you out of this country the better... including your husband and child.

Petrified by the starkness of the threat to Ephraim and Aaron, she didn't react quickly enough as his raised boot stamped down on to her unprotected midriff, its impact driving the breath from her body, leaving her gasping for air. In utter panic and sickening pain, she saw his shadowy form fumble with the front of his uniform trousers and seconds later she felt a warm wetness splatter on her bare breasts and face as he urinated on her prone body.

FIFTEEN

It was Sgt Koestler who escorted Hannah to Gestapo HQ. Following his return to the apartment, she heard the two men briefly exchange words before the Lieutenant, now fully dressed, make his exit with no more than a passing glance at her. It slowly dawned on her that the Lieutenant would have taken the car which meant that Koestler would have to wait for transport.

He gave his grudging assent for Hannah to go to the bathroom and stayed with her, watching her shower and then dress in fresh clothes. It was a trade-off she was willing to accept. At least she felt clean again. As for Koestler, he made no attempt to touch or molest her, no doubt warned off by the Lieutenant.

The journey to Prinz Albrechstrasse took longer than expected. She thought she recognised the driver as the soldier who had driven her and Max Feldman back to her apartment just days ago but he showed no sign of recognition when she got into the vehicle.

Despite the trauma of her experience with the Lieutenant, she was, in an odd way, unafraid by the prospect of being arrested knowing that Ephraim too was imprisoned in the same building. Both sides of her face had now become swollen and she was still unable to breathe deeply. Fortunately the Lieutenant's boot had struck her below her rib cage and although her stomach muscles were exceptionally painful, she knew a fractured rib would have been much worse. Glancing at her hands, she gave a rueful smile... at least her fingers were still intact!

Unlike the previous visit there was no registration formality to undergo. Instead, she was taken to the basement and roughly pushed into a holding cell. Surprisingly, the overhead ceiling light remained on. Hearing footsteps stop outside her cell door and then go away again, she realised that the light being on was not an oversight but to allow the guards to observe her. The cell was larger than the one in which she and Ephraim had been interrogated in just days before; probably to accommodate the iron frame bed at one end of the cell but a bed devoid of mattress or blankets. The sight of the bare bed frame made her think longingly of her own comfortable bed in the apartment and whether she would ever sleep in it again. Whether by omission or order, the guards had not confiscated her watch and from it she saw the time was now approaching 11pm.

From his position in the corridor, SS Major Oskar Nagel spent several moments studying Hannah through the aperture in the door. Despite its restricted view and the bluish swelling to her face, he could see that the prisoner was an extremely beautiful woman. The Major had an eye for attractive females. Since being assigned to Gestapo HQ some three months earlier, he had become a frequent visitor to the less salubrious night clubs and bars in the capital. War-time Berlin had quickly regained its former notoriety for licentiousness; more so now than in pre-war days. Paradoxically, the mounting resistance and attrition being exacted on its Eastern front by Soviet forces together with the increasing number of Allied bombing raids seemed to lend even greater urgency for military personnel especially, to enjoy life with scant regard for tomorrow. Although food rationing was becoming more stringent, alcohol was still in plentiful supply, especially in the clubs and cabaret bars. And it was this night life which drew Oskar Nagel like a bee to honey. And tonight would have been no exception had he not been forced to delay his plans for the evening in order to interrogate the Jewish woman he was now scanning through the spy-hole in the door of the holding cell.

Deciding he had seen as much as he needed to, the Major entered the cell and noticed with a touch of smug vanity that the woman immediately stood up from the iron bedstead she had been sitting on. Whether through fear or apprehension mattered not; if it induced a sense of passiveness, it would make his job that much easier.

'We seem to be short of chairs... just the one I see. I'll take this and you will sit on the bed. Now let me see,' he glanced down at the paper in his hand, 'you are Hannah Bergmann aren't you?'

'Yes, that is my name.'

'My name is Major Oskar Nagel and it was my intention to interview you. How long would have depended on what you would have disclosed of course. I understand you have already had the pleasure of meeting with Lieutenant Heinz earlier today; I trust it was not a too unpleasant experience for you?'

'It was extremely unpleasant as you undoubtedly know. But isn't that his job, to make life unpleasant for people like me?'

'In this report he states that you were uncooperative, that you resisted arrest and needed to be restrained. Is that correct?'

'Did he also tell you that he tried to have sex with me?'

A brief smile flitted across his face. 'There is no mention of that in this report so clearly he wasn't successful.' Looking up from his report, he slowly appraised his prisoner. 'Mind you, I can't say I blame him; apart from the bruising on your face you are a fine looking woman'.

'You forgot to add "for a Jew" Major.'

'Not only are you extremely attractive for a Jew but you also appear to be very spirited. That could be most unwise in this place.' Arising from his chair, he approached the bed and looked down at her. 'Now, let's get down to business. The purpose of your arrest was for me to question you about your relationship with Colonel Von Hartmann and with a little persuasion,' he hesitated in mid-sentence, 'I think you would have told me whatever it was I wanted to hear. But it seems that your Colonel friend is not only assigned to the General Staff unit here in Berlin but, surprise, surprise, he is also an Abwehr officer, and therefore out of reach from Gestapo jurisdiction. Not only out of reach, but a man with influential friends it would seem. So, tonight you will sleep in your own bed... at least for a little while longer.'

A feeling of relief and anger took over as she attempted to comprehend what she was hearing. 'If that's the case, then why don't you ask the questions you were going to put to me or would you prefer to 'persuade' me instead?' Seeing a smile appear on Nagel's face brought her anger dangerously close to the surface. 'Both you and your Lieutenant seem unable to understand why a senior Army officer like this Colonel Von Hartmann would help a Jew like me to find out about my husband, without expecting something in return. Well, thank God there are still decent people left in this world and one or two of them may even happen to be German.'

Hannah knew she had gone too far but amazingly the Major, an officer in the dreaded Waffen SS Gestapo, did not react. Instead, his face broadened into a smile, lifting each corner of his mouth.

'Tell me Bergmann, there is one question I will ask while you're here; do you really have what we soldiers call the 'clap'?'

Bolstered by her unexpected change of fortune, Hannah met the Major's enquiring gaze full on. 'If I did have what you soldiers refer to as the 'clap', then don't you think I would have been more than happy to have passed it on to such a pleasant man... with my very personal compliments!'

SIXTEEN

After the fetid atmosphere he'd been breathing for the past three days, the cold morning air felt good to Ephraim. There had been two further interrogations with the same Nazi inquisitors which had provided him with slightly more information than was disclosed at the first grilling.

He now knew that Thereisienstadt was to become a camp for prominent Jews to accord with the Nazi Government's resettlement policy to the occupied territories of Eastern Europe.

As the camp's intending Medical Officer, he felt inwardly excited at the prospect of being able to practice medicine again but deeply saddened at the thought of being separated from Hannah and Aaron. Both interrogator's had spoken about the possibility of a reunion at a later date subject to him fulfilling the role in a submissive manner but he knew he would be a fool to believe any undertaking made by men who at the first sign of non-compliance could facilitate his death with a simple stroke of a pen.

From his holding cell in the basement, Ephraim frequently heard the agonised screams of other prisoners being tortured; possibly on the orders of the same men offering him the prospect of a reunion with his wife and child! With his tempory release drawing closer, he desperately needed to dispel the doubts still lingering in his mind about Hannah and this military officer; doubts which centred on whether she really did have an involvement with a man sufficiently influential to ensure her continuing freedom. If that was the case then would she even consider leaving Berlin and her career with the orchestra to live in the middle of nowhere?

When the moment for his release came he was inexplicably blindfolded and roughly marshalled through a labyrinth of dark passageways in the bowels of the building with no way of knowing where he was until being halted by a firm hand on his shoulder. In the same moment, the blindfold had been removed and strong hands roughly pushed him down the steps at the entrance of the once majestic building.

It took him a few moments for his eyes to become adjusted to the grey drabness of late morning. Looking up, Ephraim saw flocks of gulls wheeling in the sky, their raucous screeches seeming to taunt him with their mobility and freedom.

It took nearly an hour to walk to the apartment. His keys and other personal items taken by the guards had not been returned so he was forced to bang on the front door of the building hoping to attract the attention of other tenants. Almost at the point of giving up, he thankfully heard the deadlock mechanism being activated and he was able to push the half-glazed front door open. The hallway felt unusually strange, no longer exuding that feeling of security and warmth he normally experienced within its familiar interior.

With his pulse racing from the effort of climbing the stairs to the third floor, Ephraim hesitated in the small hallway to catch his breath and to summon sufficient nerve to ring the bell. Waiting there, it seemed forever before he detected the sound of footsteps in the hallway of the apartment.

'Hannah; it's me... Ephraim. Open the door.

He heard the familiar click of the lock being disengaged and watched impatiently as the door opened as far as the security chain would allow.'

Cautiously releasing it, the door swung open to reveal his tearfully beautiful wife. From the bruising on her face, he could see that she too had been 'interviewed' but at least they were together again... if only for a brief time.

Later, sitting together on the sofa, the same sofa from which she had tried so desperately to escape from the harrowing assault of Lieutenant Heinz, Hannah felt too numb to recount what had occurred. Instead she chose to sit quietly in Ephraim's strong arms, listening to him recount details of his confinement and content to let him believe her facial bruising had occurred during her second interview at Gestapo Headquarters. They spoke at length about Aaron and both felt deep gratitude to Frieda for her willingness to shelter him, a Jewish child, despite the beating she had experienced only days before

But burning in the mind of Ephraim was the thought of his impending transportation to Thereiseinstadt and whether he would be able to persuade Hannah to accompany him even if it meant having to leave Aaron in Berlin.

The prospect of being able to practice medicine again was particularly appealing, especially when compared to the insurmountable restrictions he currently faced in Berlin. But realistically he knew that the worsening atrocities now being openly committed by the Nazis would be no different wherever he was.

Whilst confined in his cell, he had attempted to compare life in Berlin with what little he knew about Thereiseinstadt and which of the two locations might offer the best chance of survival for both himself and Hannah assuming of course that he could persuade her to accompany him.

Fully aware of the consequence of refusing to go to Thereiseinstadt, his concern still centred on the insidious inferences put to him by the Gestapo interrogators regarding her relationship with a Nazi officer. But looking at her bruised face he drew a crumb of comfort. If such an influential friend existed then why had that person allowed her to be interrogated in such a vicious manner? But on the other hand, why had she been released without charge or the threat of transportation?

The mounting turmoil raging in Ephraim's mind was uncharacteristically stilled by Hannah easing her body away from his embrace. With a deft movement of her fingers, she skilfully unbuttoned her silk blouse and gently directed his hand onto the softness of her breast. In a barely audible whisper, she kissed him gently and murmured 'Ephraim... I need you to make love to me.' Putting her finger to his lips to silence his response, she added, 'don't say a word my poor darling; just do it for me.' The urgency in her voice was reinforced by her hand reaching downwards seeking physical confirmation of Ephraim's compliance.

'Hannah, please. Can we wait until later or at least go into the bedroom?'

'I don't want to use the bedroom or do it later. I want you to have me now... on this sofa.' To emphasise her desire, Hannah slowly moved her hand down below the waistband of his trouser, his slim waist narrowed even more by lack of food. The sensation of her probing fingers stifled the need for any further words or resistance. The same urgency propelling Hannah now began to drive his increasing desire. Slowly easing himself onto her eager body, he was immediately drawn in by her frantic fervour. In their years of staid love-making he had never experienced this level of animated passion before. This was sexual passion at a level which Ephraim had never known either with Hannah or any other woman.

She too was experiencing her own transformation. Eyes closed, she was responding to a growing awareness of her sensual attraction to men other than Ephraim. She thought of Von Hartmannn and even the thuggish Lieutenant Heinz who only hours before, had wanted to rape her on this very sofa, the thought of which now drove her to a level of desire she had never experienced before.

SEVENTEEN

It took Ephraim a whole day before he felt able to break the news of his imminent re-settlement to Theresienstadt. Still mortified by their recent encounters with the Gestapo, their discussion was surprisingly devoid of emotion. Telling her as gently as possible it took Hannah only seconds to realise that he had been given no choice other than to accept the Gestapo ultimatum which meant that their only real decision was whether she and Aaron should, or even could, go with him. The thought of taking Aaron away from the relative safety with Frieda became the deciding factor, at least for the moment but if conditions at Theresienstadt proved to be less dangerous than in Berlin then Hannah agreed she would attempt to follow him.

But realistically they both knew they would have little choice in the matter of a reunion. They were Jews, a people without status or rights. Jews being re-settled in increasing numbers to concentration and slave labour camps far beyond the boundaries of Germany.

Later that day they arranged to meet with Frieda in the local Lutheran church. She had already told her neighbours that Aaron was the child of her younger sister killed in a recent air raid; an explanation becoming increasingly plausible as the intensity of the Allied bombing raids reached unprecedented levels. In the awful realisation that transportation to Eastern Europe would probably mean they would never see their precious son ever again, they begged a reluctant Frieda to return home to collect Aaron and meet them in a heavily wooded picnic area once popular in pre-war days but now deserted and overgrown. Hugging their baby son, they were .barely able to contain their emotions as they made their silent farewells. Not even the sight of Aaron walking happily away, hand in hand with Frieda with barely a backward glance could ease the unspeakable sorrow in their hearts.

Returning to their apartment, Ephraim busied himself preparing a traditional Shabbat supper which included hamantaschen... small pastries filled with poppy seeds, and offered a Sephardic prayer which he had learned as a boy.

'We should have eaten these at Purim, but I guess we were too busy entertaining our Gestapo guests.' Ephraim's quip drew the faintest of smiles from Hannah.

'Purim is a happy festival so we shouldn't mention it in the same breath as those evil men.'

'I stand rebuked... sorry, my little girl.'

'A genuine look of loving warmth appeared on Hannah's face. 'Ephraim, you haven't used that expression since how long? After our marriage you would say that to me every day. What made you remember it now?'

'Perhaps I was simply reflecting on those happy days compared with what we are now facing.'

'In which case we need to be a little more positive about then and now? Our son is as safe as we can make him; you have an assignment where you can be a doctor again and for the moment I'm still free. If we compare that to what you say is happening to other Jewish families, then we should be grateful.'

Moved to tears by her chastening words, Ephraim went to the small oak cupboard where Hannah kept her violin. 'Sweetheart, will you do me the honour of playing something for the man who loves you more than life itself?'

Barely able to hold back her own tears, she reached out and ran her fingers down the side of Ephraim's face before taking hold of her beloved Bellini.

'Of course I will... would you like to choose or shall I?'

'Play something which captures this moment for both of us.'

Too upset to speak, Hannah tucked the violin under her chin and looking into Ephraim's eyes, she played a haunting

Russian lullaby which she had last played to Aaron in a vain attempt to send him to sleep against the competing sound of air raid.sirens. Finishing with a traditional Russian flourish, Hannah practically threw her violin down and poured herself into her husband's waiting arms. Neither spoke nor could speak... it wasn't until hours later when utterly spent from their emotional love-making that they fell into something reminiscent of a natural sleep.

EIGHTEEN

The following morning Ephraim returned to the same grim building he had been released from two days earlier. Locked in a cold basement cell, it seemed a long three hours before he was taken to the yard at the rear of the building where he joined a large group of people who from their dress and mannerisms Ephraim guessed were prominent Jews from upper class districts of Berlin.

Ordered to stand in the bitterly cold yard they were finally herded on to two open-backed military trucks under the watchful gaze of two SS guards. It took the best part of an hour to reach the rail siding at Schlesischer railway station by which time most of the detainees were chilled to the bone by the freezing wind. Ephraim had been first to clamber on to the second truck and had positioned himself behind the back of the driving cab, hoping it would provide some form of shelter from the icy wind when the truck began its journey to the railhead. Crouching down, he watched as the remaining internees climbed aboard. In the unseemly melee he noticed one elderly woman being pushed towards the side of the truck. Reaching out, he touched the arm of her coat and wordlessly offered his sheltered position to her. Moving to make way for her he was roughly shoved aside by a burly middle-aged man forcing himself into the space he had just vacated.

Pulling his fur-lined collar over his ears the man remained unresponsive to Ephraim's angry shouts. Watching this happen, the SS guard stepped forward and ordered the man to move to the side of the truck. Seeing no sign of compliance, the solder raised the butt of his rifle and struck the crouching man a glancing blow to the side of his head. Watching the dazed man crawl away, the soldier hit him again; this time between the shoulder blades and lashed out with his boot for good measure before returning to the rear of the truck.

Arriving at the railhead siding, the detainees were shepherded into a cold brick building, its asbestos roof pimpled with dark shapes of moss looking for the world like small mounds in an icy field of hoar frost. Here they were given a bowl of warm celery soup heavily peppered in an attempt to inject some flavour into its watery content. Warming his frozen hands around the soup bowl and lost in thoughts of Hannah and Aaron, Ephraim dimly became aware of angry shouts coming from the table near the door. Looking round he saw the same burly man, this time belligerently remonstrating with an SS Officer, probably the person in charge of the transportation. From his expressive hand gestures, Ephraim guessed the man was complaining about the soldier who had struck him during the journey to the railhead. In the general hubbub, Ephraim wasn't able to hear the conversation but watched transfixed as the man was roughly pulled out of the building by two tough-looking SS Guards followed by the urbane Captain. Seconds later the sound of a pistol shot reverberated through the room before the officer reappeared, holstering his Luger firearm.

'Does anyone else have a complaint about my soldiers?' He paused. 'Or about the food, perhaps?' He raised an eyebrow as if hoping for a response. 'If not, then you will make your way to the train.'

Having experienced the cold-blooded murder of his elderly neighbour just days before, Ephraim was not wholly shocked by the sight of yet another gratuitous execution being meted out but inwardly he felt profoundly relieved that Hannah had chosen to remain in Berlin and not have to witness this latest act of mindless brutality.

The 385 kilometre rail journey from Berlin to Theresienstadt which in pre-war days normally took just six hours, took four days to complete. Each day their train was forced to give priority to military transports on their way to the Eastern front and overnight the train would be shunted into a siding; sometimes not moving until mid-morning. The overcrowded compartments lacked any form of heating and by the second day, the toilets had ceased to function due to lack of water and the sickening smell of human faeces quickly pervaded every compartment of the train. No further food was made available and the single bucket of water allocated daily to each carriage was exhausted within the first hour of its distribution.

By the time the train finally arrived at Theresienstadt some 50 kilometres north of Prague, seven detainees had succumbed to dehydration and lack of food; their bodies callously thrown off the train whilst it was on the move.

The camp bore the hallmark of it being a former military base with its brick-built barracks now being hurriedly refurbished by gangs of foreign labourers working under the direction of Czech supervisors.

Surprisingly, the camp was policed not by German soldiers but by newly appointed Jewish guards, who Ephraim later discovered, reported to Czech Gendarmes. The Camp Commandant and his immediate subordinates were German SS officers but they appeared to maintain a deliberately low profile leaving both the day-to-day administration and security duties to non-German personnel.

The newly painted notice board at the entrance to the camp described it as 'The Reich Home for the Aged.' Ephraim would have liked time to explore the Camp more fully but within an hour of his arrival, he was summoned into the office of the SS Adjutant, Captain Hugo Kernick.

Attired in a uniform tailored to fit his overweight frame, his standard issue jack boots reflected the care bestowed on them by his Hungarian batman, their highly polished toe-caps and leather calves positively gleaming under the desk.

Ushered into the main office by a bespectacled clerk, there was an unnerving silence before the Adjutant chose to look up from his paperwork, his close-set eyes and pudgy features critically surveying the man who stood before him. Leaning back, he made no attempt to introduce himself.

'So, you are the doctor who will apply the balm of Gilead to all these poor, down-trodden Jews who have the good fortune to reside in this camp.'

Unsure whether a response was required, Ephraim opted for silence.

'Let me tell you what I expect. Firstly, you will report directly to me. I report directly to the Camp Commandant so that will be your line of authority. Clear so far, doctor?'

'Perfectly clear. Do I address you by your title of Adjutant or your rank of Captain?

'You will address me at all times as Captain and I will refer to you as 'doctor'. I will want to know who attends your clinic and what medication you have prescribed so you will maintain accurate records on a day-to-day basis. Should it be necessary for you to treat a German officer or soldier, then they will of course be given priority over other patients. I trust that won't be a problem, doctor?'

'Of course not, Captain, your instructions are chrystal clear. Can I assume you were a physician before you joined the armed forces?'

'That is of no our concern to you. Just accept that you will do precisely what I tell you to do... to the very letter.

There was no mistaking the growing angst in his voice.

'As you wish, Captain. I merely asked because if you aren't a qualified physician, then how can you know whether the medication I have administered during the course of each day is appropriate.'

A look of exasperation appeared on the Adjutant's face. 'I was hoping to have an intelligent relationship with you doctor, despite you being a Jew. But I'm now beginning to think you are deliberately choosing not to understand what I'm saying to you.' The iciness in his tone was not lost on Ephraim. 'You are being offered the chance to separate yourself from those other Jews who will pass through this camp and I have just outlined in very simple terms what you are expected to do in return for this opportunity. You will obey orders... my orders. Nothing more. Can you bring yourself to do that, doctor, or should I ship you out to the next camp?

Despite the recent trauma with the Gestapo in Berlin and the ever constant threat of dire consequences at the first sign of insubordination, Ephraim still felt tempted to prick the pomposity and arrogance of this bull of a man staring at him from across the desk.

'Look Captain, I have no problem with accepting orders, either from you or any other German officer. If you are a qualified doctor, that would be extremely helpful for a second opinion from time to time. But if that is not the case, then please be assured you can rely on me to comply with your order.' Ephraim hoped that the Adjutant would recognise the submission in his response but the Adjutant's next words urged even greater caution in the way he was expected to relate to this man.

'Dr. Fischer, I am not a doctor but neither am I as unintelligent as you seem to think. I can accept pragmatism on your part but if I detect, even for one moment that you are attempting to make a fool of me, then I will personally save the Reich the cost of transporting you elsewhere and terminate your miserable life here in Theresienstadt. Do I need to say more, doctor?

Forcing himself to return the Adjutant's malignant stare for what seemed an eternity Ephraim's reply succeeded in masking his true feelings. 'I understand perfectly Captain and thank you for answering my question.'

NINETEEN

Despite the barely concealed threat made by the Adjutant during their initial conversation, Ephraim threw himself into doing what he had missed for so long... being a practising physician once more.

Situated in a self-contained block away from the main administrative building, the camp clinic was surprisingly well equipped despite the competing demand for medical supplies for the Eastern front. Neither were there any shortage of patients. The Jewish inmates flocked to the clinic in droves as did the Czech nationals employed within the camp but only occasionally was he required to treat the small number of servicemen cynically disregarding the Nazi Government's decree forbidding Jewish physicians from treating German nationals

As the first week drew to its close and satisfied that the new camp physician was accepting his authority, the Adjutant chose to broaden Ephraim's remit and allow him to treat the various groups of patients without the need to report back to him at the end of each day. Almost despite himself, Ephraim began to develop a degree of sympathy for the man; a career officer assigned to a non-combatant administrative role. But conversely, he perhaps wondered whether the Adjutant was content to sit out the war in comparative safety.

As for himself, it had taken just a matter of days to realise that Theresienstadt was not what it seemed. A number of newly-arrived Jews had told him they had been forced to assign all their possessions, wealth and former homes to the Nazi Government in return for them being provided with accommodation, food and medical services beyond the borders of the Third Reich. Additionally, they were to be provided with a weekly allowance, payable in a currency unique toThereisenstadt which could only be used within the confines of the camp.

Of more immediate concern was the 'invitation' which came in the second week for him to dine with the Camp's senior German officers; an invitation conveyed personally by the Adjutant himself. Entering the clinic during the busy morning session the Adjutant surprisingly chose to wait in the anteroom until Ephraim had completed an examination of an elderly Jewish patient suffering from chronic anaemia no doubt caused by the lack of nourishment and essential vitamins prior to her arrival. Sadly, he also knew she would not recover but in the short term the better food being provided in the camp should at least help to prolong her life a little longer. The only remedy he could offer were words of comfort and for this Ephraim was rewarded with a grateful smile.

Hardly had the door closed before the burly figure of Captain Kernick strode in. 'Good morning doctor. I'm pleased to see you are a busy man.' He tapped Ephraim's desk with his cane. 'These people should be grateful we have their welfare at heart.'

Resisting the urge to respond other than formally, Ephraim drew a deep breath. 'Good morning Captain. I trust you are not in need of my services?'

Instead of taking the seat directly opposite to him, the Adjutant chose to position himself on the edge of the examination couch. 'Of course not but thank you for your concern; you will be the first to know should that become necessary.' Although appearing outwardly relaxed, Ephraim could sense from the Adjutant's languid body language that he wanted to speak informally which he noticeably felt uncomfortable with. Easing himself up from the edge of the couch, he positioned himself in front of Ephraim's desk. 'Doctor, the Commandant wishes you to join him for dinner this evening. In accepting what amounts to an order to attend I trust you will not repeat the truculence you initially displayed when we first met. This is, after all, an unusual request.'

'Unusual in what sense, may I ask?'

'Doctor, I warned you when we first met that I have a low level of tolerance which includes responding to stupid questions. It is highly unusual, if not against military regulations, for German citizens, let alone senior officers, to consort with Jews. Personally, I think it wrong for the Commandant to want to do this but I take my orders like the good soldier I am.'

Hearing the Adjutant's self-effacing words, Ephraim found it difficult not to smile; wondering whether the man's arrogant pomposity was an affectation or whether it came naturally to him.

'That being so Captain, can I ask whether there is a specific reason for this invitation. I wouldn't wish to be responsible for you or your Commandant to breach regulations.'

Although a burly man, Ephraim was alarmed at the speed with which the Adjutant threw his body weight forward, smashing his heavy cane down on the desk as he did so. The blow, delivered with lethal vehemence, caused the silver SS emblem on the end of the black ebony staff to snap off, ricocheting off the top of the desk before striking Ephraim just below his left eye. Within seconds, he felt warm blood begin to flow down his cheek.

Regaining his self-control, the Adjutant drew back and made to leave the room. Pausing in the doorway he checked his stride and glared back at Ephraim. Seeing the blood beginning to stain the front of his white gown he gave a satisfied smile. 'Be ready at 20.00 hours doctor and clean yourself up, you loathsome man.'

TWENTY

Purposely arriving some minutes early, Ephraim was dismayed to find that the other guests, all SS officers, had arrived before him. He had dressed the wound on his face with a small plaster which looking in the mirror did not appear too unsightly.

The Commandant's aide-de-camp, a youngish-looking Lieutenant, greeted him with distinct coolness and mutely ushered him into a large ante-room.

'Doctor Fischer... do come in.' The greeting came from the same officer who only hours earlier had done his best to remove his eye with the dismembered end of his staff cane. 'Gentlemen, allow me to introduce our camp physician. This is Dr. Fischer who hails from Berlin, husband of the celebrated violinist, Hannah Bergmann, soloist with our Berlin Symphony Orchestra.'

Ephraim noted the emphasis the Adjutant placed on 'our' and wondered whether any of those present had ever attended a concert at which his wife had performed. He was aware that military personnel were not generally known for an appreciation of classical music but in a war-time environment who could really determine just who attended what?

Earlier in the quietness of his room, he had attempted to understand the reason for him to be invited to a dinner at which he would almost certainly be the only non-military person present. Nor was he was under any illusion that the men he would be dining with this evening held the power of life and death not only of himself but every other Jew within the precincts of Theresienstadt. For him to unnecessarily antagonize them, particularly at such close quarters, could be tantamount to him signing his own death warrant. But why had he been invited? Idly he wondered whether he was being accorded a form of privileged status similar to that of Hannah but surely it wouldn't stretch to being invited to dine with men implementing the murderous policy of genocide to eradicate what their Fuhrer referred to as the 'cancer' at the heart of Aryan Germany.

'Line of least resistance;' wasn't that Max Feldman's recipe for survival? Unable to answer his own question, Ephraim turned to the officer he now knew to be the Commandant and thanked him for the invitation.

'No need for thanks doctor, delighted you could join us.' Perversely, the mollifying tone of the greeting had the effect of actually increasing Ephraim's nervousness.

'Gentlemen, now we are all here, we shall proceed to dinner.' To his surprise, Ephraim found himself being shepherded into the dining area alongside the senior officer of the Totenkopf SS Unit at Theresienstadt camp.

'Dr. Fischer, you will sit there,' motioning Ephraim to the chair opposite to his own. The other officers were left to select their places and Ephraim noticed that the chairs furthest away from the Commandant were hurriedly filled by the junior officers. Never in his life had he ever been in such close proximity with military personnel and despite the feigned sense of bonhomie being exuded by the Commandant, it did little to dispel the growing sense of unease forming inside him.

Sitting quietly as the officers settled down in their chosen seats, Ephraim wondered whether they would offer a form of blessing as a prelude to the meal or worse, propose a toast to their Commander-in-Chief, Adolf Hitler?

As if reading his thoughts, it was the Commandant who arose and offered a perfunctory blessing on the food. Lost in thought and caught off-guard, Ephraim quickly lowered his head at the last moment. At the conclusion of the blessing, he noticed that the waiter offering wine to each of the officers pointedly passed him by, a deliberate snub for which he was grateful having already decided he did not want to have a glass in front of him should a toast be offered at some stage of the dinner.

Any toast offered by a group of Totenkopf SS Officers would be anathema to him, a Jew.

As a medical student living and working within a largely Gentile environment, Ephraim had departed from the strict orthodox rites of his childhood and since marrying Hannah, neither had subscribed to a program of living they both thought had more to do with the ancient Talmudic code than the present day. Neither of them had been regular attendees at synagogue, using the excuse that the professional demands on their time prevented them from attending. However, the advent of war and the Nazi government's unbridled policy of institutional hatred towards Jews had caused both of them to question the liberal way they were addressing their religion but despite this, neither he nor Hannah had shown any real inclination to follow the level of orthodoxy their parents would have wished.

'How long have you been a doctor, Doctor?' The enquiry was put by a sallow-faced Lieutenant sitting at the far end of the table. Although the question was directed to him, Ephraim noticed the Lieutenant glance at the Commandant as if seeking his approbation for a remark which he no doubt hoped his senior officer would find amusing.

'How long? Let me see. Sometimes it feels for ever whilst at other times it seems like it was only yesterday that I left medical school. In reality it was nearly eight years ago.

'And which university did you graduate from? Was it Berlin?'

Wondering where this conversation might be leading; he glanced at the Commandant who appeared to be taking an interest.

'No, it was Heidelberg for my first degree. I then completed my post-graduate training in Berlin.'

'Heidelberg you say? How did you manage to gain admittance there? I thought Jews were barred from'... his voice trailed off in mid-sentence.

'You didn't finish your question, Lieutenant. You were about to say something about Jews being... being what? This time it was Ephraim who left the question hanging in the air.

The unexpected directness of Ephraim's response caused the junior officer to again glance towards the Commandant who wordlessly motioned him to silence with a dismissive wave of his hand. 'Come now Dr. Fischer, you know full well that the Lieutenant is referring to the fact that Jews are precluded from attending institutes of learning but unfortunately, his inability to calculate that you had completed your graduation before that decree was enforced obviously escaped him. An easy mistake I'm sure you will agree.'

'I have no problem with the Lieutenant's inability to calculate dates with decrees... especially those pertaining to Jews.'

Having expected a compliant response from their guest, the temerity of Ephraim's reply clearly surprised the other diners.

'Dr. Fischer, I apologise for my error; I assure you no offence was intended.' The peace offering, muttered by the Lieutenant fooled no one, least of all Ephraim who sensed that it would actually antagonise the other officers sitting around the table. Apologising to a Jew was not something that they as SS officers would have much experience of.

It was the Adjutant, Captain Kernick, who decided to change the subject. 'Dr. Fischer, in 28 days' time, we will be having an inspection of this establishment by the International Red Cross. They are coming here at the invitation of our Government so they can see for themselves and to then inform the world at large, that we are providing Jewish people with good accommodation, food and medical care in each of our camps. Before they get here, a Government Film Unit will factually record daily life in this camp which the Red Cross representatives will then take away with them. This film will repudiate the lies and propaganda which the enemies of Germany are spreading. And you, doctor, will have a key role in this exercise. The reason you have been invited here tonight is for us to assess whether you are deemed compliant enough to participate in this project. And perhaps that is the reason why our young Lieutenant here chose to test your attitude sooner than planned. So having outlined our objective, we would like to hear your view doctor. The stage is yours.'

The enormity of the deception coldly outlined by Kernick momentarily shocked Ephraim into silence but an inner sense warned him of the yawning danger contained within the Adjutant's innocuous invitation.

Clearly impatient, the Adjutant spoke again before Ephraim could bring himself to answer. 'Do we take your silence as being in agreement or not?

Looking at each of the officers around the table, Ephraim sensed their growing wish to hear his response.

'It would have been nice to have got beyond the first course before having to make such a decision but clearly that is not to be.' Ephraim noticed a glimmer of a smile appear on the face of the Commandant. 'As you stated earlier today Captain, the real choice you appear to be proposing is for me to comply with your wishes and in return, live beyond the visit of this Red Cross delegation or I can decide to decline your offer, in which case I will be shipped out to an extermination camp and certain death. Isn't that is the real choice before me?'

At his mention of an extermination camp, Ephraim saw the Commandant perceptibly stiffen and lean back in his chair. But it was the Adjutant who chose to pursue the conversation. 'Your analysis of the situation does you credit, Dr. Fischer. You already appear to know what happens to those Jews who no longer have a place in our society. But tell us, what do you know about these so-called 'extermination camps;' it's a term my fellow officers are not entirely familiar with.'

Ephraim heard a nervous snigger carry from the end of the table.

'Taking the good doctor's point, can we have the second course served;' it was the voice of the Commandant cutting across the debate. He nodded to the waiter, an unsmiling SS corporal.

'I'm sure we can manage to eat and talk at the same time.' Glancing round the table, he gave a half smile at his own terse comment. Encouraged by the Commandant's words, a new voice entered the debate. 'I think we should hear what Dr. Fischer has decided.'

'Gentlemen, I'm sure you don't need reminding of the Fuehrer's General Order to all military forces engaged in the war against Russia, in which the Bolsheviks are likened to Jews and therefore regarded not only as racially inferior sub-humans but to be exterminated regardless of international convention. Does that not summarise the policy and attitude of your Fuhrer toward people such as me? And as you are the physical means whereby that policy is being pursued I hardly think you need me to explain my reference to extermination camps.' Ephraim stopped, knowing he had again said too much but driven by the growing anger within him.

It was the Commandant who broke the silence. 'Carry on doctor; I believe my comrades are finding this highly informative and perhaps even educational? He looked at each of his subordinates for affirmation but none was forthcoming.. ''So tell me doctor, how is it that you are so well versed in our military communiqués; to the point of being almost word perfect?' The Commandant's raised eyebrow gave no clue as to whether his question posed an immediate threat to Ephraim's well-being or simply an expression of genuine curiosity.

'It's no great mystery, gentlemen. Medical colleagues... not Jews but your own German Army doctors returning from the Russian front have spoken openly about it, especially the Einsatzgruppe units operating behind the front line. Whilst very few of them expressed what their personal views of this policy were... in today's climate that would be most unwise, it was spoken of quite openly which is why I am aware of it.' As he finished speaking, Ephraim knew that he had now gone beyond the point of recall. Like a cat playing with a mouse, he guessed the Nazi officers would soon tire of the game being played for their entertainment but for the moment the game was allowed to continue.

'Doctor... ' the strident voice of Captain Kernick cut in. 'As you appear to know so much about our operations in Russia, perhaps you will enlighten us with your own view on the policy you have so clinically illuminated.'

Throwing aside whatever caution remained, Ephraim gave a long hard look at each individual officer around the table before fixing on his inquisitor. 'Captain Kernick,' he unconsciously lowered his voice. 'As an officer in the Totenkopf SS and Adjutant of this establishment, your responsibilities and authority are second only to that of the Commandant. To the troops you command, you represent a line of authority which stems directly from your Fuehrer. So in simple terms, you are instrumental in ensuring compliance with those policies and orders which flow down that particular chain of command. That is a very simple analysis of how the military machine works... at least to my non-military understanding.

But then look behind the uniform to you, the man.' Glancing directly at the Adjutant, Ephraim saw a look of undisguised hatred. 'I know you are married and I believe from the photograph in your office that you have a child... just as I do. But there the comparison ends. And why? Although we were both born in Germany, you are deemed to be an Aryan whilst I am a Jew. A distinction which you clearly believe in.' Fingering the plaster covering the cut on his face, Ephraim waited for the inevitable reaction.

But even those officers aware of the Adjutant's unconcealed hostility to Jews were shaken by the vehemence of his response.

'You filthy Jewish scum! How dare you compare yourself with an officer of the Reich! Jews and vermin like you deserve to be burned alive and even that is too good!' As he spoke, Kernick jumped to his feet and made to move towards

Ephraim, prevented only by the chair of the young Lieutenant getting in the way.

'Sit down Captain Kernick... now!' The cold anger in the voice of the Commandant had the required effect. The Adjutant, anger exuding from every fibre of his body, fell rather than sat back onto his chair. 'I'm sorry Commandant but can we have this man removed; his very presence offends me deeply.'

Before the Commandant could voice his reply, Ephraim stood up. 'Captain Kernick. I am sorry you take exception to my words. As you find my presence so offensive, then I will gladly leave.' Looking at the Commandant, Ephraim inclined his head in what he hoped would be seen as a gesture of regret and made to push his chair back.

'You will do no such thing Dr. Fischer. You too will stay in your seat and all of you,' he paused while his eyes slowly scanned those around the table, 'calm down... and that is an order. And no, Captain Kernick, I will not ask Dr. Fischer to remove himself or have you forgotten the overall objective of why we are here tonight. I want no more discussion on whether Dr. Fischer will or won't be a member of the staff who meets the Red Cross. I will deal with that matter tomorrow. But for tonight, I want you to conduct yourselves as officers of the Third Reich and if that makes you feel uncomfortable Dr. Fischer then you have my permission to go to your quarters... but only after you have finished the meal.'

TWENTY ONE

Having missed two performances, Hannah knew it was imperative for her to meet with Max Feldman. She had managed to get a written note to him and felt somewhat disappointed that he had not responded. Neither had she heard from Ephraim since his transportation to Theresienstadt but with her recent experience of the Gestapo still vividly etched in her mind, she could at least understand why communication between them would be difficult, if not impossible.

Knowing Ephraim had been assigned to a specific job at Theresienstadt had initially given her a modicum of comfort but as time elapsed she began to feel a growing sense of despair.

She had twice made the journey to Frieda's home in the past week but the anguish and tears when it came to say farewell made Frieda's counsel to stop punishing herself as the only sensible decision.

Walking to the rehearsal hall, the damage and destruction from the latest overnight bombing raid was much in evidence. Breathing was difficult with strong winds carrying stinging dust particles from piles of rubble which only hours before had been homes to countless Berliners. Despite taking shallow breaths, the acrid smell of burning stung her nostrils and it wasn't until she reached the green parkland alongside the River Spree that the air became clearer to breathe.

A number of roads had been closed off and it took longer for her to find the new rehearsal hall due to their usual practice room having been requisitioned by the military. By the time Max Feldman arrived, a number of musicians had still not found their way to the hall which gave her an opportunity to speak with him in the room he was using as his office.

Effusive as ever, Max greeted Hannah with an affectionate hug. Remembering the emotions that their last embrace had evoked, she was careful to angle her face to one side to avoid the possibility of letting Max think that a repeat was on the cards.

'My dear girl... how wonderful to see you.' Sensing her changed mood, he reluctantly relaxed his hold. 'I received your note but as we were due to rehearse today, I hoped you might be here. He gave an expressive gesture with his hand; 'and lo, here you are. When I heard that you and your husband had both been arrested, I naturally feared the worse so tell me, has Ephraim been released as well?'

Although not wanting to excite Max or indeed herself, she had welcomed the warm embrace proffered by her long time mentor and friend. It felt vaguely comforting to be in the arms of a man again even if it wasn't her husband.

'It's good to see you too, Max. I must confess there were times when I didn't think I would. Ephraim was arrested and I think he's having a bad time compared with what happened to me. I'm told he's been sent to a camp in Czechoslovakia to work as a camp doctor.' Easing herself from Max's loose hold, she glanced nervously at herself in the long mirror on the far wall and was pleased to see that the dark shadows beneath her eyes had almost faded. But the dress she had hardly glanced at when taking it from the wardrobe earlier that morning made her look unusually dowdy.

Seeing Hannah scrutinise herself, Max again extended both hands and held his protégé at arm's length.

'Considering what you have been through, my dear girl, you look truly exotic.'

'Max, it was the dress I was looking at. I can't believe how awful it looks in this light. And look at the colour for God's sake... its wartime grey!'

'It may be grey but it does nothing to hide your stunning figure, my dear.'

'Thanks Max. I can always rely on you to say the right thing at the right time. I need cheering up. I can't tell you how much

I miss having Ephraim around. My life has changed from having a husband and baby son at home to where I am now entirely on my own. I know things could be a lot worse but I hate it, Max... I truly, truly, hate it.'

Never really comfortable when discussing her family or personal matters, Max nodded in a manner he hoped Hannah would construe as comforting.

'Sorry Max, I guess I'm going on a bit. Being on my own doesn't suit me.' Taking her violin from its case, she changed the subject. 'Tell me... how is the orchestra performing? Are we still on programme?'

'We are, but only by re-arranging everything. We lost two performances due to the bombing; the Wagner concert was lost in its entirety and then the Mozart evening came to a crashing halt, together with the ceiling in the foyer sometime during the second movement. So yes, we are still on a programme of sorts but short of rehearsal time but as you are blessing us with your presence today this will hopefully give a lift to the orchestra.' He smiled. 'I think it's the way you stand up to me that they secretly admire.' He smiled at his own admission.

'Max, if you weren't such a bully, I wouldn't need to react.'

'Come here, you belligerent, adorable female. One quick hug and then we'll get down to the serious stuff.'

'Oh? And what might that be?' For the first time in days, Hannah felt a sense of relief and laughingly stepped forward, allowing Max to fold his arms around her; experiencing for a brief moment a fleeting sense of security.

She had no way of knowing what emotion, if any, Max Feldman might be feeling but the subsequent rehearsal which followed was uncharacteristically relaxed. Not having played nor practised for over a week, she actually relished the chance of once more being part of the orchestra and as Max had predicted, her presence did seem to lift the other musicians.

The evening's concert, Beethoven's Third Symphony, the Eroica and Egmont Overture, required no virtuoso performance from her and for once it felt comfortable to simply be part of the violin section and able to free her mind from the worldly happenings outside of the concert hall. As usual, the audience were a mixture of military personnel with a number of civilians interspersed among them but unlike the two previous occasions, she was able to leave the concert hall at the conclusion of the evening's performance without having to cope with uninvited admirers in her dressing room.

Having declined the opportunity to have supper with Max, Hannah soon began to feel a sense of nervousness at finding herself alone once more in an apartment which no longer felt homely or secure. The flat itself was unchanged from when Ephraim and Aaron were last there but tonight it had an air of depressing emptiness.

Entering the lounge, she sat on the sofa, the sofa where she had aroused her bemused husband to a level of love-making which had plainly shocked him. She also wickedly reflected on what her reaction might have been had her Gestapo tormentor seen through her subterfuge and forced her to have sex with him. 'Can you experience something like that and not react' she wondered. And to what extent had the terrifying experience with him driven her to such extreme passion with a bemused Ephraim soon after? Choosing not to dwell on her own searching questions, instead she hurried in to the bedroom.

The curtains were still drawn back from when she had opened them earlier that morning and even though the blackout was in force, there was sufficient light coming off the street to cast dim shadows in the room.

Recalling Ephraim's warning of the danger from windows blown inwards from the blast of exploding bombs, she hurriedly pulled the curtains together.

Once in bed her thoughts turned to Ephraim and Aaron, realising just how much she missed them both. Finding it difficult to relax she let her mind drift to Von Hartmannn and the events which had drawn him to her. Why, she wondered, had he put himself at risk to help her, a stateless Jew. Had he been attracted by her seductive posturing on the concert platform or had his intervention been motivated simply out of sympathy for her wish to be reunited with a man he had never met? But without his intervention, she knew she would now be incarcerated in a cold Gestapo cell instead of the warmth and comfort of her own bed.

It was the starkness of this comparison which caused the greatest concern. Aware of Von Hartmann's imminent departure from Berlin, she again questioned whether it might have been sensible to have accompanied Ephraim to Theresienstadt after all.

Unable to sleep, she began to count sheep... something she last did as a child until eventually her overworked brain finally drifted into a fitful slumber.

Several times she imagined she could hear the sound of authoritative knocking on the front door of the building followed by the tread of heavy footsteps approaching her apartment but on each occasion the sounds faded into nothing. Later, it was the mournful wail of an air raid siren which caused her to abandon hope of further sleep. Peering through a gap in the heavy black-out curtains, her eyes were drawn to the cold fingers of light probing upwards into the night sky above, seeking to detect and expose enemy bombers in their illuminated embrace.

From a nearby park an Army artillery unit suddenly opened fire, unleashing a torrent of tracer into the night sky; their rapid rate of fire competing with the crump of heavy eruptions as each deadly payload unleashed by unseen Allied bombers fell to earth.

As the explosions drew inexorably closer, she stared at the street below and in the dim light she imagined she glimpsed two people sheltering in the doorway of the building on the opposite side of the road. Overhead, an almighty explosion lit up the night sky as an anti- aircraft battery found a target and for an infinitesimal second the area below was illuminated with a brilliance exceeding that of a mid-summer day. In that briefest of moments Hannah clearly made out the figure of a uniformed serviceman and a girl and in panic realised the danger they were exposed to on the open street.

Impulsively dashing to the ground floor, she opened the front door and tried frantically to attract the couple's attention. Outside, the intermittent noise was deafening and it was several moments before either of them spotted her waving arms. As the blast from a nearby explosion rent the air, the couple were able to run into the shelter of the hallway where she saw that the serviceman was in fact a young soldier with a very attractive girlfriend. She appeared to be a little older than him with a heavily made-up face topped by a head of blonde hair. Her short dress emphasised her shapely legs, one of which was bleeding profusely from a deep abrasion just above her left ankle.

In her mad dash to the ground floor, Hannah suddenly realised she was garbed only in her nightdress. Clasping her arms around her chest, she gave an involuntary shiver. 'Look, I'm getting very cold standing here and you need to have that wound dressed so come up to my apartment. It's not much warmer but you can stay there until this air raid is over.' Without waiting for a response Hannah turned and made for the stairwell. By the time she reached the third floor, she was quite breathless but relieved she had time to put on her dressing gown before the soldier and his limping companion arrived at the front door.

'Come in and take a seat. I'll warm some water and clean that cut; the last thing you want is for it to become infected.'

Before being forced to leave his position at the General Hospital,, Ephraim had managed to garner a supply of sterile military field dressings and it was one of these that Hannah now unwrapped from its brown paper covering. The woman had removed her stocking whilst the soldier, kneeling on the floor, was attempting to stem the flow of blood seeping from wound with a piece of greyish material which she guessed might be the soldier's handkerchief.

'For heaven's sake, don't dare use that.' The authority in her voice stopped the soldier in mid-wipe. 'You will contaminate the wound with whatever germs may be in that cloth.'

Sheepishly, the soldier stood up and smiled at Hannah. 'Sorry, I didn't want the blood to run on the carpet. I'm Pieter Gunter by the way and this is my friend Olga.'

'Elsa... my name is Elsa.' Her interjection was immediate.

'Sorry... this is Elsa.' The apology was unnecessary in light of the girl's correction but it told Hannah that the couple barely knew each other; probably having met only an hour or so before in a club or bar or wherever else soldiers went for entertainment in war-time Berlin.

'Pieter, would you go into the kitchen and run the hot tap into the enamel dish you'll find on the table. And then bring it here please.' Examining the gash more closely, she was concerned that the wound was still bleeding copiously. 'I think you will need a stitch or two in this... unless we can pull it together with a bandage and stop the bleeding. How did it happen?'

'We were walking home from the Hoffenblute Club when the air raid started. The bombs weren't falling too near us then so I must have been struck by a piece of home-grown shrapnel; there's a lot of it flying about down there. It didn't hurt at first but now I've stopped walking my leg feels painful.'

'I'm not surprised. It's a fairly deep cut and you appear to have a burn which is weeping.' Taking the water from the soldier, she used a piece of sterile gauze from Ephraim's medical kit to stem the flow of blood. In the distance she heard the air raid sirens finally signal the end of the bombing raid which seemed somewhat premature as the sound of exploding bombs could still be heard in the fading distance..

Included in the field dressing was a small safety pin and she used this to deftly fasten the end of the bandage in place. Standing up, she admired the neatness of the dressing and.

wondered whether Ephraim, always the perfectionist, would have approved.

Glancing down at Hannah's handiwork the woman drew in a deep gulp of air and expelled it slowly in obvious relief. 'Thanks for this. I can feel my leg pulsating but the cut itself feels less painful. And thanks for letting us into this building. It was getting very scary on the street. I don't know your name but I'm Elsa Seilhamer.' Reaching out, she took hold of Hannah's hand to formalise the introduction.

'Oh, I'm Hannah Bergmann and you don't have to thank me; I'm sure anyone would have done the same in the circumstances. It was the merest chance I happened to see you in the black-out.'

From the corner of her eye, Hannah could see the young soldier beginning to fidget. Catching her glance he rose to his feet and reached for his greatcoat.

'Now the air raid has finished, I really need to go.' He glanced at Elsa to see whether she was also preparing to leave. 'My pass expires in two hours' time and I can't afford to be late getting back to barracks. The Provost Marshall gets a kick from putting low-rankers like me on extra duties so bang would go the rest of my free evenings in Berlin.' He nodded towards Elsa before extending his hand to Hannah. 'Thanks again for what you did tonight; it was very kind of you especially for patching up Elsa's leg.'

Hannah thought how confident and well-spoken he sounded for a private soldier and instantly chastised herself for such a snobbish thought

'Pieter, you go.' Elsa gave him a half-smile. 'I won't be able to keep up with you so I'll make my way home in my own time. Go on... off you go.'

'Are you sure? I did promise to see you home safely and if we hurry, I can still do that.'

A hint of irritation came into Elsa's voice. 'I just told you, I won't be able to walk at your pace so I want you to go.' She raised her voice, imitating a military command. 'On your way, soldier. 'Rising painfully from the sofa, Elsa Seilhamer stumbled rather than moved towards him and gave him the semblance of a hug. 'Off you go now and perhaps we'll meet again on your next visit to the Hoffenblute? OK?'

With a barely concealed sigh of relief, Private Pieter Gunter needed no further encouragement and moments later Hannah heard the front door of the building close, followed by the faint sound of his receding footsteps in the street below.

'I gather he's not your regular boyfriend.'

'No. I met him this evening at the Club where I work. I probably won't even remember his name tomorrow.' Still standing, Elsa attempted to walk across the room and Hannah could see from the grimace on her face that her leg had stiffened considerably despite the dressing.

'Look Elsa, you can't go anywhere on that leg tonight. Why don't you sleep on the sofa and see how it feels in the morning. And try to raise your leg when you lay down; that will help to alleviate the throbbing and prevent your ankle from swelling.'

'You seem to know a lot about injuries; are you a nurse or something?'

'Good heavens, no,' Hannah suppressed a laugh. 'My husband is a doctor so I suppose I may have picked up one or two things from him. If you would like to stay I'll get you a couple of blankets and then we can both get some rest.'

In reply, Elsa Seilhamer hobbled back to the sofa and gingerly laid herself down.

'Thanks, Hannah. I think I will stay. I don't think I could make it to my apartment anyway.'

By the time she brought the blankets back to the lounge, Elsa's eyes were closed and her shallow breathing indicated she was already in the first throes of sleep.

TWENTY TWO

'Here you are then, a cup of hot coffee. Hope you don't mind but I helped myself to a coffee as well.'

Through eyes heavily shrouded in sleep, the figure of Elsa emerged at the side of the bed, holding a cup of what she knew must be the last of the coffee given to her by Frieda.

'Elsa... what time is it and how is your leg?'

'It feels less painful than it did last night and I can't see any sign of fresh bleeding so I guess it will be OK to take the bandage off later today? What do you think, nurse? Elsa's clipped accent had an amusing lilt to it which Hannah had difficulty in placing.

'I'll take a look at it when I get up and thanks for the coffee.' Peering at the small travelling clock on the dressing table Hannah was shocked to see it showed 12.25.

'Oh dear God! I was due in rehearsal at 10.30 for tonight's concert.' Squirming upright, she freed her legs from the sheet which had wrapped around them during the night.' You should have woken me earlier, Max will be spitting blood.'

'Whoa, don't panic. You'll still make it. That clock appears to have stopped. According to the one on the kitchen wall it's just passed 8.00 am.

Relieved, she gratefully sank back into the enfolding warmth of her bed. 'I normally wind this clock when I come to bed but I guess I forgot to do that last night; hardly surprising I suppose.'

Looking at Elsa, Hannah could see that she was even prettier than she had first appeared the previous evening. Her freshly washed face, now devoid of make-up, positively glowed in the early morning light, the fairness of her naturally wavy hair glistening with tiny droplets of water from the shower.

Wrapped in one of Hannah's large bath towels, Elsa looked the epitome and image of the Aryan model whose face adorned thousands of street posters promoting membership of the Hitler Youth organisation.

'How long have you been up for heaven's sake? You've obviously showered and made the coffee and it's still so early' Forcing herself to sit up again, she wrapped her fingers around the hot cup and sipped the caffeine-laden drink. 'M'mmm, this is a good way to start my day. Thanks Elsa.'

'No need for thanks. I appreciate what you did last night, particularly for letting me sleep on your sofa. I remember what you said about anyone doing the same? You might think that but believe me, it simply isn't true. Everyone seems to look out just for themselves these days. I can't think of too many people who'd let a complete stranger stay overnight in their home.'

Hearing the sincerity in Elsa's gratitude caused her to experience a twinge of embarrassment. 'I suppose it's a matter of instinct, isn't it? You either trust people or you don't. And there was no way I could let you attempt to get home after your friend had gone, not with that gash in your leg. By the way, I hope you didn't get your dressing wet in the shower; that could cause it to bleed again.'

'Hannah please... my leg isn't going to drop off. It's just a bad cut... isn't it?' The enquiring tone in Elsa's voice was appealing.

'No it isn't just a cut. I think you were struck by a fragment of hot metal which is why the flesh around the wound appears to be burned. And the force of its impact may have damaged either your muscle or the bone itself. That's why you couldn't walk on your leg last night. Let me get showered and dressed and I will look at it again and we can decide whether you go to your apartment or to the hospital. Does that sound sensible?' Without waiting for a reply, she threw the bed clothes to one side and made a dash for the bathroom.

Luxuriating in the warmth of the hot shower, Hannah decided on two objectives for the day ahead. Firstly, she would attend rehearsal in preparation for that evening's concert and secondly, she would ignore Frieda's advice and spend some precious time with Aaron. Closing her eyes, she again tried to visualise Ephraim; his face, his mannerisms, the sound of his voice but very little would come to mind.

Stepping from the shower, she realised that the large white bath towel was missing from the chrome rack... probably still wrapped around the shapely form of her overnight guest.

'Elsa, can you get me a fresh towel from the cupboard next to the room heater please. You appear to be using the one that was here.' The slight irritation in her voice softened at the last moment but the gentle reproach wasn't lost on Elsa.

'Oh, I'm sorry, Hannah. I should have asked first but I used the bathroom while you were still sleeping and when I saw the shower I couldn't resist it. There isn't one where I live.' With a touch of contrition, she took hold of Hannah's towel; 'here, let me dry your back for you... turn round.'

Timidly, Hannah found herself obeying. Oddly, the sense of intimacy being shared with Elsa did not disconcert her. The last time she had openly displayed her nudity with other females was as a teenage schoolgirl after weekly swimming lessons.

'You have a fantastic figure, you know.' Stepping back, Elsa let out a sigh of admiration. 'God, if I had a body like this, I'd earn a fortune.'

Laughing to herself, Hannah turned and took the towel from Elsa and draped it round herself. 'Elsa, if you had my body, you wouldn't be allowed to earn a fortune. I am a Jew and you must surely know how this country treats people like me. My husband, a doctor, is not allowed to practice medicine and any day now, I expect to be told I cannot remain with the orchestra I have been a member of for five years. So maybe I should consider doing what I think you do and afterwards tell my pure-blooded Aryan clients that they have just consorted with a stateless parasite'

It took Elsa several moments to think about Hannah's words.

'Oh dear, I have touched a nerve haven't I.' Now it was her turn to remonstrate. 'Listen to me my friend in need; stop feeling sorry for yourself.' Snatching the towel from Hannah's body, Elsa slowly removed her own covering. 'Look carefully at my body... can you see any difference between us? I might be a bit older than you and yes, you're stunning to look at but apart from these differences,' she smiled, 'we're the same aren't we? Can you see anything which says you're a Jew and I'm a Gentile? Open your eyes, Hannah, and look at me. Do I look different to you?'

The blunt impact of Elsa's words, delivered with the finesse of a hard slap made Hannah's senses reel. Suddenly oblivious of her own nakedness, she reached out and pulled Elsa to her, feeling warm tears run down her face and fall on to the bare shoulders of the woman she had met only hours before.

It was Elsa who broke the charged silence. 'So I take it you don't wish to change places with me after all? And here's me thinking that a nightclub hostess was what every young girl aspires to.'

The feigned seriousness of Elsa's statement coupled with the absurdity of two virtual strangers nakedly hugging each other was too much for Hannah. For a brief moment, the tensions and anxieties of the previous days were swept away, replaced by a burst of girlish laughter.

Over a sparse breakfast of matzos' and weak tea Hannah learned that Elsa's apartment was just a few minutes' walk from her own building. Elsa's leg was still painful so leaning on Hannah's arm they made their halting way along Charlottenburg's busy tree-lined streets. Their eyes took in the damage and destruction resulting from the overnight bombing raid; the dust and sulphurous smell of burning making the morning air unpleasant to breathe. Pathetic items of furniture recovered from shattered buildings vied for a place on the pavement amid the heaps of rubble being piled up by gangs of labourers, many wearing an obligatory yellow armband on their sleeves.

Entering a quiet side street, Elsa stopped to relieve the strain on Hannah's arm and to take the opportunity to sit down on a low wall above which were an ornate set of painted railings. Catching her breath, she gave Hannah a quizzical look. 'The yellow armbands on those workers, don't you have to wear one too? I thought all Jews had to wear them in public.'

'They do but I have a special dispensation but for how much longer, I have no idea.' She gave a cynical laugh. 'But it makes no difference whatsoever, believe me. The restrictions on Jews are precisely the same whether you wear a yellow armband or not. But for the moment I'm just not so obvious.'

'Why do you think Hitler dislikes you Jews so much? Every time I listen to him on the radio, he blames the Jews for everything whether it's sabotage, food rationing, the bombing and so on; he puts all of it down to you people.'

Elsa's directness appealed to Hannah. 'So do you think we're responsible for all those things you've just mentioned?'

'Of course not but I get the impression he's jealous of Jews because they're so successful in business. My dear old Dad, bless him, worked for a Jewish tailor for years until the workshop was looted by a mob while the Police stood by and watched. And guess who suffered most?' She didn't pause long enough to give Hannah the chance to answer. 'People like my father who then had no job to go to the following day. How stupid was that? It's alright for people like Hitler and his cronies; politicians always look after themselves.'

Listening to Elsa's harangue, Hannah wondered how many other Germans felt the same; more so with the war now being brought to the capital itself. 'I'm afraid we all know stories like that. But if you feed enough hatred to the general public, then in time they will believe whatever they are told. We can only trust that one day this war will be over and life can go back to something approaching normality.'

'Who do you want to win... us or the Allies?'

'I'm not going to answer that Elsa. I just want this miserable war to end. But whether life will ever get back to how it was in pre-war days, Lord only knows.'

Elsa looked thoughtful. 'I can understand why you say that Hannah but many of these anti-Jewish laws were passed before the war. I remember the night when the synagogues were burnt and that was two, three years before the war began? The reason I remember it so clearly was because it was the day before my Dad's workplace was smashed up. He couldn't get another job for months after that.'

Glancing ahead, Hannah spotted a street clock above a jeweller's shop, its weight supported by two buckled metal brackets. The Allied bombs had badly damaged the premises but inexplicably, the clock was still working. Seeing the time, she felt a mild touch of panic. 'Elsa, can we talk as we walk. I'm very conscious of the time and I daren't be late for my rehearsal today.' She didn't want to aggravate Elsa's injury but the thought of invoking the scathing wrath of Max didn't bear thinking about.

'Look, I can make it from here, really.' As if to emphasise her growing confidence, Elsa quickened her pace and disengaged her hand from Hannah's arm. 'See, I can manage OK now. And we're very near anyway.'

'How near is near?'

'Near enough for you to be on your way.

'Well if you're really sure you can manage on your own, then I'll say goodbye here but you know where to find me if you want to stay in touch.'

Elsa, thankful to stop again and ease the throbbing pain in her leg reached out and wrapped her arms around Hannah. 'Thanks for taking me in last night and for dressing my leg. For a Jew, I must say you're a pretty decent woman!'

Thrown by her comment, it took a moment for her to appreciate the irony in Elsa's humorous remark.

'And you take care of that leg; have it looked at as soon as you can.'

Giving Elsa a farewell hug, she hurriedly retraced her steps back to her apartment to collect her violin and to then begin the long walk to the rehearsal room located at the rear of the Kroll Opera House on Konigsplatz.

Entering the normally noisy dressing room, she intuitively sensed something was amiss. The sound of chatter and instruments being tuned, always a feature of dressing room activity abruptly fell away as other musicians spotted her and hurried into the rehearsal room. Several members of her own violin section, fellow musicians who had played alongside her for several seasons, seemed to deliberately avoid eye contact as they too hurried away. Puzzled, she glanced round and caught sight of Irene Schumacher, a gifted cellist who occasionally had given her small gifts of food for Aaron. Seeing Hannah standing on her own, Irene Schuman hurried over. The concern on her face was obvious.

'Good God Hannah. What are you doing here? I thought you'd be with Max and the others.'

Sensing the worst, she grasped her friend's arm. 'Irene, what are you talking about? What others? Why wouldn't you expect to see me?'

Embarrassed, Irene Schumacher's complexion darkened. 'Because Max Feldman was arrested yesterday morning during rehearsals. Gestapo Police came in and took him and four other members of the orchestra away. They were taken out and thrown on to a truck with lots of other people. It was shocking; one minute we were rehearsing normally and then suddenly there were Police everywhere. They had a list with names of the people they wanted to arrest and when Max tried to intervene, they beat him with truncheons and dragged him out with the others.'

'Oh dear God.' Feeling her legs would give way at any moment, she hurriedly sat down. 'I suppose they were all Jews, weren't they?'

'I think they must have been although none of them wore the yellow star on their coats.'

Feeling a band of pain tightening across her chest, Hannah forced herself to think logically. 'Irene... please try and remember. Was my name on that list?'

Wordlessly, Irene Schumacher turned her head away in a gesture that confirmed Hannah's worst fear.

'So that's why you were surprised to see me here this morning wasn't it. You thought I had been picked up too.'

The increasing pain in her chest began to impinge on her breathing and she knew she had to get out of the over-heated building and fill her lungs with cold air. Stumbling past the cellist and into the street, her pace quickened. By the time she reached Konigstrasse she knew she was drawing attention to herself. In her panic to leave the Opera House, she had left her coat in the dressing room and the silk blouse and lightweight skirt, put on that morning in anticipation of a warm rehearsal room, were now soaked by a sudden cloudburst, the force of which was driving what remained of the melting ice into the wide gutters.

As her panic began to subside, Hannah slowed her steps, realising that further flight would be foolish. Sheltering under a leafless linden tree she reasoned that if her name had been on the list mentioned by Irene Schumacher then why hadn't the Gestapo come to the apartment to arrest her? Brooding on this, she steeled herself to turn round and return to the Opera House to recover her warm coat and violin.

It took a supreme effort of willpower to re-enter the building she had fled from only minutes before. Ignoring the questioning stare of the Security Guard, she made her cautious way through the auditorium and re-entered the dressing room. She spotted her coat, lying shapeless and abandoned on the tiled floor. The warm air blowing through the large fan heaters immediately began to penetrate the clamminess of her silk blouse. Thankfully, the dressing room was now empty. From the rehearsal area she could hear individual musician's running through various passages in preparation for that morning's rehearsal. With her composure now under control, the awful realisation that her career with the orchestra was finally at an end suddenly dawned on her. Resisting an almost irresistible urge to leave the building, instead she forced herself to calmly sit on the hard bench, her coat across one arm and her violin case in the other. From the rehearsal room she heard the distinctive tap of the baton striking the metal edge of the conductor's music stand signalling the arrival of the orchestra's new conductor followed by the plaintive tuning note of an oboe and quickly picked up by the rest of the orchestra. Duly tuned, an expectant hush descended upon the orchestra. Listening intently, she heard the familiar voice of Claus Mueller, a capable cellist now cast in the role of temporary stand-in for Max Feldman. As for Max, she wondered whether he was being held for questioning in the same Gestapo building on Prinz Albrechstrasse where she and Ephraim had been interrogated or was he even now on his way to a concentration camp in the East. 'So much,' she thought acidly, for Max's futile efforts to ignore what was happening to Jews elsewhere throughout Germany and the occupied territories.

Stepping out of the Kroll Opera House, she was relieved to see that the rain had stopped and rays of bright sunshine were now breaking through the heavy cloud overlay. Retracing her steps through the same bomb blasted streets, she puzzled as to why the Gestapo should have her name on a list of detainees yet so far had made no attempt to arrest her.

Lost in thought, she found herself heading in the direction of her apartment. 'Why not' she reasoned? 'If I'm to be arrested it may as well be in my home.' As she walked, she offered an inaudible prayer of thanks that both her parents were no longer alive to experience the increasing terror facing Jews in the maelstrom created by Adolph Hitler and his anti-Semitic acolytes within the Nazi Government. Her father, a strong minded man had died a year after the birth of Aaron following the death of Hannah's mother two years earlier. His burning anger and resentment at every new restriction placed on Jews had been partially tempered by the arrival of his first grandson especially when Aaron took his very first steps in the spacious home her parents had lived in for most of their married lives. Following the excesses of Kristalnacht, her parents had decided to move to Switzerland but a debilitating illness to her mother had prevented this happening. Ironically, she knew that permission for her parents to leave Germany would have been granted provided they were able to pay the Nazi Government an exorbitant levy to emigrate and to find a country which would accept them. 'If only that was still possible' she thought.

Arriving in Goethestrasse, she was relieved to see no obvious sign of Gestapo or Police activity. Letting herself in to the building she was grateful to see the lift at ground floor level. As it slowly ascended, she experienced a moment of panic, not knowing what to expect when the door next opened on the third floor. Stopping with a slight judder, the opening door revealed the familiar hallway between her apartment and that previously owned by Mr. Glickstein. Approaching her front door, she even wondered whether the Gestapo might be waiting inside the apartment or whether they had already looked for her there and changed the front door lock before leaving.

Inserting her key into the mortise lock, she was relieved to feel it turn smoothly. Checking each room, she was reassured to see that no one had entered the apartment since leaving earlier that morning with Elsa Seilhamer.

In the kitchen, she saw the crumbly remains of the breakfast she had shared with her. Opening the small cupboard above the gas range she saw it was empty other than for a packet of stale biscuits. Resisting the urge to nibble, she threw the biscuits into the waste bin and settled instead for the remains of a matzo which did little to ease the pangs of hunger in her stomach.

Eating the small morsel only served to make her hunger worse and it wasn't long before the draining effects of her disturbed night and the long walk to and from the Opera House began to take effect. Reluctant to return to her bed, she settled into a comfortable position on the sofa, stretching her tired legs along the length of its three cushions.

Realistically, she knew she had little chance of avoiding arrest in a city as militarised as Berlin let alone escape from it. And if by some miracle she could evade arrest and get out of the city then where could she escape to? And who would give shelter to a fugitive Jew at the risk of losing their own freedom? Having been present when Mr. Glickstein had been murdered and remembering Ephraim's comment about the cemeteries being filled with increasing numbers of Jewish dead, she had little doubt what her fate would be if arrested. Frieda had told her that the Nazis Government were openly broadcasting details of its intention to re-settle Jews and other so-termed undesirable groups to areas within Eastern Europe in order to accommodate those German Nationals returning to the Fatherland from the newly occupied territories. The transported Jews and other undesirables were to be accommodated in slave labour camps to provide a work force for the host of new German industrial factories now being built throughout Eastern Europe.

Despite her increasing doubts she began to think positively about people who may be persuaded to provide her with temporary shelter. Clearly Max was now out of the question. She thought too of Inga and Claus but promptly dismissed them. The thought of endangering them and their beautiful young daughter for aiding her, a wanted Jew, was out of the question. She also realised that this same reason would also prevent her from contacting her other German friends; even those she had known since childhood. In growing desperation she even thought of Elsa, a girl she barely knew or even where she lived. Casting her eyes round the room only brought back the many happy moments she had shared with Ephraim in this lovely old apartment; memories which had multiplied many times over with the arrival of baby Aaron. She remembered it was on this very sofa she had broken the news to Ephraim of being pregnant; a joy now marred by the thought of having brought an innocent young child into a world hell-bent on the genocide of her race.

Having decided not to contact any of those people who might have been prepared to help her, she thought again about Elsa. She was single with no family or children to think about so would she agree to provide temporary accommodation until she could plan something more secure? She remembered her saying that she worked in a club. But which club and where?

Elsa had several times mentioned the name of the club but galling to think it hadn't registered with her. Looking down on the street below she recalled that Elsa and her soldier friend were walking to her apartment so hopefully both the club and her apartment might be close by.

Becoming increasingly frustrated at being unable to recall the name of the club she gave up and set about packing a suitcase with several changes of clothes and toiletries. In the hanging wardrobe, she let her fingers dwelt longingly on the silken folds of her concert dresses in the knowledge she was probably seeing them for the last time. Taking a deep breath, she closed the mahogany panelled door with a dismissive shrug.

Pressing down on the packed suitcase lid, her acute hearing picked up the sound of men voices coming from the ground floor. Warily opening the front door she immediately recognised the gruff voice of the ground floor tenant in animated conversation but with whom she wondered. Hoping beyond hope that it wasn't the Gestapo, she cautiously peered over the balustrade and was relieved to see he was speaking to a slightly built man wearing the distinctive green uniform of a Postal Delivery worker

Thinking quickly, an idea came to mind. 'Excuse me.' Hearing her voice she saw both men look up. 'Do you know this neighbourhood very well?

Luckily it was the Postal worker who responded to her enquiry. 'If you're addressing me, young lady, how may I help you?'

Not wanting to say too much in front of her neighbour, her reply was guarded. 'I'm seeking a friend's address and thought you would be the best person to ask.' Even in the dimly lit hallway below, Hannah detected a hint of smugness appear on the man's face.

'I have a special telegram for number 11 on the fourth floor; you're on the floor below aren't you?'

'Third floor; shall I wait for you?'

'If you will. I'll get the lift to the fourth and then use the stairs. I can use the exercise.'

Returning to her apartment she was careful to leave the front door fully open and it wasn't too long before she heard the man announce his presence with a faintly called 'hello there'. The Postman, an elderly man clearly too old for military service, was breathing heavily from the effort of carrying his heavy post bag down from the floor above. His moulded helmet bearing the Bundesposte Imperial Crest reminded her of a photograph of her Grandfather wearing a similarly shaped helmet during the Great War; a Pickelhaube she seemed to recall.

'Thanks for stopping by, I know you must be extremely busy.' The man's weathered face took on a pained expression ostensibly to justify her sympathetic observation.

'Doing twice as much but what else can you expect at a time like this. Now, what can I do for you?'

'I'm trying to contact an old friend who came to Berlin to work in a nearby club. But I'm afraid I don't know which club or its address so I was wondering whether you could help me?

Would you know the names of clubs in this immediate area and where they are located?'

The pained expression was immediately replaced by one of paternal concern. 'I know of several clubs and bars around these parts but they're not the type of place a girl like you would want to go to, believe me.' Giving her a broad wink, he added 'I'm sure you get my meaning, young lady.'

'I think so and thank you for your concern but all I want to do is to contact this person and I'm afraid this is the only information I have.'

Satisfied he had discharged a moral duty to impart due caution, the man's brow furrowed. 'Let me think now; there is the Hermitage Club or has that been closed?' The question was self-directed. 'That would be the nearest but it was always full of men, if you follow my drift?'

Resting his mail bag on the floor and beginning to now warm to the challenge, he raised his hand and cupped his chin. 'Then there is Heidi's Bar which is not the place I think a friend of yours would work in and then there is the Hoffenblute on Brookestrasse.' He got no further.

'That's it... the Hoffenblute!' Hannah's memory clicked into gear. 'That's where she said she worked.'

'Well that's one of the better clubs. Not that I would know of course but you pick these things up as you walk your round. Now let me see.' The lips on the elderly face pursed. 'As I say, it's on Brookestrasse and very close to the Army barracks; I can't remember the exact number but you can't miss it.' Reaching down for his bag with one hand and adjusting his uniform jacket with the other, the Postman looked at his watch. 'Is there anything more I can do for you before I go?

'No thanks; you have most helpful.' Walking to the door, Hannah put a guiding hand on the Postman's elbow. 'Do be careful as you go down the stairs; some of the lights aren't working.'

'I will, and good luck with your friend. I hope you find her.'

TWENTY THREE

Entering the dimly-lit interior of the Hoffenblute Club, her keen sense of smell instantly detected the unmistakeable odour of stale beer and tobacco. Earlier, she had waited until dusk had settled on the city and then forced herself to wait a further hour, resisting the temptation to switch on any light in the apartment for fear of attracting the attention of the Gestapo. Even with the heavy curtains fully closed, she knew it was still possible for chinks of light to be seen from the street below.

Following the elderly Postman's directions she had no difficulty in finding the oddly-named Hoffenblute club. Peering through its half-open doorway she stopped, unsure whether to enter or look for a bell push to attract attention. During the short walk from her apartment she again puzzled why the Gestapo, having failed to arrest her at the Kroll Opera House, had not turned up at the apartment. Thinking back to her conversation with Irene Schumacher, it occurred to her that she would not have actually seen the names on the Gestapo list but in witnessing the arrest of the other Jewish members of the orchestra she had probably assumed it did which would account for the distraught look she had given in answer to her question. 'But suppose my name wasn't on that list' she thought; 'then I would have no reason to hide.'

Failing to find any external means of attracting attention, she pushed the door fully opened and entered the club's brightly-lit interior. To her left was a cloakroom and beyond that, partly obscured by a stained red velvet curtain, was the entertainment area. Reluctant to go any further, she called to attract attention.

Moments passed before her call elicited a response from somewhere behind a small staging area.

'What can I do for you;' the voice belonged to a short overweight man, his collarless shirt open at the neck and the waistband of his trousers straining against his corpulent girth.

'We're not open for another two hours.' Approaching Hannah, she saw his calculating eyes looking her up and down. 'What is it you're after?'

'I'm looking for a friend of mine, a girl named Elsa... Elsa Seilhamer. I understand she works here.'

'And if she does, what d'you want with her?'

'That's my business; I just want to know when she will be here.' The terseness of her reply appeared to take the man by surprise.

'She does work here but she won't be around until about 10 o'clock; she likes to turn up when the customers are well lubricated does Elsa.' He gave an oily smile. 'Is she a friend of yours?' There was no mistaking the man's less aggressive change of tone.

'Yes she is but with the bombing we've lost touch.' Pushing her luck further she added the one other detail she was able to recall. 'Would you know her address by any chance? I believe she sometimes shares her apartment with two other girls but having moved several times in the past few months I've mislaid it.'

'Does that mean you're looking for a job?' His eyes ran over her figure. 'With your looks you could earn good money working here.'

Smiling at the very obvious meaning of the man's remark she decided to play him along. 'And what exactly would I have to do to earn this good money?' Lowering her eyes, she gave what she hoped would be seen as a seductive smile. 'I wouldn't be very good serving drinks; I can't add up which means I would be giving your customers the wrong change.'

Quickly assessing the apparent naivety of the attractive woman standing before him, the man began to scent the smell of easy money. 'How well do you know your friend Elsa? Has she ever told you how she earns her money?'

'I know Elsa entertains customers and I assume she gets paid a commission on the drinks they buy?' The uncertainty in her voice was straightaway picked up by the man.

'You don't know do you? How do you think girls like your friend earn what they do without having to work during the day?' It wasn't so much a question, more like being invited to draw a logical conclusion.

'If you are about to tell me that Elsa is a hostess then of course I knew that. I just told you, we've been friends for years.'

'Then your 'friend' would have told you that she earns her money not just by commission on the drinks she persuades her customers to buy but from what she can squeeze out of them upstairs.'

'For sex? You mean Elsa sells herself for money?' This time there was no hiding her gullibility.

'What else would she do it for? It's the best currency in town right now; especially with so many people looking for a good time.'

'Elsa was with a soldier when I last saw her; does that mean you get lots of servicemen in here?' She hoped this question would deflect the man's attention from herself.

'Of course we do; where else d'you think all these boys go to when they're off duty? Hannah chose to let the question pass.

The man volunteered a few more titbits. 'We get a mix of people in here; a few civilians of course but mainly soldiers from the barracks down the road plus a few sailors and airmen passing through this part of town. They're all looking for a good time with lots of cash to throw around.' Glancing at the watch on his wrist to indicate he had more pressing things to do, he tried one final shot. 'Look, I'll tell you where to find Elsa so why don't you talk it over with her and if you decide you'd like to give it a try, then come back and talk to me again. OK?' He turned to leave but paused in mid-stride. 'By the way, what's your name?'

Instantly cautious, she blurted out 'Emma – Emma Schmidt.'

'Right, well I'm Kaiser Wilhelm so maybe I'll see you later.'

It took just a matter of minutes for Hannah to walk the short distance to the barely legible address written on a stained beer mat. Approaching the building, she recalled Elsa mentioning that she occasionally let other girls from the club stay at her rented apartment and wondered what reason she would give for her visit if Elsa wasn't at home and the door was opened by a stranger.

It took several rings on the bell before she heard the front door release give access to the inner hallway. A single low watt light bulb in the hallway served only to emphasise the general dowdiness of the building but worse was the pungent smell of stale cooking.

From the rack of numbered mail boxes she saw that Elsa's apartment was probably located on the second floor with the entrance to the stairwell barely visible in the gloom.

Entering it, the smell of cooking was even more overpowering and looking up, she saw the stairs had no natural light. Gingerly negotiating her way past a bicycle and the undercarriage of a pram, both chained to the metal balustrade, she reached the second floor. After the gloom of the stairwell the brightly-lit hallway took her by surprise. Glancing to her left she spotted the number on the door of Elsa's apartment.

It seemed ages before a heavy eyed Elsa responded to the doorbell.

'Hannah.' A questioning expression immediately replaced the sleepiness in Elsa's eyes. 'What are you doing here? C'mon in.' Turning, she led the way into a deceptively spacious lounge.

'Take a seat or would you prefer to go in there?' Without waiting for a reply, Elsa led her into the warm kitchen. 'Sorry I took so long to open the door. I was in the process of getting up; very busy at the club last night so I was trying to catch up on my beauty sleep before this evening. Can I make you a coffee?'

Nodding grateful acceptance, she watched as Elsa filled a large enamel kettle and saw again just how attractive she was.

'I had to call at your club to get your address; I think the barman I spoke to was somewhat reluctant to let me have it so I had to pretend we were friends of many years but I don't think he believed me.'

'I'm surprised he gave it to you. He's a miserable wretch and normally he won't help anyone unless there's something in for him.'

After several attempts with a spluttering match, the gas finally ignited with a mild whoosh causing blue flames to lick hungrily around the base of the kettle. From a wall cupboard, Elsa produced two large mugs, putting a generous spoonful of coffee in each one. 'Did he also tell you what I did at the club?'

'He said you were a hostess and that you were very popular with his customers.' She thought it prudent not to expand further.

Elsa gave a wry smile; 'the 'barman' as you call him is the owner; Otto Hirsh. He's owned the Hoffenblute for years but I've only worked there for six months. He treats me OK but I wouldn't trust him further than I could throw him. He'd sell his own mother if he thought there might be some profit in it.'

'I rather formed that opinion of him myself. But I suppose when you run a night club then you need to be focussed on the business. After all, it's not a charity is it?'

Elsa's reactive laugh took Hannah by surprise. 'I've heard the Hoffenblute called many things but never a charity.' Still chuckling, she turned and gingerly touched the top of the kettle as if to test whether the water was hot enough. Moving to the small window overlooking the rear of the building, Elsa appeared to deliberate before speaking. 'So tell me... ' she hesitated; 'why are you here?' As she turned to face her, Hannah saw that all trace of friendliness had disappeared from Elsa's face.

'I think I am about to be arrested and I need a place to stay. The Gestapo came to the rehearsal room two days ago and took away all the Jewish members of the orchestra and I think my name was on their list too. I'm afraid to go to my apartment in case they are waiting for me so I'm here because I have no one else I can turn to in Berlin. I remembered your kind words about a Jew being the same as any other person and stupidly perhaps, I thought you might help me.'

Looking into Elsa's face, Hannah could see no perceptible change of expression and she knew then that she had been overly optimistic. 'I'm sorry Elsa, I have no right to ask you that. I'm sorry; truly sorry.'

Appearing to disregard the contrition in Hannah's voice, Elsa faced the woman she had met only hours before. When she spoke her voice was devoid of warmth. 'I don't suppose you've thought about what would happen if I was caught sheltering a Jew? And how do I explain you to my neighbours let alone any of my club mates who stay here from time to time?'

'Look Elsa, I have already said I'm sorry for coming here. I simply didn't think it through but when you are as scared as I am then you don't think very clearly. I'm ashamed to say I was only thinking of myself which must sound extraordinarily selfish to you. So other than to repeat how sorry I am, what more can I say?'

Seemingly unmoved by Hannah's apologetic words, Elsa continued to stare nervily. 'Let's go into the other room, finish our coffee and talk about this a little more.'

With Elsa heading back to the sitting room, Hannah tried not to show her disappointment. The comfortably furnished lounge was untidy with an opened magazine and several odd shoes lying on the floor.

'Sit down and try not to look at the mess; I usually tidy up once a week but in a matter of hours, it looks just the same again. And the bombing doesn't give you any incentive to keep the place tidy when you know it could all be blown away in an instant.' Stretching from her chair to open a draw, Elsa drew out a packet of cigarettes and pushed them across the small table. 'Do you smoke Hannah?'

'No I don't; in fact I've never even tried them. Even the smell of cigarettes makes me feel heady; much the same with alcohol too.'

A look of incredulity appeared on Elsa's face. 'Are you telling me you've never touched alcohol or smoked a cigarette in your whole life?' Lighting her own cigarette, Elsa inhaled deeply. 'I can't believe a girl can get to your age without at least having had a drink or two.' Laughing to herself, Elsa leaned back in the leather armchair. 'I don't suppose you tried sex either did you? Before you got married I mean?'

Strangely enough, Hannah didn't feel embarrassed by the directness of Elsa's question. 'No of course I didn't. For a Jewish girl to get pregnant was a fate worse than death.

Elsa smiled. 'But didn't you tell me that your husband is a doctor so surely he would know what to do if you slipped up?'

This time it was Hannah's turn to laugh. 'For that very reason, Elsa, doctors are usually more cautious. But the biggest deterrent I suppose is what parents and friends would think so we were pretty cautious I guess.' Inwardly, she marvelled at how easy it was to talk with Elsa and to share such intimate details.

Drawing on her cigarette before extinguishing most of it in the empty ashtray, Elsa threw another direct question. 'Now that you're no longer working, what will you do for money?

'I have some savings but why do you ask? Surprisingly, Hannah felt more sensitive to discussing money than she had about her pre-marital life.

'Because dear girl, if I let you live here, you will have to pay your share. And you will also have to share my room. Fortunately I have a large bed and I don't usually get home until the early hours so on most nights you shouldn't be too disturbed..'

Confused by Elsa's apparent change of mind, she knew she had to clarify the situation. 'Look, I may be clutching at straws but only a moment ago you pointed out the dangers of sheltering a Jew but now you're saying I could stay here if I can manage my share of the rent. That would be wonderful from my point of view but what about your friends here... won't they inform on me once they know I'm Jewish?

'How will they know? Are you going to tell them?'

'Of course not but they will find out because my papers say I'm Jewish.' A note of despair crept into Hannah's voice.

'Then get a different set of papers and a new identity; that would solve your problem.'

'So what do I do? Go along to the appropriate Government office and tell them I want to change my identity? I wouldn't even get out of the building before being arrested.'

The expression on Elsa's face darkened, reflecting the fact that she was about to say something which she felt uncomfortable with. 'There are ways of doing such things but invariably there is a cost attached which is why I asked you about money.'

'Elsa, I know you mean well but if it was only a question of money then surely all the wealthy Jewish people would be doing it; wouldn't they?'

'You've got it wrong Hannah. The wealthy Jews, as you call them, are paying to leave Germany. Not to change their identity and remain here. But that door is now closed with the Swiss turning refugees back at the border.

'How on earth do you know about that? And fake identity cards too?'

'Which of those two questions would you like me to answer first?

'Start with the obvious one; is it possible for a Jew to obtain false papers good enough to pass scrutiny particularly by the Gestapo? Do you know anyone who has actually managed to do that?'

'That's another question Hannah and any more like that could cause me problems.'

'I don't understand. How can my questions cause you problems?

'Because if I tell you too much and you get arrested you will be interrogated and 'coerced' by the Police to tell everything you know which would then involve me.'

Instantly the senseless murder of neighbour Glickstein and her own experience with the two Gestapo thugs at her apartment sprang to mind and she knew that Elsa's concern had terrifying substance.

'You're right' she acknowledged; it's better I don't know. I really need to think this through before getting you involved or without knowing whether my name was on that Gestapo list. But I won't know that without going back to my apartment and waiting to see what happens but then of course it could be too late.'

Leaning back, Elsa folded her arms across her chest. 'Sensibly, I think you should assume your name was on that list and do all you can to avoid arrest.' She drew a deep breath. 'Look, you know what I do for a living and I get to meet lots of men who are usually well lubricated servicemen if you get my meaning. And soldiers talk; sometimes about home, sometimes about where they've been fighting and sometimes about what's happening to Jews in those countries occupied by our troops.' She paused for breath. 'I think your musician friends were arrested as part of a new order from the Government and they're probably now on their way to Eastern Europe to work in whatever it is they are building there. At least, I think that's where they're sending you people.'

Listening to Elsa, Hannah felt the muscles in her throat constrict. Unable to speak, she felt her eyes moisten but dabbing them with a hastily produced handkerchief, she was able to prevent herself from crying. Knowing she had said too much, Elsa pulled Hannah into an embrace.

'Look, don't worry; you can stay here until you decide what you want to do. No hurry so take your time and we'll try to work something out.' Easing herself back, Elsa softly dabbed at the moistness on Hannah's face with her own small handkerchief. 'But no more questions otherwise I may hand you over to the Gestapo myself!'

Elsa's misguided attempt at humour failed to provoke a reaction from Hannah but within herself she felt the stirrings of two quite bewildering emotions; outward relief at the prospect of sanctuary coupled with a strange inner feeling of indebtedness to this woman she barely knew.

TWENTY FOUR

The International Red Cross delegation's visit to Theresienstadt passed off much as the German authorities had planned. The Jewish inhabitants of the Camp, mainly from Berlin, appeared to the casual observer to have not only accepted their lot of being resettled but against the backdrop of wartime rationing and general shortages, they actually appeared grateful to be well fed and cared for. Housed in the former barracks of the Czech Army, the newly refurbished single storey accommodation units provided visible evidence of the comfort and security offered to displaced persons by a benevolent German Government.

The Swiss lawyer leading the international delegation was particularly impressed by the medical facilities as dispensed by a former Berlin medical practitioner... a Dr. Ephraim Fischer.

His surgery was open on a daily basis other than after sunset on the Jewish Shabbat and even then access was available in the event of an emergency. Dr. Fischer himself had appeared to be thoroughly professional though reticent even when a member of the Red Cross delegation, a Swiss professor of medicine insisted on speaking with him out of earshot of the ever-present German officers.

But had this same professor spoken to this same Jewish doctor just days before, he would have gained a less favourable impression of Theresienstadt and perhaps a fuller understanding of the gross deception being employed with Teutonic thoroughness as part of the Nazi Government's Final Solution to the Jewish Question; a chilling euphemism for nothing less than the systematic extermination of the Jewish race.

But this was a very different Dr. Fischer, a man much changed from the spirited and erudite physician who had dared to question the doctrine of Aryan superiority. Retribution had come swiftly to Ephraim just hours after leaving the dinner attended by the Commandant. Awoken from a deep sleep by a burning sensation in the centre of his forehead, he instinctively attempted to push away the source of the pain but as if in a bad dream, he felt both arms constrained by the sheet being held firmly down on both sides of the bed. Now fully awake, his eyes focussed on the hate-filled features of the Camp Adjutant bending over him holding a lighted cigar. Puffing hard to ensure the tip was red hot, the cigar was again pushed into his face, this time burning into the skin of his upper temple.

'You snore very loudly Dr. Fischer so my comrades and I have decided that we must correct that with the help of your surgical instruments of course. But that's not the only reason why we are here; is that not so, gentlemen?' By inclining his head slightly back and raising his eyes, Ephraim became aware of three other uniformed officers in the room, two holding the sheet taut and the third person no doubt ready to react if he showed any sign of resisting. Peering more closely, he recognised the young Lieutenant who had sat at the end of the dining table earlier that evening.

'You didn't listen, did you Doctor, when I told you never to cross me; so now we have to teach you a lesson. Our caring Commandant wants you alive for the Red Cross inspection but as long as you can talk when spoken to, he will be quite indifferent as to what happens to you in the meantime.'

The Adjutant leaned closer to Ephraim; so close that he could detect the strong smell of alcohol on his breath. 'Does that surprise you doctor, seeing how friendly you two were over dinner?'

Ephraim, his initial surprise now replaced by stark fear, heard ingratiating laughter from the other officers. Looking up, he saw the Adjutant nod his head to his fellow compatriots and felt the sheet around his shoulders slacken and his arms pulled above his head and tied to the metal bed end. At the same time his legs were similarly coupled to the end rail and the sheet removed from the bed.

'So my loquacious man of medicine, it's time we began. But before we do, I notice you have been singularly silent for a man who had so much to say earlier. Perhaps we shall succeed in helping you regain your voice. In fact I personally guarantee that will be the case.' The venomous hatred in the man's voice sent a shiver of added fear coursing through Ephraim's body.

Standing up to his full height, the Adjutant slowly unbuttoned his uniform jacket and carefully laid it on the back of the wooden chair. Next, he undid each of his two gold cuff links which Ephraim saw were embossed with the SS symbol and purposefully began to roll up the sleeves of his white dress shirt in a slow and deliberate movement designed to maximise the already unbearable tension within him.

'I wish there was something I could like about you Dr. Fischer but I have not been able to detect one single aspect which commends itself to me.'

Despite the paralysis of fear clutching at his innards Ephraim involuntarily reacted. 'The feeling is mutual I assure you Captain.'

'Ah, so you can speak.' He laughed in an unnaturally falsetto voice. 'That's good because we are about to give you an opportunity to express yourself even more.'

Even in his fearful state of mind the threat within the Adjutant's sarcasm was not lost on Ephraim. 'Is that why it takes four of you to inflict this 'opportunity' on me? But I forget myself.' He gave a mirthless laugh. 'You gentlemen are all members of the Waffen SS so the odds may be about right.'

Being aware of the Adjutant's notoriously quick temper, Ephraim knew he would never be closer to death than he was at that moment. But to his surprise, the Adjutant simply smiled and turned his attention to the metal tray being carried from the surgery by his accomplice. Blinking fear-induced sweat from his eyes, Ephraim saw to his horror that the Adjutant was holding a pair of surgical forceps in the jaws of which was a glowing piece of red hot metal.

'Now doctor,' he paused deliberately, 'earlier you impressed us all with your knowledge of High Command field operations but this is one order which you will not be aware of.

From tomorrow, all Jews working for the Reich will be given a number which will be tattooed on their forearms and therefore not removable. However, because you will have the honour of being the first Jew in Theresienstadt to bear this mark, we thought you ought to be a little different from those other creatures; which is why we are here tonight.' With exaggerated deliberation the Adjutant slowly held the forceps over Ephraim's face.

'Do you recognise this symbol, doctor?' He paused to let Ephraim focus on the hot metal object. 'It will be a pity if you can't recognise it because it will remain with you for the rest of your life... however short that may be.'

Through eyes smarting from the salty sweat streaming from his raised forehead, Ephraim recognised the crude symbol of the swastika, rapidly losing its red glow as the heat dissipated.

'I think we may need to put this in the burner again, doctor. They say the hotter the metal, the less pain. What do you think? Shall we try and see what happens? We can always do it again if we don't like the result.'

Despairing of any form of compassion, Ephraim closed his eyes and inwardly began to recite a verse from the Talmud, memorised as a child but fixated in his memory ever since.

On the edge of consciousness, Ephraim felt the burning metal sear the flesh on his chest and held there for interminable seconds before being withdrawn. Despite his body being restrained by the bonds holding his hands and feet he felt his back arch in an uncontrolled spasm. Above the roaring in his ears, he heard himself scream out in indescribable pain and several times he thought his heart was about to fail. As the intensity of the pain receded, he once more became aware of the voices of his tormentors.

Mercifully, a douche of cold water struck his fevered face, and he felt the ropes holding him to the bed being removed.

'Welcome doctor; you are now a fully accredited member of the Untermenschen; an endearing term which accurately describes parasitic creatures like you.'

Sitting up, Ephraim saw that only the young Lieutenant had remained with the Adjutant; of the other two there was no sign. The sickening stench of burning flesh was overbearing and looking down Ephraim saw a pool of his own excrement between his inner thighs... voided from his bowel at the height of the torture.

No longer caring whether he lived or died, Ephraim reached down and scooped his hand in the revolting discharge. 'You see this, Kernick? This is Jewish shit and it will still be here when you and your kind have long gone; mark my words well, you evil Nazi bastards.'

For the second time that night, the Adjutant did not respond as Ephraim expected.

'Come now doctor; be a little circumspect. You could get yourself in a lot of trouble with that loose mouth of yours. Let me tell you the point of this exercise?' Several seconds of silence elapsed before he continued. 'If you so much as say one word out of place when the Red Cross delegation visit this Camp then you will be brought back here and I personally will go somewhat further than your Rabbi did with your circumcision. To be precise, I will use a gas torch to burn off your Jewish bollocks and watch with utmost sympathy as you slowly bleed to death with not so much as a single Aryan bullet to ease the pain of your journey into the next world. I trust I make myself clear?' Without waiting for a response, he strode towards the door beckoning the Lieutenant to follow. Stopping in the doorway, he turned once more to savour the pained distress of his tortured victim. 'Clean yourself up and see a doctor about that burn. It looks quite nasty to me!' He gave a shrug. 'But what do I know about such things? As you know... I'm not a doctor.'

TWENTY FIVE

'You would have to be living on a different planet not to know what's happening to the Jews in this country. Everywhere you look they're being rounded up, shoved into special areas and then packed off on cattle trucks to God-knows where. Thank goodness you're here with me.'

The flow of words from Elsa brutally encapsulated the grim events daily taking place in Berlin and other German cities.

Several days earlier and unbeknown to Hannah, Elsa had made a point of visiting her friend's former apartment building off Goethestrasse. Using her well-honed talent of being able to elicit information from men, it did not take her long to strike up a conversation with the pompous individual living on the ground floor. On the pretext of being a stranger to Berlin and seeking accommodation, Elsa's tactile approach to men of all ages obviously rekindled distant memories in the mind of the older man. Invited into his comfortable apartment and displaying a length of stockinged leg that that would have been revealing even in the soft lighting of the Hoffenblute, it wasn't too long before her newest admirer informed her that the Gestapo had visited the flat on the third floor just a day after Hannah had fled. The apartment was now occupied by an official who worked in a Government Ministry.

Tentatively enquiring about the previous tenants, she did her best to display moral indignation when he told her that they were Jews; very bad Jews, who had now gone their separate ways. The husband, a doctor, was now in Switzerland earning huge amounts of money from Jewish refugees while his wife, a musician, had moved in with a high-ranking German officer and was living in high style despite the shortages and privations elsewhere throughout the country. Unfortunately he didn't know the whereabouts of the couple's small child but he believed they had placed him in care so as not to be burdened in their new environments. As the man drew his rancorous litany to a close, she recalled Hannah briefly mentioning a child on the night they had first met but not since.

Adjusting her skirt to a less revealing level she thanked the man profusely and rewarded him with a kiss on the cheek, deliberately leaving the rosy red imprint of her lipstick as a memento of her visit. On her way to the door Elsa innocently enquired whether the man had a wife. 'Oh yes; I'm expecting her home at any moment.'

In which case,' she thought, 'you will be in very deep shit!'

Over breakfast the following morning Elsa casually mentioned her visit to the apartment building in Charlottenburg and was relieved by Hannah's positive reaction to her news.

'So it's nice to know I got out in time; the question is, what do I do now?'

'There was something else, Hannah. Your nosey neighbour told me you had a child. I remember you mentioning something about your baby when I first came to your apartment so where is your child now?'

Seeing tears begin to fill Hannah's eyes, Elsa took her hands in hers. 'Don't say anything now but if you want to talk about it later then I'll be happy to listen.'

'You're right, Elsa; it's not something I can even think of, let alone talk about without floods of tears but when I feel able to do so then you will be the person I will unload on... I promise.'

'Releasing Hannah's hands Elsa leaned back in her chair. 'On another subject, how's your money holding up?'

'It's holding up for the moment but disappearing fast because I'm not earning anything to top up my savings. I need to find a job but I can't do that until I get my new ID card.'

Lighting a cigarette, Elsa blew a smoke ring towards Hannah. 'I spoke to the man handling that last night. His work is good but he has had to change your photograph slightly as you have a well-known face in some circles. Not that the Police on the street will recognise a world famous violinist of course!' Her irrepressible humour was never far from the surface.

'As we are talking about money, can I ask whether you are losing money because I'm sharing your room?'

Elsa's infectious laugh kicked in. 'What you really mean is whether I'm losing business by not being able to bring men home to my bed because you're already in it. Well the short answer to that is 'no'. I generally do enough business at the Club so when I get home then all I want to do is sleep; nothing else. So don't give it another thought.' Reaching for the ashtray, Elsa stubbed out her cigarette. 'By the way, you can skip your rent this week. I've had a lot of good evenings at the Club lately. Apart from the usual crowd of soldiers and airmen, we've had shiploads of sailors in and they spend their money like they're never coming back on dry land again especially the submariners. Can you imagine being under the sea in a rusty steel tube?' She grimaced. 'Personally I couldn't do it but their money is good so why should I worry.'

'That doesn't sound like you Elsa. I've never met a kinder person than you so I can't really believe you don't care. Each one of those sailors will be someone's husband, brother or son so imagine how you would feel if one of them was a member of your family.'

Stung by her words, Elsa impulsively jumped to her feet. 'You self-righteous bitch! You don't know the first thing about me other than how I earn my money so don't presume to impose your moral judgements on me. OK?' Standing up, Elsa disappeared into her bedroom.

Mortified by Elsa's unexpected outburst and too shocked to know what to do next, she felt an acute sadness. Elsa was risking her own liberty to provide her with a safe haven in a city where Jews were now being hunted like animals. Not only that, she was also her only lifeline to survival. Without her continuing friendship, she would undoubtedly be sharing the same fate as countless other Jews either being murdered or transported to Eastern Europe.

From the bedroom, she heard the sound of sobbing... an intensely distressing sound made worse by knowing she had been the cause of Elsa's reaction. Quietly entering the bedroom, Hannah saw Elsa lying across the still unmade bed. Looking up, she beckoned Hannah to her. Her eyes, swollen with tears made their own emotional appeal. Reaching down, she cradled Elsa's moist cheek with her hand.

'My dear sweet girl; what did I say to hurt you so much? I can't bear to see you like this.'

Covering Hannah's hand with her own, Elsa attempted to stem the flow of tears. Sitting up, she leaned towards Hannah and hugged her close. 'You know Hannah, there are times when I look at you and weep. You are so innocent and yet there are times when I would willingly swap places with you.' Straightening up, she withdrew her arms from around Hannah and instead held her by her shoulders. 'You remind me of all the things I wanted to be when I was a young kid growing up. Just look at yourself for a moment; you're twenty six or seven and you've had only one man in your life who just happens to be your husband, for God's sake! And then I look at myself in the mirror, particularly after a heavy night and what do I see? Someone who sells herself for money and booze and where will it get me? I'll be old before my time and already I can see lines appearing on my face.' She pulled her hand away from Hannah's shoulder and lightly drew a finger around her own mouth. 'Sorry my innocent little cherub but hearing you say how nice I am to everyone was just too much. But be assured; hard-nosed Elsa Seilhamer is once more in control of her emotions and I promise it won't happen again.'

Leaning forward, Elsa cupped Hannah's chin in her hand and raising her head she gently kissed her moist lips. The suddenness of Elsa's impulsive move and the electrifying sensation it caused stunned her like nothing she had ever experienced before. Instead of pulling away, she reached out and pulled Elsa closer... their lips reluctant to part. She heard herself begin to moan and felt her body begin to tremble uncontrollably. Falling back onto the bed, she became aware of Elsa's hand, still moist from her tears, enter her loosely buttoned pyjama top and begin to stroke her breast and tease her hard nipples. Gasping for air, it was Elsa who finally pulled her lips away. 'My God! What did I just say about you being so innocent? Are you about to tell me you've never kissed a woman before because if you are, then I just won't believe you?'

'No, I have never kissed a woman before. In fact, I've only ever kissed two men in such a way... Ephraim and a man you don't know, which I regretted immediately.'

'Was that the Army officer you told me about?'

'No, it wasn't him; he wasn't that sort of man or rather I don't think he was that sort of man. I think if I had kissed him I would have regretted that too. He may have got the wrong impression about me.'

'You mean he may have thought you were easy meat... like me?'

'No, please Elsa, don't say that. I didn't mean it that way. This war makes people do all sorts of things just to get by so please don't think I'm being judgemental again. I know people who think musicians are strange creatures which in a funny way, I suppose we are.'

As she continued speaking, Hannah was unashamedly aware that Elsa's warm body was still embracing her own. 'Without you, Elsa, I would probably be on my way to the East, or even dead like my dear old neighbour so I am truly very grateful to you from the bottom of my heart.' Closing her eyes, she again sought Elsa's mouth with her lips; eagerly venturing into the erotically charged world which had suddenly opened to her.

TWENTY SIX

Two evenings later an excited Elsa returned from the Hoffenblute earlier than usual. 'Is there a woman here by the name of Kristine Keller? If there is, I may have something for her.'

Hearing Elsa's voice, she eased herself off the bed, dropping the book which had lost her interest before the end of its first chapter. 'I'm here in the bedroom but now coming.' Tidying her hair with her open fingers she joined Elsa in the lounge. 'Why are you home so early?'

'Because I have your new identity papers my darling. From tonight you are no longer a Jew by the name of Hannah Bergmann but a pure Aryan by the name of Kristine Keller. Welcome to the Fatherland!'

Nervously taking the envelope from Elsa's outstretched hand, she took a deep breath and drew out what she hoped might be her passport to a normal existence within the Jew-hating Nazi State. Scrutinising the document closely, Hannah saw that the identity card produced by Elsa's contact looked impressively authentic. The forger had given her the identity of a woman of similar age who Elsa informed her had been killed in a recent air raid in Hanover but whose death had not been reported.

Cleverly, the forger had partially sealed the identity card within a cellophane cover designed to give the impression of added care by its bearer but in reality putting an opaque layer between the photograph and the eye of a casual scrutiniser.

'Sorry but I opened the envelope before I got here. I wanted to check it was what you were paying for.'

'So what do you think, Elsa; will it pass inspection?

'Why not, it looks very good to me. When you get used to your new name we'll go to the Hoffenblute for a celebratory drink.'

'Kristine Keller... ' Hannah let the name roll off her tongue. 'It won't take me long to get used to it but going to your Club is out of the question. You've probably forgotten that I've met the man who runs your club and he would recognise me in a moment whatever name may be on my identity card.'

'But you didn't give him your name, did you?'

'No I didn't but all I really want to do is to be able to get around this city confident that my new identity will stand up to examination if I'm questioned.'

'I understand that but what will you do for money? You aren't earning money from your orchestra job so what are you going to do?'

Hannah was amused by Elsa's description of her soloist career as a 'job'. 'I need to think about that. At the moment I have no idea except I do know I wouldn't be able to work at your club. I remember you telling me that I'm the original one-man woman so there is no way I could bring myself to... '

'Do what I do for a living? Is that what you were about to say?'

'Elsa, I'm not criticising what you do for a living. What I really meant to say was that I am simply not able to do it. If for no other reason, I would be hopeless trying to small talk strange men. Basically I'm a very shy person unless I know what I'm talking about; my music for example.'

Expecting a volatile response, Hannah was relieved to see a look of puzzlement cross her friend's pert face.

'Can you play any instrument other than your violin... the piano perhaps?'

'Of course I can. Most musicians have the ability to play across a range of instruments. Why do you ask?'

'Because I think I may have just found the perfect job for Kristine Keller. Let me speak to the Boss this evening but before I do, would you fancy playing in the club?'

'I'm not sure. What type of music do they have there? I thought it would be a cabaret with a small band or am I out of touch with that as well?' Her deprecating remark brought a smile to Elsa's face.

'Hannah, you really are original. Thank God there aren't too many like you in this world.' Taking Hannah's hands in her own, she gave a kiss to each extended fingertip. 'So, do we give it a go or not? If you think you can handle it, we can go to the club tomorrow afternoon when things are quiet and you can see the set-up for yourself. Maybe have a tinkle on the piano to see whether it's up to your standard. If it isn't, don't tell the Boss it needs tuning. He's a tight fisted bastard who doesn't like parting with money... especially his own.'

Warming to the thought of being able to see and mix with people again, she gave a nervous smile. 'I feel apprehensive but you're right, I need to earn money and I can't do that by staying in your apartment all day. So let me give it a try but promise you won't leave me when we get to your club.'

'OK, I promise but right now I'm going to take advantage of this early night and get some sleep. Tomorrow morning I will re-introduce you to what passes as everyday living in this big city of ours. It's been a long time since I've treated myself to lunch so we'll do it together and then make our way to the Hoffenblute.'

'Elsa, I've never had a friend like you before. You've let me live in your home at huge risk to yourself; you've obtained a new identity for me, and now this... an opportunity to earn some much needed money. And what have I given you in return? Absolutely nothing. I wish there was something I could do... truly! You told me last week that you envied me but without you I would most likely be dead by now.'

'Hannah!' The sharpness in Elsa's tone took Hannah by surprise.

'What?'

'Shut up!'

Walking towards the bathroom, Elsa stopped. 'And there is something you can do for me when you've stopped feeling sorry for yourself. You can make me a coffee whilst I have a wash. And then warm up the bed for me. I'm determined to get a good night's rest for a change without some drink - sodden, sex-starved serviceman pounding me into sexual oblivion.'

'In which case, let this naïve, unworldly, non-drinking refugee from the real world prepare your path to the land of nod. I'll have your coffee ready when you've had your wash'.

Disappearing into the bathroom, Elsa made one last comment. 'And here's me thinking there's nothing you can do for me.'

That night, lying alongside Elsa, she wondered, not for the first time, where her life was taking her. Far removed from Ephraim and Aaron and owing her continuing freedom to this worldly woman for whom she felt such deep affection; an affection which in her heart she realised was unnatural and yet an emotion without any semblance of guilt. Even now, tantalisingly close to Elsa, she felt an urge to reach out and let her hands run over her still form, feeling each curve of her sumptuous body. Barely daring to breathe, she let her fingers extend towards the softness of Elsa's lips and gently pressed her finger against them as if it were her own lips making intimate contact. She felt Elsa stir, purse her lips and respond with the lightest of kisses to the tip of her extended finger.. Encouraged, Hannah eased herself closer and made contact with the warmth of Elsa's naked body. Lying there, for the first time since leaving her apartment, she felt a sense of peace which she desperately wanted to savour for as long as possible. Lost in her thoughts, she felt Elsa's hand move upwards and close over her fingers. Silently, she guided their joined hands downwards to her breast and a nipple which conveyed her growing excitement with its hardness.

Groaning in her excitement and now wanting Elsa to fully awaken, she squeezed the nipple as hard as she could and heard a sharp intake of breath escape from Elsa's lips. Resisting the urge to press even harder, she released her hold and pulled Elsa's yielding body onto her back. Wordlessly, she leaned over and pressed her lips over Elsa's partly open mouth.

'Dear God, Elsa... tell me what to do; I've never done this before but I don't want to stop.'

Wordlessly, Elsa sought Hannah's hands under the sheet and placed them on her breasts. 'Squeeze me hard and hurt me and don't stop if I cry out... .do it.'

The plaintive need from Elsa lent even greater urgency to her. Moving her head down, she cupped Elsa's firm breast in her mouth, her teeth easily locating each hard nipple in turn. Biting hard, she felt Elsa's body frantically react to the pain and heard her scream in ecstatic agony. Falling into a darkening abyss, Hannah felt her body being engulfed and finally overwhelmed in a wave of forbidden passion.

TWENTY SEVEN

The piano was in a surprisingly tuneful condition and even better, positioned at the rear of the area reserved for the small combo, making it easy to access and leave the stage via the curtained side wing without having to step onto the open dance floor. From this position she would be able to see into the dimly lit bar area without exposing her own self to the clientele. The owner, none other than the person she had encountered on her previous visit, demanded she play several pieces from a tattered score sheet produced from beneath the lid of the piano stool. Working her way through both numbers with several ad-libs of her own, she watched as the owner signified his satisfaction by way of an expressive grunt.

'OK, that will do. You can start tonight. I'll pay you the same as the last piano player and you'll get paid in cash at the end of each week.'

True to her word, Elsa had remained close by and she now suddenly interjected. 'You do it every time, you mean old bastard. Do you think my friend would work in a dump like this for that sort of money? That's why your last piano player walked out so you'll need to up the ante if you want to employ my friend.'

'Elsa, I'm talking to her... not you. And why should I pay more when she's not working the customers like you and the other girls do. That's where the money is and if she's that hard up then she knows what she can do. With her looks she could probably make as much as you with a bit of practice.'

Faintly amused to hear herself being discussed as though she wasn't there, it was several seconds before she spoke. 'Elsa's right; thank you for your offer but the money isn't what I was expecting so I'll try somewhere else but thank you for your time.' Raising herself from the stool, she retrieved her coat from a nearby chair and looked for the exit gap in the dark red curtain.

'If you won't employ my friend then I'm out of here as well so you won't be seeing me tonight.' The firmness in Elsa's voice took Hannah as much by surprise as it did the Bar owner.

'Elsa, please... you don't need to do this. I can find a job easily enough. There are plenty of bars and cafes who employ musicians so I just need to look around.'

'Then we'll do it together so let's get out of this place.'

'Wait. Wait... the two of you, just calm down will you.' Recovering from the suddenness of Elsa's ultimatum and facing the prospect of losing a positive contributor to his burgeoning profit, the owner opted for judiciousness.

'OK then.' He took a deep breath. 'I didn't realise you two were joined at the hip so this is what I'll do. I'll pay you half of what Elsa earns so the harder she works, you more you earn. You play the piano; she plays the customers. And that's my final offer... take it or leave it.'

Hannah's immediate reaction was to accept the offer before the man changed his mind but she was beaten to it by Elsa, who unpredictably as ever, reached out with both arms and gave the man an embracing hug.

'There, you mean old sod; that wasn't too difficult was it? Now we can go home and get ready for tonight's performance.' Walking towards the exit, she paused and inclined her head towards the owner. Thanks Boss... you won't regret this, I promise.'

'I already am.' Looking directly at Hannah he gave a wink before raising his arm in mock anger. 'Get out of here and take that conniving woman with you before I do something I regret. And don't be late tonight otherwise I'll deduct your earnings... from both of you!'

Outside the Hoffenblute, the two women gleefully embraced.

'Thanks Elsa, you really didn't have to do that but on the other hand, I'm pleased you did.'

'In which case you can buy me a drink later from your first night's earnings and I should warn you I am quite partial to a tot of champagne; or what passes for champagne in this city of ours.'

Musically, the job presented no difficulty. From her position behind the upright piano she was able to observe the various groups of customers, mainly servicemen with a sprinkling of civilians. With Elsa, there were five other girls employed to entertain them. They did this by dancing with them on the small dance floor in front of the bar, all the while encouraging their customers to keep the alcohol flowing. In regular procession, girls would disappear for short periods of time before returning to repeat the cycle once more albeit with a different man.

From her vantage point, Hannah noticed that Elsa appeared to be the most popular girl in the club particularly with the civilian regulars. Guiltily, she was aware that her aversion to the selling of sex had been all but overcome in the realisation that her friend's numerous clients were adding to her own earnings. She even accepted those nights when she was forced to sleep on the sofa in the lounge when Elsa occasionally engaged in extracurricular activity with a client brought back to the apartment.

And this was one of those nights. Elsa had asked her to sleep on the sofa and despite wanting to lose herself in sleep, she found herself consciously listening to the sound of sexual activity coming from the bedroom. Her recent arousal with Elsa had introduced an entirely new dimension to her life and listening to Elsa now expressing very audible pleasure to someone else caused an unnatural pang of jealousy in her mind.

Unable to sleep, Hannah's mind inevitably turned once more to the events of the recent past. In a matter of weeks she had gone from being the principle soloist with Berlin's leading orchestra whilst living with her husband and child in an exclusive area of Charlottenburg but now compelled to earn a living by working with a false identity in a salacious night club. Worse, she had no way of knowing whether Ephraim was still alive or whether Aaron was still safe with Frieda.

Once again, the sound of renewed activity from the bedroom disturbed her train of thought. Knowing that sleep wasn't going to happen she decided to get up and make herself a warm drink. Looking out through the darkened kitchen window she was able to see fingers of intense light from a nearby searchlight battery piercing the night sky. In the distance Hannah heard the drone of approaching aircraft in the vanguard of yet another air raid by Allied bombers. The sudden crescendo of anti-aircraft fire made her jump and in the distance she saw a flaming orb of fire fall from the sky before exploding with a searing flash which for a brief moment exceeded the brightness of the searchlights.

'That will be one bomber which won't be making it home tonight.' The voice came from the doorway, startling Hannah who had carefully closed the door when she had entered the kitchen.

'Close your black-out curtain. If the windows get blown in, we'll be cut to shreds.'

Soundlessly obeying the instruction, Hannah turned to face Elsa's bed companion just as he turned on the light.

'Kristine... what are you doing up? You were fast asleep when I came home.' We didn't wake you up with our noise did we?' The innocence in Elsa's voice was beguiling. 'Sorry... let me introduce you. Kristine, this is Oskar. Oskar, this is Kristine.'

Hannah saw a look of instant recognition cross the man's face.

'No need for an introduction, Elsa. I believe I may have already met your friend. Its Bergmann isn't it? Hannah Bergmann... the violinist?

Staring at Hannah from across the kitchen stood the naked figure of SS Major Oskar Nagel.

The two Gestapo Police arrived within minutes of Nagel's call to his office at Prinz Albrechstrasse. Earlier, Elsa's frantic pleading on behalf of Hannah had been cut short when Nagel, who moments before had been enjoying Elsa's full repertoire of sexual tricks, coldly informed her that she too risked being arrested for giving material aid to a Jew. But if he was expecting the menacing coldness in his cultured voice to intimidate Elsa, he was wrong.

'You bastard! You could have walked away and no one would have been any wiser. And why would you pull me in. I'm not a Jew?'

'Indeed you aren't but your friend is. And she seems to have acquired a new identity and I suspect you may know how she managed that.' His raised eyebrow reinforced his question. Coolly dressing, he gave Elsa a cruel half-smile as he buttoned up his shirt.. 'And by the way... if you ever address me like again, let me show you what will happen to that entertaining body of yours.' Now fully dressed, he withdrew his black leather belt from around his uniformed waist. With menacing deliberation he slowly folded the belt in half leaving the end with the heavy silver buckle, swinging loose. Looking straight into Elsa's eyes, Nagel swung the belt down on to the seat of the chair next to where she was standing. The impact of the blow caused the chair to recoil backwards; its padded leather seat torn open, exposing the grey horse-hair infill beneath it.

'So take care my lovely, because if you open your mouth just once more you will be next to feel the end of my belt; it would be a pity if I had to spoil that pretty face of yours.'

Looking at the deep gash in the chair seat, Elsa numbly sat down, shocked by Nagel's display of crude viciousness. Unable to stop herself, she began to shake uncontrollably.

Seeing Elsa, strong street-wise Elsa break down, Hannah realised that she too couldn't hope to withstand the physical treatment she would receive at the hands of the Gestapo.

'Major Nagel!' the pleading tone in her voice was very evident. 'When you last interrogated me at that awful building which you operate from, you told me my release was due to my friendship with Colonel Von Hartmannn, head of the Abwehr unit here in Berlin. You might need to think about that.' To her surprise, Nagel did not attempt to interrupt.

'What you didn't know then or now is the extent of my relationship with him, a man obviously able to exert influence even within the Gestapo at a level which I suspect is somewhat higher than that of a major like yourself.' In his mind, Nagel admired the woman's ability to make his rank sound more like that of a junior subaltern. 'And he did that for me. So would you like him to know about your weakness for prostitutes like her and the use he might wish to make of it from an Army intelligence point of view?'

It was difficult to assess what effect this had on Nagel, more so as he showed no reaction to her threat.

'This person,' she nodded towards the still shaking Elsa, 'is just someone I share this apartment with. My Identity Card was provided for me by the Jewish underground for a price. The reason why this woman introduced me as Kristine is because she has always known me by that name since I came here last week.' Again she paused and again the Major maintained his unnerving silence. 'You already know I was a classical musician so do you really think I would willingly associate with a trollop who sells herself for sex like she does? Would you know what it's like having to listen to her banging away with people like you, night after night? So if you want to make a fool of yourself and in the process, have your card marked as a regular user of prostitutes, then go ahead and arrest her. Perhaps she deserves to be arrested for the whore she is, but don't try and associate her with me.'

It took a thunderstruck Elsa seconds to react.' You stuck up cow. How dare you! I might be what you say I am but at least I'm a German... unlike you! If I'd known you were a Jew, I would never have let you in here. As it is, I'm going to have to have this place fumigated the moment you're out of it.'

'Spoken like the whore you are.'

Without warning, Elsa leaped out of her chair and launched herself at Hannah. The burly form of Major Nagel was too late to stop Elsa grabbing Hannah by the hair, pulling her head back and delivering a bruising slap across her face. Before she could strike again, Nagel was able to roughly shove Elsa back, preventing her from striking Hannah a second blow. Visibly out of breath from his intervention, he glared at Hannah. When he spoke his voice was devoid of feeling. 'You are obviously a highly talented woman even for a Jew but don't try and take me for a fool or try my patience any further tonight. If you try that on me again, I will ensure you never actually get to the detention unit which would be a pity because I'm looking forward to dealing with you personally. I may even decide to spare you the necessity of being transported.'

'You,' pointing to Elsa, 'you open the front door and then sit down' pointing to a chair in the lounge.'

Still in shock by the suddenness of Elsa's attack, Hannah looked across the lounge and saw the two uniformed Gestapo Police officers staring in obvious confusion.

'Take this woman to HQ and put her in the detention unit. I will deal with the paperwork tomorrow.'

Looking up, Hannah saw a look of puzzlement cross the face of the younger of the two Policemen. 'Which woman are you referring to, Sir?'

'This woman, pointing at Hannah... the Jew.'

'Wait'... it was Elsa. Running into the bedroom and appearing moments later carrying Hannah's warm coat with a scarf tucked in the inner sleeve. 'Take this filthy coat with you; one thing less to contaminate my apartment with.'

Stopping in the doorway and feeling utter despair, Hannah turned and took one final look at Elsa... both women intuitively knowing they would never see each other again.

TWENTY EIGHT

Except for the absence of the iron bedstead which she remembered from her previous detention, the holding cell was grimly familiar. As her eyes adjusted to its interior gloom, she was glad to see a chair in the far corner of the cell. Sitting down, she pulled her coat tightly around her, expressing silent and grateful thanks to Elsa for her quick thinking. Even wrapped in the warm coat, it didn't take long for the cold to seep into her body. She remembered Ephraim once telling her that the best way to overcome this sensation was to energise the blood circulation by vigorous exercise. 'If he was here now, he would have me running round this room' she mused and despite the grimness of the surroundings she forced a wry smile.

Not for the first time since their parting, she wondered whether he might still be alive and if so, would they ever meet again? Irrationally, she drew a crumb of comfort from not having received any communication from him but in her quieter moments she knew this was unrealistic. She recalled seeing an official letter addressed to Mr. Glikstein's family which Ephraim had intercepted, stating that their gentle neighbour had died of a heart attack. Why, she wondered, did the Nazi government bother to communicate, let alone pervert such information to the point where a premeditated murder had been officially sanitised to become a statistical heart attack? She recalled Elsa telling her of gossip gleaned from several clients, one a senior Nazi officer, boasting of a new anti-Jewish programme now being communicated to special units within the military whereby all Jews were to be forcibly removed from Germany and transported to Poland and other points East. Once there, they would be forced to work in factories now being set up by the Government to supplement Germany's beleaguered war economy. Elsa had quickly changed the subject when she asked what was happening to those older Jews and children who were not able to work leaving her to draw her own chilling conclusion.

Sitting alone with her thoughts, she realised that she was now about to find out for herself just what does happen to Jews in Gestapo custody.

Despite the intense cold, Hannah realised that she must have drifted off because she was awakened by the cell door swinging open. The overhead light had been turned on and by its glow she saw a smiling Major Oskar Nagel looking down at her; this time fully dressed in the uniform of the SS Gestapo.

'Good morning... I see you managed to get some sleep.'

Hannah, her brain still sleepily befuddled, got to her feet but remained silent.

'I see we have only one chair in here; excuse me for a moment.' Turning, Nagel tapped on the door with his foot and patiently waited for it to be opened. Glancing back at Hannah he attempted to lighten the tension. 'Room service here is not what it used to be.'

The levity of the man's approach did nothing to lessen Hannah's caution. She heard the external lock click back and saw the door opened by a soldier dressed in the same black SS uniform as that of the Major.

'We need another chair in here. And fetch a glass of water too.'

The very mention of water made her realise how thirsty she was. She estimated it must be about five hours since she had last had a drink; in Elsa's kitchen she recalled, just before the entrance of the man now standing in front of her.

Turning to Hannah, the Major indicated with a slight nod of his head for her to sit down again. 'I will arrange for you to have something to eat when you have answered my questions. Ok?'

'Thank you.'

'You told me last night that you have known Elsa Seilhamer only since you moved into the same apartment; is that correct?'

'Yes. That is correct.'

'So if I ask you where you got your false Identity Card from, you will tell me that it was provided by your former neighbour Salomon Glickstein shortly before he died, will you not.'

Bemused by Nagel's approach, she was about to challenge it when the cell door swung open admitting the same soldier holding a wooden slatted chair in front of him on the seat of which was balanced a single glass of water.

'Put it down there and pass the water to her; and don't spill it!' Hannah noticed a slight shake in the young man's hand as he passed her the glass.

Straightening up, the soldier looked at Hannah with what she took to be a degree of apparent sympathy before asking the Major whether he required something more.

'No. Leave us and close the door behind you.' Exiting with obvious relief, the soldier slammed the cell door behind him.

'Now... where were we.' He glanced at his papers. 'I believe you were about to confirm that your former neighbour provided you with your forged Identity Card, were you not?'

'Major, I don't understand. I never told you that last night. I said it was provided by a member of the Jewish underground in return for a payment.'

'So who was this person and who introduced you to him? Or did this person simply walk up to you in the street and ask whether he could provide you with false papers? Or would you prefer me to think it was your fellow tenant Elsa Seilhamer who obtained it for you?'

The implication behind the Major's threat suddenly became chillingly clear.

'Would you wish to implicate your friend and expose her to questioning and certain execution or name a person who is already beyond the reach of justice? I will be guided by your decision Bergmann; the living or the dead? It's your choice.'

Putting the glass of water to her lips, she let the cold liquid slake her dry mouth and throat. She thought of Elsa who had given her shelter and friendship at great personal risk to herself. For her part, she had done nothing more than to dress her injured leg on the night they had first met. So was Nagel playing a game which only he was aware of and using his overnight bed mate as leverage?

'Major, I don't know what your reasons are for wanting to protect Elsa Seilhamer; only you would know that. But I'm confused because only last night you were prepared to have her arrested yet now you appear to want to absolve her from any involvement. If that is the case, then I am extremely grateful. So yes, it was my neighbour Mr. Glickstein who provided me with false papers.' Lowering her head she quietly added 'and may my God forgive me for saying that.'

'I'm sure he will, Bergmann. A Jew dies and a Gentile lives. That seems to me to be an equitable arrangement especially as the Jew in question is already dead!'

'I'm not in a position to question your logic Major or your reasoning but please understand I knew Mr. Glickstein and he was a gentle man and as far removed from criminality as you could wish for.'

'Bergmann, listen to me.' He gave an expressive sigh. 'I want you to forget your neighbour and move on to yourself which is why I'm questioning you instead of those two gentle souls you met on your last visit to this building.' Raising his head, the Major looked directly into Hannah's eyes. 'Thanks to a mutual friend telling me about your husband, I took the trouble to make an enquiry before I met with you this morning.'

Hannah tensed, her body instantly galvanised by the Major's comment. The absence of news to date had at least enabled her to retain a degree of optimism but was this bewilderingly contradictory officer about to now dash that hope?

Sensing the import of what he was about to say, the Major attempted to lighten the atmosphere by giving the barest hint of a smile which through her tearful eyes looked more like a grimace.

'Subject to the vagaries and limitations of field communications, I spoke with our unit at Theresienstadt earlier and I am told that your husband... is he called Fischer, Ephraim Fischer?' Hannah nodded in confirmation. 'Well, he appears to be alive and well and functioning as a Camp Doctor in one of the better camps in the East. That's all I can tell you I'm afraid.'

'Thank God.' More tears of relief flooded her eyes which she hastily tried to brush away with the end of her cashmere scarf. 'And thank you too Major; that was kind of you to take that trouble.'

'And you should also thank your unnamed friend too. Should I ever meet up with this person again I will pass on your thanks?'

'Thank her with all my heart.'

'Now, we need to talk about you.' Still digesting the news of Ephraim's continuing survival, she found it difficult to focus on what the Major said next, as though he was speaking to her from a distance.

'What I am about to tell you is not public knowledge, at least not yet. A new General Order has just been issued to special units in the Army whereby all Jews are to be arrested and transported to the occupied countries in the East. Jews from Berlin are being sent to holding camps such as Sachsenhausen and Ravensbruch whilst some have already been transported further east to camps where your husband is now located. I have no control as to where you will go or where you will end up. So whatever happens to you from now on is outside of my control. And more importantly you will now forget what I have just told you. I hope that's clear?'

'Very clear but why did you feel it necessary to arrest me? Couldn't you simply have left Elsa's apartment and forgotten about recognising me. After all, I'm not a criminal or any danger to the State or to your precious Nazi Party. I'm a musician for God's sake; nothing more than that.'

'But you are a Jew Miss Bergmann, albeit a beautiful Jew but still a Jew. And I am a Gestapo officer charged with arresting Jews. So having arrested you and ensured you have not been interrogated by officers less understanding than myself, then I have done my duty and I can do no more. At least when you leave here you will still be in one piece.' He looked up but she could not detect any obvious sympathy on his cold features

'And what if you were ordered to kill all the Jews arrested by your Gestapo; would you have come here this morning and murdered me?'

'Of course... and you would be making a fatal mistake to think otherwise.'

TWENTY NINE

Whether SS Major Oskar Nagel had chosen to use whatever influence he may have had, Hannah would never know. Following her interrogation she had been moved to a single cell and held for a further two days in solitary confinement. A watery soup plus a piece of stale bread had been pushed through the hatch in the cell door on each of those mornings but at no time did she ever see the person serving it. Thankfully the cell had a small toilet and hand basin which enabled her to ease her thirst from the constantly dripping tap but apart from the regularity of what served as a meal, she had no way of knowing whether it was day or night.

On what she calculated to be her third day in custody, the door of the cell was thrown open by a tight-lipped Guard and she was hurried to the ground floor and ushered into a grim looking yard at the rear of the building. There she joined a group of other inmates, many of whom wore the obligatory yellow stars on the arms of their coats. Like her, some were carrying nothing whilst others had either a small suitcase or a pathetic bundle of belongings tied together with hemp string.

Surrounding the group were yet more black-uniformed SS guards, each holding a truncheon which they used to prod their prisoners into an ever tighter group. More prisoners appeared from the building and she saw one elderly man stumble on the heels of the person ahead of him. Clearly hurt, the man tried to rise to his feet but it was obvious that his leg or ankle had sustained either a severe strain or fracture from the fall. The SS guard nearest to him shouted for him to get up but the man was plainly unable to do so. Holding out his hand for assistance, Hannah saw several men within the nearest group move to help him but prevented from doing so by other guards. Watching as though in slow motion, Hannah saw the guard point his rifle and aim with slow deliberation at the stricken man's head. Pulling the trigger; the noise of the gunshot reverberated around the high walls of the yard. Unable to draw her eyes away from the macabre horror taking place in front of her, Hannah saw the old man's head burst open, his body impelled downwards on to the grey cobble stones. Blood which moments before had been coursing through the man's body now began to run in dark rivulets between the stone courses.

From behind her, she heard an authoritative voice which had the effect of wrenching her eyes away from the murderous scene she had just witnessed. Looking up she recognised the figure of Major Nagel striding towards the group with a military bearing she had not previously associated him with. Slapping the folds of his greatcoat with his silver capped swagger stick, he stopped just short of the body of the murdered man, carefully avoiding the large pool of blood in front of him.

'Let this be a lesson to you people. Disobey an order and you will die.'

Glancing round and seeing the shocked expressions on the faces of the Jews nearest to him, Nagel moved on with a satisfied smirk. 'You will now be transported to Sachsenhausen where you will be fed and given accommodation and required to work for which you will be paid. You will also receive good health care. In return for which I expect you to cause my soldiers no further trouble. ' Having just witnessed the brutal contradiction of Nazi intolerance, Hannah knew Nagel was lying.

Looking at the cowering group, Nagel's searching gaze alighted on Hannah. 'You will remain here. You will not be going to Sachsenhausen so stand over there away from these people.'

Numbly, Hannah stumbled rather than walked to the spot indicated by Nagel's pointing cane.

Turning to the NCO who moments before had coldly murdered the injured man, Nagel gave the order for the loading to commence. Although each of the two Army trucks had canvas tops, there were no seats and she watched as each person was forced to either take hold of the metal side supports or clutch each other for support as each vehicle started forward with a sharp jolt. As the second lorry exited the yard, the heavy metal gates slid shut leaving Hannah in the company of the murdered Jew and the Nazi officer responsible for her arrest.

Approaching her, Nagel undid the buttons of his greatcoat and produced a leather-bound cigarette case from an inside pocket. Selecting a brown cigarette, he lit it with an expensive gold lighter. 'Davidoff' he explained; 'last of my French souvenirs.'

Watching Nagel savour the cigarette with obvious relish, Hannah forced herself to remain silent. Standing within yards of the murdered corpse, she waited until Nagel finally flicked the remains of his cigarette into the gutter

'You no doubt want to know why you are still here.'

'I'm sure I will find out in due course, Major.'

'Sachsenhausen would not have been a healthy place for a friend of Elsa's. I'm sure you understand what I'm saying to you?' Numbly, Hannah nodded her head.

'Later today, you will be taken to Ravensbrück concentration camp to the north of Berlin where you will join other Jews being transported to Theresienstadt. But my influence ends here, Bergmann. Once in Ravensbrück you will be just another Jew.'

Trying to assimilate the information imparted by Nagel, Hannah forced her mind back to his reference to Elsa. 'So is Elsa the reason I'm not being sent to Sachsenhausen with the others/ Is that what you are saying?

'That is precisely what I'm saying. You owe that woman more than just your warm fur coat' He gave a sardonic smile. 'Which I find puzzling bearing in mind how much you two alley cats appeared to dislike each other so intensely when I had you arrested. Or am I being naïve.'

'Major, you may be many things to many people but being naïve would not, I suspect, be appropriate in your case. So if you should meet up with Elsa again, please convey my heartfelt thanks.'

Watching Nagel disappear back into the building, she glanced up at the forbiddingly high walls and the equally daunting steel gates, their standard military grey paint showing streaks of rust. Above the high walls of the yard, she saw dark rain clouds gathering and she could see there would be no protection in the yard should the heaven's open. A small bird, possibly a sparrow, flew into the yard, nervously pecking at miniscule grubs secreted in the runnels between the cobble stones.

Feeling utterly alone, she pressed her back against a wall and let her body slide down its course granite surface. Lowering her head in her hands, she tried not to cry but failed. Unchecked tears coursed down her cheeks onto the stone cobbles just a metre away from the dead Jew. Looking at his body, she felt saddened to know whether anyone would say Kaddisch for the poor man. Recalling the barefaced lie stated earlier by SS Major Nagel to the departing Jews, she wondered whether his death would ever be reported or worse, ascribed to 'natural causes'.

Numbed by the cold radiating from the stone wall, she realised that her back had lost any sense of feeling and her legs were now beginning to do the same. Recalling how the elderly man had been shot for being unable to get to his feet, she forced herself to stand up. She felt a tingling sensation in her legs and for a moment thought she might fall over as her lower limbs seemed to have only a disjointed connection with the rest of her body. Slowly, very slowly, she began to regain her equilibrium and to hasten the process she began to gingerly move around the yard. Staring at the steel gates, she enviously thought of those Berliners on the other side of them for whom life would be going on as normally as possible within a wartime environment without regard for what might be happening within the grim walls of the open yard.

'Stand clear of the gates! Back against the wall.'

The booming voice from an unseen loudspeaker startled her. Stiffly, she returned to the spot she had occupied for the past hour.

She heard a loud metallic click and watched transfixed as the gates slowly opened to reveal an SS soldier manning the Guard Post in the street. She saw him manfully lift the wooden barrier to allow an Army staff car to enter the yard. Stopping alongside her, Hannah watched the driver sharply exit the vehicle and pull open the rear door for the passenger in the rear seat to alight. Seconds passed before he appeared. Leaning awkwardly to get out of the vehicle without bumping his head, she immediately recognised the young Abwehr officer she had met at the Operations Centre in Spandau. The braided bars on his uniform epaulettes indicated the rank of captain but his name eluded her.

'I can tell by the look on your face... you don't remember me.' Standing in front of her, he spoke quietly in a friendly voice. 'I have to sign a release note and then we'll be out of here.' He turned to go into the building but paused at the foot of the stone steps. 'By the way, my name is Captain Heidrick and the Colonel wishes to be remembered to you.'

The reference to Von Hartmannn surprised her. From the corner of her eye, she saw the driver wordlessly beckon her to get into the car. The fabric covered bench seat was surprisingly soft, unlike the last car she had ridden in, from the Kroll Opera House to her apartment in Charlottenburg in the company of Max Feldman.

Hearing a loud shout from inside the building, she heard the driver mutter an expletive before alighting with obvious disgruntlement and disappear into the building. Looking beyond the still open gates, she saw countless Berliners going about their daily routines; some looking in to the prison yard with curiosity whilst others deliberately lowered their eyes as they passed beyond the wooden barrier.

Gazing wistfully at the normality of daily life, she didn't immediately see the approach of the driver but she instantly recognised what he was carrying. The black leather case which she hoped would contain her treasured Bellini violin. She heard the driver open and close the boot lid of the vehicle before resuming his position next to the rear door.

It was a further 20 minutes before the slim figure of Captain Heidrick emerged from the building. Sitting alongside her, he removed his cap and unbuttoned his greatcoat. From an inside pocket he produced a pack of cigarettes. Flicking the top open with his thumb, Heidrick deftly extracted a cigarette with his lips but made no attempt to light it.

'Get me out of this place, Soldier but let them raise the barrier first.' His attempt at informality brought no reaction from the driver. 'And hand this release note to the Sentry but don't talk to him. OK? I don't want to stay in this place a moment longer than necessary.'

Clear of the building, the Volkswagen staff car gathered speed and Hannah saw Heidrick visibly relax. Lowering the rear window he took the still unlit cigarette from his mouth and tossed it out of the car before shutting out the blast of cold air.

'So, Bergmann... we meet again. Your circumstances appear to have changed somewhat since we last met so how are you bearing up?'

'Better now I'm out of that awful building but I have no idea what to expect at Ravensbrück. But thank you for asking, Captain.'

Turning towards her, Heidrick delivered what he hoped would be good news. 'We are on our way to Ravensbrück but once there, you will join another group leaving for Theresienstadt where I believe you will be reunited with your husband.'

It took several charged seconds before the link between Ephraim and Theresienstadt registered in her mind.

'Did I hear you correctly? You did say my husband and Theresienstadt didn't you?'

'Yes to both questions but I cannot tell you anything more because I don't know anything more. If I did I would tell you of course..'

'I want to believe you Captain but I'm having difficulty taking in what you've just told me.'

'Don't get too excited Bergmann. Theresienstadt is still a concentration camp but you must try and stay there as long as you can. How you manage to do that in the current climate I simply don't know.' Leaning towards the driver, Heidrick issued a sharp order. 'Pull over and take a smoke.'

'Sir, we aren't allowed to stop on a main highway so we'll have to wait until we can pull into a side road.'

A look of annoyance crossed Heidrick's otherwise handsome features. 'In which case wait until we are clear of the city but hurry it along.' Easing back into the seat, it was clear he was unwilling to speak further in the confined space of the vehicle with the driver present.

Passing through Blankenfelde, the suburbs gradually gave way to open fields and heavily wooded areas where in pre-war times Berliners would picnic and relax amid the scented pine and beech trees but now sadly overgrown with weeds and scrub as nature began to reclaim the land.

Finally able to stop in a slip road leading to more open parkland, the driver turned the engine off and applied the ratchet handbrake with an exaggerated firmness probably to make the point that he wasn't too enthused at the prospect of leaving the warmth of the car with the onset of heavy rain now gusting through the leafless trees.

Raising his greatcoat collar, the driver made his disgruntled exit and hurried towards a rotting wooden seat with green algae discolouring the original timber.

Alone in the car and aware of her growing apprehension, Heidrick waved his hand in the general direction of the driver. 'He's a conscript provided from a motor pool and I don't want him overhearing what I am about to tell you.' Lowering his voice Heidrick turned towards her. 'Concentrate on what I am about to tell you Bergmann because we haven't much time.'

'Take my word for it, Captain; I am fully concentrated.' She gave him the glimmer of a smile.

'When you came to our HQ at Spandau I don't suppose you noticed which particular Army unit is based there did you?'

'No, I didn't but then my knowledge of the military is extremely limited so what is the point of that question?'

'Colonel Von Hartmann and I are attached to the Abwehr. Its role is to gather intelligence from various sources and collate this data into strategic reports. In this role, the Colonel has established a network of like-minded officers who share his view on the way this war is being conducted.'

Having taken precious seconds to absorb the news about Ephraim, Hannah could hardly believe what the young Captain was now revealing. 'I think I understand what you are saying but aren't you putting yourself at risk by telling this to a Jew?'

'This is precisely why I am telling you. The Colonel has instructed me to contact certain officers including that indoctrinated pig of a Major at Gestapo HQ to try and safeguard you as much as possible. That's why you aren't on your way to Sachsenhausen with those other Jews.'

'But why would the Colonel do this for me; I've only met him twice and...' she blushed, 'nothing happened between us.'

'I can't answer for Von Hartmann but only for myself. I joined this Army to fight for my country against the Bolsheviks and Communists. I did not become a soldier to murder innocent people like you, Bergmann. I am a soldier, not a Nazi.'

'So what does this mean for me? Will I ever get to Theresienstadt?'

The increasing sound of heavy rain on the metal roof followed by the driver hurriedly re-entering the car prevented any further response from Heidrick. Turning back in his seat, the Captain issued a curt order for the driver to remove his wet greatcoat before starting the car. 'It mists up the windows and I would prefer you to see where you're driving.'

In the rear of the vehicle, Hannah's mind was in turmoil. Even with the covert assistance of a man she barely knew, it was clear that her life beyond Ravensbrück, let alone Theresienstadt, would be in extreme jeopardy.

THIRTY

Ravensbrück concentration camp north of Berlin was a truly terrifying place. Originally built as an internment camp for long-term political prisoners, Ravensbrück was now an integral part of the Nazi Government's extermination policy operating specifically for women.

At the main gate to the camp, the driver was directed towards the Reception Centre where Heidrick left the vehicle without a word; presumably to present the document he had received earlier from Gestapo HQ. Returning to the car, he motioned Hannah to get out. Curtly dismissing the driver, Heidrick turned to face her.

'This is where I depart, Bergmann. I understand from inside there'... he nodded towards the building, 'that within a few days you will be transported by rail to Theresienstadt with a number of other internees. I doubt we shall ever meet again but at least you travelled in some comfort on this stage of your journey.' He stopped as if trying to remember something. 'Oh yes... when you eventually get to the train, it will probably be an enclosed freight wagon with no seats. Make sure you sit at the side of the wagon so you can lean on it and more importantly, stay as far away from the shit bucket as you can possibly get.' His face coloured in embarrassment. 'Before I leave you there is one other thing. Von Hartmann instructed me to recover your violin; it's in the trunk. That's why I was so long in the office when I collected you.'

The unexpected prospect of being reunited with her beautiful instrument brought a fleeting touch of happiness, immediately dispelled by the thought of having to enter the forbidding hut in front of her. Passing the soldier guarding the entrance, she felt an icy stab of fear lodge in the pit of her stomach. Clutching her violin, she was unceremoniously pushed by a pock-faced second soldier towards a wooden table behind which sat an unsmiling female SS guard reading the document given to her by Captain Heidrick. Several times she glanced up, fixing Hannah with a penetrating stare before returning to the document. Grossly overweight, the girth of her midriff strained against the buttons of her uniform blouse.

'This document states that you're a special prisoner; in what way are you special?'

'I don't know the answer to that question. I wasn't aware I'd been given that category.'

'So why were you were granted 'privilege Jew' status before your arrest?'

'I'm unsure of the reason for that too but probably because I was a musician with the Berlin Philharmonic orchestra. I was a soloist so that may have had something to do with it.'

'Were all Jews in the orchestra given the same status as you?'

'No, I don't think so.'

'So you were given a privilege denied to other Jews and you claim not to know why. Is that correct?'

'That is correct.'

'Then explain why you arrived in a military vehicle when other Jews are transported in trucks?

'I don't know why that happened either. I was taken from the interrogation room in Berlin and ordered into a car. That is all I know.'

Clearly not believing one word of what she was being told, she gave Hannah a frigid stare and changed tack. 'What have you been told about this Camp?'

Wanting to terminate the interview as quickly as possible, Hannah elected for discretion. 'I know nothing about this Camp other than its name.'

'And you expect me to believe that too?' Standing up, she glared at Hannah. 'You arrive under personal escort and you want me to believe that the accompanying officer didn't say anything about Ravensbrück?

'That is exactly what I am saying.' Sensibly she knew she should stop there but something impelled her to go on. 'I'm a Jew so why would a Gestapo officer talk to me.'

By wrongly assigning Captain Heidrick to Gestapo status, Hannah hoped it would divert the line of questioning being put to her by this awful woman.

'I suppose this same officer never mentioned where you are to be transported to, did he?'

'No he didn't. Does that mean I am to be moved to another Camp?'

'It means whatever I want it to mean.'

Holding the document in her fat stubby fingers, the woman appeared to be studying it but this time in much fuller detail. Watching her, she felt a sense of rising dread as she made a number of notations with a green fountain pen.

Eventually looking up, the woman's face conveyed an exaggerated air of authoritarianism as she stared wordlessly at Hannah. It seemed an eternity before she next spoke. 'Take her to the Selection Centre.'

Feeling the prod of the soldier's rifle in her back, she turned to follow him as the woman threw one last comment. 'As you seem to know so little about this Camp I will leave you to find out what happens when you get to the selection centre.' With a dismissive wave of her hand, the woman sat back and glared with envious eyes at the beautiful woman in front of her. 'Take her away' she barked.

The terminal building looked like a busy rail station except for the overwhelming presence of Gestapo guards and Camp workers, the latter group weirdly garbed in black and white striped uniforms. From a distance they reminded her of oversized pyjamas. Some also wore floppy hats made of the same material. Two separate rail lines terminated at a set of massive hydraulic buffers, each glistening with liberal coatings of grease.

Directed by the escorting soldier to move to the far end of the terminal, she joined a small group of other prisoners.

Ordered not to speak, the only noise in the cavernous building came from the low hubbub of conversation between the Gestapo guards. Although expecting a transport to arrive at any moment, the sudden wail of a siren seemed to take them by surprise. Hurrying away from their various groups, they quickly formed a single line alongside the track. From her position at the far end of the terminal she heard the familiar sound of a steam engine seconds before it appeared, billowing clouds of grey smoke into the enclosed roof of the terminal. Behind the engine Hannah counted thirteen freight wagons. Transfixed, she watched as the engine came to a sudden halt a metre or so from the buffers. The repercussive effect rippled through each of the wagons causing them to lurch forward and then recoil back before finally stopping.

Unable to look away, she watched as the heavy wooden doors of each freight wagon were unlocked and opened to reveal a solid mass of people tightly packed together. From within, a surge by prisoners in the centre of the wagon forced those women standing in the open doorway to either jump or fall onto the unforgiving hardness of the concrete below. Some, unable to rise up were immediately set upon by SS Guards and for the first time Hannah noticed a number of large dogs on long leashes being encouraged to attack these hapless people. The yellow star on the clothing of each prisoner told its own story.

Driven forward by the Gestapo guards, the uniformed camp workers pulled the fallen women upright and marshalled them into groups close to where Hannah was standing. The gaps created by the fallen prisoners were quickly filled by Camp workers climbing into the crowded transports, each armed with a wooden club which they used to viciously force the remaining prisoners from each wagon. To her horror, Hannah saw that among the adults were a number of children, some of them crying while others were attempting to hide behind their mothers coats from where they looked on in silence at the scene unfolding before their innocent eyes, perhaps sensing with a child's perception that something bad was about to happen to them.

As each freight wagon discharged its human cargo an even more macabre sight met her eyes. Lying on the floor of the wagon nearest to her were the corpses of women and children who had died during the journey. Unceremoniously, each body was picked up by camp workers and thrown out, landing with a dull thud on the hard standing. Other prisoners, some transfixed and in shock, stared at the lifeless bodies before being roughly herded into two lines. Old and disabled women were marshalled to one side and the younger women, many with children were made to form another column. Those prisoners carrying small cases or bundles were roughly ordered to leave them in a growing pile at the side of the rail track.

An unnatural silence descended over the general mass of people, disturbed only by the harsh recriminations and shouted orders from the Gestapo guards. In this atmosphere of terror even the children were subdued and silent.

With her eyes intractably drawn to the bodies of the dead women and children she barely heard the Guard order her small group to remain at the rear of the two columns from where she was able to witness first-hand the grim selection process taking place before her.

The sight of a Gestapo officer accompanied by two NCO's making their way to a raised dais drew her attention. From his elevated position, the officer signalled for the able-bodied women in the left hand column to approach him. With a deft wave of his stick, each of the prisoners were ordered to either the left or right of the wooden platform where they were quickly hustled out of the terminal building through one or other of the two exits until eventually all had passed through the grim portals.

Next it was the turn of the remaining column of younger women and children and as the column moved forward

Hannah heard the pitiful cries coming from many of the younger children, aroused from their temporary stupor by the short walk towards the selection point. She also noticed that the number of female Guards had visibly increased in number. This time each individual inspection took marginally longer but again, the majority of women including most of those with children were selected for the same left exit, closely marshalled by the female Guards. Unusually, two women, each holding a small child were selected to leave by the right exit and she watched mesmerized, as their infants were snatched from their grasp by camp workers and physically taken out of the building through the same exit as the other children. Oddly, whether through shock or sheer terror, the whole scenario taking place before her was carried out in silence other than for the cries of the small infants gradually receding as they disappeared from view.

With the last of the women now removed, the fear among Hannah's small group visibly increased as the Gestapo officer signalled for them to approach him. Ordered forward by the Guard, she found herself walking behind a well-dressed middle-aged couple. Behind her she could hear the footsteps of the remaining detainees, understandably disinclined to get ahead of her.

'Halt!' The shouted order came not from the Guard but from the NCO standing to the left of the dais. Pointing with his gloved hand to those at the rear, he waved them to come forward. Seeing their reluctance to do so, he strode towards them and roughly shoved the four laggards several paces further forward until all twelve detainees stood in a roughly formed line under the critical eye of the senior Gestapo officer.

'Who are these people and what are these men doing here?' The tone of his enquiry did nothing to alleviate the feeling of dread growing with every second..

'These are Jews from Berlin, Major.' It was the second NCO who responded. 'They are all assigned for transportation to Theresienstadt.'

'Then what are they doing here and who said they will go to Theresienstadt?'

'Their transportation orders were issued by the Resettlement Office in Berlin. They're waiting here for two other groups to arrive before being shipped out sometime tomorrow.'

Staring at the fearful group before him, Hannah sensed for one awful moment that the Major might be debating whether to detain them within Ravensbrück rather than comply with the order to transport them on to Theresienstadt. Clearly irritated, the officer wheeled away from the dais and strode towards the exit. Watching him move away created a fleeting sense of relief within the group. But without warning the Major dramatically reappeared. 'Those two' pointing at the elderly couple who had preceded Hannah to the dais. 'They stay here; I decide who leaves this Camp. Not some arse-licking bureaucrat in Berlin.'

Having already witnessed the grim spectacle which had unfolded in front of her only minutes before, she intuitively knew that the couple's death sentence had just been pronounced. Whether in ignorance or stilled by fear, neither of them reacted. Instead, the man protectively extended his arm round the shoulder of his wife and gently ushered her towards the exit taken only minutes before by those women and children who too had been selected for extermination by this same Gestapo officer.

THIRTY ONE

With many of Germany's major cities and industrial centres under increasing aerial bombardment by Allied Air Forces, it was another five days before the transport for Theresienstadt was ready to leave. Berlin had experienced its heaviest bombing raid to date causing extensive damage to the rail marshalling yards bringing in turn consequential delays to the transportation programme. No trains arrived at the Camp for four days and looking out through a grimy window of the locked dormitory Hannah was aware that the feverish activity of the first two days had now ceased. Camp workers were confined to their quarters whilst a group of younger women prisoners spent their time sorting through a mountain of clothes, shoes and other personal effects. Of the children there was no sign.

Meals consisting of a concoction tasting vaguely of turnip with a piece of grey looking bread were provided twice daily. Knowing she would soon be facing the long rail journey to Theresienstadt and guessing that no food would be provided en route, Hannah forced herself to eat despite the revolting smell emanating from the metal food container.

Whimsically, she recalled the wonderfully appetising meals prepared by Ephraim. Closing her eyes in order not to look at what she was eating, her thoughts drifted to the prospect of meeting him again. Knowing that a reunion could still be denied on the whim of any Gestapo official, she let her mind turn instead to Aaron. Offering her silent gratitude to Frieda, she wondered if he still called out for her when he awoke during the night as he sometimes did at their apartment in Charlottenburg... now just a fading memory.

The dormitory was equipped with a separate toilet and cold water wash basin. Thinking back to the hellish conditions and lack of sanitation she had witnessed in the confines of the freight wagons, she took every opportunity to enjoy the simple pleasure of being able to wash. At night, when the other prisoners were in their wooden bunks, she would quietly go to the washroom and scrub her body from head to toe. Without soap, she used a piece of rough towelling and the coldness of the water to invigorate her aching body. On the third night she was startled to see a camp worker staring at her from the unlocked doorway. Calmly explaining she wouldn't be much longer, she marvelled at the unconscious change in her outlook. In the past, the thought of a strange man looking at her partially clothed body would have been hugely embarrassing but now she felt unaffected by it despite the laviscious look on the man's face.

On the fifth morning, Hannah was awakened by the sound of a blaring klaxon relayed through the Camp public address system. The previous day had seen the arrival of three of the delayed trains, each bringing increasing numbers of women and children to the camp, this time from Cologne and Hanover. Watching through the barred windows of the detention hut, she saw columns of women, elderly and young, many with children, leaving the Selection Centre in a procession which she knew would lead to their immediate slaughter. Closing her eyes she once more offered silent thanks to Von Hartmann. Without his intervention, she knew her life would in all probability have ended here in Ravensbrück in company with those now making their way to the gas chambers and death.

As the wail of the siren faded the dormitory door was thrown open through which four robust female guards appeared, supervised by the overweight SS NCO she had first seen in the Reception Centre.

'Outside in 5 minutes. And I do mean five minutes!'

Hearing this, a mild panic ensued as each of the prisoners reacted to the order. Hurriedly, the room emptied as they filed out and formed a nervous line outside the hut. It took two attempts at a roll call before the senior guard was satisfied and then a further period of waiting followed before the order was finally given for the detainees to retrace their steps back to the railhead terminal.

Arriving at the central spit of land between the two rail lines, her eyes took in a sight reminiscent of the scene she had witnessed five days earlier. An empty freight train with its wagon doors fully open stood in the left hand siding with no trace of its earlier cargo of human flotsam. Camp workers, playing water hoses into the empty wagons were attempting to shift excrement from the floor of each wagon until being halted by an angry bellow from a Gestapo NCO striding towards the train.

'You lazy shit-heads! Use the brooms or I'll make you eat the fucking stuff.' Still bawling obscenities, the NCO strode towards a wretched camp worker sorting through a pitiful heap of personal effects on the hard standing. 'You! Get into that wagon and replace that man there.' Wielding a heavy baton, he pointed to another worker on board the freight wagon, a man whose life was now in the hands of this pugnacious bully.

Watching the luckless victim nervously climb down, she was reminded of an animal locked in the glare of headlights from an approaching vehicle. Watching him approach the NCO and expecting the worst, Hannah tried to avert her eyes but found herself locked in morbid fascination. Expecting the man to be punished or worse, she was astonished when instead, the NCO pointed to the pile of suitcases lying on the hard standing. 'You... sort through those cases and bundles and bring what you find to me; understand?'

It took her a few moments to realise what was taking place; that even here in what she now knew to be an extermination camp, a man's life had just been spared in return for what he could find in terms of money or jewellery hidden in the personal effects of those poor souls already on their way to the gas chambers.

'So that's what this is all about?' The angry outburst came from behind her. Turning, Hannah saw a middle-aged woman trying to remonstrate with an elderly man.

'Don't try and hush me, woman: these people are nothing more than thieving murderers. Have you forgotten what happened to that man in the prison yard; shot dead because he couldn't get to his feet. And where are the people who those cases belong to?' Gesturing with his hand to emphasise his rising anger, Hannah instinctively knew that the man's outburst had taken him beyond the point of recall. From the rear of their group, a female guard within earshot of the outburst, forcefully pushed her way into the group and stood in front of the man. Without speaking but with exaggerated menace she slowly drew a weighty truncheon from her belt. Anticipating the expected blow, the elderly man straightened up to his full height and drew his shoulders back with a semblance of military bearing.

'Point out your wife to me.' The obvious threat sent a cold shiver through Hannah's body.

'Why do you want to know who my wife is? I was the one who shouted.'

Unused to being disobeyed, the guard moved even closer. Reaching out with her truncheon, she touched the shoulder of the woman standing to the man's right. 'Is this her?' Before the man could react, Hannah saw the truncheon impact with astonishing force into the midriff of the woman. Gasping for breath, the truncheon struck twice more, this time to the woman's head, driving her luckless body down onto the unyielding concrete. The effect of the last two blows had clearly disorientated the woman, her glazed eyes staring up at her husband without recognition. Watching in speechless horror, the elderly man threw himself down alongside his wife, attempting to shield her from further blows. Beyond the small group the commotion had attracted the attention of two other female guards. As they came running across the hard standing, the burlier of the two guards roughly pushed Hannah aside in her rush to join in the affray. Wielding similar clubs, all three guards stood in a menacing trio staring down at the prostrated couple.

Struggling to regain her senses, the woman attempted to rise up but was restrained by her husband's hand across her chest. Looking up at his wife's assailant, he slowly began to stand up.

Ominously, all three guards edged closer making it difficult for him to stand without touching them. Aware of what might happen if he did, the husband hesitated but then with an uncaring effort, he pushed up to regain a standing position.

'Well done old man, now help your wife up.' Placing the end of her truncheon under his chin the first guard forced his head up so that she could look directly into his eyes. 'And if I hear so much as a squeak from you again, you will both finish your journey here in Ravensbrück.' Jabbing viciously upwards, Hannah saw the old man's head snap back as he again fell to the ground. Laughing at the spectacle, the three guards walked away.

Watching him stumble painfully to his feet, Hannah reached out and touched the elderly man's shoulder and together they helped his bemused wife to her feet. Looking closely at her head, she could see that neither of the two blows appeared to have broken the skin though she could see a darkening area developing just above the temple. Reaching into her pocket, she retrieved a soft silk handkerchief which had been given to her in happier times by Ephraim. Pressing it into the woman's hand, Hannah felt a responding squeeze.

It was a further two hours before the group were ordered to climb aboard the solitary freight wagon detached earlier that morning. With surprising agility, two camp workers scrambled into the freight wagon and assisted each of the detainees to board. Once inside, she became aware of an overpowering stench which vaguely reminded her of the carbolic acid Frieda had occasionally used for clearing a blocked drain in the apartment.

Taking stock of her surroundings she remembered the advice given by Captain Heidrick and positioned herself against the end wall of the wagon as far from the slop bucket as she could get. As the large wooden door slid shut and the steel latch noisily engaged, the interior of the wagon was cast into darkness except for slivers of light penetrating through cracks in the timber sidewalls.

With her eyes gradually adjusting to the gloom, she was able to see that most of the internees had seated themselves either on the floor of the wagon or on small cases which several had been allowed to bring with them. Clutching the violin case recovered by Heidrick, she eased herself down with her back pressed against the rough wooden boards. The closing of the wagon door had brought a noticeable sense of relief as each person realised that they could now speak without fear of being overheard by the guards.

Outside, they heard more bawled commands from the Gestapo guards ordering camp workers to 'push'. Slowly, very slowly, they felt the first movement of their wagon being man-handled along the track until being halted by another truck and the sound of coupling chains being hooked up could be heard in the wagon. Then all went quiet for a matter of minutes until without warning, the train jolted forward on the first stage of its journey to the East.

Prior to the outbreak of war, the rail journey to Theresienstadt normally took approximately six hours to complete subject to the time it took to change trains at the former border between the two countries. But this was wartime and for Hannah Bergmann and the 42 other Jews confined within the stinking freight wagon, the nightmare journey would seem without end. With priority being given to military trains travelling to and from the Eastern front, their train seemed to spend most of each day halted in sidings. Having had their watches confiscated at Ravensbrück, they had no means of knowing the time of day other than for the morning routine when the door of the wagon would be slid open by one of the numerous guards escorting the prisoners. The overfilled slop bucket would be emptied alongside the track and two military food canisters separately containing water and a ghastly foul-tasting soup would be brought to the wagon by the two guards. An Orthodox rabbi in the group took it upon himself to pronounce a traditional Hebrew blessing on the 'meal' they were about to partake of. Whilst respecting his faith, Hannah wondered, not for the first time, how any Jew could maintain their faith in religion when their very existence as a race was being subjected to institutionalised genocide. Before the war, she had most times accompanied Ephraim to the synagogue and dutifully observed Shabbat and Jewish Holy Days but since her arrest, what little testimony she had retained from childhood had all but disappeared. At Ravensbrück she had further questioned the existence of a God who allowed the slaughter of innocent women and children. But despite her many anguished prayers for enlightenment, the Heaven's had remained implacably sealed to her supplications.

Each time the train halted, she felt an irresistible urge to get out of the stinking wagon and to breathe fresh air again. But the presence of the armed Guards ensured that no prisoners were able to alight from the train and by the third day she began to lose the will to go on. During the night two more prisoners had died making five in total since the hellish journey had begun. Unlike earlier transports, Teutonic bureaucracy now required that all 43 Jewish internees must be accounted either dead or alive at the end of the journey so the corpses were placed close to Hannah's position in the wagon. The indescribable stench coming from the overflowing slop bucket now pervaded every square centimetre of the wagon's interior space before being overridden by an even more sickening odour... that of decomposing bodies.

Needing to use the bucket on the first day to relieve herself, Hannah had forced herself to wait until darkness to hide her embarrassment. Stumbling from the motion of the train and tentatively feeling her way towards the bucket she sensed rather than saw that it was already full to overflowing. In utter misery, she turned and leant against the wooden planked end wall and buried her face in her hands.

'Just do it my dear... don't be embarrassed'.

Looking towards the sound of the voice, she dimly recognised the woman who had been assaulted by the female guards at Ravensbrück.

'I'll stand in front of you if you like. Tip the bucket with your foot – that way you won't splash your legs.'

Numbly obeying, Hannah eased the bucket sideways allowing a measure of the foul slop to spill onto the floor. Grateful for the scant cover provided by the woman, she relieved herself by squatting down, careful not to touch the steel rim of the bucket. Finished, she stood up, hardly daring to breathe because she knew that the overwhelming stench would cause her to vomit.

Regaining her position at the far end of the wagon, Hannah let her exhausted body slide down into a sitting position, her head sinking low onto her chest.

Through a slatted vent, she saw that outside of the wagon darkness had descended and in her numbing tiredness she became vaguely aware that she was drifting into an unwelcoming blackness to awake just moments later in familiar surroundings. She was once more in her Charlottenburg apartment and in the kitchen she could hear Ephraim preparing a meal. On the woven rug in the middle of the lounge she saw Aaron playing quietly with a wooden truck given to him by Frieda on his first birthday. Looking at him, she felt the urge to run her fingers through his blond locks. She recalled the questioning looks of family and friends when they first set eyes on this blond haired Aryan-looking infant born from the union of two dark-haired Jewish parents.

Slowly, the image of Aaron began to fade, replaced instead by the sound of distress from other prisoners and she felt herself being inexorably drawn back to the coldness and noise of the wagon. Despite pressing the collar of her coat against her nostrils as a crude filter, she barely prevented herself from gagging at the worsening smell within the compartment. During her brief interlude of sleep her body had moved sideways with the motion of the train. Forcing her eyes open it took several seconds for them to focus. To her horror, her head was just inches away from a grey lifeless face locked in the riga mortice of death with eyes staring sightlessly into her own. Horrified, and despite having little feeling in her lower body, she forced herself into an upright position. Slowly, painfully, her circulation returned and she was able to stand up. Unwilling to drink for the first two days from the water bucket, she knew her body was suffering the effects of severe dehydration. With the vividness of Ephraim and Aaron still lingering in her mind, she knew that to have any chance, however slight, of seeing them again, she had to stay alive. Making her way towards the water container mercifully positioned at the opposite end of the wagon to that of the slop bucket, she cupped her hands together and thrust them into the dark recess of the bucket. But instead of water, her hands grasped nothing more substantial than air. Overwhelmed and devoid of energy and the will to go on, Hannah felt her legs give way at the knees as she fell to floor of the wagon.

How long she lay there she would never know. Time appeared to lose all meaning as the train continued its interminable journey eastwards. Drifting in and out of consciousness her mind finally succumbed to a blackness so dense that medically speaking, there could be no return to the world she was about to leave.

THIRTY TWO

'So, Dr. Fischer, I'm told your wife was among the last intake of Jews from Berlin. I see from the shipment notes that five of them did not finish the journey in the same condition as they commenced it; too much inbreeding among you people. As a doctor you should know all about that.' He paused to see whether Ephraim would react. 'Was your wife among the five or the thirty seven?'

'She was hours away from the former group. As you will have seen from my daily report, my wife is presently in the clinic where I am treating her for dehydration with a saline drip.'

'I did not ask you for a clinical report, doctor, only whether your wife was alive or dead; the overt threat in his voice never far from the surface. 'If I had seen your daily report I would not have asked that question... you arrogant man.'

Taking the seat normally occupied by patients, the Adjutant fixed Ephraim with a look embodying the contempt he felt for him. 'Tell me doctor, do you consciously try to annoy me or does it come naturally to you?'

Quelling a growing anxiety, Ephraim took a deep breath before replying. 'Assuming that isn't a rhetorical question and being fully aware that you hold the power of life and death over every Jewish person in this camp, why would I deliberately seek to annoy you?

'I will tell you why, doctor. You are clearly an intelligent man and it is that which leads you and others of your persuasion to believe that you are always right and everyone else is wrong. So it is your intellectual arrogance which offends me; a conceit which marks you and all other Jewish misfits for special treatment.'

Even with the threat contained within the Adjutant's words, Ephraim fought unsuccessfully to constrain his response.

'Special treatment as defined by the Third Reich and for what? Being intelligent? I can't think your own intelligence actually lets you believe that, Captain.'

'That is because you are not listening, doctor. Intelligence in itself is not a fault. It is the arrogance which you parasitic Jews couple with that intelligence. Jews use intelligence as a means to acquire assets and influence which is why they controlled the real wealth in Germany and it took the Fuehrer to recognise this.'

'And to then apply the solution of genocide?'

'Be careful doctor; the fact that you and your Jewish wife are still alive presently belies that statement.' Rising quickly to his feet the Adjutant strode towards the door. Stopping, he looked back at Ephraim. 'But who knows, doctor, perhaps in another time and in different circumstances I believe I might have enjoyed meeting you. But this is neither that time nor place so for the sake of your continuing good health I suggest you learn to use what intelligence you have to express yourself in a less provocative manner; especially to me. Do I need to say more or can I take it that you may at last have learned that lesson?'

Alone once more, Ephraim felt cold beads of perspiration begin to form on his forehead. Staring at the chair just vacated by his antagonist, he knew that the psychotic Adjutant had given him a final stark choice; comply or die. A warning which if unheeded would inevitably result in the death not only of himself but Hannah too.

Riven by the thought of the Adjutant's menacing threat, Ephraim hurried to the small room at the side of the clinic where Hannah and two other patients were being cared for. Following her arrival the previous evening, Ephraim had spent most of the night attempting to arrest her descent into a level of coma from which he knew there could be no return.

Overnight, her body had at last begun to respond with infinite slowness to the energising effect of the saline fluid now coursing through her body. Within her level of growing consciousness, dark shapes had begun to flit across her inner vision only to quickly disappear from whence they came. Slowly the shapes began to take more tangible forms and with it came the dull realisation that she was looking at the blurred image of a man.

She saw an indistinct hand reach down and take hold of her wrist and she was able to feel slight pressure being applied. Unable to focus, she once more began to draw back into an aura of protective blackness halted only by the sound of a familiar voice attempting to rouse her from a sleep from which she had no inclination to awaken from.

Summoning up what remained of her willpower, she heard herself murmur 'who are you?'

'Hannah, its Ephraim, your husband.'

She heard the same sound repeated several times more. With failing willpower, she struggled to understand what was happening to her.

Vaguely, she saw a man's muzzy shape lean over her and felt the outward coolness of something brush across her forehead. 'You can't be Ephraim; my husband was taken from me.'

'Hannah... you've had a long journey and you are still very weak. I want you to lie still and rest and I will explain everything later.' Taking her hands he placed them under the starched sheet and gently caressed her cheek as the debilitating effects of the journey slowly lessened, replaced by a will to live which mercifully began to draw her into the realm of natural sleep.

It was another 48 hours before she was able to stomach a weak broth and to recall the memory of the journey from Ravensbrück. The reunion with Ephraim was tearful but strangely constrained with both making Aaron the focus of their stilted conversation. It was a further four days before she felt strong enough to get up and take her first bath. The two bed-washes given by Ephraim had done little to dispel the awful smell lingering from the nightmarish rail journey.

Recuperating in the hot water of the bath she attempted to clear her mind of recent events and focus on what might lie ahead.

So much had happened since she had last seen Ephraim, some aspects of which she knew she would never be able to share with him. Elsa, for example... what was she now doing? And the Hoffenblute; did I really work there, she wondered? And the German officer... Von Hartmannn; where was he now? Would I have slept with him as the price of Ephraim's release? And the SS Lieutenant intent on raping me; was he the reason I become so aroused with Ephraim only hours later?

Pondering questions to which she had no answers, she decided to abandon the bath and return to her bed. Wrapping herself in a large green military-issue towel, she spotted a small mirror positioned above the hand basin in the corner of the room. Critically examining the face staring back at her, she appeared to be in remarkable good shape other than for the heavy shadows under each eye. Ironically, the starvation diet of the past two weeks had removed the slight pudginess from her hips and thighs resulting from the sundry potato-based meals prepared by Ephraim prior to their arrest.

Entering the ward Hannah found Ephraim waiting by her bed.

'You didn't tell me you were leaving the ward. I presume you went to the bathroom?'

'Of course. Why else would I walk around wearing only a towel?' She gave Ephraim a caustic look. 'I could still smell the awful stench from the train and I badly needed to wash my hair. Does that cause a problem?' Glancing across the room at him, she saw his obvious agitation.

'Sweetheart, we need to talk. You having a bath could cause us both a problem, a major problem and you need to understand that this camp is not what you may believe it to be. You've already seen for yourself what happens to Jews in places like Ravensbrück. They are being murdered in their hundreds, probably thousands if we did but know it. And

Ravensbrück is just one of many such camps used either to supply slave labour for the Nazi war factories in the East or to systematically murder Jews, Slavs, Bolsheviks, homosexuals and anyone else whom this Government cares to put in the frame. It's far worse than anything we could ever have imagined in Berlin.' His face took on a pained expression. 'How the civilised world can let this happen simply beggar's belief.' He stopped... emotionally drained.

Seeing the obvious stress he was under, a cold chill ran down her back.

'Ephraim, I need to get in bed before I catch cold.' Sliding back between the white linen sheets and glancing at Ephraim, she saw his shoulders droop and his body relax.

'Hannah, I'm sorry. This is not an appropriate time to talk about such things. You need more rest so let's leave it until later.'

Smoothing out the sheet in front of her, she looked up and smiled. 'Darling, I'm happy to talk now or later but can you try talking to me as my husband and not as my doctor?'

Laying her head against the hard pillow, she followed Ephraim's example and let her body relax. 'Am I surprised by what you have just told me? How can I be surprised after what I witnessed with my own eyes? You came to this camp directly from Berlin whereas I came via Ravensbrück so I've seen precisely what you've just described. In that awful place, I witnessed with my own eyes, hundreds of women and children daily being murdered in the gas chambers. But what I don't understand is why this camp is so different from Ravensbrück and what are we doing here?

'Perhaps I am the person who should answer that question.' Engaged in their own whispered conversation, neither had seen the portly figure standing in the open doorway. 'Allow me to introduce myself. I am Captain Kernick; Camp Adjutant and you must be Dr. Fischer's wife?

'Captain Kernick... I'm Hannah Bergmann.' Giving him the sweetest of smiles, she added 'Dr. Fischer's wife.'

'Welcome to Theresienstadt.' Sitting himself on the edge of the bed he chose to look directly at Hannah, deliberately ignoring the presence of Ephraim. 'I believe your husband was about to tell you about the camp you now find yourself in. Is that not so, doctor?'

Hearing no response from behind him, the Adjutant rose to his feet with feigned slowness. Still looking at Hannah, he repeated his question; 'is that not so, Dr. Fischer?'

Acutely aware of Hannah's close proximity to this dangerously volatile man, Ephraim elected for prudence. 'I'm sorry Captain, my mind was temporarily elsewhere.'

Seating himself back on the bed, Hannah saw Kernick tapping the fingers of one hand on the swagger stick lying across his knees. 'You can play at being a doctor when you have answered the two questions put to you by your wife... and need I remind you that I am not the most patient of men.'

Forced to recount the official version as relayed to him by the Adjutant during their first meeting was not easy. Since that meeting, Ephraim now knew that every aspect of Theresienstadt as a Nazi show camp was a cruel deception, created solely to deceive the International Red Cross and through that reputable organisation, the world at large.

'When you are alone with him, I'm sure your husband will tell you something quite different because he is an arrogant man who thinks he knows best. But be careful, both of you. Never forget you are both inmates here and if you step out of line, you will be punished as your husband has already learned to his cost.' He turned his head and looked at Ephraim.

'Doctor, show your wife what happens when you challenge authority. And you' jabbing his short ebony cane into Hannah's chest, 'look closely.'

Behind him, Hannah saw Ephraim's pallor darken, a sign she recognised as suppressed anger. Slowly, he began to unbutton his grey shirt and with an exaggerated flourish he exposed his bare chest. The swastika, luridly outlined in burned flesh, was shocking to look at.

Unable to absorb what her eyes were seeing, Hannah attempted to reach out to Ephraim. Anticipating a reaction, the Adjutant struck down hard on Hannah's outstretched arm. Leaping to his feet, the Adjutant turned and faced Ephraim. 'Don't even think of it, doctor, or you will die; both of you; painfully and very slowly!'

Fighting to suppress an almost irresistible urge to hurt or even kill the man standing before him, Ephraim turned and walked out of the small ward.

'Your husband's stupidity will be the death of him. He's extremely fortunate that he reports to me and not to one or two of the other officers here otherwise he would be dead by now.'

Staring at the brutish man before her, she was struck by the irony in his words, knowing they probably described his own characteristics more accurately than those he ascribed to her husband. Whilst Ephraim had a number of faults, being stupidly arrogant was not one of them.

Seeing no reaction Kernick tried again. 'I understand you are a classical musician; what is it you play?'

The sudden change of subject momentarily threw Hannah. 'Violin, I play the violin. Until my arrest I was a principle soloist with the Berlin Philharmonic.'

Guarded as to what to say next, Hannah lowered herself further into the bed and closed her eyes for several seconds in feigned tiredness.

That is most interesting; would that be the same orchestra once conducted by a Jew named Max Feldman?'

Hearing her mentor's name took her by surprise. 'Yes it was but how do you know Max Feldman?'

Kernick gave a snort. 'I don't know any Jew personally.' The distaste in his voice was unmistakeable. 'He passed through here in transit to Auschwitz only last week. Another man with the same arrogant characteristics as your husband,'

'Having known him for eleven years, I can understand why you should think that.'

Hardly had the words left her mouth before she knew she had made another mistake. The Adjutant's face muscles stiffened causing his lips to almost disappear.

'Don't patronise me, woman. I don't need you to confirm what I think.'

If she hoped that would be the end of the outburst, she was wrong.

Standing menacingly over her with his stick pushing hard into the fold of the bed covering, his voice became truly frightening. 'You people are a disease in our Fatherland; you are all parasites sucking the blood of our great nation and we have been forced into this war to eradicate people like you.' Shocked by Kernick's vitriolic outburst, Hannah's vocal chords froze.

Clearly disappointed by his inability to provoke a reaction to his taunting diatribe, the Adjutant delivered an irritated smack to the bed cover with his stick.

'Tomorrow, you will report to my office... without your husband and I will decide whether you are to remain in this camp or whether you follow your leader.' He hesitated, savouring his own unwitting attempt at humour; 'or more correctly whether you follow your late leader... to Auschwitz.'

THIRTY THREE

The next few days passed in a bewildering haze. The meeting threatened by the Adjutant was either forgotten or postponed; she never found out why. Allowed to walk freely around the camp, she quickly realised that she was probably the youngest internee in Theresienstadt other than for a small group of children who seemed unattached to any particular family. Looking at them, she wistfully thought of Aaron and silently implored her God to ensure his continuing safety with Frieda.

Following her discharge from the clinic and despite them being allowed to share the same quarters her relationship with Ephraim continued to be strained. She remembered the initial nervousness they had both experienced during their brief honeymoon but afterwards, their undoubted affection for each other had not resulted in the kind of lovemaking she had anticipated, especially after the birth of Aaron. She had long since accepted that Ephraim was not particularly tactile nor outwardly affectionate though her own experience with Elsa, now but a dark memory in the back of her mind, shamefully reminded her that she did not conform to this pattern of behaviour when sexually aroused.

Lying together on the first night of their reunion and feeling Ephraim's strong arms around her, she felt an overwhelming sense of relief. In hushed tones they exchanged kisses but neither of their bodies reflected a desire for intimate consummation. Fully aware that his wife had witnessed more horrors of Nazi genocide than himself, Ephraim felt a sense of deep trepidation as he related the true function of Theresienstadt as a show camp designed to demonstrate to the world at large just how well the Nazi Government treated its Jewish population!

Easing himself away from the warmth of Hannah's body, Ephraim recounted the night he had been burned with the hated insignia of the swastika to ensure his compliance with the Nazis orchestrated plan of deception.

Gingerly running her hand across the raised scarring, she felt Ephraim wince as her fingers probed too deeply. Pulling her hand away, she gave him the gentlest of kisses. 'Sorry darling, I didn't mean to hurt you.' Quickly changing the subject, she decided to ask the question which had been in her mind since regaining her sense of memory. 'Ephraim... when the Red Cross inspection has finished and they have their propaganda film to show to the world, what will happen to those Jews and children who are here now?'.

Turning on to his back it took him several moments to compose his reply. 'Well at the moment, the original internees are still here but it will be only a matter of time before they are transported to camps like Auschwitz so God alone knows what will happen once the Red Cross visit is completed.

'I've already told you what I saw before coming here so it will be the same fate that those poor people faced at Ravensbrück.' Sitting up, she pulled the top cover over her shoulders and looked at her husband. 'Auschwitz is a death camp, Ephraim. That is what really awaits all these people including the children.' Her litany of words was so devoid of feeling it was as though she was offering a comment on the weather.

Disconcerted by her bluntness, Ephraim tried to regain control of the conversation. 'How do you know, Hannah... who told you that?'

'I overheard it from the guards in Ravensbrück. Apparently there are two camps. Auschwitz which is the extermination camp and Birkenau which supplies slave labour for the new factories which the Nazis have built in that region.'

'So with this camp having served its purpose then I suppose that will be our next destination.' Pulling himself upright, he drew Hannah to him, feeling the warmth of her body through the rough material of his pyjamas.

Against all odds both she and Ephraim had been reunited. Responding to his closeness, she felt an overwhelming sense of affection for him. Kissing his unresponsive lips, she knew he was lost in his thoughts; concerned as always for her and the world at large.

'Sweetheart, if we could live our lives over again, you would still be the man of my dreams. Let's hope we at least share the same transport... wherever it may take us.'

'Hope and Captain Kernick are strange bedfellows. I'm afraid it will be Kernick who decides where each of us will go.'

'Is he really as nasty as you say he is? Hasn't every person got a good side if you look for it?

By way of reply, Ephraim gave a caustic laugh. 'Good side? Kernick is pure evil so never think otherwise,'

'That's a contradiction Ephraim... pure is the opposite of evil.'

Plainly irritated by her flippancy, Ephraim, pushed himself away and held Hannah at arm's length. 'For God's sake, woman, I don't need a lesson in semantics at a time like this.'

'And I don't need an angry husband... at a time like this.' Moving herself closer, she snuggled into the folds of his body. 'Hold on to me my little cherubim and don't say another word.'

Locked in each other's warm embrace and lost in their separate thoughts, she and Ephraim drifted into an uneasy slumber. Distantly, she imagined she felt Aaron's little hand in hers. Looking down at the pale innocence of his baby-like features, she saw no sign of recognition in eyes once delightfully mischievous but now dulled. Bending down, she attempted to embrace Aaron but her arms simply passed through his empty frame. Slowly drifting from her view, she saw a fading Aaron wistfully looking back in puzzlement as his small figure disappeared into a nebulous background. Desperately, she tried to follow him but her legs refused to move as though ensnared to the floor. Her voice too was powerless, no sound issuing forth or penetrating the backdrop of silence between herself and her dear child. As the image of Aaron faded, the space was filled with a cloying blackness. From afar, she heard a voice calling out in obvious distress repeating Aaron's name and growing increasingly louder.

She felt herself being gently shaken and a different voice replaced that of the voice she now recognised as her own.

'Hannah; wake up... wake up.'

'Ephraim? Is it you?'

'Yes, it's me; you were calling out.'

'It was Aaron. I was dreaming about Aaron. It was frightening. I couldn't touch him and he couldn't hear me when I called him.' She felt tears begin to run down her cheeks. 'Why can't he be here with us? There are other children here so why can't we have our child with us?'

Startled by Ephraim's reaction, Hannah felt the bedclothes pulled away from her shoulders.

'Hannah, listen to me for God's sake. Those children you refer to will soon be as dead as those you saw at Ravensbrück. Their parents never came here because they are already dead. They are window dressing purely for the Red Cross visit together with everyone else in this camp. There will be no more Red Cross inspections after this; they will have their damn film so they won't need us anymore. It's only a matter of time before we are all shipped off to Auschwitz and you already know what will happen when we get there.'

Feeling goose bumps on her bare arms and shoulders from the cold chill of the bedroom, Hannah pulled the bedclothes over herself. 'When will the Red Cross inspection take place?'

'The first visit has already happened the week before you arrived. There will be a follow-up visit to discuss their report with the Camp Commandant which I guess will take just an hour or so which may have already happened for all I know. Why d'you ask?'

'Then why did they allow me and the other internees to come here if the inspection and follow-up visit has already taken place. It simply doesn't make sense.'

'They're bureaucrats Hannah. They work by the book and follow their last order and any changes to those orders takes time to implement. They have a new policy. They call it their final solution to the Jewish question. That's what you overheard the guards speaking about at Ravensbrück.'

'Final solution for what? Do they want to kill everybody who they don't like or disagree with?'

'In a word... yes! They have this insane plan to purify the German race which means that non-Germanic people... people like us who were to be resettled in the East are now to be exterminated.'

In the darkness of the room, Ephraim heard his wife gasp in horror. Feeling under the bedclothes, Ephraim located Hannah's warm hands. 'Promise me you will never ever mention Aaron in this place again. We have to believe he's still safe with Frieda and will survive this war... even if we don't make it.'

THIRTY FOUR

The malevolence in his tone was unmistakeable. 'Your wife and other selected internees will be transported to Auschwitz and they will leave tomorrow. But you doctor, you will remain here until further notice; you have unfinished business '

With the safety of Hannah foremost in his mind, Ephraim knew this was not the moment to antagonise a man with an unstable temperament invariably balanced on a knife-edge. Instead, he nodded his head in feigned acceptance.

'The less able internees will not be transferred. They will stay here and you will remain with them until such time as you all leave together.' He gave a sardonic smile. 'One way or another.'

Again, the temptation to react was nigh on impossible to resist. But dredging up what remained of his depleted will-power, he forced himself to remain silent. Within his chest he felt his heart begin to race as he sought to control his anger. Taking a deep breath, he expelled slowly and let his shoulders drop in an effort to relax.

'Will that be all, Captain? With your permission I would like to go to the clinic; I have a number of patients waiting.'

'They are Jews doctor so let them wait. I'm surprised you don't want to dash off to break the news to your wife. It may be a long time before you see each other again... at least in this life.'

Swallowing hard, Ephraim sucked more air into his lungs and expelled it with obvious trepidation. Seeing this, a smile of satisfaction crossed the Adjutant's face. 'So, you are human after all. I was wondering what it would take to get a reaction from you. Now I know. It's your wife, doctor. She is your Achilles heel... your weak link.'

'Interesting that you regard a person you love as a weak link.' I can't relate to that philosophy, Captain.'

'Then let me explain, doctor. If I wanted to punish you, say for being arrogant or perhaps even for displaying signs of dumb insolence, I could inflict more hurt on you by physically punishing your wife rather than you. Surely even you can understand that?'

'Of course I know what you're alluding to but why would that give you a sense of pleasure?'

'You continue to misunderstand me. It's not about pleasure, doctor, it's about control; the means to control errant people like yourself. You may be foolish enough to consider death as an option to following an order from myself but would you still disobey if it was the life of your wife that was at risk?'

'I just told you Captain, I can't relate to that kind of thinking. As a doctor I'm dedicated to healing people; not threatening to kill them.'

'Then you may have to change your thinking on that subject. If you were to tell me you have never helped a terminally sick patient to die to avoid unnecessary pain then I would not believe you. All doctors have done that when necessary, including you. Am I correct?'

'Yes I have done that but only to spare a patient further pain and when that person is close to death anyway.'

'D'you know doctor, I do believe I'm beginning to make an impression on you after all.' He let out an expressive sigh. 'That's very encouraging so let me extend this lesson a little further. If I tell you that those inmates who will not be transported to Auschwitz will either be shot or starved to death then their position becomes much the same as those terminally sick people you have helped to die in your murky past, does it not?'

The enormity of what the Adjutant was proposing struck Ephraim like a thunderclap, stopping any form of reply.

'And if I were to promise your wife not only safe conduct to Auschwitz but also exemption from the selection process upon her arrival there, would that make you more agreeable to assisting in my proposal?'

Still struggling to find his voice, Ephraim reached out for the chair on the opposite side of the desk from Kernick. 'That would be cold blooded murder Captain and you know it.'

Kernick sighed again, this time more audibly and Ephraim saw a gleam of satisfaction appear on his chubby features. 'Of course it would, but how would you prefer to die if you were in their shoes. Imagine being lined up with members of your family, seeing soldiers with rifles facing you and knowing you are about to be executed... how would that make you feel? Before Ephraim could respond, the Adjutant went on, 'I saw this happen in Russia and believe me it does cause unnecessary panic and its messy' adding these final words as though it was the recollection of the latter which offended him more than the enormity of the murderous crime.

'Captain, I need time to consider what you have just suggested. May I come back to you later today... please?' Stumbling to his feet, Ephraim looked to the Adjutant for a reply.

'No, you may not. I want your decision now before you leave this office. Otherwise your wife will remain here and face the same fate as those we are speaking of.' He raised a quizzical eyebrow in expectation of Ephraim's reply. 'Once you leave here, doctor, the die will be cast so it's yes or no... your choice.'

Breaking the news to Hannah of their impending separation was heart-rending enough but what followed was worse.

'But why would this man, this Adjutant, give me dispensation from the selection process at Auschwitz? You told me he was a thoroughly indoctrinated Nazi; the 'epitome of evil' were your very words so why would he do this for me? And why can't we go together?'

'Because I have to remain here to look after those older inmates who aren't well enough to be transported. Sweetheart, you know better than I do what those cattle trucks are like.'

'Ephraim, when you call me sweetheart, I know the situation must be dire. So stop trying to protect me and just tell me the truth. What have you been forced to agree to in order to get this special dispensation for me?'

Unable to respond to her searching question, Ephraim dropped his gaze, unable to maintain eye contact with Hannah.

'They intend to murder all those inmates who are not fit enough to work in the factories at Auschwitz. They want me to examine them and determine who will go and who will stay. That is what I have to do so please don't ask any more questions. You are my priority; not those other people. They will have to look out for themselves.'

'But those 'other people' you so blithely refer to are your patients, Ephraim. They're weak and elderly and what about the children... what will happen to them?'

To her dying day Hannah would never forget the visceral cry of anguish which escaped from her husband's tortured soul.

'God Almighty, Hannah! Wake up to what is happening! You told me that the Nazis are killing people like us. Men, women and children too are being murdered in their thousands each day. And if I as a doctor can help a few souls cross over in peace as the price to get you away from here then I will do it. Don't dare question my reasoning or my ethics or I'll lose my resolve and we will both die in this awful place.' Placing his hands gently round Hannah's face, he leaned forward and kissed her.

'Hannah I want you to listen to me because we may not get another opportunity. We have had good times together especially when Aaron came into our lives. We have to hope that he is still safe with Frieda and as we sit here, you have the best chance of getting out of this place. You have to take that chance for his sake so please don't question what I do.'

Covering Ephraim's hands with her own, Hannah returned her husband's kiss. 'Are you telling me you won't be leaving here?'

'There is no way that Kernick will let me leave here alive but I promise you, my dear sweet girl, that none of those innocent children will suffer.'

Releasing her hands, she clasped herself to her husband, bereft and utterly lost for words.

Feeling the strength and passion of Hannah's embrace, Ephraim's mind again turned to something he had been mulling over for several days. A plan so extreme which would inevitably result in his own death but before that moment could occur, he intended to exact his own form of retribution on his Nazi tormentor.

Later that morning, with the burning memory of his farewell to Hannah still vividly impressed in his mind, Ephraim reported to the Adjutant's office. Sitting behind the large oaken desk reading a Berlin newspaper several days out of date, Captain Kernick fixed Ephraim with a look of annoyance. 'Doctor, I do not like to be disturbed, especially when I have a chance to catch up with the news.' Putting the newspaper down with an exaggerated air of resignation, he carefully removed spectacles which Ephraim had never seen him wear before. 'But now you're here I may as well tell you what will happen today. The children and the other inmates will leave together because I understand that Auschwitz has a special facility which will dispose of them within hours of their arrival. I've given orders that no water or food be provided for the two day journey; there's no point in feeding them when our own people are suffering so badly.'

Listening to these chilling words, Ephraim felt his resolve chrystalise. 'I will need to draw a supply of diamorphine from the dispensary Captain and I also need the key to the drug cabinet please?'

Opening a desk drawer the Adjutant drew out a bunch of keys, checked the tag on several before casually tossing a key across the desk before returning back to his newspaper. 'I must say I find your attitude much more agreeable, doctor. Pity it has come about all too late.'

Not trusting himself to respond, Ephraim quickly gathered up the key and hurried to the well-stocked pharmacy. Unlocking the refrigerated drug cabinet he carefully studied the contents. Finding what he wanted, he unfastened the two lower buttons of his shirt and secreted a small glass vial of sodium chlorate and one of d-tubocurarine, a muscle paralysing drug extracted from the highly toxic curare plant and used in anaesthetics to keep a patient pain-free and fully conscious during surgery. To avoid suspicion, he left the three fastenings on his white overall undone. Gathering up the brown cardboard box containing the diamorphine, he closed the cabinet and exited the pharmacy, remembering to lock the door after him.

Returning the key, Ephraim was relieved to see the Adjutant still in his office ostensibly engrossed in the same newspaper. Placing the key on his desk did not cause Kernick to look up or speak.

Making his way back to the surgery, Ephraim retrieved two syringes from the boiling water of the sterilisation cabinet. Carefully, he filled the first syringe with the muscle paralysing drug, letting the needle remain in the vial, sealed by its rubber collar. The other syringe, unfilled, he put in the same overall pocket containing the sodium chlorate.

Knowing what he was about to do, Ephraim knelt behind his desk, silently contemplating what he knew would be his last day in his life. He couldn't remember when he had last sought comfort in prayer. Closing his eyes in an attempt to induce a sense of spirituality, he found the emotion of that difficult to simulate. Instead, it was the face of Hannah with her languorous beauty, black lustrous hair and full-lipped sensuous mouth, which filled his thoughts. Desperate to focus on what lay ahead, Ephraim began to recite the Shema Yisroel but immediately rejected this, preferring instead to offer a childhood prayer he had memorised for his bar mitzvah. Drawing comfort from this, he stood up, reassured himself that the syringes and drugs were in place and began his short journey with destiny.

Entering the Administration Office, Ephraim could see that the Adjutant, having finished with his newspaper, was now engaged in a meeting with his Lieutenant, the same officer who had assisted Kernick on the night they had branded his chest with the hated symbol of Nazism. Of the Adjutant's clerk there was no sign. Looking up, the Adjutant beckoned him into the inner office. 'Did you get what you wanted from the dispensary, doctor?'

'Yes thank you Captain. Shall I wait in the Surgery until you are ready?'

Looking at his Lieutenant as though unwilling to address Ephraim directly, the tenor in the Adjutant's voice displayed a level of ill-concealed excitement. 'Before you disappear doctor, let me tell you a little more of what we intend to do today. There will be two transports leaving for Auschwitz. The first will take those inmates deemed capable of work in our factories in Silesia. The second transport will take those incapable of work and they will be disposed of immediately after arrival as will the Jewish children who will also travel in this second transport. That will leave a group of 23 inmates too old to travel so your task will be to put them to death by injection. I don't want them shot... the noise will cause panic.'

The Adjutant's dispassionate manner of delivery reminded Ephraim of a man arranging a holiday excursion rather than an organised plan to murder 23 human beings.

'And when... ' he paused, 'my task is finished, what will happen to me?'

'Doctor,' he gave an exaggerated sigh, 'you are an inveterate recidivist and in danger of falling back into your old ways again. What happens to you will depend on how well you obey my orders. You will just have to trust me as I would you if I were in need of medical attention'. He laughed loudly.

'Provided of course that the Lieutenant here was standing over you with his Luger pointing at your head!'

'The oath I took when I qualified as a doctor requires me to administer to the sick, regardless of their race or origin so the presence of the Lieutenant would be unnecessary.'

Leaning back in his chair, Kernick's face assumed a picture of smugness. 'Doctor, yet again you insult my intelligence. Do you really think I would place my life in the hands of a Jewish doctor, without taking the most elementary precaution?'

'Fortunately, Captain, the matter is academic because you are never likely to be in need of my assistance,'

'Oh but you are wrong again, doctor. You seem to make a habit of getting things wrong today. The Lieutenant is here for a reason. I have a damaged cartilage in my right knee which requires surgery but that will not be possible until this camp has been closed down. So in the meantime I need you to keep me mobile and pain-free which is the reason I have kept you here instead of sending you to Auschwitz with those other people.'

Standing in front of the two seated Nazis officers, Ephraim could barely believe what he was hearing, his agile brain already amending his previous strategy to incorporate this unexpected twist of fortune.

'Look Captain, if you expect me to treat you, as I would any other patient, then can we at least have an understanding. I won't knowingly harm you and I can assure you I will work much better without a gun pointing at my head.' He stopped, hoping at least for a nod of assent but Kernick remained impassive.

Ephraim persevered, knowing he had to draw a response from this normally loquacious man. 'Captain, tell me, if anything should happen to you whilst I am treating you, then what would happen to me?'

The ploy worked. 'You would be shot... immediately.'

'So what better guarantee could you have than that?'

'Doctor, I follow your logic but you forget one essential element. The inbred hatred which you Jews instinctively harbour towards us Germans will always override any thoughts you may have for your own personal safety. Your ingrained adherence to your Mosaic law is another reason and one which I cannot afford to ignore.'

His next words sent an icy chill down Ephraim's spine. 'You are an intelligent man and you know that neither you nor your wife will survive once you arrive in Auschwitz. Sending two more Jews to their death really means nothing to me but you doctor, you may be thinking, old man Moses had a point when he proclaimed his eye for an eye philosophy so why not take one or two Nazis with me before I die?

Hearing this, Ephraim realised his thinking only seconds before had been premature.

'Very well Captain, you tell me how you would wish me to manage your pain relief and we'll proceed accordingly with revolver at the ready if that is what you insist upon.'

Inside his overall pocket, his fingers closed around the syringe charged with the curare-based drug.

'Would you like to come to the surgery before or after the transports leave? The injection will take just a moment and you should get almost immediate relief.'

'Should or will.'

'You will get immediate relief.'

'In which case I will come to the surgery. Go and get ready. I don't want to waste any more time with you today.' Dismissively, he waved Ephraim towards the exit.

Turning to leave, he stopped in mid-stride. 'Captain, the children.'

A hint of impatience crept into Kernick's voice. 'And what about the children, doctor?'

'You mentioned wanting to avoid panic so wouldn't it be sensible to separate the children from the adults and keep them in the Nursery until they can be loaded in the transport.' Ephraim knew that the Adjutant's response would determine how twelve innocent children would die. He was also relying on the Adjutant's arrogance to facilitate the answer he wanted.

'Doctor, when I want your advice I will ask for it.' Then without a trace of embarrassment, he added 'I was about to give that order to the Lieutenant so carry on walking and get back to the surgery.' Ephraim could not resist one final word. 'I'm sorry, Captain. Unlike you, I'm obviously unable to think in military terms. I will be at your disposal when you have finished your deliberations.' For a brief second he thought he had again gone too far and inaudibly cursed himself for his sarcastic temerity; a habit he seemed unable to contain. Detecting the growing sense of malice from the seated Adjutant, Ephraim turned and rapidly left the presence of the man he intended to kill.

Walking back, he looked towards the area in the camp reserved for recreation. This had been the backdrop for the Nazi propaganda film showing happy Jewish families at play; these same people now destined for certain death at Auschwitz. Standing at the rear of the first of three groups assembled by the Czech guards, Ephraim immediately recognised the forlorn figure of Hannah, her distress all too obvious. Putting caution aside and relying on the perceived authority enshrined within his white overall, Ephraim strode past the unquestioning guards.

To embrace his wife he knew would invite the attention of the German Overseer so he stopped just short of the woman whom he had shared the best years of his life with. Looking into her tearful eyes, he took courage from her calmness.

'Sweetheart, be strong for both of us. Do anything to survive not only for your sake but for Aaron too. It's only a matter of time before the Nazis are defeated so think of what your friend Max said... 'make it through to the end'. Remember always

Hannah, you have been the love of my life and my last thought on this earth will be of you, my dear sweet wife.'

Choked with emotion and unable to speak, Hannah threw herself into Ephraim's arms and clutched herself to him. As she did so, she heard the harsh shout from the Overseer ordering the Czech Guards to intervene.

Before they could act, Ephraim gently eased himself back. 'Go in peace Hannah and remember my words. Do anything to survive.' Knowing this would be their final moment together, Ephraim leaned forward and kissed Hannah's upraised face. 'Shalom my darling girl and may our God be with you always.'

Unable to bear the moment any longer and conscious of the approaching Guards, he turned sharply away and strode towards the clinic. The Czech guards, strangely hesitant about clubbing the man they recognised as the camp physician, lowered their truncheons and watched as he walked away.

Reaching the Clinic, Ephraim let his pent-up emotions drain away. Tears withheld in Hannah's presence now began to course down his face, unchecked. Conscious of what still lay ahead, he sat down and buried his face in his hands. He thought of the sweet innocence of their young child; of Hannah bringing enjoyment to untold thousands of people with her musical talent and he, a physician, endeavouring to alleviate suffering when being allowed to practice. And not just Hannah and himself but thousands of Jews like them; a race of people traditionally enriching their communities with their talents and industry. He thought yet again of the sheer insanity of a cultured European nation seeking to exterminate such people for no other reason than being Jewish while the rest of the civilised world looked on.

Taking a succession of deep breaths, Ephraim was able to bring his agonised emotions under control just in time to see the bulky frame of Captain Kernick limping towards the clinic. And Kernick was alone.

Brushing past him, Ephraim waited for the man who embodied the very essence of Nazism to speak.

Unbuttoning his uniform jacket, the Adjutant stopped in the centre of the room. 'Do I lie on that couch or sit in this chair?'

'The couch will be best but you will need to either remove or lower your uniform trousers so I can examine and then inject your knee.'

'There's no need for an examination; just inject my knee and stop wasting time.'

'Fine Captain, I'm happy to do that. Whilst you are removing your uniform I will prepare the injection.' Opening the enamel door to the small sterile cabinet, Ephraim withdrew the vial labelled to show the content to be diamorphine but which he had earlier discharged into the sink and replaced with the curare drug. Inserting the needle through the rubber seal, he filled the syringe with a rock-steady hand. Aware that the Adjutant was watching his every move, Ephraim went through the procedure with deliberate slowness.

'Let me see that drug bottle, doctor.' Sitting on the side of the couch with his uniform trousers neatly placed on the chair beside him, the Adjutant presented an amusing picture. His white legs were muscular and Ephraim could see that the right knee was swollen, no doubt caused by water retention.

Holding the empty vial of diamorphine, the Adjutant scrutinised the label. 'How much of this will you need to inject?'

'Judging from your body weight and the size of the swelling, I will inject 10 mg. That will give you the relief you want.' Inwardly, he could feel the mounting tension begin to increase his heart rate. 'Will your Lieutenant be much longer, Captain?'

'He won't be coming. He has other duties to attend to so go ahead with the injection.'

'Fine, if you are happy to for me to proceed without him then let's do it.' For added effect he raised the syringe and theatrically squirted a small amount of the muscle paralysing drug knowing Kernick was watching his every move. 'I would like you to lie flat to enable the drug to get into your system as quickly as possible.'

Looking at the odious figure now ostensibly at his mercy, Ephraim felt no sense of remorse. Feeling the opening in the knee joint, he carefully directed the needle through the soft tissue. Glancing up at the man who personified all that he had come to hate, he held Kernick's eyes with his own as he exerted pressure on the syringe, feeling the plunger smoothly inject a small amount of the lethal drug into the Adjutant's leg. For a few timeless seconds there was no reaction. With eyes still locked on his adversary, Ephraim began to feel a sense of growing panic and tempted to push the plunger fully home. Instead, he injected a further 3mg and waited for the reaction he knew should follow. Almost imperceptibly, he saw Kernick's leg relax.

For Ephraim, this was to be the redeeming moment. Leaning over the immobile figure of the Adjutant he mouthed each word with slow deliberation. 'I know you can hear me but you can't react because I have just injected you with a muscle paralysing drug which as I increase the dosage, will paralyse your vital organs and kill you in about five minutes or sooner if I so wish. In simple terms Captain, you are about to die at the hands of a Jew.'

Looking intently into Kernick's eyes, Ephraim could see that both pupils had already dilated as his body began to tremble and go into spasm. No sound escaped his lips as the curare wreaked its paralysing effect on his vocal cords.

'However, before I administer your last rite, Captain, there are two minor operations I wish to perform on you.' Reaching into a surgical side tray, Ephraim extracted a silver scalpel and held it in front of Kernick's face just long enough for him to recognise the instrument.

With a deft downward movement, the scalpel slashed through the fine cotton of the Adjutant's shirt exposing the same whiteness of his chest as in his legs. Looking at the man lying helpless before him, Ephraim recalled the night when he too had been constrained by Kernick's accomplices before being branded with a red hot iron.

'Captain, I know you can hear my every word so I want you to remember the night when you and your comrades scarred my body with the symbol of your Nazi Party. I now intend to return that favour and initiate your body with a similar mark of recognition. However, before I do that you will need to become a fully-paid up member of the Jewish race. Can I take it you are happy with the plan so far?'

Pausing to allow time for his words to register, Ephraim again used the scalpel, this time to cut the two tie-strings of Kernick's undergarment. With unhurried deliberation, he donned a pair of surgical gloves, watching with fascination as minute particles of white talcum powder fell onto the dark green cotton material. Exposing Kernick's genitals, Ephraim grasped his penis and pulled the foreskin over its head.

Despite the paralysing effect of the curare drug, Ephraim felt a satisfying tremor of fear run through the otherwise inert body. 'Can I take that as an indication of your approval, Captain?' Feigning disappointment at getting no reaction, Ephraim pressed on. 'As you Aryans are so much more intelligent than Jews like me, you've probably guessed what I am about to do. I am going to circumcise you and place the redundant foreskin in your mouth. I will then embellish your chest with the mark of Judah and there was something else... now what was it?' Ephraim looked up at the ceiling as if seeking to remember the answer to his question.

'Ah yes, now I recall... the final stage or would you prefer me to use the term 'final solution' as being more appropriate? I am going to send you off to that Aryan Valhalla where all good SS men go but first a word of caution Captain; when you get there, remember to keep your mouth closed and your trousers buttoned up otherwise your comrades will not let you in.'

Looking down at the pathetic figure of this indoctrinated Nazi, Ephraim felt an acute sense of shame begin to overwhelm him. The words of his Hippocratic Oath floated through his mind causing a feeling of revulsion to well up in his stomach. Releasing his hold on Kernick's penis, his fingers located the syringe and angrily he injected the remaining drug into the Adjutant's leg.

Withdrawing the needle, he took a pace back from the couch. Kernick's breathing began to labour as his lungs gasped for air. Standing back from the couch, Ephraim saw his eyes roll into his head as his heart gave up the unequal struggle. With a final expiration of air, the Adjutant of Theresienstadt, Captain Hugo Kernick, Iron Cross 2nd Class, died. Not on the field of battle but in utter ignominy at the hands of a vengeful physician dedicated to the sanctity of life.

THIRTY FIVE

To those within earshot of the clinic, Ephraim's clamorous call for help caused consternation. The first to respond was the German Overseer but the scene which met his eyes was too much for him to take in. Bemused, he drew his service revolver, pointed it at Ephraim and barked an order to an unseen guard to fetch the Lieutenant.

Ignoring the Overseer, Ephraim leaned over the dead Adjutant and began to administer heart resuscitation.

Only with the arrival of the Lieutenant did Ephraim look up and speak. 'The Captain is having a heart attack. Nodding towards the corner of the room, he barked 'get that oxygen cylinder over here and fetch that face mask... quickly!'

The urgency in Ephraim's voice caused temporary bewilderment to the young officer before his military training kicked in. Taking hold of the cylinder and mask, he positioned himself on the opposite side of the couch.

Looking down at the immobile form of his superior officer, he could see Kernick's chest heaving in time with the rapid pressure being exerted by Ephraim.

'Quickly... turn the cylinder on and place the mask over his mouth and nose.'

Satisfied that the mask was correctly positioned and functioning, Ephraim issued a further instruction. 'Place your hands over mine and get into the rhythm. I will withdraw my hands and I want you to take over. Can you do that?'

Looking at the sweat on Ephraim's brow, the Lieutenant nodded assent. Working in tandem until he was satisfied that the pressure and rhythm were correct, Ephraim slowly withdrew both hands.

'I am going to get my stethoscope from my desk and then I will ask you to stop whilst I check for a regular heartbeat. Are you comfortable with that?'

Totally caught up in the deception being choreographed by Ephraim, the Lieutenant signified his agreement with another brief nod.

Stepping back, Ephraim arched his body, bringing welcome relief to the mounting pain in his lower back. Wiping the perspiration from his forehead, Ephraim took his time to collect the stethoscope before returning to the couch.

'When I say stop, take your hands away and step back. Are you ready?'

'I'm ready... say when.'

'Stop now!'

Placing the stethoscope against Kernick's still chest, Ephraim's mind was racing. For his plan to succeed it was imperative for the Lieutenant to believe that Kernick was still alive when he arrived at the clinic but he knew there was a limit as to how long he would be able to maintain the deception?

He would never know the answer to that question. While appearing to concentrate on listening for a non-existent heartbeat, Ephraim saw the figure of the camp Commandant appear and testily summon the Lieutenant to his side with an impatient gesture. Their hurried whisperings were lost to him before the Commandant strode over to look at the now dead figure of his Adjutant.

'I'm afraid we have lost him, Commandant. I'm sorry. Both the Lieutenant and I tried our best but to no avail.'

'What was he doing here; was he unwell?'

It was the Lieutenant who replied. 'He had a problem with his knee, Commandant; something to do with a torn cartilage I believe.'

'And what was he expecting you to do, doctor?'

Ephraim knew his life would depend on the plausibility of his explanation.

'I was intending to give the Adjutant a pain-killing injection as a temporary measure. He saw me prepare the injection and he checked the description of the drug and dosage but when I cleaned the area to make it sterile, he appeared to have a fit and fell back on the couch. Medically speaking, some people do have a violent aversion to injections and this could cause fainting or in cases of extreme stress, even a heart attack. I simply cannot say what caused this Officer to collapse.'

'Did you actually inject this pain-killer?' The Commandant again, this time his tone was questioning.'

'No, I was about to when he collapsed.'

'Show me the syringe and drug you had prepared.'

'The remains of both are there, Commandant' pointing to a broken syringe lying in a pool of minute wetness. 'When the Captain collapsed he knocked the syringe onto the floor and either I or the Lieutenant must have trodden on it when we were attempting to resuscitate him.' Ephraim silently hoped that the Lieutenant wouldn't contradict his involvement.'

'Was the Adjutant still alive when you arrived,' the question this time directed at the Lieutenant.

'He was still breathing when I applied resuscitation sir.'

Inwardly, Ephraim breathed a sigh of relief.

Digesting this information, the Commandant looked at the dead figure of his Adjutant for the last time before turning away.

'Lieutenant Halder, arrange for Captain Kernick's body to be taken to his quarters and advise the Czech undertaker to make the appropriate burial arrangements.' Turning to Ephraim, he gave a curt nod and without uttering a further word, strode from the clinic.

Within minutes of the Commandant leaving, the Adjutant's body was removed from the clinic. Four German soldiers arrived carrying a wooden coffin crudely made from bare pine boards. Under the expressionless supervision of the Lieutenant they each took a limb and prepared to lift the heavy corpse. As they raised the body off the flat couch it sagged, causing expelled air in the lungs to emit a loan moan. Startled, the soldier holding the Adjutant's left arm let it go and jumped back causing the lifeless limb to fall to the floor. Embarrassed, he regained his hold and with a muffled grunt sufficing as an apology, all four soldiers lowered the Adjutant's body into the coffin. As the wooden lid was positioned in place, Ephraim realised he was seeing Kernick's detestable face, a face even now beginning to reflect the grey pallor of death, for the last time.

In spite of his loathing for this arrogant man and his murderous creed, he felt a growing sense of revulsion and guilt welling up within him. An involuntary heave from the pit of his stomach forced the taste of acidic bitterness in his mouth. Knowing he was about to vomit, Ephraim quickly made for the lavatory on the far side of the corridor, barely making it before expelling the remains of his earlier breakfast into the gaping toilet.

Straitening up, he took several deep breaths to regain his composure before flushing his mouth with cold water. Looking into the small mirror positioned above the basin, Ephraim saw beads of sweat glistening on his forehead. Splashing cold water on his face had the desired effect of calming his jangling nerves. Returning to the clinic, he saw that the Lieutenant was still there, waiting for him..

'Ah, so the doctor returns; what was the reason for your sudden exit?'

Remembering an old adage taught to him by a former patient, Ephraim injected an element of truth into the web of lies surrounding the death of the Adjutant.

'I was sick; throw-up sick. No doctor likes to lose a patient especially a youngish person with no apparent illness. I'm afraid it's something you never quite get used to.'

'Come now doctor, this wasn't just any youngish person; this was a Nazi officer who detested Jews in general and you in particular. And if you can bring yourself to admit it, I'm sure the feeling on your part was mutual. So why would his death have that effect on you, a man used to seeing death on a daily basis?' The question hung in the air like a poised sword.

'I look beyond the person, Lieutenant and focus on the medical challenge. Here was a man who should not have died, yet who did. And without the benefit of a post-mortem report, I don't know why.'

'Doctor, look at me.' The tone in the Lieutenant's voice took on an accusatory note. 'Stop this bullshit and answer a simple question. Did you kill Captain Kernick with that injection? Yes or no?'

Surprised by the Lieutenant's direct question and suddenly overwhelmed by the enormity of what he had done, Ephraim drew himself to his full height. 'Yes, I did and given the opportunity I would like to kill all of you insane, murdering bastards.'

Anticipating immediate arrest and summary execution, Ephraim waited for the Lieutenant to make his move. Instead, came another question.

'So was the Adjutant dead before I came into the clinic?'

'Yes he was.'

'And the attempt to resuscitate him... was that a charade too?'

'I had to convince you so you in turn could convince the Commandant... as you did.'

The faintest hint of a smile crossed the Lieutenant's face. 'Yes I did... like putty in your hands.' Clearly undecided what to do next, the young officer moved closer to Ephraim. 'Tell me doctor, what was your reason for wanting the children moved to the Nursery?'

Now it was Ephraim's turn to exercise caution. 'Before answering that question Lieutenant, can I ask whether you have children of your own?

'You can ask but what is the relevance of that to my question?'

'Because if you have children of your own you will understand what I have to do.' Ephraim saw the young officer straighten up, his hand hovering over the leather holster of the sidearm strapped to his belt.

'Doctor Fischer... I want you to listen to me carefully. You have just admitted killing a German officer the penalty for which is death, execution by a bullet in the back of your skull. I'm sure you didn't need me to tell you that?. Which means that in 15 minutes you will be dead so answer my question before I shorten that deadline even more? And don't test my patience any further because you are already on borrowed time.'

'Then go ahead Lieutenant. Shoot me now and may your soul rot in hell for being an accessory to the murder of those innocent children. Left where they are, they will be transported to Auschwitz in a cattle truck, in the dark, with no parents to comfort them, terrified, hungry and thirsty. Once there they will be gassed or shot. That's why I asked whether you have children of your own because you will then understand what I need to do and why?

'War is no respecter of people, doctor. Children as well as adults get killed.' He hesitated and stared at Ephraim. 'But you have a point.' Turning towards the door and looking out towards the buildings on the far side of the recreation area, the Lieutenant appeared to be considering his options.

'The children are located in the Nursery and you have an hour before they are due to be shipped out. And doctor... two final things. Firstly, in answer to your question... yes, I do have a child of my own. Secondly, if you are still alive when the soldiers come for the children then you will be shot. I trust we understand each other?'

'Perfectly, Lieutenant; may your own child grow in wisdom and peace... unlike those poor mites in the nursery who will be dead within the hour.'

The four-man squad of soldiers tasked with the evacuation of the children arrived at the Nursery within the stated hour. Forming up outside the Nursery they stood at ease awaiting the arrival of the Lieutenant. Seeing his approach, the Czech NCO ordered the squad to come to attention.

'Form up in a line but do not present arms.' Not knowing what to expect, the Lieutenant's order was whispered to avoid panic-stricken children running off in all directions.

Ordering the Sergeant to follow him, together they approached the door of the Nursery, emblazoned with a newly painted caricature which neither recognised as a dreidel doll nor did they understand the Hebrew caption beneath it... 'Nes Gadol Vaya Sham'. 'A Great Miracle Happened Here.' The door yielded easily and both men had to peer into the interior of the large room, darkened by the drawn blinds.

Activating the light switch revealed a picture of peaceful tranquillity. Six beds each bore two children, all of whom appeared to be sleeping. Looking more closely, the Lieutenant noticed the absence of breathing and knew then that with his approbation, Dr. Fischer, had spared each child, the innocents of Theresienstadt, the trauma and terror of the journey to Auschwitz and death once there. Of the doctor there was no sign, despite a thorough search of the entire camp. The evening roll call tellingly revealed that two Czech camp guards had also disappeared together with their rifles and a supply of ammunition; the same two guards who had ignored the Overseer's order to assault the doctor earlier that morning. But any sympathy felt by the Czech NCO towards his erstwhile comrades brought its own vengeful consequence.

The following morning, on the order of the Camp Commandant, he and the other three members of the missing men's squad were executed by firing squad under the command of the newly promoted Adjutant, Captain Werner Halder.

THIRTY SIX

Numbed by the emotion of their final parting and realisation that Ephraim was now almost certainly dead, the journey to Auschwitz passed as in a tormented nightmare. No water had been provided in the rail wagon and by the end of the second day Hannah began to hallucinate.

Unable to find a space at the side of the wagon, she had been forced to sit on the foul smelling wooden floorboards, a surface saturated with urine slopping from an overfull slop bucket. Sitting there for hour after interminable hour her mind began to drift away into a merciful black morass. Looking beyond the imposing darkness she thought she recognised her mother and father as they walked alongside a glistening lake, it's cool water causing her to salivate in the hope of slaking her raging thirst. In a voice which was barely audible even to herself, she attempted to call out to both parents but in despairing frustration, she watched as they slowly faded from view only to be replaced moments later by numerous kindergarten children, each one identical to Aaron. Reaching out, she felt her fingers touch hair... not the fine silken hair of a child but hair coarsened with age. Forcing her eyes open, she saw that her hand was fingering the grey locks of an old woman; a woman too tired to even notice. Slipping her hand down onto the elderly woman's shoulder, she gave a slight squeeze in silent apology.

With priority being given to countless military trains to and from the Eastern front, it was three and a half days before the journey finally ended at the Birkenau rail head. From her grim experience at Ravensbrück, Hannah knew this was where the final selection process would take place.

It began with the wagon door sliding open, flooding the interior with natural daylight and releasing the ghastly stench of fetid air into the atmosphere. Shielding her eyes from the glare, she unsteadily regained her footing and drew several deep draughts of fresh air into her lungs. Through the widening gap of the open door, she saw a phalanx of SS Guards wielding heavy wooden clubs and a senior officer holding what appeared to be a riding crop. Alongside them in even greater numbers were people she now knew to be camp workers dressed in the same black and white striped uniforms she had first seen at Ravensbrück.

Letting the awful stench disperse, neither the SS Guards nor the camp workers approached the wagon until the shrill blast of a whistle, magnified through an unseen PA system, signalled time to begin the disembarkation.

Unlike Ravensbrück where the internees were ordered to either climb down or be thrown from the freight wagon, here at Auschwitz a wooden platform leading to a long ramp had been provided. In the daylight, she managed to locate her violin case and the small toilet bag given to her by Ephraim before stumbling to the opening on legs just beginning to regain some feeling.

Outside in the chill morning air, Hannah saw that the train had halted at a large marshalling area overseen at the far end by an arched gateway. As each wagon disgorged its human cargo, the internees were roughly shepherded towards the centre of the ramp and formed into two lanes; one lane for men, the other for women and children.

The growing sense of apprehension was further heightened by a disembodied voice coming from speakers mounted on lighting poles positioned on each side of the single rail track.

'Attention!... Attention!' Immediately the increasing hubbub died as the internees, now full of apprehension awaited the next pronouncement. They did not have to wait long.

'This is the Medical Officer speaking.'

Peering towards the end of the ramp, Hannah recognised the person speaking into a hand-held microphone as the officer she had seen moments before, the man holding a riding crop.

'By order of the Fuehrer you have been resettled from the Fatherland to this, your new home here in Eastern Europe. You will be housed and fed and in return you will be required to work in one of the new factories built to provide you with gainful employment.'

'First, you will be assessed by me to determine your suitability. Those of you fit enough for such work will be directed to their quarters whilst those not well enough at present will be taken to the shower block for de-lousing before going to the medical centre. One last instruction. You must leave all personal belongings here; they will be returned in due course.'

Handing the microphone to the guard standing alongside him, the Medical Officer walked to the raised platform and lowered his corpulent buttocks on to a stout wooden stool.

From what she had seen at Ravensbrück, Hannah knew she was yet again witnessing the black art of Nazi deception, designed to instill a sense of false security in those about to die.

Responding to a signal from the SS Overseer, the camp workers began to move among the lines of bemused prisoners, removing each pathetic bundle of property. Dehydrated and feeling increasingly weak, Hannah allowed the violin case containing her treasured Bellini to slip to the ground. Partially shrouded by her long coat it escaped the searching eyes of an already overburdened camp worker. Later she was to realise that this unwitting touch of fortune had briefly extended her life beyond the selection ramp.

As each column of human jetsam slowly edged towards the point of selection, her sense of anxiety tangibly increased. Peering over the shoulder of an older woman immediately ahead of her, she was able to see that the majority of prisoners, the elderly and infirm, women with children and those with obvious disabilities, were being directed to the de-lousing chambers with barely a cursory glance from the inspecting Officer. A smaller number, those he visually adjudged as being fit for work, were given a slightly longer inspection.

Signalled to approach the inspection point, Hannah saw the Officer's eyes immediately fasten on to the violin case before transferring his appraising gaze to her.

'Why are still holding that case?' The question was edged with curiosity rather than a threat. Reaching forward, he tapped the case with his riding crop. 'I'm intrigued; it looks like a violin case but show me what's inside it.'

Balancing the case on one hand, Hannah nervously undid its two retaining clips and opened the lid to reveal the mahogany instrument crafted in a bygone age.

'So... it is a violin.' His voice expressed surprise. Giving the case a final tap, the Officer glanced up at the pressing wave of prisoners. 'Close the lid and follow that line there' indicating with a casual wave for Hannah to join those selected for work.

'And leave your violin case here.'

Only too anxious to get away from the selection area on legs still trembling from the emotional trauma of the past few moments, she dropped the instrument case without a second thought. Glancing to her left she saw those internees selected for apparent delousing being expertly marshalled to their almost immediate death. Against that comparison the loss of her treasured Bellini violin was of no import.

Quickly ushered through the entrance to the main camp of Auschwitz she looked up and read the crude metal sign welded to the iron portal over the gate; 'Arbeit Macht Frei... ' 'Work Brings Freedom.'

THIRTY SEVEN

Once inside the main Auschwitz complex, Hannah and the other new arrivals were marshalled into an area between two accommodation blocks and subjected to a more detailed inspection; this time conducted under the pitiless scrutiny of SS NCO's. The type of work assigned to each prisoner determined their accommodation block. For those inmates assessed as being fit for physical work in the factories and mines outside of the camp, each day of unremitting labour and poor food soon took an inevitable toll. At night, in bunks designed for single occupancy but now crammed with four times that number, some would use whatever means they could find to slash the veins in their wrists, their warm lifeblood slowly seeping into a putrid mattress. Others would make a rudimentary noose from their threadbare prison garments and hang themselves in the darkness of the stinking cell block.

For Hannah, after two days in the female prison block, all vestige of family and professional life had all but been extinguished. The Kapo in charge of the accommodation block, a callous Latvian woman in her mid-forties was particularly vicious towards the Polish and Russian women thereby giving the German internees a degree of relief from the threats and beatings suffered by the other prisoners.

On the third day there was a noticeable change. Instead of dispersing after the early-morning roll call, the women were ordered to remain in the open yard. The heavy rain which had fallen for much of the night had eased but large pools of water still remained; slow to drain away through the porous grey shale.

A flurry of movement at the far end of the block signalled the arrival of an SS guard. To avoid getting mud on his highly polished jackboots, he carefully stepped around the deeper puddles before halting in the centre of the assembled women.

With legs astride and hands on hips he theatrically ran his gaze over the women before speaking.

'The German women will to move to the right; you others will move to the left except the Poles... you will remain in the centre. Now move... quickly!'

Despite the urgency of the command, it took time for some of the bewildered women to form in their respective groups. Whilst this was happening she noticed a male Kapo position himself just behind the German NCO. Having achieved the required separation, both men approached the group of Polish prisoners. Oddly, it was the Kapo who now assumed the initiative. Walking among the fearful women the Kapo took his time. Despite the shapeless form of their drab prison overalls, it was clear he was interested only in the more attractive women. Finishing his inspection he roughly pulled seven women out of the group, pushing them to the rear of the yard, closely watched by the Latvian Kapo. Within minutes, the Polish women were shepherded from the yard.

With their removal the focus switched back to the NCO. Using his heavy pace stick as an extension of his right arm, he directed the non-German group to close up with the remaining Polish women.

'You women are all assigned to work in factories outside this camp so you will now be taken to your new quarters and begin your labours later this morning.' With a casual flick of his pace stick, he impatiently directed two camp workers to begin removing the women.

Addressing the remaining women, all German, Hannah saw what she took to be a leer run across his lean features.

'Now... what does the Fatherland have in store for you? Reaching into the pocket of his uniform tunic he pulled out a yellow card. Studying it for what seemed an eternity, he at last looked up. 'Right... let me have your attention... ' an injunction entirely superfluous as each of the remaining women were only too anxious to hear what he had to say next.

'Unlike those other groups, you have all been chosen to work within the camp; in the Central Administration Unit or to give it its colloquial name; 'Kanada'... the 'Land of Plenty.''

Looking up, he was clearly disappointed at failing to see any perceptible appreciation for his attempt at humour. Dropping his voice to ensure he would not be overheard, he tried again. 'Take my word for it, it's the best assignment in this shit-hole of a camp.'

Later that morning, she and the other women were moved to Block 22; a brick built two-storey building accessed from the tarmacked road leading from the Main Gate. Immediately adjacent to the building was a combined shower block and small laundry unit next to which was a similar building housing Kapo's and other camp workers.

Beyond that was Block 24, a smaller one-story building, the purpose of which remained a mystery until a loose-lipped Kapo disclosed its purpose. It was a brothel which according to rumour had been ordered by Reichsfuhrer-SS Heinrich Himmler, following a visit to Auschwitz five months earlier.

It also explained what had happened to the Polish women selected earlier that morning, each having been 'chosen' to service the sexual needs of camp workers. Hannah later learned that with typical Germanic organisation, admittance to the brothel was regulated by a voucher system issued by the SS Officer in charge of Administration with stipulated times of entry and a maximum of 15 minutes per visit! Military personnel were strictly forbidden to use the facility as the Polish women were all Jews and as such, a danger to the purity of their Aryan blood.

THIRTY EIGHT

It took Hannah just a matter of hours to appreciate the material benefits attaching to working in 'Kanada'. Unlike many other prisoners in the camp, workers in this facility were spared having their heads shaven nor were they required to wear the striped uniform worn by other inmates. Within the Central Sorting Area, her task was relatively simple; as each train arrived at the camp, all personal belongings would be confiscated and brought to the sorting area where every case, valise and bundle would be opened and searched by workers adept at finding valuables, cash and other items secreted by their former owners. Her task was to gather jewellery, rings and watches from each of the other women and place them into large wooden boxes and to sort appropriated money into national denominations watched at all times by a steely eyed SS Overseer. At the end of each day, these would be collected and placed in even larger steel boxes... probably destined for Nazi coffers in Berlin. Included in the recovered booty were surprising amounts of alcohol, much of which would find its way to the military barracks other than that stolen by the Kapo's. Edible food found in cases and valises was allowed to be taken back to the women's quarters and shared with the other inmates.

It took her less than a day to realise that the irregular shape of the sorting room made it difficult for the SS Overseer to adequately supervise the growing piles of wealth on each of the sorting tables. Knowing this, increasing numbers of SS military personnel would regularly wander into the building and help themselves to a watch or piece of jewellery or whatever else took their fancy. Seeing this happen on a daily basis filled her with a sense of irony in knowing that Hitler's vaunted SS troops, standard bearers of the Nazi creed of purity and integrity, were little more than common thieves in the face of temptation.

Another aspect of daily life in 'Kanada' was the distinct pecking order which she had no wish to challenge. She had been accepted by the other women and had done nothing to displease the SS Overseer. An older inmate, Miriam, had quietly befriended her and it was she who told her that the Kapo's too were as much prisoners as themselves. They retained their supervisory roles only as long as it suited their SS masters and to do this they were expected to be ruthlessly sadistic towards those prisoners in their charge. If for any reason they displeased their German masters then according to Miriam, they would be marched back, usually at night, to the same accommodation block they had previously supervised. Once there, and encouraged by the SS guards, they would invariably be beaten to death by the other inmates. But alive and well, a Kapo was a person to be feared and she was strongly advised by Miriam to keep a low profile and do nothing to draw attention to herself.

On overcast days and without the benefit of a strong wind the stomach churning smell of burnt human flesh spewing from the crematory chimneys would drift to every part of the Auschwitz complex, clinging to hair and clothes alike.

On Miriam's request and the unexpected consent of the Overseer, Hannah and the newest intake of women were each allowed to select various garments and underwear from the mountain of clothes recovered each day from those thousands of women forced to strip naked before entering the gas chambers.

Showered and with freshly washed clothes now replacing the filthy garments she had worn for the past two weeks, she felt a glimmer of self-esteem for the first time since her arrest.

The lay-out of Block 22 was much the same as other accommodation units within the main Auschwitz complex. The ground floor comprised a large open area housing crudely assembled wooden two-tier bunks with an ablutions room at one end of the block and a wooden stairwell situated at the opposite end of the building. This gave access to an upper floor with yet more bunks contained within wooden screens giving a semblance of privacy notably absent on the ground floor. The Kapo's sleeping area was to the left of the centrally placed entrance door from where she was able to scrutinise inmates exiting and returning to the block. The Kapo in charge of the building was a Hungarian woman who rarely spoke except when administering a savage beating with a thick bamboo cane to some unfortunate soul.

To her surprise, Hannah was assigned to the first floor where she slept in the top bunk, the lower one thankfully occupied by Miriam.

Before falling asleep each night she would endeavour to think about Ephraim and Aaron. Following their traumatic parting at Theresienstadt she accepted that Ephraim was now probably dead but when she thought about Aaron she was invariably filled with sadness and apprehension for his continuing safety in a city which thankfully was hundreds of kilometres away from the daily horror of Auschwitz.

She recalled the parting words of Ephraim; 'do whatever it takes to survive... for Aaron's sake.' But lying in her bunk at night she spent endless hours wondering what she could possibly do or hope to achieve in her present situation to fulfil his wish. Fate had dealt her a fortunate hand with her placement in 'Kanada' but always in her mind was the threat of summary punishment or death at the whim of the SS guards or their subservient Kapo's.

On this particular night and with thoughts of Aaron pressing on her mind, her weary body finally gave in to sleep. But almost immediately she was disturbed by a sudden noise and the sound of an obvious struggle taking place at the far end of the room. Half awake and with the clamour growing louder, she swung her legs over the side of the bunk and prepared to jump down.

'Stay where you are Hannah... don't get involved.' From below, the calming voice of Miriam temporarily allayed her growing alarm.

Now fully awake, it took several moments for her to realise what was happening. The repeated cries of alarm had stopped as suddenly as they had begun, subdued by the sound of two heavy slaps followed by a series of low moans. All had gone quiet for a while before she became aware of a rhythmic creaking noise coming from a wooden bunk. Lying back, she heard the sound progressively increase until she heard what even she realised was the climactic moment of two people having sex. She heard a second sound, a groan escaping from the woman followed moments later by an unidentified rustling and the sound of fading footsteps on the wooden staircase.

Peering over the edge of her bunk, Hannah dimly saw Miriam's head above the grey blanket.

'Miriam... are you still awake?' Without waiting for a reply Hannah reached down and touched Miriam's shoulder. 'Shouldn't we go and see whether she's alright?'

'Hannah, listen to me and stay where you are. Whatever may have happened is now over so go back to sleep... OK.'

'But who was that and why didn't the Kapo stop him coming into the block?'

For a few seconds there was no reaction but then in the gloom she saw Miriam throw back her blanket and ease herself out of her bunk. Standing close to her, she felt Miriam's cold breath on her face.

'Whether you can bring yourself to face up to reality or not is up to you but all of the women here are prisoners in a camp where thousands of Jews and other women like us, are being murdered every single day. The fact that we are still alive is because we work in a unit which is producing millions of marks for the Nazis. But almost any prisoner can do what we do so consider yourself fortunate that it's you and not someone else.' For a moment she stopped speaking and Hannah heard her take a deep breath.

'I know you give the impression of being a little girl lost but even you must know what has just happened. Either a soldier or a Kapo came here for sex. They don't ask... they take and tomorrow it could be you or someone else. And the unfortunate girl you wanted to run to? Do you hear her complaining? She's probably fallen asleep already. And by the way... in case you forget, we are just temporary residents here so think of it like a hotel.' Miriam gave a mirthless chuckle.

'But why don't they use the brothel if they want sex?

A sound of exasperation escaped Miriam's lips. 'If it was a Kapo then their visits are controlled by the SS. If it was a soldier, they are forbidden to have sex with Jews. And the Polish women in the Puffhaus are Jews.'

'But we are all Jews in this building. So what's the difference?'

'The difference? Miriam repeated her words. 'Hannah, are you being stupid or do you really need me to spell it out for you? To them we may be Jews but we are also women. To a man wanting sex there is no difference particularly at this time of night when they can't see who they're fucking. They're happy to kill us in our thousands during the day but they have no qualms about having sex with us at night. They fuck us because there are no recriminations and they know no one cares what they do. So please, no more questions... we both need our sleep.'

Clambering back into her bunk, a last thought entered Miriam's mind. Straightening up, she again drew close to Hannah's ear whispering 'some women here may actually welcome male company in the night, depending on who the male might be. And the need for sex pays no regard to camp rules or regulations. You want it... you do it whether you're a German, Jew or Gentile so take that thought with you as you drift off into your sweet little world of fairies and make-believe. Sweet dreams my friend.'

Lying back on the hard paillasse Hannah thought about Miriam's parting shot and again the words of Ephraim flashed into her mind; 'do whatever it takes to survive.' Instantly her thoughts turned to Aaron. 'What' she wondered 'would I do if it meant I could see my baby son again?'

THIRTY NINE

As the weeks became months, the number of trains arriving each day dramatically increased. In the central sorting area, the amount of foreign currencies, gold, silver and jewellery began to assume mountainous proportions as did the level of theft now being perpetrated by SS personnel. Not all the property ending up in the Central Sorting Area came from those prisoners consigned to death in the gas chambers. Similar amounts of confiscated booty was also taken from those new prisoners adjudged able to become slave labourers in the burgeoning industrial complexes, some within walking distance of the camp. Major corporations such as Krupp Weschel Union, I.G Farben, Daimler, Puch, Steyr and numerous other companies had been attracted to the region by the Nazi Government's promise of unlimited slave labour sourced from the nearby camps of Auschwitz and Birkenau. As well as enabling these industries to manufacture and supply the mounting needs of the Nazis voracious war machine, the supply of labour was also an essential element in the German Government's policy of ethnic cleansing. Cynically, the Nazi's exacted a fee for each prisoner supplied from either camp which each of the major organisations would then recoup by providing starvation-levels of food to their labour force until death inevitably intervened, only for these newly dead to be replaced by yet more slave labour in a never-ending cycle of horror

For Hannah the monotony of work at the Central Sorting Area barely managed to compensate for the fact that she was still alive. Though outwardly hardened to the dire conditions surrounding her and the other inmates, inwardly she was becoming more and more vulnerable to periods of self-doubt. The forlorn hope of somehow being able to survive the war kept her going on a daily basis but all hope of Ephraim still being alive had now gone. Even her cherished memories of Aaron were becoming blurred but without being able to cling on to the hope that he may still be safe, she knew she would have no reason to carry on living. But even this optimism was becoming ever more doubtful as news filtered through of Allied air raids being increasingly targeted on Berlin with cargoes of death which drew no distinction between Nazis and those oppressed by them.

In an effort to retain even a semblance of sanity, she purposely tried to blank out her revulsion of what was happening elsewhere within the Auschwitz complex where daily, thousands of innocent victims were being brought to this hell on earth for one purpose only... their indiscriminate extermination. The location of 'Kanada' away from the immediate killing areas in no way helped to sanitize the unspeakable horror taking place every hour of every day.

Her job in the Central Sorting Area required no cerebral input, just mind-numbing routine work made worse by the SS Overseer forbidding the women from speaking to each other. So it came as a surprise when he suddenly announced that they would not be required to work late into the evening as they were usually required to do.

'Can I ask why?' Hannah knew without looking who was posing the question. It was the irrepressible Miriam of course.

For a moment there was a worrying silence before the Overseer deigned to reply. 'Because tomorrow is Christmas and tonight there will be a carol service in the military Chapel.'

'Are we invited?' Miriam's dangerously absurd question had the surprising effect of bringing a smile to the Overseer's normally miserable countenance.

'I think not. Jews don't celebrate Christmas... or so I'm told.'

Knowing she had been fortunate thus far in not incurring the Overseer's anger, Miriam sensibly shut up.

Looking up, his face took on a haughty expression. Peering at each woman in turn, he gave Miriam an especially hard stare,

'So if there are no other questions,' a look of self-assuredness crossed his face, 'carry on working until I tell you to stop.'

Later that evening and alone in the shadow of Block 22, Hannah recalled the numerous Christmas concerts performed by the Berlin Philharmonic in various European cities at this special time of year. Being orthodox Jews her parents did not observe Christmas; instead they celebrated Hanukkah and she wistfully remembered them giving her a small present on each of the eight nights of the Festival. After their death she and Ephraim had on several occasions spent part of the Christmas period with Gentile friends, enjoying the experience but always with a slight touch of guilt. 'Oh happy days' she recalled.

Standing alone in the crisp winter evening but with her thoughts far away, her keen hearing detected the distant strains of a tune she recognised as 'Silent Night' which she guessed could only be from the carol service spoken of earlier by the Overseer. As the sound of voices carried on the still night air she wondered how people committing mass murder on a daily basis without qualm or conscience, the greater majority of whom were Jews, could now be celebrating the birth of Jesus Christ, himself a Jew.

Lost in personal melancholy, she gazed beyond the brightly lit electric fence and thought of the world beyond its boundary; a world largely oblivious to what was happening in camps like Auschwitz and elsewhere. Saddened by her memories and beginning to feel the chill wind bite into her body, she decided it was time to return to the accommodation block. Taking a final, longing look at the world beyond the wire she became conscious of a slight movement further along the yard. Shading her eyes from the harsh security lights, she was able to make out the slight figure of a small child walking slowly towards the electric fence. As the child entered the illuminated area in front of the wire, she saw it was a young boy... probably no older than six or seven.

Alarmed, she recalled Miriam telling her that many prisoners, desperate to escape the daily horror of what passed as life within Auschwitz, would throw themselves on to the high voltage electric fence as an instant means of death in open defiance of their hated captors. Fearful for the child's safety but anxious not to scare him, she tried to adopt as casual approach as her nervousness would allow. Approaching him, she saw the boy pull something from his head and then move his tiny hand through the spacing of the electric fence. Now within touching distance, she knelt down to his level and placed a gentle hand on his shoulder. 'You shouldn't be here... this fence is very dangerous for children.'

Glancing up, his face illuminated in the harsh glare of the security lights, Hannah saw his grimy face and wind-bitten cheeks. Taking his cold hand, she led him gently away from the danger area and headed towards her own accommodation block. Tugging his hand away, he pointed towards Block 23... the brothel and Hannah realised his Polish mother was probably working there. As he walked away, she heard him say 'wolnosc... moje wlosy sa wolne.' Watching as he disappeared in the gloom, she memorised the young child's words. Later, when repeating them to Miriam, she saw her friend frown. 'Freedom?' I don't understand. The child said 'freedom... my hair is free.'

***

The world had entered a New Year but for those within Auschwitz, it passed unheralded. For the slave labour gangs forced to work in the burgeoning factories outside of the camp there was no respite from the daily back-breaking toil. By way of contrast however, workers in 'Kanada' were allowed one half-day off each week to coincide with the Overseer's rest day. It was Miriam who realised that this highly unusual concession was probably due to the Camp Commandant's reluctance to trust other SS personnel from gaining access to the booty within the Sorting Area in the absence of his trusted NCO.

The rest period gave Hannah an opportunity to prepare her clothes for the week ahead and sometimes read a book which like everything else in her personal effects had been 'acquired' from the Sorting Area. Much of the reading material had strong religious overtones and was of little interest to her. But as Miriam pointed out, people on a journey to death did not usually bring trashy novels for comfort!

As month succeeded month, Hannah learned more and more to appreciate Miriam's philosophical approach to life as a prisoner in Auschwitz. Despite the suffering and organised killing taking place within the camp, Miriam always seemed able to remain unaffected by the sheer enormity of it.

Sitting in the area between Block 22 and the security fence surrounding the Auschwitz complex, both she and Miriam were appreciating the warmth of the early spring sun on their pallid skins. Looking beyond the fence, she watched a flock of small birds and quietly envied them their freedom. Conversation between the two of them had dried up and glancing at her friend, she realised that Miriam had quietly fallen asleep; the one sure way to escape from the heinous crimes happening just a short distance away.

To exercise her brain, Hannah attempted to remember a musical score she used to play as a warm-up exercise before rehearsal but failed to get her mind to concentrate. 'There's no point' she thought, 'I'll never play a violin again.'

Giving up, she felt the wearying tiredness accumulated throughout the past week begin to take over and within seconds she felt herself drifting off in an intermittent slumber despite the intrusive noise of shunting engines coming from the Birkenau rail head. Quietly at first, the sound of peoples voices began to encroach and beside her, she felt Miriam begin to stir and gently touch her shoulder.

'Hannah, wake up. It's time we weren't here. We have to clean our room before roll call so we need to go.' Standing up, Miriam stretched her arms above her head and pretended to engage in a form of physical exercise.

'We have plenty of time for that so let's enjoy the sun for as long as we can.'

Her words clearly amused Miriam. 'Just where do you think you are, Hannah Bergmann? In some kind of holiday camp? This isn't a tourist hideaway my innocent little friend. It's a death camp for God's sake.' She laughed at herself. 'Ok, you stay here but I need to visit the toilet block so I will see you upstairs when you've had enough of doing nothing. And watch out; this Polish sun shrivels your skin and turns lazy Jews like you into goblins!'

Laughing at the absurdity of Miriam's remark, she heard herself say 'I don't see too many goblins around here but maybe that wouldn't be such a bad thing compared to this.' She waved her hand expressively towards the numerous crematorium chimneys belching out dark grey smoke.

Watching her friend enter the accommodation block, she realised how fortunate she had been to have met Miriam. Apart from knowing she had been arrested in Hanover and had now been in Auschwitz for about ten months, she knew little else about her.

Earlier that day, Miriam had told her how every six weeks or so, SS guards would round up the prisoners working in the Gas Chambers and Crematoria and callously shoot them before replacing them with another batch of prisoners from among the new arrivals. Why this policy had not been applied to the women in the Central Sorting Area was puzzling. Philosophical as ever, Miriam thought it was because their experience and skills built up over many months continued to generate ever increasing amounts of cash and valuables, so much so that the Nazis did not wish to interrupt an important revenue stream. How Miriam could rationalise between death and economics was beyond her imagination but her friend's ability to do so only increased the respect she felt for her.

FORTY

The Rapist returned to Block 22 and this time he chose her. From a sleep already disturbed by the volume of noise coming from the main Camp, she was awakened by a weak torch beam being shone on her face. Raising her hand to shield her eyes from the light, she felt her wrist firmly gripped as her unseen assailant attempted to roughly pull her out of her bunk. His other arm encircled her back and effortlessly he lifted her down to the wooden floor. In total shock, she felt herself being picked up and carried towards the stairwell. The strong smell of stale alcohol on the breath of her attacker stifled any thought of calling out.

Sensing this, she heard the man mutter 'if you scream I'll kill you; understand?'

Too shocked to react, she knew there was no point in resisting as no one would respond to any cry for assistance.

Outside the building, she was able to see the face of her assailant and instantly recognised him as the Kapo who had selected the Polish women for work in the brothel.

Terrified by the man's obvious intention, she managed at last to find her voice. 'Where are you taking me?'

Without replying, the Kapo hurried across the open area between the two adjoining blocks. Entering the darkened building, he quickly made his way to a room on the ground floor. Closing the door with his foot, he dropped her on to the mattress of a steel framed camp bed.

'Strip off,' He gave an irritated gesture with his hand... 'if you want to get back to your own bed after I've finished with you.'

In her mind she recalled the distressing sound of the prisoner who had been raped just metres from her bunk and Miriam's advice not to interfere. Was this the same man? If it was then why had he brought her to his room and not raped her in her own bunk?

Mutely she undid the three buttons of her night dress and pulled it over her head and let it fall to the floor before moving back to the dishevelled bed.

Looking up, she watched as the Kapo removed his clothes and in a daze, she forced herself to move over to allow him room to lie beside her. The bed creaked as he lowered his weight on to the mattress and roughly pulled her naked body to him. Despite the chill night air, the Kapo was sweating profusely and the smell exuding from his body was revolting.

'Hold me, Jew girl.' He spoke in halting German which she knew wasn't his natural tongue. Moving on to her side she put her arm round the waist of the Kapo. Angrily, he took hold of it and pushed her hand down towards his groin.

'I said hold me... here.' The growing anger in his slurred speech was coldly terrifying.

Slowly she forced her hand down towards his groin. In her stomach she felt the first gagging heave of nausea caused by the fear of what was about to happen. The smell of body sweat and stale alcohol added to her mounting distress.

She felt the Kapo push his body upwards and her fingers closed around his enlarged penis. In desperation she began to move her hand up and down and heard him groan.

'What do you want me to do?'

By way of a reply the Kapo swung his leg over Hannah's thigh and forced her back onto the mattress, heaving his muscular body on top of her. The compressing effect of his weight on her stomach coupled with the overpowering smell of alcohol and stale tobacco from his breath plus the rancid body odour was too much. Gagging, she tried to push the Kapo off her.

'Stop! I'm going to be sick.' Her chest began to involuntarily heave and she knew there was nothing she could do to prevent herself from vomiting on to the bed of a man who would probably knock her senseless in frustration and rage.

She felt the Kapo push himself up, stare at her heaving chest and then roll off the mattress and pull her towards an enamel bucket produced from under the bed. He was still holding her head over the bucket when her next convulsion threw a mixture of vomit and saliva into the receptacle. Two more heaves followed and she realised she was now sweating profusely. Listlessly, she fell back onto the bed.

'I'm sorry... sorry... sorry.' Struggling to sit up she searched with her free hand for the nightdress she had thrown to the floor moments earlier. Finding it, she used it to wipe the beads of sweat from her face and upper chest. 'I need to splash some water on my face and rinse my mouth out otherwise I'm going to be sick again.'

Feeling utterly wretched, she thought for one awful moment he was about to return to the bed. Instead, he straightened up and she sensed his anger. 'Get out of here you filthy bitch. 'I'll come for you again, Jew girl and when I do you'd better improve on tonight... understand?'

'I understand.' Rising off the bed, Hannah quickly draped the damp nightgown over her shoulders, hoping it would cover her bare breasts.

'Take that bucket and clean it out before you go. Now get out!'

Hurriedly finding the washroom at the end of the corridor, she frantically sluiced the bucket and tiptoed back to the Kapo's room. Fearful that his frustration may have caused him to change his mind, she was relieved to find him lying on the bed, breathing heavily as sleep enveloped his drink-addled senses.

Returning to her own darkened quarters, Hannah was relieved to see that her abduction had not been noticed other than for Miriam's soft voice floating up from the bunk below. 'Tell me about it tomorrow... OK?'

'The Kapos are usually recruited from German prisons but the animal who came for you last night is a Romanian.' Miriam's knowledge of her assailant only served to make Hannah feel even more uneasy. The threat of his intending return would now make every night a terrifying prospect.

Relaying the events of the previous night to Miriam had not provided either the comfort or sympathy she was hoping for. 'You've probably aroused him even more so just get it over with. He'll soon tire of you and then go on to another woman.'

'Miriam, you don't understand. I was prepared to do that just to get out of that filthy room but my body reacted. I couldn't help what happened. He was revolting and stank like a sewer. Even without the smell and the alcohol, he would have made any woman sick.'

An undisguised look of exasperation flitted across Miriam's face 'Hannah, tell me... how many men have you had in your life; five, ten, twenty maybe... how many?'

'I'm not answering that because it's totally irrelevant. I wouldn't dream of asking you the same question.'

'You would be very surprised if I told you.' Turning to face Hannah in the quietness of the empty room, Miriam took her friend's hands in her own.

'Look, you can't compare the situation here with anything you may have experienced before your arrest. In here we have no rights and nobody cares whether we live or die. Stuck in this hell-hole, we have a choice. It isn't much of a choice but none the less it's a choice. We can do whatever we can to survive each day or we give up and die. That's the choice we have to make.'

'You sound like my husband; those were almost his parting words to me.'

'Then heed what he told you for God's sake.' Miriam's animated words seemed to strike a chord. 'If you have something to live for then fight for every second of the day and do whatever it takes to achieve it.

If Germany loses this war then all this Hitler-shit and horror will be swept away and I badly want to be around to see that day. If that means being raped by that foul-smelling excuse for a human being, then so be it. I would do it. I may not enjoy it but I would do it.' Releasing Hannah's hands, Miriam sat upright. 'The last comment about enjoying it was a joke but at least I wouldn't throw up on him even though he's a stinking Romanian!'

Hannah's face reddened in embarrassed amusement. 'Miriam, you're priceless.'

'Priceless? I don't think so but thank you anyway.' Her voice softened. 'Just try to be at peace with yourself Hannah and you will find life here may become a little easier. And whatever you may be forced to do, don't have a conscience about it, OK? If there is a God then he will understand.'

'I often doubt that Miriam.'

'Doubt what?'

'Whether there is a God.' In a gesture of futility she waved her hands in front of her. 'If there is, how can he allow this to happen?'

'But who else do we have to believe in? Maybe the Rabbi in the synagogue perhaps or even Winston Churchill as a long shot?' Hannah saw her friend's eyebrows lift. 'You tell me someone better than God because I have just exhausted all my candidates.'

'It's a comfort being able to talk to you Miriam. I guess my life has been totally sheltered before all this happened. I still can't comprehend the scale of what's happening and how so many lives have been affected.' Looking around the empty room to assure herself that their conversation wasn't being overheard, she drew closer to her friend. 'I've never been entirely sure about God nor have I ever possessed that same degree of faith that my parents had. And worse than that. I'm even unsure about my own sexuality. I'm not quite as innocent as you seem to think I am.'

Sensing her friend's wish to unburden herself, Miriam guided her towards their own small section of the room and sat her down on the lower bunk 'You want to tell me about it or should I try and guess?'

'You couldn't possibly guess what troubles this strait-laced woman with a beautiful child and loving parents has encountered. For a start, I'm supposed to be a pillar of sobriety but I now regret not having slept with other men. At least I would be better prepared for this.'

'Hannah, if you were the biggest whore on the face of this earth you would still be utterly unprepared for what is happening in this awful place. If anything will help you to survive, it's your very innocence, believe me.'

'My innocence?' She repeated herself. 'Is it that noticeable?'

'It is, and you should thank your God for that... unless of course you don't believe in God in which case you should thank Winston Churchill!'

FORTY ONE

The Romanian came for her again two nights later. Completely sober, he came an hour after the lights in Block 22 had been doused and most of its inmates asleep. Fully awake, she sensed his presence before feeling his hand on her shoulder. Without waiting to be pulled from her bunk, she eased herself over the side and slipped down onto the wooden floor. Without a sound, she followed his large frame down the stairs and out of the building. Crossing the illuminated yard she entered the Kapo's block and passively retraced her steps.to his room.

Closing the door behind her, he began to remove his clothes and nodded for her to do the same. Pulling her nightdress over her head, she heard the Kapo expel his breath in anticipation. Reaching out he pulled her naked body towards him; not roughly but with a firmness which surprised her, conveying as it did, the futility of resisting..

Reaching down, she let her fingers locate and take hold of his stiffening penis. The revulsion experienced on the first occasion was still there but subdued by a growing awareness of what was about to happen. In her mind she heard Miriam's injunction... 'Get it over with' and slowly moved her hand up and down. Feeling his mounting excitement, she began to increase the momentum and felt his penis grow even harder in her grip. In her loins she felt the first stirrings of expectation which she guiltily tried to suppress.

Expecting the Kapo to take her to the same revolting bed from which she had escaped from just forty eight hours earlier, she was frightened when he effortlessly lifted her up and moved towards an armless chair in the centre of the room. Her previous experience of love-making with Ephraim had been wholly confined to their marriage bed but here in the unyielding grip of a man determined not to be thwarted again, she guessed what the Kapo wanted her to do. Sitting down with Hannah facing him, the Kapo eased her legs apart forcing her into a position where she was astride him. Closing her eyes she sensed his hands reaching out before his fingers actually touched her breasts, fondling them with surprising gentleness. No amount of self-control seemed able to prevent the growing excitement now beginning to course through her loins. It seemed so very long ago since she and Ephraim had last made love and now her body, if not her mind, was about to experience sex with this brute of a man

'Tell me when you want to do it.'

Mirthlessly, she saw the Kapo frown; 'you'll know when I'm ready so listen to me, Jew girl. If you don't perform tonight then I'll make damn sure you end up in the gas chamber in the morning.' With that, the Kapo cruelly squeezed both nipples hard causing Hannah to scream out in sudden pain. Letting go, he put his hands around her waist and smoothly lifted her slight frame up and towards him. Effortlessly lowering her down she felt the tip of his erect penis push against her moist vagina. Teasing her, the Kapo easily held her in this suspended position.

'Open your eyes and look at me, you Yiddish bitch.'

Unable to bring herself to look at him, she kept her eyes closely shut. Enraged, the Kapo reacted by viciously thrusting upwards whilst roughly pulling Hannah down onto him. The sudden and brutal penetration was excruciating and her scream echoed beyond the small room.

With both eyes still firmly closed and her body reacting to the intense pain, Hannah did not hear the door being flung open nor was she immediately aware of the light from the corridor suddenly flooding into the room. Feeling the Kapo's vice-like grip on her waist lessen she threw herself off him. Losing her balance, she fell onto the floor and in desperation began to crawl towards the door. Looking back at the Kapo, she didn't immediately see the two soldiers who had entered the room. She did see the Rumanian leap from the chair and make a despairing grab for his trousers before being roughly pushed back by the shorter of the two soldiers whom she recognised as the NCO who had deferred to this same Kapo when he had selected the Polish women for the brothel. To the right of the NCO stood an Officer calmly appraising the situation without appearing to dwell on her naked figure.

It was the NCO who spoke. 'So, what have we here?' Without waiting for a reply, he jabbed his pace stick into the Kapo's midriff. 'It seems you might have overstepped yourself this time.'

'I can explain Corporal.'

'Keep your stinking mouth shut and only speak when I tell you.' Using his stick, he pushed Hannah's dishevelled nightdress towards her. 'Did this man force you to come here tonight?'

'I had no choice. He threatened to beat me unless I did what he wanted.'

'What is your name?' It was the Officer who put the question.

'Bergmann. Hannah Bergmann.' Averting her eyes downward she reached down and recovered her nightdress and hastily pulled it over her shoulders, shivering as she did so.

'And you are a German?' This time it was the NCO putting the question

Nodding assent, she began to move furtively towards the door, hoping to be ordered to leave. Instead, she saw the officer appraising her more closely whilst the NCO turned his attention to the Kapo.

'So a Romanian prisoner raping a German woman. Even a scum-bag like you must know what the penalty for that is.'

Hannah saw a look of utter bewilderment appear on the face of the Kapo.

'But she's a Jew for fuck's sake. She's not a German so what are you talking about?'

'And you're a prisoner. That's what I'm talking about. And if you open that big mouth of yours once more, I'll have you taken to the punishment block'

'You don't frighten me, you two-faced greedy bastard! Haven't I given you enough gold teeth from these fucking people to keep you off my back?

Angrily the NCO struck out with his heavy pace stick, slashing the Kapo across his face. Stunned by the suddenness of the attack, it was several seconds before the man reacted. Grabbing the end of the stick with one hand, the Kapo pulled his tormentor towards him and with his bunched fist, struck the NCO senseless with two ponderous blows to his head. As the soldier slumped to the floor the Rumanian leapt to his feet. Wielding the stick like a sword, the Kapo targeted its pointed end into the eye socket of the immobilised soldier, forcing it into his skull to penetrate the brain. With his last dying effort, the hand of the NCO appeared to wave an incongruous farewell before falling back onto the floor.

Unable to pull her eyes away from the macabre scene unfolding before her, she barely witnessed the blurred action of the Officer drawing his sidearm pistol and firing twice into the chest of the advancing Kapo. In the confined room space, the double discharge was deafening with the pungent cordite fumes adding a surreal touch as they rose towards the high ceiling. In slow-motion she saw the unsteady figure of the Kapo vainly trying to stem the flow of blood pumping through his open fingers as he lurched towards the officer with his other hand raised as though to ward off further injury.

Calmly, the Major fired again, the 9mm bullet hitting the stricken man in the middle of his forehead. Crumpling at the knees, the Kapo collapsed and was dead before he hit the floor.

Re-holstering his Luger pistol, the Major lightly touched her on the shoulder: 'Get back to your quarters as quickly as you can before the camp guards arrive.'

Mortified by the shocking violence, Hannah pointed helplessly at the two bodies. 'But what about these two men?'

'They will be attended to but it looks as though they are both beyond help.' Turning away, she gripped the nightdress and pulled it closer to her body. Looking round, she saw him stop in the doorway.

'By the way' he said calmly. 'I'm Major Kurt Steiner and after morning roll-call tomorrow, you will receive a Transfer Order to report to my administration quarters. The Order will get you out through the Main Gate so make sure you don't lose it nor the directions attached to it. You will make your own way there so bring what personal belongings you may have; but not that nightdress.'

Turning on his heel, the Major took two paces towards the door before looking back at a bemused Hannah. 'You will never speak of this to me or anyone else. Is that clear?'

Stunned and unable to speak, she could only nod in agreement.

FORTY TWO

The road from the Camp was deeply rutted, damaged by the endless stream of heavy military vehicles lumbering along its tarmacadam surface. For much of the way she found herself having to walk on the very edge of the busy road to avoid deep puddles on the unmade pathway. Several times she was forced to stand aside as groups of prisoners were marched by under armed escort presumably to work in the nearby factories, the silhouettes of which she could see in the far distance.

Being on the outside of the camp and alone for the first time since her arrest felt odd; more so because not once was she challenged or questioned by the numerous military personnel and SS camp guards who simply ignored her as they passed by on the road.. She reasoned it was probably because she wasn't wearing prison clothing nor did she have a shaven head but despite the air of deceptive freedom, she knew that to try and escape was all but impossible. Too far from Berlin and even if by some miracle she did manage to avoid her German captors then there were growing numbers of Polish partisans roaming the countryside who according to Miriam were even more anti-Semitic than the Germans.

Following the indistinct directions written in pencil on the back of what looked like an Army Requisition Form, she managed to find the turn-off to the unmarked lane which she hoped would lead to what was shown simply as an 'X' on the vague directions. At the point of thinking she had taken a wrong turn she finally spotted the isolated administration building situated in a grove of silver birch trees, their lime green leaves about to herald in a Spring which had barely arrived.

The house was built in typical Polish style. Outwardly functional in appearance but visibly lacking the architectural neatness and symmetry she normally associated with rural

German properties. At first sight the entrance looked imposing with its interlocking brick archway below which hung a heavy oaken door weathered by years of harsh Polish winters. The windows at the front of the building were each flanked by a pair of green slatted shutters which from their lop-sided appearance had not been moved in years. The concrete rendering below the limestone brickwork was heavily streaked with green algae giving the three storied building an unkempt, non-military appearance.

Her approach was watched by a dumpy looking woman standing at the front of the entranceway, staring but with no discernible sign of warmth. As she got closer, the woman dropped the yard broom she had been using to sweep the forecourt and took a halting step towards her.

'Who are you,' she quizzed as Hannah drew nearer. 'Are you from down there' nodding in the direction of the camp? 'What are you doing here?'

Determined not to let her inquisitor get the upper hand, Hannah responded in similar vein. 'Which of those questions would you like me to answer first? And by the way, my name is Hannah Bergmann. And yes, I have come from the camp. So having answered your questions, can I ask your name?'

'That's my business. Who told you to come here?'

Listening to the woman's dialect, she thought she recognised the inflections of the Czech language.

'You're Czech aren't you... whatever your name might be?'

The woman straightened up and moved aggressively towards her, close enough for Hannah to feel her cold breath on her face. Stepping back, she saw that the women was clad in extra clothing as protection from the bitterly cold wind and the reason for her apparent shapelessness, unlike her own threadbare garment appropriated from the camp clothing store. Looking more closely, Hannah was able to see that she was much younger than she first appeared despite the grey balaclava hat which enveloped her head and ears except for a fringe of fair hair protruding from beneath its woollen peak.

Without warning, the woman reached out and grasped Hannah by her shoulders. 'Corporal... Corporal Erlich, come quickly; I think there's an escaped prisoner from the camp here!'

Despite the stridency of her call, it clearly did not carry the immediacy the nameless woman was hoping for. Several long seconds passed until from the corner of her eye, Hannah saw a mature and somewhat portly soldier emerge through the doorway and from the expression on his face, a man clearly not relishing the thought of leaving the warmth of the house.

'Danuta, why in God's name do you think that every person who comes to this house is an escapee? Use your head for once. If she was on the run she'd be heading in the opposite direction.' Now his exasperation came to the fore. 'Let her go, woman, and just get on with your work otherwise it will be you going back to the camp... and staying there! That would give us all a rest.'

Expressively rolling his eyes skywards he looked at Hannah, 'I suppose you must be the woman Major Steiner told me about last night. A musician if I remember correctly?'

'I am a musician and my name is Hannah Bergmann. I was told to report here this morning by an officer whose name I can't now remember.'

'Well I'm Corporal Erlich and I run this house for Major Steiner. He's the officer you met last night. Get yourself in the house out of this cold and I'll show you where you'll be staying.'

From his accent she guessed that the corporal might originate from Southern Germany, an impression comically heightened by his sad looking face, trimmed moustache and portly midriff reflecting the popular image of Bavarian manhood. He also appeared older than the average conscript. Turning towards the house, the Corporal nodded for her to follow him. 'You're

German aren't you, unlike that one, pointing to Danuta. 'Where do you come from?'

'Berlin... I am a Berliner.' Stepping into the house, Hannah felt the building's comforting warmth immediately envelope her shivering body. Pausing by a floor mounted heater, she let its heat waft up around her legs and hands, both of which had been exposed to the bitingly cold wind during the long walk from the camp.

'This way young lady. I'm putting you on the top floor away from that Czech woman. She's the cook by the way and she sleeps in the basement. She's been here for several months now and if I had my way I'd send her back to the Camp. She came here with her sister who went down with some fever or other so I reckon you must be here to replace her'.

'What did Danuta's sister do here'?

'She helped with the Major's personal paperwork and kept him looking smart by pressing his uniforms and washing his clothes'.

'I thought they did that in the Camp'.

'They do but Major Steiner is very particular as you will find out'.

'How long have you worked for the Major'?

Hearing this, Erlich turned and faced her.. 'Let me tell you something Bergmann for your own good; call it a house rule if you wish but I'm not supposed to talk with you like this as you are no doubt aware. In the Camp I hear you're not even supposed to look the guards in the eye but fortunately for you I'm a soldier... unlike those specimens you came across in the Camp.'

Chastened by the Corporal's admonition and on the point of apologising, she saw him wrinkle his nose and sniff loudly. 'You smell young lady. When did you last have a bath or shower?'

'About four days ago. I'm sorry but the stench from the chimneys sticks to every piece of clothing as well as your hair. I must be used to it because I'm afraid I can't smell it.'

'Well Major Steiner will so I suggest you get yourself up to the bath room and I'll have Danuta bring you a change of clothes.'

'Corporal Erlich, can I say just one more thing before your house rules apply?'

'You may, but a word of warning young lady. Be very careful when the Major's staff officers are around. Some of them won't accept you people as human beings let alone the same as them.'

Tears began to well up in Hannah's eyes. 'All I wanted to say, Corporal, was thank you; you have a good heart.'

Clearly embarrassed, the portly NCO turned sharply away. 'That may be so, young lady, but don't try taking advantage of it. Get yourself moving and report to me when you're more presentable. I'll be in the downstairs office so off you go and wash that awful smell away.' And with those words, Erlich was gone.

Refreshed by the hot bath and feeling brighter in the clean clothes provided by a surly Danuta, Hannah looked around the smallish room assigned by the Corporal on the top floor of the building. The small window overlooking the rear of the building let in sufficient light and Hannah was pleased to note the absence of bars on the outside. The curtains had seen better days but at least they looked clean and capable of being drawn together at night. The mattress on the single bed was firm and overlaid top and bottom with white sheets and grey army blankets. Standing in the centre of the room she was aware of a pleasant masculine smell but unable to identify its source.. The walls and door were a pale shade of blue with the architrave around the door painted in what had once been a glossy white finish but now dulled with age and yellowing at floor level where it butted against the pine floor boards. Opening the wardrobe door, Hannah saw several field grey uniforms presumably for daily use and a black dress uniform with its collar and epaulettes edged in silver. Stepping back quickly, she hurriedly closed the wardrobe door.

'They're German uniforms in case you didn't recognise them.'

It was Danuta standing in the door well.

'Danuta... I didn't hear you come upstairs.'

That's because you think you've escaped from the Camp. But make the most of it because you won't be here for long.' Entering the room, Danuta stood in front of the window and looked into Hannah's eyes. 'So how long do you think you'll last here?'

'I have no idea but how have you managed to last as long as you have?'

A look of anger crossed Danuta's face. 'Look at me; do I look like you and those other Jews in the Camp? The only thing we have in common is that we are both prisoners of the Germans but thank God I don't share your loathsome religion. If I did, I would willingly walk into the gas chamber on my own. I hate Jews for what they have brought this world to.'

Stunned by the sheer vehemence of Danuta's outburst, Hannah felt an irresistible urge to launch herself at the Czech before rationality returned to hold her back.

'In the name of your God, what have we ever done to you? It's not us Jews who have brought the world to this hell but the Nazis and their demonic leaders. How can you exonerate people who daily kill innocent children in their thousands?' Catching her breath, she turned away from the Czech. 'You don't know what you're talking about, you sad woman?'

Hearing a slight commotion behind her she saw Danuta's eyes fill with alarm.

'I was rather hoping you two would manage to get on better than this. I see I'm badly mistaken.'

Hannah turned, her anger subsiding as she stared at the tall figure of the man she now knew to be Major Steiner.

'So having made such an error, I guess it falls to me to correct it? Glancing at Hannah, he appeared to deliberate before continuing. 'Should I decide by assessing who prepares the best meals in which case it will be you who will return to the Camp, my little Jew girl or should I decide that I have had enough of your unending dullness and send you, Danuta, to the gas chamber you so obviously wish for? Tell me ladies, who is it to be?'

Steiner lowered himself gently onto the bed and looked impassively at Danuta and Hannah, neither one detecting the touch of humour in his question.

It was Danuta who broke the silence. 'Please Major; I was simply repeating what your Fuehrer has said about Jews. I have been happy working for you until this woman appeared. She has been here for barely an hour or so and already she has brought much trouble with her. Please have her returned to the camp before she can create even more mischief here.'

A look of exasperation crossed the Major's face and it was several moments before he spoke. 'Corporal Erlich tells me you're a Jehovah's Witness. Isn't that a Christian religion?' His voice framed the question softly. 'So what do you have against people like this woman who believe in the same God as you?'

Fearfully, Danuta attempted to reply but no sound emerged. In despair, her shoulders drooped and her body slowly slid to the floor. Deep sobs began to rack her frame and impulsively, Hannah found herself kneeling to comfort the wretched woman.

Rebuffed instantly by Danuta, she heard herself say 'Look my coming here has obviously brought back memories of this woman's sister which I can understand.' A wistful look showed in her eyes; 'at least I've had a warm bath and clean clothes.' She gave a wry smile. 'For that at least, I'm very grateful.'

Now clearly irritated, the Major stood up. 'Am I supposed to take your selfless gesture seriously or are you simply being cleverly astute'

Puzzled by his words, it took her a few moments to collect her thoughts. 'I don't understand why you think that, Major. I have many faults but being 'cleverly astute' would not be one of them.' Daring to go on, she added 'can I ask why you think that.'

'Because it's not for you to say who goes or stays; that will be my decision. By volunteering to go back, are you hoping I'll be touched by your selfless gesture and send this woman in your stead? That's why I referred to you as being astute or would you prefer words which you can understand?'

Having delivered his caustic rebuke, Steiner eased himself up to his full height and towered over both women. Danuta, with downcast eyes was still sobbing but catching a look at her face, Hannah could see no evidence of tears.

'Danuta, you will serve dinner at the usual time and you Bergmann, you will remain in this house until I say otherwise. And while you remain here you will be responsible for taking care of my daily admin duties together with keeping me looking presentable.' He smiled as he saw Hannah frown. 'And perhaps there will be times when I require you to entertain my occasional guests with the same level of virtuosity you apparently displayed in Berlin where I understand you met my cousin, Hauptmann Von Hartmannn.'

'Your cousin?' Her voice registered total surprise. 'You mean Colonel Von Hartmannn... he is your cousin?'

'Was my cousin.' The Major corrected her. 'He was apparently killed in a plane crash heading to the Russian front.'

'Oh dear God, no!' An involuntary gasp escaped her lips. 'I am truly sorry to hear that. He was very kind to me when we met in Berlin.'

Well he certainly remembered you. Being Jewish, he knew you would almost certainly end up in this stinking place. So you could say your arrival here today was to a certain extent pre-ordained.' Steiner smiled at his pained remark. 'So, having had the opportunity to be washed and laundered and no longer smelling like a dead cow, you now also know the reason why you're here and no longer in the Camp. Like Danuta's sister you will act as a general factotum where you will work to the orders of Corporal Erlich and who knows,' he gave a slight shrug of his shoulders and smiled. 'You might even give me the benefit of hearing the occasional musical interlude.' His smile broadened further, softening the stern features of his handsome face. 'But not tonight' he said. 'I am tired and tomorrow I have many meetings. So, I want no more trouble between you two... is that clear?'

Without waiting for a response, Steiner strode from the room, slamming the door behind him.

Danuta, a look of plain relief on her face struggled to her feet. 'Don't expect me to be grateful to a bitch like you. The Major will soon tire of you and your fancy music and that will be the end as far as you're concerned. Better you had gone back to the Camp tonight than wait for that to happen. But while you are here you will keep out of my way because I intend to remain in this house long after you and all those other Jews are just ashes in the wind.'

The impact of Danuta's hate-filled words struck Hannah with the force of a blow and this time she could not hold back. As Danuta turned to leave she reacted. Grabbing hold of the Czech's hair, she pulled her head back with a savage jerk. Unprepared, Danuta fell heavily to the floor, her head striking the edge of the metal bed frame. Straddling her prone body, Hannah looked down at the woman's shocked expression before striking hard to the unprotected side of Danuta's head, so hard that her hand stung from the force of the blow.

'Listen to me, you obscene woman! If I ever hear you say anything like that to me again, I will kill you and to hell with the consequences.' She rose to her feet. 'Now get out and don't ever come into this room again unless I say you can.'

Standing up, she watched as the dazed Danuta rose unsteadily to her feet, hurriedly catching hold of the washbasin to stop herself falling back. With her anger still close to the surface, she fought to overcome the urge to strike the Czech again while she was still unsteady but the sight of Danuta's bloodied head and rapidly closing eye stayed her hand. Instead she forced herself to calmly watch as Danuta staggered from the room.

Alone, she fell on to her bed and felt her whole body shaking with anger and sheer fatigue. Inwardly she felt ashamed; ashamed of having resorted with such violence and coarse language... the language of the gutter as her dear Father would have said, to deal with Danuta's shocking words. 'Why didn't I just tell her to get out of this room? Dear God, am I becoming like everyone else in this hellish world?' A question to which she had no answer.

***

The following morning she rose early and after dressing made her way to the ground floor with some trepidation. Danuta was already preparing breakfast and once on the ground floor Hannah detected the familiar aroma of real coffee pervading the kitchen and beyond. Danuta looked up and Hannah saw that the area around her right eye was discoloured and dark. Her lower lip was also swollen. Wordlessly, Danuta picked up a large knife with a serrated edge and moved towards her. Brushing past, she busied herself cutting slices of bread from a freshly baked loaf.

'Am I expected to help you with the food preparation and do we eat here or somewhere else?'

Danuta continued cutting bread, choosing to ignore Hannah's question.

'Look, Danuta, I'm sorry about your sister. I never asked to take her place so can we at least be civil to each other. For my part, I am sorry, truly sorry, for what happened last evening.'

This time Danuta did stop cutting and turned round to face Hannah. 'So you're sorry are you? Look at my face, you Jewish bitch. You did this to me and now you're sorry.' A look of revulsion crossed her battered face. 'Well let me tell you something Jew girl... you'll be even sorrier before I finish with you.

Without warning, she suddenly raised the knife in her hand and impaled it into the pine table where it quivered like an arrow.

'You eat with the Corporal in there and don't come into this kitchen unless you are told to. And be careful what you eat, Jew girl. Remember... I prepare it.'

Stopping herself from reacting to Danuta's outburst, she coolly reached out and grasped the bone handle of the knife. Wrenching it from the wooden surface she calmly held it at stomach level. 'Come and get your knife Danuta.'

The coldness in Hannah's words made Danuta start. 'So what is it now? I meet you for the first time yesterday and you do this to my face. So what are you going to do for an encore this morning; stab me to death in my own kitchen?'

Moving quickly to ensure the broad table was safely between them, Danuta spoke again. 'Tell me Bergmann; are you on some divine mission to kill me?'

'Very good Danuta. At least you remember my name.' Casually tossing the knife back on the table, she looked the Czech squarely in the eye. 'Here, take your knife and don't dare threaten me again because if you do, your words may well become self-fulfilling. She took a deep breath and when she spoke there was a hint of conciliation in her voice. 'Look, I have already said I'm sorry for what I did to your face and what I said last night. But understand this; just like you and your sister, I never asked to come here either.'

Danuta stared silently for what seemed an age. All of a sudden, her shoulders drooped and her battered face seemed to soften. 'Go and eat your breakfast and don't worry about what's in it... at least for today!'

FORTY THREE

The rest of that morning passed in a haze. Corporal Erlich gave a brief run-down of her household duties which though mundane weren't too onerous. The dexterity of fingers skilled in playing the violin came in good stead when faced with familiarising herself with the keyboard of the Olivetti typewriter. Quickly acquiring a passable level of proficiency, she was soon able to relieve the Corporal from the task of preparing the reams of official reports and requisition forms which the military machine seemed to require in triplicate for every conceivable item.

In addition to acting as a secretarial 'gopher' she was required to ensure that the Major's uniforms were reasonably presentable and ready to wear each day. Having regularly pressed her Father's trousers as a teenager and Ephraim's too after their marriage this aspect of domesticity did not pose any difficulty. With Hannah now assuming responsibility for the daily office routine, this left Corporal Erlich with more time on his hands to take care of the Major's military kit including several pairs of jack-boots which she was grateful for as she had no idea how he achieved such a high gloss on the weathered leather.

Major Steiner had apparently left the house before dawn and she had no idea when he would next reappear. And Corporal Erlich didn't seem to know either. 'He will get here when he gets here' was his blinding insight as to the Major's pattern of coming and going.

During the course of that first morning she found herself constantly thinking about Danuta. Was it an olive branch she had offered earlier or merely words to get her out of the kitchen? Whatever her reason, the breakfast had been delicious and her stomach was now reacting to the richness of the food compared to the awful slop that her body had become accustomed to in the camp. 'Weren't the Czechs renowned for their intellect and guile' she wondered? 'Wasn't that why they were such excellent chess players or am I confusing them with the Russians' she wondered? 'Time will tell' she reasoned but in the meantime she decided she would remain outwardly friendly to the Czech woman and see how it worked out.

Later that day and still familiarising herself with the layout of the house, she heard the gruff voice of Corporal Erlich summoning her to his small office. Tapping on the door before entering, her disbelieving eyes were straightaway drawn to the familiar object in front of her. There on his desk lay her open violin case with the portly corporal gingerly holding her beloved Bellini in his overlarge hands.

'Ah, there you are young lady, I understand this belongs to you. The Major ordered this to be returned and here it is.' His admiring gaze was that of a man who understood craftsmanship. 'It's a beautiful piece of wood and well put together.'

Hearing Erlich's admiration for her instrument and overjoyed at what she was seeing, Hannah was temporarily lost for words..

'You know, I've never held a violin before; beautifully crafted and very old I would imagine.'

With his earlier reproach regarding house rules foremost in her mind, it was several moments before she found her voice. 'You have an eye for good craftsmanship, Corporal.' She knew it was stating the obvious but Erlich seemed pleased with the compliment.

'Yes I do, young lady. Before I became a soldier I was a wood turner so I know good craftsmanship when I see it.' Continuing to fondle the violin in his rough workman-like hands, Erlich turned it several times to examine the instrument from different angles.

Warming to his unexpected appreciation, her pride of ownership came to the fore. 'It was made in Italy sometime around 1760 and if you look inside it you can see the name of its maker.'

'Well that may be so' he said gruffly holding out the violin for her to take. 'Look after it and make sure you keep that piece of old wood in a dry place.' Returning to his paperwork an amusing smile crossed his ruddy features.

It was a moment to savour. Quickly finishing what remained of her infinitely boring household duties, she managed to restrain herself from actually running to her room but once there, she impatiently tuned her treasured instrument and let her fingers gently familiarise themselves with its polished contours.

Since purchasing the Bellini from a collector in Vienna some seven years before her arrest, she wondered how many times had she visualised the making of this beautiful instrument. How Angelo Bellini would have chosen with exquisite care, maple wood with a beautiful grain which he had allowed to dry naturally for many years in some corner of his dusty Venetian workshop. Peering inside the violin, she looked at the sound post which Italians referred to as the 'anima'... the heart of the instrument. Placing the violin to her shoulder, she again felt the familiar feel of the polished maple as she nestled it between her slender neck and shoulder. Before letting the bow touch the violin's strings, she tried to calculate how long it had been since she had last played with the orchestra. She thought back to that awful morning at the Kroll Opera House on Konigsplatz where she had first learned of the arrest of Max Feldman and the other Jewish musicians and the frightening belief that her name too had been on that same list.

Caressing the violin with her left hand, she realised just how much she had missed her music, even the surfeit of Wagner and other German composers forced on the orchestra by its servient Trustee Board.

It took several intensely pleasurable minutes to fine tune the violin. She always associated her instrument with the warm sunshine of Italy but today, its wondrously mellow sound would resonate within the colder climes of Eastern Europe.

Forcing herself to concentrate, she quickly ran through a series of musical exercises and scales until she was satisfied that her hands and ear were as coordinated as she could expect after such a long period of inactivity. She briefly toyed with the idea of playing part of the concerto that had apparently captivated Von Hartmannn but chose instead to play a less difficult score by Vivaldi, penned while a choirmaster at a small church on the Venetian waterfront. The piece, full of zestful brio reflected as it did the very essence of the composer's love of his country. As her dexterity and fluidity increased, she felt her whole being taken up by the exuberance of the score and for the first time in recent memory she began to feel a growing sense of inner peace. From Vivaldi, she moved on to several shorter pieces by Mozart until finally, with fingers aching, she chose to finish with a slower piano movement by Chopin, scored for violin by the composer himself. Letting her tired arms relax, she gently placed her violin back in its case and reluctantly closed the lid. The sound of the catch clicking shut was sufficient to break the uplifting spell induced by the music. Looking at herself in the small mirror in the corner of the room she noticed her eyes, dulled in recent weeks, were once more beginning to reflect a suggestion of their former iridescent sparkle. Dashing cold water on her flushed features, she reflected yet again on the importance of music in her life and its rejuvenating ability to lift her inner spirit even in the midst of the unspeakable horror that was Auschwitz.

Surprisingly, the melodic sounds coming from Hannah's room had made an impression on Ernst Erlich. Living in a small rural community in Southern Bavaria he had never attended a classical concert in his life. But as a young apprentice wood turner he vaguely remembered his father tuning in the old accumulator-powered radio in their dusty workshop and now listening to the haunting sounds emanating from Bellini's beautifully crafted instrument, it brought back memories of his dear old father and his appreciation of similar music. So engrossed was he in listening to Hannah's accomplished artistry, he didn't hear Steiner enter the room behind him.

'I trust she presses my uniforms as well as she plays that violin, Corporal?'

The sudden appearance of the Major took Erlich by surprise and several moments elapsed before he spoke. 'I don't think you will have any complaints about Bergmann's duties, Major... trousers or otherwise. This is her stand-down time in preparation for any entertainment you may be planning. Incidentally, that is the reason why she's here, isn't it?' The innocent innuendo within Erlich's question wasn't lost on Steiner.

'Never lost for words are you, Corporal; not bad for a man from Bavaria.'

The informal and relaxed relationship between Steiner and Erlich was not one encouraged within the strict hierarchical ranks of the Wehrmacht. But their association stemmed from the time of Erlich being posted to Steiner's reconnaissance unit during Operation Barbarossa some two years earlier. It was at Stalingrad that the bond between the two men had been sealed. Retreating from the advancing Red Army and seeking refuge in a freezing, waterlogged cellar, Steiner had been badly wounded in the chest by fragments of a grenade fired into their bolthole by pursuing Russian infantrymen. Believing the Germans to be dead, the Russian soldiers had moved on and it was Erlich, resisting the temptation to escape, who had stayed to tend to Steiner's wounds with what remained of their field dressings. Drifting in and out of consciousness and with a raging thirst quenched only by melting snow dribbled into his mouth by Erlich, the two of them had remained in their freezing hideaway for five seemingly endless days and nights before being able to make their perilous way back to German lines.

Hospitalised in Germany, it took Steiner eight pain-filled weeks to recover from his wounds. Though barely fit, he was assigned to his present command in Upper Silesia, tasked with defending the increasingly important manufacturing units set up in the region to supplement the Eastern front war effort. The workers for these essential industries were drawn from the two nearby concentration camps of Auschwitz and Birkenau which also functioned as death factories for the thousands of new arrivals perfunctorily adjudged as being unfit for work.

'She plays well, Corporal; how long has she been up there?'

'Can't say I've really noticed, Major... not the type of music I'm used to.'

Steiner grinned like a small boy and slapped his thigh in mock sarcasm. 'Of course; how stupid of me! I forgot you Bavarians prefer brass bands, lederhosen trousers and steins of beer served by big busty women.'

Erlich appeared unamused. 'Is that really what you think happens in Bavaria, Major? If that is the case then I wouldn't mind some of that now instead of what's going on down the hill.'

Erlich's oblique reference to the concentration camp caused a look of consternation to flit across Steiner's face. 'I've told you before, Corporal. That's not a subject we discuss in this house. Don't let me remind you again... OK?'

'Sorry Major, I won't mention it again.' Turning to leave the room, Erlich was halted by Steiner's next words.

'Stay where you are, Ernst;' a softer tone came into Steiner's voice. 'This is your office and I'm on my way to my room so I'll leave you in peace.' Reaching the open door, Steiner stopped and looked back. 'Ernst, you're a good man and what is happening down there sickens me as much as it does you, so never think otherwise. But realistically there's nothing we can do about it other than carry on and do what soldiers are supposed to do... obey orders; whether we think them right or wrong. Correct Corporal?'

'Right Major; but if we soldiers lose this war then I hope those bastards down the hill get what they deserve.'

'I'd like to think so to, Ernst, but if the Red Army get here first then make no mistake; they will draw no distinction between them and us. To the Ruskies we are all Germans and all guilty.

***

It was Corporal Erlich, with a measure of paternal pride that relayed the news to Hannah and Danuta. 'Ladies, I have some news which will be of interest to you both.' He looked up to ensure he had their attention. 'Major Steiner has been promoted to Colonel and he'll be returning later today from Berlin.'

Neither woman was sure whether to comment so Erlich's announcement was acknowledged in silence. Masking his disappointment he then announced that a dinner would be held at the house that evening, attended by officers from Steiner's own field unit. Danuta was instructed to procure additional food and Hannah was told to prepare a short programme of music 'but nothing too heavy, mind,' cautioned Erlich.

Despite disliking anything remotely connected with food or cooking, Hannah offered to assist Danuta in the kitchen but thankfully the Czech declined.

Grateful for the opportunity to escape from the mind-numbing preparation of endless reports and requisitions, she made a dash to her room and began to prepare several pieces which she hoped might entertain servicemen whom she guessed may not be too acquainted with classical music! She was also mindful of Erlich's gentle reproach. Practising for an hour, she at last felt satisfied she had the right balance; a composition loosely based on a well-known German folk song interwoven with tantalising refrains from two popular melodies which she knew most servicemen would be familiar with. For her second piece she decided on a little-known Hungarian Gipsy Dance; a clever blending of gusto and nostalgia intended to show-case her newly revived virtuosity.

After running through each of her proposed arrangements and committing both to memory, she looked at herself in the mirror. Thankfully, the fresh colouring in her cheeks had partially replaced the grey pallor of the camp. Her hair however, was another matter. Still showing traces of the awful cut given during her first week at Auschwitz, she decided to attempt to even up its irregular length. This meant asking Danuta for a pair of scissors.

She found the Czech in the large pantry preparing piles of vegetables for the evening meal.

'Have you come to help me or to beat me up again?' The touch of humour from the normally dour Czech brought a smile to Hannah's face.

'Neither... we have a truce, remember?' She saw Danuta's face soften.

'Do you have a pair of scissors I could borrow?'

'What do you want them for? Are you going to stab me with them?' Smiling more broadly now, Danuta probably guessed what she wanted them for but still felt compelled to ask.

'I need to cut my hair, it looks awful.'

Danuta looked up and walked around Hannah, closely examining her hair and feeling its texture between finger and thumb. 'You're right, it does need cutting. Are you planning to do it yourself?'

'I've never tried but I can't make it worse than it is now, can I?'

'You can and you probably will.' A further examination followed. 'Would you like me to do it for you? I used to cut my sister's hair so I will make a better job of it than you will.'

'That's very kind of you Danuta but aren't you too busy preparing tonight's food?' The thought of Danuta standing over her with a pair of lethal scissors also flashed into her mind.

'Give me ten minutes and I will come to your room so go and wash your hair but don't dry it; wet hair makes cutting easier.' Without waiting for a reply, Danuta turned back to her vegetable preparation, the conversation summarily terminated by the busy Czech.

It took only a minute or so for Hannah to realise that Danuta really could cut hair despite the overlarge scissors she was using.

'You have nice hair, Hannah; I suppose you always had it cut professionally?'

'Yes I did until my arrest.' She expressively turned the palms of both hands upward in mock despair.

'What happened to you husband and child; were you all arrested together?'

'My husband was arrested first. He was sent to a camp near Theresienstadt and I haven't heard from him since. He's a doctor and he was ordered to work in the camp medical unit but whether he is still there I have no way of knowing. He hasn't been in touch since his arrest.'

'And your child; what happened to him?'

Danuta's directness disconcerted her and despite the Czech's apparent change of heart she didn't want to tell her too much, especially about Aaron.

'He disappeared when Ephraim and I were arrested and we never saw him again' she lied.

Hannah's shocking statement brought no reaction from the emotionless Danuta. Instead, she changed the subject. 'I'm familiar with the town of Theresienstadt but not the camp of course. My family lived in a small village close by. In those days it was a former Army barracks but as we never had much of an army it became a police training centre until the Germans invaded and turned it into what it is now.'

Hearing Danuta speak of her family somehow made Hannah feel more comfortable.

'What are you planning to wear this evening?' Half-smiling, she nodded towards the wardrobe. 'You won't find anything suitable in there unless you're into Army uniforms and greatcoats?'

The laugh which exploded from Hannah's lips was spontaneous, causing her head to jerk back and collide with Danuta's scissors.

'I have just the clothes you provided me with when I arrived. Corporal Erlich had my camp clothes burned so maybe I should wear an overcoat.'

Danuta stepped back and looked at her handiwork from several angles. 'There... I think that is an improvement even though it's much shorter than I imagine you were used to. At least it will now grow evenly again. Dry your hair and then come to my room in the basement.' Without another word, Danuta slipped the scissors in the front pocket of her apron and by the time Hannah turned to thank her, the Czech had gone, her footsteps echoing down the passageway.

Looking at herself in the mirror, she was pleasantly surprised to see how neat her hair now looked and how well the shorter style actually suited her.

Making her way to the basement, she tentatively tapped on Danuta's open door and receiving no response, stepped into the room which until this moment had been forbidden territory. Although it had taken no more than 10 minutes or so to dry her hair and descend to the basement, she saw that Danuta had already laid out a clean set of work clothes to replace those she was wearing. But lying alongside the austere grey skirt and top was a plain black dress.

'It belonged to my sister.' Danuta had quietly reappeared. 'She was smaller than me and about your size so with a bit of luck it may fit where it touches on you. It will certainly look better than those garments' nodding towards the work clothes lying on the bed.

'I'm surprised your sister was allowed to wear a dress in the house. Every person around here seems to be in a uniform of some kind or another, including us.'

'The Major allowed Blanca and me to have free time on a Sunday morning. It was an opportunity to get out of our work clothes and change into dresses and then we would hold a service in this room; just the two of us.'

'You and your sister, Danuta... the Major told me you were Jehovah Witnesses?'

'I still am. Do you know anything about my religion?'

'Hardly anything and probably less than you know about my religion. Maybe we could learn something from each other perhaps?' Her invitation was broached as a question.

The Czech gave a non-committal reply. 'Maybe... who can say?' Clearly anxious not to dwell on the subject, Danuta picked up the dress and unzipped the side fastening, ready for Hannah to slip into it.

Looking at herself in the mirror, she wondered how Danuta must be feeling seeing her sister's dress now being worn by her. Standing up, the dress felt right and she had to admit it fitted well though in style, it did reflect the dowdy end of the fashion spectrum. Seeing Danuta looking at her critically, she began to feel a sense of disquiet. Unable to contain herself a moment longer, she turned and faced the Czech. 'Look, I know you don't want to talk about it but I feel we should. When I first came to this house, you wished me dead. I reacted to that by becoming unforgivably violent yet here you are, cutting my hair and now lending me Blanca's dress: I'm having difficulty in understanding your sudden change of heart towards me. I feel nervous, Danuta and when I feel like this I just have to talk about it... so can we?'

'You feel nervous of me... of me?' Danuta's raised voice was a mixture of amusement and astonishment. Taking hold of Hannah's shoulders she spun her round so that they both faced the mirror. 'Look at us, you the newly arrived woman brought here to entertain German officers and me, a cook. Whilst Blanca was alive, the Major tolerated me because my sister was attractive and she amused him. Now she has gone, how long do you think it will be before Erlich will be told to return me to the camp? And we both know what that will mean. And now you ask why I help you instead of wanting you dead. If you can't guess then let me spell it out for you. I'm hoping he will find you as amusing as Blanca and continue to keep us both here.' Letting her arms drop, Danuta turned away. 'That shouldn't be too difficult to understand.' Her tone of voice dropped even lower. 'I want to survive, Hannah, nothing more than that and you being here can make that a possibility.'

'Danuta, you must know I have no influence over Major Steiner but provided we both do what is expected of us then I'm sure neither of us will be sent back.'

Even as she was speaking, the implication behind Danuta's statement slowly dawned on her.

'Is that the reason why you are lending me Blanca's dress? So the Major will draw a connection between me and your sister?'

'You must draw your own conclusion but trust me; you look far more attractive in Blanca's black dress than in those grey work clothes.

Later, waiting nervously in her room she heard the sound of animated discussion and merriment from below gradually increase in volume, no doubt commensurate with the amount of alcohol being consumed. Earlier that afternoon she had watched as crates of beer and several cases of wine had been delivered to the house.

As the minutes ticked by, she began to feel increasingly tense at the prospect of playing to a group of German officers; a cadre of men led by a Fuhrer dedicated to the daily slaughter of thousands of innocent men, women and children.

Even in the quietness of her room, she imagined she could hear the distant roar of the furnaces and she knew that if she could bring herself to look from her window she would see thick palls of grey smoke billowing out of the crematoriums blackened chimneys; a shocking testimony to Danuta's hate-filled words.

The summons from Erlich broke her sombre mood and together they made their way to the large dining area on the ground floor. Whilst waiting to be introduced by Steiner, his uniform jacket now displaying the insignia of his promotion, she counted some fifteen officers including a number of SS personnel. Taking her place on the temporary rostrum in the centre of the room, she noticed that Steiner appeared to be fully engrossed in a conversation with an officer she guessed might be the Camp Commandant. Her arrival in the room did not attract too much interest from the diners around the table and it wasn't until she saw Erlich lean over Steiner's shoulder and whisper to him that he became aware of her presence. Glancing round, she saw him get awkwardly to his feet. Tapping on the side of a glass with a knife brought the various conversations to an end.

'Gentlemen, I have a treat for you. We are about to hear from the former principle soloist of the Berlin Philharmonic Orchestra. Playing especially for us this evening we have the pleasure of being entertained by Miss Hannah Bergmann.'

Rising from the chair thoughtfully provided by Corporal Erlich and looking up she saw that Steiner had turned his seat in order to watch her performance. Thinking back to the occasion in Berlin when she had unwittingly focussed her performance on Von Hartmann, she decided that for this evening it would be wiser to concentrate on the chandelier at the far end of the room!

Laying the bow across the tuned strings of her violin, she played the opening stanzas of the German folk song she had chosen earlier. Glancing up, she was gratified to see that several heads were nodding in time with the music. Weaving an intricate tapestry, she progressively introduced the unmistakeable strains of 'Lili Marlene' to the score, causing several of these same nodding heads to look somewhat perplexed until a number of the younger officers showed their approval by tapping their hands on the table. By maintaining the underlying folk song as the predominant theme, there was even more participation as she introduced the haunting refrain of 'Falling in Love Again'. As the tune became recognised the majority of those present took up the melody and began to hum the familiar chorus line, perhaps with thoughts of wives or girlfriends in mind. As she brought the music to a flourishing conclusion, a number of officers showed their appreciation by banging on the table with the palms of their hands whilst others clapped. The Camp Commandant, she noticed, did neither.

Encouraged by their appreciation, she decided to attempt to get a reaction from the Commandant. Standing up, she took a step forward and adopted her familiar stance of performing on her feet. Her final piece, the Hungarian Gypsy Dance, was difficult to play with its fast tempo and frequent changes of key but the music adapted perfectly to her style of delivery. Centre stage with her beautifully tuned Bellini nestled into her body, it felt almost like old times. She also knew that every officer in the room could not only see her but be aware that the plain black dress did nothing to hide the sensuality of her lithe body. Naughtily, she also wondered whether despite being a Jew and therefore forbidden fruit to their Aryan purity, she was instilling in some of them a desire to do more than just listen to her accomplished virtuosity. Whether it was this or her syncopated fluidity of movement or the effect of the spirited finale which brought the audience, including the Commandant, to their feet she didn't know or care but she knew she had won her audience over.

Despite calls for an encore, she was mindful of Erlich's instruction, presumably from Steiner, to leave at the conclusion of both pieces.

Gaining the sanctuary of her room, she threw herself down on the bed. From past experience she knew that the exhilaration induced by her performance would not last but whilst it remained she was determined to hang on to its every last second. Still feeling euphoric her thoughts inexplicably turned to Ephraim. If he was still alive, she wondered what he might be doing at this same moment. Since their traumatic parting at Theresienstadt she hadn't received any news about him but realistically she knew that any form of communication from him would be extremely unlikely.

Down below, she heard the diners singing a tune she recognised as the 'Horst Vessels Marching Song' though with somewhat different words to those she remembered when it was played at several of the concerts she had attended. Eventually the laughter and chatter diminished until the only sound heard was that of crockery and cutlery being cleared away.

The knock on her door took Hannah by surprise. It was Erlich, his green uniform tunic unbuttoned and his white collarless shirt undone at the neck, a sure sign that the Corporal had consumed more than a few steins of beer during the course of the evening.

'The Major wants to see you in the Dining Room, Bergmann. I told him you may well be asleep so it's up to you whether you go or not. By the way, from tomorrow, you will address the Major as Colonel; is that understood?' He didn't wait for an acknowledgement. 'So, are you asleep or will you be going downstairs?'

Realising she was being given an option by this kindly man, she had to think quickly. 'No, I'm happy to go down and see what he wants. And thank you for advising about the Major's change of rank.'

Her response brought a disbelieving shake of the head from Erlich. 'Bergmann, you're a strange one, you really are. I wasn't advising you; it was an instruction.' With a feigned look of despair, he added 'I'll tell the Major you're on the way and I'll see you in the morning.' Stopping at the door, he gave her a look which instantly reminded her of her dear old father. 'By the way, that piece of old wood sounded wonderful this evening. Well done, girl.'

As she listened to Erlich's ponderous footsteps recede down the stairs, she immediately began to regret her decision. Dashing a douche of cold water on her face, she tidied her short hair and again looked at herself in the small mirror. The effects of her performance had abated and she could now see distinct signs of tiredness in her eyes. Since reaching her late teens, she had harboured the belief that not only her moods but her level of health could be assessed by the brightness or otherwise of her eyes; 'windows to the soul' her Father had once told her and tonight they were telling her that she should have chosen sleep. Instead, she found herself once more re-entering the large dining room now thankfully minus its earlier guests.

'Bergmann... come in and take a seat.' She saw that Steiner was already sprawled out in his favourite chair by the fire. 'That was a very spirited performance you gave tonight. Jurgen was right about you being a very talented person.'

The mention of Von Hartmann's name caused a trace of sadness to flash into her mind. By some bizarre twist of fate, that unexpected meeting with him in Berlin had brought her into contact with this complex man but only having first experienced the hellhole of Auschwitz on the way. But thanks to Von Hartmann and now Steiner, she was at least still alive.

Switching back to the present, she thanked Steiner for the compliment adding, 'it was a joy for me to be able to perform again.'

'How long has it been since you last played professionally and why did you not play in the Camp orchestra?' Without waiting for a reply he stood up. 'Let's go to the other room while Danuta clears away. I think even she was enchanted by your rendition this evening.' Glancing down the room, he sought confirmation; 'isn't that so, Danuta?'

By way of reply, Danuta gave a brief nod and continued to stack the used crockery on to the small wooden trolley, its wooden joints ominously creaking with the weight.

Leading into the comfortably lounge, Steiner directed Hannah to take the chair nearest to the still glowing fire. 'Erlich tells me you're somewhat averse to this cold Polish weather so you'll be more comfortable sitting there.' Choosing a chair for himself, Steiner spread out his long legs and eased into a slouching position, always hoping to ease the nagging pain in his lower back. 'You haven't answered my question Bergmann; why did you not play in the camp orchestra?'

A cautionary note triggered in her mind. Dare she tell him, a senior German officer, her reason for not wishing to do so? Taking a deep breath she decided to follow her instinct.

'Because the camp orchestra is part of the deception that you Nazis use to deceive new arrivals into believing this awful place is something other than what it really is... a death camp.' She stopped, her courage melting away, fearful that her words would cause a violent reaction from him. Instead, his reply was surprisingly urbane.

'Bergmann, listen to me. You call me a Nazi and I can understand why you think that but do you really believe I am the same as some of those other officers you entertained here this evening?'

'I would like to think you are different but you all wear the same uniform and as soldiers, you are bound to follow orders which translate into the systematic murder of innocent people. I know you don't actually work in the Camp but have you any idea just how many innocent little children are murdered each day by soldiers wearing the same uniform as yourself?'

'I think you should stop there, Bergmann.' From his ice-cold tone, she knew she had stepped over the line.

Taking a deep breath to calm his rising anger, Steiner let several seconds pass before replying. 'Do you think we Germans are the only people who do such things? Would it surprise you to know that it was the British who invented concentration camps in which hundreds of Boer women and children died from starvation and disease? And the Americans too; would you care to know how they treat their black people? Like third class citizens in much the same way as we Germans treat you Jews yet does the world at large ostracise America as they do us Germans?'

'That is because the Americans, unlike you Germans, do not actually murder their black population so that is an unfortunate comparison Major.' Suddenly remembering Erlich's instruction, she quickly corrected herself. 'Sorry, I should have addressed you as Colonel.'

Ignoring her correction, Steiner changed tack. 'You may have a point Bergman but as a Jew you must know from your childhood days just how the Russians and the Poles treated Jews in their pogroms. They massacred thousands of Jewish people over long periods of time.'

Torn between caution and the urge to respond, she settled for reticence.

Taking her silence for acquiescence, Steiner rose from his chair and stood with his back to the fire.

'The trouble with Jews are that they have never regarded themselves as Germans. As a race, they have never assimilated, whichever country your people have lived in. Jews have always chosen to separate yourselves from the world at large so first and foremost they are Jews who just happen to live in Germany or wherever else on this earth. Being a Jew is not just your religion, it's your heritage and nationality. That's why the Fuhrer made you stateless. Why can you not understand that, Bergmann?'

Giving what she hoped Steiner would construe as innocent coyness, she smiled as sweetly as she could. 'Am I able to speak freely Colonel or am I expected to simply agree with your view of the world.'

'That depends on what you say.' Listening to him, she detected the growing condescension in his voice. 'I think you must agree that I've given you more licence than you would get from many of those other officers who were here tonight.'

Choosing not to pick up on Steiner's ingratiating remark, she thought it prudent to agree with him. 'Yes you have and for that I am grateful but the sadness is that there is nothing I can say or you can do, to change what is happening in this awful world.'

'Again, I can but agree with that too so why not accept it and just try to survive what is happening around you. Not just here in Auschwitz but elsewhere in this damned world.' Staring into the glowing embers of the fire, it was several moments before he spoke again. 'You also need to understand that you are far safer here than where you came from.'

'I am only as safe as you wish me to be, Colonel. You can have me sent back just as easily as you brought me here and I would be dead within hours; we both know that.'

As though not hearing her words, Steiner moved awkwardly closer to the fire. Still staring into the hearth he stooped down and gathered up two logs from the nearby stack and carefully positioned them on top of the dying embers. Staring intently, he saw orange and blue-tipped flames began to curl around the dry logs until they became fully engulfed. In the ensuing silence Steiner was also thinking how to respond to this woman.

'Why would I do that, Bergmann? I like having you here.' He turned to face her. 'Not only for your musical talent which you ably demonstrated tonight but you are beginning to make this place seem almost normal. Can you imagine what it was like when it was just Danuta and her sister here? The place was like a morgue. Corporal Erlich also likes you. He won't say so but I've known him long enough to know when he takes to a person. Also, I've never met a Jew whom I could talk to before so perhaps I may even learn something from you. Or perhaps you may even learn something from me; who can say?' Again, he turned and stared into the fire.

'Colonel, I am extremely tired; may I have your permission to go to my room please?'

'You will go when I say you can go and not before.'

Looking at him closely, she saw Steiner stand and reach forward and steady himself by resting his hand against the oak mantelshelf. She had no idea whether he was tired like her or whether it was the amount of alcohol he had undoubtedly consumed during dinner which caused him to hold on.

'In which case, can I get you something; another drink perhaps?'

'No, I have had enough drink for one night but tell me,' his voice picked up; 'are Jews allowed to drink alcohol? Danuta's religion doesn't seem to allow it.' Without waiting for a reply, Steiner released his hold on the mantelshelf and turned to face her again. Framed by the orange glow from the burning logs, he seemed even taller.

'I hardly know you Bergmann but already I think you are not long for this world. Not only are you naïve but I think you are just not equipped to deal with life as we face it today.'

'When you say I am not long for this world,' she could barely force the words out, 'does that mean you have decided to return me to the camp?'

'Listen to what I am saying to you, Bergmann.' A note of impatience was evident in his tired voice. 'You are just too weak to survive especially in this environment. You are right of course; thousands of people are being killed daily. And not only Jews but Bolsheviks, gypsies, old people, homosexuals; all being murdered in their thousands and those not being gassed are being worked and starved to death in the factories and mines both here in Auschwitz and in many other similar camps too. And do you know why? It's happening to purify this mythical Aryan race so fervently believed in by Adolph Hitler.' He paused for a reaction but none came. 'Look, I can't be telling you anything you haven't seen for yourself when you were in the camp. So if I hadn't arranged for you to be transferred here, how long do you think you would have lasted? A week perhaps... a month maybe? How long, Bergmann... you tell me?'

Looking down at her, Steiner seemed to lose the thrust of his question. Reaching out with both hands, he pulled Hannah to her feet. Instinctively she drew back and saw a look of pained anguish flicker across his weary features.

'Please Colonel.' She tried to pull her hands away. 'You must be extremely tired so please think what you are doing.'

'Think!' The anger in his voice was now unmistakeable. 'Why should I think? That's your trouble my little Jew girl, you think too much. Do you think this God of yours will come to this terrible place and smite us Germans dead? Is this what you hope will happen? Then where was he today Bergmann, and yesterday and every fucking day in this god-forsaken hell?'

Shocked by the crude suddenness of Steiner's outburst, she felt a sense of panic and turned to leave the room, her heart pounding in her chest.

'Where do you think you're going? Just stay where you are until I say you can leave. D'you hear me?'

She stopped, halted by Steiner's shouted order.

'I said 'do you hear me? Look at me when I speak to you.'

Steiner's faltering voice lowered and he appeared to regain control of himself again.

'I understand you perfectly, Colonel. I'm sorry I caused you to get so angry. It wasn't my intention.'

Slumping back into his chair, his head sank down on to his chest. Seeing his eyes begin to moisten took her by surprise, reflecting as it did, the emotions and stress the man was obviously feeling. When he next spoke it was in a conciliatory voice.

'Look, you must understand that I am as much a prisoner here as you are. I am supposed to be a soldier of the Wehrmacht yet I find myself assigned to this stinking shit hole. Do you think I'm immune to what's happening here or that I can change anything? What do you think would happen if I had told the Camp Commandant earlier tonight that I didn't agree with the policy of exterminating these people?' He stopped abruptly, hoping that she would say something to help to salve his conscience. But her damning silence spoke louder than any words she could offer.

'I'll tell you what would happen. I would be immediately summoned to Berlin and shot without trial: it's what all good armies do. They shoot the dissidents to keep the rest in line.'

'At least you appear to accept that Jews like me are people.'

'I'll tell you what you are, my fragile little Jew girl. You are beginning to become my conscience and reminding me of what this world was like before this madness overtook every last person in it.'

Encouraged by his calmer demeanour, she took up the seat opposite him.

'Are you saying that you are so far away from common decency that you can't recover it?'

'No. I'm not saying that. I would just like to close my eyes and open them to find this was all a terrible dream. But it isn't, so we do what we are ordered to do and hope that one day we can return to a life of normality or whatever that may mean in the future.'

This time she did engage albeit with trepidation. 'I'm sorry you feel like that Colonel; if you lose hope then what else is there to hold on to.'

Without warning, Steiner heaved himself out of his chair and she feared he was about to lose his temper again. Instead, he walked to the end of the room and turned abruptly.

'I don't understand you. You speak of hope but realistically what hope do you have? Do you really think you will leave this place alive when every day, Jews like you are being murdered in their thousands?' He emphasised his words with an angry slap on his knee. 'So tell me in terms which even I can understand... what hope do you think you have?'

'I think you misunderstand me. Hope isn't a means of changing what we face today; it's simply hoping things will become better in the future. In many ways, it's the same as faith, something you can't see or touch and therefore intangible.'

'So we're back to your faith again? To the great hereafter and the avenging God of the Israelites; the hammer of us Huns. Is that what you describe as hope?'

'Colonel, please understand, I have never renounced my religion but that doesn't mean I hold a deep conviction about it. I simply hope for a better future in this life, particularly for my son. If it doesn't happen and if there is a God and a life after this, then perhaps that is where we will find what I speak of.'

Appearing to reflect on Hannah's words his face showed no visible reaction before he slowly stood up. 'Bergmann, come here.'

Petrified, she rose from her chair and moved towards him. This time it was she who reached out and gently touched his arm. Their eyes met and she once more saw the emotional strain on Steiner's face, his eyes registering what she recognised as mind numbing fatigue.. 'Please Colonel, you are extremely tired and you need to rest.'

Ignoring her plea, Steiner lurched forward and grabbed hold of her shoulders in order to steady himself. 'Go to your room my little Jew girl and trust that when you reach that beautiful place you hope for, it will be a better world than the one you find yourself in tonight.'

FORTY FOUR

Lying in her bed but unable to sleep, she tried to put her muddled thoughts in perspective. She had difficulty in believing that within the military, let alone the Gestapo, there were officers like Von Hartmannn and perhaps even Steiner; men capable of thinking and acting like human beings despite their allegiance to a creed fanatically dedicated to the slaughter of her people. Thinking of Von Hartmannn, she remembered how he had wistfully spoken of home and family. And now Steiner too; the man to whom she owed her continuing survival but only on his terms.

She thought back to when she had first met Steiner and consciously shuddered, recalling the awful chain of events on that horrific night in Block 23. Knowing Steiner's kinship to Von Hartmann and from him the expectation that she would end up in Auschwitz, she also wondered whether her selection for survival had been as coincidental as she had first imagined.

If not at the selection ramp then perhaps it might explain why he had arranged for her to be brought to his personal quarters? Looking back, she remembered Ephraim, Max and even Elsa telling her on numerous occasions that she had no idea of the effect she had on men so was it her naivety and innocence which attracted them to her? She remembered Elsa laughing in disbelief when she told her that Ephraim had been the only man she had had sex with and then only after they were married. Thinking of Elsa caused an emotional lump in her throat; what a wonderful friend she had been.

Her thoughts were interrupted by the sound of Steiner unsteadily climbing the creaking stairs to his room further along the corridor. When Corporal Erlich had assigned her to this room on the top floor she had experienced a degree of anxiety at being so close to Steiner's bedroom. But that concern had gradually lessened to the point where she now welcomed the safety which came from being in close proximity to a man who clearly had no interest in her as a woman. Thinking back to the nightly terror she had faced in the accommodation block in Auschwitz it was, in the oft-repeated words of Ephraim, 'a no contest'.

Despite the drowsy warmth of her bed, she recalled again the chilling words spoken by Steiner earlier that evening. 'Do you really think you will leave this place alive when thousands of Jews like you are being killed daily?'

Before her sudden removal from Auschwitz, Miriam had told her that the war appeared to be turning against Germany especially in Eastern Europe. News gleaned from recent batches of Russian prisoners appeared to indicate that the Red Army had not only halted the German advance but was now beginning to go on the offensive. She knew her survival would depend on a number of factors, all of which were utterly beyond her control. But having now adapted to life in Steiner's Administration Unit, she realised that her chance of surviving the war would be infinitely better if she was able to remain where she was. But if by some miracle she did survive then how would she fare when the Red Army liberated Auschwitz? To Russian soldiers, aware of the atrocities committed by the invading German Army in their homeland, she was a German woman... a woman to sate the pent-up frustrations of soldiers bent on revenge.

It seemed she had been asleep for just a matter of minutes before being startled by a distressing cry seeming to come from along the passageway. For a brief moment the noise stopped only to be repeated moments later by a low moaning sound. Now fully awake, she heard the sound of Erlich's heavy footsteps pounding up the stairs. Seconds later, she heard her name being called.

Scrambling out of bed, she frantically searched for her dressing gown before hurrying in the direction of Steiner's room. Entering it for the very first time she dimly made out the stocky figure of Corporal Erlich kneeling by the side of Steiner's bed.

'Fetch a bowl of cold water but don't turn the light on. And be quick girl!' There was noticeable panic in Erlich's deep voice.

Hurrying to the bathroom, she quickly found an empty bowl and let the cold water run for a moment before returning to Steiner's room.

'Open that drawer and let me have the brown bottle with the white label and then fetch a spoon from the kitchen.' The sense of urgency in Erlich's voice added to the apprehension she was beginning to feel.

'I have one in my room; I'll fetch it.'

'Ernst, where's that damn medicine!' Steiner's voice was barely audible. Weakly reaching out for the bottle offered by Erlich, she watched as Steiner put it to his lips and heard several gulps as he swallowed the liquid. Falling back onto his pillow, Hannah saw that his face and chest were glistening with sweat.

'Bergmann, get a flannel and bathe the Colonel's face and chest. He's in a fever and we need to bring his temperature down as quickly as we can.'

Running back to the bathroom, Hannah grabbed hold of several hand towels and flannels from Danuta's clean linen basket, soaking each one under the cold tap before retracing her steps. With a pained look of relief, Erlich stood back to let her take up his position before exiting the room; probably to get dressed.

Standing over Steiner, she could feel the heat rising from his fevered body. Using a wet towel she dabbed his face and then laid it over his heaving chest. Repeating this at regular intervals, she was relieved to hear his breathing gradually become less laboured as his fevered temperature slowly dropped. Instead of gulping for air, his breathing became more regulated.

Removing the last of the wet flannels she carefully dried his face and chest; exposing his upper body to the cold air in the room. With the darkness of the room adding to her growing sense of awareness, she let her sensitive finger tips feel their way across Steiner's bare chest to check whether the fever-induced sweating had fully subsided. Towards his upper rib cage her probing fingers detected an irregular skin formation just below Steiner's left breast. Despite the dimness of the room, she was able to make out an ugly lacerated wound which even to her unpractised eye, she could see had been badly stitched, probably in a first-aid station or field hospital. She let her soft fingers dwell on the protruding tissue and wondered whether he had sustained the wound during the time she now knew he had spent in Russia. It was the sound of Erlich's approaching footsteps in the passageway which broke the spell and the realisation of what she was doing. Guiltily she jerked upright and pulled her hand away, just as Erlich re-entered the room.

'How is he now; has he cooled down yet?'

'I think so. The fever appears to have subsided as quickly as it came on. I think he's now sleeping.' Rising to her feet, she gathered up the towels. 'I'll take these back to the bathroom and go back to my room. I'll listen out in case the Colonel has a re-occurrence but he seems to be OK for the moment.'

'You do that... and Bergmann.' Erlich's voice was barely a whisper. 'You've been a great help.'

Returning to her room, Hannah eased herself into her still warm bed and took a deep breath in what proved to be a futile effort to quell the pulsating beat of her heart. Inwardly, she knew her brief encounter with Steiner would intrude upon her thoughts unless she could find refuge in sleep. But how to find sleep when her mind and body were still racing with thoughts she knew no respectable Jewish girl should be thinking.

FORTY FIVE

It was the sound of squawking chickens which aroused her the following morning. She knew Danuta usually fed them with scraps left over from breakfast which could only mean that the other members of the household had not only risen before her but had breakfasted as well.

Leaping out of bed and grabbing her crumpled dressing gown from where she had thrown it just hours before, she ran to the bathroom and in sheer panic threw ice cold water on her face to dash away the last trace of sleep. The bare wooden treads on the rear staircase seemed to magnify the sound of each hesitant step as she tentatively approached the ground floor... there to be confronted on the very last step by a stern faced Corporal Erlich.

Giving the military timepiece on the wall an exaggerated glance, he struck an unfamiliar pose with both hands on hips. 'And what time of day d'you call this, young lady?'

'I'm sorry Corporal. I have no excuse. My alarm failed to wake me. I promise it won't happen again.'

'The reason why your alarm didn't wake you Bergmann was because the Colonel turned it off before he left this morning.' Nodding his head towards the kitchen he looked at Hannah with a faint smile on his face. 'Go and have your breakfast and turn in for work when you've finished.'

'Sorry Corporal but did you say the Colonel came to my room this morning and turned my alarm off so that I could sleep in?'

'That is exactly what I am saying so run along now and get some food in you otherwise you'll still be here at lunch time!'

In the kitchen Danuta was her usual bustling self and Hannah noticed that she had prepared a space on the crowded table for her to have breakfast.

Still puzzling over Erlich's statement, she failed to acknowledge the 'good morning' greeting from Danuta. 'Did you hear what Corporal Erlich said to me? He told me that the Colonel came to my room and turned my alarm off; can you believe that?'

'If the Corporal said that then it must be true.' She gave Hannah a questioning look. 'Tell me, what happened on the top floor last night? I heard shouting and lots of footsteps but then it all went very quiet.'

'The Colonel had a bout of fever so that would probably account for the shouting you heard. Thankfully Corporal Erlich knew what to do and I simply helped out with towels and cold water.'

'He'd be dead without that man to look after him. He's had these attacks before but he won't go to see the Camp doctor and who can blame him for that?' Turning from the stove, Danuta brought an enamel pot over to the table and poured out three cups of steaming coffee, its strong aroma bringing back nostalgic memories of mornings spent with Ephraim in their now barely remembered Charlottenburg apartment.

'I suppose you realise that if something should happen to the Colonel whether him being killed or transferred away from here then that would be the end for you and me... kaput!' She brought her hand down sharply on the surface of the table.

'We would be sent back to the Camp and the Corporal would go back to the Russian front again. So remember what I told you recently Hannah, you must do everything you can to keep us here. The Colonel obviously likes you which could be the reason why he let you sleep in this morning' wistful adding, 'something he never did for my sister.'

As Danuta disappeared from the kitchen with Erlich's coffee, the implication of her words struck home. Since her horrifying arrival at Auschwitz, she knew her death was just a matter of time. Only the curiosity of the Gestapo officer at the selection ramp had spared her life that day. His likely intention to assign her to the Camp orchestra had probably been forgotten in the sheer number of prisoners arriving that morning but in her mind it had merely postponed her inevitable fate. But now Danuta... strong minded, sensible Danuta, was telling her that if they could remain in these quarters until the Camp was liberated, then a glimmer of hope might possibly exist. But for that to happen, Germany would have to lose a war which in August 1943, it showed little sign of doing despite the Red Army unexpectedly halting the Wehrmacht's renewed offensive.

It was after midnight before Steiner returned. Uncertain whether she was expected to wait up, she decided to remain in her room, waiting to be summoned. His arrival had been announced by the sound of tyres on the gravel and the slamming of a car door which had the effect of snapping her tired mind back to the present.

Not having been summoned and increasingly uncertain what to do, she decided to join Danuta in the kitchen. Once there she heard the familiar voice of Steiner talking on the telephone.

'Take this coffee to the Colonel and tell him that his supper will be ready in 10 minutes.'

'Will he want supper this late at night? Won't he be too tired to eat?'

'Have you ever known a soldier turn down the chance of a hot meal?

'I haven't known any soldiers so I wouldn't know. Will he be having the stew you prepared earlier?'

'Of course; what else can I prepare in 10 minutes at this time of night?' With Danuta, she realised you could always expect a logical response

Making her way to the first floor office, she caught sight of Steiner emptying his briefcase on to the hearth and with his foot then push the contents into the blazing fire. As the flames began to lick through the wad of papers, Steiner straightened up, pressing both hands into his kidneys as he arched his back beyond its normal curvature.

Seeing Hannah approach with the coffee he smiled in anticipation. 'Ah, the coffee lady cometh. Put it down there will you' nodding in the general direction of his desk.

'Danuta asked me to remind you that your supper will be ready in ten minutes. And by the way, drinking strong coffee so late at night won't help you sleep. The caffeine in coffee actually keeps you awake and after your disturbed night I think you need all the rest you can get.'

Settling himself in the high-backed wooden chair at the side of the fire place he gave Hannah a puzzled stare. 'Should I believe what I'm hearing, Bergmann.' A contrived look of puzzlement appeared on his face. 'Last night in this very room you told me I was as much a Nazi as those other officers from the camp. Yet tonight you are concerned for my welfare. Care to explain that contradiction and your change of heart?'

Embarrassed by her own boldness, she attempted to recover her poise. 'I can't believe I said that either so please forgive me.' Feeling her face beginning to colour up, she turned to hurry from the room.

'No wait. I'm still puzzled as to why you're so concerned whether I sleep or not?'

Swallowing hard to compose herself, she took a deep breath. 'Because last night you woke the entire household with your moaning and groaning. I know you couldn't help doing that so tonight you need to get a good rest. That's why I mentioned the coffee. No other reason, believe me.'

'You disappoint me, Bergmann. I thought it was your husband who was the doctor but you seem know a thing or two about such things too. Or maybe you are just a caring person; even to a German who happens to wear an army uniform.'

Reflecting on his words, it took her tired mind several seconds to realise that Steiner was actually engaging her in conversation without any sign of the irascibility he had displayed the previous evening. Emboldened, she reached out and took hold of the coffee cup. 'I'm returning this to the kitchen; can I get you something else; a whiskey perhaps?' Without waiting for a reply, she quickly made her exit. Watching her leave the room, something akin to a smile appeared on his face. Leaning forward he took hold of the metal poker and pushed the remaining papers into the flames. Torn muscles in his chest, a painful reminder of Stalingrad, had troubled him all day but now, seated in the high backed chair, he felt the throbbing ache begin to ease as the heat from the fire gradually warmed his body. Faintly aware of his head jerking forward onto his chest he remembered nothing more until hearing a distant voice encroaching into his relaxed slumber. The intermittent voice ceased only to be replaced by a persistent shaking of his shoulder.

In his tired brain, he was once more in the stinking cellar of the wrecked building in Stalingrad and the hand shaking him awake was a Soviet soldier. Instinctively, he grabbed his assailant's wrist and roughly pulled him towards his balled fist, poised to strike his imaginary protagonist.

Standing alongside him and shocked by his reaction Hannah struck out at Steiner's unprotected face. The grip on her wrist instantly lessened and she saw recognition dawn on his face. Leaning back, she saw his hand gingerly examine his rapidly colouring cheek.

'Bergmann... you struck me by God!

Filled with the enormity of her impulsive act, she quickly backed away. Overcoming an urge to run, she felt her legs begin to weaken. In utter despair she slipped to the floor knowing she had just committed the ultimate crime.

From somewhere behind her, she recognised the forceful voice of Ernst Erlich before feeling his brawny arms take hold of her and pull her upright.

'Go to your room... now!' The level of anger in the voice of this normally placid man only added to her growing sense of dread;

'Corporal, I was... '

'Bergmann, I won't tell you again... just go!' Roughly propelled through the open doorway brought her face to face with an anxious looking Danuta.

'Hannah, what on earth has happened in there and why was the Corporal shouting at you?'

Too distressed to answer, she pushed past the querulous Czech. Reaching her room, she slammed the door shut, hoping Danuta wouldn't follow her. Through tear-filled eyes, she took in the room which since her arrival had become her personal sanctuary from the world at large with its familiar furnishings and the small personal touches she had since added but all now in dire jeopardy. Drawn to the window, she peered through the blackness of the Polish night towards the Auschwitz complex. From the luminescent glare emanating from the sodium lights on the forefront of the crematoria buildings she dimly made out the silhouettes of the various chimneys separating the two camps. With a sense of impending dread her thoughts turned to Ephraim. She recalled his foolhardy courage and his reckless defiance when being questioned at Gestapo Headquarters in Berlin.. 'If there is a God' she thought, 'then please let me be reunited with him soon.' Unable to stem her emotions any longer she began to cry uncontrollably and felt tears begin to flow unchecked down her face. Sobbing, she turned towards the marble topped wash-stand with its jug of water and bowl; ironically given by the man who had just ordered her to her room; the normally mild mannered Corporal Erlich.

Soaking a flannel in the water she dabbed her face, its coldness acting as an astringent on her flushed features. Reaching for the large towel kept on the rail at the side of the wash-stand she enveloped her head and took a deep breath before slowly expelling it, seeking a fleeting moment of peace before steeling herself to face the reality of what lay beyond her temporary shelter.

'Bergmann, why are you hiding beneath that towel?'

The shock at hearing Steiner's voice was total. Frantically pulling the towel from her head she automatically began to straighten her hair.

'Leave your hair alone and sit down here.' Nodding towards the bed, Steiner swung the only chair in the room to face her and sat down. 'Tell me what happened when you came back into my office. Was I asleep?'

'I took your coffee back to the kitchen and came back to tell you that your supper was ready. You were asleep so I spoke to you but you didn't wake up. Stupidly, I shook your shoulder. You were startled; you grabbed hold of my arm and went to hit me with your other hand. As you pulled me on to you I raised my hand and... ' she stopped in mid-sentence, the damning admission trapped in her throat.

Steiner's raised voice reflected feigned impatience. 'Bergmann... get to the point; did you deliberately strike me... yes or no?'

The discoloured imprint of her fingers on Steiner's left cheek ruled out any hope of denial.

'Yes I did but not intentionally. I reacted to what was happening. I can't tell you how sorry I am.'

Striving with difficulty to maintain his unyielding façade, Steiner leaned back in the old pine saddleback chair causing its rickety joints to protest.

The sound induced even greater panic in her. 'Colonel, don't lean back. The wooden joints on that chair are loose and it may collapse under your weight.'

Cautiously Steiner slowly rose to his feet.

'Bergmann, you are a paradox, a complete paradox. Last night you tended me during my fever and tonight you try to knock me unconscious! What am I to make of you?'

Sensing the question to be rhetorical rather than humorous, Hannah judged it prudent to steer the question to the previous evening. 'I didn't do very much last night other than to cool you down with cold towels. It was the medicine which appeared to do the trick.'

'Erlich told me you spent nearly an hour with me; is that correct?'

'I'm not sure how long I stayed with you, the important thing was to get your temperature down. I just did what Corporal Erlich told me to do.'

Pushing the chair away with his foot, Steiner seated himself alongside Hannah on the side of the bed. 'I trust this bed is stronger than that chair?' Finally a smile slowly creased his face.

Feeling his closeness, a barely suppressed ripple of relief began to course down her back.

'If I set what has just occurred against your nursing skill of last evening I reckon they just about cancel each other out. Would you agree with that?' A teasing grin appeared on his unshaven face.

Realising she had been holding her breath Hannah relaxed and felt her shoulders slump in relief. 'I'm grateful for your understanding Colonel.'

Perhaps I'm the paradox here, Bergmann. One moment I act like the soldier I was before this war started and then I see the fear in your eyes and wonder whether I've become like those brain-washed thugs you met in the camp.' Turning to face her, Hannah imagined she could feel the heat radiating from his closeness.

'Tell me Bergmann, which of those two personalities do you think I am?'

'How can I possibly answer that question? The fact that I'm still here and not in the camp tells me you are not really like those other officers who were here last night. But as I told you when we last spoke, you all wear the same uniform and you all follow orders; whatever those orders may be.' Expecting a rebuke or at least a response, Hannah was surprised by his reticence to reply.

'Colonel, we've talked about this subject before so you are obviously bothered by it but in reality it's a question which only you can answer.'

In the silence that followed, Hannah began to gently edge away from his brooding form. Sensing the movement, Steiner clamped his large hand over hers.

'Don't move away... please.' The wistfulness in his tired voice was touching. 'Let me tell you something I will never understand. Every one of those SS officers who came here last night were ordinary citizens before they became soldiers; normal people with wives and children who could have been your next door neighbours. Capable of killing people? Not in a million years! But look at these same men now and you see people who are utterly transformed into mindless killers. So what has caused them to act as they now do? You say it's the uniform but you are wrong, Bergmann; very, very wrong. It's the poisonous indoctrination poured into them by a leader who has cynically manipulated the entire nation.' Steiner continued to gaze at the floor but retained his grip on her hand.

'When truth is laced with fiction it becomes a powerful cocktail, particularly when you have a receptive population. The reparations demanded by the British and French after the Great War were an act of revenge to ensure we would never again threaten the peace of Europe. But when you humiliate a nation as the Allies did to Germany, then you will get a reaction and when a man like Hitler appears, promising to restore our Aryan manhood and make us strong again, then people will listen. Not only to listen but to believe too so the only ingredient now required is power; the power that comes from the ballot box which has enabled the Nazis to act in the name of the people. But to get people to give him that power, Hitler needed a scapegoat to blame for the mistakes of the past and you Jews were obvious candidates for that role.'

Although unsure whether Steiner was being deliberately provocative, she knew she had to retort. 'How can you say that? You sound as though the Jews are the enemy of your exalted Fatherland but you know that to be complete nonsense.' Anticipating a reprimand for her candour she was relieved when Steiner remained silent, continuing to stare at the threadbare carpet on the floor. Emboldened by his passiveness, she felt she must say more before his irascibility returned. 'Why are we so different from other religious groups or peoples and why did Hitler choose us for extermination? Having made us stateless then why not just let us leave Germany and go elsewhere in this world?' Animated by own words, she realised that she was actually having a rational discussion with Steiner the man and not the German officer.

Turning his head to look at Hannah, she saw the corners of his mouth lift as he attempted the briefest of smiles before responding. 'Because he needed an easy scapegoat and the Jews with their economic power and ownership of international industry were an obvious target. Or to be more precise, Hitler effectively harnessed the jealousy factor in people and used it to turn the majority of the population against Jews like you.' Steiner's tiredness was beginning to have a noticeable effect but he was determined to finish his point. 'And unlike other religious groups, you Jews never really assimilated with us Germans. First and foremost you are always Jews, whichever country they may happen to live in but I'm only repeating what I told you last night. Put it down to age or tiredness, my little Jew girl.'

Ignoring his last remark, Hannah pressed on. 'Could the reason for that be the fact that Germany took away our citizenship and declared Jews like me to be stateless?

'It's a chicken and egg situation Bergmann, but the evidence of other countries is against you. Jews have become a separate people by choice and you know that to be true. But whether they have been driven into that state of mind by the various pogroms inflicted upon them is a far deeper question.'

Releasing his hold on her hand, Steiner rose to his feet. 'I've had a long day and I'm tired but getting back to my original question which you failed to answer. I am a soldier in the German Army and like your friend Von Hartmannn, I am not a Nazi nor will I ever be. So as long as I remain in this posting both you and Danuta will be safe. Beyond that, I cannot say. But I want you to listen to me Bergmann and remember these words. I don't ever want to see that look of fear in your eyes again because it reminds me of all the things I am ashamed of within my country.' He stopped abruptly, realising he had said more than he intended. Instead he reached down and cupped Hannah's cheek in his hand. 'You're a beautiful and caring person, Bergmann, and in different circumstances, who knows.' His voice trailed off leaving any further words unstated.

Later, wrapped in her warm bed, she thought of the qualified assurance of safety offered by Steiner but inwardly, her mind turned again and again to his parting words.

FORTY SIX

Hannah saw nothing of Steiner for the next two weeks. Knowing her safety was totally dependent upon his continuing presence both she and Danuta began to feel increasingly anxious until Corporal Erlich provided the reason for his absence.

'Stalingrad has fallen and our troops have surrendered. I just can't believe it.'

Clearly shaken, Erlich had broken the news during breakfast. 'God help those poor buggers. As if they haven't been through enough in that hell-hole. The Ruskies are worse than animals.'

'You mean they're worse than German troops?' It was Hannah asking the question.

'Careful Bergmann... you know what I mean.'

Sensing discord, Danuta quickly interceded. 'The Corporal is referring to his fellow soldiers, Hannah, so stop playing games.'

Ruffled by the Czech's open rebuke, she sensibly opted for silence.

Looking at both women Erlich chose to be conciliatory 'I forget that for you two girls our defeat in Stalingrad will sound like good news. The sooner this war is over, the sooner you can both go home.'

Hearing Erlich refer to her and Danuta as 'girls' brought a smile to her face. 'I guess that's something we can all agree upon Corporal; an end to this war, I mean.'

'Does this mean that you and the Colonel may have to go back to the Russian front again?' Danuta's quavering voice reflected the anxiety she was feeling for her own safety.

'I hope that won't be the case. We'll all know more when the Colonel returns from Berlin.'

Looking at Erlich sitting at the opposite end of the breakfast table, his uniform shirt open at the neck and his grey military braces unfastened, Hannah felt a wrench of sadness for this kindly man. Conscripted in mid-life, he almost certainly hated the war as much as she did and would no doubt like nothing more than to return to his small Bavarian village and pick up his former life again. But then she thought, 'wouldn't we all'.

Hoping for Erlich to expand on her previous question, Danuta tried again, her voice still reflecting her concern. 'So can we expect the Colonel back soon, Corporal?

'You will know when he gets here, Danuta, so no more questions from either of you. I'm afraid my chrystal ball doesn't show beyond the next hour or so.' Rising from the table, Erlich went to the stove and refilled his mug with coffee.

'If you two ladies will excuse me I have work to do.' With a shrug of his broad shoulders, Erlich walked out of the kitchen.

'He speaks to us like a father Danuta. Can you imagine any of those SS soldiers referring to us as ladies?'

'Don't fool yourself Hannah. What the corporal says is meaningless. I'm more concerned with what will happen to us if the Colonel is sent elsewhere. We are safe only as long as we remain here and we have no control over that. If we were to be sent back to the camp I swear I would kill myself rather than return to that awful place.'

'Stop talking like that. So far as we know we aren't going anywhere, least of all back to the camp. The Colonel gave his word, remember?'

'And you believe him of course.'

'Yes I do.'

'Then you're a fool, Hannah. He's a murdering Nazi just like the rest of them so stop dreaming.' Rising quickly, Danuta headed for the door before Hannah could reply to her outburst.

Left alone, she resisted following the unusually garrulous Czech, preferring instead to remain in the warm kitchen mulling over the events of the past few minutes. Realistically, she knew Danuta was correct; their fate did depend on events beyond their control and any return to Auschwitz would be a certain journey to death. 'But if that that were to happen, would I have the courage to follow Danuta's example' she wondered?

Two days after his return from Berlin Steiner summoned Hannah to his office. Since his late night arrival and his departure before dawn the following morning, she had not seen nor spoken with him. The summons came by way of Corporal Erlich and with Danuta's dire forebodings still filling her mind, she was understandably nervous.

Seated behind the long pine table he used as a desk, Steiner glanced up as she entered. Nodding her towards the chair opposite to his own, he slouched back into his favourite pain relieving sprawl. 'Tomorrow I will be meeting with two fellow officers, both of whom have seen you perform in Berlin. Their names won't mean anything to you but they would like the opportunity of hearing you play for them. Will you do that?'

'Of course Colonel, it will be my pleasure.'

'You will be pleased to know that neither are members of the SS. Just plain ordinary Wehrmacht soldiers except that one is a retired general so no wrong notes because retired or not, he still has the authority to have you shot on the spot!' Glancing at her nervous expression, his features softened. 'Sorry Bergmann, that wasn't funny.'

Touched by his unexpected apology, she felt herself begin to relax. 'Did the General express any particular piece of music, Colonel? And being retired should I address him as Mister or General?

'You will address him as General. Officers at his level always retain their military status and no, he didn't request any specific piece of music so you may thrust in your sickle and make your own choice.'

Puzzled by Steiner's odd comment, she queried its meaning. 'That sounds almost biblical, Colonel... is it?'

I'm impressed, Bergmann.' It refers to missionary work but I have no idea why I quoted it.' His face took on a pained expression. 'My God, what am I saying? I'm not even religious.'

Seeing Steiner in such a light hearted mood she knew she could relax a touch more.

'I suggest you lay off anything by Wagner which shouldn't distress you too much. I'm told his works are anti-Semitic and therefore beloved by the Fuhrer or did you already know that?'

'I wouldn't know what type of music appeals to Hitler but I have never liked Wagner anyway. His music is too martial and lacks the fluidity of say Mozart or Brahms.' But then again, I don't understand how music by itself can express a particular philosophy or belief. Words can do that but not music.'

'Bergmann, your logic shames me. It was Wagner's anti-Jewish remarks which I was referring to so I stand corrected.' Putting both hands behind his head and leaning further back in his chair, Steiner disregarded the piles of paperwork lying on his desk and focussed his full attention on her. 'Tell me, what's been happening while I've been away?'

'Corporal Erlich told us about Stalingrad falling to the Soviet army and the huge number of German troops taken prisoner. He thinks they'll be treated badly.'

'He's right to think that. They will be lucky to ever see Germany again.' She saw his gaze fall away and a look of undisguised contempt crossed his face. 'It's the price they will pay for being led by a madman.'

Stunned by his frankness, she quickly attempted to change the subject. 'Does this mean more troops will be sent to the Eastern Front, Colonel? Will you have to go there again?'

Having dared to express her innermost dread, she waited for Steiner's inevitable rebuke. It never came. Instead, he leaned even further back in his chair and gazed at the ceiling.

'I would rather die than go back to that damn country, Bergmann. The Russians are one of the few nationalities you can generalise about with some degree of accuracy. Under the Tsarist regime they were little more than serfs and now under the Bolsheviks they are treated as cannon-fodder. Occasionally you might meet a half-decent specimen but in the main they are little more than animals. God help our women should they ever cross the Oder. The Ruskies will want revenge for what those murderous bastards in the Einsatzgruppen have done to their people in the name of Germany.'

'Einsatzgruppen?' Hannah's face expressed genuine puzzlement. 'I'm not familiar with that term.'

'Nor would you want to be. They're groups of soldiers recruited from the dregs of Germany's gaols that follow up behind the main front and murder civilians in their thousands; .particularly Jews and Slavs.'

Becoming even more encouraged by his continuing openness, Hannah could not resist another question. 'So are these people, these Einsatzgruppen as you call them, doing anything worse than what is happening here in Auschwitz, Colonel?'

'I'm tempted to say yes but what could be worse than what is happening here and in other camps too. But as I've told you before, there is on the one hand, the true German Army... the Wehrmacht, and then there are those indoctrinated fanatics, some of whom you have already come across in the camp. But you must never, ever, confuse the two, OK?'

Unused to Steiner's continuing frankness, her instinct told her to go no further. 'With your approval Colonel, may I go to my room and decide what to play for your guests tomorrow?'

Still locked in his thoughts, Steiner did not reply. Instead he gave a half-hearted wave of dismissal and continued to stare into the ceiling, trying not to think about his own nightmarish experience of Stalingrad to which could now be added the pointless loss of so many fellow German soldiers and comrades. In the very deepest part of his mind, the part which no other soul was privy to, his loathing for the Fuhrer increased beyond measure.

FORTY SEVEN

General Beck, accompanied by his aide de campe and a Colonel Claus Von Stauffenberg arrived promptly at 1800 hours. Greeted at the door by Steiner, all four officers hurried into the long dining room with the heavy interior door closed behind them by an unusually terse Corporal Erlich. Only Danuta with her creaking food trolley was allowed to enter the room and she too was ushered out as soon as the various dishes had been served.

Waiting nervously in the adjoining room Hannah began to sense an air of mounting tension. Even the usually imperturbable Erlich seemed on edge.

Eventually the door was thrown open and Steiner himself appeared to summon her into the smoky candle-lit room.

'Gentlemen... this young lady is Hannah Bergmann who tonight will play especially in your honour, General.'

Rising from the far side of the dining table General Beck walked round and extended his hand. 'Miss Bergmann, Ludwig Beck. I saw you perform in Dresden with the Philharmonic last year though I'm ashamed to confess I can't remember what you played but I certainly remember you.'

Taking his hand, Hannah was impressed by his firm grip. 'Thank you General; I can't recall what I played either.' Laughing, she turned towards the younger officer. 'And you sir, you are?'

'Claus Von Stauffenberg. The General and I are from Army Group Centre. I regret having missed your concert in Dresden so I cannot remind either you or General Beck what you played that night but I promise to be most attentive this evening.'

Looking directly at the witty young Colonel, Hannah couldn't help but notice the black patch covering his left eye and the empty left sleeve tucked into his uniform pocket. Embarrassed, she quickly looked away.

Turning back to the General, she asked 'do you have a particular piece of music you would like me to play for you this evening?'

'I would prefer it to be your choice Miss Bergmann. What would you suggest?' Relieved at knowing she could now play what she had rehearsed earlier, she tucked her violin into her soft neck. 'In which case I would like to begin with a light-hearted polka by Johann Strauss which I will follow with something a little more reflective by Puccini. It's from his opera 'Gianni Schicchi.'

Seeing a look of puzzlement flit cross Steiner's face, she added 'I'm sure you will recognise the melody if not the title.'

For the next ten minutes Hannah lost herself completely in the exuberance and gusto of the Polka before moving on to her interpretation of 'O Mia Caro Bambini.' Not knowing what reaction to expect from Steiner's guests she chose to close her eyes as her bow made its final draw. The silence which followed was disconcerting. Slowly opening them again she was relieved to see that General Beck was clearly entranced.

'Dear God, that was memorable, truly memorable.' Turning to Steiner, he pointed to the bottle of red wine on the table. 'Would you allow me to pull rank on you Colonel and offer this lady a drink?'

'You can try General but be aware... this lady is quite capable of speaking for herself.'

Attempting quickly to analyse Steiner's probable attitude to the General's invitation, she opted for caution. Inclining her head towards the senior soldier, Hannah gave an almost imperceptible bow. 'General Beck, Colonel Von Stauffenberg, Colonel Steiner and the unnamed gentleman in the corner;' she nodded in the direction of the aide de campe sitting at the far end of the table; 'my thanks to each of you for allowing me to entertain you this evening but I will reluctantly decline your kind invitation, General. If I were tempted to accept then I would be breaking the habit of a lifetime.'

The General appeared disappointed. 'Far be it for me to expose you to the perils of drink so instead allow me to propose a toast which we can all participate in.' Raising his glass, the General waited for Steiner and Von Stauffenberg to get to their feet and raise their glasses. 'Gentlemen... to music and a better world.'

Overawed by the unexpected courtesy extended by this hardened soldier, she made a second bow, this time deeper and more prolonged and quickly made her exit from the room.

Gaining the privacy of her room, she placed her violin on the bed and moved to the window, staring moodily at the inky blackness of the Polish night. The exuberance experienced just moments before was quickly dissipating leaving in its stead a sense of deepening sadness. Turning the light off, she stared into the cloudless Northern Hemisphere sky, her eyes simply not able to take in the countless array of stars shining in the universe above as they had since time began. She spotted the crescent shape of a new moon just rising above the forbidding silhouette of dense woodland on the distant horizon. Staring at the stars, she lost track of time until the sound of a vehicle at the front of the house, its heavy tread tyres noisily dislodging the gravel as its driver accelerated too hastily, drew her back to the present. The vehicle's fading sound lingered in the still night air for many seconds before all became quiet once more.

Compared to the sheer magnitude of the cosmos above and beyond her gaze, it suddenly came to mind just how insignificant mankind is when compared to the universe and the eons of time since its creation. Still gazing upward, she began to feel her mood not only lighten but take on an extraordinary sense of reassurance. A cold shiver ran down her spine as for the first time in her life she was able to contemplate an existence beyond the present and to look beyond, to a time when Hitler, the Nazis and their insane perversions would fade into history and the world would move on. Just thinking about this was sufficient to cause her innermost spirit to soar beyond the present, borne by the knowledge that even the horrors and evil being perpetrated in this life were but a grain of sand in the desert of time. Placing both hands on the top edge of the window frame and taking deep breaths, she induced her body to relax. She did not hear the soft tap on her door, becoming aware only when it was repeated for a second time.

'I was afraid you might be asleep Bergmann so I'm glad I caught you before you turned in.' Entering the room Steiner closed the door behind him and fumbled in the darkness for the old pine chair. 'Why are you standing in the dark; and still fully dressed? You aren't planning to escape are you?'

Realising that Steiner was still in a jocular mood induced a sense of ease. 'I was planning to slide down the drainpipe and hide in the trunk of the General's car but I lost my nerve. Besides, why would I want to leave here? Good food, good company and the offer of a glass of champagne in the company of an appreciative German general. What more could a girl want?'

'Your sense of humour does you credit, Bergmann. I was pleased you turned down the General's offer; it would not have been appropriate.'

'Oh really? In what way would it have been inappropriate?'

In the darkness of the room, she imagined she could see the all too familiar look of exasperation appear on Steiner's face.

'Bergmann, you are a Jew, a prisoner in this house and the General is a very senior officer. The two cannot mix. As much for your sake as his; trust me.'

Chastened, she chose not to say more.

'There was another reason why I didn't want you to accept the General's offer so let me show you.' Rising from his chair, Steiner made for the door and with the deft skill of a magician, returned carrying a tray holding a bottle and two glasses.

'I'm assuming your reply to General Beck was a polite excuse and you actually do drink alcohol?'

Astonished, Hannah could do no more than mumble. 'Yes I do but I haven't drunk anything other than coffee and water since my arrest.'

In which case, why not have a mild reunion with something a little stronger and see what happens. And don't turn the light on, it will disturb the ambience.'

'Colonel, you will forgive my puzzlement but a moment ago you were reminding me that Jews and senior officers do not fraternise so what has changed in the last few moments to alter that view?'

'Downstairs, Bergmann, you were a Jew. But here in this room, you are a woman... a very attractive woman.'

'But you are still a German officer, Colonel. And in the cold light of morning I think you will see that I am still a Jew.'

Laughing, Steiner rose from the creaking chair, looking out of the small window. 'How long have you been here, Bergmann?'

'In this house or in Auschwitz?'

'Both.'

'I was arrested some five or six months ago and came here via Ravensbrück and Theresienstadt. I'm sorry to be so vague but you lose track of time in the camps. I think I spent five, possibly six months in the Auschwitz camp before you brought me here... about four weeks ago?'

'It was four weeks and two days to be precise.' Reaching for the bottle poised on the edge of the marble washstand, Steiner poured two glasses of red wine, its deep ruby colour appearing black in the darkness of the room.

'And do you think our relationship has changed in these past four weeks and two days?'

Hannah forced a smile. 'Our 'relationship' as you put it, Colonel, is invariably governed by the mood you are in. Sometimes you can be very intimidating or like now, surprisingly charming. Does that answer your question?'

Instead of replying, Steiner passed Hannah a glass of wine. Raising his own glass, he tapped the two together. 'To life and the living.'

Repeating the toast, Hannah took a sip and let the smooth red liquid slip down her throat. After months of enforced abstinence the taste of alcohol felt strangely unfamiliar. Only once, following a concert in Saltzburg, had she ever been close to becoming inebriated and she had no wish to experience that sensation again.

Steiner clearly had no such inhibitions. Re-filling his empty glass he returned to the window and motioned for Hannah to join him. Together they gazed out into the forbidding darkness and the stars above.

It was Hannah who broke the awkward silence. 'After I came back to my room tonight I spent almost an hour looking at these stars. It made me realise just how insignificant we humans are and in a strange way I found that to be uplifting. Can you possibly understand that, Colonel?'

'I understand only what I can see and touch, Bergmann; not those nebulous bodies floating in space.' Steiner moved closer and she felt his hand take gentle hold of hers. 'Tell me... does your star-gazing help you to forget or maybe even ignore what is happening to mankind at this very moment?'

'How can any civilised person not be horrified by what's happening in this terrible place.' Releasing her hand, she moved slightly away from him. 'I'm also very afraid of where this might be leading; surely you can understand that?'

'Of course I do but tell me, why shouldn't we ignore the outside world however briefly and enjoy this moment and let the future, whatever it may hold, take care of itself.'

Hannah felt his hand reconnect and tighten its grip.

Guiding her arm behind her Steiner drew her towards him, his closeness causing her to involuntarily shiver.

With just the faintest glimmer of moonlight penetrating the room, the charge of sexual tension became very tangible. Steiner's uniform, exuding the now familiar smell of starch and masculinity pressed against her bare arm. Turning to face his taller figure, she knew she would be powerless to resist whatever overture he might make or to even control her own rising desire. Closing both eyes, she guiltily tried to justify what her body was feeling with the words of Ephraim. Had he guessed that a moment like this might arise when he had told her to 'do whatever you must do to survive?' Trembling with apprehension, she reached up and touched Steiner's face, her fingers barely caressing its rugged features. Within her chest, her heart felt as though it was about to burst. Outwardly powerless to control her emotions any longer, she raised her head and sought Steiner's mouth with her lips and felt herself drawn firmly to him as he encircled her yielding body with his powerful arms.

With one last desperate attempt to pull away and stop what was happening, she tried vainly to imagine the inner guilt and recrimination which she knew would inevitably follow but to no avail. Despairingly, she made a final pleading effort for him to stop. 'Please Colonel' but her voice lacked conviction. 'I'm begging you... please stop now before it's too late. Remember what you said only moments ago about German officers and Jews

'Tonight Hannah, I'm not a Germans and you're not a Jew; just a man and a woman... just you and me.'

Guiding her towards the small bed, he stopped and held her at arm's length, slowly undoing the zip on the side of her dress and inching it off her bare shoulders, letting it slip noiselessly to the floor. Leaning forward, he kissed her neck, deftly unfastening and removing her bra as he did so. Moving his hands lightly over her breasts sent shivers of excitement coursing down her spine. Engulfed by unstoppable waves of desire but trying desperately not to reciprocate, she stood helplessly as Steiner removed her silken pants. Lifting her naked body onto the bed he hurriedly threw off his own clothes, tossing them on top of her own.

'What is it that's holding you back, Bergmann? Is it because you can't bring yourself to do it?

Hardly daring to breathe, she whispered, 'no, it's because I want to do it which frightens me.'

Lying alongside him on the narrow single bed with their naked bodies barely touching, the sexual tension increased until Steiner broke the spell. Turning on his side, he leaned across to kiss her, his tongue brushing across her passive lips. As if possessed by a will of its own, her body began to press in slow rhythmic movements against the hardness of his muscular body. Now beyond the point of recall, she began to return Steiner's kisses, slowly at first but then with a passion she could never remember ever experiencing with Ephraim. She let her fingers purposely move down his body to find that part of him she now wanted to feel inside her.

As her fingers enveloped his hard penis, she heard Steiner utter a low moan but he was not about to hurry. With his hand he gently eased Hannah onto her back. As their bodies parted she closed her eyes, expecting him to move on top of her. Instead, she felt him begin to kiss her neck and then move to her breasts. Rolling his tongue around each hard nipple, he gently bit each one in turn and felt her body instinctively react as though charged by an electric shock. Feeling as if she would burst, she experienced her first orgasm of the night, welling up from within the very depth of her body. Unable to contain her emotions any longer, she heard her own pleading voice crying out in a jumbled mix of ecstasy and desire.

'Oh dear God... do it... do it.'

'Patience my little girl... we have all night.'

Hearing the calmness in his voice, she tried to regain a semblance of control over her own rampant emotions. In a futile effort to slow her racing heartbeat she began to breathe deeply.

Positioning himself above her, his weight borne on his elbows, he enveloped her breasts in his large hands, sending more shimmering waves coursing through her body. Moving downwards, his mouth lingered around her navel before letting his tongue discover that area of her body which until now had been the exclusive preserve of just one other man.

Never in her most intimate moments with Ephraim or even with Elsa Seilhamer had she ever experienced anything remotely like the emotions now enveloping every fibre of her being. With all semblance of control now lost, she allowed her legs to be gently drawn apart by Steiner's head easing its way between her soft thighs. His darting tongue began to tease the lips of her moist vagina, triggering a succession of seismic orgasms to erupt; each more intense than the previous one. With his own need for fulfilment drawing closer, Steiner pulled himself to the top of the bed and positioned himself above Hannah's prostrate body. Reaching down, she let her exploring fingers find his throbbing hardness. In total submission and wild desire, she eased her legs further apart and guided Steiner into her body.

For Hannah, the remaining hours of darkness passed in a haze of excitement, exploration and fulfilment, utterly overwhelming the sexual repression and strictures of her Jewish upbringing. Bizarrely, her marriage vows made within the sacred canopy of the Huppit flashed through her mind but then disappeared just as quickly. Desperately tired after the exertions of the night she fell into a deep slumber, neither feeling nor hearing Steiner rise from her bed and make his way along the narrow corridor to his room.

Thankfully both Steiner and Erlich had departed before Hannah awoke the next morning. Struggling to arouse herself after what she guessed was barely an hour or so of uninterrupted sleep, she felt truly awful as she stood in the newly installed shower room on the ground floor and let the hot water attempt to energise her tired body.

Hurriedly drying herself, she wiped the steam from the large mirror above the washbasin and peered at herself in the watery reflection. The wholesome food prepared by Danuta had restored her body to its former shape and more pleasingly, the dark shadows under her eyes had now completely disappeared as had the hollows in her cheeks. Stepping closer and looking down she saw that her breasts too had recovered their previous fullness and inexplicably, the brown areolas around each nipple had also regained their original dark colouration.

Dressing quickly she thought about Danuta. Would the wily Czech be aware of the overnight liaison between Steiner and herself? And Erlich too? More importantly, what would Steiner's reaction be to the realisation he had slept with a Jew; a capital offence in the depraved code of conduct enshrined within German military regulations.

In an effort to assuage her growing anxiety, Hannah hoped that Steiner would have fully calculated the risk he was taking before entering her room. Why else would he have done so? Or would he now regret what had happened even though he had clearly planned the seduction; complete with wine and glasses?

Nor had Steiner shown the slightest hesitation or reluctance to have sex with her. She vividly recalled two occasions during the night when she had momentarily drifted into a restless sleep only to be awaked by a freshly aroused Steiner again wanting to engage her tired body in yet more feverish activity.

Fully dressed and knowing she could wait no longer, she made her way downstairs and entered the breakfast room with a feigned air of confidence which she really did not feel. With Danuta aware that her own continuing presence within the unit was to some extent dependant on her relationship with Steiner, she did not anticipate any reaction or hostility from the Czech even if she was aware of what had occurred just hours before.

But thinking about Erlich did cause a pang of concern. At times she thought he looked on her with an almost paternalistic approach. Whilst his outward manner would mostly be influenced by Steiner's attitude, perhaps the mild Bavarian with his own sense of family values might well deplore the seduction which had occurred at the instigation of his senior officer.

But within minutes of entering the kitchen and exchanging pleasantries with her, she convinced herself that Danuta had no inkling of what had taken place three floors above her room in the basement.

'We have the house to ourselves, Hannah. The Colonel has taken the Corporal with him and neither will be back until late evening. Does that change your plans today?'

Relieved by Danuta's small talk and the knowledge of not having to face Steiner so soon, her immediate thought was to return to her room with its warm bed.

'I had a bad night last night. I don't know whether it was nerves or not but after I finished my performance, I just couldn't rest or get to sleep and this morning I feel totally washed out. So unless you can think of something you would like help with here, I may try and catch up with my sleep.'

As guarded as ever, Danuta did a quick visual inventory of her kitchen. 'No, I don't think so but thanks for the offer. Make the most of today. It doesn't happen too often in this house and it's unusual for both of them to be away together.'

'Are they together or just doing separate things on the same day?'

'They had breakfast together and left in the same car so presumably they are on the same mission.' The sight of Danuta busying herself around the kitchen exuded a sense of wellbeing so removed from the horrors happening less than four kilometres away within the charnel camps of Auschwitz and Birkenau. Thinking about this, she gave no thought to Danuta's next seemingly innocuous probe.

'If you're going to catch up on your sleep this morning, will you be working in the Colonel's office later?'

'I don't think so. I'm up to date with my work; at least until the Colonel returns with the next load of paperwork.'

'I thought I would clean the room while it's free of people.

'Good idea; can I help at all?'

'No thanks. You go and catch up on your sleep and I will see you later.'

It took just minutes after slipping into her still warm bed for her to fall asleep. The evocative aroma of Steiner still lingered on the single pillow they had shared and closing her eyes she could almost imagine him still lying beside her. The glowing warmth of their encounter still coursed through her body and despite her earlier shower, she could detect the moistness of Steiner's latent semen beginning to seep from her now calm body.

It was the sound of a voice, a male voice raised in anger which broke through her blissful slumber. Half awake, she thought it could only be Steiner and Erlich returning earlier than expected but listening more intently she realised that the voice was that of a stranger.

Intrigued and now fully awake, she tried to identify where the sound was coming from. Guessing it might be from the office on the first floor, she decided to get up and investigate, fervently hoping the voices were not those of Nazi officers. Without Steiner or Erlich in the house, she knew how quickly life could change for a vulnerable Jew in the Third Reich.

Approaching the small ante-room next to Steiner's office Hannah realised that the men weren't speaking in German but in what she hardly recognised as Polish. Unsure whether to enter, she hesitated in the doorway. Alerted by her footsteps on the uncarpeted floor, she found herself suddenly confronted by a burly individual dressed in an ill-fitting coarse weave suit and wearing the traditional leather cap favoured by Polish workers.

Still speaking in Polish, he directed a question to someone behind him. To her astonishment, it was the voice of Danuta who replied... in Polish!

Unsure of what was happening, she attempted to look beyond the man's burly form, calling for Danuta as she did so.

Appearing from the inner office, Danuta spoke sharply for the man to move aside. For a moment the man remained where he was, fixing Hannah with a penetrating stare before sullenly stepping to one side. Motioning her forward with a wave of her hand, she followed Danuta in to the office.

Sitting behind Steiner's desk, a second man gave her a brief nodding smile. Dressed in similar clothes to his glowering companion, the man beckoned her to ait down.

Reverting to fluent German, it was Danuta who spoke. 'You were supposed to be asleep. I thought you told me you had had a bad night and needed to catch up.'

The accusatory tone in Danuta's voice rankled Hannah. 'I was asleep until being woken by your visitors. Who are these men and why are they here in the Colonel's office?'

Obviously understanding German, the surly Pole spoke rapidly to his companion emphasising each word by pointing aggressively at Hannah in a manner which needed little interpretation.

'Hannah, for my sake please go back to your room. These men mean you no harm. If you stay here, you will make life difficult for both of us.'

'Do you mean difficult or dangerous?'

'Both! So please leave and forget you came here, OK?' The pleading tone in Danuta's voice was tangible.

'I'm not leaving until I know what these men are doing in Colonel Steiner's office and why are all these military documents spread out on his desk?'

It was the second of the two Poles who spoke. 'Danuta is right, we mean you no harm.' Taking the chair from behind the desk, he pulled it closer to Hannah. 'My name is Henryk and my friend and I are Polish and we were political prisoners here in Auschwitz before it became the death camp it now is.' Knowing he was about to go beyond the point of recall, he stopped and glanced at his companion. 'Jan and I are members of the Polish resistance and we have coerced your friend to let us have access to these military papers. Whether they will be of use I don't know but that is why we are here. As a Jew, you are as much a prisoner of the Nazis as are the Polish people. So in that sense we are on the same side fighting against the Fascists.'

Looking beyond the man calling himself Henryk, Hannah glanced up at Danuta. 'And where do you stand in all this? And to what extent have you been 'coerced' by these men?'

'Coerced?' Danuta gave a knowing smile. 'He's being kind, Hannah. I hate the Nazis as much as you so I will do anything I can to help in their defeat.'

'I find that difficult to believe. Weeks ago you told me that you couldn't wait to see Jews like me exterminated so why should I believe what you say now?'

Suddenly reverting back to Polish, Danuta spoke sharply and for a brief moment, Hannah feared for Danuta's safety.

'At least one of these men can speak German so use it so I know what they're saying.'

'I was telling them to leave and forget what they came for. I also told them I would try to convince you to forget about them too; as if this had never happened. If you then wish to report or betray me to the Colonel then at least these two people will be well clear by then.'

'Betray you! How dare you say that to me?' Struggling to control the anger in her voice she stepped closer to the Czech. 'Danuta, listen to me; every person whether Jew or Gentile, murdered by these evil people is a crime against humanity so don't dare think I would betray anyone with the courage to resist these murderers.' The pent-up vehemence in her voice was becoming difficult to contain.' You don't need to convince me to forget this meeting took place. I just wish there was something I could do to help you.'

Exchanging glances with the two Poles, Danuta turned to Hannah. 'There is something you can do. Just go back to your room and remain silent on what you have seen this morning. Think about it but don't ever mention this ever again. If you still wish to help in future then I promise there will be other things you can do to help.' The calmness in Danuta's demeanour impressed Hannah.

Employed as a cook it was clear that Danuta was also engaging with a local resistance group and evidently commanding respect from these two dangerous men.

'If I agree to do that Danuta, I want you to make me a promise.' She waited just long enough to allow Danuta to nod her assent. 'You and these two men must promise no harm will come to either the Colonel or Corporal Erlich. Without the Colonel, you and I both know what the outcome will be for both of us.'

Danuta gave one of her rare smiles. 'Outcome?' her voice became edged in mock incredulity; 'is that a new word for death, Hannah? If that's what you mean then say it.' You must know that I'm of more use to the resistance alive than dead so of course I will promise that.'

Breathing a sigh of relief, she turned to leave the room but Danuta's voice stopped her in mid-stride. 'Before you leave, Hannah, would you have any idea what the Colonel and his two guests discussed here last evening?'

Again impressed by the Czech's directness, Hannah measured her response carefully. 'I was in the room for about 20 minutes, playing for most of that time so no meaningful discussion took place while I was there. What they discussed either before or after my performance, I have no idea so I can't help you or these men.'

'But if you had overheard anything of importance, would you feel able to tell me?'

'I will need time to get used to the idea but if I decide to help then you won't need to question my commitment. You either accept it or you don't.'

'We want to believe you but we have to be careful.' It was Henryk who spoke. 'We need to know how many troops are stationed in this area. Not the soldiers in the camps but those assigned to the industrial units in this region and where they are located.'

It took Hannah a moment to consider the implication behind the Pole's question. 'That level of information would be restricted to military personnel and not to me or Danuta.'

'But you work for the officer who commands these troops so you might see a document or hear something which could be helpful to us.'

'That is extremely unlikely and even if I did, how would I be able to pass any such information to you?'

'Danuta knows how to contact us so that would not be difficult; you simply tell her what information you have.'

Anxious to get away from the office before becoming more involved she almost ran to the welcome sanctuary of her room. Still glowing inwardly from her overnight tryst with Steiner, she seriously questioned whether she would be able to divulge information garnered from a man who had risked not only his military career but his very life in consorting with her. Could I betray that trust, she wondered?

***

The Colonel returned earlier than expected accompanied by a small cadre of Wehrmacht officers. Of Corporal Erlich there was no sign. Seating themselves round the long pinewood table in the centre of the room, Steiner wasted no time in getting the meeting underway.

Waiting in the adjoining ante-room, she could not help but overhear the obvious discord being voiced by a number of Steiner' subordinates in being required to strengthen the regional defences but with fewer men to counteract the new Soviet offensive

Listening as each officer spoke, it became clear to even her non-military mind that the defeat of the German Army at Stalingrad was being seen by a number of outspoken officers in the room as an ominous turning point in the Russian campaign. One particularly vociferous voice warned that should a resurgent Red Army force the German Army to retreat, then this could well signal the beginning of the end of the war. Listening intently in the ante-room, Hannah was surprised by the noticeable lack of dissension from the other officers to this opinion.

Equally surprising was Steiner's marked disinclination to express his own thoughts as the speculation gained ground but at the conclusion of the meeting he made a point of speaking privately to those officers who had done so.

As quickly as it began, the meeting ended with a call for Steiner's driver to bring in the drinks trolley. But unlike previous gatherings and despite the flow of alcohol, there was a noticeably sombre mood among the majority of those present. Sensing this, Steiner called his fellow officers to order and proposed a toast. 'To our comrades in the Sixth Army; may God help them.'

As the last of the officers finally departed, Steiner made his way to his office. Hearing his shouted summons, she hurriedly joined him, trying to suppress her growing apprehension which had visibly increased during her long wait in the ante-room.

'Ah, there you are, Bergmann. Close the door and sit down. We need to talk.'

With Erlich not in the building, she wondered why Steiner wanted the door closed. She did not have to wonder for long.

'There were two visitors here today. Did you see either of them?'

Petrified by the bluntness of Steiner's question, she did no more than nod her head in confirmation.

'Where did you see them; was it in this office?'

Still unable to speak, she this time affirmed Steiner's question with a downward glance.

'Had you seen or met either of these two men before today?'

Swallowing hard, she finally regained her voice. 'No Colonel. I was in my room when I heard voices. Thinking it was you I came down to this office and found them here.'

'Did you speak to them?'

'Yes I did. I asked them what they were doing in your office. They told me they were Polish Police officers but their rough clothes made me think that that was improbable. As an inmate here, I wasn't in a position to challenge them but I did ask whether they were here with your knowledge?' They spoke together in Polish, pushed me aside and left.'

'And were you going to report this to me?'

'Of course but as you know, I haven't had an opportunity since you arrived back.'

Steiner leaned back in his chair, fixing Hannah with a quizzical look. 'Tell me, was Danuta with them? And a word of caution, Bergmann, be careful how you reply because I may already know the answer.'

Under Steiner's steely gaze, she once again felt her vocal cords constrict with fear. Nodding dumbly in silent assent, she felt her eyes begin to fill with tears.

'Was she already here when you came into the office?'

'Yes she was.' Her reply was barely audible.

'What was she doing? Was she speaking to them?'

'She spoke to them in Polish so I couldn't understand what was being said but from her tone I gather she was challenging their presence here too.'

'When these men left this office, did Danuta go with them?'

'Yes she did... presumably to see they left the building.'

'And did you speak to Danuta after that?'

'No, I didn't. I went back to my room and went to bed. I felt unwell after... ' her voice trailed off.

'After what, Bergmann?'

Even with her mind in turmoil, she was able to decipher the tantalising nature of the question.

'Ah... the Jew and Gentile encounter. Is that what are referring to?'

Before Hannah could respond, Steiner rose from his chair, slowly allowing his aching back muscles to straighten up before walking to the far end of the office. Stopping, he turned and faced her.

'What happened last night was a mistake... an aberration on my part and something which must never happen again. I trust you understand why.'

Hoping that Steiner had moved on from the Polish intruders, Hannah was happy to agree. 'Of course I understand.'

'You say you understand Bergmann but do you agree?'

'I'm not in a position to agree or disagree, Colonel. It's your decision... not mine.'

Animated, Steiner strode back to his chair, letting the upper backrest take his weight as he leaned forward. 'I told you when you first arrived here that you would not last long in this world. But you settled in well and I gave you an undertaking that as long as I remained in this posting both you and the Czech woman would be safe. Do you recall that conversation?'

'Of course I do and I remain deeply grateful for that promise.'

'Then why did you agree to help those two Poles who were here today?'

Steiner's unexpected reversion to the Poles and his deadly accusation struck with heart stopping force. Struggling to regain a semblance of self-control, she felt her heart begin to race to the point where it seemed about to explode within her.

'Look at me Bergmann; why were you prepared to help those damned Poles.'

Despite knowing her next few words could jeopardise her very life, she could only offer a mumbled response. 'How did you know?'

'Because Danuta's two friends were arrested shortly after leaving here and under questioning they talked. Too much for my likening which is why we are now having this discussion?'

Forcing herself to look directly into the eyes of the man who only hours before had taken her body to heights of unknown passion, she dared to pose the question which would seal her fate. 'What will you do with Danuta and me?'

Sucking air through his teeth, Steiner returned her stare. 'That's a good question Bergmann. Tell me; are you as involved as Danuta appears to be?'

'Involved with those men or the Resistance?'

'Either.'

'I have already told you what happened, Colonel. I had never seen either of those two men before today and I wasn't aware there was a Polish Resistance.'

'And Danuta? Did she let them into the house and into this office? They couldn't have gained entry without help. And how did they know that Corporal Erlich wouldn't be here?'

'I'm not able to answer either of those questions, Colonel. I'm sorry.'

'As well you might be, Bergmann.' Clearly agitated, Steiner stood upright and angrily kicked the chair away from him. 'Look, I want to believe what you tell me but I'm also aware that a member of this household is involved with the Resistance and that is a major problem for me.'

Sensing a change in Steiner's manner, Hannah hoped he might be wanting to bring the intrusion to a conclusion. 'Would it help if you could accept that Danuta is a Czech and not a German? Why should she not want to help to resist those who have invaded her country? If she was a soldier, she would become a prisoner of war and kept alive whereas if you send her back to the camp she will be murdered.'

'You ignore one important precept Bergmann. Danuta is a civilian... not a soldier and therefore not covered by the rules of war. Danuta has allied herself to the Polish Resistance who are invariably shot when they are captured.'

'That's barbaric; she doesn't deserve to die. And who will cook your food if you send her back to the camp?'

Raising his hands in feigned supplication, Steiner's grim countenance broke into a smile. 'I swear to God that only you would use that excuse to spare a death penalty.'

She knew she had to keep him talking. 'I seem to recollect Napoleon once saying that Armies fought on their stomachs. If he really did say that then it becomes a perfectly good reason not to punish someone who prepares such excellent meals for you.'

Looking at her with amused disbelief, Steiner tried not to laugh. Sitting down, he drew a deep breath, held it for several seconds and then noisily expelled it. 'Bergmann, I want you to listen to me very carefully. You need to grasp the fact that both you and Danuta are on the opposite side of this war to myself. Any act committed against the Fatherland and deemed treasonable is punishable by death. That is why Danuta must be sent back to the camp for knowingly assisting a Resistance group who are sworn enemies of Germany. By saying she is a good cook is quite absurd and not worthy of your intelligence.'

'Then why are you still smiling.' The audacity of the question instantly replaced the expression of humour on Steiner's face with a look of amazement. Seeing this, she realised she had gone too far. It was Steiner who spoke first.

'The fact you were a musical prodigy probably allowed you to say and do what you liked in your exclusive world of classical music but you no longer live in that spoiled environment. It finished when you were arrested. Wake up to that fact and you may survive; forget it and you will die. And one last thing;' he paused, as if to add gravitas to what he was about to say next; 'if you ever dare speak to me like that again, then you will accompany Danuta back to where you both came from. Is that clear?'

'You make yourself perfectly clear, Colonel. Can I be equally clear? Not only will you lose a good cook but you will also lose your clerk, nurse, entertainer and Jewish bed mate. But as such a coupling must never happen again, then I suppose the latter service won't be too much of a loss.'

Fuming with anger, Steiner leapt to his feet, his tired body seeming to explode as he strode round the desk and struck Hannah hard across her face. With her senses reeling from the force of the blow she fell to the floor, frantically trying to regain her equilibrium. Clutching at the chair for support she managed to pull herself upright and through eyes displaying a myriad of whirling stars she looked to see where Steiner was. She felt her mouth filling with a mixture of warm blood and bitterness as her stomach went into shock. As her vision slowly cleared, she saw he had retreated to the far end of the room. Strangely, she felt no pain from the blow, only the befuddled effect of being disorientated. Instinct told her to get out of the room but with her head still spinning, she knew she would probably fall down again. In despair, she closed her eyes and began to take deep breaths; advice given by Ephraim seemingly light years ago as a cure for dizziness and nausea.

She vaguely became aware of Steiner approaching and expecting further blows, she wrapped her arms around her head in a futile gesture of wanting to protect herself. Instead, she felt his strong hands take hold of her shoulders and roughly pull her to her feet; his face a mask of unedifying anger.

'You deserved that and more, you spoiled bitch. Maybe Goebbels was right about you people; treat a Jew with kindness and they spit in your face.' Pushing her roughly back onto her chair, he stood over her, glowering, as if deciding what to do next. Turning her head to avoid looking at him made Steiner even angrier. Forcing her head upward he leaned closer. 'You appear to have forgotten that you are a prisoner here, Bergmann; and more to the point, a Jewish prisoner held by a Government systematically eradicating people like you from the face of this earth. Do you understand that grim reality or do I have to knock it into that arrogant skull of yours?' Steiner stopped speaking, his temper still very much to the fore.

Meeting his eyes, Hannah knew that all was lost with this man. 'Do what you must, Colonel. There's nothing I can say that will change whatever you decide to do so go ahead and do it. If you want me out of here then send me back now; frankly I've got beyond the point of caring.' Defiantly returning Steiner's threatening stare, she rose to her feet. 'Unless you have something more you wish to add, Colonel, then may I remove myself from your presence and go to what used to be my room?' In the icily cold silence which followed she hoped that Ephraim would have been proud of her had he been here.

Listening to Hannah's declaration of intent, Steiner realised he was no longer in control of the situation. By openly stating her wish to return to Auschwitz and inevitable death she had nullified whatever threat he could use to save her from herself. His mind went to Danuta and the events of that day and it was several long moments before he spoke. 'No you may not go to what 'used to be your room'.' You will stay here and listen to what I have to say.' Seeing Hannah give a barely perceptible shake of her head as if to say' I've heard all this several times over but go ahead' was sufficient to cause the hackles on his neck to rise but this time he managed to control his anger.

'Unlike Danuta you told me you were an innocent party when these two Poles came here today. I choose to believe you Bergmann because as much as you hate us Germans, you like life more and you are sensible enough not to jeopardise it. Is that a fair interpretation of your emotions?' Grim faced, he stared at Hannah, not expecting her to reply. 'So when you say you want to voluntarily return to that death camp down the road then I am disappointed.'

'Why would you be disappointed, Colonel? One less Jew in this world isn't likely to cause a German like you to lose any sleep or am I misreading something here?'

The silence which followed was almost physical. Knowing he could not control himself, Steiner again retreated to the far end of the room where he lashed out with his heavy boot against an unyielding bookcase. 'Damn you, woman; have you not absorbed a single word I've said? I ask the questions here... not you.'

'Is that because you are German whereas I am a prisoner?... Sorry, I should have said a Jewish prisoner or is it because you can't bring yourself to admit you are as much a Nazi as those other animals in the camp.'

Hearing this, Steiner realised he was being given two distinct choices by this infuriating woman. Not only was she now controlling the discussion but the implications stemming from it too.

'Bergmann, come her.' The tone of his voice was truly frightening. 'For my sake if not your own, do not say one more word.' Watching as she approached him he was still unsure as to which of those two choices he would make.

Stopping at what she hoped would be a safe distance in case he resorted to further violence, she never once lost eye contact with him.

Taking a deep breath, he closed the gap between them. 'Look, there can be no excuse for hitting you and I am deeply sorry. I could say I've had a long tiring day, I could tell you of the increasing pressure I'm under as the Red Army gets ever closer but the truth is that I am a violent person. I try hard to contain it but it seems to be part of my make-up and I suppose it's that which make me a good soldier.' He took a deep breath feeling strangely relieved at being able to unburden himself.

'You and I come from vastly different backgrounds and maybe that makes our relationship difficult. But in future I will do my level best whatever the circumstances to control myself so there can be no question of you going back to the camp. Can we agree on that, Also, it wouldn't be too sensible to lose two members of my personal staff in a single day.'

'So does that mean you have changed your mind about Danuta?'

Hearing Danuta's name, she saw Steiner pull away and walk back towards the desk. Intuitively she sensed danger.'

'That will not be possible. Danuta and her two Partisan friends were executed two hours ago... on my personal order.'

FORTY EIGHT

For the next two days her emotions vacillated between grief and anger. Thoughts of the many kindnesses extended by Danuta kept coming to mind. She recalled her misgivings before allowing Danuta to cut her hair and how the initially antagonistic Czech had given her the black dress which had belonged to her dead sister. And now Danuta too was dead; killed on the order of the man whom she had shared her body with. Thinking about it in the quietness of her room, the stifling parameters of her Jewish upbringing seemed almost something to be yearned for. 'If only I could turn the clock back' she thought.

Erlich too was unusually quiet to the point of being almost morose. Normally a well-ordered man by nature, even he now occasionally railed against the loss of Danuta in the smooth running of the household even though he had never previously shown any noticeable appreciation of her contribution to it.

For her part, she went about her duties as before, carefully avoiding any reference to Danuta whilst in Steiner's presence. For his part, Erlich had taken upon himself the task of preparing the household meals but even the availability of fresh vegetables and eggs from Danuta's chickens could not hide the fact that many of his offerings were invariably overcooked or barely edible.

On the third day, salvation appeared at the front door of the house in the form of Miriam Karlinski. Escorted by a soldier and breathless from his quickened pace, Miriam could only throw her arms around Hannah's neck as they greeted each other with genuine affection. The exuberance felt at seeing her friend momentarily subdued the wretchedness she continued to feel at the shocking fate which had befallen Danuta.

Ordered by Erlich to take Miriam to the basement room previously occupied by the Czech, Hannah could barely contain herself. 'Miriam, I just can't believe it's you. Of all the people who could have been sent here. When did you know you were coming?'

Having regained her breath, Miriam looked round the tidy room which still contained many of Danuta's personal items.

'I was told earlier this morning. I had no idea I would be coming to the same house as you.' Placing her hands on Hannah's shoulders, she quickly appraised her. 'Look at you, girl; you seem to have blossomed since coming here so maybe it's going to be a good move for me as well.' Looking over her shoulder, Miriam asked the question which Hannah was dreading. 'So what happened to the woman who was here before me?'

'Can we talk about that later, Miriam? I want to enjoy this moment a little longer.' Clutching at Miriam's hands, Hannah pulled her former room-mate to her. 'It's so good to see you again. We never had time to say goodbye and I thought I would never see you again. But suddenly, here you are.'

Returning her friend's hug, Miriam tried again. 'Now tell me, what did happen to my predecessor in this place?'

'Your what?'

'The woman I'm replacing; what happened to her?'

'She was shot. The Colonel had her executed for being involved with the Polish Resistance. I still can't believe it happened, Miriam; it was all so sudden.'

'Any more sudden than what's happening down the hill?'

'You mean in the camp?'

'Of course I mean the camp. Have you forgotten what's happening down there? Since you came here, the transports have increased ten-fold.' Miriam waved her hands to dramatise the point she was making. 'That means more people than ever are being murdered every day. So if your friend was mixed up with the Resistance then what's one more death in this place?'

Shocked by Miriam's callousness, it took her a few moments to come to terms with it. 'I suppose it was because we lived in this house together. She was a decent woman and why shouldn't she want to help those fighting against the Nazis?'

'No reason at all Hannah but if you get caught then you must expect to pay the price. I take it you were fond of this woman?'

'We weren't close but she didn't deserve to be shot especially as the Colonel had the power to prevent it.'

'But why should he. He's a German officer and if she was mixed up with the Resistance then her mistake was getting caught. Compare her death with those thousands of innocent people and particularly the children who are being slaughtered every day, Do they deserve to die?' Miriam paused. 'I think you've lost your sense of perspective, Hannah.'

'Keep talking like that Miriam and you should get on well with the Colonel.'

'Well you seem to have managed fairly well for a Jew. You must tell me how you do it.'

Slightly irritated by Miriam's cold rationality she decided to change the subject. 'Can I make you a coffee; its real coffee if you can remember what that tastes like? Then I think you should report to Corporal Erlich. He's responsible for everything that goes on in this house, including us.'

'What's he like... this Corporal?'

'He's a thoroughly decent man but don't get on the wrong side of him. He's also fiercely loyal to the Colonel.'

'And what about you, Hannah; where do your loyalties lie?'

'It's not a matter of loyalty Miriam, it's about survival. Remember giving me that advice in the camp?'

'I do and it seems to have worked in your case. At least you're still alive!'

'We both are and long may that continue. At least I think we are safer here than we were in the central sorting office. Has much has changed since I left?'

'It was called 'Kanada' or have you forgotten that too? To answer your question, everything has changed including the SS Corporal. He wasn't too bad but all the women and the two Kapo's have gone plus a lot of the inmates who replaced the women you would have known.'

'When you say 'gone' you mean they've been murdered too?'

Miriam gave a snort... a habit Hannah had all but forgotten. 'The amounts of cash, gold, jewellery and other valuables going through that Centre is just unbelievable so the Nazis now change the inmates every few weeks so no one can keep a check on it. It's no longer the refuge it was when you were there. There are now thirty huts doing what we did and they still can't keep up with the mountains of stuff pouring in to the camp.'

'So how have you managed to survive if all those inmates we worked with have been killed?'

Taking hold of Hannah by the shoulders, Miriam fixed her with a steely stare. 'You don't ask questions like that in Auschwitz, Hannah. You do what you have to do to survive.'

'Miriam, you can have no idea of what I may have done and I don't want to even guess at how you have managed to survive so let's drop the subject, shall we?'

Miriam's reply was opaque. 'Knowing how naïve you were when we last worked together, I doubt whether you have actually done anything to still be alive; you haven't had to.'

Standing up, Miriam circled Hannah. 'Just look at you; despite all that shit we were forced to eat in the camp you somehow managed to retain your attractiveness and since coming to this place, you are even more beautiful.'

Blushing, Hannah gave an embarrassed wave of her hand.

'But now look at me, Miss Beauty Parlour. I'm middle-aged and look much older so what have I got going for me after ten months in that hellish place?'

Unsure whether Miriam was expecting her to respond, Hannah said nothing.

I'll tell you what I've got; it's called a brain, a street-wise brain. I make connections with the people who count; the Kapo's, the guards and tell them what they want to know. Which inmates are stealing food and valuables from Kanada; which women the men can take when they come calling at night? These are the things the guards want to know so I use my eyes and my head, Hannah, and as these people are due to die anyway, what's wrong in bringing their date with death forward by a few weeks?'

Listening to Miriam's cold, analytical logic, a feeling of revulsion swept over her before an even more chilling realisation dawned on her. 'So was it you who arranged for the Kapo to rape me?'

With arms folded in front of her frail frame, Miriam exuded belligerence. 'Yes it was me and I'll tell you why? You probably won't want to remember this but the Kapo who selected those Polish women for the brothel that morning also wanted you as his personal woman but once he tired of you, you would have been passed on and fucked by Rumanians, Latvians, Slavs and God knows who else before being replaced and sent off to the gas chamber. So your short journey to Block 23 that night was a price worth paying to keep you alive and out of the Puffhaus. So spare me your anger and maybe show a touch of gratitude instead.'

For a brief moment she was unable to fully grasp the significance of Miriam's admission.

Staring at her erstwhile friend, she gave her the coldest of looks. 'I'm going to my room to think about what you've just told me. In time I may come round to being grateful but at this very moment I want you to know that you caused me to experience the most horrific happening in my life and because of that I may decide I never want to speak to you again.' Turning away, she threw one final jibe. 'And one more thing. However much you attempt to justify your actions, you are nothing more than an informer and that is probably the reason why you've been sent to this house.'

Leaving the room, Hannah almost collided with the pensive figure of Corporal Erlich quietly standing in the shadow of the lower staircase. Wordlessly, they passed without either of them acknowledging the other.

Following her charged conversation with Miriam, the atmosphere in the house for the next few days became edgy and difficult. Steiner and Erlich were spending an inordinate amount of time behind the closed door of the office whilst Miriam kept a discreet distance within the kitchen area. In the small ante-room, Hannah attempted to relieve the boredom by occupying herself with mundane office work until that too ran out.

Wondering how to occupy her time for the next few hours, she was relieved when Erlich appeared and told her to tell Miriam to provide a pot of coffee after which she was free to go to her room.

Passing the order on to Miriam without comment, she chose to go into the garden before returning to her room on the third floor.

The pleasant warmth of the sun on her bare arms served to emphasise the coldness of the house. Unlike Ephraim whose skin was pale and susceptible to sun-burn, her own golden toning reflected a lineage of forebears probably from much warmer climes.

Seated on the bench at the far end of the garden, she watched Danuta's chickens scratching around in their enclosure. Still dazed by her sudden death, she bitterly recalled the qualified promise of safety given to her and the Czech by Steiner; a promise which had been disbelieved with uncanny prescience by Danuta.

Closing her eyes, she turned her face to the sun and attempted to clear her mind. Overhead, creamy windblown contrails marking the passage of aircraft flying at high altitude laced the Polish sky. From the nearby woods the raucous sound of crows disturbed the stillness of the morning, competing with the clucking sounds coming from the dozen or so chickens forever searching for grubs behind the wire fence of their pen. As much prisoners as herself she thought moodily.

'So... what have we here? I hope you aren't sleeping on the job Bergmann? Does that mean I'm working you too hard?' It was Steiner, approaching silently by walking through the unkempt grass.

Hearing his voice she irrationally felt a sense of guilt. 'No, I wasn't sleeping, Colonel; just resting my eyes and enjoying the warmth.'

She noticed that Steiner too had discarded his uniform jacket and had also removed the detachable collar of his white uniform shirt thereby creating the appearance of relaxed affability made more pronounced by the red non-military braces he was wearing. Carrying two cups, he offered one to Hannah.

'It's coffee; Erlich thought you might need a drink.' Sitting down, he offered the cup to her and gingerly leaned back against the weather-beaten crosspiece bearing a strange crest carved by some long forgotten turner or carpenter.

'Can you bring yourself to speak with me or am I still in purdah?'

'I'm not sure what you mean by purdah but as I work for you, you can say whatever you like to me.'

'But you're still angry with me.'

'I think upset would be more appropriate but yes, I am angry as well because it was all so unnecessary. Danuta was a good person' adding with a degree of acidity, 'unlike us Jews!'

A faint trace of amusement spread across Steiner's face. 'Are you about to tell me we shot the wrong woman? If that's the case then we can easily rectify that mistake. But only in part of course.' He laughed at his own mocking humour. 'Because there's no way we can restore the Czech woman back to good health.'

'That wasn't what I meant Colonel and your attempt at humour is misplaced too. Danuta died for no other reason than wanting to help free her country' stopping herself from adding 'from barbarous people like you.'

Expecting Steiner to react with his customary anger, she was relieved when he merely looked at her with an expression which reminded her of a father about to remonstrate with a small child for some minor infraction.

'Knowing what a delicate and soft-centred woman you are, I can understand why you were so upset at what happened to the Czech woman but what you won't know is that she was more heavily involved in the Resistance than she ever revealed to you, if indeed she ever did tell you of her extra-curricular activities.'

Guessing he wanted her to react to his remarks, she first waited to gather courage. 'You try and make the poor woman seem like some sort of Mata Hari whereas in reality Danuta was a cook for God's sake.' She hoped she had correctly remembered the name of the woman executed by the Germans for being an alleged spy in the Great War.

Unperturbed by her remarks, Steiner pressed on. 'I don't expect you to understand this but there are a number of other very critical things happening in the wider world and the last thing I can afford is to have a member of my household identified as a spy and then be seen to do nothing about it.'

'As always Colonel, you are unarguably correct so there isn't much point in you saying anything more. Danuta is dead and that's the end of it.'

'The end of Danuta but I want to speak about Miriam. How well do you know her?'

Puzzled by his question, she decided to be non-committal. 'We worked together in the Sorting Centre but apart from that, I know nothing about her.'

'But I understand you had an argument with her when she told you she had informed on other inmates; is that true or not?'

'It is true but then who wouldn't do that if it kept you alive.'

'Is that a rhetorical question or would you like me to answer it?'

'No, please... go ahead.' Since their sexual encounter, Hannah felt more comfortable in making conversation with him; subject always to his mood.

Finishing his coffee, Steiner balanced his cup on the wooden arm-rest. 'I've mentioned before that there are a number of officers like myself and your friend Von Hartmann who joined the military to fight the Bolsheviks and the British but in the wake of our advances, there are thousands of innocent people, not just Jews, who are being systematically slaughtered by gangs of criminals masquerading as soldiers. This isn't what we are fighting for. But as Germany conquers more and more countries, the harder it will become to get rid of a leader who will eventually overreach our military resources and bring Germany to the edge of utter destruction.' He looked at Hannah for a reaction but none was forthcoming. Perturbed he asked, 'you do understand what I'm telling you, Bergmann?'

Unsettled by Steiner's frightening admission, she heard herself blurt out 'why are you telling me this? How can you forget the thousands of innocent people who are daily being slaughtered in German concentration camps so forgive me if I fail to understand the difference.Its murder whichever way you care to look at it.'

'I'm telling you because I may require your help.'

As Steiner's words assumed focus, Hannah could barely stop herself from wanting to laugh out loud. 'Colonel, you seem to forget another important fact. I am a prisoner here... and a Jew... remember?' She waited for this to sink in. 'So how on earth do you think that I can be of help in any meaningful way? It's just too ludicrous for words.' She gave a nervous laugh which died in her throat.

Stung by her mild rebuke, Steiner reasserted himself, the soft tone now laced with a hint of abrasiveness. 'Stop talking and listen. I need you to re-establish your connection with the new woman. Gain her confidence and find out what she's up too and who she is reporting to. That shouldn't tax your integrity too much.' His face attempted to mask his concern. 'Our new housekeeper is an informer who I think has been placed here for a purpose.' Hoping for a glimmer of interest he paused but wisely, Hannah chose to remain silent.

Annoyed by her reticence, Steiner tried again. 'You appear to have lost that normally loquacious voice of yours?'

'No, Colonel, my voice is as loquacious as it ever was but to answer your question, why not have Miriam sent back to the camp; surely that would be the simplest solution.'

'And what reason would I give to justify that?'

'You could say she can't cook which wouldn't be too far from the truth.'

Unable to hide his amusement, Steiner' face broke into a boyish grin. Taking a firm hold on Hannah's hand, he squeezed her soft fingers together. 'Bergmann... have you understood the import of anything I've just said to you or do I need to repeat myself?'

Aware of his increasing annoyance and realising she may have already pushed his patience to the limit, she gave a quick nod of understanding.

'Since Hitler came to power there have been a number of attempts on his life. They have either failed or been detected with predictable consequences to those who have tried' He looked up with the air of a school teacher about to address an errant child. In any democracy there must always be room for dissent but this isn't a democracy. What we have in our country is a one-man dictatorship with military decisions now being taken by a madman who will ultimately lead Germany to defeat.' Steiner released Hannah's hand and lifted her chin, his piercing grey eyes boring into hers. 'Can you now begin to understand what I am saying to you?'

Hearing Steiner, a senior Army Wehrmacht officer speaking to her, a Jewish prisoner, in such detail had a numbing effect on her. Jerking her hand away from his, she moved further along the bench, trying to put space between them. When she spoke there was alarm in her voice.

'Colonel, what you've just told me is pure madness. The world is at war and do you really think a small number of officers, however well intentioned, will be able to change what is happening? Even if you managed to kill Hitler, someone else will simply take his place and the killing will continue as it does now. Why can't you can understand that?'

Distressed, she stood up and moved away from Steiner. 'Colonel, please listen to me. If the wrong person heard what you have just told me then we would both be killed... instantly!'

Calmly, Steiner beckoned to her; 'come back and sit down.'

Fearful and uncertain, she remained rooted to the spot but then found herself complying with Steiner's summons. Sitting down, she made a conciliatory move towards him. 'I can tell from your expression that you aren't going to listen to me, are you.'

'No I'm not. In fact I can't. Unless someone takes action then our country will perish; swallowed up by the Russians, Poles and God knows who else.'

Becoming slightly more comfortable by Steiner's disarming frankness and with her own confidence beginning to grow, she couldn't stop herself disputing his last remark. 'It's not **'our'** country or have you forgotten telling me that Jews like me have no country; made stateless because in your opinion we never assimilated or has it slipped your mind.

'Stop playing politics and answer my question. Will you assist me or not?'

'And if I say no... what will you do?' The chilling realisation behind her own question struck home before Steiner could reply. 'You would kill me, wouldn't you?'

'Don't make me answer that.' His voice became conciliatory. 'Look, you Jews must hate the Nazis more than any other people on this earth so don't fight me.'

'Why would I fight you? If you hadn't arranged for me to come here, I would have been one of those women from Camp Kanada who are now dead, thanks to friend Miriam.'

He gave out a long sigh. 'Dare I take that as an affirmative 'yes', Bergmann?'

Still in shock by the candour of Steiner's admission, she couched her response with a degree of caution; 'how much more affirmative would you like me to be?'

Pushing himself upright, Steiner took a long moment to apprise the woman he was now entrusting with his very life. 'For the moment Bergmann, that will be sufficient.'

***

Re-establishing a relationship with Miriam proved easier than anticipated. The morning after her discussion with Steiner and with him again in Berlin, Miriam brought a peace offering to the office.

'I thought you might like some nibbles to have with your coffee, Hannah. I'm also making choulent for our supper this evening so I hope you aren't a vegetarian.' Without waiting for a reply she placed the small wooden tray on the side of Hannah's desk and made to leave the room.

'Miriam... do you have a moment? I would like to speak with you.'

Halted by the softness of Hannah's request, Miriam turned and removed several files from the chair in front of Hannah's desk. 'Would you like me to sit or stand?'

'You'll be more comfortable sitting down so just pass those files to me.'

Sitting down, Miriam waited for Hannah to speak.

'Look, I'm sorry I reacted as I did when we last spoke. Since living here, I've tried to put the horror of the camp out of my mind but when you told me that every one of those women we had worked with were dead, it just brought everything back again.'

'I guess I read you wrong Hannah. I thought you were upset because of what I told you about the Kapo.'

Hating what she was about to say, she looked away from Miriam's gaze, pretending to adjust the strap on her shoe. 'How can anyone be judgemental in a place like this? It's all about survival. Nothing else matters. I realise that now.'

'So does that mean we can be friends again?'

'Miriam, how can we not be friends?' Raising her coffee cup, Hannah proffered a mock toast... 'to friendship and survival.'

'I'll drink to that later but for now, can you answer my question. Are you a vegetarian or not?'

Relieved at the success of her duplicity, her reply was jovial. 'Provided its beef and not pork then choulent will be fine!'

FORTY NINE

Never in his life had Ephraim Fischer felt more apprehensive and vulnerable as he approached the main gate of Theresienstadt camp. Looking beyond the barrier, he could see no sign of life other than for several off-duty personnel chatting to each other, one drawing on an old fashioned clay pipe, its brown tobacco-stained bowl puffing out clouds of grey smoke. Dressed in the uniform of a Czech camp guard, Ephraim knew his life would depend on the next thirty seconds or so.

Approaching the pedestrian exit gate he tried not to make eye contact with the German sentry manning the barrier who for his part displayed little more than bored disinterest in him. As the camp physician, he had treated many of the German military personnel and as he drew closer to the elderly soldier, he hoped this man had not been one of them. To be recognised now would mean arrest and instant reckoning for his calculated murder of the Camp Adjutant.

Fully aware of Ephraim's crime, the young Lieutenant, himself a parent, had granted him a tacit stay of execution to allow him to painlessly end the lives of twelve young children who he knew were destined for the horror of the train journey to the gas ovens of Auschwitz. Like a lonely sentinel Ephraim had stood alongside each child and watched as their innocent young lives had painlessly ebbed away; ensuring that no more earthly harm could be inflicted upon their innocent souls.

With a final glance at the children, he had quietly closed the door and began the short walk to his appointment with the Nazi Lieutenant and his inevitable death. Instead he had been intercepted by one of the two Czech guards who had earlier been reluctant to obey the German Overseer's order to assault him during his distressing farewell to Hannah. The Czech had offered Ephraim a proposition. He and a fellow guard were preparing to desert, complete with their Mauser rifles and ammunition, to join the growing number of Czech partisans. In addition to their weapons, both had been ordered to procure or steal a supply of scarce medical supplies to take with them. By breaking into the camp infirmary they knew they risked being discovered and shot. How much simpler they reasoned, if the Medical Officer, rumoured to be under imminent sentence of death, were to give them access to a harvest of medical supplies in return for his own freedom. It was a decision which took Ephraim just seconds to make.

Smiling as though he hadn't a care in the world, Ephraim had brandished a folded piece of paper purporting to be his Czech identity card at the bored soldier who barely nodded in return. Once past the gate, he had to force himself to walk normally and not break into a run. Clear of the camp, he had met with the two absconding guards and for the next ten days they were moved from location to location in a number of safe houses provided by members of the partisan group.

The need to lie low to avoid recapture for the first two weeks or so occasionally caused him to wonder whether he had merely exchanged one form of prison for another but for the first time in his life, Ephraim began to feel an increasing sense of purpose in being part of an organised group fighting back against the hated German occupiers. And being a stateless Jew more than offset any suspicion pertaining to his former German nationality. Unlike their Russian and Polish neighbours, the Czechs had more readily accepted and assimilated many of those Jews escaping from the murderous pogroms committed by close neighbouring countries in Eastern Europe.

As Partisan resistance became more organised and better equipped, the Germans military resorted to murderous reprisals against the civilian population. Villages in the vicinity of Partisan activity were frequently razed to the ground with their populations either shot or incarcerated in communal halls and buildings which were then set on fire. Those managing to escape from the blazing infernos were murderously cut down by machine guns strategically positioned around the burning pyres.

Within his own Partisan group, Ephraim had quickly organised a small medical team which included a young Jewish medical student, Tomas Lampl, and two women with varying levels of nursing experience. Without access to hospital equipment or operating facilities they were forced to administer treatment literally 'on the hoof' to the growing number of casualties. But despite the tiredness and ever-present threat of capture and execution, Ephraim Fischer, MD, had never been more committed to a cause.

Following its bitterly fought victory at Stalingrad, the Red Army was growing in confidence and with renewed supplies of aircraft, arms and munitions supplied from its manufacturing bases in the furthermost parts of the Soviet Union and supplemented by its Western Allies, it began to push the German Army back towards the German/Polish border. Ephraim's unit was ordered to move eastwards to engage the stubbornly retreating Wehrmacht, each step unwittingly taking him closer to Auschwitz and Birkenau.

FIFTY

Following her rapprochement with Miriam, Hannah was relieved to be once more on friendly terms with a woman who like herself, was doing everything within her control to find safety against a backdrop of mayhem and murder. The penetrating stench of burning flesh incessantly pouring from the blackened chimneys of the crematoria bore silent testimony to the ceaseless and unremitting slaughter of innocent lives.

Pushing the knowledge of Miriam's duplicity to the back of her mind, she once more found her former friend an easy person to like. In many ways she reminded her of Frieda; the same no-nonsense approach to life which conversely gave a chilling insight as to why she was still alive.

When it came, the approach was disguised in such a subtle way that she almost missed it.

'Do you ever wonder what it would be like to get away from this place, Hannah?

Miriam put the question while she appeared to be busying herself in the vegetable garden with Hannah taking a break from her office routine.

Caught off-guard, her reply bordered on the absurd. 'Oh I think of nothing else, Miriam. One day I'm in Italy, the next day Monte Carlo and where else?' Laughing at her own vivid imagination she took a seat on the bench she had so recently shared with Steiner.

Undeterred, Miriam tried again. 'I'm being serious Hannah. The Colonel is always going somewhere and as you are his secretary cum general factotum, wouldn't you like to go with him?'

Undecided whether Miriam was simply being friendly or pursuing a quite different agenda, her reply was circumspect.

'Don't let life here delude you into thinking we can come and go as we please. We are as much prisoners here as we were in the camp.'

'I'm not forgetting that or where we are. How can I with that stench in my nostrils every second of every day. But for you, I'm sure the Colonel could arrange whatever he wanted to.'

Cautiously, Hannah rose from the bench and approached Miriam. 'But why would he do that for me? Or even for you?'

'Not me Hannah; it's you he will do things for.' Placing her hand on Hannah's shoulder Miriam lowered her voice. 'Look in the mirror, girl. You are so beautiful yet so innocent about men. 'Do you really believe the Colonel just happened to be in Block 23 that night or that it was purely a coincidence that he stumbled upon you and that Romanian pig or do you think there was some other reason?'

Sensing this was the approach which Steiner had spoken of, she cautiously decided to lace truth with a degree of subtlety. 'You ask whether there was a reason for him being there that night and then bringing me here. Of course there was but you are wrong in thinking it was down to my looks. Frankly, I don't think he has any interest in me as a woman.'

'If that's the case then what was the reason?'

'I met his cousin, a senior officer at one of my concerts in Berlin. He knew I was a Jew and likely to end up here so he asked the Colonel to look out for me. Ironically, if it hadn't been for the curiosity of the SS guard at the selection ramp, I would have been dead long before the Colonel could act on his cousin's behest. So whatever you may think, you could not be more wrong.'

'Hannah... d'you mind if I sit down?' Moving along the bench to make room for her, the sense of urgency in Miriam's demeanour began to ring alarm bells in Hannah's mind.

'Look, whatever the reason may be, I do know a thing or two about men and from the way the Colonel looks and speaks when you are in the room it's obvious that he's very attracted to you so why not use that to our advantage?

A tolerant smile flitted across Hannah's face. 'Miriam, I think you may have lost your grip on reality so please listen to what I'm about to say.' He's a senior German officer and I'm a Jew; a prisoner just like you. Surely you can understand that?'

'So d'you think he's not like other men?' She gave Hannah time to ponder on her question. 'For God's sake girl, it's you who may have lost touch with reality!' Her voice reflected her growing exasperation. 'His wife died a year before the war began so he's a lonely man; a man you can use to our advantage.

'I don't understand what you mean when you say to 'our' advantage. And how did you know about his wife?'

An uneasy look briefly flitted across Miriam's face causing Hannah to feel even more perturbed. 'I've worked for Colonel Steiner for several months now and I never knew anything about his personal life so how do you know what happened to his wife?'

Sensing this to be a critical moment in her ploy to involve Hannah, it was several seconds before Miriam answered. 'Hannah, you need to believe me when I tell you this is our best chance to remain alive... at least until the Russians get here then we will need to play a new game.'

'Game!' She couldn't contain her exasperation any longer. 'How can you use that word? This isn't a game for heaven's sake. It's a matter of life and death even this far outside the camp or have you forgotten what happened to Danuta? So exactly what game are you referring to?' The forced brusqueness in her voice surprised even herself. 'I'm waiting Miriam... you either answer my question or I'm returning to the house.'

Miriam drew a deep breath and glanced round the small garden area as if to assure herself they were alone. 'I've been told to record who the Colonel meets, their names and rank and if possible get him to become attracted to you for obvious reasons. However, knowing your naivety that may be easier said than done.'

Unconsciously holding her breath, Hannah attempted to digest Miriam's words. 'But why would anyone want to spy on the Colonel. He's a senior officer loyal to his country?'

'But not all the military think like that, Hannah. Some would like to make peace with the Allies and draw them into the fight against Russia.'

'I think you've been fed a lot of stuff and nonsense.' Her tone was harsh. 'The Allies will never agree to any deal whilst Hitler remains in charge.'

'And that is precisely why the Nazis can't afford to have dissident groups within the military planning to do just that. It would mean they would have to get rid of Hitler before any talks could take place. And that's why they see plotters everywhere and since Stalingrad I'm told certain people have become more paranoid than ever.'

Hearing Miriam speaking so knowledgeably on strategic issues which could only have come from a person of senior rank, sent a cold shiver down her spine. In revealing so much to her, Miriam was obviously feeling confident that she could persuade Hannah to help entrap the very man to whom she owed her continuing survival.

'When you say you want the Colonel to be attracted to me, what you really mean is that you want him to have sex with me.' Innocently, she added 'but isn't that a serious offence within their military regulations?'

'Probably, but that would give them a lever to use against the Colonel. They could then question him about those other things I've just mentioned.'

'By 'under pressure' I presume you mean torture?'

'For heaven's sake Hannah... stop being so pedantic! Whose side are you on in this fucking war?' The crudeness of her outburst emphasised the mounting pressure being felt by Miriam.

Sensing an advantage, Hannah turned the screw even more. 'If the Nazis can punish one of their own senior people for fraternising with a Jew, then what do you think will happen to that Jew? Should I guess or will you spell it out for me?'

Anxious to regain her composure, Miriam's reply was modulated. 'My dear girl, you are being unnecessary antagonistic. D'you think I would I be doing this if I thought it would damage our chances of survival?'

Miriam's condescending tone caused even more anger to well up inside her. 'I think you are the one being stupidly naïve. Can't you see you are being manipulated by whoever it is you are working for and when you've served that purpose you and I will be disposed of. It's what the Nazis do to Jews like us... or have you forgotten?'

'No I haven't forgotten but what else could I do. It was either to do this or join those other women in the gas chamber. What sort of choice was that?'

Looking into Miriam's face, she saw what she hoped might be the first sign of regret. 'Look, no one can blame you for making the choice you did but you need to think this through. This war can't last for ever and you need to think whether the Nazis can actually win it. Now that the Americans are increasingly involved I think it will be the Allies who will eventually win. So we should be thinking how we can survive until that happens. We are lucky because we have a choice of sorts, unlike those thousands of poor souls being slaughtered in the camp.

'Hannah, you are deluding yourself. Shut away in that little office has given you a false sense of optimism.'

'Ok, so you tell me, Miriam Karlinski, what choice do you think we have?'

'We have the choice of whether we assist the Nazi or not. That seems to me to be the only realistic options we have.'

'And you think any decision we make will possibly change anything in this war?'

'That's the wrong question Hannah. Of course we can't influence let alone change anything so the right question is how we can survive what's happening; Listen to what I'm telling you and stop being argumentative.' Pausing to reflect on her own words, Miriam's brow puckered in concentration. 'I think I've been wrong about you' she said quietly. 'I marked you down as a spoiled young woman, beautiful but naïve and extremely vulnerable. Yet here you are, imparting words of wisdom to me, streetwise Miriam Karlinski, on how to stay alive but unfortunately for both of us, your strategy has a fatal flaw, my dear. The Allies may well win this war but I doubt whether we will be around to see it happen. It's like an opera... the goodies win in the end but the heroine always dies!'

Pretending to tire of Miriam's growing pessimism, Hannah stood up as though to return to the house. Her manoeuvre worked.

'Hannah, look; I'm not stupid so I know what you say is sensible. But unless I can come up with some meaningful information, then I'll be replaced with someone who can.' Her voice reflected her mounting anxiety. 'I'm not too concerned with who wins this war if I won't be around when it happens. It's not this year or the year after that I worry about but how to survive today and next week and worse, how to extricate myself from the mess I've got myself into.'

Convincing herself that Miriam's plaintive plea for help was genuine, she sat down and took hold of her friend's hands. 'I think you should have a quiet word with Colonel Steiner when he returns and be guided by what he says. Will you do that?'

Alarmed, Miriam pulled her hands away and unconsciously pulled her shawl across her chest, reminiscent of a woman at the end of her tether. 'That won't help, Hannah. From what I've seen of him, the Colonel would have me shot on the spot. These Nazis don't need an excuse to kill people... especially

Jews!' Grimacing in anguish, she attempted to absolve Hannah from its implications. 'I wish now I hadn't burdened you with it.'

'Trust me Miriam and do what I suggest. If you tell Colonel Steiner everything you know, I'm sure he will find a way to help you. And if you want me to be with you when you meet him then I will be happy to do that.'

Brooding and unable to think clearly, Miriam rose and without saying another word, made her way back to the house and the familiar territory of its kitchen.

FIFTY ONE

Steiner's three day strategic mission to each of his Wehrmacht units in the region had been frustrating. Reinforcements of both men and materials to replace increasing losses were being withheld by Berlin whilst supplies of raw materials to Upper Silesia were drying up as an increasing number of trains were being commandeered for the transportation of Jews from the occupied countries of Europe. As a consequence, German forces along the entire Eastern Front were suffering from chronic shortages of fuel, ammunition and replacement of vital equipment. This in turn was causing even heavier and unsustainable losses among front line units with countless numbers of irreplaceable troops either surrendering or being captured by a buoyant Red Army equipped from industries located in remote regions of the Soviet Union, far beyond the reach of a depleted Luftwaffe.

The fact that all major military decisions in the Russian campaign were now being taken personally by Hitler without input from front line commanders was an added cause of resentment among senior officers but even against this depressing scenario, Steiner found that very few would speak openly or question the Fuhrer's conduct of the war.

Returning to the house that evening, it was clear that Steiner was in a belligerent mood. Signalling his arrival by slamming the rear door of his staff car, he followed this with an unnecessarily hard kick to open the heavy front door. Hearing his arrival, Hannah hurried to the office on the first floor arriving just seconds after Steiner.

'Pour me a drink... and make it a large one.'

'And what drink would you like, Colonel? Wine, gin or whisky?'

Emptying the contents of his bulging briefcase onto the desk, Steiner appeared not to hear the question. Swiftly looking through his papers he appeared to find what he was looking for. Reading it, he unbuttoned his uniform jacket and stiffly eased it from his shoulders. Absorbed in the paper in front of him, he attempted to place the jacket on the back of the chair where it hung for a few seconds before falling to the floor.

Retrieving the jacket, Hannah hung it on the coat stand by the door.

'I asked you to pour me a drink... where is it?'

'I'm waiting for you to tell me which drink you would like,' adding 'Colonel' almost as an aside.

'Pour me a whisky... that much,' indicating a measure between his forefinger and thumb.

'And water?'

'What?' Looking up from his paper, he gave Hannah a quizzical look. 'What did you say?'

'I asked whether you wanted water with your whisky.'

'No, make it neat.'

Pouring the drink, Hannah caught the strong vapour exuding from the gold coloured spirit as it swirled in the bottom of the lead chrystal glass. How people could drink a liquid smelling so distasteful was beyond her ken. At no time in her Jewish upbringing nor as an international traveller had she ever felt tempted to try whisky, a drink she knew was enjoyed by many, including her own husband.

Pouring the drink she placed it within his reach and remained standing alongside his chair. Tossing the paper aside he reached out and took a long sip from the very full glass. Smacking his lips together in appreciation, he leaned back in his chair and closed both eyes.

'I get the impression you've not had the best of days, Colonel?' Being able to converse so freely with this hot-tempered man was now so different from their earlier one-sided conversations.

Peering through tired eyes, Steiner could only mutter a fatigued reply. 'I've had better days, Bergmann, but then again I've had worse. It only becomes a problem when you can't tell the difference!'

Looking at the signs of tiredness and stress etched on Steiner's face, she remembered his tenderness on the night they first came together. With deliberate slowness she leaned forward and took the half-filled glass from his hand and placed it on the desk. 'Close your eyes and think of home... and try to relax.' Moving behind his chair, she drew a deep breath and placed both hands firmly on Steiner's shoulders and let her strong fingers begin to massage the knotted tendons and muscles in his broad shoulders. Stopping only to unbutton his shirt, she worked non-stop for twenty minutes before realising that Steiner was falling asleep. Opting for caution she retreated to the other side of the desk, and called him repeatedly until he finally stirred.

Sitting up, he rubbed his neck. 'You have strong fingers, Bergmann. I suppose that comes from being a violinist.'

'Possibly, but I'm pleased it relaxed you. I'm sorry you fell asleep here and not in your comfortable bed.' Instantly regretting the unintentional innuendo, Hannah's face reddened. 'I'm sorry, Colonel. I didn't mean it to sound like that.'

'No need to apologise, Bergmann, what with my tiredness and your therapy, I would be asleep for the next 36 hours.'

Sitting up, he pushed his papers to one side, leaned his elbows on the desk and joined his fingertips together, forming a pyramid.

'Tell me, have there been any developments with your friend in the kitchen while I've been away?'

Recounting every detail of the conversation with Miriam took time and despite his obvious weariness, Steiner's concentration was impressive; not only listening intently but interjecting several times to clarify certain points.

Taking a sip of whisky, he looked into the glass as though the golden liquid was some form of oracle. 'The acid test will be whether she now talks to me, Bergmann. D'you think she will?'

'I hope she will. She certainly didn't commit herself but who can say.'

'But even if she does speak to me, how can I be sure she isn't doing it under orders from whoever it is she's reporting to?' Tiring of the subject, Steiner abruptly stood up. 'The simple answer is for this bloody woman to just disappear. To let them think she has run away.'

Concerned by the sudden change in his manner, it was several seconds before his alarming words fully registered.

'By 'disappear' you mean to have her killed.'

Showing signs of exasperation, Steiner turned on Hannah. 'Perhaps you can suggest a better solution?'

Unable to find words even remotely adequate to convey her growing trepidation, her reply was barely audible.

'Did you say something, Bergmann?'

'I tried to but what can I possibly say that would make any difference to what you decide to do?'

'Is that a question or a statement?'

'Neither. It's frustration... pure and simple frustration.' She truncated each word to add greater emphasis.

'You're wrong, Bergmann. It's prevarication... pure and simple.' Steiner parroted her words. 'You know it's the right decision but you can't bring yourself to think about it which is to ignore the wider implications of letting her live.' Rising from his chair he walked towards the fireplace where the logs placed there earlier by Erlich were now glowing embers. Turning to face her, he leaned his shoulder against the wooden lintel. 'Look, if the strategy I told you of earlier actually succeeds then this damn war could end sooner, sparing thousands of people, including Jews, from what's happening now. So this might be the time to get your pretty little arse off that fence and face up to life.'

Stung by his callous appraisal, Hannah knew Steiner was right but still felt unable to acknowledge, let alone agree, to the killing of a woman as desperate to live as herself.

Taking her silence as acceptance, Steiner tenderly traced his fingers down her cheek. Clasping her own hand over his, she moved fractionally closer before speaking. 'Can you at least wait and see whether she comes to you; will you at least allow her a few days?'

The pleading tone and her upturned face, its beauty made even more tantalising by the glow from the fire, was too much for Steiner. Impulsively, he pulled Hannah to him. 'Look, I wasn't expecting you to pull the trigger but I'll give her three days before I decide what to do. In the meantime, don't speak to her about this again; let her decide her own fate. Can we agree on that?'

Before she could voice her consent, Steiner's lips closed over hers. The conflict between guilt and desire briefly resurfaced within her conscience before she reacted. Placing both arms around Steiner's neck, she drew him closer and unashamedly returned his kiss with fervour. Only the thought of detection by Erlich made her pull away whilst still in control of her emotions and she was thankful to feel Steiner move away too.

'Sensible move, Bergmann but aren't you just postponing the inevitable?'

'Maybe, but it's not for me to decide, Colonel.'

Well maybe you should decide. That will tell me something about you.'

'Tell you what exactly?

'That despite your Jewish background and your monogamous relationship with your husband, you are tempted by the thought of more sex with a German officer whose

Government persecutes Jews like you.' He smiled; 'you have no idea how seductive that is to a man like me.'

'You mean it actually arouses you?' Her querulous voice expressed surprise. 'I find that very strange.'

'Then let me explain, When I think of that virginal Jewish woman who first came into this house compared to how you were when we came together on that night; there's just no comparison. And it's that difference which I find arousing.' He half-smiled at the frown which appeared on Hannah's face.

Surprised by his unexpected frankness, Hannah felt a tinge of embarrassment. 'I think we have both changed, perhaps more than we realise. And we both know when the turning point came... at least I do.' Nervously, she glanced towards the door. 'I think we should move back to the other end of the room in case Corporal Erlich should come in.

Seemingly unwilling to conclude the interlude so quickly, Steiner gripped Hannah by her shoulders. 'Only if you tell me you have understood what I've just said to you.'

Unwilling to openly commit herself, Hannah simply brushed her hand across Steiner's cheek. 'C'mon, you have work to do.' Gently easing away, she walked towards the desk with Steiner reluctantly following.

Later that evening with her emotions still in turmoil, the temptation to go to Steiner's room was becoming increasingly enticing. After picking at a supper shared with Erlich, she had excused herself and spent the next hour seeking solace in her music. Playing with the same level of intensity which had attracted Von Hartmannn, she attempted to blank out the temptation at the other end of the darkened corridor. She had no way of knowing whether Steiner would be awake after his long journey or whether he would even be receptive if she did accept his thinly veiled invitation but the uncertainty just added to her desire to find out.

Unable to clear her mind and tiring from playing, she undressed quickly and fell into bed. With her brain still wrapped in the musical exercise she had just subjected it to, sleep was a long time coming. At one stage she heard Steiner make his way to the bathroom and heard the water pump running for several minutes before his footsteps padded past her door once more.

Lying in bed, the same bed in which she had succumbed to his rampant sexual overtures her emotions ranged from deep shame to that of mounting temptation. In a vain attempt to suppress her increasing desire for Steiner, she tried urgently to induce a feeling of guilt for her deeply shaming indiscretion with him but within her conscience she knew she would do the same again were he to come to her room now. In a vain attempt to salve her nagging conscience, she recalled Ephraim's parting words at Theresienstadt; 'do whatever it takes to survive?' Or am I using that as a pitiful excuse to justify my sexual inclination she wondered? Sporadically drifting in and out of sleep, her mind jolted back to the shockingly erotic experience she had experienced with Elsa Seilhamer and before that the provocative kiss she had tempted Max Feldman with. And worse, her abject surrender to the rapacious demands of the Rumanian Kapo. And now it was Steiner, her protector on that terrifying night, who was occupying her every thought. 'Am I a woman escaping from my stifling upbringing or a repressed whore; or do they both amount to the same thing?' The questions kept coming before sleep finally intervened, taking her mind into a dreamless vacuum of silence.

FIFTY TWO

Next morning Hannah's sleep was rudely awakened by an agitated Corporal Erlich bursting into her room.

'Bergmann, get downstairs... quickly!' Gone was the quiet bearing of the middle-aged soldier and in its stead stood a clearly agitated Wehrmacht NCO.

Knowing better than to question Erlich in this mood, Hannah had to force herself out of her warm bed. Sleepily making her way to the marble washstand, she doused her face with cold water and quickly dressed.

Making her way to the ground-floor dining room, she saw that neither Steiner nor Erlich were fully dressed. Steiner, looking tired and unshaven, wore his uniform shirt open at the neck with his red braces hanging down around his waist whilst Erlich wore his comfortable non-service shoes instead of standard-issue boots.

Facing them were two uniformed SS soldiers; a youthful-looking Lieutenant accompanied by a burly thick-set Sergeant.

Noticing her arrival, Steiner brusquely introduced her by name. Without acknowledging her presence, the Sergeant spoke to her directly. 'When did you last see this Karlinski woman?'

'Karlinski? Do you mean Miriam?'

The stinging slap across her face took Hannah by surprise and briefly distorted her vision. As it cleared she saw a look of anger flash across Erlich grim features but Steiner's face remained impassive.

'Well?'

'It was last night at supper.'

'And the time; what time did you last see her?'

'About 7pm.'

'And did she say anything about wanting to escape?'

'Escape?' The word stuck in her throat. 'Of course not. Why would she tell me?'

'Because you both work together and presumably you talk to each other?' This time it was the Lieutenant who spoke.

With her face still stinging, Hannah looked towards Steiner for reassurance but his face gave no hint of comfort. 'Of course we speak to each other but never once has she ever talked of escaping.'

'I think you're lying.'

Not knowing whether to answer, Hannah remained silent.

'You can answer my question here or I can take you back to the camp.' The chilling menace behind the threat was terrifying..

'Lieutenant... ' It was Steiner, aware his authority was being challenged by a subordinate officer, who intervened. 'You've asked your questions and I don't think you will get any further with this prisoner so if you have no other business here, I have work to do.'

Unsettled by Steiner's unexpected intervention, it took the SS Lieutenant a few moments to compose his reply. 'You will forgive me, Colonel, but as an SS officer I am carrying out an investigation with this woman which I have not yet concluded. So with your permission I will carry on with my questioning.'

From her position directly in front of the Lieutenant, Hannah could see the other two men in the room. The SS Sergeant, clearly enjoying the confrontation, stepped forward and struck Hannah another stinging blow before she could react.

'I think we should take this Jew back to the camp, Lieutenant. We'll get more out of here there.'

Whether galvanised by the second blow or the spoken threat, Steiner made his move with surprising coolness. 'Lieutenant, remove this piece of garbage from my office and take yourself with him!' Moving closer to the junior SS officer, he added 'and if you dare challenge what I say again, your career will take a distinct turn for the worse. Do I make myself clear?'

Chastened, the Lieutenant took a step back. Wordlessly, he turned on his heel and moved as though to leave but then stopped. 'Colonel; I apologise for my apparent insubordination. I assure you it was unintended.'

Steiner's response was unequivocal. 'Get your slimy arse out of here and take that bullying prick with you. And soldier... if you so much as fart, let alone say another word, I will personally stuff your balls in that arrogant mouth of yours. Now, get out... both of you!'

Watching as the two men exited the room, it took a moment or two for Hannah to recover from the stinging slaps to her face and the base crudeness of Steiner's dismissal.

'Did I shock you?'

'A little but I think you made yourself perfectly clear.'

'It was soldier talk; it leaves no room for misunderstanding.'

'But won't the Lieutenant complain about your treatment of him when he reports back.'

Throwing his head back, Steiner broke into a laugh. 'If you were a soldier, would you report what I said to him? He would become a laughing stock in his unit. Trust me; we'll hear no more from him.'

Erlich, feeling out of the conversation spoke up. 'Your face is red, Bergmann; does it hurt?'

Touched by his concern, Hannah fingered her smarting cheek. 'It's stinging but it will be just fine in a moment.'

'In which case, Ernst, what's the news of this damn woman? When did you know she was missing?

'At about five thirty this morning. That's when the Lieutenant called me on our field radio. She was here when I locked the house last night at 10.45 and assuming he called soon after she was caught then she had a window of about six hours.'

'So is she dead?'

Hannah tensed, concerned for her friend and fearful to know the answer.

'Sorry, Colonel, I thought I'd told you. She's alive and lying in the basement. She was brought here by the guards who caught her.' She's been badly beaten; probably by the same bully-boy who slapped Bergmann.'

'Why has she been brought here and not taken back to the camp?'

'Because camp records show she's on our establishment.' Erlich hesitated. 'This means you will need to decide what to do with her.'

'What usually happens to inmates who get caught trying to escape?'

'They're either shot on the spot or executed in the camp as a deterrent to other prisoners. I'm surprised the guards bothered to bring her back here.'

'In which case Ernst, contact the camp and tell them to collect the prisoner and do what they normally do.' Laughingly, he turned to Hannah, 'you see, Bergmann, there is a God after all. This will resolve the problem of our in-house informer for a reason which even her controller will understand. It's a perfect solution.'

'But not a very smart solution, Colonel.'

From the corner of her eye Hannah saw Erlich's eyebrows rise up into his creased forehead. 'Mind what you say, Bergmann.'

'It's OK Ernst; let her speak.' Steiner's conciliatory tone was encouraging. 'What's wrong with my solution?'

'It's what Miriam's controller would expect you to do: her escape and recapture has given you the perfect reason to have her shot. So why not confound them by sparing her life. That will convince them you aren't aware of their plan and by the same token, you gain Miriam's gratitude and loyalty.' Hannah looked at Steiner for his reaction.

For a long moment he returned her stare before turning to Erlich. 'Ernst, what do you make of this woman?'

'She talks a lot of sense, Colonel: which is surprising for a Berliner.'

'Did you mean to say 'for a Jew', Corporal?'

Seeing the pained look of consternation on Erlich's weathered face, Hannah instantly regretted her words. 'Sorry, Corporal, I didn't mean to say that.'

'But you did so let me answer you. I'm a simple Bavarian and to me, people are people without the need for labels. So remember that before opening your mouth again.'

Duly shamed, Hannah looked to Steiner. 'While you are thinking about your decision, can I go and see if I can help Miriam?'

'No, stay where you are. Ernst, bring her up here and stay with her while Bergmann sees whether she can patch her up with the medical kit. Then put her back in the basement until I get back later today and make sure she gets something to eat and drink.'

FIFTY THREE

The harshest winter in living memory and the frozen landscapes of central Poland, once the breadbasket of Eastern Europe, had yielded little in the way of food for a population facing near-starvation. The frozen ground had prevented the planting of spring crops whilst the invading German military had seized whatever food they could pillage. And where the invaders found livestock, these too were slaughtered to supplement the Wehrmacht's own dwindling food reserves.

Denied provisions from a starving population, Ephraim's group of Partisans were forced to take extreme risks in order to replenish not only food but ammunition and medical supplies.

With thousands of troops in transit to and from the Eastern front and increased numbers of German units patrolling throughout the region, it was becoming extremely hazardous to sabotage even unguarded rail lines, junctions and other 'soft' targets. Every raid carried out by the Partisans invariably brought a murderous response from German SS units. Countless small towns and hamlets were razed in retribution, their inhabitants slaughtered as a message to Poles everywhere. Against this backdrop, an increasing number of Poles, villagers and townsfolk alike, refused to assist the partisans or worse, informing the Germans of their whereabouts. The last two sorties involving Ephraim's group had been compromised by Polish informers and the group had suffered heavy casualties. With few medical supplies remaining from those taken from Theresienstadt, Ephraim had done what he could for the wounded but he knew some would die due to lack of medication. One of the two Czech Gendarme deserters from Theresienstadt had been badly wounded in their first raid in Polish territory. Without morphine to ease his pain and drifting in and out of consciousness, his death was only a matter of time so with

Ephraim's grudging assent, his fellow deserter had mercifully ended his comrade's life with a shot to the head as the Partisans retreated into the dense Polish forestland.

Three nights later and desperate to obtain further medical supplies, Ephraim and two German-speaking Partisans, each wearing Wehrmacht uniforms purloined from dead prisoners, drove to a Wehrmacht Field Hospital Dispensary Unit. From his knowledge of Teutonic bureaucracy gained at Theresienstadt, Ephraim knew that paperwork, correctly completed and signed off by a senior officer, were paramount in the military mind. So equipped with such a document ironically bearing the signature of a Captain Hugo Kernick for some minor medication but now substantially added to by himself, Ephraim and his two comrades approached the heavily guarded Dispensary.

Each of them carried authentic ID papers previously issued to former Wehrmacht soldiers but since skilfully altered to reflect their own identities. Ephraim's papers showed him to be a Captain attached to the Medical Corps.

Stopping at the closed barrier giving access to the unit a visibly bored soldier barely glanced at the requisition form in Ephraim's hand before nodding to a second soldier to raise the barrier. Standing back as the vehicle moved forward, the soldier gave Ephraim a perfunctory salute which lacked the usual military crispness.

The Dispensary was clearly signposted by crudely painted wooden signs. With one man remaining with the vehicle, Ephraim and the other Partisan entered the portico of a building which despite its requisition and use by the military, still reflected the faded grandeur of its imposing past. Two Corinthian pillars, each pock-marked and scarred by bullet holes flanked what had once been the imposing entrance to the stately building. Inside, their eyes were drawn to a red-carpeted staircase leading to a mezzanine floor. Further access to the imposing hallway was halted by a wooden counter, its entrance flap securely bolted in place. Aware that their two previous operations had been compromised by informers,

Ephraim, his nerves jarring with apprehension, wondered whether this too might be another trap. Undecided whether to beat a hasty retreat or shout for attention, he was relieved when an attractive blond woman wearing a white non-military coverall appeared, taking Ephraim by surprise.

'Sorry, I was expecting a soldier' he muttered

'Well you've just found one, Captain, because underneath this coverall there is a conscripted soldier who also happens to be a pharmacist which is why I'm here.' In referring to his rank so informally, Ephraim recognised the manner of a civilian unused to military convention. Reaching for a clipboard, she leafed quickly through the sheaf of papers attached to it. 'Have you come for the requisition from General HQ?' Without waiting for a response, she turned and indicated a pile of boxes immediately to the right of the stairwell. 'They've been ready for collection since yesterday.'

With his initial fear held in check and balanced by growing optimism, Ephraim's brain clicked into gear. 'I will need to check the original requisition order to ascertain what was ordered is in fact all here, soldier.'

'Of course. I wouldn't expect you to do otherwise. Shall I read out the order as you check through the boxes?'

Anxious to now get clear of the building as quickly as possible, Ephraim decided to be bold: 'Look Soldier, we've been badly delayed getting here so give me the form and you bring the boxes to this counter so that I can check them off.' He nodded to the Partisan standing alongside him. 'This man will load them directly on to our truck and we'll be on our way and out of your hair.'

Within her own domain, the Orderly was clearly a woman who needed to stay in control. Petulantly grabbing the requisition form from the paperclip, she let it fall onto the counter rather than pass it to Ephraim's outstretched hand. 'Whatever suits you best, Captain,' making no attempt to disguise the annoyance in her voice.'

Glancing through the extensive list of medical supplies, Ephraim could barely contain his excitement. The contents on his own list were meagre in comparison to what he was now staring at.

As each box was first brought to the counter and then taken to the waiting truck, it seemed to all three men as if time stood still. With the loading finally completed, a relieved Ephraim signed off the receipt proffered by the surly Orderly. But looking at the woman as she studied his signature, he realised he had just committed a cardinal error.

'Fischer.' She repeated the name again. 'You wouldn't be the same Dr. Fischer who worked in Berlin would you? If so... ' her voice trailed off in growing alarm. 'You're a Jew aren't you? You're not in the Army... you can't be.'

Mortified by his mistake, Ephraim attempted to bluster. 'You're wrong Soldier and you are also insubordinate.'

If he was hoping to intimidate the woman then he was sorely disappointed.

'I'm not wrong. I worked at the same hospital as you once did in Berlin. I thought you looked familiar but I couldn't place where I'd seen you before.'

Knowing his bluff had been called, Ephraim knew he had to act quickly or lose the priceless bounty of medical supplies now secured on the waiting vehicle.

Faced with the awful decision of whether to murder the Orderly in cold blood or to try to escape, Ephraim wavered. Behind him he heard the hurried footsteps of his comrade re-entering the Dispensary.

'Captain, we need to leave now...' a growing sense of urgency in his voice.'

'Return to the truck and wait for me.'

Surprised by Ephraim's response, it took the Czech just seconds to assess the situation. 'Captain... you go. I will deal with the problem.' Vaulting over the wooden counter, he spun the transfixed Orderly round and clamped his large hand over her mouth. With his free hand he unsheathed a serrated knife and drew his arm back to plunge it into the helpless woman's chest.

'Stop!' The authority in Ephraim's shouted order barely stayed the blow. 'Let her go. And get outside!'

Confused, the Czech hesitated, the point of the knife pressing into the white coverall. Slowly, he took his hand away from the Orderly's flushed face and stepped back, watching as the stricken woman slid to the floor. Looking hard at Ephraim, he slowly shook his head as he strode past him. 'She'll scream the fucking place down as soon as we leave.'

Alone with the prostrated figure lying on the black and white tiled floor, her saw her begin to tremble with delayed shock. Inexplicably he noticed the contrast in colour between the woman's blond hair and her reddish complexion. Seeing Ephraim move towards her, the Orderly tried to slide away. When she spoke her voice was hoarse and barely audible.

'Don't touch me. Get as far away from me as possible. You've got two minutes before I raise the alarm so go.' Raising herself onto her knees, her natural truculence reasserted itself. 'And Jew boy,' she paused to catch her breath, 'my life for yours so we've even. Now get out before I change my mind.'

Backing towards the exit, Ephraim heard running footsteps behind him. He turned to see the Czech driver roughly push past him, a Luger in his raised fist. He heard the deadly plop, plop from the silenced pistol and saw the woman's body jerk backwards, two round holes appearing in the front of the white coat. Her face convulsed with shock and she mouthed a silent curse as her eyes rolled upward with the onset of death.

Shocked, it took Ephraim a moment to recover. 'You murdering bastard. She was giving us a chance to get clear.'

'And you'd believe a German?' His voice was coldly dispassionate. 'Get outside before I shoot you too.'

That night, huddled in a small forest clearing some 20-odd kilometres from the Field Dispensary, Ephraim found himself constantly recalling the face of the murdered woman; someone's daughter, perhaps a wife or even a young mother but now a cold lifeless body reflecting yet again the madness of this war.

FIFTY FOUR

Despite his request for his Cook to be returned to the Admin unit, Steiner's entreaty was refused by the Camp Commandant of Auschwitz. At the conclusion of the morning roll call all available camp workers were forced to witness the execution of Miriam Karlinski and three other prisoners; each paying the ultimate penalty for attempting to escape. They were hanged with a course hemp rope around each of their necks, the other end fastened to a metal rail slung between two wooden posts .Standing on the stool before it was kicked away, her face bore silent witness to the vicious beating she had already endured. Even in her final moments, Miriam Karlinski fought against death but it took less than a minute before her uneven struggle came to its inevitable end.

It fell to Hannah to yet again gather and dispose of her meagre belongings. In a small leather wallet, probably stolen from the Central Sorting Area, she found two sepia photographs. The first showed a young Miriam in her graduation robes but giving no clue as to the nature of her qualification. The second photograph posed a further mystery. Flanking Miriam was an elderly man who could have been her husband or even her father. But sitting on her lap was a child, a young girl. The reverse of the photograph was inscribed 'my darling Zigi' but offered no explanation as to the child's identity or parentage. She could not recall Miriam ever mentioning a child or any other aspect of her life before being transported to Auschwitz so with her death, the photographs would retain their mystery. Looking at the upturned face of the child, she once more experienced the deep burning hatred she felt for all Nazis. In the lonely quietness of her room, she fervently wished success to men like Steiner; plotting to remove Hitler, the architect of Nazism and the man at the very heart of darkest evil.

Since divulging his involvement in the plot to kill Hitler, Steiner had become noticeably reticent and with Miriam now gone, she wondered whether she too might now be in danger. Having witnessed the cold-blooded manner in which he had killed the Kapo on that savage night in Block 23 and more recently giving the order for Danuta's summary execution, she knew he would not give a second thought to her own death in order to preserve the knowledge of his involvement, however slight, in the plan to bring the war to an earlier conclusion.

It was two weeks before the new cook arrived. Like Danuta before her, the new inmate was a Jehovah's Witness. Perversely, the SS seemed to liken followers of this religious sect and their adherence to a strict biblical code as being akin to their own veneration of their Aryan creed.

Agnetta was Danish and her background was touching. She and her German husband had been living in Hanover when war was declared. Following their arrest, the husband had immediately renounced his Church membership and unlike his foreign wife, had been duly released by the Gestapo. Despite resolving not to become too attached to her, Hannah found herself liking Agnetta's positive attitude to life despite the sheer awfulness of her experience in Auschwitz.

It was a further two days before Steiner met with Agnetta Larssen. Following a long and often discordant session with his military support team, it was becoming increasingly clear to Hannah, that the war was now undoubtedly beginning to turn against Germany; at least on the Eastern Front. With his attention span becoming shorter by the minute, Steiner abruptly halted proceedings and called for Hannah to arrange coffee for those present. In an unguarded fatherly moment, Erlich had told her that her presence in such meetings would invariably attract a degree of ribald comment normally associated with soldiers. She knew this annoyed Steiner; perhaps with the same hint of possessiveness she had detected on the night when General Beck had proposed a toast to her in this very room. Later during that same fateful evening, Steiner had come to her room and turned her fettered world upside down.

Demurely moving from the meeting room, Hannah made her way down to the kitchen and passed Steiner's order to Agnetta.

'Will the Colonel be there?' Her voice reflected a touch of nervousness.

'Of course he will.' Sensing the Dane's apprehension at the thought of entering a room full of German officers for the first time, Hannah volunteered to help the new woman. 'You make the coffee and I'll prepare the cups. We'll do it together and I'll give you a hand when you take the tray upstairs. Can you manage that?'

'Thanks Hannah, I appreciate that.'

Liking Agnetta's easy manner, Hannah took a long look at the pretty young Dane as she poured hot water into the enamel coffee pot. Endowed with piercing blue eyes and blond hair so typical of Scandinavian women Hannah could see that Agnetta, with her diminutive frame and pleasant manner, was an extremely attractive woman. She also wondered whether Steiner would be attracted to her. She knew Danuta's sister had found favour with him but whether that had ever been consummated she had no way of knowing and asking Steiner was out of the question. What she did know in every detail was her own encounter with him leaving her in no doubt that Steiner could be sexually aroused when an attractive woman was in close proximity.

Re-entering the meeting room, the level of conversation died down and several officers were on their feet, one obviously keen on taking the tray from Agnetta and placing it on the table at the far end.

Drawing closer to the nervous Dane, she whispered 'you need to take the tray round the room yourself and I will bring the milk and sugar. Take a deep breath and don't be nervous.'

Following her round the room, Hannah was able to see the reaction Agnetta had on men who had been away from their wives and girlfriends for too long. Thinking about this, it occurred to her that with her blond hair and blue eyes Agnetta, just like Elsa Seilhamer, was the epitome of Aryan womanhood; the symbolic figure of the Third Reich which every red-blooded soldier of the Wehrmacht was pledged to defend. And even better, the attractive Dane wasn't Jewish!

Coming to Steiner's desk, Hannah saw him glance up from the report he was reading. Raising a quizzical eyebrow, he gave Agnetta an appraising look.

'You must be the new cook?'

Too nervous to speak, Agnetta nodded in response.

'Well let's hope you last a bit longer than the last one did. Dismissing her with an unthinking wave of his hand, Steiner dropped his voice and spoke quietly to Hannah. 'Let her do that Bergmann; your place is here,' tapping the chair next to him.

Placing the tray down for Agnetta to recover, she took her seat at a discrete distance from Steiner's chair. Waiting for the assembled officers to finish their coffee and cigarettes gave Hannah an opportunity to study the men in the room particularly those sitting directly facing her. Two were quietly speaking to each other but next to them was a youngish-looking Captain unabashedly staring at her. Returning his half-smile and knowing that Steiner was aware of their visual exchange, she marginally eased the hem of her resisting skirt back over her knee line and slowly crossed her legs. Daring to look up, she saw a broad smile appear on the officer's face which she found difficult not to respond too. A sharp tap on the desk by Steiner brought the meeting to order and the mild flirtation to an end.

During pauses in recording action points, she once more rekindled in her mind the circumstances which had led Steiner to risk his career and come to her room on that fateful night. Could he possibly have been jealous of General Beck and was he now becoming irritated at the innocent exchange between herself and the smiling young Captain? Did Steiner regard her as his personal property with a need to assert his ownership when another man showed an interest, however innocent such an approach might be? Or was it simply a case of old fashioned jealousy rearing up inside a man whom she knew so little about. And more worryingly, was she too beginning to feel symptoms of that same jealousy in not wanting Steiner to show an interest in Agnetta.

To clear her mind, she attempted to think about Ephraim. Realistically she knew she should accept the fact that he was dead; murdered at Theresienstadt along with those other inmates not shipped out on the same hellish transport which had brought her to Auschwitz. Despite his oft-spoken exhortation regarding the need for her to survive by whatever means, would his understanding have extended to forgiveness if he had known she had broken every word of her sacred marriage covenants and worse, with a German officer? Could he possibly understand the overwhelming temptation she had faced on that fateful night when her innermost emotions had been aroused to a level she had never before experienced.

Engrossed in her thoughts, she didn't hear Steiner actually close the meeting. It was the sound of his chair being pushed back which dragged her mind back to the present. Giving a crisp salute to his gathered comrades, all of whom were now standing, he called out the names of three officers he wished to stay behind while the remainder were dismissed in a hubbub of noise.

'Tell Erlich to make sure we aren't disturbed and tell the new woman to bring some more coffee in. And get yourself something to eat because you will be working late.'

'So what time would you like me to report back, Colonel?'

'Come here after supper, say around 1900 hours. And Bergmann... knock before you come in.'

Adopting what she hoped would be seen by the remaining officers as a deferential pose, she exited the room, adding to herself, 'I always do, Colonel.'

Returning at 1900 hours, she was alarmed to hear the sound of raised voices including that of Steiner. Knocking as instructed, the oak panelled door remained firmly closed until Erlich, appearing from the stairwell, told her to return to her room until being sent for.

Not knowing how long she would be expected to wait, she quickly refreshed herself with cold water and feeling like a naughty child playing truant, took her violin from its velvet lined case, tuned it and proceeded to run up and down a series of scales. The soft mellow sounds resonating from her treasured Bellini had the same refreshing effect on her mind as the cold water had on her face. Tiring of scales, she turned to playing a slower piece, a melodic adagio, part of which had been plagiarised into a popular song. The words which had been added to the original composition by a modern songsmith kept popping into her mind and soon she was quietly humming them as she played the classical score composed more than a century before.

Outside her window, the spring-like day was drawing to its close, the rays of the setting sun casting deepening shadows through the trees and tall hedges. Looking at the tranquil scene, Hannah wondered if the world would ever again know a peace to match the beautiful landscape she was now looking at. Still gazing out of the window and lost in thought, she heard the door of her room open to admit a stern looking Steiner, one eyebrow raised as he eased himself down on the side of the bed.

Surprised by his sudden appearance, Hannah guiltily laid her instrument back in its case.

'I'm sorry Colonel. I was told to wait here until you sent for me.'

Ignoring the apology, Steiner came straight to the point. 'I want to know why you were casting your spell over that hapless young Captain today. And don't try and deny it; I saw you.'

'Was I?' Her buttery coyness seemed to have little effect on Steiner. 'I wasn't conscious I was casting any spell, Colonel.'

'Whether you were or not isn't the point, Bergmann. You are like a honey pot to these lonely young men as well you know. Even my ultra-conservative cousin, Von Hartmann fell under your spell which explains why you are still in this unit with me... and still alive.'

Choosing not to pick up on his unconcealed threat, instead she gave Steiner the sweetest of smiles. 'But obviously you feel immune to whatever it is you believe I do to these men.'

Staring hard at her, Steiner patted the blanket next to him. 'Come and sit here.'

'Are you sure you will be safe, Colonel? I wouldn't want you to go the same way as your cousin.' Even speaking to Steiner in jest was always something of a gamble; one wrong word and his mood could change in a flash.

'I'll take a chance; sit here.' This time it was less of an order.

Sitting next to him, she immediately became conscious of the man's physical attraction..

'Ok, I'm here as instructed. Now what?' To her surprise, Steiner made no move to touch her.

'What do you expect to happen or more to the point what would you like to happen?'

'That depends on whether I can speak freely without incurring your wrath or whether I remember to keep my place and act like a dumb Yid and take what comes from my German master?'

Steiner gave a long drawn out sigh. 'You disappoint me Bergmann, you really do. I had hoped that you could finally recognise the difference between me and those brain-washed Nazis you constantly refer to.' In obvious annoyance Steiner stood up and looked down at her; his composure on the very edge.

Alarmed by his mood swing, Hannah spoke quickly. 'Of course I recognise the difference Colonel but you are still a German officer whatever your personal feelings may be and I am still a Jew. And you may have forgotten but the last time I thought I could speak freely, you knocked me down and... .' Knowing she had said too much, her words tailed off.

'Finish what you were started to say, Bergmann. And what happened next?'

'You don't need me to tell me; you know perfectly well what happened.'

Sitting himself back on the side of the bed, his large hand overlaid hers. 'I seem to remember we had a long discussion during which I expressed profound regret for slapping you... twice wasn't it?'

'No. You gave me three very hard slaps with your open hand.'

'Three slaps you say... with an open hand.' He appeared to consider this. 'Well just consider yourself lucky that it wasn't with my fist! Perhaps I'm managing to control my temper somewhat better than you give me credit for.' Laughing to himself, he turned to face Hannah. 'I also recall we touched upon the several occasions when it was you who struck me or have you chosen to forget those moments.'

'No, I haven't forgotten them or the understanding you showed to me afterwards. But when I see you dining with people such as the Camp Commandant and his SS officers all my fears come flooding back to the surface; more so since you told me of this plan to remove Hitler. Since that conversation I have become a liability, a very dangerous liability which you can dispose of with a simple stroke of your pen especially when you lose control of yourself. That's when I think you will send me back to the camp as you did with Danuta and Miriam.' As each impulsive word poured out, she felt her legs begin to weaken. Moving quickly, she reached for the chair and quickly exchanged places.

She saw Steiner rise to his full height and gingerly massage the muscles in his lower back. Unable to disengage her eyes from his, Hannah felt trapped with nowhere to hide or run to.

'Hannah... stand up.' His voice was commanding and chilling. In her abject fear, she failed to notice Steiner had used her given name.

'You appear to suffer from a form of selective recall so let me say this to you one last time. Other than for my occasional loss of self-control which I have already admitted to, you have nothing to fear whilst I remain in this unit. I know I gave a similar undertaking on behalf of Danuta but we both know the reason why she was executed. If she hadn't involved herself with those Polish partisans then she would still be here. So take that anxious look off your face... it doesn't suit you.'

Desperately wanting to believe what she was hearing her shoulders slumped in obvious relief.

Looking at her dispirited form, her head bowed and utterly drained, evoked mixed feelings of guilt and sympathy in Steiner's mind. Resisting an urge to take hold and comfort her, instead he tried to lighten her mood. 'Tell me Hannah, have you never been tempted to hit someone; other than myself that is?' The conciliatory tone was back.

'No, never! I detest violence of any kind.'

'Even when it's a German officer on the receiving end?'

Sensing his further appeasement, Hannah reached up and let her fingers touch Steiner's cheek. 'Especially when it's a German officer.'

With her hand still touching his face, Hannah hoped for a reaction but Steiner's passive look offered no hint of encouragement. 'What can I do to make amends, Colonel?'

'I can think of several areas of mitigation we might explore later but not at this precise moment.' Reverting quickly back into military mode, Steiner turned to leave but halted in the doorway. 'By the way, Corporal Erlich will be going on leave tomorrow and he'll be away for ten days. During his absence my driver will stay here and will sleep in the basement, next to the new cook's room and I've ordered him to lock her door overnight: I don't want any more of these damn women doing anything to bring those goons from the camp to come here again. And Bergmann,' his voice dropped to a whisper, 'I won't tolerate any deviation from my instructions. You are to stay away from the basement. I don't want you feeling sorry for her and compromising yourself. Do I make myself clear?' His raised eyebrows served to emphasise the point.'

'Of course.'

'Sure?'

'Very sure, Colonel.'

'Good girl.' With that, Steiner turned and was gone.

FIFTY FIVE

In-mid July, Claus Von Stauffenberg returned to Steiner's HQ, this time accompanied by two senior Wehrmacht officers, a Von Gersdorff and a Von Kleist. Days before their arrival, the German offensive at Kursk, code-named Operation Citadel, had rapidly developed into the largest tank battle of the war before ending in a decisive defeat for the Axis forces whilst providing a morale-boosting victory for the Red Army. The earlier Soviet victory at Stalingrad had effectively halted the German invasion of the Soviet Union and Steiner suspected that from Kursk onwards, the Wehrmacht would now be forced into a bitter and stubborn retreat from a resurgent Red Army.

Over dinner it was Von Kleist who posed the question, a question at the forefront of their collective minds. 'How could we lose so many men and so much of our best equipment to a rabble army?

Listening to him, Steiner forced himself to take a deep breath before replying. 'Rabble army?' He repeated Von Kleist's words. 'In numerical strength you are undoubtedly correct but this 'rabble' you refer to have just beaten two of our most formidable Panzer Armies equipped with our newest tanks and equipment, so doesn't that tend to question your statement? Steiner's retort was purposely provocative. Sensing conflict between the two men, it was Von Gersdorff who reacted first.

'Our comrades fought well but they were let down by Berlin. Von Manstein wanted to close the Kursk salient in March before the Russians could prepare their defences but he was overruled by Hitler.' He waited for a rebuke or at least an admonishment but none came. 'It was the Fuhrer's decision to wait until 5 July to attack by which time the Russians had turned the whole area into a defensive death trap.'

Noticing that Von Stauffenberg had not reacted to the unconcealed criticism of Hitler, Steiner decided to push the boundary even further. 'I wonder how many of our Wehrmacht comrades share that opinion of our Commander-in-Chief and more to the point, how many would dare to express it so openly'

It worked. Von Stauffenberg's riposte was instant and direct. 'I would hope that in this room, Colonel, we can express whatever view we wish especially about Hitler and those bootlickers he surrounds himself with in Berlin.'

'I don't have a problem with that but I presume that's not why we are here?'

'You are correct, Colonel, but let me explain further.'

Seeing Von Stauffenberg move with a pronounced limp towards the desk at the far end of the room reminded Steiner yet again of the grievous wounds this man had suffered in the service of his country. The black patch covering his sightless left eye gave his aristocratic features a piratical look, drawing attention away from the loss of his right hand and two fingers from the left hand. Sitting down, Von Stauffenberg motioned the others to do likewise. Nodding towards Von Kleist and Von Gersdorff, he turned his attention to Steiner.

'During our journey here, I took the opportunity to brief our two comrades so they already know what I am about to tell you.' He paused to loosen his tie and Steiner noticed that in doing this simple task, his breathing had become laboured. 'At dawn yesterday, the Allies landed in Sicily and our forces are already withdrawing. High Command believes the Allies will use Sicily as a staging post for other landings on mainland Italy in order to launch a two-pronged assault from both the North and South of that region with our forces trapped in the centre.' He paused, allowing Steiner to fully digest the information. 'Without doubt, the tide is turning against us. El Alemain and North Africa have been lost; our Russian campaign has been halted at Stalingrad and I personally believe our defeat at Kursk will now signal the beginning of our retreat from the Soviet Union. Bolstered by these victories, the Allies are clearly on the offensive both on this Eastern front and now in Italy with every prospect of the Italian Government surrendering and throwing in their lot with the Allies.'

Von Stauffenberg appeared to be speaking directly to him so Steiner thought he ought to reply. 'To do that, they would have to depose Mussolini and his cohorts.'

'Mussolini was arrested yesterday.' Von Stauffenberg let his dramatic announcement carry. 'So gentleman, the European front has entered a distinctly critical phase where sensibly, Germany should now be seeking an accommodation with the Allies. But we know the Fuhrer will not countenance any such proposal because he knows the Allies will promptly hang him and his like-minded gang as war criminals. Meanwhile, our cities are being subjected to day and night bombing by the Allied air forces with our Luftwaffe increasingly unable to stop them. In short, we are reaping the whirlwind which Germany unleashed on the world in 1939. So unless we, the military, take action, our Fatherland will be destroyed to become nothing more than a wasteland or worse, a satellite of the Soviet Union.'

It was Von Kleist who broke the uneasy silence which followed Von Stauffenberg's analytical assessment. 'None of us can dispute what you say but even if Hitler were to be deposed, why would the Allies agree to even meet with us let alone make peace?' Expecting an interruption, he scanned those present but the room remained silent. 'In the space of twenty five years Germany has instigated two major wars invading or involving each of those countries now opposing us and causing the deaths of untold millions in the process. So why would the Allies consider anything even remotely resembling a peace overture from us when they are now in the ascendency?'

Not wanting to be left out of the discussion, it was a thoughtful Von Gersdorff who attempted to reply. 'That is a telling question to which we may not wish to know the answer to.'

'Explain yourself, Willie.' Stauffenberg's informality brought a wry smile to Von Gersdorff's lined face.

'I was about to do just that so please bear with me. If I were Stalin I would see this as a gilt-edged opportunity to extend the Soviet Union by ensnaring most of Eastern Europe to create a defensive buffer against any future German incursions in to Russia. And it gets worse. If on the other hand I were in Winston Churchill's shoes, I would wish to see Germany utterly destroyed so it can never again be in a position to threaten the supremacy of the British Empire. So for once, the interests of the Russians and the British converge with both wishing to see Germany made powerless. Against that backdrop I cannot see the Allies demanding anything other than unconditional surrender. Realistically, why would they seek anything less?'

Listening intently, Von Stauffenberg stroked his chin. 'I notice that you have not mentioned Hitler. Do you believe his continuing presence will prolong this war?'

Suddenly all three officers attempted to speak at once but Steiner's voice won through. 'That's a simple question to answer, gentlemen. Our Armed Forces have invaded and conquered most of Western and Eastern Europe because we are better trained, better equipped and led by professional officers. In some countries we have actually been welcomed as liberators.' Steiner gave a cynical smile knowing he was pushing plausibility a touch too far. 'But in the eyes of the civilised world, our military achievements will count for nothing; absolutely nothing,' emphasising each last word by repeating himself. 'Instead, we will be seen as a malignant military force which has allowed a madman to implement this insane policy of Aryan conquest coupled with unrestrained genocide.'

'You're referring to the Jew policy? It was Von Kleist who posed the question.' Don't mince your words, Colonel. Be specific so we all know what you're referring to.'

Ruffled by Von Kleist's interjection, Steiner reacted aggressively. 'The 'Jew policy' which you so disengagingly refer to, Colonel Kleist, is nothing less than the wholesale slaughter of innocent civilians being exterminated in their thousands. Mainly Jews but other groups too; people defined by our Nazi leaders as non-Aryan.' He stopped speaking and looked at each man in turn. 'Ask yourselves, is this what we are fighting this war for?

Plainly uncomfortable, Von Kleist attempted to bring the discussion back to military necessity. 'But without these people working in our factories, we couldn't produce or replace the equipment we need to fight this war.'

'You aren't listening, Colonel. The people I'm referring to aren't working in factories. They are being gassed, murdered in their thousands, buried in mass graves because the crematoria, which you can see if you care to look out of that window, cannot keep pace with the thousands of daily victims.'

'But not every Wehrmacht officer will be aware of what you are referring to.'

'I doubt that very much but can anyone around this table say they're not aware of what is taking place especially on this Eastern front by Einsatzgruppen units operating behind our front line troops. German, Ukrainian and Latvian SS units with specific orders to massacre entire villages on the pretence that these people... old men, peasant women and children, armed with shovels and hoes will become resistance fighters and a threat to the German military machine.'

'Steiner! Cut out the cynicism and make your point.' Von Stauffenberg was clearly becoming annoyed.' Look; none of us are comfortable with what these so-called pacification units are doing but we need to understand who ordered this policy in the first place. What we do know is that nothing happens in the Nazi Party or the military without the knowledge and approval of Hitler and that, I would remind you, is why we are here.'

Bridling at Von Stauffenberg's rebuke and looking directly at Von Kleist, Steiner was not to be thwarted. 'You referred to the 'Jew policy', Colonel. Are you seriously expecting me to believe that you don't know what's happening in camps like Auschwitz? If so, then let me enlighten you. These camps are nothing less than mass killing factories; our Government's solution to ridding Germany of what our leaders euphemistically refer to as undesirables... the Untermenschen.' Steiner stopped, wondering whether his outburst would provoke a further response but an unbroken silence prevailed in the room.

'Can any of us imagine what the rest of the world will do when they discover what has been done in the name of Germany? Will any of us be able to say we knew what was going on but were powerless to stop it because Hitler and his henchmen were too powerful? Well, I don't accept that because Hitler is wholly dependent on the military. Without us, he is nothing.'

'Colonel Steiner... ' It was an impassioned Von Gersdorff who interrupted him. 'I was under the impression that Jews were simply being transported to the East to make room for Germans living in those regions which were taken from Germany in reparation after the Great War. But you say that isn't so. More than that, you say they are being murdered but have you actually witnessed this with your own eyes?'

For a long moment, Steiner attempted to ascertain whether Von Gersdorff was trying to exonerate his conscience or was genuinely ignorant of the genocide being perpetrated by his country.

'Yes, I have seen it and thousands of others are seeing it too and knowing how soldiers talk, I'm surprised you haven't picked up the scuttlebuck, Colonel.' The sarcasm in Steiner's voice did little to mask his accusatory anger.

It was Von Stauffenberg who again interceded. 'Whether the Colonel knew or not isn't important. What we must focus on is how to stop this madness from destroying not only the Jews but the German people. And to do that we need to kill Hitler!

Operation Valkyrie – the plot to assassinate Adolph Hitler had gained a new convert... Colonel Kurt Steiner. Wanting to get to know him better, Von Stauffenberg surprised Steiner by electing to stay overnight. Accompanied by his aide de campe, he first bid a brotherly farewell to his two fellow officers before joining Steiner in the long dining room. Earlier, Erlich had lit the kindling and logs in the steel grate and the fire's warmth gave a welcoming feel to the room.

'Don't be too judgemental of Gersdorff and Kleist, Colonel. Both are excellent comrades and persuading them to join me is proving difficult... particularly Von Kleist'

Stated so openly in front of his aide de campe, Steiner realised that he too must be a confidante of the aristocratic young Colonel who had now seated himself in Steiner's favourite chair, letting the heat of the open fire suffuse his aching limbs.

Staring through the glass of red wine thoughtfully provided by Erlich, Von Stauffenberg no longer appeared so animated. 'Sitting here, it's difficult to believe there is a war going on. But if there wasn't a war, then I suppose we wouldn't be sitting here.' Musing at his own logic, Von Stauffenberg took a sip of wine and smacked his lips in mock appreciation.

'It's the oath of loyalty that many of our comrades appear to have difficulty with; that and their consciences. But you don't seem too concerned about breaking your oath, Colonel. Why is that?'

'Are you referring to the oath of loyalty we swore to the Fuhrer?'

'I am referring to the oath you swore to Adolph Hitler in person; not to the Fuhrer which is the office assumed by the head of state. Many of our fellow officers follow the creed of Von Manstein namely that Prussian field marshals do not mutiny. Fortunately there are some among us who are neither Prussian nor field marshals so our numbers are growing.'

Chastened but undeterred, Steiner advanced his point. 'It's not just the oath, Colonel: the Fuhrer has a following among many officers. They give him credit for restoring our national pride and rebuilding our armed forces between the wars and Germany's major land conquests since this war began; so whether deserved or not, that is how many of our comrades still perceive him.'

'I believe it's worse than that, Steiner. Many of our leading generals have mistrusted him for various reasons but have done nothing about it which is why it's now up to us, the colonels, to bring him down.'

'To bring him down you mean to kill the Fuhrer.'

Von Stauffenberg was unequivocal in his reply. 'Yes, I mean precisely that. I intend to kill Adolph Hitler and the gang of thugs around him.'

'Meaning who exactly?'

'Meaning Himmler, Goebbels, Goering, Bormann, Ribbentrop,' he paused for breath, 'the list is by no means exclusive, Steiner.'

'By speaking to other officers about this plan, you obviously understand the risk you are taking and the danger of being denounced. Not only will this mean that the plot will fail but it will also bring instant retribution by the Gestapo?'

'That will always be the primary risk, Colonel, but what is the alternative? What other option do we have to save our country and stop this madness?'

Looking at Von Stauffenberg, Steiner recognised the deep conviction in his earnest features. He saw a man grievously wounded whilst serving his beloved Fatherland only to belatedly realise that its leadership was incorrigibly corrupt and evil.

'Personally, I think the risk is too high. By widening the network of like-minded officers you also increase the risk of exposure and you only need one informant to blow the whistle for your plan to fail with terminal consequences for all those involved. But to answer your question, I believe there is no realistic alternative other than to let this war take its course. Even now your efforts may be too late.'

Continuing to stare into the fire, Von Stauffenberg seemed preoccupied with his own thoughts, letting Steiner continue his assessment. 'Predictably the Allies will demand nothing less than unconditional surrender and then God help Germany. If the reparations which followed the last war are anything to compare with, then the Allies won't content themselves with just seeking justice. They will look for revenge in every sense of that word. Some will want Germany broken up and for this to happen I expect France will want the Rhineland and Saarland ceded to Paris with the Ruhr turned into an international zone. That would suit Roosevelt and his isolationist pals; no more American involvement in any future European war.'

'And the Russians... what will they demand?' The question came from Von Stauffenberg's aide de campe.

'If by Russia you mean Stalin, then who can say what that man will want. But if I were him, I would want Germany divided into dozens of small regions, each with insufficient power to ever again be in a position to threaten his Mother Russia.'

Evidently unfazed in the presence of senior officers, the ADC tried a new angle. 'But wouldn't that raise the spectre of some future Hitler-figure attempting to reunite those same regions into one powerful state and the cycle would begin once more.'

'It may well be but what would your solution be?'

'As the Russians push us back, I believe their aim will be to retain a military presence and to occupy each of those countries in Eastern Europe which we have conquered and to then subjugate them as satellites of a greater Soviet empire.'

'But if that were to happen then the Soviets would become a greater threat to the Allies and the West than we do?'

The young officer gave a disarming smile. 'You need to remember, Colonel, this war has always been a conflict between Fascism and Communism and at the moment the tide appears to be turning against Fascism.'

'I can't disagree with you, Captain, as much as I would like too. But the Allies must surely resist the spread of communism as much as we have attempted to do.'

'But will they resist to the point of going to war against Stalin? The Commies have the largest army in the world with seemingly limitless manpower compared to their Allies who are not only weakened but sick of war so perhaps the Fuhrer was right in seeing Communism as the real enemy; not only of Germany but the rest of the free world as well.'

'Then why has he tried to enslave what you term as 'the rest of the free world'? You appear to forget that Hitler came to power on the promise of redressing what we Germans saw as the injustice of the 1918 Armistice agreement. In part, he fulfilled that undertaking but he should have stopped when we regained the Sudetenland from the Czechs. But he became carried away with his belief that Germany could conquer the world. Not just the French and the British empires but the Russian territories as well. As a consequence, we now have conflict on numerous fronts and again we have stupidly forced the Americans to fight against us.' Seeing the Captain's growing impatience, Steiner paused to give him a chance to respond.

'Colonel, whilst Communism and Fascism are radically opposite in philosophy, their aims are identical inasmuch they both want to dominate the rest of the world so whether Hitler or Stalin wins this war, the end result will be the same.'

'Do you really believe that?' It was Von Stauffenberg breaking into the conversation.

'Captain Schoning makes an excellent albeit depressing point, a view which I am increasingly coming around to as this damn war grinds on regardless of its eventual outcome.' Turning to face the junior officer, Steiner raised his near-empty glass; 'I'm grateful for your comments Captain. Who knows, in a different life you could have been a political analyst.'

Taking this as a cue for a break in the discussion, Steiner leaned across the table and refilled each of their glasses with the last of his palatable French red wine. Sipping from his newly charged glass, he remembered the discussion with Hannah which had been the prelude to their subsequent sexual encounter. 'I overheard one of the Jewish inmates express an interesting thought recently. Looking at the stars, this person drew comfort from the fact that nothing lasts forever and if I remember correctly, this same person said that 'men and their works shall pass away and become as mere grains of sand in the desert of time' so perhaps we shouldn't worry too much about this damn war or even our mad Fuhrer who believes his Third Reich will last for a thousand years.'

Von Stauffenberg smiled; 'do I detect a touch of mysticism or is it cynicism in that comment, Colonel?'

'Probably a touch of both if I care to think about it but how can we be anything other than depressed at what is happening on all our fronts? Because Hitler is convinced he knows better than his generals, we are now in the throes of losing this war. And his insane policy of Aryan superiority coupled with the systematic slaughter of Jews and others of such ilk will mean that Germany will become a pariah in the eyes of the civilised world long after this war has ended. Can either of you see anything to be cheerful about?'

'Your prognosis, Colonel, is gloomy beyond words, so I suggest we stop talking about this damn war and enjoy a quiet supper together.' The lines on Von Stauffenberg's forehead, indented by the thin black strap holding his eye-patch, came together in pensive thought. 'Tell me Colonel; the last time I was here, you surprised General Beck and myself by introducing your in-house violinist to play for us. Is she still here or has she been moved on?'

'By moved on, are you asking whether she is dead?'

'Colonel Steiner, unlike Von Kleist, I have no illusions about what happens to Jews in a place like Auschwitz. So you do not have to impress that point on me. I was simply enquiring whether she remains in your household and if so, I was about to ask whether it might be possible for her to play something for us during supper, perhaps?'

Forever the aristocrat thought Steiner; couching his wish in a velvet glove.

'Yes, Hannah Bergmann is still here and I'm sure she would be delighted to entertain us after dinner. But before then she will be busy preparing the food we are about to enjoy so you will have to curb your expectation until after the meal is concluded.'

From the corner of his eye, Steiner noticed that the young Captain had emptied his glass. Mischievously, he raised his own half-filled glass. 'Let me propose a toast to the success of Valkyrie.'

Painfully, Von Stauffenberg stumbled to his feet. 'To Valkyrie gentlemen... and your good health too, Colonel.' Embarrassed, the aide de campe followed suit and raised his empty glass: 'to Valkyrie... and to the end of this damn war.'

***

Surprised by the order to entertain Steiner's guests after dinner, Hannah quickly excused herself from the kitchen and made for her room. Changing into the now-familiar black dress, she ran through a series of preparatory scales before deciding what she would play.

Summoned finally to the dining room by a breathless Erlich, severely winded after climbing three sets of stairs, she was delighted to recognise the much wounded officer who had recently accompanied General Beck. As on that occasion, her eyes were once more drawn to the visible evidence of his many injuries so she tried not to stare, focussing instead on the black eye patch which she thought added a sense of intrigue to his autocratic features.

Rising to greet her, Von Stauffenberg extended his left hand in a token of welcome which took her by surprise. 'We meet again, Madam. Thank you for agreeing to play for us this evening.' Still holding Hannah's hand, he introduced his aide de campe. 'This is Captain Raul Schoning. On-duty, he assists me in my day-to-day tasks and off-duty he plays what he calls jazz wherever he can find a piano.'

Nodding to acknowledge the Captain, Hannah saw a blond-haired young officer with startling blue eyes and a ready smile looking at her with very obvious apprehension. Returning his smile, she saw an expression she had seen many times before and one she was now able to recognise... a mixture of subdued admiration coupled with a hint of something more sensuous.

As if reading her thoughts, it was Steiner who spoke. 'There is a piano in the storage room next to the kitchen. If my corporal and your driver could manhandle it in here, then why don't you play some jazz for us, Captain?'

'I would be happy to do that but I was rather hoping to listen to a professional performance from Miss Bergmann.' Looking towards Von Stauffenberg, he sought adjudication. 'I'm sure the Colonel would prefer that too... wouldn't you Colonel?'

Von Stauffenberg's reply took everybody by surprise. 'Why not have a jamming session?'

Startled, Steiner voiced his surprise. 'What on earth is a jamming session?'

Delighted at being able to display a knowledge of such things, Von Stauffenberg's reply had a touch of smugness. 'I heard a small group of musicians do this in Paris before the war and it was highly entertaining.' Looking at Hannah, he asked, 'would you be happy to try it?'

'I would love too provided Captain Schoning leads off.' Encouraged by Von Stauffenberg's informality, it was to Hannah reminiscent of pre-war times when no longer was she a Jew in the company of Wehrmacht officers but among fellow musicians having fun around their world of music. Glancing at Von Stauffenberg, she saw a look of boyish delight on his face. In his mind, the war and its deadening backdrop pushed to one side if only for a brief interlude by this stunningly beautiful woman.

It took longer than expected for a puffing Erlich and Von Stauffenberg's driver to bring the upright piano into the dining room during which time Hannah and Raul Schoning agreed upon several numbers and keys. She hoped the experience gained whilst playing the piano at the Hoffenblute night club would stand her in good stead but until they struck out together, she had no idea whether the young Captain could actually play and to what standard.

Within seconds of beginning their first number she had her answer. The slow tempo strains of 'Stomping at the Savoy' filled the room before Schoning quickened the tempo, nodding to Hannah to take the next riff. Raul Schoning was indeed a gifted musician and for the next four minutes they shared individual solos only coming together for the finale. Having played three numbers in quick succession, she was secretly delighted when Von Stauffenberg insisted they continue with their impromptu programme. His face mirrored a look of almost child-like happiness reflected by the remaining fingers of his left hand tapping out a syncopated rhythm on the arm of his chair. Erlich too had discretely positioned himself at the far end of the room and Hannah was amused to see his large booted foot attempting to keep in time with the music.

Ending with an extended version of 'Sweet Georgia Brown' it was Steiner who eventually brought the musical interlude to an end using Von Stauffenberg's proposed early start the following morning as the reason for calling a halt. Not being a lover of music, she guessed he had tolerated rather than enjoyed the session but disturbingly, at one point during their third number, Raul Schoning had playfully put his arm around her waist whilst she was playing an unaccompanied solo and the look on Steiner's face was one which Hannah instantly recognised. 'My God' she thought... 'the man is seriously jealous!'

In quiet moments after their first sexual encounter, she had frequently wondered what had prompted his sudden desire for her on that fateful night. She had dismissed the thought that it may have been the innocent accolade accorded her by General Beck but having seen what she now recognised as barely disguised jealousy, she wondered afresh. If her notion was correct, would it bring Steiner to her room later tonight or would the thought of Von Stauffenberg sleeping in close proximity on the third floor be a sufficient deterrent to ensure an undisturbed night?

FIFTY SIX

Whether through pique or sheer tiredness, Steiner resisted the temptation to come to her room that night despite knowing that the worsening situation on the Eastern front would take him away from the Admin centre and Hannah too, for the next ten days or so.

'So much for my theory of jealousy begetting sexual activity' thought Hannah.

At Debica, some 120 kilometres from Auschwitz, Steiner's staff car came under attack from a marauding Russian fighter aircraft intent on strafing vehicles on the highway leading to Krakow. Having spotted the German vehicle too late, the Yakovlev Yak-3's machine guns chewed up the surface of the road some 40 metres ahead of Steiner's vehicle.

Shocked by the suddenness of the attack, the young conscript driver momentarily froze before bringing the vehicle to an emergency halt. Leaping from the stationary staff car, both he and Steiner sought cover in the ditch alongside the road and watched as the Yak came around in a tight turn to line up for another strafing run.

'We're too close, soldier. If the car goes up we'll be roasted alive. Run back that way but stay in the ditch.' Steiner's coolness helped the driver overcome his rising panic and together they retreated further away in a half-crouching run. Throwing themselves flat as the Russian fighter approached, they waited for the deadly chatter of its guns. Instead, it was the note of the plane's engine, spluttering instead of roaring, which made Steiner look up. As the Yak flashed by, he saw the face of its Russian pilot frantically wrestling with the plane's controls. Rapidly losing height, the heavy fighter hit the centre of the road in a belly-landing, its metal propeller bending under the engine as it made contact with the road. Sliding to a halt in a shower of sparks, Steiner heard a dull explosion and saw the plane becoming enveloped in flames as its fuel tank ignited. From the burning wreck, he saw the pilot stumble from the cockpit and attempt to drag himself away from the shattered wreck of an aircraft which only seconds before had been a deadly war machine. Barely clear of the plane, Steiner saw the pilot fall down, still perilously close to the burning fuselage.

Rising from the ditch, Steiner pulled his shocked driver to his feet and together they ran towards the figure of the pilot, now lying very still. Even from a distance, he could feel the intense heat coming from the burning aircraft. Shielding his face with his cap, Steiner got to the barely conscious figure of the pilot ahead of his driver. Pulling on the straps of his unopened parachute, he pulled him clear of the burning wreck. Behind him, he heard the sound of exploding ammunition as the fire reached the drums of encased ammunition in the wings.

Steiner knew that the black smoke billowing from the blazing aircraft would inevitably attract a German patrol so together with his driver and the injured pilot, they sat on the grass verge and waited. The pilot, slowly recovering from the initial impact, had removed his leather flying helmet and Steiner saw the shocked features of a fresh-faced young man with a thatch of dark hair damply compressed by his tight-fitting leather helmet. Bleeding profusely from a deep cut just above his forehead, he was attempting to stem the flow of blood with the sleeve of his brown flying jacket. Behind German lines with a Wehrmacht officer standing over him, the young pilot reached into his uniform pocket and extracted a card bearing his name and service number and with a shaking hand, cautiously offered it to Steiner. With his upraised palm, Steiner indicated that he was to retain it and instead, opened his cigarette case and took out a small cheroot. Lighting it, he passed it to the Russian. Hesitantly, the pilot reached out and put the cheroot between his lips and drew deeply, savouring its flavour before exhaling and mumbling his thanks... in German!

Intrigued, Steiner crouched down to the pilot's level. 'You speak German?'

Through trembling lips he mumbled... 'a little.'

'And where did you learn to speak 'a little' of my language?'

Still in delayed shock from his narrow escape he could only mutter 'as a prisoner I can only tell you my name and number; nothing more.'

Hearing this, Steiner rocked back on his heels and with a smile, patted the Russian on his shoulder. 'Good man; your political commissar wouldn't want it any other way.' Glancing up, he noticed his driver had brought the medical kit from the staff car and was frantically searching for a dressing from among the tin's depleted contents. 'Give the box here.'

Relieved it would be the Colonel who would apply the dressing to the pilot's injury, the driver passed the box to Steiner; never once taking his eyes off the young pilot.

Detecting his nervousness, Steiner smiled. 'Is this the first Russian you've met in this war, soldier? How long have you been at the front?'

'Two weeks' sir, and yes, he is the first Russian I've seen.'

'Then say hallo, he won't bite you' Speaking in fluent Russian, Steiner spoke to the pilot. 'This is my driver who thinks you may have horns in your head. And yes, I know a little of your language too.'

Despite himself, the Russian's blood-streaked face broke in a half-smile.

Finding a dressing, Steiner tore off its paper wrapping and firmly pressed the sterile gauze over the bloody cut. 'Driver, wrap this bandage round his head but don't move the dressing. When you've done that, use another dressing to clean the blood from his face. Can you do that?'

'I can sir but shouldn't we take his pistol first.'

Hearing this, the pilot's right hand moved quickly down to his side holster and in one fluid movement, drew out his standard-issue Tokarev automatic pistol and pointed it to cover both

Germans. For a frightening moment, time stood still. Then spinning it round he grasped the loaded gun by its barrel and offered it to Steiner.

Taking the weapon, Steiner stood up and examined it. Although heavy by hand-gun standards and lacking the engineering precision of his own Luger, Steiner knew from his experience at Stalingrad that it rarely jammed, even in the most extreme weather conditions and in the hands of a competent soldier, it's automatic rate of fire could be deadly at close quarters. And with typical Russian foresight, it could also fire German 7.63mm ammunition!

Looking at the young airman, Steiner knew that in the hands of the Waffen SS, he would be interrogated and tortured before being despatched with a bullet in the head. Aircraft could always be replaced quickly but it took much longer to train and replace dead pilots. Knowing this and looking at the young pilot who moments before had tried to kill him, Steiner made his decision.

Still speaking in Russian, Steiner ordered the pilot to get to his feet. Shakily, the Russian did so.

'Can you walk?' By way of reply, the pilot took a stumbling step forward before stopping. 'I can walk... which way?

'Good. Head towards that car.'

Hesitantly, the Russian stumbled twice more before Steiner's driver took him by the shoulder and helped him reach the vehicle, its engine still running following their rapid abandonment moments earlier.

'Put him in the back and be careful as you do so. He may have damaged something in that crash. And when you've done that, pass me the map for this area.'

With the Russian pilot safely seated, Steiner clambered in alongside him. Thrusting the military ordnance map in front of the pilot, he again reverted to Russian.

'Look at this map and tell me the best place for you to try and make your way back to your own lines. D'you understand what I'm saying to you?'

Not quite believing what he was hearing, the pilot leaned away from Steiner in order to be able to look into his face. 'I understand what you say but I do not understand why you would do this. We are enemies and we are told that Germans kill captured pilots.'

'For once your Commissars are telling the truth, Ivan. That's why I'm going to help you avoid that fate.

Realising that he had nothing to lose, the Russian looked at the map and pointed to an area which Steiner guessed was some 25 kilometres from their present position. 'Here would give me a chance without placing you too close to our lines.'

Taking the map back, Steiner made a mental note of key reference points before addressing his driver. 'We're about to make some Russian mother very happy, so just follow my directions.' Seeing the incredulous look on the conscript's face, he added, 'and think how you would feel if you were in Ivan's shoes... OK?'

It took longer than Steiner had reckoned to reach the point on the map indicated by the Russian pilot. Several times their car was halted by wrecked vehicles and in the distance, they could hear the sporadic sound of artillery fire. Stopping the car near an abandoned farm outbuilding, Steiner turned to his silent and still disbelieving passenger. 'If I were you, I would hide in that building until your forces take the area which I suspect will be very soon. Take this canteen of water and these field rations and stay under cover.' Extending his hand, he grasped the Russian's shoulder and half-pushed him out of the car. 'And good luck!'

Turning, the young pilot stared at Steiner. 'I shall remember you, Colonel.'

'Please do and if you're looking through a gun sight at the time then remember to aim high!'

Walking unsteadily, the Russian reached the entrance to the outbuilding, turned once more and then disappeared.

'Ok soldier, let's get out of here. We have work to do and it's not here, believe me.'

FIFTY SEVEN

Hannah was relieved when Steiner returned safely from his mission. Being in the company of the kindly but dour Corporal Erlich for ten days had taxed her patience almost beyond measure. She knew the middle-aged Bavarian must be like thousands of other servicemen in hating the war but patriotically feeling they had a duty to serve their country. The elderly Corporal could talk for hours on his passion for wood and its workings without once noticing when her eyes would begin to glaze over. However, knowing from Steiner that his leave had been cancelled at the very last moment elicited s degree of sympathy towards him which Erlich was not unaware of.

On the second evening of Steiner's absence and firm in her resolve of not wishing to get too close to Agnetta, she decided to spend an hour or so playing for her own pleasure. Her session with Raul Schoning had stimulated her musical senses to the point of making her realise how fixated she had become with classical music. Before leaving the following morning, the amiable young captain had given her an album of sheet music so tonight she decided to play her way through it. One number in particular, 'Serenade in Blue' particularly appealed to her, more so when she increased the tempo. Midway through the number, she heard a faint tap and thinking it might be Erlich, she opened the door to see Agnetta standing there.

'I heard you playing from down below and hoped I might come in and join you. Do you mind?'

Surprised by the normally shy Agnetta's presence, Hannah stepped back and nodded her in. 'Actually I'm nearly finished but take a seat on the bed and make yourself comfortable.' Staring out of the window to avoid looking at Agnetta, she ran through the rest of the sheet music before concluding with an exaggerated flourish and mock bow to acknowledge the

Dane's enthusiastic clapping. 'That's it for tonight Agnetta; not my usual repertoire but fun to play around with.'

'Well that sounded pretty special to me; I feel extremely privileged... almost like being at a private audition. Corporal Erlich told me you played with a Berlin orchestra? Is that where you lived?'

'I did before all this happened but it all now seems so long ago.' Taking time to put her violin away she noticed that Agnetta was showing no sign of wanting to leave. 'And what about you; do you play any form of music?'

'Afraid not. I'm told I'm tone deaf whatever that may mean.'

'It's a term usually applied wrongly to describe a person who has no aptitude for music rather than a hearing difficulty. Believe me, it's not something to worry about especially in a place like this.' Pouring cold water into the washstand basin, Hannah splashed her face and towelled it dry. 'Tell me, what did you do in the Camp before you came here?'

'I was assigned as a cleaner in the SS Blockhouse with several other women of my religion.'

'That must have been pretty awful for you. Were the other women as pretty as you?'

Agnetta thought about the question before responding. 'I suppose they were and I can guess why you ask that question.'

'Was it that bad then?'

Agnetta's reply surprised Hannah. 'It was worse than bad, it was truly awful. We were raped almost daily and one girl was shot in front of us for refusing to show pleasure while it was happening. So we did just that but they never realised it actually strengthened our faith by being tested in such a way. They told us we were chosen because we weren't Jews.'

Hearing Agnetta's unintended gibe reminded her of Danuta's vitriolic belief that Jews were the cause of the world's problems. She recalled the memory of her own horrific experience, so similar to that of Agnetta which had brought both of them to this place of temporary sanctuary. But unlike Agnetta who claimed her faith had been strengthened by her experiences, her own belief in God, never strong in the orthodox sense, had been all but extinguished following her encounter with the Romanian Kapo. Added to which, she was also an adulteress, a willing participant in an act of sexual gratification. To her own surprise, she felt no sense of guilt and knew she would probably do so again if tempted. Even the eroticism of her brief and tender relationship with Elsa caused no sense of shame.

'Would you like me to go, Hannah? You seem lost in your thoughts.'

'Sorry, I was far away.' Looking at an uncertain Agnetta poised on the edge of the bed and ready to leave, she felt a growing sense of admiration for the young Dane. Like herself, she had undergone similarly horrific experiences and yet, unlike her, had managed to keep her faith intact.

'No, please stay because there's something I want to tell you. Something that could even save your life.'

Intrigued by Hannah's dramatic pronouncement, Agnetta coolly repositioned herself on the bed. 'Anything that can save my life I just have to hear.'

'Well cut out the jocularity and listen. The last two inmates in your position died in tragic and unnecessary circumstances and I don't want you to become the third?' She positioned the chair so she could sit facing Agnetta. 'Danuta who was here when I arrived became involved with the Resistance and was shot on the order of Colonel Steiner. She was followed by a woman named Miriam who tried to escape but was caught by the SS and executed in the camp. Like you, both were very intelligent women who each stood a chance to survive this war but who chose to follow different paths and consequently paid for that choice with their lives. So my advice is very simple... choose what you do very carefully because your life will depend on it. End of sermon.'

Listening to Hannah's sobering words it was a thoughtful Agnetta who finally spoke. 'I knew the last woman had been killed but I never knew why. Of course I want to get through this war so thanks for the warning. Presuming it was a warning?

'I'm not sure I understand why you say that but I've said my piece and the rest is up to you. I now need to get ready for bed so you will have to excuse me.'

'That sounds as though I'm being dismissed.' She rose from the bed. 'But tell me before I go... how have you managed to survive for so long?'

The directness of the question unsettled Hannah. 'Look Agnetta, you came here uninvited and you now need to think about what I've just told you, but in the quietness of your own room. We can talk again tomorrow if you wish but for now, I need to get some beauty sleep. So off you go and please close the door as you leave.'

Lying in bed, she had the uneasy feeling that the Danish newcomer had the necessary characteristics and chutzpah to cause even more problems in the household than either of her two predecessors.' Only time will tell' she thought as she drifted into a world of embraceable sleep.

The return of Colonel Steiner was akin to the house coming out of hibernation. The Polish summer had brought pleasant days of warm weather tempered by cool winds blowing from the East. The hedgerows surrounding the Polish fields and smallholdings on the distant horizon were in in full bloom though crops throughout the region were sparse due to the unusually cold winter coupled with the dire shortage of manpower. The garden at the rear of the house, once lovingly tended by Danuta but neglected by Miriam, was now overrun by weeds and thistles making it a perfect place to quietly sit and think.

But from the moment Steiner returned to the unit, all thought of relaxation disappeared. Sitting for hours taking endless notes, she slowly became aware of a subtle change in his attitude. Gone was the ill-tempered manner which had been so much a part of his persona, replaced instead by a more thoughtful trait which if anything, made his decision-making ability even more incisive.

That evening, Steiner took the unusual step of dining with Erlich and his driver who had been assigned a permanent billet in the unit next to the trusted man from Bavaria. Believing the meal would take up much of the evening, Hannah enjoyed a quick supper of latkes; fried potato pancakes usually eaten for Hanukkah.

Shamed by Agnetta's recent testimony of her strengthened faith compared to her own moments of inner guilt, she had resolved to read the Talmud more regularly in an attempt to resuscitate what remained of her fraught testimony. Tonight, engrossed in its labyrinthine Hebrew text, she felt her eyes beginning to close and she knew her ability to absorb any further spiritual uplift was improbable. From the fields around the property, the sound of cicada beetles began to intrude, adding a final knell to her well-intentioned endeavour. Closing the heavy tome, she made her way down to the small anteroom on the first floor where she knew she could hear whether the dinner was still in progress. Oddly quiet, she decided to check whether Steiner wanted to continue working but hoping he too would be too tired.

Knocking gently, she was dismayed when his summons to enter sounded as energised as ever. Entering, she saw that Erlich and the driver had departed and the dinner table cleared away except for two glasses and a half-full decanter of red wine.

'I came down to see whether you wanted to continue your reports, Colonel.'

'But hoping the answer might be no... correct?'

'Correct.'

'Good call Bergmann because I'm too bushed for any more work tonight. There's a time for work and a time to relax so I am going to have another glass of wine while you tell me what's been happening whilst I've been away.' Without asking whether she wanted to join him, Steiner casually poured the plum-coloured wine in to both glasses and pushed the second one towards her. Half smiling, he raised his own glass and proposed a toast. 'To you... Shana Madela.'

Astonished at his use of Yiddish, Hannah raised her own glass to hide her embarrassment. 'I can't toast myself. Do you understand what it means?'

'Of course I do. It means 'pretty girl'.'

Blushing, Hannah sipped her wine. 'Thank you Colonel for a most unexpected compliment but I would prefer 'le Chaim... to life.'

'Well I prefer 'Shana Madela' as its highly descriptive. You're a beautiful woman Hannah Bergmann.' Taking a deep swig of wine, he looked into its redness as he held it level with his eyes. 'I saw the way my two fellow officers looked at you when you entertained us the other evening. Von Stauffenberg was especially enchanted by you.

'Then I'm pleased. That poor man must have been through hell with those dreadful injuries.'

'To hell and back I would think.' Unwilling to dwell on the subject of other men, Steiner quickly changed the subject. 'I understand the new housekeeper is another religious crank; a Jehovah's Witness so Erlich tells me. Did you know that?'

'Yes I did. She told me that her faith had actually been strengthened because of her experiences in the camp which I find disturbing. I wish I could feel the same but it just doesn't happen for me I'm afraid.'

'I wouldn't be too concerned about that. History is full of religious fanatics who seek persecution in order to purify their souls.' Raising an eyebrow, Hannah saw he was having difficulty in suppressing a grin. 'I'm afraid that kind of religion is not for me.'

'Do you have any belief at all?'

Leaning back in his chair, Steiner put both hands behind his head. 'Do you really want to discuss religion with a German when you know what we are doing to your people?

'Maybe tonight you can relax and just be a man and not a German... remember?'

Steiner laughed. 'Of course I remember except I did say those words in a somewhat different context.' Rising to his feet in one easy movement, Steiner picked up the decanter. 'Bring your glass Hannah; let's move to somewhere more comfortable.'

Following Steiner into the lounge area, he allowed Hannah to go ahead of him and with his foot, closed the inter-communicating door with a firmness which signified he did not wish to be disturbed. Hannah thought this unlikely as she guessed that Erlich would now probably be in his bed following the earlier supper and the inevitable flow of Bavarian beer. The prospect of Agnetta appearing too was also highly improbable with her being confined to her room on the ground floor.

Beckoning Hannah to sit in the padded leather armchair opposite to him, Steiner recalled her question. 'You asked whether I have any belief in a religious sense or whether I am simply a non-believer.'

Unused to alcohol and not wishing to befuddle her brain, Hannah took the merest sip of wine while she pondered Steiner's comment. When she spoke, her answer was to the point. 'My question was whether you believe in God? A simple question which I would have thought you could answer without too much difficulty.'

'Ok, let me think about that for a moment.' He smiled, knowing his lack of an immediate response would irk Hannah and to extend the delay even longer he reached out, re-filled his own glass and topped up Hannah's barely touched drink.

'To answer that question, I need to say something about the nature of religion. Would you like me to do that?'

'Provided you can do so without losing your temper.'

'Look, I want you to get one thing perfectly clear in that beautiful head of yours. Some weeks ago, I spoke to you on a subject which would have placed not only my career but my life in some jeopardy. I'm sure you don't need me to remind you of that conversation. But whether that was foolhardy or not should at least have conveyed the fact that I trust you implicitly.' He picked up his glass but oddly, replaced it on the table without drinking from it.

'So having given you an opportunity to take advantage of that indiscretion you have not so much as mentioned it since.' This time he did take a sip from his glass, his brow furrowing as he did so. 'So why am I reminding you of this?'

Knowing he wasn't expecting her to reply, she watched as Steiner fiddled awkwardly with the stem of his glass before placing it neatly in the centre of the wooden coaster in front of him.

'Because, Hannah Bergmann, our relationship emphatically changed the night we came together in your bed. Maybe that doesn't answer your question but I think you know by now that my temper is usually the cumulative result of many things; the job, the war, the waste of young lives and for what? I try hard, very hard, to control it but I don't always succeed as you well know.' He looked up, hoping to see a degree of understanding on Hannah's face. 'Or is that just a pathetic excuse for an answer?'

Astonished by his open frankness, she was briefly lost for words. When at last she did speak, her reply was thoughtfully moderated.

'Colonel, I have to accept what you say because I'm not in a position to say otherwise. But I think you are prevaricating because you haven't really got an answer or perhaps you haven't even thought about it. And being a soldier I guess doesn't help very much.'

Puzzled by her comment, Steiner looked bemused. 'I can't follow your thinking. I'm not sure being a soldier influences my thinking one way or another?'

Feeling more like a seminary teacher than the reality of being a Jewish prisoner conversing with a senior German officer, she looked Steiner in the eye. 'Because as a soldier you will have seen some truly dreadful things, especially at Stalingrad, which could well cause you to doubt the very existence of God just as I now do after seeing what is happening in camps like Auschwitz.'.

Pondering her words, he took his time before replying. 'I think I'm beginning to understand.' He hesitated as though reluctant to reveal something deeply personal. 'My answer is this. I do not believe in God so I suppose I am a cynic but hopefully not an agnostic.'

'If you have no belief in God then you are an agnostic'. She wavered, suddenly unsure of herself. 'Isn't it the same thing?'

'No it isn't the same thing. To me, religion isn't a fact; it's nothing more than a hazy act of faith in a world yet to come or so you and the world at large would like to believe.' Steiner smiled knowing his next comment might cause Hannah to think that the agnostic cynic sitting opposite her was about to become philosophical. 'Throughout the centuries it has been mankind which has created the image of God. A God incidentally who has chosen never to appear to mankind nor ever likely too, based on the evidence so far. So mankind's belief in God must remain just that; a belief and nothing more.' Steiner stopped speaking, expecting Hannah to interject but unusually she remained silent.

'I also have difficulty with the concept of this God being the creator of all mankind. If that is true, then this God of yours must accept accountability for both good and bad in this world, such as wars and all the wickedness which man inflicts upon his fellow man including that which is happening to Jews like you.'

'But surely it's something more than just a belief. Isn't faith a part of the equation as well?

'I think you are wrong, Bergmann. In my book, faith and belief are one and the same thing.'

Animated by Steiner's smugness, Hannah threw caution to the wind. 'No, I believe it's you who is wrong. A belief is a fundamental part of faith but they are not the same. You can have faith or a hope in that which is to come without actually believing in the means to attain it.'

'I'm not sure I understand that distinction; it sounds too Rabbinical for me and similar to debating how many angels can dance on the end of a pin.'

It was Hannah' turn to look puzzled. 'Now it's me who doesn't know what you are talking about. In fact, I don't even know why I'm arguing with you on matters which I too have doubts about.'

'In which case let's move on to yet another nebulous aspect of religion and see whether you or I can understand what is hidden from the rest of mankind.'

'I was under the impression we were having a serious conversation so can you stop being cynical and tell me what you're referring too.'

'I'm referring to this fairy-tale world of life after death' and the difference between heaven and hell... a concept invented by ancient church leaders of a mythological paradise to which they alone hold the key of entry to or conversely, everlasting damnation which again, only they can consign you to. But it helps if you are wealthy because it then doesn't matter how bad you are because you can buy indulgences from the Church and in you go, straight to heaven with no questions asked.' He laughed aloud, knowing he had strained his philosophical argument to a ludicrous point.

'I think you're referring to a practice which went out of fashion with Martin Luther in the Middle Ages.'

'Well done, Bergmann. I wouldn't have expected a Jew to know about him.' Looking up at the ceiling, he tried again. 'Look, forgive my flippancy so let me be serious. I was thinking about people who do whatever they choose in this life in the belief that redemption awaits them in the world to come. If that is the case, then what is the point of trying to live a good life here if all will be forgiven in the hereafter? Frankly, I think death is the end of the line. Bang, you're dead and that s it! Do you agree or disagree with that?'

'I disagree profoundly! The overriding principle of religion is that of a judgement with punishment and reward meted out in accordance to how we have conducted ourselves during our time on this earth. And the evidence showing that this one single principle is sufficient to cause the greater part of mankind to lead good lives is overwhelming to the point where the evil committed by men like Hitler is confined to a small minority.'

'But Bergmann, you are missing the point. If there is no life to follow this one, then monsters like Hitler need have no fear because sanctions hold no dread if there is no possibility of retribution.'

Having hoped for a simple and direct answer to her original question, Hannah was struggling to find words to further dispute the temporal logic of Steiner's reasoning.

'I really don't know how to respond to your points, Colonel. I now wish I hadn't asked you that question.'

Scenting victory, a touch of superiority crept into Steiner's voice. 'Come now Bergmann, you can't really mean that. I think you were hoping for an admission of belief on my part sufficient to strengthen your own flagging testimony so I'm sorry to have disappointed you.'

Finishing off his wine, Steiner surveyed his empty glass. 'This is a fine red which doesn't leave you with a thick head in the morning. Standing up, he made for the wine cabinet at the far end of the room and returned with a new bottle. 'About the only thing the French are good at.' Smirking, he skilfully uncorked it and produced two fresh glasses. 'Never mix wines from different bottles... take my word for it.'

Whether it was the effect of the small amount of wine she had drunk or Steiner's earlier comment relating to their changing relationship she had no way of telling but for the first time in his presence, she began to visibly relax.

'If you are about to follow your pyrrhic victory on religion with a further discourse on wine then save yourself the trouble because I concede immediately. My knowledge of wine is fairly minimal.'

'In which case let me savour my victory.' Slowly he filled each of the two glasses. 'Let the wine stand for a moment.' Laughing at his further injunction, he couldn't resist adding 'that will be my final comment on the subject of wine for tonight. While we wait, can I ask you a personal question?'

'Of course; will I be allowed to do likewise?'

Steiner leaned over from his chair and looked into her eyes. 'You may ask whatever you wish but whether I will be able to reply will depend on your question.'

'I assure you my question won't cause you to breach military secrets.'

'In which case, go ahead... try me.'

Knowing she was about to enter into unchartered territory, she took a deep breath before speaking. 'If you feel able to talk about yourself, I would like to know what you felt after you left my room that night. You told me very clearly that what had occurred between us must never happen again but in the same breath you then almost broke that decision albeit in extreme anger.'

Taking time to reflect on his reply Steiner suddenly sat upright. 'Listen... do you hear that?'

Listening intently, Hannah's keen hearing picked up a sound she had last heard in Berlin. 'It sounds like an air raid siren to me but why would the Allies bomb this area?'

'They wouldn't bomb the camp but the industrial factories in this area could be key targets but surely their bombers don't have the range.' His comment was self-directed.

In the distance they heard the siren's doleful wail continue with growing intensity. As if linked to the sound of the siren, the two ceiling lights began to flicker before cutting out, casting the room in total darkness. She heard an unsteady Steiner grope his way to the door and call out for Erlich but without success. Disappearing into the office, he returned moments later holding a lighted candle with several more in his other hand. 'That bloody man will wake up tomorrow and not even be aware there was an air raid.'

'But we're not sure it is an air raid.'

'Then why have all the lights in the entire area been shut off?' Lighting two more candles, Steiner placed them on either side of the wooden mantelshelf and settled back into his chair. 'They say that war is the engine of change but sitting here in comparative darkness, you would have to doubt that.' Picking up both glasses, he handed one to Hannah. 'So let's make the most of it.'

'I think in this war you have to live for the moment, Colonel. Anything else is a bonus.'

'I'll drink to that so tell me, Hannah Bergmann, what would be an appropriate toast in Hebrew?'

'I gather from that that you have exhausted your Yiddish cum Hebrew vocabulary... true?'

'Very true.'

'In which case repeat after me... Mazel Tov'

'Mazel Tov.'

Listening to Steiner, a senior German officer repeating the toast in Hebrew caused Hannah to wonder whether she was actually hearing correctly. By saying earlier that their relationship had changed she had assumed he was referring to its physical aspect but here was this same man, not only talking to her as easily as Ephraim once did, but now pronouncing a toast... in fluent Hebrew!

Quietly encouraged, she decided to test Steiner's intentions further. 'Now we can see each other again, would you like to answer my question?'

'Which was, how did I feel after we made love on the first occasion?

'Not love, Colonel; it was sex; plain simple sex.'

To her astonishment Steiner became extremely animated. Falling out of his chair on to his knees, he propelled himself across to Hannah. Grasping her two hands he pulled her close. 'I want you to listen to me very carefully. First, when we are alone, you will address me either as Kurt or Steiner... OK? Secondly, I know you were probably wracked with guilt after what happened and to salve that Jewish conscience of yours you would prefer to think of it as just sex, perhaps even with a touch of alcohol as an added palliative to ease the guilt.'

Studying his face in the soft candlelight, she fully expected to see him smile but instead his face was expressively serious.

To me, it certainly wasn't just sex. I accept that my referring to it as love was maybe too strong a word for what actually happened but for me, it wasn't just sex. But thinking back to that night, that is the one word and emotion which keeps coming to mind.' His hands gripped hers more tightly. 'I hadn't been with a woman since my wife died and that has been my choice and not through lack of opportunity. So whilst love may be the wrong adjective to describe what happened, it certainly wasn't just sex. Can you possibly understand that?

Looking at the man kneeling before her, his frame dimly outlined in weaving candlelit shadows, Hannah felt her eyes fill with tears. Emotionally overwhelmed and unable to speak, she could barely nod her head to show her understanding.

Overhead, a group of US Air Force Boeing B17 bombers were overflying the darkened landscape of Auschwitz am Birkenau en-route to Russia, their young American aircrews unaware that just 9000 metres below the camouflaged wings of their four engine war machines, lay the most horrific death factory known to mankind. To save weight their bomb bays were empty as each aircraft was flying at the very limit of its range; a tangible product of the American Lend-Lease programme to the Soviet Government.

Aware of the enemy aircraft above them and knowing their own depleted Luftwaffe lacked the resources to engage them in combat, the camp authorities chose to enforce a black-out for the rest of the short summer night.

In the Administration quarters a very unsteady Officer I/C Defence, Upper Silesia Region, was helped to his room. The candle held by Steiner became extinguished soon after leaving the lounge and together in total darkness they made their laboured way to the top floor of the building. Once there, Hannah helped Steiner to his bed where she covered him with his Army greatcoat. Leaning over his passive form, she planted a gentle kiss on his damp forehead and whispered 'goodnight Kurt Steiner. Thank you for a most interesting evening.'

FIFTY EIGHT

Wearing a slip of a nightdress leaving little to his imagination, the coffee hurriedly prepared and served by Agnetta failed to curb the growing impatience of the young Abwehr Lieutenant. Unable to rouse the household with his first tentative knock, it took a solid thump on the heavy oak door before being admitted by a sleepy-eyed driver. Increasingly aware of the growing disturbance, Erlich meanwhile was frantically stirring Steiner into life and assisting him into his uniform.

Exactly 15 minutes after the Lieutenant's arrival, Steiner made his appearance looking as though he had been up for hours.

Acknowledging his crisp salute with a casual nod of his head, Steiner imposed himself immediately. 'Lieutenant, I hope what brings you here so early is more important than the briefing you have just interrupted.' From the corner of his eye, he saw Erlich raise an eyebrow, his face a picture of incredulity.

'Colonel, I apologise for my untimely arrival but the news I bring is critical. Italy has withdrawn from the war and surrendered to the Allies and Mussolini has been arrested by his own people. The Fuhrer will be making an announcement later but General Staff HQ require all senior officers to know before the official announcement.'

Already aware of this information from Von Stauffenberg, Steiner resisted the temptation to prick the young officer's smugness.

'That's very considerate of HQ but having informed all senior officers, what are we now expected to do about the 'new' situation?'

Ruffled but still on-message, the Lieutenant replied with equal coolness. 'You will wait for further orders, Colonel. In the meantime you may wish to inform those other officers you are presently conferring with in order to avoid unfortunate rumours later.'

Steiner laughed aloud. 'Tell me Lieutenant, with the Allies now firmly entrenched in Northern Europe and ready to jump out of Sicily and Allied landings expected anytime on Italy's Mediterranean freeboard, what room will there be for rumours in the face of so much fact. The only surprise is that the Italians didn't switch sides before now. They know their war is lost and... '

Erlich's heavily accented Bavarian voice broke in, interrupting Steiner in mid-flow. 'Colonel, the call from Berlin is due any moment.'

Hearing Erlich's interjection, he nearly missed the discreet wink on the face of his stout minded protector. 'You're right Ernst, thank you.' Turning to the Abwehr officer, Steiner could see from his body language that he was anxious to leave. 'My thanks to you as well, Lieutenant. Be assured I shall await those further orders with great interest.'

Left alone following the Lieutenant's departure, Steiner slapped his old comrade across his broad shoulders. 'What would I do without you, Ernst?'

'It cuts two ways, Colonel. Without you, my soldierly career would have ended at Stalingrad. We both know that.'

'And mine too, old friend, if you hadn't pulled me out,'

Embarrassed by Steiner's words, Erlich's face reddened. 'I need to have a word with our cook. She served coffee to that young man looking as though she had come straight from the camp brothel.'

'You mean the Puffhaus, Ernst?'

'Probably but I think we're speaking of the same place.'

Enjoying a relaxed moment with his trusted comrade before the pressures of the day intervened, Steiner recalled something else. 'Didn't you tell me that she was the same religion as that Czech woman and her younger sister?'

'I did Colonel but she certainly has a different way of expressing it. Even when she's dressed she shows more of herself than Danuta and her sister ever did... collectively!'

'And you don't like that?'

Erlich thought about it. 'I suppose I must do really, otherwise I would have had a word before now, wouldn't I.'

'Ernst, just remember; she's a Scandinavian woman and they have a reputation for free love so just watch yourself in that basement at night.'

Laughing to himself, Erlich made to leave. 'And you need to be careful too, Colonel, with all these young Abwehr pipsqueaks round every corner. Give me a half-dressed Dane anytime.'

Not aware of the earlier meeting and having sacrificed breakfast to gain an extra 15 minutes in bed, Hannah duly reported to the first floor office at 07.55am. Steiner was already there speaking on the field telephone with news on the Italian situation. Seeing her in the doorway, Steiner waved her in to the office and bade her sit down in the same gesture.

Finishing his call, Steiner stood up and came round his desk. Motioning her to stand he gently kissed her on her forehead before sitting her down. 'And you thought I was asleep when you left, didn't you.'

She blushed; 'yes, I was convinced you were dead to the world.'

'There's a lesson there Bergmann; never underestimate a dead soldier.'

'Lesson understood, Colonel.' She gave a mock salute.

Quickly briefing her on the morning's happenings, Steiner seemed markedly relaxed. 'The war in Italy, though not over, is lost. We will have to replace the Italians which will mean we will be further weakened elsewhere so hopefully it will hasten the inevitable.' He didn't elaborate further but Hannah could guess his conclusion.

'As a result of what has happened in Italy, I will be attending a briefing meeting with my team so may not be back tonight. But if I do manage to return then I would like to know whether I will find a contrite Jewish woman, regretting what has happened between us in which case I will accept that and go quietly. Or a woman who will reciprocate what I feel and want to experience life to the full and to hell with what else is happening in this damn world.' Holding his hand up before Hannah could reply, he added, 'no need to answer now; just think about what I've just said. It has to be your call and I promise I will respect your decision... whatever it may be.'

By mid-afternoon, Hannah's mind was in turmoil, vacillating between the ingrained parameters of Jewish morality and continuing faithfulness to a husband who was almost certainly dead contrasting with the physical desire to experience and enjoy yet more sexual fulfilment with a man to whom she was becoming increasingly drawn to.

Throughout the morning she tried desperately to expunge the memory of the passion she had experienced with Steiner by thoughts of her matrimonial lovemaking with Ephraim but each time it was the unbridled sex with Steiner which forced its way back into her mind.

By early evening she had at last cleared her mind and made her decision. Joining Erlich for supper she was amused when he recounted the earlier conversation he had had with Agnetta which clearly had had little effect as the Dane appeared in her short grey overall with no obvious dress beneath it. Seeing Erlich's face redden in embarrassment, Hannah decided to step in. Excusing herself, she followed Agnetta back to the kitchen. Whether it was the mental anguish of the previous few hours or a desire to help Erlich, she didn't know. Without further thought she angrily seized hold of the Dane's left shoulder and spun her round to face her. In the same movement she grabbed hold of the lapels of her overall and ripped it downwards, fully exposing the Dane's nakedness beneath it. In the same movement she slapped the startled Dane across her face and again with the reverse of her hand.

'Go to your room and get yourself dressed and never appear like this again! Is that clear?

Bemused and shaken, Agnetta held her hand to her face. Stepping back, she recovered quickly. 'Perhaps I can't compete with your looks Hannah but maybe you could use a few lessons from me in how to get a man, particularly with the assets you have.'

'You little tramp!' Her anger boiled over. 'How dare you try and embarrass a man old enough to be your father. Don't you realise how lucky we are to be here.'

Instead of being cowed, Agnetta's response was remarkably unabashed. 'So what's wrong in making the most of our luck? In case you haven't realised it, there are men in this house and we are women. Get the picture?'

'Listen to me Agnetta. The one sure way of remaining in this house is not to become involved but simply keep your head down and survive each day as it comes. Why on earth do you think a middle-aged man would be interested in what you have to offer?'

Agnetta's reply took Hannah's breath away. 'I wasn't aiming for the Corporal. It's the Colonel I want. Get him sucked in and he can make things happen for me unless of course you are already there in which case, you may have a rival... darling!'

Trying hard to control her rising anger, Hannah chose instead to be icily cool. 'You obviously learned a lot from your time with the SS,' but whether the Dane heard was doubtful as she was already heading to her room.

Arriving back just after 10.00 pm, Hannah knew within minutes that Steiner had had a disappointing day. With just a cursory greeting, he launched into an angry tirade directed at those officers he had met earlier. 'Even now, they think the

Fuhrer will pull a rabbit out of his hat and overnight, the war can be won.'

Interrupting him, she asked 'would you like a coffee or would you prefer something a little stronger?'

Annoyed by Hannah's interruption, Steiner's reply was barely more than a grunt.

'I'm sorry, Colonel but I'm not sure what that means so I am going to pour you a whisky unless you grunt twice more in which case I will make you a coffee.'

Seated behind his desk Steiner blinked, his face a parody of disbelief but he remained silent.

'So it's a whisky then.'

Slowly relaxing and taking minute sips of the fiery amber liquid, he fixed Hannah with a quizzical look. 'Well... what have you decided?'

'Why don't you wait and find out. Just sit there for a while and enjoy your drink, then take a shower and I will give you my answer later; provided you aren't too tired of course.'

'I have already told you, Hannah, never underestimate this soldier.'

'I think you said to never underestimate a dead soldier but as I detect some form of visible life from your side of the desk, then I am obviously mistaken in thinking you were referring to yourself.'

'When I said our relationship had changed, I was correct. But what I have only just realised is by how much it has changed.' He took a further sip of whisky. 'I actually believe it's you who now controls it or at least the emotional part of it. Would you agree with that?

'Would you accept one or two grunts by way of reply to that question?'

Slowly placing his glass on the desk, Steiner's voice was quietly composed. 'Come here.'

Moving round to his side of the desk, she stopped inches away. Reaching out, Steiner gently pulled her on to his lap and caressed her hair away from her face. Looking up, his lips met hers and Steiner inwardly thrilled as her tongue gently parted his lips. With one arm around her waist, Steiner used his other hand to unbutton her blouse and let his fingers slowly enter and explore the soft, silky flesh above her breasts. Inching her bra strap off her shoulder, he let it slip down her arm. Hardly daring to breathe, Steiner eased his lips away and gazed intently into the face of Hannah Bergmann. He saw her lovely iridescent eyes aflame with passion as she returned his look. Covering his hand with her own, she eased her bra aside and placed his warm hand on her breast. 'Does this answer your question or would you prefer me to grunt instead?'

Unable to prevent a smile crossing his tired features, Steiner let his hand dwell on her warm body. 'I swear I have never known anyone like you.' Reaching up to her eager lips, he let his mouth savour the sensuality of this incredible woman.

This time it was Hannah who gently eased away. 'I'm always afraid of being disturbed in this office.' Let's save it for later when we can relax in my room.'

Hesitating for a second, Steiner nodded his assent. 'But before we go, I need to know something.'

Hannah could guess what Steiner's question would be.

'When we came together on that first night, you were torn between physical temptation and Jewish guilt. The second time when I tried to force myself on you, you fought against it despite me striking you. But tonight, you appear to want me as much as I want you. Tell me my little Jewish girl, am I reading this situation correctly.'

Turning her head, she kissed him again. 'Absolutely correct, Colonel.'

'Then tell me why?'

Forcing herself into an upright sitting position but letting Steiner's hand dwell on her breast, its nipple now even harder under the sensuous feel of his fingers, she took a deep breath. 'I have had lots of time to think about you, me and the circumstances which have forced us together but in truth, the answer only came to me today. Since my arrest, and even before, you are the one person I have met who makes me feel there is some true goodness in this awful world. You aren't perfect by any means and sometimes you can be extremely crude but to me, you are the only reason I am still alive today. So I am in your debt and how better to repay my thanks.'

'But I thought... '

'Wait... let me finish. I have no idea whether my husband is still alive and I accept the odds on that as being extremely unlikely but even if he were, would I still want to make love, and I did say love, to you? And the answer is yes, I would.

'But doesn't this go against that moral code you fought so hard to maintain?'

'Of course it does but I thought very deeply after our discussion the other evening. '

'What part of what discussion are you referring to?'

'Our discussion on religion and your belief in there being no God. Thinking about it since, I'm forced to that same conclusion because how else can anyone explain, let alone justify, the horrors being committed in camps like Auschwitz, particularly to thousands of sweet innocent children while this illusionary God remains silent. So if there is no God and if this is the only life we have then why shouldn't we make the most of it and cling to whatever vestige of goodness and love we can find.'

Stopping, she looked at Steiner, 'Does that help to explain my change of heart?'

'Partly but it also makes me feel somewhat embarrassed too.'

'Why on earth should it cause you to feel embarrassed for God's sake?' Realising her unintentional pun, she laughed.

'Because of what you give me credit for. Yes I do rail against what is happening in this goddamned war but never forget I am still a soldier who obeys orders. But my resistance to Hitler and this war isn't a sign of goodness or love. The truth is, I am simply a German officer who hasn't swallowed the propaganda and bullshit served up by Hitler and Goebbels.'

'And that's why I hold you in such deep esteem, Kurt.' This was the first time Hannah had used his given name.

Releasing his hold, he eased Hannah to a standing position and fastened the buttons on her blouse. 'Let's meet in your room in say 30 minutes. No more eulogies for tonight; let's just enjoy the moment and each other.' Regaining his feet, he took Hannah by the shoulders. 'And before you ask, l need to tell you this. The feelings you have expressed for me are much the same as I feel for you and the problem we now have is how to hide or disguise them from the rest of this damned world.'

Slightly later than planned, Steiner made his unobtrusive way to her room. As on the first occasion, he brought an unopened bottle of wine... another fine red from the Bordeaux region of France. 'A present from an old comrade I met earlier today.'

Before his arrival, she had carefully positioned two candles on the marble washstand and their glow now threw dancing shadows on the walls as she and Steiner moved around the room.

'Did you bring the wine because you thought I might be nervous?'

He gave a rueful grin. 'Your nerves? Have you thought I might need a glass or two to ease my own nerves?'

'I doubt that very much but whatever; to us.'

'To us... whatever the future may hold.'

Completing the toast, Steiner leaned forward and ran his lips across her cheek, a tender prelude to the passion to come. Looking closely, she noticed that he had shaved off the dark stubble from the previous 24 hours and his whole person exuded an aroma of masculine freshness. Sitting together and content to let the silence add to the growing expectation building in each other, it was Hannah who wickedly increased the tempo. Slipping off her shoe, she raised her leg and placed her foot in Steiner's lap, just close enough to feel the growing hardness in his groin. Taking hold of her foot, he fingered each of her toes as she sensuously moved her heel to increase his excitement. Looking at him leaning back in his favourite slouched position, Hannah broke the charged silence. 'Where was home before you joined the Army, Kurt?'

'My home?' He sounded surprised. 'I haven't heard that word in years. I was born in a small town called Quedlinburg in the Harz Mountains. It's a small medieval town with lots of old timber-framed buildings and good country folk and a wonderful place for kids to grow up. My father was killed in the Great War but we were provided for by my mother's parents.'

Sipping her wine, Hannah slowly increased the movement of her foot and felt an immediate response from Steiner's groin. 'Do you like that, Kurt' she asked innocently?

'No, I hate it but if you stop I will probably have to kill you. Understood?'

'Understood.' Another highly charged silence followed before she once more broke the spell. 'And why did you join the Army?'

'Because our country had been humiliated after the Great War and I wanted to be part of the new Germany which Hitler promised to deliver. And in the beginning he kept his word but then like most dictators, he overstepped himself.'

'But on one pretext or another, Hitler then invaded other countries like Austria, Czechoslovakia, Poland, which as a soldier, meant war. Surely you knew what you were letting yourself in for?'

Steiner stirred, becoming slightly agitated. 'Look, you need to understand that young men want war, they hunger for war. To them it's a glorious concept. But in reality, young men don't understand war with its horrors, terror and death. All they see is the glory and the triumphalism until that awful day when war finds them. And when it does, then that is when they become as boys again and cry for their mothers.'

'And does that include you?'

'It would have done if Ernst Erlich hadn't risked his own life to pull me out of that stinking cellar in Stalingrad.'

'He's a good man, the sort of man I would have liked for an uncle.'

Emptying his glass, Steiner noticed that Hannah had barely touched her wine. 'Enough about your uncle, let me top up your glass?'

'No, I'm fine, thanks.' Peering at him through the mellow softness of candlelight, she saw that Steiner appeared more relaxed despite the strain of his long day beginning to reflect in his evident tiredness. Removing her foot, she stood in front of him. 'Before you get to the yawning stage would you like me to show you how far I have come from my repressed Jewish upbringing?'

'I'm not sure what that will entail or whether I should be worried but go ahead. You have my undivided attention.'

'In the knowledge that there isn't an instruction book to cover the situation we are about to explore, you can either take my word for what happens next or we will need to rely on our common sense and instinct. OK so far?'

Her deadpan style of delivery was intoxicating and Steiner knew for the first time that this woman had him in her total control.

'If there was an instruction book then chapter one would say that in order to make our intentions perfectly clear, it will be necessary to remove every stitch of clothing from our two bodies. Then you will lie on my bed, face down while I massage the stress from your neck and shoulder muscles.' Folding her arms in what she hoped might be interpreted as a lecturing pose, she introduced a cautionary note. 'At this juncture I should point out that depending upon how relaxed you actually become, there is a fair chance of you falling asleep. However, if you are still awake when we reach this point then this will be where you will be required to turn onto your back in order to... ' Hannah stopped. 'At this juncture we will pause and you will have to wait to see what happens next.' Raising her glass, she coyly asked 'what do you think of the plan so far?'

Steiner feigned puzzlement. 'I'm a very slow learner but if it helps this particular exercise, should I be the one to strip off first and then do the same to you?'

By way of reply, she wrapped both hands around Steiner's neck and let her mouth engage his lips. 'I'm ready when you are, Colonel,' she whispered.

The massage to Steiner's neck and back muscles took longer than expected but instead of inducing sleep, it actually seemed to invigorate his tired frame. Turning over, he looked up at the extraordinary woman bestriding him, her black lustrous hair loosened and falling over her shoulder, glinting in the soft candle glow. Gazing up into her deep set eyes and full lipped sensuous mouth, Steiner's world felt full. 'If I could choose my moment to die, then this would be it' he muttered, more to himself than to Hannah.

'Touched by Steiner's words, she leaned down and kissed the scar tissue on his upper chest, the same tissue she remembered fingering when Steiner was in the throes of his fever. 'Even though the best is yet to come?'

'Sweetheart, I can't believe this is actually happening. I'm afraid to even close my eyes in case it's a dream and you will have disappeared when I open them again.'

'Would you like me to pinch you to prove it's not a dream or do something more in keeping with the evening's program?'

'Like what?'

'How about this for a start?' Sliding her body forward, Hannah pushed Steiner's hard penis down onto his stomach and stopped. 'So close my darling man but not quite there.' Moving sensuously forward and back she simulated the sexual momentum but without allowing penetration. Looking at her through half-closed eyes, Steiner emitted a low groan and began to match her rhythm. Reaching up, he pulled Hannah on to his beating chest and attempted to kiss her. But raising her head, she evaded his lips only adding further to his overwhelming desire for this beautiful temptress.

'Patience, my little soldier boy. You can only advance when you hear the trumpet sound.'

'And when will that be?'

Inching her body slightly forward, she felt the head of his penis brush the lips of her vagina. 'Any moment now so keep listening and tell me when you hear it.'

Knowing he would not be able to contain himself much longer, Steiner began to increase his own rhythm.

Raising herself upright, Hannah lifted her body, allowing the bulbous head of Steiner's penis to barely penetrate before stopping.

Steiner got the message. 'I hear it, sweetheart... not just the trumpet but the whole fucking orchestra!'

With her own last vestige of control nearly gone, Hannah let herself slide down, feeling his pulsating hardness completely fill her yearning void. She felt his hands reach up and squeeze her breasts, cupping and lifting them in the same pulsating movement. With his fingers he squeezed each hard nipple, sending spasms of sheer delight coursing through her body. Looking down at him, she saw the same look of passion which she herself was now experiencing. Having achieved full penetration, he had stopped all motion, content to enjoy this moment of supreme intimacy.

Sitting astride him, his throbbing penis creating waves of sensational spasms throughout her body, she felt her first orgasm course through her loins. Rising slightly, as though being lifted by a wave about to tumble on to the beach, she pushed down hard in time to feel her whole body explode as Steiner pushed upwards. Falling onto his heaving chest, she rained kiss after kiss on his lips and cheeks. Slowly, very slowly, she began to regain control of herself; her breathing slowly subsiding to somewhere near its normal level.

'I guess my need was greater than yours so let's call that a warm-up for the main event,' she said.

'You can call it what you like provided there's more to come.'

'Oh there is but you must now control what happens next.'

'You mean I get to conduct the music this time?'

'You have the baton, maestro, so when you're ready, you may proceed.'

Needing no second bidding, Steiner with surprising agility, rolled Hannah onto her back and eased on top of her. Unbidden and with renewed arousal, she drew her legs apart and guided him into her body. Expecting him to remain in this position, she was surprised when he placed both legs outside of her own and closed them, creating a tunnel for his increasing fervour. Sensuously moving in and out of her receptive body, he reached up and placed both her arms above her head and held them there, creating the feeling of being cocooned within his powerful frame. Gradually, his pumping motion began to quicken. Deep down inside her, she could feel her own vaginal muscles gripping and relaxing in time with each thrust. As his pace quickened she felt as though he was growing even larger and she knew she was about to implode yet again.

From a distance she heard herself screaming 'I can't hold it... I can't hold it' and felt her body involuntarily convulse under Steiner's weight as waves of hot juices akin to an electric current ran through her lower body. Utterly lost in her own orgasm, it was several seconds before she became aware that Steiner had slowed his frantic pumping and with great deliberation, she felt him ejaculate into her. For a full 30 seconds more, Steiner continued to drive and withdraw, thrust and withdraw, increasing and prolonging her mind-blowing orgasm as he did so. Gradually the momentum slowed until eventually, he pulled away and fell onto his back alongside her, grateful for the cool air wafting over their hot breathless bodies.

With Steiner lying on his back, Hannah laid her head on his outstretched arm and nestled into his body. With her free hand she ran her fingers over his chest seeking to touch the raised scar tissue. Gently following its raised outline, she leaned over and kissed the damaged area.

'In medical terms this is known as cicatrix.'

'Cica... what?'

'Cicatrix... old scar tissue.'

'So what term would doctors use to describe what has just happened, Hannah?'

'I think they would describe it as an irregular occurrence requiring further investigation.'

'Investigation by whom?'

'By doctors of course.'

Reaching over, Steiner began to lazily fondle her left breast, its charged nipple still radiating warm sensations throughout her body.

'Do you still wonder what happened to your own doctor? Remind me again Hannah, what was your husband's name?'

'Ephraim... his name was Ephraim and of course I think about him and what may have happened to him.'

'And what conclusion did you arrive at?'

'I think he was probably murdered at Theresienstadt. He was tortured and branded by a psychotic Adjutant and denied access to the transport which brought me and the other Jews to Auschwitz so it's the only conclusion I can reach.'

Turning to face Hannah, he stroked her hair away from her face and gently kissed her closed eyelids. 'Tell me and be brutally honest. Is that how you used to make love to your husband?'

Raising herself on to her elbow, Hannah reached out and touched Steiner's face. 'Look at me when I say this because it's important for you to understand. I have only made love to one man in my life and that man was my husband. And I have never, repeat never, made love to him like that. We were both repressed by our Jewish upbringing and sex was always something to do and then forget. Does that answer your question?'

'So how come you are so... ' he struggled for the right word. 'So controlled and so experienced?'

'Because it took a man like you to bring out what has obviously been latent in me.'

Blushing in the soft candle light, Steiner could not resist feeling smug. 'I would like very much to believe that?

'Well it's true, whether you believe me or not.'

'What about your foreign tours; were you never tempted to go with other men?

'Short answer? No.'

'You didn't need to think about that, did you?'

'That's because I was rarely in one city long enough to form any sort of relationship or attachment so it never happened.' Teasing him, she asked 'would you prefer it if I had been with lots of other men?'

'You told me I'm now in control so let me answer that in my own way.' Placing her hand on his penis, she felt it begin to swell. 'Hold me and when you think I'm ready, I want to have you again. Is that what you would like?'

By way of reply, Hannah gave Steiner a lingering kiss and moving her body closer to him she raised her leg above his waist. Guiding him into her, she felt Steiner push hard. Easing her onto her back, he came on top and pulled her legs up, pinioning them with both arms but still allowing access to her breasts. Unable to move other than for her arms, Hannah gave herself up to Steiner who rode her body as though he was a man starved of affection. In the timeless period which followed, Hannah had numerous orgasms but the most sustained moment came when Steiner again filled her Jewish body and Hebrew soul with his Aryan seed before subsiding with fatigue

Lying together afterwards she felt an overwhelming affection for the man who in three short hours had now become more than her lover.

Guiltily, she thought again about Ephraim'

As though reading her mind, she heard Steiner murmur 'You must have loved your husband very much but he's not here and I am.'

Hearing this, Hannah felt an urge to have Steiner again but this time a cautionary doubt crept into her mind.

She knew from her Mother's constant exhortations in her teenage years that unprotected sex invariably ran the risk of an unwanted pregnancy and tonight, with the passion and frequency of their couplings, she knew that risk would have been perilously high. But with fate having brought both her and Steiner this far, this was not the time to think of such things unless that same element of fate should decide otherwise in the future

FIFTY NINE

It was the sound of sporadic gunfire in the distance which broke through Ephraim's sporadic sleep. Awake in seconds, he opened his eyes to see the Partisans grabbing their weapons and taking up well-rehearsed defensive positions. The raid on the Field Hospital Dispensary Unit and the gratuitous shooting of the Pharmacy Assistant had sickened him to his very core, so much so that he had decided he would no longer carry a weapon. Instead he chose to lug two heavy canvas satchels containing essential medical equipment and medication.

Watching from the rear of the group, the sound of approaching gunfire made him feel distinctly uneasy. The common thread binding this disparate group of Poles, Czechs, Russians and a solitary Ukrainian was their hatred of Germans and their Romanian and Hungarian allies. And here in dense woodland, some 10 kilometres south west of Wodzislaw, Ephraim watched as the Partisans prepared for action without knowing who it was they were facing. The barbarity inflicted by the Einsatzgruppen not only to captured Partisans but to innocent hostages and villagers had appalled Ephraim. As a doctor dedicated to saving life he had become increasingly sickened by their unbridled cruelty and slaughter of defenceless civilians. And worse, he knew his fellow Partisans were no better.

Three days earlier, two Wehrmacht deserters from a front line unit, had unknowingly stumbled into the Partisan camp in the same area of forest which they were now preparing to defend. The two soldiers, both in their late teens, appeared to be in a state of shock. Their glazed eyes had the look of men desperately in need of rest and their replies under interrogation were halting and repetitive. Ephraim knew that persistent sleep deprivation could kill more quickly than hunger and recommended that they allow the two soldiers to sleep before further questioning. But to men bent on gratuitous revenge, such advice went unheeded and Ephraim watched in sickening horror as one of the two soldiers, his hands trussed behind him and hoisted from an overhanging branch was slowly lowered onto a bayonet mounted on a Mauser rifle held in the steely grip of a Pole who Ephraim knew had witnessed his wife and children being murdered by a passing SS unit. Unable to tear his eyes away from the scene, Ephraim saw the soldier slowly lowered with the tip of the bayonet penetrating deeper into his rectum as his body fell to the ground. Screaming in agony before mercifully losing consciousness, the momentum of his falling body tore the rifle from the Pole's grasp as the soldier's weight carried him to the ground where he lay in a crumpled heap. Pulling the bloody bayonet from the body of the young soldier, the Pole plunged it again and again into the back of the German. Spitting on the lifeless body, he turned and faced the other soldier. To his dying day Ephraim would never forget what happened next. Instead of being intimidated or pleading for his life, the teenage soldier powerfully shook off his captor's hands, pulled himself upright and faced his tormentors. Smiling tersely, he signalled for the Pole to attack, his beckoning fingers taunting his murderous adversary. Enraged, the Pole charged at the German, attempting to skewer him with the same bayonet still dripping with the blood of his tortured comrade. Side-stepping the lunging thrust, the soldier grabbed the barrel and stock of the Mauser and with a skill owing more to martial arts than basic training, he snatched the rifle from the grasp of the Pole and clubbed him viciously to the side of his head as his momentum carried him forward. Stumbling to the ground, the Pole tried to rise up but not before the same murderous bayonet drove into his broad back; not once but twice more before the other Partisans could react. Dropping to one knee the German soldier fired off two rounds, killing one of the two Russians who had lowered the rope and wounding the other before he was himself cut down in a hail of bullets.

Watching the horrific scene unfolding before his eyes, Ephraim knew he had to get away from these depraved killers. As a physician he had been forced to accept that in warfare, people kill and get killed. But the escalating brutality now being meted out by both sides was more than he could stomach. His influence within the original bunch of Czechs had lessened as other nationalities had joined the group with several of the newcomers openly questioning his loyalty as a German, albeit a Jew, fighting against the Wehrmacht. His decision to not carry a firearm had rekindled the question of his commitment, lessened only by a grudging awareness of their need for his medical skills.

With the sound of gunfire drawing closer, Ephraim felt a sense of grudging admiration for the Partisans as each resisted the temptation to return fire. Short of a major retreat, Ephraim believed the area to be occupied by the Wehrmacht so he assumed it would be German troops attacking their camp but the lack of workable communication equipment and political differences between the numerous Partisan groups meant there was little shared intelligence so in reality the attackers could be any one of several different forces... including other partisans!

Ephraim's group did not have long to wait to discover the answer. Within minutes, their clearing was swept by a hail of bullets calculated to draw a response and reveal the location of anyone foolish enough to return fire. As the seconds ticked by, the sound of troops moving through the undergrowth became louder. More gunfire, again aimed in their general direction ripped through the trees and bushes at waist height. Suddenly, a ricocheting bullet found a target. Ephraim saw a Partisan leap up, clutching at his face, vainly attempting to hold his shattered jaw in place. His agonised scream brought the game of cat and mouse to a deadly conclusion and Ephraim witnessed more Partisans die as the attackers poured murderous bursts of heavy machine gun fire into the small clearing from where the Partisans were now attempting to fight back.

A barked command eventually brought the firing to a halt and through the smoky grey haze of cordite fumes, Ephraim saw Red Army soldiers pour into the clearing. Holding his hands above his head, Ephraim stood up from his concealed position and allowed himself to be pushed towards the small group who had survived the overwhelming onslaught. Standing with his shocked and forlorn comrades, he saw wounded Partisans being dispatched by a bullet in the head. With all resistance now suppressed, other soldiers were shamelessly turning bodies over, looking for watches and other personal items to steal.. Standing apart from his men, a young Red Army officer quietly surveyed the prisoners. Breaking his silence, he asked 'do any of you speak Russian?

Marius, a former language graduate from Brno University, nodded his head and half-raised his hand in weak acknowledgement.

'You will tell me who you are and what you are doing in this area. If you and these men are sensible then you will cooperate otherwise you will all be shot. To make sure you have understood what I said, you will repeat back to me in Russian. Go ahead.'

Dutifully, the young Czech did as instructed and then repeated the same message in both Czech and German.

'Marius, ask this man why we were attacked and being treated like prisoners when we are both fighting the Germans?' It was Ephraim who asked the question.

The translated answer was chilling. 'In this area every man carrying arms is an enemy of the Red Army.' Looking closely at Ephraim, the Russian spoke to a burly soldier standing alongside him who nodded his understanding. It was Marius who spoke. 'They intend to question our comrades but they will start with you.'

Roughly pushing Ephraim away from the pitiful number of surviving Partisans they made their way to a secluded part of the clearing within sight of three dead Partisans. Once there, the soldier placed a folding canvas seat for the Officer. Unbuttoning his rough serge uniform blouse, he sat down and beckoned Ephraim and Marius to stand before him with two armed soldiers immediately behind them.

'What is your nationality and how long have you been in this group?'

Ephraim thought it odd that he wasn't interested in his name... at least at this stage of questioning. 'I am a German... a German Jew and I joined the Czech Partisans after escaping from Theresienstadt concentration camp some four months ago.' He stopped and listened to Marius translate his answer.

'And before you went to... ' the officer attempted to repeat the name of Theresienstadt but failed so he tried again 'Before you went to this camp what did you do for a living.'

'I was a doctor.'

'But a Jewish doctor.'

'Is there a difference? It took Marius a few seconds to translate and Ephraim saw a look of anger cross the Officer's face. Speaking sharply to the soldiers behind him, Ephraim tensed, expecting to be struck by either one of them. To his surprise nothing happened.

It was Marius who explained. 'He said you are to be made an example of but only after he has finished questioning you.'

Looking at the bodies of the dead Partisans lying just metres away... men who had risked their lives to free their country from German oppression, Ephraim felt a surge of anger well up inside of him. 'If he means I am to be shot like those poor devils, then he'd better do it now. I'm not answering any more of his questions so tell him that.'

Marius hesitated, wondering how he could soften Ephraim's apparent death wish. Sensing this, the Officer stood up. Standing inches from Ephraim's face, he locked eyes before speaking in perfect German. 'You are a man of some spirit, doctor. I'm surprised you have lasted this long knowing how much your own Gestapo love to get their hands on Jews like you.' Breaking eye contact, he faced a nervous Marius; 'it makes their day to capture a defiant Jew. Oddly, they appear to get little satisfaction from murdering a bunch of whimpering, passive Jews so when they meet someone like you, doctor, a man who tells them to go fuck themselves then what a pleasure it is for them to rid their beloved Fatherland of such a person.' Returning to his canvas seat, the Officer stared at Ephraim. 'Should I satisfy the wish of a man who seeks his own death as much as you seem to or should I induct and engage your services as we head for Berlin like avenging angels? Tell me, doctor, if you were sitting in my place, what would you have me do to a loose-lipped, foolhardy Jew like you?'

SIXTY

Some eight weeks after her fateful liaison with Kurt Steiner, Hannah knew she was pregnant. Following her arrest and internment at Auschwitz, her periods had stopped but with the better food and living conditions since leaving the camp, they had resumed although intermittently. It was the occurrence of morning sickness, the same symptom which she recalled from her pregnancy with Aaron, which confirmed it. Sitting in her room after the initial sickness had abated on the second morning, the realisation and magnitude of her predicament struck home; a Jewish prisoner carrying the child of a senior German officer. The minute embryo in her womb was a death sentence in waiting.

She realised that whatever emotions Steiner had expressed during their last sexual encounter, he could dispense with her at any time simply by sending her back to the camp and a predictable outcome.

She cursed her own weakness in wanting to share her body with him. Since their coupling on that fateful night some eight weeks ago she had gone to his room on countless other occasions, indulging in the sheer joy of uninhibited love-making; something she would never have dreamed of doing with Ephraim but where at least any resulting pregnancy would have been explainable.

She wondered whether her sexual desires had been driven by a need for love and affection or whether they stemmed from an instinctive need to survive. Thinking this through in her mind, she concluded that she had been living for the moment with little regard for a future which now was even less likely to materialise. Looking at herself in the small mirror above the wash basin, she was aware that the effect of so much fulfilled arousal had actually increased her attractiveness. Her hair, dulled before coming to the Admin unit, had regained its lustrous sheen and her honey-coloured skin now radiated its former softness and warmth. Her eyes shone with their former sparkle which even Steiner, jealous man that he was, had begrudgingly conceded made her appear irresistible to men. But she knew these same features would count for nothing when exposed to the deadly Zyclon B gas within the gas chamber; the same killing area which Danuta had hatefully referred to as 'the great leveller.'

Wanting to reason things out in her mind before facing Steiner, she threw the bedroom window open and stared out beyond the overgrown garden now showing sparse evidence of Danuta's labours. The vegetable garden which just week before had been a well-tended source of fresh vegetables sufficient to feed the entire household was now barely recognisable, overgrown with weeds and thistles.

Beyond the garden, the woods were in full leaf with the lighter hues of green on the silver birch trees making a colourful contrast to the darker leaves of the mature oak trees on the shadowy horizon.

She thought back to the night when Steiner had stood on this same spot and how together they had looked at the stars in the timeless cosmos above the killing ground of Auschwitz. That was the night she had first given herself to him which he had accepted with a hunger and desire quite unknown to her. She recalled the difficult conversation three days later when a contrite Steiner had told her that such an occurrence must never happen again. Yet since that moment, he had obviously changed his mind or had become increasingly addicted to their couplings despite the risk of extreme punishment for consorting with a Jew. But whatever the reason, he was now a willing partner; a man wonderfully experienced in aspects of lovemaking beyond her wildest imagination.

More and more she thought about Ephraim and was inwardly grateful that he would never discover her shame. And if by some miracle he had survived, she knew there wasn't the remotest chance of him being able to accept that she had become the mistress of a German officer despite his despairing exhortation to do whatever she could to survive.

Worse, not only was she this man's willing mistress but now carrying his Gentile seed in her Jewish womb. Knowing Ephraim almost as well as he knew himself she realised he would react with shocked repugnance. But of more immediate concern was how Steiner would react when she broke the news to him.

Placing her hand on her stomach as if seeking to hide the fact of her pregnancy, she dared to compare her feelings and emotions for both Ephraim and Steiner. Her marriage to Ephraim had seemed to be all that a good Jewish girl could ever wish for. Entirely supportive of her flourishing musical career even as his own medical practice diminished, she remembered how well he had adapted to the enforced changes in their lives. As a father he had loved Aaron dearly and being restricted from practising medicine other than to Jews, he had taken on the role of child-minder whilst she spent increasing amounts of time travelling with the orchestra on its frequent tours to the capitals of occupied countries. Ephraim was not outwardly affectionate but never had she doubted his love for her which had made it easy for her to reject the occasional invitations from men whom she suspected wanted more than just dinner. Had this war not so dramatically intervened in their lives, she was certain that she and Ephraim would have remained happily married in much the same way as they had before their arrest. But that was before she became the willing lover of Steiner and even if the war did come to an abrupt end and if by some miracle Ephraim was still alive she wondered whether she could go back to him and pick up their lives as before?

She was still unsure whether the feelings she felt for Steiner was the genesis of real love or merely an infatuation against the deadly backdrop of Auschwitz and her inborn instinct of simply wanting to survive... whatever it took! If it was love then did she love Steiner more than Ephraim? If both men were here now with no war raging in the background then who would she wish to spend her life with? Guiltily knowing the answer to her own searching question but fearful of its consequences, she tried to clear her mind and decide how she would break the news to Steiner. But with her emotions still in turmoil, she knew such a conversation would be tantamount to sealing her own inescapable fate within the charnel camp that was Auschwitz.

Tentatively making her way downstairs she heard the sound of Steiner's raised voice on his field telephone berating an unfortunate subordinate. She now knew him well enough to appreciate that he was at his sharpest in the mornings particularly when addressing strategic objectives rather than having to react to events which had already occurred. When taking notes at his weekly briefing sessions with his Wehrmacht officers she was particularly impressed at the concise manner with which he quickly raced through the strategic agenda covertly knowing that this same highly professional soldier had only hours before taken her consensual body into the realms of wild sexual fulfilment.

Their lovemaking was now so intense that all inhibitions between them had long since disappeared. Her initial shyness had been replaced with openness; a feeling she had never experienced with Ephraim. Aware of Steiner's impatience to have sex as soon as they were alone she would frequently tantalise him with prolonged foreplay. Afterwards they would lay naked and spent on the threadbare rug in front of the open window letting the warm night breeze with its fragrant scents of the forest cool their hot bodies, often without a word passing between them. Sometimes lying inches apart, she would occasionally reach down and take hold of Steiner's overworked penis and hold it quite still before beginning a slow rhythmic movement. Sometimes he would feign sleep but his growing hardness would invariably tell its own story. Groaning, he would move on top of her compliant body and they would make love yet again. On numerous occasions Steiner had told her that he could never get enough of her and his insatiable performance throughout each long night bore true testimony of this.

She had known for some time that she had become besotted with the man whose nascent child she was now carrying. Not only besotted but unashamedly addicted to the world of intense sexual pleasure he had introduced her to. But this morning, seated in the austere office across the desk from each other, it was business as normal.

'You're late and Ernst tells me you missed breakfast. Anything I should know about?'

'Know about' she thought. Did he already have an inkling of her pregnancy?

For a split second she was tempted to tell him but instead she simply murmured 'I felt queasy when I got up and was sick. Sorry for being late.'

Raising one eyebrow in a quizzical gesture, Steiner asked 'are you OK now?'

Looking at the amount of paperwork in front of him, she decided this was not the moment to test his reaction to impending fatherhood so shuffling a few more papers across the desk; she nodded her willingness to carry on.

The next few hours passed excruciatingly slowly and several times Hannah felt more faint stirrings of sickness in her stomach. When Agnetta brought in coffee at 11.00 am, she excused herself and made a hurried dash to her room. Returning minutes later she was irritated to see the curvaceous Dane sitting in her seat. Seeing Hannah reappear, she stopped speaking and nervously glanced away. From the expression on Steiner's face she guessed that he too was plainly annoyed.

'Speak to Corporal Erlich. And Larssen, if you wish to remain in this unit then never speak directly to me again. Do you understand?

The threat contained in Steiner's rebuke did not stop Agnetta from displaying her natural coquettishness as she slowly rose from the seat. Looking at her from across the desk, Steiner was allowed to glimpse her tantalising cleavage emphasised by the low vee-neck of her drab overall. Maintaining eye contact with him, Agnetta placed both hands on the desk and leaned forward. 'Thank you for your time Colonel: I'm sorry to have bothered you' as she slowly backed towards the door.

Looking at the calculated scene unfolding before her, Hannah felt an irresistible urge to take hold of the outlandish Dane and slap her senseless. Instead, she stood stock still and watched as Steiner, not only oblivious to her presence but seemingly unable to take his eyes away from the departing Agnetta. The noise of the closing door broke the transfixation. Belatedly looking away, he became aware of her standing there but not knowing for how long, his face took on a deepening hue. Whether for her benefit or to disguise his all too obvious interest in Agnetta, she heard him bark 'I want that woman out of this unit within the hour. Tell Corporal Erlich to see me when we've finished here.'

Resuming her seat opposite to him, Hannah took a calculated gamble. 'Is that for your benefit or mine, Colonel?' Her reversion to formality was not lost on Steiner.

'I don't understand your question. When I give an order I expect it to happen. It has nothing to do with you so tell Erlich to come and see me when we've finished here. In fact do it now.'

Still unsure of his true reasoning, she decided to risk triggering the volatility she knew was always simmering beneath his deceptively calm demeanour. 'Can it wait until we finish the paperwork? After all, that 'woman' will still be here then and who knows... you may have changed your mind by then.'

It slowly occurred to Steiner that he was being drawn into a game of Hannah's choosing. To spare further embarrassment and inwardly relieved, he decided to play along. 'Tell me one good reason why I would change my mind.'

'I can give you two good reasons but I'm not sure you are ready for either one.'

'Bergmann, you are the most annoying woman I have ever known. Stop playing games and tell me what is it you want to say?'

'Alright, but try not to lose your temper.' She saw the semblance of a scowl appear on Steiner's face. 'Firstly, not many prisoners get the opportunity to speak with their captors so you can't blame Agnetta for seizing her moment as she just did. And you know as well as I do that to send her back to the camp will mean the end for her. Unlike Danuta and Miriam, she hasn't broken any rules so why do it? She's not even a Jew, for God's sake.'

Interrupting her, Steiner seized on Hannah's unintended slip. 'You do realise what you have just said?

'I do but if you interrupt again I will lose my train of thought.' Thinking back to their previous one-sided conversations, she again marvelled at the transformation in their relationship which allowed her to speak to Steiner in such a manner hopefully without incurring his anger or rebuke.

Touching his forehead in a gesture of feigned apology, Steiner's body language showed a growing impatience. 'And what was your other point?'

'I'm expecting your baby so you may want to keep Agnetta around to satisfy your re-awakened sexual needs. That by the way was her job application but I'm sure you realised that.'

The shock to Steiner was total. As if disbelieving his own ears, he sprang up and came around the desk and squatted in front of Hannah. 'Will you say that again, please but this time say it slowly.'

'I believe I am pregnant and as you are the only man I have had sex with since I've been imprisoned, then it can only be your baby. I can't tell you anything more than that.'

'You say you believe you may be pregnant so how sure are you?'

'Having had experience of my previous pregnancy, I am very sure.'

Standing up, Steiner paced to the far end of the room before retracing his steps. 'Hannah, I need time to think this through. In the meantime, you are to tell no one, not even Ernst Erlich. Is that clear?'

'Very clear, Colonel but you do realise it's not something I can keep secret for too long; especially with Agnetta waiting in the wings.'

The lines on Steiner's brow knitted together. 'Look, I've told you several times now that I'm a Wehrmacht officer and not one of those murderous Nazi bastards you keep referring to from your time in Auschwitz. And yes, I admit I was angry at Nilssen but there was never a chance I would send her back to that damn place?'

Moving closer, he lowered his voice. 'And tell me this; why you think I would let a woman who has been fucked by dozens of SS camp guards take your place, assuming there is a place to take.'

A growing sense of annoyance began to overcome Hannah's earlier anxiety. 'Colonel, be realistic. As my pregnancy becomes more noticeable then you will come under immediate suspicion for consorting with a Jew and that fact alone will place you in grave danger. So the sensible thing to do would be to send me back to the camp. End of story. I can't make the position any clearer because realistically, you have no other option.'

Slowly beginning to come to terms with Hannah's dramatic announcement, Steiner needed time to think so he changed tack. 'So is this what Gentiles would refer to as the wages of sin, Hannah?'

'Not being a Gentile, I have no idea but I prefer to think of it as the outcome of a loving relationship. The pity of it all is that we shall never know or see the baby we have made.' Leaning towards Steiner, Hannah turned her tearful face upward and gave him a gentle kiss. 'Kurt, by taking me away from that awful place you have enabled me to live something akin to a civilised existence. By coming together as we have done, I have come to know a form of physical love so very few women ever experience. For both these blessings, I thank you with all my heart; without guilt or regret. You are a good man Kurt Steiner and I'm sure you would have made a good father.'

Looking down at her tear stained cheeks, Steiner reached out and attempted to gently brush them away. 'And you, Hannah Bergmann... not only are you a pessimist but you are also wrong. I do have a choice, albeit a dangerous choice, which is why I need time to think this through.

Rising from her chair, she pressed herself against his body, standing on her toes to draw her mouth close to Steiner's ear. 'Listen to me, Kurt Steiner, Colonel of the Wehrmacht and holder of the Knights Cross. Realistically we both know there is no other alternative open to you. I don't want you to say there is because that will cause me to build up hope where, realistically, no hope can possibly exist. I am pregnant and very soon that will become obvious and that will point responsibility firmly at you. So sensibly you must send me back to the camp before those two things happen. If you hadn't rescued me from that dreadful place I would have been murdered long ago so let's be thankful for the time we've enjoyed together. Can we agree on that?'

Gently pushing her from him but retaining hold of her shoulders, she noticed a moistness appear in his eyes.

'I think a woman in your condition needs to sit down and for once in your life I want you to curb your argumentative nature and just listen to me.' Easing her back into her seat, he positioned himself on the edge of the desk.

'Since your arrest in Berlin, the war has moved on.'

Hearing Steiner's depiction of her arrest, the two horrific train journeys which followed and the lottery of the selection process encapsulated within five brief words made her think his succinct description would have been more appropriate in a military report.

'You won't know this but our cities are being bombed to rubble. Hamburg was virtually destroyed last autumn and many other cities, including Berlin are being increasingly targeted. The Allies have made landings in Italy and they are expected to invade France any time soon. The newly equipped Red Army is pushing us back on the Eastern Front which means that Germany will be fighting on three fronts. At best we can only delay the end of this war but we cannot win it.'

He swivelled round and picked up the cup of nearly cold coffee before continuing. 'Our losses in manpower, armaments and equipment are not being matched by replacements from within Germany which is the reason why this area has become so crucially important to our war effort. The Russians know this too which is why I expect their next major thrust to be in this region. If they overrun Krakow then they will be here within a matter of weeks.'

Slowly, it dawned on Hannah why Steiner was summarising the current war situation. 'So are you are saying I should stay here until the Red Army arrives? But what then? There were rumours in the camp that the German army has massacred thousands of Russian civilians so surely they will do the same to German people, whether Jew, Gentile or whatever; to Soviet soldiers bent on revenge we are all Germans.'

Before Steiner could respond, she went on. 'And what about you, Kurt... what will happen to you?'

Steiner became pensive. 'Hannah, listen to me because we need to be totally honest with each other. When they capture any SS personnel, men or women, or anyone associated or based near these death camps such as myself, they are shot without compunction or worked to death in a Russian gulag. Jews like you will be left to their own devices until you can make your own way back to Germany at the end of the war if of course you would want to go back to Berlin or what will be left of it.'

Hardly daring to think positively, Hannah mumbled 'of course I would go back. My son is there. But what about you; what will you do?'

Steiner's face took on a resigned expression. 'I'm surprised you ask that. I'm a soldier and soldiers are expected to fight. That's the only reason why I'm in this goddamned region.'

'But you don't believe in Hitler so why would you fight for him and those other people he surrounds himself with?'

'Hannah, I fight for my country; not for those 'other people' you refer to. When this war is over, the Allies will deal with Hitler and his lapdogs accordingly. At least I hope that will be the case.'

The realisation of what he was saying was becoming abundantly clearer by the second. 'But that will mean you will either be killed or become a prisoner of war. I remember what you said about those soldiers who surrendered at Stalingrad, that death would be more preferable than becoming a prisoner of the Russians.'

'And that's even truer now than it was then. The Russians have limited food supplies and with so many of our military personnel captured, priority is being given to their own troops so thousands of German prisoners are being deliberately starved to death. That for me is a good enough reason not to be captured. It's unfortunate we aren't on the Western front and facing the Americans or British.'

'What's the difference between them and the Russians? I would have thought every one of the Allies hate the German military in equal measure?'

Steiner's response reflected a hint of irony. 'They probably do but generally speaking, neither the Yanks nor the Brits are known to deliberately murder their prisoners.'

Taking hold of her hand, Steiner's face reflected the growing compassion he felt for this spirited woman. 'Tell me, if you could make a wish, what would it be?

Annoyed by his flippancy, she pulled her hand away. 'You're making fun of me for wanting to talk about a serious situation. A situation which you say could well be upon us in a matter of weeks.'

'In which case would you prefer to wait until it happens?'

'No, that isn't what I want. You asked me a question so at least let me answer it.' Drawing a deep breath to steady her nerve, she stood up and took a pace back.. 'I would like you and me to leave here and make a dash towards the American front. Once there you could give yourself up which will mean that not only you and I will be safe but our unborn baby too. And when this war is over and you are repatriated, we will be reunited. What happens then will depend on a number of things but that is what I would like to happen.'

Listening to her, Steiner was once again struck by the innocent naivety enshrined within Hannah's heart-felt words; words which touched him deeply. However, for those words to come to fruition would require him to ignore the current reality facing them both; a reality which he knew would effectively disillusion her childlike proposition. Attempting a half-smile which instantly died on his lips, he moved towards her and placed his hands on her shoulders. 'Hannah, I want you to listen to me and be honest with yourself; OK?'

Unwillingly to agree to something which might affect not only her immediate safety but her future life as well, she chose to nod in apparent assent.

'Let's just suppose we did manage to escape from here and reach the American lines and follow the scenario which you've just outlined. The war ends and we become reunited. You say what happens next will depend on a number of things so this is where you need to be utterly frank with yourself. Firstly, we have nothing in common other than being excellent bed partners. Sweetheart, I'm not denigrating what has happened between us but would it be enough to base our future lives on? Seeing Hannah about to respond, Steiner put a finger to her lips. 'Don't answer that just yet.

Secondly, you are a classical musician and will hopefully return to that world again. Me? I will be an unemployed ex-soldier like many thousands of my comrades. How long do you think I could accept being kept by you and what do you think that would do for our relationship or my own esteem?'

Easing his hand from her face, she spoke with feeling. 'May I say something now? I promise I'll be very frank.'

'I haven't finished but go ahead.'

'What you choose to refer to as 'excellent bed partners' I would prefer to think of as something more akin to being lovers. Being utterly frank with you, yes it was just sex to begin with but what has since happened between us has taken my emotions way beyond that initial infatuation to the point where now the question for me is whether this Jewish woman with very limited exposure to life is experiencing a meaningful form of love or something much deeper?'

'Do you want me to answer that?'

'No, not yet. I'm simply asking myself a question which I've mulled over endlessly but whether you share or even like my conclusion will be for you to decide.' Looking at his craggy features, she ran a hand down his cheek. 'For my part I believe I am deeply in love with you. And whatever your feelings may be, nothing will change or alter that.

The fact I am now pregnant I regard as a wonderful blessing whatever difficulties it may bring in the future. My sole regret is that in all probability neither of us will survive this war to see our baby but because this world is such an evil place, this too may be a blessing in disguise.'

Temporarily silenced by the sombreness of her words, Steiner swallowed hard and sought to gain time by posing an innocuous question. 'And have you thought how this ex-soldier could keep and maintain you in a lifestyle you were once accustomed to?'

'And what lifestyle are you referring to? Would it be my pre-war existence as a classical musician but existing within the constraints and restrictions of being a stateless Jew? Or perhaps you mean my wartime lifestyle as a prisoner here in Auschwitz? What I do know is that if I do manage to outlive this war, then other than to find my son in Berlin, I have no intention of staying in Germany. Whether I will ever be able to pursue my career again will depend on where I go. In a country like America or even England I suppose I can earn a good living particularly with a good agent to look after my interests; a man with presence and authority used to dealing with people. It would be a different lifestyle to what you do now but it could be a realistic backdrop to a life together with our baby and my son.'

Steiner looked amused. 'You do realise the implication of what you have just said; an internationally acclaimed musician managed by her former Nazi gaoler. It would be you that became the story... not your music. And what concert platform will engage your talent against that background? Without me the world of classical music can become your oyster once more but with me alongside you, you would become a pariah.'

Visibly hurt by Steiner's cold assessment, she sought to think of an appropriate response but failed.

'Hannah, it's a nice thought but unlikely to happen for a number of reasons. First, there is the small matter of being able to successfully escape from this place alive which in my case is extremely unlikely bearing in mind my aversion to Russian prison camps and Siberian Gulags. Secondly, even if we were to survive and able to find each other in a post-war Europe teeming with millions of displaced people, there remains one more fundamental hurdle.'

'Which is?'

'What if your husband somehow manages to survive this war too; what then?'

'Kurt, I want you to understand and believe what I said a moment ago. I told you I am deeply in love with you. Not as a means of surviving in this fearful place but here in my heart,' emphasising her words by placing Steiner's hand on her throbbing chest.

With surprising tenderness, Steiner eased his hand away and gently caressed her cheek. 'Look, I don't doubt how you feel towards me but I'm simply pointing out how unlikely it would be. And another thing too. Whatever we decide upon for the future, must be based upon being able to expedite your escape from here and get you to Berlin. In present circumstances, that would not only be extremely dangerous but we would also need a huge slice of luck to overcome various elements which will be beyond our control. Don't ask me now what these are because without thinking about it, I really can't say.' Seeing the disappointment on Hannah's face Steiner knew he had to say something positive. 'Give me time to think and then we'll have another discussion. At this moment, I'm uncertain what we will need to do to get you to Berlin but let me think about it; if only to evaluate the difficulties we will undoubtedly meet and how we might overcome them.'

Hannah tensed. 'This plan you speak of. Apart from assisting me to escape this awful place, what would your reason be for wanting it to succeed? Would it be to simply escape Russian imprisonment or to make a life together with me and our child?'

With slow deliberation, Steiner took up his familiar position behind the large desk. 'Can we take your pregnancy out of the equation for just a moment?' He drew a deep breath and placed both hands behind his head before continuing. Can you recall me telling you when you first came here that I thought you would not be long for this world with your innocence and naivety? I'm sure you remember that conversation?'

'Of course I do. Every word and syllable but I'm still here so your timing is somewhat adrift even if your prognosis may well turn out to be correct given time.'

Angrily, Steiner slapped the table. 'Stop being so damned irritating and just listen.'

Instantly regretting her words, Hannah allowed her head to drop and stared at her shabby shoes; a poignant reminder of her time in the Central Sorting Area.

Regaining his composure, Steiner leaned back and took a deep breath. 'Well my little Girl, that was the night I began to fall in love with you and since then it has reached the point where I now have similar feelings to what you say you feel for me. But unlike you, I have to take a more pragmatic view on how we could realistically get you away from here, which at this moment looks extremely unlikely let alone to think of sharing a life together.'

Tentatively, Hannah raised her hand like a child seeking to get attention. 'May I speak without being slapped down?'

Half-smiling, Steiner nodded his assent.

'I believe anything can be possible if you really want it to happen. The biggest problem is your commitment to the Army when in reality you not only despise Adolph Hitler but everything he stands for. So how far does that commitment extend? Do you have to die to discharge that duty or at what stage do you begin to think of yourself?' She waited for Steiner to respond but this time it was he who chose to remain silent.

'Kurt, I was hoping this would be a joint discussion so can you please answer my question?'

'I wasn't aware you were asking a question. I thought you were in rhetorical mode.'

Ignoring the temptation to retort, Hannah pressed on. 'Look, for me to try to escape on my own would be nigh on impossible. But together, it could happen especially in the confusion created by thousands of refugees fleeing ahead of the Red Army. So for this to happen, I need to know if you will come with me.' She paused before daring to put the question. 'Will you?'

Squirming in obvious discomfort, it was several long seconds before he spoke. 'Do you have any idea what you are asking me to do? You want me to break my oath as an officer of the Wehrmacht and if that isn't serious enough, you want me to leave my unit and my men in the face of the enemy and become a common deserter.' He paused to let Hannah consider his words. 'Sweetheart, you must know I cannot do that.'

Utterly dejected, she sank lower in her chair. By refusing to even consider escaping together, she realised that Steiner had in effect passed a death sentence, not only on her but also on their unborn baby.

SIXTY ONE

Adjusting to the ways of his new Red Army comrades was not easy for Ephraim. Whilst most of them grudgingly accepted the benefit of having a qualified doctor within their ranks, a number of individual soldiers showed undisguised hostility towards him. To many of them, he was as much a German as their hated enemy. For his part, whilst able to admire their close comradeship he was mortified by their unrestrained cruelty to captured German troops. Only he and Marius of the original group of Partisans still remained with the unit, their surviving compatriots having been sent back for further interrogation and God knows what else by NKVD officers.

The unit, a forward company of the Russian 39th Guards Rifle Division were mainly of Siberian peasant stock, men who bore little physical resemblance to their counterparts in the German Army. Discipline was harshly enforced and ultimate command of the unit appeared to reside with a political commissar. On his orders, German prisoners and deserters were either sent back to the regimental HQ for interrogation or coldly shot without compunction. Either way, it resulted in fewer mouths to feed in a war zone where food rations were increasingly scarce, particularly for a forward unit detached from its regimental supply chain and its mobile food kitchens.

Despite his revulsion of the brutality of these men, Ephraim found himself warming to the Siberians. It had taken time but he believed he had finally been accepted by troops who recognised the value of a qualified medic on hand when operating far from a field hospital. In a short period of time he witnessed many acts of selfless bravery by troops whose hatred of the Axis invader knew no limits. In one desperate encounter against a well-armed group of experienced German troops, the bitter fighting had exhausted the ammunition of the Soviet troops in their forward positions. Watching from the rear of the action, Ephraim was astonished to see five Siberian troopers rise up from the comparative safety of the rubble and charge at their loathed aggressors with just their bayonets for weapons. Such was their momentum that three soldiers managed to storm the main German position before being cut down by gunfire from nearby bolt-holes. But whilst this was happening, other Red Army soldiers had followed their daring comrades and by sheer weight of numbers, overran the German positions.

Booty was always looked for from both prisoners and dead soldiers. Watches were particularly prized and Ephraim witnessed a number of men with as many as six timepieces strapped to a single forearm. SS insignia and cap badges were particularly prized but only after the German soldier had been cruelly put to death. For SS soldiers, a bullet in the back of the head was rarely used as the means of execution. If time allowed, a few prisoners would be stripped to their undergarments before being hung with a rifle strap around their neck with their toes allowed to just touch the ground. The hapless soldier's uniform would then be doused in petrol and set alight beneath his dangling feet. The Soviet troops would watch with unrestrained amusement as the German soldier would attempt to prevent strangulation by pushing his body upward with his bare toes until the agony of his burning feet became too much to bear and his dance with death would reach its inevitable conclusion.

When the momentum of battle did not allow time to exact revenge in this manner, captured SS troops would be systematically bayoneted in the throat, stomach and bowel and left to die a slow, excruciating death.

To Ephraim, time had become meaningless as the pattern of each day followed much the same as that of the previous 24 hours. But after a month since his involuntary induction into the unit, he learned they would be going back behind the constantly changing battle front for a brief rest period and for their heavy casualties to be replaced by yet more Siberian troops.

Earlier than expected, six large US-built trucks had appeared each carrying relieving and replacement troops together with boxes of captured Wehrmacht ammunition. Ephraim particularly noticed that each man carried his own field rations and water bottle. These same trucks then transported the battle-weary Siberians some 20 kilometres behind the front line to what remained of a Polish village. The main attraction for men returning from the front line were hot meals from the outdoor field kitchens, a portable canvas tent containing a shower and delousing area and inside of what had once been the village church, a regimental brothel serviced by captive Polish and Romanian women had been set up.

For the majority of soldiers, it was their first opportunity in weeks to enjoy hot food and limitless amounts of crudely refined vodka. Those still able to walk were then allowed to visit the brothel. Entrance to it was strictly marshalled, each soldier being given an allotted time with the first available woman. No distinction was made between officers and lower ranks with each man having to wait, often rowdily, for their turn.

Being a German, Ephraim was a curiosity to soldiers from other Red Army units, some of whom became dangerously aggressive especially when fuelled by vodka. Seeing this and having witnessed his medical expertise on the front line, the same officer who had interrogated him following his capture had him moved to the comparative safety of the officers' quarters.

It was there that he met General Stepan Guriev, overall commander of the Russian 39th Guards Rifle Division.

Peering at his slim figure from the rear of the temporary field HQ, Ephraim thought the Russian looked too young to hold such senior rank but later, while conversing with him over two liberally filled glasses of throat-burning vodka, he realised his initial assessment may have been hasty.

Guriev spoke flawless German. He questioned Ephraim on how he had come to be with his forward field unit and listened intently as he recounted his journey from Theresienstadt. The General made only a passing reference to the maltreatment of the Jewish population in Germany, wryly observing that 'Jews have always suffered from pogroms in Eastern Europe so perhaps your people should be used to them by now!'

Having been deprived of intelligent conversation for so long, Ephraim found himself warming to the scholarly Russian and gratefully accepted the General's invitation to share a meal with him.

Thinking back to the last occasion when he had dined with senior officers at Theresienstadt and the painful aftermath of that evening, he was surprised to see it would be just himself and the General dining together. Other officers, including the Political Commissar were seated on separate tables nearby. Fuelled by pre-dinner alcohol, the atmosphere among the group was visibly relaxed for men who only hours before had been fully engaged in bloody combat with the formidable German army.

Guriev too seemed relaxed despite frequent interruptions from a soldier conveying a constant stream of telegraphic messages throughout the meal.

'We appear to be pushing you Germans back along all fronts; other than for some isolated pockets of resistance.'

Unsure whether to express amusement or annoyance by the general pointedly allying the German Wehrmacht to himself, Ephraim prudently made no comment.

Noting this, the General gave Ephraim an inquiring look. 'It must be difficult for you as a Jew to know precisely who you are. Inwardly, you remain a German but outwardly, you want no part of what your country has engaged upon. Would that be a fair assessment, doctor?'

Unwilling to openly disagree with a man who was clearly intelligent enough to think beyond the boundaries of military terminology, Ephraim chose to respond in neutral terms.

'One's nationality is always an accident of birth so what is important is what a person does with his life regardless of where he was born. As you say, I was born a German citizen but I hold no brief for what that country has done since Hitler came to power. The real test is what each person does with their life regardless of nationality. I chose to become a doctor, which should indicate that my fundamental purpose since my graduation has been to preserve life. Not take it. That is where my former nationality and my profession part company.'

'So in essence, doctor, you are agreeing with me. Yes?'

'Yes I am.'

'And apart from wanting to preserve life, did you also hope it would lead to you becoming rich too?

'And become a member of the bourgeoisie?' Ephraim used an expression which he knew the General would be familiar with. 'Sorry but that has never been my motivation. But if you were to ask whether I sought a comfortable life for myself and my family, then yes, I would agree with that too.'

An amused expression appeared on Guriev's face. Satisfied he could have an open discussion with this likeable man, he broached the subject he really wanted to discuss. 'The Germans cannot hope to win this war nor will they. But unfortunately, they will fight to the bitter end and in the process thousands, if not millions more will die.' He nodded to encourage Ephraim to reply.

'Again I can only agree with you but it would be a mistake to dismiss the German military quite so soon. They are still extremely formidable especially when their backs are to the wall.'

'Ah, backs to the wall you say.' The General quietly repeated Ephraim's assertion. 'I like that expression but it doesn't stand up to examination. At Stalingrad your Sixth Army had their backs firmly pressed against this mythical wall but were eventually beaten. Did you know that, doctor?'

'Yes, I heard the news from several sources so guessed it might be true.'

'What sources are you referring to?'

Ephraim realised that the General, apart from taking the opportunity to speak in German, was also quizzing him in the process.

'Your troops captured a number of German prisoners, some of whom had fought at Stalingrad just before it fell.'

'And what were your feelings when you heard the news?'

'Any successful conclusion to a battle which brings the end of this war nearer must be good news, whatever your nationality.'

'I'm not sure too many Germans would share that view, doctor. They became too used to conquering all before them particularly in Western Europe so they thought themselves invincible until they were beaten at Stalingrad and elsewhere since.'

Teased by Guriev's throwaway remark, Ephraim was tempted to press him for further information but instead elected for caution.

Clearly disappointed, Guriev changed tack. 'What will you do if you survive this war? Will you return to Germany and continue being a doctor?'

'Who can say what anyone will do or where, when all this madness ends. The only thing we can both be certain of is that life will never be the same again.'

'Perhaps the world needed to go through this refining process in order to come to its senses.'

Suspecting that this wily man was still baiting him, Ephraim upped the tempo. 'You must regard life very cheaply, General, when you describe the world-wide slaughter taking place, as a refining process.' He hesitated, trying to assess whether the

Russian would react but Guriev's demeanour remained unchanged.

'Whether the world will choose to learn from the butchery now taking place is highly questionable. History has shown that war and territorial conquest are inherent within mankind and the only ingredient needed to activate a nation such as Germany is a leader who feeds those basic instincts. Hitler is a case in point.'

'And Mr. Churchill... would he fit into that category?'

Taken aback by Guriev's provocative question, Ephraim reached for his glass of vodka, gaining time before replying. 'He would, but from the opposite end of the spectrum. Churchill is endeavouring to defend the British and their Empire whereas Hitler is hell-bent on conquest and enslavement.' He took a deep breath, hoping his reply would deter Guriev from asking the one question he feared would be next. But to no avail.

'So with Hitler and Churchill at opposite ends of your spectrum, where would you place Comrade Stalin?'

'I know little about Mr. Stalin so I cannot answer that question. Other than being the General Secretary of the Communist Party and leader of the Soviet Union, he is practically unknown in the West.'

Any faint hope that Guriev would let his measured reply pass without further comment was instantly dispelled.

'Come doctor, for an intelligent man, you are being deliberately disingenuous. No man gets to become head of the greatest revolutionary party this world has ever known by being a gentle, caring soul. Stalin is an inhuman monster... at least on a par with your Mr. Hitler! But in reality those qualities are precisely what my country needs to get us through this war.' Clearly indifferent to the presence of a political commissar dining at a nearby table, Guriev made no attempt to lower his voice. 'Wouldn't you agree, doctor?'

Realising that his neutral stance was being challenged, Ephraim stood up and with slow deliberation, unbuttoned his shirt. 'General, forgive me if I appear reticent but the last time I was ordered to express a view was in the presence of a bunch of Nazi thugs and this was their idea of punishment.' Pulling his shirt fully open he exposed the burned tissue in the form of a swastika seared on the upper part of his chest, its redness contrasting vividly to the pallid whiteness of the unburned flesh.

Leaning forward, Guriev quietly examined the scarring. 'Doctor, I apologise for drawing you into a political minefield.' Picking up his glass of freshly replenished vodka, he took a deep swallow. 'Let me offer you a crumb of comfort. War throws up many unlikely coincidences so you never know whether you may meet this man again. And who knows, if there is a next time than maybe you will be able to repay him in similar fashion.'

'I already have.' Unable to prevent his instinctive reaction, he realised that he had given the General another opportunity to pursue his cat and mouse game. Looking at the Russian, he tried to inject a degree of humour. 'Even as we speak, I suspect he may well be goose-stepping with the rest of his kind in their Nazi Valhalla.'

For an interminable moment Guriev stared at Ephraim before his face broke into a smile. 'There's obviously more to you than meets the eye, doctor. I must remember not to try and upset you again.'

Reaching for the bottle of vodka, Guriev re-filled both glasses. 'A toast, doctor... to victory and a life beyond war.'

Before Ephraim could follow suit, yet another of the General's aide's hurried to Guriev's side and thrust a piece of paper in front of him. Even in the uncertain light within the tent, Ephraim saw his features darken. Returning the paper, Guriev issued a curt order causing the aide to hurry back from whence he came.

Reverting back into German, his boyish face broke into an unconstrained grin. 'My comrades have made a breakthrough at Krakov so I regret we must now part company. Beckoning another aide, he spoke quickly and Ephraim saw the man nod in silent acknowledgement. 'You will remain with my regiment as a Medical Officer so maybe we can share this pleasure again.' Standing up, he proffered his hand. Taking it, Ephraim felt a glimmer of hope within. 'Dare I ask where this unit will be heading?'

For a long moment, Guriev stared as though uncertain whether to reply but Ephraim saw his face soften before he spoke. 'We are going to Silesia to destroy the German war factories and whatever else we may find there. And if you survive the journey and the fighting, you may even find some of your fellow-Jews waiting to be liberated from their Nazi death camps.'

SIXTY TWO

Other than for Stalingrad, Kurt Steiner had had a good war. Following his graduation from Officer Cadet School and his commissioning as a junior officer in the Wehrmacht, he had experienced active service in the invasion of the Sudetenland before being assigned to Czechoslovakia and then into Poland. Like the majority of his military peers, he had been full of admiration for the insight and judgement of Adolph Hitler and the military conquests of the German military machine.

Promoted to Captain and transferred to the Western Front, his regiment followed the armoured Panzer units on their blitzkrieg through Belgium, Holland and France. After several months enjoying the sights and night-life of Paris, his unit was transferred back to Poland in preparation for Operation Barbarossa; the Fuhrer's long-planned invasion of the Soviet Union.

It was there in the endless landscape of the Ukraine, that Steiner first become aware of the rumours surrounding special SS Einsatzgruppen units and their murderous activities behind the German front lines. According to the scuttlebuck circulating among the front-line troops, townships and villages were being razed to the ground; their inhabitants, including women and children massacred or burned alive; entrapped within buildings torched by portable flame throwers.

At Stalingrad the Wehrmacht had encountered the first serious resistance from the Red Army. The aerial bombardment by the Luftwaffe had reduced much of the city to rubble which ironically prevented the Panzer tank units from operating effectively whilst creating a terrain in which Soviet troops were at last able to halt the Wehrmacht in a form of savage hand to hand fighting not seen since the trench warfare of World War 1. Such was the attrition among both officers and men that within a matter of weeks, Steiner was promoted to Major. For months without end, neither of the two sides could gain the upper hand and it was in the depths of the Russian winter, where ill-clothed German troops were literally freezing to death that Steiner was seriously wounded. For days he lay in a basement, drifting in and out of consciousness, his ebbing life saved by the care of a middle-aged NCO by the name of Ernst Erlich.

Following weeks of recuperation in Germany, he had been posted to Upper Silesia charged with organising the defence of that increasingly important industrial region with Wehrmacht units seriously depleted in terms of replacement troops, equipment and ammunition. More critically, with the breakthrough by Soviet forces at Krakov, Upper Silesia and its manufacturing industries, mines and refineries had now become the Red Army's next key objective and the battleground where Steiner's strategic defence plans were about to be put to the ultimate test.

That morning, he had addressed each of his regional commanders and by the evening, in the company of his trusted confidant, Erlich, he was a worried man. Predictably, he knew the Red Army's infantry battalions would attack from behind their armoured divisions and whilst his ground forces were equipped with limited supplies of anti-tank weapons barely capable of destroying the Red Army's seemingly endless supply of new T.34 tanks, he knew his troops would be hard pushed to halt, let alone push back the Soviet advance. Equally worrying was his awareness that his ground forces could expect little help from a Luftwaffe suffering major losses of pilots and aircraft resulting from its futile effort to supply the encircled German Sixth Army at Stalingrad.

Rising from his chair, Steiner went to the drinks cabinet at the far end of the room and returned with two bottles of beer. 'Brewed in Bavaria, Ernst; especially for a time like this.'

Looking at the label on the bottle, a wistful look appeared on Erlich's weathered features. 'It amazes me to think that whatever else may be happening in this sad old world, there are still folk brewing beer in Bavaria.' Slowly filling his glass to ensure the frothy head was kept to a drinkable level, he resisted the temptation to sip the amber liquid, giving it time to settle in the glass. 'God bless them and long may they continue.'

'Enjoy it while you can, old friend. We may not have many more evenings like this. I doubt the Ruskies serve German beer in their prison camps!'

Raising his glass, Erlich gently tapped it against Steiner's. 'Good health Colonel, wherever we end up.'

Taking a long draught of beer, it was a few moments before Steiner spoke. 'We've been through a lot together Ernst, some of which we will remember as long as we live and other times we will want to forget.'

Staring into his beer, Erlich appeared to be in deep thought. 'In which of those two categories would you place Stalingrad? For me, it was the most forgettable hell-hole imaginable; especially when I think of our comrades who died there but on the other hand will time ever allow us to forget it?' Looking at Steiner, Erlich tried to lighten the moment. 'What memories will you take with you, Colonel?'

Listening to a sombre and reflective Erlich, Steiner gauged how best to answer his pointed question. Slouching back in his favourite position, he arched his fingers and looked into the distance. 'Well for a start, I will never forget you, Ernst Erlich. You may not be the most regimented of soldiers but with a battalion of men like you, this war would have been won in a month!' Raising his glass, he offered another toast. 'To you, old friend.'

Self-consciously raising his glass in acknowledgement, Erlich reciprocated the toast and drew a deep breath. 'And what about Bergmann, Colonel; how will she rate? As a memory or your future?

Caught off-guard by Erlich's question, it took Steiner a few moments to gather his thoughts.

'I should have known better than to try and fool a canny old fox like you.' He placed his glass on the pine table.

'Bergmann is an enigma to me, Ernst. Not only has she managed to survive both Ravensbrück and now here in Auschwitz but she has also outlasted that Czech woman Danuta and the one who followed her.'

Erlich put down his glass with a meaningful thump. 'Colonel, you are being deliberately evasive to the point of rambling. You know precisely what I'm referring to. Bergmann is pregnant with your child and unless you do something, neither of you will survive the next month or so.'

Shocked by Erlich's uncharacteristic frankness, Steiner stood up and began to pace the room; a favoured tactic when needing time to think. 'Ernst, you sound very paternal... it suits you.'

Unfazed by Steiner's condescending remark, Erlich would not be deflected. 'Perhaps I did miss my vocation in life and you may think I'm a sentimental old fool but where I come from, that makes her your responsibility.'

Despite their close camaraderie, Steiner felt a growing sense of resentment begin to well up inside him. 'You sound more like a father remonstrating with the man who has wronged his daughter than a man who is supposed to be her master in this household.'

The thinly veiled reprimand would normally have stopped the elderly Bavarian in his tracks but tonight it had the opposite effect.

'I can understand why you say that Colonel because that is precisely how I feel. This is a woman who has lost her husband; her child is probably dead too and now she is expecting your baby. And we both know what will happen to her when the Ruskies get her or would you prefer not to think about that?'

Now plainly angered, Steiner strode back down the room and towered over his burly corporal. 'As you seem to care so much, then perhaps you can tell me what I can do for her. But before you do that, you will need to take into account that I am the senior officer in this region, responsible for its defence, the maintenance of essential war supplies and to ensure the two prison camps continue to supply essential labour. If I've missed anything then do please remind me.'

Unperturbed by Steiner's sarcasm, Erlich calmly drained his beer and put the empty glass on the table.

'Nothing to remind you of in that list, Colonel, you've covered your responsibilities very well.' Taking his time, Erlich poured the remaining contents from the bottle into his glass. 'Would you now like me to suggest what you might do for her?'

With his anger slowly abating, Steiner could contain himself no longer. Leaning down, he pulled the portly corporal to his feet and embraced him with both arms. 'What am I going to do with you, my old comrade?'

Instead of replying, Erlich pulled away; embarrassed by the unexpected familiarity.

Chastened, Steiner resumed his seat. 'Look' he said quickly, 'have you ever known me not to have a plan for whatever eventuality we've faced in the past?'

Erlich, feeling more at ease, smiled. 'If there have been occasions when there was a plan, then you must have been the only person to have been aware of it, Colonel.'

Steiner's face broke into a boyish grin. 'That may have been how you saw things but... ' He let his words fall away, unsaid.

'So does that mean you have a plan for Bergmann?

'It means I'm thinking about how I can get her away from here. Nothing more than that.' Re-filling his glass, he settled back. 'If we were facing the Americans or British, then it would be easy but this is the Eastern Front and we both know what the Red Army do to German women... Jews included.'

Reflecting on Steiner's words, it took a second or two before Erlich spoke. 'Then one answer would be to get her back to Berlin, where she can hide until the Allies arrive.'

Steiner gave a caustic laugh. 'Easier said than done.'

Erlich's eyes gleamed; 'but not if you have a plan.'

Puzzled by Erlich's remark, he drummed his fingers on the side of the table. 'Ernst, are you about to tell me you actually have a plan too? Or even the semblance of a plan?'

Now it was Erlich's turn to smile. 'I believe I do, Colonel unless of course, you have something better.'

'I can only decide that once I hear what you have in mind; so go ahead; enlighten me.'

Drawing a deep breath, Erlich stood up and moved to the front of the large stone fireplace to give added gravitas to his short frame.

'You won't remember this but when you were evacuated from Stalingrad, each plane had three nurses on board. And later, just before the Sixth Army surrendered, the Luftwaffe flew all female medical staff out to prevent them falling into the hands of the Russians.'

'If you're suggesting that Bergmann impersonate a nurse, then where would we get the correct paperwork from?'

'Please, one thing at a time, Colonel.' He raised his eyebrows as though dealing with a wayward child. 'First, Bergmann was married to a doctor so she will have some knowledge of medical procedures and terminology. Secondly, she won't have the problem of escaping from the camp seeing that she's already outside it. Thirdly, she had a contact in your cousin, Colonel Von Hartman and other Abwehr officers which brought her to this house albeit through your intervention.' He paused to take another deep breath. 'Unless you think otherwise, Colonel, then I believe those are all positive aspects.'

'My God man, you've really given this some thought.' Looking at Erlich who in the past had never been a man to use much initiative, Steiner began to analyse each of the points made by his loyal comrade, endeavouring to hastily adjust to the Bavarian's rational thinking. Not only adjusting to it but thinking how it could be improved upon.

'It won't fly, Ernst. There are too many things which can go wrong; any one of which will mean her arrest and execution. And what's the point in getting her to Berlin; once the Soviets breakthrough this god-forsaken country then it's only a matter of time before the Red Army take Berlin too.' Seeing the look of disappointment cross Erlich's face, Steiner knew he had to say more.

'Look, I may have mis-read you but are you thinking Bergmann would stand a better chance in Berlin because there will be more women for the Russians to fuck in the Capital than here? Is that what you're suggesting?'

Embarrassed by the crudeness of Steiner's words, Erlich shrugged his broad shoulders. 'Remember those hairy-arsed troops we fought at Stalingrad, Colonel? Away from their wives for months and seeing what our troops have done to their villagers, they will arrive here looking for revenge. The choice will be the women prisoners in the camp looking and stinking like skeletons or girls like Bergmann and the Danish girl.' He shrugged his shoulders again, becoming frustrated by Steiner's apparent lack of understanding. To reinforce his point, he added, 'they won't last a day.'

Unable to disagree with Erlich' realism, Steiner felt a tang of guilt. 'You're right, old friend, I have to do something. But whatever it is, it has to have at least a fair chance of success.' Cogitating, he rose to his feet before promptly sitting down again. Running Erlich's plan through his mind he began to critically analyse each aspect of it more fully. The obvious weakness would be when Bergmann and her ID papers were subjected to scrutiny and possible interrogation. In her naivety he knew she would not stand up to robust let alone physical questioning. So it was that aspect of the plan which had to be addressed. Stopping at the far end of the room, he grasped the top end of a saddle-back chair and outlined his concern to Erlich, half expecting or perhaps even hoping for him to drop the subject. To his surprise, Erlich agreed with him.

'So how would you suggest we overcome that, Colonel?'

'We do that by going with her to Berlin. As you can see from the calendar, I am due to attend an official briefing meeting in the next ten days at Gatow. You will become a very sick patient whom I insist is taken to Berlin for immediate treatment, accompanied by a Nursing Sister.' He threw back his head and laughed out loud. 'It's so damn simple, why didn't I think of it sooner.'

Erlich, trying to digest the new plan voiced his own thoughts. 'And once in Berlin, what then?'

'Once in Berlin you will make a partial recovery before going home on sick leave. I will ask Colonel Von Stauffenberg to recommend a Medical Officer we can trust and I'm certain he will help.' He paused, 'I will need to organise that before we leave. As for Bergmann, she will disappear into the chaos which is now Berlin; at least until the Allies arrive.'

'I need time to think about the wrinkles, Colonel, but on paper, maybe it could just work except for two small queries.' Where will you go once we arrive in Berlin?'

'And your other point?'

'What about the Danish woman?'

'Ernst, let me give you two very short, simple answers to both questions. First, I will attend my briefing meeting and then return here. Secondly, the Danish woman will stay here; her nationality may be enough to save her from the Russians and if it doesn't then she will be back on familiar ground.'

'I don't follow, Colonel. Familiar ground? What does that mean?

'For a middle-aged man, Ernst, you're naivety never ceases to amaze me. Before she came here, she was assigned as a cleaner in the SS barracks where,' he paused knowing he had Erlich's full attention, 'she was fucked on a daily basis.' He saw Erlich's face take on a pained expression, clearly unhappy with Steiner's choice of language. 'Stop frowning, old friend.

She told Bergmann that the experience actually strengthened her faith in much the same way as Jesuits wearing hair shirts.'

The explanation appeared to do little to change Erlich's disconsolate features.

'Ernst, there's something else I need to tell you; something which I have thought about for some while.' The look on the Bavarian's face remained unchanged 'When we get to Berlin, I intend to have you invalided out of the Army which means you won't be coming back here again. For you, old friend, this war is over... finished.'

Stunned, it took Erlich's laboured brain time to absorb the import of Steiner's statement. 'How can that be possible, Colonel? If it were that easy, then half the Wehrmacht would be at home?'

'Leave the arrangements to me, OK? You will be more useful at home when this war is finally over than starving in some stinking Russian prisoner-of-war camp which is where most of us on this Eastern Front will end up.'

'Do I have any say in this decision of yours?' Erlich's loyalty was touching.

Steiner's rebuff was equally as firm. 'Afraid not; I've made the decision and as far as you're concerned, it's non-negotiable.

'In which case, when do you intend to tell Bergmann?'

'Let me speak with Von Stauffenberg first,' he replied. 'I will need his help.'

Silence prevailed between the two men. But in the mind of the middle-aged NCO the unexpected realisation that he would be returning home to Bavaria was tempered by the sadness that he and Steiner would be parting company... this time for ever.

***

Steiner knew the conversation with the autocratic Von Stauffenberg would be difficult. Born into a family with strong military traditions, he straightaway rebuffed Steiner's request for assistance in expediting Erlich's demobilisation on medical grounds.

In his palatial Replacement Army Office in central Berlin, Steiner listened patiently as Stauffenberg lectured him on the duty of every good German to fight for their Fatherland, regardless of age or infirmity.

Looking at a man who had suffered grievously in the service of his country, it was difficult to become irritated with him but just such an emotion was beginning to rise in Steiner's craw.

'Colonel, spare me the lecture but not all men are in the same mould as you. This Fatherland you refer to is on a par with Hitler's mythical Valhalla inasmuch it means different things to different people. We are a bloodthirsty, warlike nation, lepers to the rest of the civilised world and a pariah state led by a madman. And the man I want to help walk away from all this is a simple wood-turner, a gentle, God-fearing man who has done his duty and more for Germany.' Stopping to draw breath, he was surprised to see Von Stauffenberg's face light up in anticipation..

'Speaking of which, have you managed to speak with your comrades on the subject we discussed at your office?

Tempted to prick Stauffenberg's air of superiority, Steiner chose instead to be factual. 'I have with somewhat mixed results.' Drawing a small notebook from his breast pocket, he glanced at his barely legible script. 'Despite the Fuhrer's meddling and our defeats at Stalingrad and Kurst, there are still a number of officers who believe Hitler will lead our nation to victory. Other officers, mainly Wehrmacht staff officers, will not break their personal oath to the Fuhrer but there are six who feel as we do.'

'Excellent' said Stauffenberg, 'that is most encouraging.' Moving from behind his antique roll-top desk, he motioned Steiner towards the adjoining anteroom furnished with four comfortable leather chairs. In the far corner Steiner stopped to admire a polished walnut drinks cabinet, its mottled texture contrasting exquisitely with the darker hued mahogany chair frames.

Quietly humming to himself, Stauffenberg opened the cabinet and drew out two glasses and a bottle of champagne. Handing the bottle to Steiner for him to open, the sound of the popping cork brought a smile to both men's features. Handing the bottle back to Von Stauffenberg, he filled both glasses and handed one to Steiner. 'To success, Colonel.'

Repeating the toast, Steiner watched the bubbles frenetically fizzing to the surface before sipping. As to be expected, Stauffenberg's champagne was first class.

'I have some news which will be of interest to you, Colonel.' He leaned forward and lowered his voice. 'I am due to be promoted Chief-of-Staff of the Replacement Army on 1 July and this will be announced in the next day or so.'

Raising his glass, Steiner felt a warm sense of respect for this much-wounded man. 'Congratulations, Colonel; a well-deserved recognition.'

A tinge of embarrassment caused Stauffenberg's face to redden. 'Thank you, Steiner but the promotion itself is not important. What is crucial is that it will enable me to personally attend the Fuhrer's regular briefings at his Headquarters.'

'And once there, what will you do?'

Still speaking in a hushed voice, Stauffenberg outlined his plan. 'The next conference will be held at Rastenburg. It's planned for some time in mid- July which is only a matter of days from now. I will attend with an explosive device in my briefcase which I will place as near to Hitler as I can get.' He took a sip of champagne. 'The bomb will have a timing device which will enable me to excuse myself to take a pre-arranged telephone call. After the explosion and with Hitler dead, our troops in Berlin and Paris will seize control from the SS and proclaim a new Government who will then declare a cease-fire and sue for peace with the Allies. As I mentioned when we last met, your role will be to ensure there will be no hostile reaction from your region.' Stauffenberg ended his analysis as abruptly as he began. 'I expect you have several questions, Colonel?'

The audacity of the plot and the closeness of its activation just mere days away took Steiner's breath away before his mind began to systematically look for the inevitable snags which he knew could so easily thwart the best laid of plans. His immediate concern centred on the bomb itself. 'The action planned for Berlin and Paris and other regions is entirely dependent on your bomb killing Hitler. If it doesn't and communication from Rastenburg becomes uncertain, whether deliberately or otherwise, then confusion will reign. Troops will be uncertain whether to rise up or stay in limbo. In that event, the one thing we can be certain of is that the Gestapo will exact terrible retribution upon us as conspirators. And you will be their immediate suspect.'

The intensity of Stauffenberg's stare was unnerving as was his silence.

'In short, Colonel, I'm saying that if you fail then the entire plot will fail and thousands of good German comrades will be murdered in the process.'

Stauffenberg stiffened, clearly not liking Steiner's synopsis. 'So what would you suggest in its stead? That we abandon the whole thing and let this madman bring Germany to the abyss of extinction?'

Hurt by Stauffenberg's rebuke, Steiner drew another deep breath to calm himself. 'No, I am not suggesting that. But since Hitler came to power, there have been numerous attempts on his life, all of which have failed. As German officers, we are trained never to undertake any operation unless we have at least two other strategies in place.' He looked at Stauffenberg for a comment but none was forthcoming. 'The weakness of this plan is whether the bomb will actually kill Hitler or not? How will we know whether you have been successful and what will then happen in Berlin, Paris and here on the Eastern Front, in the event of uncertainty?'

'Those are good points Colonel but they will become irrelevant when the bomb explodes. Hitler and the others in that room will die, make no mistake about that. And let me offer you some further comfort. We do have a well-placed comrade at Rastenburg who will telegraph directly to Berlin after the event.'

Signifying the conversation was at an end; Von Stauffenberg rose and headed towards the door. Pausing, he turned for one last word with the still seated Steiner. 'The Medical Officer you mentioned will contact you later today and will do as you request for this NCO of yours.' With that he was gone.

Staring at the departing figure of Claus Von Stauffenberg, Steiner could not know he would never see this brave fellow-officer again.

On 20 July Von Stauffenberg's bomb exploded in Hitler's conference room at Rastenburg in East Prussia. Believing Hitler to be dead, Stauffenberg hurried to Berlin only to be arrested upon his arrival. Later that day, together with four fellow conspirators, Claus Graf Schenk Von Stauffenberg was executed by firing squad. The plot had failed due to the very uncertainty spoken of by Steiner. The repercussions were immediate. Many of those arrested by the Gestapo were brutally tortured with many being forced to reveal the names of other conspirators. Some, like Stauffenberg, were shot immediately whilst others were arraigned as traitors in public show trials before being executed. Some were hung from meat hooks forced through their jaws, their grisly death throes filmed and publically shown in cinemas throughout the Third Reich.

In Upper Silesia, Steiner and six other fellow officers anxiously awaited their expected denouncement and arrest but the Gestapo's thirst for revenge appeared to have been satiated with the number of its victims plucked from Berlin and Paris.

Following his meeting with Stauffenberg, Steiner had spent time with a Major Johan Busch; the senior Medical Officer attached to the Reserve Army and left that discussion with a set of medical discharge papers in the name of a Corporal Ernst Erlich. Meanwhile, in Sandomiercz, an unnamed Wehrmacht Captain had reported the death of three members of the Medical Corps travelling in an ambulance blown to smithereens after being driven over a land mine ironically laid by the German Army as it retreated from the advancing Red Army.

Later, in the unit's Administration Office, the casualty records were covertly amended to show just two fatalities, the driver and a wounded soldier. A certain Nurse Eva Becker was restored to rude health and according to the same records, was in the process of being transferred to a unit in Berlin. The Records Officer, a young Lieutenant from the same small town in the Hartz Mountains as his Commanding Officer, was one of those six anxious men to whom the code name Valkyrie was now but a shattered dream

Having acquired a passable identity for the woman bearing his child plus a bone fide discharge document for his NCO, Steiner was ready to activate the plan for Bergmann's escape. But for the plan to have any chance of success there was one critical element still missing. And that he knew, would determine whether it worked or failed.

On the Eastern Front, the German military machine was ruthless. Deserters, stragglers, soldiers with self-inflicted wounds and even troops separated from their units in the heat of battle and found heading away from the front line, were being arrested by the SS and in many cases summarily executed without any semblance of a trial. Most were shot but some were hung from any convenient tree or lamp-post as a salutary warning to others. Against this backdrop of brutalised policing, Steiner knew it would be madness to implement his plan without the missing element.

Fortunately, he did not have long to wait. The newly reinforced Red Army's summer campaign had begun on 10 June and by the end of July, the German Army was in retreat along the whole of the Eastern Front.

Majdanek, the first Nazi concentration camp to be liberated on 23 July exposed the unspeakable horror of Hitler's murderous policy of genocide which until then had been just rumours; but rumours so gross as to be unbelievable.

Within the Auschwitz and Birkenau complex, the Nazi killing machine went into overdrive in a frenzied attempt to murder and dispose of the increased numbers of Jews being transported from every part of occupied Europe together with thousands of Russian prisoners of war. Those Russians prisoners selected as slave labour were straightway assigned to work in factories and mines but as starvation and disease took their inevitable toll, they too were then shot and replaced from the intakes of new prisoners. And so the murderous cycle of death continued unabated.

From her bedroom on the top floor in the Administration unit, Hannah could see the newly built crematoria buildings alongside the old structures, their grim silhouettes continuously obscured by thick volumes of grey smoke ceaselessly pouring from their chimneys. Alone in her room, it seemed that the world had descended into irretrievable insanity.

Latterly, she had thought constantly about Aaron. Away from the emotional pull of day-to-day contact with her baby son, she began to experience increasing pangs of guilt for bringing such sweet innocence into a world of unimaginable evil. Her strongest guilt was felt for Ephraim. Since their parting at Theresienstadt and her growing relationship with Kurt Steiner, she had found it difficult to think about him. At first, she had convinced herself that he was dead but with the shock of her pregnancy now foremost in her mind, she knew it was because of her love for another man. And because that man was a German officer made the burden of guilt almost unbearable. Worse, she now realised that Steiner would not leave his command despite his frequent declarations of his love for her. His plan to get her and Erlich to Berlin to escape from the advancing Red Army was the best she could expect but the thought of then never seeing him again was becoming increasingly agonising. Since their first discussion he had again referred to the missing element before his plan could be activated but so far he had not divulged what that essential element was.

What had surprised her was the equanimity with which Erlich had accepted the plan. She had convinced herself that Erlich, the soldier who had remained with Steiner for days in a stinking cellar in Stalingrad, would refuse to leave him but to her astonishment, he now appeared to have accepted Steiner's decision without qualm.

Since telling Steiner of her pregnancy, he had twice more spent the night in her room. His lovemaking was as urgent as ever whilst she tried to affect a mental passiveness towards him which her responsive body would quickly abandon after the first few moments. Unusually, neither spoke during their lovemaking nor afterwards in the afterglow of exhausted contentment.

But within the confines of his office, he did break the news of Von Stauffenberg's arrest and execution. Also that of General Beck, the man whom she fondly recalled had warmly expressed his appreciation of her performance on the night that Steiner had first come to her room.

Hearing the news, the hardness of her reply surprised even herself. 'Am I supposed to be upset? Isn't that what happens in war especially if you are a soldier.' She knew her harsh words were aimed at him but instantly regretting her impulsiveness, she tried to soften her remark. 'Were they close to you or simply brother officers?' It worked. The hurt expression on Steiner's face disappeared as quickly as it had appeared.

'They were more than brother officers. They were brave men trying to kill the Fuhrer but they failed. That's why they were shot.'

Her mind straightaway recalled the guarded conversation she had had in the garden with Steiner only weeks before. 'So were they the two officers you spoke about in which case I'm sorry they failed.'

'They were more than just officers. They and several others were the leaders of the plot.'

The realisation of Steiner's statement registered immediately. 'So as they were both here, does that mean that you are implicated too? Is there a danger that you might be arrested?'

'So far, no arrests have been made on the Eastern Front but that's not to say they won't happen.

'In which case, why wait? Why don't you and Ernst prepare to leave before that happens? By staying here, you not only risk being arrested but shot like those other poor souls.'

A look of resignation crossed his face. 'You know my answer to that. I can't leave my command regardless of what may happen to me.'

'So was this attempt on Hitler's life, the missing element you spoke of earlier?

'No it wasn't,' he replied. 'In fact, had it succeeded, it would have seriously compromised the plan I have for you and Erlich. The Gestapo would have restricted all personnel movements within each of the areas where the plotters were stationed.

Increasingly anxious, she probed further: 'So what is the missing element you keep referring to?'

A boyish look spread across his face. 'In a word... chaos! There needs to be an element of chaos for systems and order to break down and as the Red Army's advance brings them closer to this area then chaos will occur. Trust me, it will happen and soon.'

'And if I refuse to go?'

Clearly annoyed, Steiner took hold of Hannah's shoulder and firmly pushed her onto the edge of the single bed. 'If you really hope to see your son again you won't have a better chance than this. When Erlich leaves here you will go with him and once in Berlin, you will disappear until American or British troops arrive. Stay well away from East Berlin and once you have found your child then get as far west of the city as you can.'

The anger at Steiner's intention to stay with his command in Silesia again rose up within her but then subsided just as quickly. Regaining her feet, Hannah reached out and pulled Steiner's unresisting body towards her. 'You really do care for me, don't you?'

Self-consciously, Steiner eased her down onto the bed again; this time more gently.

'You will never know how much, my little Pumpkin.'

'Pumpkin? Where did that name come from?'

Embarrassed, Steiner blurted out 'I meant Pushkin. It's a Russian term of endearment... I think?'

Laughing at his unlikely explanation, Hannah reached out and guided Steiner's muscular frame to sit alongside her. Wordlessly, she leaned over and kissed him, letting her lips dwell on his. The clean smell of starch given off by his uniform shirt reminded her of their first night together. Shamelessly, she knelt on the floor and slid Steiner's non-military red braces off his shoulders and with deliberate slowness, undid each of the buttons on his shirt. Staring into his eyes, she pulled the shirt open and let her hands run over his bare chest, her fingers finding the jagged edges of scar tissue which had so excited her on the night when he had succumbed to fever.

Transfixed, it took what seemed an eternity for Steiner to respond. Fully aroused and lacking Hannah's finesse, he took hold of her white blouse and impatiently pulled it open.

'Slowly, Kurt; we have all night.' The softness of her cautionary whisper adding rather than dispelling the mounting tension.

'Then help me.'

Reluctantly withdrawing her hands from Steiner's beating chest, Hannah reached behind her and undid the small metal fastening holding her bra and deftly removed it. Resisting the temptation to touch her bare breasts, Steiner pulled Hannah to her feet and awkwardly undid the zip on the side of her skirt and watched as it fell to the floorboards with barely a rustle.

Knowing there was no physical evidence of her pregnancy; Hannah was content to let Steiner run his hands over her still flat stomach. Leaning forward, he pursed his lips and began to kiss the soft silky flesh around her breasts before moving his hands around her slim hips. Breathing deeply to control her emotions, Hannah felt the first stirrings of an orgasm beginning in her loins. Easing herself away from Steiner's physical enticement, she forcibly pushed him back onto the bed. Swiftly discarding her last remnant of underwear, she leaned over and undid the buttons on his uniform trousers, exposing his throbbing manhood. Straddling his inert body, she positioned herself above him and sank down on to his hard penis. Instantly lost in a swirling emotion, she heard herself cry out as the first flooding orgasm coursed through her body. Beneath her, Steiner lay totally inert. Reaching up, he gripped Hannah's arms and halted her increasingly frantic movements as she sought to extend the orgasm.

'Slow down my eager little Pumpkin. We have all night.' Moving his arms, he cupped her breasts in both hands. 'You were in this position when I first saw you... remember?'

Visions of that awful night in the Romanian Kapo's room flooded into her mind. Impulsively she struck out, hitting Steiner a sharp blow across his cheek.

Unfazed, Steiner ran his hand over the reddening mark on his face. 'Sweetheart, you look even more beautiful when you are angry.' With surprising speed, he pulled Hannah down and moved on top of her. 'But, having struck a German officer, albeit one who is besotted with you, I'm afraid there is a price to pay.' Steiner began to move his lower abdomen in a slow rhythmic movement, gently at first and barely penetrating her. Slowly increasing his rhythm, he felt Hannah's legs move up to around his waist. Still in perfect control, he reached down and clamped both arms under her knees and forced her legs up to touch his shoulders. Thrusting harder, he achieved maximum penetration and heard Hannah cry out in ecstasy and pain as she experienced another mind-numbing orgasm affecting every part of her energised body.

Steiner was relentless. Driving ever faster and ignoring her cries to stop, his movement began to verge on being demonic. Looking up, Hannah saw his eyes half-close and roll up into his head a split second before she felt him literally explode deep within her. The guttural sound which escaped his lips sounded almost primeval. Slowly, his momentum slowed and Hannah felt drops of sweat drop on to her neck from Steiner's face. Easing himself off her prostrate body, Steiner carefully moved to lay alongside the woman responsible for him to break every decree in the Nazi rule book.

Waiting to recover his breath, he felt Hannah's hand reach over and touch his scarred chest.

'I'm disappointed Kurt; this is normally when you tell me that if you could choose a moment to die then this would be it. Does this mean you want to live after all?' Moving even closer, she whispered 'I want to remember this moment for as long as I live.' Looking at Steiner's heaving chest she lightly kissed each nipple. 'Can we stay together tonight' she whispered, 'this could be the last time we make love.'

The awful realisation of her words struck Steiner with the force of a heavy blow. Impulsively, she clutched her hand to her mouth. 'Oh dear God, I don't think I can bear that.' Her body, which only moments before had been utterly lost in the ecstasy of their love-making, now began to shake with barely controlled emotion. Attempting to hide her tears, she buried her head in the soft pillow. She felt Steiner's muscular arm slide across her back and pull her closer to him but he didn't speak. For several minutes they lay together before turning to face each other. Looking at Steiner's features in the half-light, Hannah was surprised to see that he too had tears forming at the corner of each eye. Putting a finger across his lips, she leaned up and gave him an almost imperceptible kiss on his forehead. 'Don't move' she whispered: 'just lay still.'

They clung together until sleep finally overcame them. Later, Hannah drowsily felt Steiner move from her arms and lay on his back. Woken by the early dawn of another Polish day, Hannah reached out to touch him but feeling nothing but an empty space, she realised he had gone.

SIXTY THREE

The speed and ferocity of the Red Army's advance into Poland took the depleted Wehrmacht by surprise. Three days after the failed attempt to assassinate Hitler, the Red Army forced German Army Groups North and Centre back to the Vistula River; a mere 140 kilometres from the outskirts of Warsaw.

In the capital, the Polish Home Army, poorly armed but emboldened by the imminent arrival of the Red Army, rose up against the German occupiers. But in Moscow, General Secretary Joseph Stalin had a different plan... a cynical strategy which looked beyond the defeat of Germany; a plan which involved nothing less than the subjugation of post-war Eastern Europe and the Baltic States. And so the Red Army was deliberately halted within shooting distance of Warsaw but close enough to hear the sound of gunfire in the Polish capital as German troops ruthlessly crushed the Polish uprising.

In Upper Silesia, the Red Army faced stiffer opposition. General Model's Army Group North including Steiner's unit, were fighting to defend the vast industrial complex now more vital than ever to the German war effort. The Russian main offensive, Operation Bagration, had slowed after its exertions in the Ukraine but Steiner knew it was only a temporary respite. In the skies above Silesia, the Russian Air Force had introduced its new Yak-3 fighter aircraft, giving them numerical, if not technical superiority over the diminishing number of Luftwaffe aircraft.

Since returning to his Administration unit some two weeks before, Steiner had barely rested. From the bitter experience of Stalingrad, he was fully versed in the attritionable tactics of the Red Army. In the two most recent encounters, Steiner had lost a number of his most experienced soldiers; overwhelmed by countless hordes of fresh Soviet troops. His men were also aware that forward units of the Red Army did not burden themselves with prisoners. Those German troops taken prisoner were invariably shot out of hand except for those men assessed as being of military importance. These would be taken behind the main battle lines for interrogation and torture by NKVD personnel.

Meanwhile in Auschwitz, the frenzied killing went on. Even the enlarged gas chambers, capable of gassing upwards of five thousand inmates every hour could not keep up with the number of transports arriving each day. To maintain the momentum and avoid creating a backlog of victims, the SS instead utilised the same method of execution as employed by its own Einsatzgruppen. With each block of gas chambers running at maximum capacity, batches of new arrivals were now marched to deep pits sited at the very edge of the camp. Once there, they were gunned to death by merciless SS guards; their mutilated bodies then covered with layers of lime; ready for the next batch of victims. Overnight, in those pits not yet full, wounded prisoners would sometimes attempt to crawl over the dead, perhaps even members of their own family, in a futile attempt to escape only to be savagely clubbed back by Latvian camp workers put there by their SS Overseers. Because each new transport would bring new recruits for this loathsome task, these same camp workers would themselves be murdered, often shot for target practice by rifle-wielding SS troops.

In the Administration unit, there was relative calm. Since their last night together, she had barely seen Steiner much less spoken with him. During his fleeting visits to the unit, he would hold briefing sessions with various subordinates before attempting to catch a few hours' sleep before returning to the front. On the one occasion when she plucked up sufficient nerve to enter his room, she found Steiner in deep unresponsive sleep.

She was also concerned about her own condition. The sheer physical intensity of their last encounter had created spasmodic pains in her abdomen which had now lessened but only after experiencing a worrying loss of blood. Since then, there had been no other symptoms. When they had first occurred she wondered whether she was about to lose her baby or whether the bleeding was the result of Steiner's frantic love-making. In a perverse way, she hoped this was the case. 'Already', she thought, 'I'm becoming possessive about this child'.

As Steiner had foreseen, the Red Army had used the brief respite in its offensive to re-equip its forward units. From production lines relocated deep within the Soviet Union came not hundreds, but thousands of new T.34 tanks, aircraft, artillery pieces plus fresh troops sufficient to not only replace the huge number of casualties suffered by Soviet forces but enough to form yet more infantry regiments. Against these rejuvenated forces, the German military could muster only dispirited Wehrmacht and Luftwaffe troops woefully deprived of manpower reserves, essential equipment and fuel.

Tactically, the Wehrmacht Generals had recommended a series of strategic retreats to positions which could be defended in strength but as at Stalingrad and elsewhere, this was expressly forbidden by Hitler who yet again was at odds with his General Staff. Against this gloomy scenario, it was a dejected Steiner who returned unexpectedly to the Administration unit that night.

Summoning Erlich and Hannah to his office, he hungrily devoured a sandwich as he abruptly finished speaking on the telephone. Even hearing just one side of the conversation it was obvious that the news was bad. Looking up as he finished the conversation, Hannah saw the weariness and dejection in his face.

'Tomorrow morning at 0500 hours, I will be leaving for a meeting in Berlin and both of you will accompany me together with the paperwork which I assume is still in the safe?' His question was answered by a nod from Erlich. Speaking in clipped syllables as though planning a military exercise, Steiner carefully outlined his thoughts. 'My original plan was for us to get to Berlin by air. But since then the military situation has worsened and there are now severe reductions in the numbers of flights and personnel seats available. So instead we will have to travel by road which means that Shenke,' he named his driver, 'will take us there. Once in Berlin, you Ernst will use your rail warrant to get to Munich whilst you, Hannah, will disappear in the chaos of Berlin.' Leaning back, he raised his left eyebrow and looked directly at Hannah. 'Any questions?'

Since Steiner had first disclosed details of his plan, Hannah had thought of little else but because it depended on factors beyond his control, the actual implementation of the plan had always seemed too remote to contemplate. But his decision was now ending that uncertainty and she was suddenly facing the awful realisation that she and Steiner would be parting with no prospect of ever seeing each other again. Acutely aware of Erlich's presence, her only reaction was a vain attempt to stem the tears beginning to course down her cheeks.

Seeing this, Erlich reached in his pocket and extracted a white handkerchief which he thrust into Hannah's hands. Plainly uncomfortable, he turned his gaze back to Steiner. 'Well if there's nothing else Colonel, I will report to you later.'

'Yes, do that Ernst but on your way downstairs, tell Shenke not to speak with that Danish woman,' he waved his hand in a vague gesture. 'I can never remember her damn name.'

'Agnetta... her name is Agnetta.' It was Hannah who spoke.

Hearing mention of her name, Erlich halted in mid-stride on his way to the door. 'Bugger!' He blushed at his own intemperance; 'I should have thought of this before now. When the three of us leave tomorrow plus the driver, that will leave the Danish woman on her own and I'm not sure we can trust her.' He stopped to let his thoughts catch up. 'And more to the point, how will you explain Bergmann going missing when you return from Berlin.'

Despite his obvious weariness, Hannah was surprised to see a smile lighten Steiner's features.

'Ernst, my old friend, you worry too much.'

Puzzled by Steiner's retort, Erlich retraced his steps. 'In which case, Colonel, perhaps you will enlighten me.'

Looking at Hannah as though daring her to challenge him too, Steiner could not stop himself from laughing softly to himself. 'Ernst, this is a priceless lesson which you should have learned in your youth so listen carefully. Never ever underestimate the intelligence of a woman.' Working in this unit, even as a cook, Agnetta will have a fair understanding of what is happening not only in the camp but in the war itself. Whilst she remains here, she will continue to be safe so why would she do or say anything to jeopardise that?'

'Sensibly, she shouldn't but women aren't always sensible, Colonel.'

Unable to contain her simmering exasperation, Hannah finally exploded. 'Do either of you realise just how pompous you both sound?'

'Then perhaps' said Steiner, 'we could ask you to bring us back to reality. What would you do in her place? Run and tell or sit tight?

'Obviously, I would sit tight but I would also wonder what was happening when every other member of this household disappears without explanation.'

Though physically tired, Steiner considered Hannah's point. 'So are you suggesting she be told what's happening?'

'Not in so many words.'

'Then what are you saying?' A note of impatience sounded in Steiner's voice.

'Tell her nothing and she will no doubt try and guess what is happening, more so in light of the situation you have just outlined. So why not let the Corporal tell her that he will be accompanying you to Berlin and I am being taken to Ravensbrück for interrogation' adding 'it's better than saying nothing.'

It was a pensive Erlich who broke the silence. 'Bergmann's right, Colonel, I'm happy to do that but you haven't answered my question of how you intend to report Bergmann's absence when you return. And what happens if the SS question Shenke, as they surely will.'

'I have already told you, Ernst; you worry too much.' He expelled a sigh of feigned paternalism. 'With the Red Army almost in our back garden, I can't imagine the SS will be too concerned about one more missing prisoner when dozens manage to escape from outside working party's every day of the week.'

'I'm not convinced, Colonel, but let's hope you're right.'

In a gesture which touched Hannah with its spontaneity and warmth, Steiner reached out and embraced his pessimistic comrade.' 'What will I do, old friend, when you aren't around to look out for me?'

Too emotional to speak, Erlich responded by giving Steiner a hearty slap on his back before making his exit from the room.

Left alone, an awkward silence ensued until Hannah finally spoke. 'So if we do get to Berlin, then it really will be the end of our relationship?'

Sliding both hands into the pockets of his uniform trousers and clearly emotional, Steiner strode around the large table and stood in front of her 'Hannah, please don't make this harder than it is. I've told you how I feel about you and I hope you believe me but we can't just walk off into the sunset and ignore what is happening around us.' In frustration, he kicked out and connected with the unyielding leg of the table. 'Look, until this war is over, there isn't a million to one chance of us being able to remain together even ignoring our natural differences.'

'If by that you mean me being a Jew, then why don't you say it, Kurt?'

Smouldering with increasing anger, Steiner grabbed hold of Hannah by her shoulders. 'Don't you dare play that card with me.' Realising he was shouting, he instantly released his grasp. 'Without my intervention, you would have been dead months ago and you know it.'

'But instead, you brought me here, fucked me at your convenience, made me pregnant and now it's a soldier's farewell. Is that what I should be grateful for?'

Astonished by her grotesquely crude analysis, Steiner fell back into his chair. 'I truly cannot believe you said that.' For a long moment, he stared into space, recycling her bitter words in his brain and endeavouring to calm himself before replying. 'I think I need a drink and I think you should go and prepare for the journey tomorrow.'

'It will take me all of two minutes to pack what few possessions I have so may I join you in a drink before being banished to my room?'

In the silence which followed her own scarcely believed boldness, Hannah imagined she could hear the ticking of the long case clock located at the far end of the office. Quickly selecting a bottle of wine, she began to wordlessly translate its French label in an attempt to slow her racing heartbeat.

'Put the wine back in the cabinet!' His words lacked any perceptible warmth or affection.

Placing the wine back in the cabinet, she turned to face Steiner.

Expecting her words to provoke intense anger from Steiner, instead she saw a chilling coldness in his features, the intensity of which was frightening.'

'You still appear to have continuing difficulty in appreciating the difference between a Nazi officer and myself.' His delivered his words with expressive deliberation. 'You have obviously been away from the camp for so long that you've forgotten what it was like so perhaps you need to go back to appreciate the difference. Or maybe to even join the women in the Puffhaus to compare that with here.' He pulled her closer, so close she felt his breath on her cheeks. 'Or,' he leaned forward and clasped both hands tightly on either side of her head, 'you come to Berlin as planned.'

From his cold demeanour, Hannah realised that his threat of being sent back to Auschwitz was shockingly real. She felt her body begin to tremble in an uncontrollable spasm nor would any sound emerge from her constricted throat.

'You have precisely 10 seconds to make your choice... the camp or Berlin?'

Still unable to speak, Hannah made a supreme effort to pull herself away from Steiner's grasp. Wanting to get as far away from him as possible she touched the area of soft skin on her throat and gently massaged her vocal chords. Swallowing hard, she gave a short cough before managing to speak. 'I would rather die than go anywhere with a man who threatens the life of the woman carrying his child. Does that answer your question?' Still shaking, she picked up the glass of water she had been drinking from earlier and felt the cold liquid lubricate her throat made dry by fear.

With slow deliberation and apparently unmoved by her reply, Steiner went to the main door and Hannah saw him turn the key in the lock. Turning, he advanced towards her, pulling his leather belt from around his waist as he did so.

'Put the glass down.'

Turning to comply, Steiner whipped the thick belt sharply across her back. For a split second, the shock of the blow suppressed the sharp pain which followed. Before she could cry out, a second blow followed. Cowering, she fell back before her retreat was halted by the heavy table. Letting the belt slip through to the floor, Steiner followed her. Roughly seizing hold of her blouse he ripped it open, doing the same with the silk bra which for some inexplicably weird reason, she remembered she had acquired from camp Kanada. Reaching down, he tore open the waist buttons holding her skirt and ripped the material to its hem.

Wordlessly, he brushed the assortment of papers off the table and roughly pushed Hannah onto its pine surface.

Terrified, she held both hands in front of her in a futile attempt to ward off what she knew was about to happen.

Eyes blazing with rage, Steiner unbuttoned the fly buttons of his trousers and Hannah saw the manifestation of his arousal moments before he forced her legs open. Still attempting to resist, she saw the look of frightening anger in his eyes increase.

Between sobs, she heard herself say 'is this how you treat a woman you claim to love? You're no different from that that other pig who raped me in the camp.' Looking down at her helplessness he struck her across her face causing a myriad of stars to whirl in her brain.

She heard herself scream with the shock; sobbing, she tried to kick him away from her but Steiner was too strong. Knowing she didn't have the physical strength to resist much longer, she tried one last tack. 'Please... send me back; I can't stand this anymore.' Expecting more blows, she held both hands in front of her face for protection. '

'You ungrateful bitch! Not only do you want to die but you want to take our child with you.' Lashing out again but this time even harder, she was able to partially ward off the blow with her raised hand.

Nothing in their previous couplings could have prepared her for what followed. In unsuppressed anger, Steiner acted like a bull on heat. Oblivious of her screams and moaning, he remorselessly pumped her body from his standing position, both hands pushing down on her shoulders.

Hannah lost track of time as Steiner kept up his pitiless rhythm until at last she felt him begin to slow and she knew the nightmare was at finally about to end. With all sexual feeling in her own body heartlessly stifled by the sheer physicality of Steiner's assault, she felt him partially withdraw and slowly re-enter, repeating this as though seeking greater sensitivity. Despite herself, she felt the increased throbbing of his barely moving penis. Knowing this to be the prelude to his orgasm she felt his massive ejaculation fill her body. Letting go of her shoulders and with both eyes closed, Steiner pushed one last time. In the savage release which followed, Hannah realised that Steiner was as much her captive as she was his.

Exhausted by his exertion, he pulled Hannah to him and clung to her naked body. Through his uniform shirt, she could feel his racing heartbeat. Looking up, she too knew she could not live without this man.

Calmer now, she heard him whisper 'So what is it to be... the camp or Berlin?'

Still feeling the effects of his blows, it was a few sobbing moments before she was able to speak. 'I hate what you have just done to me and if I have to answer that question at this very moment, then I would choose the camp; at least I know it would all be over in a matter of hours rather than this prolonged torture of loving a man like you. You say your feelings for me are the same but how can you expect me to I believe that? You have just raped me, Kurt; brutally and without compassion or any feeling for me.' Expecting him to respond, she stopped speaking. But whether from shortage of breath or a feeling of remorse, he remained silent.

'So tell me... who is the real Kurt Steiner? Is it the man I thought I knew and loved or the brute you have just shown yourself to be? If that's the case then you won't need to have me taken back to the camp. I'll gladly walk there myself!'

Stung by her words, Steiner finally spoke. 'But if you could accept that I'm a man who does truly love you then would you still want to return to Auschwitz knowing what the consequences of that decision will be?

'Of course not but how can I believe anything you say after what you have just done to me?

Leaning down he picked up her clothes from the floor and offered them to her. As she reached for them, he snatched her outstretched hand and pulled her close. 'Hannah, there can be no excuse for what I've just done and even if there was then I doubt whether you would believe it.'

Easing herself away from his sweating body, she pulled on her skirt and blouse, not bothering with the discarded underwear. 'So why not try your excuse before you judge whether or not I will accept it?' Now partially dressed she began to feel slightly more confident in speaking to this dangerously volatile man.

As though suddenly remembering his glass of whisky he took a long swig before speaking. 'Being the caring soul that you are, you may have noticed, I am tired, very tired and under a great deal of mounting pressure which I can just about handle. But when you made that remark about you being brought here for the sole purpose of satisfying my sexual indulgence, you made me angry, dangerously angry. And when I'm that angry I tend to lose control of myself. That's why I slapped you!' Reaching out, he let his fingers run down her tearstained cheek before continuing. 'But you need to take an honest look at yourself too, Hannah.' Looking at the still-shocked expression etched on her face, Steiner realised that she was probably still on the point of wanting to get as far away from him as possible and would probably say anything simply to appease him. 'Until your arrest, you had lived a pretty comfortable life for a Jew despite all the anti-Semitic bullshit imposed on you people by the Nazis.'

Seeing her about to interject, he held his open hand in front of her face. 'Let me finish. I've listened to you so now please hear me out.'

'Since you came here, you've been treated well unlike those thousands of other women living and dying in the camp. There you would have had a life span of what; weeks, days, hours? You tell me. And you might also care to think what happened to those other women who worked in the sorting office with you.' But living here, you've been treated not as a Jew or even a prisoner but as a person in your own right but a woman who has been thoroughly spoilt in your life. Beautiful and caring, yes, but let's not forget that prima donna temper of yours.' He smiled, remembering the several occasions when Hannah had struck out at him..

'So, whatever anger or hurt you may be feeling at this moment, just remember this; we are two people from vastly different backgrounds whom this war has brought together. Neither of us are perfect but despite every unimaginable horror happening around us we have managed to form a very special relationship other than for moments like this.' He stopped to draw breath knowing his next words could irreparably change their lives forever.

'In all my adult years I have never known a woman like you and despite myself, I was drawn to you almost from the moment you came into my life. Why else am I prepared to risk my life, career and everything which goes with it to get you to Berlin? If I didn't love you it would be the easiest thing to just let you try to do it on your own; just open the gate and wave you goodbye and make no mistake, Hannah, it would be goodbye. You wouldn't last ten minutes once you step outside the perimeter of this building. So when you tell me that I'm no different from those animals in the camp then you shouldn't be too surprised when I react as I just did.' Standing back as if to give her space to think, he angled his loaded question once more. 'So what's it to be, Hannah Bergmann. It's your call?'

Moved by Steiner's remorse but still smarting from the stinging pain of his blows, Hannah let a few heart-stopping seconds pass before whispering 'Berlin of course. But hopefully without being slapped or raped on the way! Do you think you can you manage to do that, my angry tempestuous man?'

SIXTY FOUR

The first two hours of the journey passed in comparative silence due largely to the presence of the driver. Wearing the uniform of a Nursing Orderly, she shared the rear seat with her 'patient', Corporal Ernst Erlich. Sitting alongside his driver and clearly fatigued from his gruelling schedule and lack of rest, Steiner appeared to fall asleep almost as soon as the journey began.

As the vehicle pulled out of the compound, Hannah cast a furtive glance in the direction of Auschwitz and silently prayed to God she would never see that awful place again. As Steiner had coldly stated only hours before, she had a lot to be thankful for. Against all odds, not only was she still alive but now heading for Berlin and a possible reunion with Aaron. Compare that, she thought, to the thousands of poor souls who life expectancy in Auschwitz was now measured in hours.

As the first glimmer of dawn appeared over the Eastern horizon, she saw glimpses of the devastation wrought by the war. Much of the rural landscape was unworked and as the light improved, she was able to see where numerous farm buildings and even entire villages had been utterly destroyed. Nowhere did she see any sign of civilian life.

A number of military convoys containing hundreds of fresh faced youths and battle-weary troops passed them on the opposite side of the road bound for the ever-changing front line. She recalled hearing one of Steiner's subordinates relate how one convoy of front line reinforcements were driven to the map reference as ordered by German HQ only to find the location already occupied by the Red Army. In the vicious melee which followed, most of the new troops were either killed or taken prisoner.

Unusually, the Opel staff car was equipped with a heater which not only worked but made the interior positively comfortable. As the endless kilometres passed by, she had to force herself to remain awake; made more difficult by the gentle snoring emanating from a sleeping Erlich. Glancing in the rear view mirror she found herself looking into the eyes of the driver. In the Admin unit, she had had little contact with Private Shenke, seeing him only occasionally when he came into the office. He was a conscript; a young man aged about 20 whom she knew came from Wuppertal and a soldier obviously trusted by Steiner.

'Tell me when you need to stop.'

In the mirror, Hannah could swear she saw him blush. 'Sorry, Miss Bergmann... I meant if you want to stop.'

Alongside him, Steiner suddenly erupted into life from the depths of sleep. 'Shenke... pull over!'

Mystified by Steiner's shouted order, Hannah chose not to say anything.

Drawing the Opel to a smooth halt, Shenke, with a look of growing anxiety, turned to face his Commanding Officer.

'Shenke, listen to me. The name of the woman in this vehicle is Nurse Eve Becker and not Bergmann. Nurse Eva Becker.' He repeated the name.

'Sorry Colonel. It's my fault.' It was a sleepy Erlich speaking from the rear of the car. 'I forgot to mention that to him.'

Decidedly cool, Steiner half turned in his seat. 'I don't care whose fault it is, just get it right from now on.'

Understandably confused by the exchange, Private Walter Shenke, driver to a man who, unlike many other officers treated conscripts like himself with a degree of respect, was at a loss to understand what was going on. Deciding Colonel Steiner would tell him if necessary, he turned the ignition key and engaged gear.

'Shenke, turn off the engine.' Winding down the passenger window, Steiner took a deep breath of fresh air. Outside of the vehicle, the dawn chorus of unseen birds could be heard and the unmistakeable smell of the countryside assailed their senses.

'Look, Shenke. I'm sorry you weren't told before we set out but let me correct that now.' Settling down in his seat but looking at his driver, Steiner began to unfold a strictly edited version of events.

'Corporal Erlich is suffering from a disease which he picked up in Stalingrad and he has been granted a discharge on medical grounds. He looks fit but looks can be very deceptive so we are taking him to Berlin today rather than wait 3 months for an air-lift evacuation which in his case, may be too late.'

Sitting next to him, Hannah felt Erlich squirm uncomfortably in his seat.

'Because no nurse was available, my assistant, who has medical training, has agreed to accompany the Corporal but obviously as a camp inmate, she cannot do that under her own name. Which is why her papers show her to be?' He raised an enquiring eyebrow in expectation.

It took Shenke a moment to realise he was expected to complete the Colonel's statement. His brow furrowed but his recall was good.' It's Becker, sir. Nurse Becker.'

'Good man, Shenke. Don't let me down when we come to the road blocks.'

Reaching up, Steiner adjusted the driving mirror to make eye contact with Erlich. 'How are things in the back with you, Corporal?'

I'm doing as well as can be expected, sir;'

'Excellent. In which case, we need to be moving. We have a long way to go.'

In normal circumstances, the 425 kilometres between Auschwitz and Berlin could be covered in about 9 hours. But circumstances on this day were anything but normal as the Opel staff car made its way past road blocks, burned out vehicles and dispirited columns of Wehrmacht troops on the way to the front. Looking at the taut faces under their metal helmets, she was shocked to see how young most of the soldiers looked. Twice the Opel was halted by military police but the sight of Steiner's epaulettes signifying his rank was sufficient to have their vehicle passed through without inspection.

The previous evening, Shenke had filled four large metal containers acquired from a passing Panzer tank squadron with sufficient fuel for the journey. Now, with the needle of his gauge entering the reserve section, he requested Steiner's permission to pull off the road to refuel.

Looking ahead, Steiner indicated a slip road partially obscured from the main highway by dense stands of larch and birch trees and Shenke brought the Opel to a smooth stop. Grateful for the opportunity to stretch her legs, Hannah walked into the trees, filling her lungs with the clean forest air. Confident she could not be seen from the car, she quickly relieved herself in the soft undergrowth. Adjusting her skirt, she never saw the hand which clamped over her mouth and pulled her down in one swift movement. Unable to cry out, she felt herself being dragged further into the dense woodland. Through terrified eyes, she became aware of other men, their faces streaked with dark stripes effectively breaking up the contours of their facial features beneath metal helmets camouflaged with greenery from the forest.

Held in a vice-like grip by her assailant, another man deftly ran his hands over her body feeling for a weapon. The second man then produced a wicked looking knife and in a theatrical gesture, ran it across his throat whilst holding a finger across his lips. His message was chillingly clear; call out and you die!

Attempting to convey her understanding, Hannah tried to nod her head. Gradually the hand on her mouth was relaxed and she was able to gulp fresh air into her lungs but the strong arm around her waist remained in place.

Lifting her off her feet, the first assailant swung her legs up and roughly dumped her on the ground. 'How many soldiers with you' he asked in broken German?

Able at last to see his face, Hannah saw a soldier of indeterminate age with typical moon-faced Slavic features, unshaven with broken teeth and smelling of sickening body odour. Gagging, she quickly turned her head and vomited on the soft fern-like undergrowth. Unnecessarily, the second soldier again raised his finger to his lips as she continued to gag until the spasm stopped.

In the clearing, Shenke had finished the refuelling and was exercising his legs before resuming the onward journey. Some distance away, Steiner and Erlich were quietly talking and from his vantage point, it seemed to Shenke that the elderly NCO was actually remonstrating with his CO though he could not hear the detail of the conversation. At the age of ten, he remembered his own father dying from an undisclosed disease and looking at the friendly figure of Corporal Erlich, he hoped he would have a more peaceful end than his father had suffered. It certainly would not help his condition by getting irate or excited.

Looking around the clearing, Shenke could see no sign of the Jewish woman he knew as Bergmann. He tried to recall the name the CO had told him to remember but momentarily, it eluded him.

Climbing back into the vehicle, Shenke leaned over to open the glove compartment. As the driver, he was required to record the distance travelled, fuel used and purpose of the journey but since driving for Colonel Steiner, no one had actually inspected this log so he assumed this was another example of military bureaucracy but one which he was obliged to comply with.

Returning the log to the glove box he straightened up only to have his movement arrested by the stultifying feel of cold steel push into his neck and to find himself looking into the business end of a Russian automatic weapon. Through the windscreen, he saw that the Colonel and Corporal Erlich had also been surrounded by yet more Red Army soldiers. Other than for the Russian pilot released by his Colonel, Shenke had never seen enemy troops and to his surprise, he felt no fear.

Raising his hands as much as the confines of the staff car would allow, Shenke indicated in sign language his willingness to follow his captor's order to get out of the vehicle. Standing back as he climbed out, the soldier was immediately joined by another combatant who then used their weapons to force him into the cover of the trees.

Manhandled in to a small clearing, Shenke was forced to his knees and a strip of filthy cloth was fastened over his eyes. Seconds later he heard the arrival of the Colonel and Erlich. The low hubbub of Russian voices stilled and Shenke heard the rustle of footsteps. All went quiet and then a voice spoke in faltering German.

'So what have we here?'

'What you have here, Captain, are four German prisoners of war.' Steiner's voice was authoritative but it failed to intimidate the Russian.

'Indeed we do, Colonel and what a motley bunch. There is yourself, a corporal, a private soldier and a nurse. I suspect there may be an interesting story here or am I letting my imagination run away with itself?'

Steiner decided to stick to the edited version as this would check out with paperwork now being scrutinised by the Russian.

'Sad but hardly interesting, Captain.' Steiner then proceeded to relate the version he had previously outlined for Shenke's benefit.

'M'mmm,' the Russian pursed his lips, faintly amused. 'You, Colonel, will be of interest to my comrades at HQ and the nurse can provide some entertainment for my soldiers but these two,' he pointed at Erlich and Shenke, 'they are of no use and we do not take prisoners. Something we learned from you Germans.' Reverting to Russian, he issued a short command. Instantly, two shots rang out. Mercifully, behind their grimy blindfolds, neither Erlich nor Shenke felt pain as bullets simultaneously blew large holes in each of their unsuspecting skulls.

Seeing his comrade, a man who had selflessly risked his own life to stay with him in the dank hell of Stalingrad, shot like a defenceless animal, caused a burning desire for revenge in the heart of Kurt Steiner. Pulling his arms free, he lunged at the Russian officer. Momentarily caught off-guard, his captors reacted in time to roughly manhandle him to the ground. With three soldiers holding him down, Steiner was powerless to resist. Using the strength of his powerful neck muscles, Steiner strained to lift his head away from the damp peat of the forest floor and make eye contact with his captor. Speaking in fluent Russian which carried to all those within earshot, he spoke calmly, hoping to taunt the Russian officer. 'You murdering bastard. Give me a pistol and try killing me instead of manacled and defenceless men. Or does the prospect of fighting a real soldier scare a peasant like you?'

Unruffled, the Russian would not be drawn into an argument with a man whose every word could be understood by the soldiers in his command.

'Come now, Colonel, you should thank me instead of abusing me. We have merely spared your two men unnecessary suffering in what lies ahead for you Germans, armed or unarmed. And remember this. If you Germans had stayed in Poland, then your men would still be alive.'

Turning away, he issued more orders. Steiner, with hands now bound behind him and blindfolded, was pulled to his feet and led away followed by a semi-paralysed Hannah, in deep shock at witnessing the cold-blooded murder of the two men. One, a simple, elderly man who had no place in the maelstrom of war and the other, a youth not yet into manhood, who would never know life beyond this day.

At this stage of the war on the Eastern front, at a time when German armies and their Generals were being captured or surrendering in their thousands, Steiner fully expected be held by his captors until their present mission was completed. Instead, within hours both he and Hannah were escorted back to the foraging company's main unit. The journey through thick forest and dense undergrowth, was tough going for Hannah. The soldiers stopped every hour for a brief rest and smoke but neither she nor Steiner were offered a drink of water to quench their increasing thirst. One soldier deliberately stood in front of Steiner and poured the contents of his water bottle onto the ground. Twice they had to avoid German patrols. With Makarov pistols pressed against their skulls, they lay silently in the dense undergrowth as German troops passed just metres away. Lying there, Hannah wordlessly reasoned that her chances of survival as an escaping Jew were probably better with the Russians than with the Germans except for her false ID card. All too quickly she felt a heavy nudge from the soldier behind her to resume the hellish journey.

For Hannah's tired limbs, having been cooped up in the Admin centre for months without exercise, the exhausting trek to the main body of the Red Army seemed to go on for ever before darkness thankfully intervened. Stopping in a small clearing, she and Steiner were roughly forced to sit down and in explicit sign-language, told not to speak to each other. Several soldiers urinated close to where she was sitting with one simulating a very obvious act of sex whilst grinning at her. Neither she nor Steiner were given a share of the hard-tack field rations being hungrily consumed by each of the soldiers.

Barely rested, the nightmarish journey resumed as soon as the soldiers had finished their food. Most of the time they travelled in single file with Steiner guarded by one soldier leading the way followed by a second man walking behind him with his rifle covering Steiner's back. A third soldier followed just ahead of Hannah with yet another Russian bringing up the rear. Half-asleep on her feet, Hannah found the uneven ground difficult, stumbling on tree roots whilst trying to avoid low branches brushing against her face or body. Exhausted, she gratefully slumped to the ground as the Slav-faced soldier in charge signalled another halt. She didn't see the leading soldier carry on and disappear. Suffering from the effects of fatigue and hunger, she drifted off into a sporadic sleep by resting her head on a mound of damp moss. Several times she awoke with a start, taking several moments for her brain to remember where she was before slipping back into a world of darkness.

It was the sound of subdued voices penetrating her brain which woke her. Forcing her tired eyes open, she saw that the escorting soldiers had disappeared, replaced by new faces. And staring down at her were two burly troopers, one of whom nudged her body with the toe of his boot. Fearing the worst, she wrapped her arms around herself in a defensive posture. This brought a smile to the soldier's dirt-streaked face. Speaking to his companion, they reached down and pulled her to her feet and wordlessly indicated she was to walk in the direction of his upraised arm. Her pace was obviously too slow because both soldiers took her arms and between them, propelled her along for about 30 minutes before arriving at an encampment of sorts.

By the light of early dawn, she was able to make out a damaged farm building in front of which stood a large canvas tent nestling beneath camouflaged netting, effectively hiding it from the prying eyes of marauding Luftwaffe pilots. Halted under its cover, she heard a brief exchange in Russian before being ushered through the small entrance flap. Inside, the tent was illuminated by a sooty paraffin lamp by the dim light of which she made out the barely discernible face of yet another soldier. From the emblems on his shoulder boards, she assumed he might be a senior officer.

Looking up from a makeshift desk, he beckoned Hannah towards him. 'So, you must be the Jewish violinist the

German prisoner told me about?' Without waiting for a reply, he added, 'I am General Guriev, welcome to my quarters.'

Taken aback by his unexpected greeting, it took her several moments to realise the Russian was addressing her in her own language. And thanks to whatever Steiner had revealed, all pretence of being a German nurse no longer appeared necessary.

'Thank you, General. My name is Hannah Bergmann and yes, I am a Jew and before my arrest. I was a member of the Berlin Philharmonic Orchestra.'

'And presumably you were arrested because you are a Jew?'

Nodding assent, she began to wonder whether Steiner had revealed her real identity to protect her.

'And in which Nazi concentration camp did they put you?'

'I was held in Ravensbrück before being sent to Auschwitz.'

Moving from behind his desk, the General stroked his chin and gave Hannah an appraising look. Unlike many of his soldiers, he was a tall man, impressive to look at despite the drabness of his field uniform. 'And how long have you been a prisoner in both camps?

As the General framed his question, she intuitively began to experience concern. Guriev had already referred to the 'German prisoner,' but what had Steiner told this man in reply to similar questions?

'Sorry, general; your question was?'

'I asked how long you have been a prisoner in these two camps.'

'I was arrested about a year ago I think. I'm sorry to be so vague but you lose track of time in those places.'

'So tell me,' his grey eyes were unsettling, 'how have you managed to survive for so long?'

'I can't answer that. My survival, as you put it, has been in the hands of the Germans as I'm sure you know.

Beckoning her to a canvas chair, the General sat down opposite her. 'Is that entirely true? Puzzled by his question, her concern mounted. 'I'm sorry but I don't follow your question.'

'Then let me put it another way. The Red Army has now liberated Majdenek concentration camp and we have learned from there that the life of Jews in such places was measured in days if not hours. So how have you managed to survive for a year or more?'

'I told you I didn't know how long I have been a prisoner in the camps."

Showing the first sign of impatience, Guriev leaned forward. 'However long it may be, I want to know how have you managed to survive?'

'And why is she wearing a German uniform and carrying ID papers showing her to be a conscripted nurse by the name of Eva Becker?' The question came from the rear of the tent. Turning her head, she saw a second soldier whom she hadn't previously noticed.

'Let me introduce you.' It was Guriev again. 'This is the Political Officer of the NKVD. He is attached to this regiment.' Still looking at the second man, she saw a barely disguised scowl cross the man's face.

Turning back to Guriev, Hannah's heart began to quicken in her chest. 'General, not all inmates are murdered within hours. A small number are required to do the type of work which the Germans won't do themselves.' She saw Guriev's forehead crease into a puzzled frown..

'I was assigned to work in a sorting area known as 'Kanada' searching for money and valuables such as jewellery and watches from the personal effects of the new arrivals. As long as you remained fit, you survived. It's as simple as that.'

As she was speaking, the NKVD officer moved his chair so that he could see her face. 'Is that where you obtained this uniform?'

'No. This was provided by... ' she hesitated, 'by the NCO your men murdered in the forest.'

Leaping to his feet, the NKVD officer grabbed hold of Hannah's hair and forced her head back. With his free hand, he struck her a sharp blow across her unprotected face.

Above the pain and the loud ringing noise in her ear, she heard the General bark a shouted order and felt her hair released. Her head slumped forward and in the pit of her stomach she felt a sharp spasm of despair.

Guriev let a few moments pass before he spoke again. 'Tell us how you met the German prisoner; he glanced down at the paper in front of him. 'A Colonel Steiner, I believe.'

'The Colonel and another soldier heard my screams when I was being attacked by a Kapo. The Kapo attacked them and killed the soldier before the Colonel shot him and the following day I was transferred to his quarters.'

Looking up, Guriev studied the beautiful woman before him. 'How convenient... but understandable.'

Blushing at the innuendo, she realised she had walked into a trap. Just how much did this man know and what had Steiner revealed in his interrogation?

With mounting apprehension, she broke eye contact with the Russian and looked down at the trodden grass around her feet.

If Guriev was disappointed at failing to provoke a reaction, he didn't show it. Like a cat playing with a mouse, he deliberately waited before framing his next question.

'Tell me, having brought you to his quarters, did this German officer also rape you?'

Her rebuttal was instant. 'No, he has never done that.' Hardly were the words out of her mouth before she recalled the last time she and Steiner had been together. Ironically his frenzied attack then had borne all the elements of rape.

Guriev was obviously enjoying the interrogation, a faint smile crossing his refined features. 'So what is the extent of your relationship with this man?'

'Relationship?' She tried to effect a plausible laugh but without success. 'Hardly a relationship. He is a German officer and I am a Jew so if you wish to refer to that as a relationship, then who am I to disagree with you.'

'Your discretion does you credit but unfortunately it does not answer my curiosity as to why this German officer should be helping a Jew; a Jew travelling on false ID papers, to escape. Can you explain that to me?'

'No, I can't. You will need to ask Colonel Steiner that question.'

'Oh but I have and he told me he was attempting to help you escape because he felt sorry for you.'

Inwardly Hannah breathed a sigh of relief. At last some small detail of what Steiner had revealed which thankfully corroborated her response. But the Russian officer's next statement stunned her.

'So if I decide to have him shot, you will not feel any emotion for him?'

Her reply was carefully crafted. 'As a senior officer, I imagine you can do whatever you like. But to have this man shot for actually showing a degree of sympathy for a prisoner would make you no better than the Nazi animals the Red Army is seeking to overcome.'

Her response struck the target.

Impulsively leaping to his feet, the General barked a sharp command to the NKVD officer. Terrified by the sudden change, Hannah saw the man angrily glare at her before turning to leave the tent. Guriev watched him go and waited for several moments before approaching her chair. With hands on hips he looked down at her, contemplating his next move.

'I admire your spirit but if your fate was left in the hands of that man then both you and your German colonel would be shot.'

Detecting the Russian's faint hint of rapport emboldened Hannah. 'My fate?' She gave a resigned laugh. 'Whatever fate holds for me is entirely in your hands so there's no point in me believing otherwise, let alone thinking I may have some control over it?'

Hearing this, she saw Guriev's face harden; 'so what do you intend to do with me?'

Resuming his seat, the General arched his arms and fingers studying Hannah through his tired looking eyes. 'In normal circumstances that would be an easy question to answer but these are not normal times. By 'normal circumstances' I refer of course to my countries past aberrations or pogroms to be precise.' The Russian clearly enjoyed playing with words. 'Look, Russia is not at war with Jews, German or otherwise, so you should consider yourself as liberated as those Jews in Majdenek and able to leave here whenever you wish. However, as the front line in this area is in a state of flux, you could end up being recaptured and shot by the Germans or worse, find yourself providing temporary amusement for my troops. Once you leave here, then I have no control over what may happen to you.' He paused to let her think about this.

'And there is another problem which you will need to face up to.'

Puzzled, Hannah waited for the Russian to continue.

'The German Colonel admitted to me that the reason he was helping you escape was because you are pregnant with his child. Is that true?'

Caught off-guard by the question, her admission was almost inaudible. 'Yes, I believe that to be the case.'

She saw Guriev's eyebrows rise up. 'So are you not sure?'

'As sure as I can be without medical examination.'

'You told me this man never raped you so I must assume it was a consensual happening?' Guriev's fluency, couched in classic German, would have been impressive in different circumstances.

'Totally consensual. I love him and want to bear his child.'

'And that I regret may be a problem for you.'

Perplexed, Hannah looked at Guriev, wanting him to elaborate. 'Sorry, but I don't understand. What problem are you are referring to?'

'I am referring to the fact that serving within this regiment is a medical orderly; a German doctor by the name of Ephraim Fischer, a man who I believe you may already know?'

SIXTY FIVE

Steiner's interrogation was brutal. Before the Russian General intervened, he had been badly beaten by two thuggish Slavs while a cold-eyed NKVD officer looked on. Only after being repeatedly struck with blows to the arms and shoulders and punched into a semi-conscious state, did the questioning begin.

On the Eastern Front neither Germany nor Russia observed the rules of the Geneva Convention so Steiner knew his interrogator would not be satisfied with him disclosing just his name, rank and number. He also knew that whatever he revealed would not be sufficient to save him from the inevitable bullet in his skull at the end of the interrogation. 'So why should I tell them a damn thing,' he rationalised between bouts of consciousness. Twice, when a pistol was held to his temple, he had taunted them in fluent Russian for his assailants to 'go ahead, you bunch of peasants, shoot and get it over with.' But Steiner knew he had a major problem with his death wish and that problem was Hannah Bergmann. To her captors, she was a German, a German woman in a military uniform. From an experience indelibly etched in his memory from the horror of Stalingrad, Steiner knew that German nurses and female ancillaries captured by the Red Army rarely lasted more than a few hours, literally raped to death by soldier after drunken soldier, many being encouraged by their officers to take revenge on the hated invaders. Even the merciful refuge of death was no guarantee of respite from troops too drunk to know whether their victim was still alive or a newly dead but still warm corpse. And Steiner knew his captors would relish taking similar revenge on his woman.

Feigning unconsciousness brought a small measure of relief until the NKVD officer pressed the end of a lighted cigarette against his forehead. The pain was instant.

Questions followed questions; 'what is your unit?... what is its strength?... where is your unit based?... how many Hiwi traitors are with your unit?' And so it continued.

Each negative response was met with yet more blows to his unprotected face before he collapsed once again on to the dirt floor.

Lying there, with blood streaming from numerous cuts and abrasions to his head, Steiner realised he had nothing left in his armoury. In his pain-filled mind, he pictured his old comrade Ernst Erlich, and almost envied the instant death meted out to him by these animals. As a soldier, he had always imagined he would die either on the battlefield or worse, in bed, as an old man seeking a final release from having had to live on his memories. But never did he imagine it would be like this; beaten, bruised and lying on a dirt floor somewhere in Poland. He tried to remember the location of the car just before its ill-fated stop but his overworked brain refused to function. 'Christ,' he thought, 'I don't even know where I'm about to die.'

Amid the pain in both shoulders and throbbing head, he slowly became aware of a different voice somewhere in the periphery of his brain. Unlike the sneering tone of his inquisitor, the new voice was modulated and calm. Before he could adjust to it, the now familiar voice of the Political Commissar reasserted itself. He saw the raised boot coming but wasn't able to react in time and the kick struck just below his rib cage causing acute pain in his solar plexus.

Again, the refined voice broke through his level of consciousness and this time he was able to understand some of what was being said.

He felt strong arms reach down and lift him back onto the canvas seat, his head spinning from the sudden upward movement. A further exchange followed before the same arms roughly pulled him to his feet and dragged his semi-conscious body from the interrogation tent into a different and much larger area.

Seated on a chair, his jaw was expertly prised apart and he recognised the oily taste of vodka as it slid down his throat. As the alcohol took effect, Steiner slowly regained a semblance of control. Through half-closed eyes, he was able to dimly make out the figure sitting opposite him, legs crossed and smoking what looked like a small cigar or cheroot, its grey smoke rising lazily above the man's head.

Faintly at first, he heard and vaguely recognised the same voice he had heard in the other tent.

'I understand you speak Russian. Is that true?'

Through bruised and puffy lips Steiner could only muster a mumbled 'correct.'

'Excellent. Then we might have the basis for a conversation.' Stepping forward, the Russian officer closely examined Steiner's bloody features. 'But first, you need to have those cuts attended to.'

Unseen by Steiner, the Russian signalled to an aide and within minutes, his face had been bathed and the cuts treated with a stinging yellow liquid with the unmistakeable smell of iodine.

Watching from his canvas chair, Guriev patiently waited for the medical orderly to finish before scrutinising Steiner's battered face again. 'That's slightly better. Not much, but an improvement. By the way, I am General Vladimir Guriev and from your papers, I gather you are Colonel Kurt Steiner.'

Peering through half-closed eyes at the elegant man sitting across from him, Steiner was instinctively on guard. After his beating at the hands of the Commissar, he wondered whether this was the soft approach German officers were constantly warned of by High Command.'

The Russian's next words did nothing to allay his suspicion. 'Having proved yourself stubbornly resilient to interrogation, I assume I would be wasting my time by questioning you further, Colonel.' It was a statement of fact and not a question

Reluctant to speak, Steiner responded by a positive movement of his head which instantly caused a starburst of bright orange lights to flash across his barely focussing vision.

Seeing his obvious distress, Guriev smiled. 'If I were to offer you a drink, do you think you could you manage more than a nod?'

Despite the throbbing pain in his head, Steiner glimpsed the man's fleeting half-smile. 'If its whisky you're offering then I could be extremely vocal.'

'But what if the choice is just vodka... pure, refined Stolichnaya vodka; what then, Colonel? Would that still be a yes?'

Beginning to feel more at ease in the presence of the Russian, Steiner straightened his back and attempted to brush traces of earth and grass off his uniform jacket. 'As long as it's wet and drinkable, it can be horse piss for all I care.'

'Careful, Colonel, you are in danger of destroying the illusion of German sophistication which elite SS officers like you would have us lesser mortals believe.'

Even in his befuddled state, Steiner knew this to be a critical moment. Most Red Army soldiers had either witnessed or heard about the systematic extermination of populations of villages and towns carried out by SS murder squads. As a consequence very few captured SS troops survived; most being shot out of hand within minutes of capture or bayoneted to death as amusement for troops bent on revenge. Steiner noticed that all trace of humour had disappeared from Guriev's face.

'Attached to an SS unit, General, I am attached to, but not a member of, the SS.' He knew it sounded hollow and waited for the Russian's reaction but none came as Guriev leaned back, waiting for Steiner to continue.

'I am a Wehrmacht officer responsible for the defence of an area of Upper Silesia which includes industrial sites and labour camps.' These camps are manned by SS troops who do not accept orders from Wehrmacht officers but I'm sure you already know that

'Labour camps like Majdenek?'

'I'm not familiar with that location so I can't make a comparison.' Even as the words left his mouth, he knew they sounded implausible as being the predictable answer every captured SS soldier would offer up in an attempt to escape retribution.

'In which case tell me about the camp you do know about.' Guriev's question was delivered calmly with no trace of emotion in his voice. 'What are the names of these camps?'

'Auschwitz and Birkenau.' Steiner guessed this information was probably already known to this man.

'You refer to them as labour camps, Colonel, but isn't their primary purpose that of extermination camps built to murder Jews and your political enemies?'

The softness of Guriev's voice belied the accusatory nature of his statement but Steiner recognised the yawning trap being laid by his captor. With his brain at last beginning to function more clearly, Steiner realised he was about to engage in a mental game of chess with this cultivated man, the outcome of which would determine whether he survived to become a prisoner of war in some far-flung Soviet gulag or face imminent death as a member of the infamous SS corps. So his opening move needed to be bold.

'No Wehrmacht soldier can justify what is happening in these concentration camps no more than you can justify the Jewish pogroms carried out in your country.' He looked closely at Guriev for a reaction but the man's face was inscrutable. Drawing a thread of confidence from this, he became bolder. 'Or the liquidation of your country's officer class by Stalin which may have influenced my country to invade your homeland.' Still watching Guriev intently, he saw his face muscles harden but it was impossible to know whether his last remark had struck a chord or whether he had made a terrible mistake. Too late, he realised that this articulate man was undoubtedly a member of those same officer classes he had just referred to so why had he been spared death at the hands of Stalin's secret police?

But Guriev would not be hurried. Instead, he snapped his fingers and wordlessly, his aide brought two glasses and filled each with colourless vodka. He proffered one glass to Steiner who, thankful for the opportunity of additional thinking time, took hold of it gratefully with his badly shaking hand. Lifting his own glass, Guriev offered a single worded toast, a toast which Steiner did not understand.

'So you appear to support the view that however evil or psychotic our leaders may be, we as soldiers must support their actions without question?'

'No; that is not my view.' Animated by the Russian's simple analysis, Steiner knew he was being drawn into a discussion in which he could unwittingly disclose information to the enemy. But he was a player in this game too. The Russians would know about the attempt on Hitler's life but not the detail. So why not whet the man's appetite for information which in a strategic sense was worthless? As though about to impart the secrets of the universe, Steiner leaned forward and spoke with deliberate emphasis on each word. 'Nor was it the view of my fellow officers who attempted to assassinate Hitler?'

The effect on Guriev was startling. In the act of sipping his drink, he gave a discernible splutter as the import of Steiner's words registered. Taking a handkerchief from his trouser pocket, he gently wiped his chin and then carefully refolded it before placing it on his knee.

'Colonel... are you about to tell me you were involved in that attempt?'

'Yes I was; together with a number of other officers from my own unit.'

'Then why have you not been arrested with the other plotters, some of whom have already been executed according to your Herr Goebbels?'

In his mind, Steiner felt a growing sense of encouragement. Having captured the interest of the Russian, he now had to capitalise on the seemingly pathological interest most Russians showed towards matters of intrigue.

Speaking in a low voice, he locked eyes with the Russian General. 'Probably for the same reason you were not arrested during Stalin's purge of your fellow officers.'

Thoughtfully, Guriev leaned back and seemed to study Steiner with renewed interest.

'You are an interesting man, Colonel, who regrettably will be of interest to my comrades in Moscow.'

Hearing Guriev's chilling reference to Moscow, Steiner knew his gamble had failed. Once there, in the hands of Beria's secret police, he would be tortured to death to extract information which ironically had no military value. Crestfallen, he decided to play one last card.

'If I agree to disclose all I know about the plot to kill Hitler, will you agree to do something for me, General?'

Fascinated now, Guriev gave a disarming smile. 'That will depend on what it is you want from me, Colonel, but go ahead; try my benevolence.'

Gratified at not being rebuffed, Steiner revealed the true identity of Nurse Eva Becker. In disclosing his own relationship with Hannah Bergmann, he had hesitated before deciding to mention her pregnancy but the longer he spoke with Guriev, the more he became drawn to him. At Stalingrad he had met large numbers of captured Red Army officers but none that fitted the mould of this man. Further trusting his growing instinct regarding the Russian, Steiner also outlined the true intention behind the ill-fated journey which had ended with their capture by one of Guriev's forward units.

For his part, Guriev proved to be a good listener, noting with mounting interest Steiner's role in the strategic plan for the defence of Upper Silesia but without pressing him for specific detail regarding military dispositions which he knew Steiner would not disclose.

Sipping his newly replenished glass of vodka, Guriev's mood became noticeably expansive. 'So tell me, Colonel, what is it you want me to do? I can't bring your two dead soldiers back to life and I can't set you free so what is it you would like me to do for this woman of yours.'

'Realistically, there are only two things you can do. At Majdanek I believe the Red Army liberated and released the Jewish inmates.'

Guriev quickly interrupted him. 'Only those that were still alive. There were thousands who were either dead or beyond help.' He let this sit with Steiner. 'And what was your other request?'

'Let her go and make sure your soldiers don't get their hands on her.'

'That poses an obvious dilemma, Colonel.' He stood up and straightened his uniform blouse. 'I have no difficulty in liberating your Jewish woman but once free, there is no guarantee her continuing safety can be assured. As you now realise, units of the Red Army are advancing faster than the Wehrmacht can retreat so in reality there are no safe areas for her in this region. The Germans will shoot her as an escaping Jew and any troops, not just Red Army soldiers, will do to her what front-line soldiers have always done to pretty women.' He turned and walked a few paces to exercise his long legs. 'The best I can do will be to keep her within this compound until we liberate more camps and then she can go with those other liberated prisoners to... ' he waved his hand and gave an ambiguous shrug, 'to wherever such people go. At least, she will be safe whilst she remains here.'

'Thank you, General. I'm sure you will do your best.'

Embarrassed by Steiner's words, Guriev came back to his seat. 'Now you,' he said. 'Fortunately you will be easier to deal with. My orders are clear concerning captured officers who have had dealings with Nazi High Command. Whilst that may not be strictly true in your case, the fact that you had an involvement in the plot to kill Hitler, makes you a person of special interest plus whatever else you can be forced to disclose about the defences in Silesia.' He stopped the military phrasing and looked at Steiner's battered face and his voice took on a softer tone. 'As one soldier to another, Colonel, I am genuinely sorry to pass you over to Moscow because we both know what that will ultimately come to. Maybe your two comrades in the forest were the lucky ones, after all.'

SIXTY SIX

Steiner's transportation to Moscow was organised quickly. At the conclusion of his interrogation he was given a meal in Guriev's quarters before being handed over to the same NKVD officer responsible for his earlier beating. Two cuts, one on his face and the other on his left shoulder, had required further attention from a German medic who had expertly inserted stitches in both wounds to stop the bleeding.

Twice Steiner tried to engage the German in conversation but without success. Either the man had been instructed not to talk or his fear or loathing of German officer's was sufficient cause for him to remain silent.

Like the meal, Guriev had ordered the treatment to be conducted in his quarters and the General seemed to take an inordinate interest watching the two Germans together.

Comforted by Guriev's promise to keep Hannah within the comparative safety of his compound, Steiner had dismissed all thought of saying farewell to her. He knew his own battered appearance plus the overwhelming certainty of never being able to see each other again would be too upsetting to them both. He had successfully managed to mask his own feelings for Hannah but inwardly he felt a deep longing for her. He knew he was deeply in love with her; a feeling he had never before experienced at any moment of his adult years... even with his wife. In peacetime, the likelihood of them meeting in the same social circles, let alone falling in love with each other, would have been extremely remote. But this wasn't peacetime and with the world caught up in the turmoil of war, they had met and fallen in love. But the same twist of fate which had brought them together was now about to part them once more... but this time for ever.

Ruefully, he wondered what his son would be like. He couldn't imagine the thought of Hannah giving birth to a girl but quietly thinking about the parenthood he would never experience, he found himself unashamedly weeping.

Brushing his tears aside, he looked round the decrepit hut he was had been moved to after his dismissal from Guriev's tent. Through the narrow window, he watched the long summer day beginning to draw to its close; a day which had begun so well yet within hours had ended in such abject misery. Two good men had died, the beautiful woman carrying his child would remain in constant danger despite the silken assurance given by the Russian General and he would be on his way to interrogation, torture and certain death at the hands of Stalin's secret police in Moscow.

Tired of standing, he sat on the dirt floor, his back against the rough brickwork warmed from the outside by hours of strong sunlight. The planked door was the only entrance into the hut and through its large weathered cracks, he could see the indistinct form of the Russian soldier guarding his temporary prison. With his hunger temporarily assuaged by the meal and a further glass of vodka thoughtfully provided by Guriev's aide, Steiner did his best to empty his mind and within minutes he had drifted into a restless doze..

The sound of the door scraping over the earthen floor brought him rapidly awake. He couldn't tell how long he'd been asleep but glancing through the grimy window he glimpsed the lowering rays of the evening sun.

As the door swung fully open Steiner saw the hazy silhouette of the Political Commissar entering the hut followed by a Red Army soldier, a Mosin-Nagant carbine casually slung on his shoulder. With hands on hips, the Russian barked out an order for Steiner to get on his feet. Dazed but upright, Steiner chose his moment well. Lunging at his tormentor, his desperate momentum carried him forward, sending the Russian sprawling against the far wall. As he attempted to get up, Steiner unleashed a powerful kick, his boot striking the Russian between his legs. Unprepared, the man pitched forward clutching his genital area with both hands. Expecting a bullet at any moment, Steiner was astonished to see the guard backing out through the still open door, yelling loudly for assistance. On the floor of the hut, the Russian had risen to his knees. Still in pain from the vicious beating meted out to him on the order of this man, Steiner lashed out again, his boot sinking into the man's soft midriff whilst a third kick caught him on the side of his head as he pitched forward.

Standing over his sprawled form, Steiner saw the man's eyes begin to glaze over, his body slacken as if unconscious. Seeing this, Steiner spat a mixture of bloody phlegm, hitting his quarry just below his eye.

Retribution came swiftly as numerous hands pulled him out of the hut and wrestled him roughly to the ground. Held down and unable to move, Steiner heard the guard relating with relish, precisely where 'Fritz' had kicked the detested comrade Commissar.

Though his jaw was pressed against the hard ground, Steiner was still defiant. 'The cowardly bastard deserved a good kicking,' he muttered in Russian.

At least one of the soldiers laughed openly which told him that the Commissar must still be in the room. Firmly restrained and unable to defend himself, he knew he could expect little or no mercy when the Commissar did emerge. But for the second time that day, fortune smiled on him. First on the scene was not the injured Commissar but a Red Army captain. Dragged to his feet, Steiner came face to face with the same young officer in charge of the squad which had captured him earlier that morning.

Straitening himself, Steiner returned the involuntary salute thrown up by the Russian.

'As a prisoner of special interest, Colonel, we must get you to Moscow in comparatively good condition. But there are limits to our benevolence.' He gave a half-smile; 'I'm sure you understand what I am saying to you.'

Steiner's battered face broke into a grin. 'I understand completely, Captain; so much so, I'm beginning to think I may have joined the wrong army!'

'I would reserve judgement on that until after your visit to Moscow. My comrades there will not be so understanding.'

'So I believe but in war, we cannot always choose where we go or whom we meet.' He recalled the ceaseless propaganda churned out by Josef Goebbels from his safe bunker in Berlin. His vitriolic invective frequently referred to Russians and their Soviet allies as 'illiterate peasants, no better than animals, infected with the poison of politics and subjugated by their political masters.' But looking at the intelligent Russian standing in front of him, it was difficult to reconcile that description either with him or the General he had met earlier.

'Later tonight you will be taken to an airfield behind our lines from where you will be flown to an interrogation centre.' Stepping back, he gave a sharp command to the two soldiers standing either side of Steiner. Glancing at the open doorway as if expecting the Commissar to emerge at any moment, the Captain lowered his voice. 'To avoid your Luftwaffe, it will be necessary for you to leave now, Colonel. My men will escort you to the airfield but remember what I said about there being a limit to ensuring your continuing good health.' The half-smile returned. 'I'm sure you understand why I'm saying this to you.'

'Patently clear, Captain, but let me make something equally as clear to you. Like yourself, I am a soldier fighting for my country, however misguided my country may be.'

Hearing this, the Russian's eyebrows lifted in surprise. Steiner hesitated, expecting the erudite Captain to interject but hearing nothing, he continued. 'If you were headed for interrogation by the Gestapo in Berlin, wouldn't you try to escape? So whilst I appreciate your concern for my health, my overriding choice would be to die a soldier's death in battle and not in some stinking dungeon in the bowels of Moscow.'

'Then I wish you well, Colonel but go now before your words become self-fulfilling.' This time, the salute was militarily crisp but before Steiner could return it, his arms were gripped from behind and he was propelled towards a vehicle which he recognised as a Volkswagen Type 1, used extensively by the Wehrmacht and probably captured or abandoned during the Red Army's resurgent summer campaign

In the gathering gloom, it took some time to reach the airfield. Peering through the vehicle's cracked windscreen, Steiner saw that the airfield referred to by the Russian Captain was little more than a strip of flattened grass in the middle of a field. With stout hedges at either end it looked too short for the type of aircraft normally employed on military operations.

As the Volkswagen drew to a halt alongside a well-camouflaged bunker, Steiner recognised a further example of captured war booty. Just metres away stood a German-made Fieseler Storch; a single-engine light aircraft specifically designed to operate from short landing strips and employed by the Luftwaffe as a personal transport for senior officers. Interestingly, Steiner noticed that the plane still bore its Luftwaffe markings.

Inside, the bunker looked like a disused animal pen, the Soviet troops making no attempt to make it habitable. Straw littered the floor and its dark interior had a stale odour of sweat, a smell which Steiner associated with Soviet soldiers and quite distinct from that given off by German troops.

In the corner, hunched over a humming radio, an Operator with headphones clamped over his ears, was exchanging messages with a field unit. Glancing up and seeing Steiner's uniform, a look of panic crossed his round Mongol-like features before the comforting sight of the Red Army escorts came in sight. Exchanging nods of acknowledgement, the Operator pointed towards a mobile field kitchen on top of which stood a chipped enamel saucepan. Having delivered him to the bunker as ordered, the unexpected prospect of food took priority and they looked around for mugs in which to help themselves from the steaming pot.

Conscious he was no longer under their close scrutiny, Steiner glanced round the bunker hoping to detect a second exit. In the light of a flickering oil lamp he could just make out the shadowy form of a second person, a man showing no apparent interest either in him or the soldiers. Beyond him, the dim light revealed no indication of a second exit which meant his only means of possible escape would be through the same door by which he had entered the bunker. But between that and himself were several well-armed, burly soldiers concentrating on feeding themselves. Finding a wooden chair, Steiner deliberately banged the legs on the floor, seeing whether the soldiers would react and if so, how quickly. The result was interesting. Instead of springing alert, one of the three soldiers calmly placed his mug down and approached Steiner. Without speaking, he roughly shoved him down on to the slatted seat of the chair and with an unmistakeable motion of his hand, indicated that any attempt to move from the chair would bring an instant thumping from all three escorts. Whether they knew of the order to ensure his physical well-being was doubtful and still feeling the effects of his previous beating, it was something he had no wish to have repeated. But at the back of his mind, he knew any escape attempt had to be made whilst he was still within reach of German forces; once in the Soviet Union he was as good as dead.

Outside, he heard the sound of an approaching motorcycle and moments later, a man he recognised as the Political Commissar, last seen lying unconscious on the dirt floor of the hut, strode into the bunker. With eyes straining to adjust to the poor light, he fixed his venomous gaze upon Steiner. Having assured himself that the German prisoner was there, he strode past him, heading for the man at the far end of the bunker. A brief conversation took place before Steiner saw the shadowy form of the man rise, pull on a leather flying helmet, gather up what looked to be a map case and leave the bunker without speaking to the soldiers still heartily engaged in eating. With the pilot now identified, Steiner next wondered whether the Commissar would be accompanying him at least to the airbase from where he would be transported to Moscow.

Returning to the soldiers, the Commissar issued a sharp command. Roused into action, one covered Steiner with his rifle whilst the other two bound his hands behind his back. From outside, he heard the sound of the aircraft starting up, it's cold engine briefly misfiring before taking up a steady throbbing as the pilot adjusted the fuel/air control.

Bundled outside, Steiner saw the pilot glance at his bound hands and then speak with the Commissar. Clearly irritated, the Commissar ordered his hands to be undone and re-tied in front of him. This done, the soldiers half lifted and pushed their prisoner in to the rear of the four seat cabin. In front of him, the pilot had turned his attention to his map case, looking at it by the light of a torch. Climbing in alongside him, the Commissar took his seat and closed the flimsy aluminium door. Without speaking, the pilot pointed to the lap belt dangling by the side of the seat indicating he was required to fasten it.

Taxiing to the end of the strip, the pilot ran up the engine, again readjusted the fuel mixture and released the undercarriage brake. Within a matter of metres, the tail wheel lifted off the grass and with the plane now level, Steiner was able to look between the two Russians. In the darkness ahead, he saw a single torch light weakly illuminating the formidable hedge now fast approaching. Closing rapidly, the pilot waited until the last possible moment before coolly pulling back on his two-handed control column, letting the large wing area of the aircraft provide sufficient lift to clear the obstacle. Airborne, the pilot once more adjusted the fuel mixture control and throttled the engine back to cruising speed.

From his cramped seat in the rear of the cockpit, Steiner could see that the pilot had flattened out just above tree level where they would be practically invisible to prowling German night fighters, its Luftwaffe markings providing additional insurance from attack. But those same markings would provide little comfort if they were to meet a Soviet fighter plane.

As if reading Steiner's mind, the pilot half turned his head. 'Soviet fighters do not fly at night so we only have the Luftwaffe to think about.'

Surprised by this intervention, Steiner realised that the pilot had spoken in a form of classical Bohemian German. But why would he even bother to speak to a prisoner??

The same question obviously bothered the Commissar too. 'Do not speak to the prisoner in any language especially one I do not understand. And that is an order.'

The pilot's response was equally robust. 'Lieutenant, in this aircraft I give the orders; not you.'

Sullenly, the Commissar turned away and stared out of the side window, the glazed Perspex giving a distorted view of the ground below.

Having been surprised by the pilot's first statement, Steiner was astonished by his next pronouncement. To the Commissar's uncomprehending ears, the pilot could have been speaking about the weather for all he knew but with even just a slight understanding of classical German, he would have understood the pilot was in fact outlining something far more dramatic.

'In a moment, we shall develop a problem with the engine and be forced to land. That will be your chance to escape. You will need to deal with this man before we land. In the right hand pocket you will find a wrench. I guess you know what to do with it?'

Staring at the back of the pilot's head, it took Steiner only a fraction of a second to absorb the pilot's coolly delivered announcement. 'Understood... but why?'

Peering down on the battle-scarred landscape below, the pilot did not respond.

Still trying to understand what was happening or whether he could trust the man in front of him, he was unprepared when without further warning the engine began to stutter as though out of fuel and the aircraft lurched dangerously to the left and lost height. Alongside the pilot, Steiner saw the Commissar grab hold of an overhead pulley strap, his tense body in a mild panic.

Correcting the swing and in level flight once more but with the stuttering engine appearing to fail at any moment, the pilot aimed the aircraft towards what looked like a gravel farm track flanked by trees on both sides.

Casting doubt from his mind, Steiner knew he had no choice but to trust the pilot, whatever his reason may be. With both hands still tied, he reached into the small compartment where his searching fingers located and closed over a heavy metal wrench. He didn't have time to examine it. At that precise instant, the Storch, now engineless and in glide mode, hit the ground, its undercarriage failing to fully absorb the impact.

Wrestling to bring the plane under control on the unmade path, the pilot uttered just one word... 'now!'

With both hands clutching the wrench, Steiner swung it viciously at the head of the Commissar, feeling it connect with a sickening thud. One blow was sufficient. The Russian fell forward, restrained only by his safety strap. As the Storch slowed, its tail wheel bit into the gravel and it stopped in a matter of metres.

Leaping from the aircraft, the pilot pulled his seat forward and attempted to pull Steiner out of the cramped cockpit. Quickly releasing his lap belt, Steiner almost fell onto the gravel path before regaining his footing. Releasing his hold, the pilot went to the rear of the fuselage and opened a small compartment ahead of the tail assembly. Pulling out a package, he handed it to a still-stunned Steiner.'

'Take this with you, Colonel. There's a map showing where we are and the general direction of German forces. Plus a Tokarev pistol which tends to shoot high.'

Instant recognition dawned on Steiner. 'You're the Russian pilot I allowed to escape... my dear God!'

The Russian interrupted him. 'Go quickly in case we were spotted by a patrol. But take care, Colonel... don't let that man capture you again.'

Looking at the inert form of the Commissar, Steiner felt no sense of regret. 'I'm not sure whether he's sufficiently alive to capture anyone.'

'Then in which case neither of us will have a problem.'

'You don't like these Commissars?'

'They are parasites, every one of them. They murdered many of my comrades so... ' He stopped himself. 'You must go now, Colonel. My debt is repaid so don't let me meet you again.'

Coming rigidly to attention and looking at his erstwhile Russian captor, Steiner saluted with the same degree of smartness he normally reserved for very senior officers. 'Goodbye my friend. I salute you with thanks.' Swiftly turning away from a man whose name he would never know, Steiner hurried along the remaining part of the short gravel path before stopping to take a bearing from the sparse number of stars overhead. Looking back, he could barely make out the darkened silhouette of the Fiesler Storch. His chances of reaching the German lines were slim but he relished the thought that his fate was now in his own hands. And provided he managed to stay alive and free, there was always the hope, however remote that hope might be, that somewhere, someplace, sometime, he might again meet the woman who had changed his world to its very core.

SIXTY SEVEN

Guriev's calculating promise to Hannah of a reunion with Ephraim was double-edged. Having accepted that he had probably been murdered at Thereisenstadt, the prospect of seeing him again was to her mind a miracle almost beyond belief. But within seconds her joy was tempered by the awful realisation of knowing she would have to reveal her relationship with Steiner. She knew that Ephraim's hatred of the Nazis would make it immensely difficult, if not impossible, for him to accept even without his knowledge of her pregnancy.

The General had ordered the meeting to take place in his quarters; a tent devoid of any personal touches other than for one faded photograph of a middle-aged couple taken against a studio background.

In preparation, Hannah had been allowed to wash from a tin basin and a jug of murky warm water under the salacious gaze of the General's aide. Refreshed and waiting, she wondered whether Ephraim would still look much the same as when they had parted at Theresienstadt. Nervously, she brushed her hands over her stomach to reassure herself that her figure still showed no outward sign of her pregnancy. Suddenly, the thought of confessing so much so soon to a man whom she knew loved her dearly made her quail and inwardly she knew she couldn't do it.

From outside the tent, Hannah heard sounds of increasing excitement with waves of intermittent anger and laughter intruding through the canvas walls.

Minutes later, an unusually flustered Guriev strode into the tent. Taking off his cap, he aimed it at the top of his desk but missed and saw it fall on to the dirt floor. In the gloom, his eyes fastened on Hannah and he instantly regained his composure.

'Tell me again,' he said, 'what was your destination before my soldiers interrupted your journey?'

'Berlin.'

'And once there, this Colonel of yours was intending to let you escape?'

'That was the plan.'

'And was he planning to stop on the way to Berlin?'

'No, the plan was to get there as soon as possible.'

The General pursed his lips and looked thoughtful. 'In which case, there's no harm in telling you that your resourceful Colonel has escaped... from an aircraft would you believe!' Shaking his head in disbelief, Hannah heard him mutter 'God knows how he managed that.''

Recovering his cap from the floor, he dusted it off and carefully placed it on the arm of the metal framed chair. 'He apparently killed the escort while the pilot was dealing with an engine problem and just disappeared into the forest.'

Hardly daring to believe what the Russian was telling her, a wild sense of elation swept through her only for it to be rapidly replaced by a fearful apprehension of the ordeal ahead of her.

A slight shuffling of feet at the entrance of the tent caught her attention and suddenly standing in front of her was Ephraim Fischer; her husband and father of their child but now barely recognisable. His head of dark wavy hair had been shorn to his scalp and his weathered face reflected months of rough living. Momentarily transfixed, neither of them spoke.

It was Guriev who broke the silence. 'Unless I'm wrong, I believe you two people may know each other?

Clearly unaware of his wife's presence until this moment, Ephraim appeared dazed and his obvious discomfort brought a smirk to Guriev's face, plainly intent upon controlling the situation like a puppet master pulling the strings.

Wholly confused, Ephraim hesitated before moving towards his wife, brushing imaginary specks of dirt from his shirt as he approached. Encouraged by Hannah reaching towards him, he took a faltering step and embraced her. Overcome by emotion, he was unable to speak and she felt his body physically trembling.

Gently easing herself from the embrace she was able to take stock of him more closely. Reaching up with one hand, she let her fingers run over his rough bearded face, his features so very different from when they had last met. His face had lost all trace of its boyishness, replaced by a coarseness which made him appear almost thug-like. And his eyes, the same eyes which would light up with excitement when they were together, they were now dull, their former sparkle deadened.

Standing on her toes, Hannah pressed her lips against his but he did not respond. 'Ephraim, it's me... Hannah.'

Her softly spoken words seemed to trigger something in Ephraim's brain. Alone among the Partisans and latterly with the Red Army, he had always held back when his comrades indulged in the rape of captured women or when Soviet female soldiers made themselves available during rest periods away from the front line.

As though seeing her for the first time, he seized hold of Hannah and returned her kiss with a suddenness which startled her. Then holding her at arm's length, he at last spoke. 'Tell me I'm not dreaming Hannah, is it really you?'

'Yes, darling, it really is me; Hannah... your wife.'

'But how;' he stumbled for words, 'how have you managed to survive? He paused as if pondering his own question. 'You went to Auschwitz and no one survives in a Nazi death camp.' In his growing excitement he reached out, grasping Hannah tightly as though unwilling to ever let her go. 'I saw it with my own eyes when this unit liberated Majdanek. No one survives.' He repeated himself, visualising once again the sheer horror which had confronted the Red Army when they overran the first concentration camp to fall into Allied hands.

Conscious that Guriev was listening to their every word, Hannah whispered 'let's talk about that later, darling. The main thing is we are together now.' She placed particular emphasis on her last word, hoping it would stay any further questions.

Still clasping Ephraim, she looked towards the Russian General. 'As my husband and I are both Jews, are we both now liberated and free to leave here?'

Guriev looked surprised by the question and played for time. 'And why would you wish to leave here, in the middle of Poland, with half the German army between yourselves and Berlin?'

He rose from his canvas chair and lit another cheroot as he moved closer.

'As Jews you must have a very clear idea of what the Germans will do if you were to fall into their hands again?' He blew two revolving smoke rings into the still air and watched as they rolled towards the canvas roof, one chasing the other until both merged as they reached the top of the ceiling. 'So why risk it?'

'So what are our options?' It was Ephraim who asked the question.

'For you, doctor? None. You are conscripted to this unit until I say otherwise. But you,' he turned to Hannah, 'you are free to leave whenever you wish but I would not recommend it.'

'Then what would you recommend, General?'

'I would think it wise for you to remain with your husband until this unit reaches Berlin. Once there, you have my word you will both be free to leave provided we are all still alive of course.' He gave a soft chuckle, repeating his earlier admonition about qualifications. He laughed quietly and then looked as though he was trying to remember something. 'Speaking of qualification there is one other thing.' Still smiling, he looked at Hannah. 'If you choose to stay, then for your own safety, you will be attached to my personal unit.'

His face took on a mischievous look. 'You may even wish to undertake a similar role to that which you seemed to have performed so admirably before your liberation.'

Looking into Ephraim's tear stained face, she recalled his parting words to her at Theresienstadt... 'do whatever it takes to survive.' But how tolerant would he be if he realised what Guriev was alluding to? Casting caution aside, she decided to find out.

'Precisely what would that role entail, General?'

Discomforted by her question, Guriev blew another smoke ring, watching it slowly roll upwards. 'Do you really wish me to outline your previous function in every detail or would you prefer to do that in private with your husband?'

The innuendo was hard to miss and Ephraim's reaction was predictable.

'Why would my wife wish to discuss this privately? Surely it would be sensible for you both to agree what you require her to do then she can make up her mind whether she goes or stays.'

'What a simple mind you have, doctor.' Guriev's voice reflected his growing excitement. 'The duties your wife will undertake will be what I determine them to be; not something we agree by mutual consent.'

Crestfallen, Ephraim accepted the reprimand. 'I'm sorry, general; I appear to be misreading the situation.'

Beginning to tire of a game which only he knew he was playing, Guriev decided to quicken the pace.

'On the contrary, doctor; your perception does you credit.' He drew deeply on his cigar before expelling the smoke towards Ephraim.

'There is no easy way to tell you this but your wife was the mistress of the German officer you patched up earlier. Not only his mistress but now pregnant with his child.'

Hannah heard Ephraim's sharp intake of breath and felt his arms fall away from her shoulders. Confused, he took a pace back, his face registering a look of utter disbelief; a look which she knew would stay with her for the rest of her life.

'So now you understand why it may have been better for this to have been discussed in private.' Guriev again, still the circus ringmaster; still pulling the strings for his own voyeuristic pleasure.

Transfixed by Ephraim's haunted look, Hannah turned and faced Guriev. 'So when you suggest I undertake a similar role with you, was that your invitation for me to become your mistress too?' She didn't wait for him to reply. 'Because if it was, then you are no different from those animals you call soldiers outside this tent.' She looked again at Ephraim; 'darling, please try to understand what life has been like since we last met; there are no rules for these people, Russian or German; they take what they want.'

Visibly unsettled by her outburst, Guriev felt a strange stirring within him. Standing up, he issued a sharp command to his aide and within seconds, two soldiers appeared and hustled a bemused Ephraim from the tent.

As the sound of their footsteps receded, the tension within the tent increased tangibly. It was Hannah who broke the silence. 'So what happens now?' In her mind flashed a recollection of the Nazi SS Officer who had assaulted her at her apartment and the Rumanian Kapo shot dead by Steiner in the act of raping her. Was the Russian about to do the same?

'What happens now, you ask? Tell me... what would you like to happen?'

Surprised by the Russian's question, she was briefly lost for words.

'You could try thanking me for sparing you from a task which you would have found difficult.' Guriev's mastery of German was impressive. 'Thanks to my intercession, your worst moment is now behind you. You are left with the simple matter of rebuilding your relationship with your husband.'

'Well that should be easy enough,' she said sarcastically. 'A married woman with a husband and child falling in love with a senior German officer and now expecting his baby. My husband should be sufficiently broad-minded to accept that such things do happen; particularly in wartime.'

Listening to Hannah parody a situation which could effectively spell the end of her marriage only served to fascinate Guriev even more.

'I like your humour but it doesn't answer my question.'

'I think you asked what would I like to happen and as I recall, you gave me two options.' Trying to generate a level of bravado which in truth, she didn't feel, her voice was firm.

'I can choose to leave in the middle of a war zone which we both know would be highly dangerous; or I can stay with your unit until it reaches Berlin.' She paused to give the Russian an opportunity to comment but he simply nodded his agreement.

'But in reality, it isn't what I would like to happen but a case of what you would wish to do with me between here and Berlin.'

'What a tantalising thought.' He looked at Hannah and laughed gently. 'Especially for a soldier who hasn't seen his wife for nigh on 10 months.'

Strangely unembarrassed, Hannah coyly lowered her head but maintained eye contact. 'I'm not sure what you mean by that.'

Guriev felt his pulse quicken and he took a deep breath. 'What would I wish you to do between here and Berlin? I can give you a very short answer.' Moving closer, he gently raised her chin with his hand. 'You are an extremely beautiful woman and you are also a German, which makes you particularly attractive to this particular Russian field officer who hasn't slept with a woman for nearly a year. So to answer my own question, I would like you to stay with this unit and occasionally share my bed in return for my protection.'

The frankness of Guriev's proposition was disarmingly forthright.

Intrigued by the Russian's flattering analysis but anxious not to alienate a man who could still make it possible for her to return to Berlin, she knew her answer needed to be sufficiently convincing.

Moving closer to Guriev, she lowered her voice for added effect. 'You know of my relationship with the German officer who escaped and you also know I carry his child. So I can't understand why you think I would give myself to you even though it could mean you forcing me to leave your unit in the middle of Poland.' She stopped, waiting for his reaction but none came. 'Another complication is the fact that my husband is in this camp and that is something he and I will have to come to terms with.' She gave him what she hoped he would see as a appeasing smile. 'But who can say what the future will hold for any one of us? All we can do is to carry on and hope that we find what we seek most in this awful world.'

Looking at Guriev's face, Hannah had no way of knowing what was in the Russian's mind. His mask-like features displayed no outward sign of emotion and his grey eyes not only held her gaze but seemed able to bore into her innermost thoughts.

Countless seconds passed before Guriev finally broke the silence.

'I am trying to decide whether you are a whore or simply a misguided woman caught up by the circumstances you have found yourself in.'

'In which case, General, then perhaps you should tell me which of those two women you would like me to be.'

'That would depend on the type of man you think I might be?'

Thrown off balance by his question she mumbled 'I don't understand?'

'As a frustrated soldier I would prefer you to be a whore... but my whore!' His eyes grew even more intense, seeking a reaction as she struggled inwardly to hold herself together.

'But on the other hand, maybe you are simply a victim of wartime circumstances which could happen to any respectable woman' adding 'maybe even my wife.' Another pause; this time much longer and when he next spoke, his voice was barely a whisper: 'So tell me, which of the two appeals most to that waywardness in you; the soldier or the officer?

In her head, she yet again sought solace in Ephraim's oft-repeated mantra in order to survive.' But undecided, she played for time. 'Why don't you wait and see what happens between here and Berlin because at this moment, I am unable to answer that question.'

SIXTY EIGHT

As a result of Guriev's calculating disclosure of her relationship with Steiner, Hannah was fully aware that her next meeting with Ephraim would realistically determine whether their marriage would survive or not; more so with the prurient Guriev insisting they meet in his presence. With tantalising thoughts of the Jewish woman still tossing around in his mind, the Russian had ordered her to be accommodated in a small signals unit attached to his quarters. Staffed by two women interpreters, both of whom spoke a mixture of poor German and even poorer Polish, it was out of bounds to male military personnel and specifically the German doctor who on Guriev's explicit order was placed under increased surveillance.

After her meeting with the Russian, she had been escorted to her quarters and left alone to gather her thoughts. In her mind, she saw again the look of utter disbelief or was it betrayal, on Ephraim's face as he was roughly escorted from Guriev's tent.

She tried to imagine what might be going through his mind. One moment to be suddenly reunited with a wife he assumed was dead only to have his joy callously cut short by the devious Russian revealing that his wife was the mistress of a German officer by whom she was now pregnant.

Mentally exhausted from the rigours of the past 24 hours, she lay down on the spare camp bed and recalled Ephraim's tenderness and loving words when they were being questioned by the Gestapo. And how foolishly brave he had been in the face of numerous threats at the hands of their Nazi inquisitors. She had loved him then but could she love him now after what they had both been through? And what effect would Guriev's disclosure have on Ephraim's feelings for her?

She thought of Steiner. Somehow she knew he would escape or be killed in the attempt but would she ever see him again and if she did, what would she now feel for him knowing that her husband was not only alive but here in this camp. She recalled telling Steiner that even if Ephraim were still alive, she would still be his woman but how realistic was that declaration now?

Not for the first time she wondered whether her feelings for him had been the result of her overriding need to survive. She recalled Steiner telling her that had they met before the war, she probably wouldn't have given him a second glance. But that was a long time ago and she now knew from bitter experience that her days of womanly innocence had changed forever. In her mind, she imagined Steiner and Ephraim standing before her, each beckoning with outstretched arms. But which of the two would she commit to... her husband, friend and father of their son or Steiner, her imperious lover whose child she was now carrying? Mercifully, sleep overtook her before she forced herself to make a choice.

***

The following morning, over a breakfast of watery cereal and black bread and wearing the German uniform she was captured in, she met one of the two Soviet signallers. Expecting her to be openly hostile, she was relieved when Alicia, an attractive Ukrainian whom she guessed was in her mid-twenties, was surprisingly affable after first overcoming her initial shyness.

In passable German, the Ukrainian actually seemed to welcome the opportunity of relating how she and her husband had both joined the Red Army on the same day following the German invasion of the Soviet Union. After basic training, they had spent just 24 hours together before being assigned to different regiments. Four weeks later, he and many other Soviet troops had been taken prisoner and subsequently executed by SS troops while defending Rostov from experienced German Panzer units. Alicia recounted her husband's fate without any sign of outward emotion causing Hannah to wonder whether she was inured from grief by the constant horror she would have witnessed as the Red Army forced the German Wehrmacht to retreat.

'Does that make you hate all Germans' she had asked tentatively?

'Only those who have invaded our Motherland,' adding flatly; 'they must all die.'

'What about me' she asked? 'I'm a German or was, until the Nazis made Jews like me stateless.'

'Then you are no longer a German. Besides,' she gave a half smile, 'you came here as a prisoner, not an invader.' To reinforce the point, she added, 'at Majdanek I saw what the Germans are doing to Jews like you.'

Hannah's response was sensitive. 'Not only at Majdanek but in other concentration camps too. Sometimes I think this world has gone mad.' Looking at the young woman, she again saw no reaction. 'Do you think it will ever be the same again?'

Suddenly uncomfortable at having to respond to Hannah's question, the Ukrainian made to leave the table. 'I have to go on duty. Maybe I see you later.'

Alone once more, Hannah found her thoughts once more turning to Steiner; trying to visualise where he might be rather than wondering what she would say to Ephraim when Guriev allowed them to meet. And thinking of the Russian, how long would his protection last once his initial fascination for her had been gratified? Was his wish for her to share his bed simply him being provocative to test her reaction or did he really mean it? And what possible attraction could he have for the pregnant mistress of a German officer? But conversely, perhaps it was that very relationship which appeared to arouse him?

Privately, she still wondered about her own transformation. Her cloistered Jewish upbringing had implanted standards which had influenced her attitude to sex during the temptations of her late teens which in turn had led to the monogamous nature of her marriage to Ephraim. Yet against this backdrop, she had willingly entered into the forbidden world of erotic love with Elsa before embarking on her all-consuming affair with Kurt Steiner. And now, as a hostage to fortune within a front line Red Army infantry unit, she found herself coolly wondering how she would respond if Guriev did pursue his declared interest in her.

She remembered the awful night in Auschwitz when the Romanian Kapo had come for her and her decision to then do whatever it took to survive until the next morning. But with Steiner it had been different. He had not used force on that first occasion. Just him coming to her room that night had been sufficient for her to push feelings of latent guilt to the back of her mind and respond to a man who wanted her as much as she had been involuntarily drawn to him. But Guriev, a general in the Red Army and probably the only person who could now get her to Berlin, he was an entirely different proposition. She had no feelings whatsoever for this man she had met only hours before so how would she react if he insisted she become his travelling mistress too? Even more so with Ephraim just a short distance away and obviously aware of what would be happening in Guriev's quarters.

She taxed her brain but couldn't remember who it was who had once told her of the effect she had on men but whoever it was, those words had seemingly become self-fulfilling in her wilful abandonment of the moral restraints of her Jewish background and worse, her marriage vows too.

In her late teenage years and focussed on her musical studies, she had been unaware of her increasing physical attraction to men. But following her appointment as a soloist of the prestigious Berlin Philharmonic she began to develop a growing awareness that it was not just her musical prowess which men were attracted to. She had accepted a number of post-concert dinner invitations whilst on tour with the orchestra but knowing she would be leaving that city the following morning invariably precluded anything other than dinner. At home in Berlin she had for a while, dated the son of a wealthy Jewish family. Spoiled by his doting parents, he was a man used to getting his own way including a thinly veiled ultimatum for her to sleep with him. Increasingly frustrated by her unwillingness to submit to his persistent overtures, he had followed his parents to America fully expecting her to follow him. Fortunately her decision to remain in Germany was made easier by a chance reunion with a young man whom she had first met some six months earlier; a serious minded Jewish doctor by the name of Ephraim Fischer. He was so incomparably different from her previous boyfriend and a man easy to fall in love with. The birth of Aaron had sealed their marriage and in any country other than Germany, she knew she would have remained a model Jewish wife and mother. But the advent of war had changed all that in a manner which nothing in her previous years could have prepared her for.

Bored with staring at the flapping canvas roof and beginning to feel claustrophobic within the small tent, she decided to explore outside. Guriev had told her she was free to leave at any time but in practical terms she knew this was unrealistic. Lifting the exit flap, an alert-looking sentry half-raised his rifle in surprise, clearly not expecting a woman wearing the uniform of a German nurse to emerge.

Giving him her warmest smile, she saw him visibly relax. Self-consciously, he returned her smile with a big grin, his white teeth sharply contrasting against his weathered complexion.

Scattered around the small clearing were a number of well-camouflaged tents strategically dispersed as far as her eye could see and in the middle was what appeared to be a stack of felled trees. Looking more closely, she realised she was looking at a cleverly disguised gun emplacement; its alert crew constantly sweeping the sky with the quadruple barrels of what she took to be an ant-aircraft gun, its three man crew prepared to give any low flying Luftwaffe pilot an unwelcome surprise.

Feeling a gentle tap on her arm, Hannah turned to see her escort indicating with emphatic hand gestures that it was dangerous to enter the clearing, pointing instead to the cluster of tents raised within the periphery of the forest.

Reluctant to return to her quarters, she needed no second bidding. Nodding in acknowledgement, she began to walk slowly towards the main encampment area, comfortable in the knowledge that her young escort was following just a few paces behind.

Turning to face him, she stopped. Pointing to him and then to herself, she said, 'Guriev?'

It took several seconds before the sentry nodded his understanding. 'Da... Guriev' and pointed at her and then to himself. So the sentry appeared to have an order from the General to guard her. Not only within her quarters but apparently within the encampment too. Was she misjudging the Machiavellian General or was he simply ensuring she remained within his personal control?

Pointing to herself, she pronounced her name slowly; 'Hannah.' and pointing at the sentry, she raised a questioning eyebrow. 'And you?'

This time the young sentry understood immediately. Smiling, he slapped his free hand across his chest and brought his heels together.

'Vasilevski... Yuri Vasilevski.'

Bringing her hands together in a form of Asian greeting, she smiled and inclined her head in acknowledgment. 'Yuri Vasilevski... I'm very pleased to meet you.'

Seeing the happy grin on the face of Rifleman Vasilevski had the instant effect of bolstering her confidence in an encampment full of front-line, battle weary troops each with a burning hatred of Germans. Stepping out, she walked towards the heavily wooded area with him close behind.

Numerous tents, each strategically positioned to blend in with the surrounding forest held large numbers of soldiers of both sexes. Most were resting on their rainproof groundsheets, outwardly exhausted whilst those that did look up showed little interest despite her German uniform.

She recalled Steiner briefing his fellow officers on the expected offensive of the Red Army and now, just weeks later, she realised she was probably looking at Soviet troops who had been engaged in those initial battles. Thinking wistfully about Steiner's Admin unit brought Corporal Erlich to mind. If for no other reason than his brutal murder, she realised just how much she hated this never ending war.

With her escort in close proximity, Hannah began to feel a growing sense of confidence. Moving deeper into the forest she passed more temporary accommodation units, mess halls and stores which even to her inexperienced eyes was clear that the encampment was used by the Soviets as a forward base to provide a continuing supply of replacement and rested troops for the front.

In what she judged to be the centre of the encampment she spotted the specific location she was hoping to find. Three large tents, each with crude Red Cross symbols painted on their canvas side walls confirmed she was looking at the camp hospital further evidenced by a line of soldiers, some with obvious wounds, patiently awaiting medical treatment. Standing away from the wounded, three medical staff stood smoking, the grey smoke from their cigarettes swirling away in the light breeze.

If Ephraim happened to be on duty, then this would be the place to see and talk to him; away from the voyeuristic eyes and ears of Guriev. Hurrying forward, she felt her arm gripped firmly by Vasilevski, glancing anxiously over his shoulder.'

'Niet... niet!' The order was emphatic and with surprising strength, he eased Hannah back and turned her in the direction they had just come from.

Fifty paces on and hoping her young escort's bout of nervousness had settled down, she stopped and faced him. Looking beyond his broad shoulders and through the green curtain of willowy thickets, she could still make out the concealed outline of the hospital tents.

Raising her right hand, she pointed to the finger she would normally wear a wedding ring hoping that it would be the same in Russia. A look of puzzlement crossed his face before realisation slowly dawned. Raising his own hand he pointed towards the medical tents signifying he understood the connection. Still holding her arm, he steered her towards a dense clump of mature osier willows and putting a finger to his lips, signalled her to remain silent. Watching anxiously as Vasilevski walked towards the medical area she saw him stop and speak to an orderly before disappearing into the nearest tent. Moments later, he reappeared and this time he went towards an accommodation area some distance from the medical facilities.

Minutes passed before she saw the familiar figure of Ephraim emerge and converse with her escort before returning to his tent. With his mission completed, Vasilevski turned and made his way back to where he hoped his charge would still be waiting. Reaching the edge of the clearing she saw him stop for no apparent reason. Reaching into the pocket of his uniform blouse, he drew out a packet of Army-issue cigarettes and without looking back towards the medical area, he coolly managed to light the foul-smelling weed after several attempts to coerce a stuttering match into life.

Watching this, Hannah did not immediately see the sinewy figure walking from the accommodation unit and head towards Vasilevski. Seeing him, the young Russian gave another of his boyish grins and pointed to the figure of Ephraim now approaching.. Holding both hands towards her, he splayed all ten fingers, apparently indicating he was about to disappear for that amount of time.

As he turned to walk away, Ephraim gave him a friendly pat on his arm and suddenly, they were alone for the first time since being forcibly parted at Theresienstadt.

Approaching carefully, Ephraim stopped and looked at her as though disbelieving it was really her. Watching as he approached, she saw a man hardened by months of rough living. His once-fleshy physique was now considerably thinner and muscular and by a quirk of her imagination, he appeared to be taller than she remembered. But it was his face which had changed so much. His once bright eyes which had so attracted her when they had first met were now dulled with prominent age lines appearing as he frowned. His left cheek bore the scars of what appeared to be small burns and she also noticed that his left ear lobe was badly disfigured.

Looking at him, Hannah could only guess what he had been through and felt an overwhelming urge to sweep into his arms but she held back, hoping for him to react first. For his part, Ephraim remained rooted to the spot, displaying no outward sign of emotion or engagement. After what seemed an eternity, he finally spoke; his voice giving no outward sign of warmth.

'The Russian general said you had a Nazi lover whose child you are now bearing... is that true?'

Taking two steps forward, Hannah reached out and took hold of Ephraim's hands and drew them towards her. 'What would you like to hear, Ephraim? A simple answer to your question or the circumstances leading to it?'

A look of consternation appeared on Ephraim's face. 'A simple answer to my question will suffice.'

'Very well, the answer to both of those questions is yes.' In the silence which followed, she realised he made no attempt to remove his hands from hers. 'So yes, I am, or was, the mistress of a German officer and yes, I am carrying his child.'

As the fateful words left her lips, a huge sense of release flooded through her knowing that the apocalyptic moment she had been dreading had at last been divulged. But seeing Ephraim's unforgiving features, she felt compelled to add 'you should also know that neither event was planned nor was

I coerced into the relationship with Colonel Steiner who incidentally is a Wehrmacht officer... not a Nazi.'

'Which of course would make your behaviour acceptable?'

Upset by his harsh indictment, she reacted in similar fashion. 'I don't deserve that from you, Ephraim.' Trying to control herself, she took a deep breath. 'Remember your very last words to me at Theresienstadt?' She spoke slowly, emphasising each word. You said I should do whatever it takes to survive and that is what I have done which is the reason why I'm still alive and here with you, my husband.'

Pulling away from her, Ephraim took a pace back. 'If you weren't coerced into this relationship with this Nazi and forgive me if I fail to draw the same distinction as you do; to me they are all Nazis. If you weren't coerced, then you must have become this man's mistress by choice. That isn't survival, Hannah, you are nothing more than a Nazi whore!'

Stunned by the venom in his accusation, Hannah reacted. Launching herself forward, her right hand slapped Ephraim's face with all the pent-up fury she could muster. She saw his head snap sideways and watched as he slumped to his knees.

From behind, she heard a rush of footsteps and felt herself pulled back by an anxious Vasilevski.

Rising to his feet and with one hand nursing his cheek, Ephraim looked at her, a strange mix of shock and anger on his face. Without uttering another word, he turned on his heel and stumbled towards the medical tents, not once glancing back.

In despair, Hannah called after him but to no effect; her words failing to stop the man she had once loved so much. But for the strong arms of Vasilevski, she herself would have slumped to the ground. Instead, she turned away and felt his grip relax as he led her back towards her quarters.

Once there, she was grateful to find the tent deserted. Numbed by the encounter with Ephraim, she fell onto her camp bed and tried to analyse what had happened only minutes before.

With Steiner gone and probably dead, she could have told Ephraim that she had been raped on numerous occasions whilst a prisoner at Steiner's Admin unit which would explain her pregnancy but she knew she could neither lie to him or misrepresent her feelings for Steiner.

In reality, she had lived a very comfortable existence since her repatriation from Auschwitz compared to what Ephraim might have experienced since they had parted. But she also knew that wasn't the only reason for not wanting to lie to him.

Whether Steiner was still alive was almost irrelevant because her love for him had revealed what she now couldn't deny. An unbridgeable chasm now existed between what she felt for him compared to her previous feelings for Ephraim. Her experience of men prior to meeting Ephraim had been limited but to her increasingly anxious mother, the engaging Dr. Ephraim Fischer was nothing short of being 'manna from heaven'. Unquestionably, she had been attracted to him with his boyish good looks and waspish sense of humour. But whether it was the kind of love she had dreamed of as a young girl on the threshold of womanhood had never been put to the test. With nothing to compare with, she recalled how disappointed she had been with Ephraim's approach to lovemaking until her mother quietly explained that 'sex was meant to be endured... not enjoyed!'

During her pregnancy and for three months after the birth of Aaron, Ephraim had resisted her every attempt at lovemaking, sometimes quoting obscure texts from the Talmud to rationalize his self-imposed celibacy. But Hannah knew the real reason had nothing to do with ancient scripture but everything to do with modern politics as personified by the Nazis and their virulent hatred and persecution of the Jewish race. Compared to her own career which outwardly had been unaffected by the constant flow of anti-Semitic decrees, Ephraim had suffered greatly especially when he was forbidden from treating German nationals which had effectively brought his medical career to a halt.

To make matters worse, Ephraim's debarment from practising at the General Hospital in Berlin had coincided with the Orchestra's extensive tour to Russia and Scandinavia. On her return, she had noticed a marked difference in him. His light-hearted sense of humour had all but disappeared and despite her several attempts to alleviate her own growing frustration, Ephraim had remained impervious to her sexual approaches. And when some two weeks after her return they finally did make love, Hannah suspected it was more from a sense of duty rather than a heartfelt longing for her. Thereafter, that set the pattern for their infrequent couplings. That was until Steiner had entered her life and educated her body and inner soul to recognise the huge difference between dutiful sex and the wildly passionate and reckless lovemaking she had experienced with him.

Even now, lying on her camp bed in the midst of a Red Army encampment, she felt her body begin to react at the recollection of those precious moments spent in the arms of Kurt Steiner. Thinking of their brief time together, she realised that her life had taken a course of action which could not now be reversed even if she wanted it too.

The unspeakable horrors she had witnessed at Ravensbruch and Auschwitz had also dramatically changed her innocence for ever. Fully aware that her life as a Jew could be measured in hours the urge to live for the moment had seemed the only realistic path to follow. But Steiner's intervention on the night she was about to be raped had not only spared her life but had also given her a sliver of hope that she might even survive the war and perhaps be reunited with Aaron again. Whether any future life would include Ephraim was now a matter of conjecture and judging from his reaction just minutes before, that outcome looked extremely unlikely.

It was the sound of distant gunfire briefly stilling the incessant chatter of the woodland birds which cut into her thoughts. Half asleep and slow to open her eyes, she saw only the camouflaged canvas roof moving with the motion of the passing wind. Breathing deeply, she caught the pleasant smell of wood smoke; something she associated with happy childhood memories of autumn when she and her father would gather and burn the carpet of fallen leaves shed from the ash trees in the garden of their Charlottenburg home. 'Dear Poppa' she mused; 'thank God he never lived to see what has become of his precious daughter!'

Outside the tent, the sound of gunfire seemed to be getting louder. Unsure what to do, she eased off the bed just as Rifleman Vasilevski entered the tent and beckoned her to follow him. Taking her by the arm, he hustled her towards a nearby stand of birch trees and once there, forced her to kneel down. Overhead, the sound of screaming aircraft engines cut through the trees followed by the blast of exploding bombs.

Beside her, she felt Vasilevski attempt to protect her exposed body by pulling his greatcoat over her. Terrified but touched by his gesture, she wriggled closer and vainly attempted to press herself into the soft forest floor.

Lying there, she heard the deadly chatter of heavy machine gun fire and she felt Vasilevski's body stiffen as he became increasingly aware of the threat to their position. Rising quickly, he pulled her to her feet and together they raced further away from the main encampment.

Pulled along by Vasilevski, she tripped and stumbled to the ground. Seeing her fall, the Russian roughly pulled her to her feet and with surprising agility draped her over his shoulder and ran towards a compact stand of trees and scrub. Crashing through waist high brambles and ferns, he selected a tree with a particularly large trunk before setting her down beside him. Gasping for breath, she fell to her knees and looked around but Yuri Vasilevski had chosen well; their new refuge providing much denser cover. Putting a finger to his lips, he signalled silence which to her seemed odd as the sound of gunfire now seemed further away. But the young Rifleman, a prodigy of generations of woodsmen, clearly knew what he was doing. Lying still and hardly daring to breathe, it seemed an eternity before she heard the unmistakeable sound of

German voices as a strong force of infantry pushed through the forest towards the Russian base camp.

Touching her arm for attention, Vasilevski gave another of his disarming grins. Silently mouthing 'you German' he gave a thumbs-up sign. Then pointing to himself, he mouthed 'me Ruskie' and drew his hand across his throat. Pointing to the source of the voices he raised a questioning eyebrow and Hannah realised he was offering her the opportunity to return to her own countrymen.

Shaking her head vigorously, she pursed her lips in silent thanks and noticed a flush of embarrassment redden his cheeks before it creased into its familiar grin.

From the area of the camp, the sound of gunfire had dramatically increased. The heavy crump of mortar shells accompanied by the staccato chatter of heavy machine guns made it impossible to assess who might be winning the bloody clash. Overhead, yet more aircraft materialised, the distinctive throbbing sound of their diesel engines largely masked by the sound of heavy gunfire followed seconds later by ear-splitting detonations as they dropped their deadly cargoes of death. Peering through the dense screen of bushes and thickets, she caught a glimpse of large numbers of German troops slowly advancing towards the Soviet base camp.

Hardly daring to breath, the sound of mortar shells and gunfire seemed to last forever before it finely ceased except for the occasional pistol shot which as Vasilevski graphically indicated meant that the wounded were being despatched with a shot to the head. But from their sheltered position, it was impossible to guess who was shooting who? Had the Soviets managed to fight off the attack or had the coordinated Wehrmacht and Luftwaffe assault prevailed?

Anxious to find out, Vasilevski got to his knees, wordlessly indicating that she should remain where she was. Covering her with his greatcoat, he vanished like a wraith into the now still forest without a sound betraying his passing. Left alone, Hannah felt strangely calm and grateful for the daylight.

Looking up, she noticed the reassuring shafts of strong sunlight piercing through the tops of the trees; each beam drawing substance from the hazy pools of white cordite smoke lingering from the earlier gunfire.

As each minute passed, she began to wonder what she would do if Vasilevski did not return. He had obviously been ordered to guard her whilst in the encampment but that was before the German attack. And what if he were to be wounded or killed? Would she be able to avoid capture if left on her own?

She recalled Steiner telling her that if she fell into German hands again, she would face certain death if they discovered she was Jewish. That was the reason he had provided her with false papers but these had been confiscated by her Soviet captors. And without the protection of someone like Guriev, she knew her life expectancy would last only as long as she managed to avoid being seized either by the Red Army and the inevitable rape which would follow or execution by the German military for being a Jew.

Underneath the greatcoat, her body temperature was beginning to rise as the strong summer sun broke through the canopy of the trees above. Closing her eyes, she recalled Aaron trying to catch shafts of light entering through the large casement windows of the apartment and she recalled the surprised look on his face when his fingers closed on empty air.

Close by, she heard the sound of snapping twigs as people moved through the undergrowth but secure in the hiding place chosen by Vasilevski, she was reluctant to expose her face in case of being spotted. Inches from her head, a young blackbird hopped into view, the sheen of its feathers highlighted by the sunlight. Putting its head to one side, the blackbird ruffled his neck plumage as though challenging her to explain her intrusive presence in its domain. Closing both eyes for a second time, she forced herself to relax. When she reopened them the bird had disappeared.

As the sound of the advancing soldiers gradually receded, she felt a slight pressure on that part of the greatcoat covering her legs; a touch so light it could have been her imagination playing tricks or perhaps even the blackbird hopping onto Vasilevski's greatcoat. Not daring to move her head she felt the touch again, this time more firmly. Glancing down, she was relieved to see Vasilevski kneeling over her with a cautionary finger over his lips. Seeing him there, a young man she had met less than an hour ago but now her sole protector, she felt a sense of instinctive gratitude rise up within her. Without thinking, she gave the young Rifleman a playful wink and watched as his youthful features lit up.

Within their hidden enclave it seemed that even the birds were obeying the Russian's need for silence. An unnatural stillness had now settled over the glade and she began to wonder whether Vasilevski was being overly cautious and began to fidget under the warm greatcoat. Detecting this, the Russian pressed his hand firmly down on her soft bottom, preventing any further movement. Silently chastened, she heard the shrill sound of a whistle followed within seconds by a group of German soldiers racing past their shelter heading in the direction of the Soviet encampment. With the nauseous taste of bile rising in her mouth, she realised that had she and Vasilevski left their refuge just seconds before, they would have blundered into the path of the advancing Germans. As yet more troops followed their advancing comrades, Hannah saw Vasilevski signal for her to be prepared to move out. Taking hold of her hand, the Russian eased her through a small gap in the thorny bramble hedge, the same hedge which had provided an impenetrable barrier to the passing soldiers.

Pulled along by Vasilevski, they dashed towards the spot from where the German troops had just emerged from before the density of the trees and tangled undergrowth slowed their frantic pace. Small branches snapped under foot and Hannah realised why Vasilevski had chosen this moment to leave their hideaway. Any sounds made by them would be assumed to have come from their own troops should any remaining soldiers still be in the vicinity.

They travelled for at least an hour before Vasilevski halted by a small stream. Exhausted, she stumbled to the edge of the water and lay down. Cupping her hands together, she refreshed her parched throat with the crystal-clear water. Looking down at her reflected image she felt an irresistible urge to plunge into the stream and wash away the dust and tiredness in her legs. Laughing at the thought, she sat up and joined Vasilevski who had seated himself against the trunk of a large oak. Sitting in the warm sunshine, she felt a growing sense of attachment to the young Russian and his woodland skills... skills which she realised had unquestionably saved their lives so far.

As her back pressed against the rough bark of the tree, she felt her shoulder rest against Vasilevski's broad frame. To her surprise, he made no effort to move away. Nor did his face redden as he turned to face her. Leaning forward, she imitated a swimming movement which Vasilevski appeared to understand immediately. Pointing to her and then to the cool water of the stream, his slight nod was sufficient to indicate his approval.

Standing up, Vasilevski glanced around the small clearing, his eyes missing nothing. Satisfied, he took up a position which enabled him to cover the sheltered entrance to the clearing and sank down on his haunches before giving her a thumbs-up sign.

Slipping off her uniform blouse, skirt and shoes, Hannah stepped gingerly over the bracken-strewn undergrowth and stopped on the edge of the stream where she threw off her bra and pants before stepping into the water. Within four paces she was able to duck down and let the warm stream flow over her body. Lifting her feet off the sandy bottom she closed her eyes, letting her body float downstream in the gentle current. The rejuvenating effect of the water felt wonderfully cleansing, drawing much of the tiredness from her legs.

Feeling the current becoming stronger, she looked towards the bank now some distance away and saw Vasilevski waving anxiously. Turning swiftly onto her front, she lazily swam back using a powerful overarm stroke. Changing to a breast stroke Hannah matched the flow of the stream's current, easily maintaining her position with the bank. Reluctant to leave the water's invigorating effect but glancing at Vasilevski she saw he was anxious to continue their march.

Returning to the bank, she gathered up her underwear and hurriedly draped her uniform blouse over her still wet body whilst Vasilevski kept his eyes studiously fixed on the entrance to the clearing. She was relieved that the young Russian had not been perturbed by her nakedness but inwardly, she was astonished by her own transformation. The effects of her incarceration had changed the prudish Jewish girl into a woman who now had no qualms in stripping off her clothes even in the presence of a stranger albeit a stranger who radiated nothing more threatening than a boyish grin..

Some two hours later, with the memory of the cool stream rapidly fading, she saw the untiring figure of Vasilevski suddenly halt. Attempting to look around him, Hannah could see nothing unusual but she edged closer to him for safety. Reaching behind him, Vasilevski took hold of Hannah's hand and together they cautiously moved to a spot where the forest gave way to open farmland. Further on, they found cover behind an ancient willow hurdle and through one of its many broken slats they were able to look across an overgrown meadow at the remains of what had once been a small Polish hamlet.

Traditional stone cottages, the remains of their smoke-blackened roof trusses pointing upwards like accusing fingers in stark contrast to the cloudless blue sky above... each one a silent witness to the savagery of war on the innocent villagers who had lived here.

Looking beyond the desolate buildings to the untended fields and waist-high weeds in what had once been carefully tended vegetable plots, Vasilevski guessed that its inhabitants had probably fled or been murdered in the first months of the German invasion. He had witnessed this same scene many times before as the Red Army recovered territory from retreating German forces.

Sheltering behind the Russian's broad back, Hannah could see very little of what lay in front of the old wattle fence.

Rising to his feet, Vasilevski stepped forward and beckoned her to follow him. Stealthily they approached the nearest of the ruined buildings; a cottage with its burnt door frame now supporting nothing more imposing than two elongated rusty hinges vainly attempting to fill the void.

Looking down the row of cottages, Vasilevski thought he recognised the handiwork of the German invaders. If correct, he knew every building would have been ransacked for food and alcohol before being torched. He also knew that German murder squads, either to spread terror or to simply save on ammunition would frequently lock families in their cottages before setting fire to the building. Wishing to spare her from possibly witnessing the remains of former tenants, Vasilevski raised his hand and stopped her from entering. To divert her attention, he pointed towards two wooden sheds which from a distance appeared to have been spared the same fate as that of the main homesteads.

His curiosity aroused, the Russian approached the smaller shed with caution. During his basic Army training, Vasilevski had displayed no interest in the daily political lectures but realistic demonstrations by German prisoners-of-war in the art of placing booby traps in the unlikeliest of places had commanded his full attention. Pulling up a long cane once used to support runner beans, he carefully prised the shed door open. Some distance away, Hannah watched as he cautiously entered the shed. Satisfied it was safe, he signalled her to follow.

Inside, the hut had a musty smell of creosote. A wooden shelf held a number of glass jars containing a variety of nails and screws and beneath that was a tool rack holding a rusty hand scythe, a garden fork with bent tines and a well-worn spade. A wooden high-backed chair with a dilapidated cushion on its seat stood forlornly in the corner giving the impression that the owner had just popped into the cottage and might be returning at any moment.

Patting the cushion, Vasilevski motioned Hannah to sit and rest. After struggling through dense woodland and thick undergrowth for several hours the chair felt wonderfully comfortable as she leaned her aching body against it wooden back. Swallowing hard to salivate her parched throat, she thought longingly of the cool stream and the blissful effect it had had on her tired limbs.

Looking at Vasilevski, she guessed he too must be feeling tired. Catching his eye, she pointed to the floor, urging him to take a rest too. Shaking his head, he looked towards the row of empty cottages and from his hand gestures, Hannah realised he intended to check out the second shed and in a trice he was gone.

Peering through the shed's grimy window and seeing how low the sun was to the horizon, it dawned on her tired brain just why her body ached so much and why she felt so hungry. She estimated that she and Vasilevski must have been in the forest for most of the day. The tasteless meal she had shared with the Ukrainian interpreter at breakfast was the only food she had eaten that day.

Sitting in the old chair she felt her aching limbs begin to relax and suddenly she felt very tired.

Able to relax at last, she couldn't stop herself from reflecting on the grim events of the past two days. 'What would Max Feldman think,' she wondered, 'if he could see me now, sitting in a grimy shed in the middle of a war zone; hungry and thirsty and utterly dependent upon a young Russian soldier she had met only that morning.' She ran her hand across her stomach, trying to detect any sign of swelling.

She hadn't thought too much about her pregnancy other than when Guriev had shown a perverse pleasure in revealing her relationship with Steiner. Whilst a sympathetic Ephraim might just possibly have understood her pregnancy as a consequence of being raped, she realised there could never be the remotest possibility of him being able to accept her willing relationship with a German officer whether SS or Wehrmacht. In his own words, they were all Nazis.

During their brief time together at Theresienstadt, she remembered Ephraim telling her that it was naïve to believe that German field officers did not know what was happening in the concentration camps which in his mind made every one of them complicit in the killing of Jews. More to the point, he now knew she had willingly consorted with a Jew-killer and nothing she could now do or say would make him change his mind. So in affect their marriage was now realistically over. As dead as the proverbial dodo.

The raid by German troops on the Soviet camp earlier that morning had thankfully dispelled any prospect of finding herself in Guriev's bed but it also meant she now had no possible means of getting to Berlin. She wondered too whether Ephraim might have survived the ferocious assault or was she now a widow of a man who had shown no understanding or sympathy towards her predicament despite having heard Guriev proposition her.

Lost in thought, her eyes were drawn to the deepening shadows creeping across the wooden floor boards as the evening sun approached the point where it would quickly disappear over the distant horizon. Reflecting on Guriev's outlandish proposal, she ruefully acknowledged the futility of being able to expect any promise of safety to be honoured by a man perversely attracted to her on the basis of her being the mistress of a German officer. Added to which, the grim prospect of recapture by the Germans was a distinct possibility as the tide of war ebbed and flowed on the ever-changing Eastern Front.

The return of Vasilevski thankfully interrupted thoughts that were becoming gloomier by the second. But his cheery features now showed a worrying sign of concern; his gesture signalling Hannah to follow him adding to her growing anxiety.

Forcing her reluctant body from the comfort of the old chair, she followed the Russian wearily. Thinking they might be moving to the larger shed, she was surprised when Vasilevski hurried towards one of the smaller cottages. He waited for her to catch up before entering through what remained of its scorched rear door.

In the main room on the ground floor, she watched as he lifted up a threadbare carpet in front of a large fire hearth housing an ornate cooking range. Poignantly, a brass poker and shovel set stood where the former occupants had last placed them together with a small brush and dustpan on the tiled area to the side of the range.

Watching as Vasilevski crouched down, she could only marvel as the Russian prised up a hidden trapdoor in the floor. Grunting with the effort, he pointed to the end of each wooden board and smiled. Bemused by what he was trying to convey, he lowered the trap door back into the floor and only then did she understand the cleverness of its fitment. Instead of the usual square hatch door, she was looking at the irregular ends of boards which neatly slotted into the normal floor boards making the opening difficult to distinguish. Wondering how on earth Vasilevski had spotted the opening, she found herself yet again impressed by the boundless talents of this lowly ranked soldier.

Entering the cellar down a steep set of wooden steps, she saw Vasilevski lower the trap door after first laying the old carpet across it to lend additional concealment. Blackness immediately engulfed the cellar and she felt, rather than saw him descend and stand close to her. Reaching out, her hand fastened on to the serge material of his uniform blouse. Sensing her unease, the Russian took hold of her hand and together they inched away from the wooden steps before being halted by a solid object. She felt Vasilevski fumble in his uniform pocket and after three loud clicks, the flint wheel of his Red Army-issued lighter finally ignited the petrol wick. By its flickering light, she was able to dimly make out the shape of a solid work bench with a dusty oil lamp hanging from a hook in the low ceiling. Vasilevski had seen it too. Removing the lamp's filler cap, he peered in and his familiar grin confirmed it had a quantity of paraffin remaining in its brass tank. The sliding glass wind shield made lighting the lamp difficult but after adjusting the wick, the lamp gave out a surprising amount of light.

The cellar was a single room with a dirt floor and much larger than it had initially appeared. There were two chairs similar to the one in the shed but it was the far end of the cellar which drew the Russian's attention. The cellar had obviously been used for the preserving of produce and neatly arranged on a rack of steel shelves were jars each clearly labelled... in barely legible Polish! On a lower shelf, standing upright like soldiers at attention, were unmarked bottles which when held against the light of the paraffin lamp appeared to contain something akin to red wine whilst to the left of these bottles were three wheels of identical cheeses.

Examining them, Vasilevski pointed to Hannah and rubbed his stomach. Tonight, neither of them would go hungry.

The cellar was also equipped with a cold water tap piped from the cottage above which was plumbed to fill a large zinc bath supported on two wooden trestles. The drain emptied into a waste pipe which disappeared through the bottom of the cellar floor. In sign-language, Vasilevski indicated that he thought the bath was used to wash the produce before bottling but looking at the size of it, Hannah thought this questionable.

However, what didn't require too much guesswork was the knowledge that she and Rifleman Yuri Vasilevski would be spending the night in this underground bolthole. She also realised that she ought to make an effort to prepare a meal of some description, if only to contribute something to their relationship. Without him by her side that day, she knew beyond doubt that by now, she would probably be dead... several times over.

Spotting a rack of plates on the lower shelf, she washed them under the cold tap to remove the thin layer of dust which had accumulated and began to look through the various handwritten labels on the jars, all of which were utterly incomprehensible to her. Behind her, she heard the sound of water running into the bath and looking round she saw Vasilevski, stripped to the waist washing his upper body, face and arms with a vigour her tired limbs could only envy. Disregarding his puzzled look, she took the small piece of wet towelling from him and pushing him round, washed his broad back. His youthful physique reminded her of Steiner's more mature body.

Handing the flannel back to the grinning Russian, she set her mind once more on attempting to visually decipher what each jar contained. Certain that one contained sweet peaches, she prised off its lid and was delighted to see she was correct. Next she examined one of the three cheese wheels and using a wire cutter attached to the end of a scarred cheese board, she sliced through the creamy ripe cheese and managed to detach two large segments. From over her shoulder, an interested Vasilevski was following her every move. Draining the peach juice into an empty jar she apportioned the soft peaches to each plate followed by the cheese. Looking up, she smiled and signalled for him to take his plate. Using the bench as a table, he arranged both chairs and sat opposite to her, both hands neatly tucked into his lap. Puzzled, she stared at him only to realise they had no cutlery to eat with.

Not able to control himself any longer the young Russian laughed aloud as he held both hands up in feigned supplication. Hearing his infectious laughter, she did her best to maintain a straight face but failed. Wordlessly, she wiggled her finger at him in silent admonishment and together they set about eating the food in much the same way as their forebears had done in centuries past.

Later that evening with their hunger pains eased by a second helping of cheese, this time varied by a jar of preserved pears, Vasilevski confirmed that the dusty bottles did in fact contain a coarse red wine probably fermented from locally harvested grapes.

Two sips were enough to discourage Hannah from wanting to finish the overfull jar. Vasilevski however, had no such inhibitions. Holding his glass jar up to the oil lamp like a practiced connoisseur he sipped it for flavour. Expressing his satisfaction, he tipped his head back and downed the fiery red liquid in one swallow. Placing the empty jar back on the table, he shyly caught sight of her look of astonishment and instantly blushed. Wishing to spare his embarrassment, she quickly refilled it and proposed a toast with her own jar. Tapping the two jars together, she sipped her own drink and hoarsely whispered 'le chaim' as the rough wine passed down her throat.

By the time her jar was finally empty, Vasilevski had drained two more, each time replenished by her. Holding the dark green bottle against the light, she saw that it held just enough wine to fill one more glass but this time Vasilevski declined the refill.

On a pre-war visit with the orchestra to Stockholm, she had joined several friends for an evening which had finished in a waterfront bar where she recalled seeing a group of Russian seamen drinking a clear liquid straight from bottles and thinking how very masculine it had looked. Wanting to impress Vasilevski as a woman of the world, she struggled to her feet and seized the bottle from his startled grasp. Throwing her head back she took a deep gulp which strangely did not feel as fiery as the first sip had done. Passing the bottle back to Vasilevski, she watched as he too took a further mouthful before passing it back to her. One more gulp and the bottle was finally empty. Letting it slip through her fingers, the bottle fell onto the hard dirt floor but did not break. She saw Vasilevski jump out of his seat and felt his strong hands take hold of her shoulders and gently lower her back into her chair. She felt the room begin to spin and suddenly there were two Vasilevski's in front of her. She heard a voice calling out for someone called 'Yuri' but had no idea who it was. Slowly the spinning stopped and she remembered no more until waking much later with a dreadful taste in her mouth.

Above her head, the oil lamp was still burning; its wick turned low. As her eyes adjusted to the gloom, she realised she was lying on the stout bench which had served as the meal table. Vasilevski had placed his greatcoat over her with a seat cushion for a pillow but he was nowhere to be seen. Listening intently, she detected the sound of light breathing but trying to peer furtively around the cellar whilst trying not to move her throbbing head proved difficult. With no sound coming from the cottage above, Hannah pursed her lips and in a voice barely more than a soft whisper she called Yuri's name.

From beneath the bench she heard a faint stirring and very soon the tousled head of Vasilevski appeared. Rising quickly, he made his way over to the zinc bath and without any sense of embarrassment, proceeded to urinate in it. Flushing the bath with the cold tap he looked across to Hannah and raised his eyebrows which she guessed was an invitation to do likewise. Having bared her naked body when taking a swim the previous day and recalling the awful experience of using the stinking slop bucket on the cattle truck to Auschwitz, she had no qualms and followed suit.

Watching the cold water flush the bottom of the bath, Hannah couldn't resist. Since that cleansing dip in the river she and Vasilevski had travelled a considerable distance at the hottest time of day. She had sweated profusely and could still feel the dust from yesterday's journey sticking to her body.

Plugging the bath, she watched it fill up surprisingly quickly. Quickly undressing, Vasilevski's initial puzzlement turned to unabashed admiration. Easing herself into the cold water, she saw her young protector watch with acute interest as she slowly let her body adjust to the cold water. Lying full length, she saw the Russian looking at her almost as a young boy would stare at his first sight of a naked woman. Returning his infectious grin, she sat up and signalled for him to take her place in the bathtub. Understanding immediately, Vasilevski required no further encouragement. Quickly stripping off his uniform shirt and trousers, he was left wearing just a pair of green underpants bizarrely stamped 'U S Army Property' across the waistband. Casting her mind back to the wall maps in Steiner's office, she knew that the American and Russian troops were fighting on different fronts so she guessed her youthful protector's underpants were part of a military aid programme.

Approaching the bath, Vasilevski stopped and stared in open admiration at her naked body. Putting fingers to lips, he blew an imaginary kiss of appreciation. Not knowing how to respond, she cupped her hand and flicked cold water at him causing him to hurriedly step back.

Since her modest teenage years, only two men had seen her fully unclothed and both, Ephraim and Kurt Steiner had been her lovers. But then she remembered the Rumanian Kapo in Auschwitz and the SS Lieutenant in her apartment in Charlottenburg and a cold chill ran down her back. They too had seen her naked body but only after subjecting her to threats and force. Glancing across at Vasilevski, she smiled, knowing she could now add him to her expanding list.

Hauling herself out of the bath, she dressed quickly; studiously avoiding looking at the Russian who was now in the bath splashing its cold water over his well-muscled body.

She recalled Ephraim explaining that women have unusually high levels of sexual libido during pregnancy but casting a furtive glance at Vasilevski's prone body she doubted whether this was true in her case. Running her hand across her still flat stomach, she wondered yet again whether she really was pregnant despite the early symptoms she had experienced at Auschwitz.

Looking up suddenly, Vasilevski caught her eye before she was able to look away. With a dripping hand he beckoned her to approach him. As she did so, he sat up sending a miniature wave down the bath and offered Hannah the piece of towelling he had been using as a flannel.

'Back... you want me to wash your back?'

Nodding, he closed his eyes as Hannah vigorously applied the flannel to his shoulders and lower back. Teasingly, she let the flannel drop into the water and she began to massage the tense knots in Vasilevski's shoulder blades. Applying greater pressure, she heard him grunt with pleasurable pain.

Working both hands upwards, her deft fingers moved to Vasilevski's neck muscles.

Half closing her eyes, she recalled the night Steiner had been gripped by fever and the unforgettable sensation she had experienced when touching his naked chest. Slowly, very slowly, she moved Vasilevski's head and upper body back to a horizontal position and kneeling forward, Hannah began to massage his upper chest muscles letting her strong fingers playfully pass over his raised nipples. Looking down the bath, she saw Vasilevski hurriedly recover the floating flannel and surreptitiously place it over his genital area but even in the dim lamplight, there was no hiding the large bulge beginning to rise beneath it.

Smiling to herself, she used a chipped enamel mug to pour water over the Russian's thick head of hair. The water was surprisingly soft and with the remains of a bar of carbolic soap, she managed to generate a healthy lather. The hair wash lasted only as long as the lather remained and with a final flourish, she rinsed his hair and roughly towelled it. Lying back in the cold bath without a trace of embarrassment, Vasilevski reminded her of bath nights with Aaron. Although she guessed she was perhaps only a year or so older than Vasilevski, she felt a degree of maternal warmth towards him; a young man barely out of his teens yet who had chosen to remain with her rather than find his way back to Red Army lines and personal safety.

Later, after a meal of yet more cheese and preserved fruit, Vasilevski scouted the area before returning for her. Despite its claustrophobic mustiness, the underground storeroom had afforded a sense of temporary refuge. But now, emerging into the early morning brightness, she began to feel vulnerable again. Using the outlying buildings as cover, they made for the same forest area which had served them so well the previous day. Once there, Vasilevski made several laboured attempts to communicate and she could only guess at what she thought he was trying to say. Hoping her interpretation was correct, she thought he was offering two choices. They could either stay in the vicinity and wait for the Red Army to overcome what was left of German resistance or they could head off in an easterly direction avoiding German units before meeting up with advancing Soviet troops. After several more frustrating attempts to converse, she believed Vasilevski had decided upon remaining in the same area, forage for food during the day and use the cellar at night. But increasingly frustrated by her inability to understand his language, she knew she could be wrong.

Once more in the forest, the dense undergrowth made for slow progress and after several hours they had found no other villages or dwellings around the perimeter of the dense woodland. Thankfully the temperature in the forest was cool and several times they came upon small streams of chrystal-clear water; probably tributaries to the river which she had swum in the previous day

'Was it only yesterday' she wondered? In her exhausted state of mind, it seemed much longer than just one day... a day in which so much had happened. After their closeness in the cellar, Vasilevski seemed more at ease and on several occasions he literally half-carried her when she felt as though her legs could not walk one step further.

They frequently heard the sound of distant artillery fire and listening intently, Vasilevski used a twig to sketch the familiar outline of a tank and then added matchstick figures to illustrate infantry support. Using both hands to illustrate the shapely curve of a woman, the boyish-looking soldier pointed at her.

Puzzled, Hannah pointed at herself; 'me?'

Nodding enthusiastically and slapping the palm of one hand into the crook of his elbow, Vasilevski executed the universal sign for rough sex. 'Ruskies... fuck, fuck, bang, bang!'

It took a moment for the awful realisation to impact in her tired brain. With recapture by German troops spelling certain death, her one slim hope of reaching Berlin had rested with Guriev and his unit. But with that option now seemingly closed coupled with Vasilevski's warning to avoid his rapacious comrades, her chances of surviving the war had all but disappeared. And the thought of attempting to live out the war in an area of Poland completely foreign to her was beyond her imagination. From early childhood, she recalled the horror stories of Jewish pogroms in Eastern Europe so the prospect of surviving in Poland would be as improbable as being recaptured by the Germans.

Studying Vasilevski's tender years, she felt that her life had just entered a cul-de-sac. Without him, she knew she would now be dead. Sensing her mood, Vasilevski uneasily pulled her closer to him and muttered a few consolatory words in Russian. Silently, she again cursed her own ignorance in not being able to communicate with this selfless young person.

Easing herself away from his embrace, she managed to produce a genuine smile which seemed to relieve Vasilevski's growing anxiety; at least she hoped it would. Minutes later they were once more on the move and by mid-afternoon, she realised they had traversed the entire area of open farmland on the edge of which the same blackened village was once more in view.

Skirting the rear of the cottage which had been their overnight refuge, Vasilevski made his way to the overgrown vegetable garden before moving on to each of the adjoining garden plots. Beckoning her to follow him, she was surprised to see clusters of tomatoes, runner beans and peas, borne on self-seeded plants from the previous year's windfalls. Harvesting the ripe pickings revived yet more happy childhood memories of visits to her grandparent's garden at their country home in Potsdam.

The gunfire heard earlier had stopped and sitting on the warm ground and screened by rows of last season's old growth entwined with new season fruit, it was difficult to imagine they were in the middle of a war zone. The late afternoon sun still retained much of its warmth and having walked for most of the day she knew she could easily fall asleep. Vasilevski, ever sensitive to possible danger and no doubt feeling vulnerable in their exposed location beyond the cover of the forest, had disappeared minutes before. Consciously fighting the drowsiness which was slowly enveloping her tired body, Hannah tried to take stock of her bleak situation.

'It really comes down to three options,' she reasoned. 'If I am captured by either German or Soviet troops the outcome will be the same. The Germans will kill me for being a Jew or I will be raped to death by Red Army soldiers because I am a German.' She allowed herself a grim smile at the irony of this conclusion.

Looking around the small settlement, she considered her third option. 'How long could a German woman, a woman wearing the uniform of a German nurse, expect to survive in a Polish village destroyed by German troops; its villagers either massacred or forced to flee? Not liking the answer, she closed her eyes and let her senses take in the familiar sounds of the countryside. In front of her, a speckled thrush expressed its raucous irritation at her presence in his part of the garden. Cautiously opening one eye, Hannah saw the reason for the fuss. Partially hidden among the stalks of bolted cabbages, a newly fledged thrush was busy snatching at a tasty morsel provided by its noisy parent. 'Perhaps' she supposed, 'I could make out here for a month or two' but instantly dismissed the thought. No nearer to a positive solution, Hannah threw back her head, let her shoulders relax and recited the mantra which had carried her through even darker days during the nightmare train journey to Auschwitz; 'live for this moment... tomorrow will be worse.'

Without warning an eruption of small arms fire from within the forest startled her. Alert and frightened, she looked for

Vasilevski but he was nowhere to be seen. The gunfire was getting closer and suddenly, the overgrown screen of bamboo canes and foliage seemed less protective. The safety of the earthen store room in the nearby cottage was temptingly close but she knew she must stay where Vasilevski could find her. Without him, she had no realistic chance of survival.

SIXTY NINE

Using high definition Leica binoculars, a trophy recently acquired from the body of a dead Wehrmacht lieutenant, the Partisan leader scanned the open areas of the village for any sign of movement. The protracted engagement in the forest with German troops had been costly in terms of losses. The eleven partisans who had awoken that morning were now reduced to just five and they badly needed to find shelter as far as possible from units of marauding German troop's fighting a ferocious rear-guard action against the advancing Soviets and their partisan allies.

Seeing no sign of life, the Polish leader again checked each building to satisfy himself that the area was clear of German troops. The burned-out buildings were a familiar sight; a sight he had become grimly familiar with since his own village had been overrun in the days following the unstoppable German blitzkrieg in late 1939. He had been lucky. When the Wehrmacht Panzer units passed through the village in mid-September they had pillaged for food and water but had not harmed the villagers. But rumours of SS murder squads following the Panzer units quickly began to circulate so he and his brother had left their distraught parents and young sister only hours before their worst fears were realised. Every person remaining in the village, including his family had been pitilessly slaughtered and their homes torched before the murder squads moved on.

Satisfied it was safe to move, Wojciech Lukaszek softly whistled to his remaining comrades to follow him. In the general melee following the German ambush, they had had no opportunity of recovering their dead compatriots. But now, in the quiet aftermath of that bloody encounter, each man bore an even greater hatred for the German invader.

From her prone position between rows of overgrown bean supports, Hannah heard the soft whistling sound and looking through the tangled weeds, she thought she spotted what appeared to be a well-armed man heading in her direction.

Petrified, she tried to flatten herself between two furrows but too late, she realised that her movement was causing the canes on either side to move. Spotting this, the approaching man instantly dropped to his knees and barked out a warning.

Transfixed and hardly daring to breathe, Hannah saw two more similarly armed figures followed moments later by a further two. Watching them approach her eyes were drawn back to the first man, now very close and using his machine pistol to indicate he wanted her to stand up.

Stumbling to her feet, her arms were immediately seized and she felt herself dragged towards the rear of the cottage and pushed through its open door space.

Once inside, her arms were released and she felt the tension lessen.

'Polski?' It was the man with the gun who spoke.

'No. I am a Jew' adding quickly 'a German Jew. I have escaped from the Germans.'

'Is that so?' The same man again, picking up on Hannah's language and attempting to respond in barely understandable German. 'In which case tell us more but wait until we find a safe spot to talk.'

Since her arrest and the many harrowing things she had experienced, the thought of survival now came naturally and her brain instinctively recognised a chance to not only ingratiate herself with these desperate men but to also pinpoint their position to Vasilevski.

'I know a place where we can talk,' pausing to let the translation register. 'It's where I've been hiding since my escape.'

From the excited gabble which followed, Hannah suspected that each of the partisans probably had a basic understanding of German before the leading Pole nodded his assent.

'Ok... lead on.' He pointed the muzzle of his pistol towards Hannah's chest; 'but no tricks.'

Inside the cottage, Hannah lifted the worn carpet and saw each of the Poles study the floor boards, their eyes searching for the trap door. Taking a flat-edged coal shovel from the hearth, she inserted it between the dividing boards and levered the hatch cover open. Strong hands took over and seconds later all five Poles were peering into the dark cellar.

Once below, by the dim light of the oil lamp, a quick inspection took place, followed by a heated exchange.

'My comrades prefer a position where they can see the enemy coming. If we were trapped down here,' he gave an expressive sigh; 'we would be shot like fish in a barrel... or worse.'

'I don't understand? What could be worse?'

Staring at her with a look of disbelief, it took the Pole a moment to realise it was a genuine question.

'Flame throwers; the Jerries use flame-throwers to save on ammunition. When the SS enter a village, they herd our people into the local church or barn and then burn it with flame-throwers. If anyone manages to get out of the building they are shot like dogs' adding, 'get the picture?'

Mortified as much for her naivety as by the horror of the explanation, Hannah nodded her understanding. 'I'm sorry. I shouldn't have asked you that.'

Studying her intently for any trace of sarcasm and seeing none, the Pole relented.

'As you're hiding from the Germans too then we're on the same side. You can't stay with us but if you do get captured, then forget you ever met us... OK?

'If I get caught by the Germans then you would be the very least of my worries.'

Thinking he detected a hint of flippancy in her comment, the Polish leader caught hold of her arm and forced her to look at him. 'Listen to me.' Despite his obvious irritation he spoke calmly. 'Jews and the SS are a bad mix and if they catch you then you can expect a quick death.' He relaxed his grip. 'You've been in one of their camps so you know what I'm telling you is true. But if the Nazis find out you met up with us,' he pointed to his comrades , 'then you will be tortured for days even though you won't be able to tell them a single damn thing.'

'And what do you think will happen if I fall into the hands of Soviet troops hell-bent on revenge for what has happened to their women?'

A querulous look appeared on his lined face. 'Look, this war has made some strange bedfellows with Poles fighting on the same side as the Red Army and the Soviets offering a form of amnesty to Jews like you... at least while this war lasts.'

'So what are you telling me?' It was her turn to be puzzled.

'I'm saying you may be better off with the Ivans than you would with the Jerries.'

'By Ivans and Jerries you mean Russians and Germans?'

'That is exactly who I mean.' Looking at the woman standing before him, her dishevelled uniform actually adding to her obvious attractiveness, Wojciech Lukaszek experienced a sense of pity for this doomed woman. Her simple helplessness seemed to cry out for protection but looking at the faces of his comrades anxious to move out of the cellar, he knew this was not possible. A woman as attractive as this would be a recipe for trouble among a group of men who had lacked the closeness of women for months. But could he just leave her here knowing that it would only be a matter of time before the village again became the front line between the armies of Fascism and the Bolsheviks?

Undecided, Wojciech turned away and froze in his tracks. Standing above the rim of the hatch, a Russian soldier was covering both him and his comrades with the business end of his machine pistol. With the daylight silhouetting his bulky frame, the Red Army soldier looked immense to the Poles below, his sudden presence exuding frightening menace.

A shouted command in Russian needed no interpretation nor room for misunderstanding and each of the partisans slowly and purposely placed their weapons on the table before taking a pace back.

Another command and this time three Poles squatted on the earthen floor while the two remaining Partisans stood behind them and placed their hands on their heads. Only then did the Russian soldier carefully climb down the wooden steps into the cellar for Hannah to recognise Rifleman Yuri Vasilevski.

Peering in the gloom, Vasilevski motioned to Hannah to step behind him and she thought for one awful moment, he was about to shoot the entire group. Instead, the Russian quietly spoke to them, ordering the two standing Poles to sit on the floor with their comrades and designating Wojciech Lukaszek to be their spokesman.

Hannah could only guess what was being said but several of the partisans obviously had an inkling of Russian. Vasilevski's boyish manner was now replaced by a cool commanding presence which clearly intimidated the Poles. Even Vojciech seemed subdued.

Vasilevski knew he had to quickly decide whether he could trust these men or whether he would have to execute them. As a Soviet soldier, he had been indoctrinated to believe that both the Poles and Germans were the enemies of his homeland. He also recalled the endless lectures from Political Commissars telling him and his fellow conscripts how the treaty between the Soviet Union and Germany to carve up Poland between them had been treacherously abrogated by Hitler with Operation Barbarossa from which time the Polish partisans had been fighting both armies. But since the defeat of the Wehrmacht at Stalingrad and the growing ascendency of the Red Army, the Polish Home Army had thrown in its lot with the Soviets. But Vasilevski had no way of knowing whether this particular group were aware of this. If so, they were comrades... if not, they were enemies.

Sensing his doubt, Hannah recalled overhearing a briefing given by Steiner to his fellow officers which touched upon this very subject. Taking a deep breath to calm her nerves, she coughed to clear her throat. Speaking slowly in the hope of being understood by each of the Poles, she outlined the dilemma facing the Russian. As her words were interpreted, the tension felt by the sitting partisans began to diminish. Raising himself to knee level, Vojciech Lukaszek placed one hand on his chest and closed his eyes followed immediately by each of his comrades. In unison, they quietly began to recite what Hannah took to be a Polish prayer.

Sheltering behind Vasilevski, she wondered how he would react as an atheistic Bolshevik, to this outward manifestation of religion. The answer came in a millisecond as the machine pistol in Vasilevski's hand exploded. In the confined space of the cellar its percussive noise was truly shocking. The partisan kneeling behind Vojciech jerked back as a hail of bullets tore into his chest, killing him instantly. Horror-stricken, Hannah watched as his body slowly slid sideways in grotesque slow motion. Only then did she see the revolver still clasped in his lifeless fingers.

In the stupefying silence which followed, she saw Vasilevski step forward and calmly kick the pistol away from the reach of the nearest partisan.

Fearing for their lives, the surviving Poles sat and waited for their execution. It was the youngest member of the group, a young thick-set boy perhaps no older than a teenager who stood up and tearfully addressed Vasilevski in Russian.

Hannah didn't understand what he said but watched as the youth turned and knelt down and clasped the dead Pole to his bosom. In that awful moment, she intuitively guessed they were brothers.

Looking down at the two men, Vasilevski's mind was sickened. The fleeting glimpse of the revolver had caused him to react but was the man about to kill him? And if this small group of partisans were allies of the Red Army why had this man not surrendered his weapon when ordered to do so? Or was he about to hand the weapon over before his machine pistol made his decision shockingly irrelevant?

Glancing round, he sought Hannah's eyes and she could see the indecision on his face but still shocked by the violence, she could only reach out and touch his arm. It was the strong voice of Vojciech speaking in German who broke the silence.

'Please take your friend and yourself out of this cellar and leave us with our dead comrade' before repeating himself, this time in Russian.

Undecided, she took a halting step towards the ladder, hoping Vasilevski would follow but instead, she watched in stark amazement as he dropped his weapon and fell to his knees on the earthen floor alongside the two brothers. A quick babble in Polish followed and Hannah watched in fearful silence as the partisans regained their feet and recovered their weapons from the table. Then upon a command from Vojciech, they gathered up the body of their dead comrade and gently eased him and themselves through the wooden hatch to exit the cellar.

Kneeling before her, the distraught figure of Vasilevski stared into a sightless distance, mortified by the consequence of his instinctive reaction. Moving towards him, she rested her hand on the back of his head and let her fingertips run through the short hair on the nape of his neck. In the poor light, she could see the soft gleam of wetness on the cheeks of his boyish face. Spontaneously, she attempted to brush them away only to see more tears begin to gather. Looking at him in the gloom, she saw the face of a young boy and again had a flashback of Aaron's beautiful face looking up at her. How she would love to be with him now; to hug and kiss him and to let him know how much she had missed him.

The surreal moment passed quickly and it was Vasilevski who interrupted the awful silence. Regaining his feet, he recovered his weapon and cautiously led Hannah and himself out of the cellar. Once clear, he reconnoitred the village from an upstairs window seeking the whereabouts of the partisans, convinced that once they recovered from their shock they would return to wreak revenge for the killing of their comrade. Gazing over the untended fields, he looked for signs of birds suddenly taking flight which to his practised eye could indicate the presence of passing humans. Looking intently for several full minutes he detected nothing to cause alarm.

Expecting to return to the forest, she was surprised when Vasilevski led her some two kilometres through open countryside to what appeared to be an abandoned barn, it's open doors leading to a large storage area. Peering into its cluttered interior she recognised the unmistakeable shape of an old tractor, standing on wooden blocks with no sign of its four wheels. The barn, its timber cladding mottled with splotches of green algae, was surrounded on three sides by dense woodland and practically hidden from view until approached by a gravel driveway heavily overgrown with dense ferns and brambles.

Inside, the barn was strewn with dusty spider webs attaching to every nook and cranny. On the overhead beams, swallows had built mud nesting boxes and listening to the occasional cheeping sounds, Hannah guessed they were still feeding their hungry, unfledged young.

She realised that Vasilevski must have discovered the barn earlier that morning and peering towards the far wall she spotted a ladder leading to what looked like a hay loft. The Russian climbed first, inspecting the loft before beckoning her to follow him. Unable to match the agility with which he has ascended she saw Vasilevski give a wry grin before extending his hand to assist on the last three rungs. Safely up, he nodded towards a small hatchway cut in the bottom of a planked wall and gestured for her to follow him through it. Doing so, she found herself standing in a timber-framed chamber, almost sumptuous in comparison to the gloomy cellar they had just vacated. With natural daylight coming through two algae-tinged windows set in the roof the chamber was positively bright.

One wall contained a row of shelves on which stood yet more bottled preserves similar to those found in the cellar. But there the similarity ended. On adjoining shelves Hannah was delighted to see tins of meat products and fruit including peaches and apricots. Below the shelves stood a hand-carved wine rack containing bottles of various red and white wines which according to their labels, had incongruously originated from wineries in Northern Italy and now inexplicably stored in a remote tractor loft in a forest somewhere near the Polish/German border!

Holding a bottle of red wine, Hannah turned to Vasilevski and wagged her finger in self- admonishment, remembering her embarrassing inebriation of the previous night. But the Russian's face showed no trace of humour and she realised he was still wracked with anguish over the death of the partisan. Replacing the wine on the rack, she reached out and put her arms around Vasilevski, a young adult barely out of his teens who had acted so manfully since following his General's order to escort her in what was supposed to be nothing more dangerous than a stroll through Guriev's Base Camp. For a brief moment, Vasilevski's body was absolutely rigid but slowly she felt him relax and heard the first of many sobs escape from his laboured soul. To spare his embarrassment, Hannah avoided looking at his face by pressing him even closer to her. When she held Steiner this close, it would have been the prelude to them making unbridled love but with Vasilevski, she felt only maternal stirrings. Whatever happened to her beyond this moment, she knew she already owed a huge debt to this caring man. But no longer was she a naïve, straight-laced Jewish girl but a woman now tempered in the ways and desires of men and holding her young Russian protector so close, she knew she risked him misinterpreting her gesture. She fondly remembered how self-consciously aroused he had become when she had gently teased him by massaging his upper body in the cold bath tub in the cellar.

But neither on that occasion nor when he had seen her repining in the cold bath had he shown any interest in her other than to protect her until such time as they could re-establish contact with the Red Army.

Not knowing what thoughts might be going through his mind, she was relieved when it was Vasilevski who eased himself away from her, making an obvious effort to control his emotions.

That evening, they fashioned a meal from the well-stocked food store and opened a bottle of white wine from the Veneto region of Northern Italy, coincidentally close to where her treasured Bellini violin had been made centuries before. By nightfall and feeling relaxed for the first time in days, Hannah watched with growing amusement as Vasilevski battled to remain awake by singing softly in Russian before his head finally slumped and sleep overtook him. In the dwindling light, he looked impossibly young; more like a teenage school cadet than the deadly combatant he had shown himself to be.

Moving to the raised platform which she had decided would be her bed for the night, she lay down with her head cradled in her arms. Nearby, the steady breathing of Vasilevski reminded her of the nights when an exhausted Steiner would fall asleep before she crept back to her own room. How she would love him to be here now. To feel his powerful body fusing with her own. Since their first sexual encounter, he had taken her mind and body to undreamed heights and seeing Ephraim again had unwittingly reinforced the difference between the two men. Increasingly aroused, she fought against the unfeeling sleep inexorably closing in on her, reluctant to lose the awareness of Steiner from her mind. But within seconds she too had drifted into a dreamless void. Little could she know that within the same vicinity, she too was in the mind of two men with very different motives?

SEVENTY

Operation Bagration, the massive Soviet offensive which began in Byelorussia in late July 1944 was gathering renewed momentum after being briefly halted by desperate Wehrmacht troops, chronically short of fuel, ammunition and reinforcements. By comparison, the Red Army, its exhausted front-line units now reinforced with newly equipped infantry and tank regiments recruited from within the vastness of the Soviet empire, were looking at objectives far beyond the Polish border and into the very heart of the Third Reich itself. Eastern Poland fell quickly and by early August, Warsaw itself was poised to fall. The arrival of the Red Army east of the Vistula River was the signal for the poorly armed Polish Home Army to launch an ill-timed attempt to liberate their capital before the arrival of Soviet forces. But General Secretary Joseph Stalin, secure in his Moscow bunker, had a quite different agenda. Cynically bringing the Red Army's advance to a halt, the uprising was murderously suppressed by ruthless German SS units as Comrade Stalin knew it would. The fewer Poles to survive the war would mean fewer Poles to resist the Soviet Union's occupation after the war.

In Western Europe the Allies had fought their way beyond the bridgehead of their June landings in Normandy and by early August had liberated most of Northern France with Paris falling in late August. The battle for Germany and Berlin itself was about to enter its final bloody phase.

Without his service watch, now a souvenir on the wrist of some nameless Red Army soldier, Steiner had to rely on occasional sightings of the stars for direction. In the dense wooded terrain he needed a point of reference, a village or some other landmark to be able to ascertain his position with the map given to him by the Russian pilot. Having spent much of his youth trekking and camping in the clean air of the Hartz Mountains, the forest held no fears for him but unlike now, he always knew where he was in those far-off boyhood days. He knew his life would be measured in the time it took for a Soviet soldier to squeeze a trigger if the Soviets recaptured him but he also knew that Wehrmacht forces in this area had been reinforced by Panzergrenadiers of the elite SS Division Das Reich with orders to execute any troops found suspiciously adrift from their units.

As the first rays of dawn began to lighten up the night sky, Steiner looked for a suitable place to rest. Overnight, he had stumbled upon a fresh water stream which had temporarily slaked his thirst but without the means to carry water he was again feeling thirsty. Away to his left, he spotted a stand of mature pine trees, many covered by wild climbing ivy which together with dense scrub around the base of the trees would provide his exhausted body with a much needed refuge during the hours of daylight..

Scrambling underneath the overhanging ivy wasn't easy but once inside its protective screen, Steiner knew he had found a perfect shelter. Not only was it cool but seasons of undisturbed pine needles provided a soft bed on which to lay his greatcoat. Sleep came quickly and even the sound of distant gunfire sometime during late afternoon failed to arouse him.

It was gnawing hunger pains and a growing thirst which eventually caused him to stir and as the forest began to darken around him once more, he reluctantly left his shelter and set off in the direction of what he hoped would be the German front line. Above the forest a bright harvest moon penetrated through the tree canopy allowing sufficient light for him to find his way through the dense woodland. With no way of knowing the time, he stopped when his body needed to rest and as the night wore on he realised he was having to stop more frequently. Despite his leaden legs and a throat parched dry by lack of water he knew he had to keep moving and cover as much distance as his strength would allow during the short hours of darkness.

Occasionally he glimpsed unidentified stars through gaps in the overhead foliage and to keep his mind off food, he tried to remember the name of the school teacher who had attempted to teach astrology to bored young students more interested in joining the Hitler Youth movement. Giving up on the name, he turned his mind to recalling whether this time of year was known as the solstice or equinox before accepting he couldn't recall the answer to that question either.

Frustrated at his lack of memory, Steiner knew he had to press on before the soft light of dawn would reveal his presence to others. He guessed that those Polish villagers who had managed to escape the murderous clutches of the SS murder squads might also be sheltering in this same forest as would groups of Partisans, both of whom would give short shrift to any German soldier unfortunate enough to fall into their hands.

Stumbling with fatigue, his energy draining away through lack of nourishment, Steiner didn't see the algae-covered timber fence which suddenly appeared to rise up in front of him. Too close to stop, he noisily clattered into it. Fearful of being detected in the stillness around him, he froze before convincing himself that all remained quiet. Cautiously peering over the obstruction he had stumbled in to, he recognised the shadowy outline of a building, its silhouette diffused by a screen of yet more pine trees.

Reaching into the pocket of his greatcoat for the pistol given to him by the Russian pilot his searching fingers found nothing but dry pine needles. Neither did his other pocket yield the missing gun. Conscious of being unarmed Steiner warily made his way around the barn until he came to an entrance partly obscured by weeds and scrub growing through the gravel of a path which crunched noisily underfoot. The interior was several shades darker than the forest and peering through the gloom Steiner thought he recognised the shape of a farm vehicle parked in the centre of the barn and despite the area being open to the elements, his nostrils detected the unmistakeable smell of petrol.

Entering cautiously, he squeezed behind a small trailer and settled down to wait for the dawn light to improve. Being inside the farm building, especially one so remote would make him more vulnerable to capture than in the dense forest but he knew he had to find food and water before moving on.

As the light slowly improved, Steiner was able to see a small opening at first floor level but no obvious means of gaining access to it. Confident that the barn was uninhabited, he stood up but then immediately froze. Outside, the distinctive sound of vehicle tyres on gravel penetrated his tired brain, its throbbing engine note suddenly stilled some distance away. Despite deadening fatigue his military instinct sensed danger and he knew he had to get out of the barn as quickly as possible. Hurrying through the open exit, he stumbled into the thickets at the side of the barn's yawning entrance. Finding what he hoped would be adequate cover he settled into a position where he could still see the entrance to the building.

For endless minutes nothing happened and Steiner wondered whether his hearing had played tricks. With hunger pains again beginning to influence his judgement and the possibility, however optimistic, of finding food somewhere in the barn, Steiner was on the point of retracing his steps when he saw them. Hardly daring to breathe, he spotted three shadowy figures moving towards the entrance with a fourth person covering their rear. All were armed with short stubby automatic weapons which from his vantage point he thought he recognised as British Sten guns. Worse, he recognised the men as Partisans... men intent on killing any German soldier unfortunate enough to fall into their clutches.

The leading group moved into the barn whilst the fourth man stationed himself at the entrance. No sound came from within and several times the man on guard disappeared inside only to reappear moments later.

Looking out into the forest, the man lazily nestled his gun between his knees and Steiner watched as he took a tin from his trouser pocket and proceeded to roll a hand-made cigarette. Feeling in another pocket, he produced a box of matches and Steiner saw him make several attempts before he finally succeeded in lighting it. In doing this he saw the gun fall to the ground. But instead of retrieving the weapon, the man, drawing hard on his cigarette, moved towards the trees opposite to where Steiner was positioned and began to urinate

Realising he was closer to the dropped weapon than the Partisan, Steiner's instinct for self-preservation kicked in. Flinging himself forward, he grabbed hold of the gun before the man could react. Stopped in mid-stride, the man's mouth fell open but the sight of the German uniform was the catalyst for him to bravely charge at Steiner. Despite his fatigue, Steiner struck the man a savage blow to his head with the metal butt of the gun. A further kick to his prostrate form ensured the man would remain unconscious for some time.

Pulling him towards the trees, Steiner extracted the man's belt and used it to bind his hands behind his back. Tearing the back off the Partisan's shirt, he stuffed a portion of the grubby material into the man's mouth and tied it in place with a strip torn from the remaining material. Breathing heavily but gratified to be armed again, Steiner was about to head into the forest when he heard the unmistakeable report of a shot from within the barn. Quickly taking cover, he looked back towards the still darkened interior of the barn where only moments before he had been hiding. The shot was followed by the sound of a violent scuffle culminating in a woman's tortured scream.

Torn between staying or seeking safety in the forest, Steiner's curiosity and hunger made the decision for him. If there was a woman living in the barn then there might also be some food or drink once the Partisans had left. The unconscious man lying alongside him would obviously present a problem when they discovered he was missing but at least he was now armed and the thought of pitting himself against the remaining Partisans didn't unduly worry him.

As a hardened soldier, Steiner thought he was immune to shock but the sight of Hannah Bergmann being forcibly dragged from the barn proved him wrong. Even in the full light of day he again doubted what his tired eyes were seeing before his brain registered the reality of what was happening just metres from his concealed position.

With one arm twisted behind her back and her head forced downwards, Steiner watched as she was pushed to the ground by the muscular Partisan holding her. Recovering his gun from his shoulder sling, he pointed the barrel at her unprotected head. Behind them came the two remaining Poles supporting a dazed Russian soldier bleeding copiously from a head wound. Releasing their hold, Steiner watched transfixed as the young soldier staggered forward, almost stumbling over the hapless form of the woman at his feet. Defiantly, he turned and faced his attackers before bending down and offering his outstretched hand to assist her to her feet. Angrily, one of the Partisans ran forward and struck the Russian a vicious blow to his head knocking him down on to the gravel path alongside Hannah.

Watching this unfold in front of him, it took precious seconds for Steiner to realise that he was about to witness the cold-blooded execution of the woman who had changed his life.

Leaping up, a frightening roar of hatred escaped from his throat as he aimed the strange weapon at the three startled men before him. Squeezing the trigger, he felt the gun recoil and saw the bullets spray around his targets. The two Partisans at the rear fell instantly but the leading Pole, unwounded, reacted with the feral instincts of a man experienced in killing. Dropping to one knee he aimed his weapon at the rushing German and Steiner knew he was about to die. The gun exploded but instead of bullets tearing at the flesh and bone in his chest, he heard them pass harmlessly over his shoulder as the leg of the Russian soldier lashed out, kicking the spitting barrel upward. Angrily, the Pole rolled away and committed the cardinal error which would cost him his life. Instead of directing his weapon back to Steiner, he loosed off a burst which tore into the body of the half-conscious Russian. Reprieved, Steiner's second fusillade found its mark, shattering the face of the Pole.

Ignoring Hannah, Steiner turned towards the two men felled by his initial volley. One man was beyond visible recall, his chest oozing profuse amounts of blood from three separate chest wounds. But his companion, wounded in the groin and beginning to moan with the delayed onset of pain, stared up at Steiner, his hand held up in subjugation, wordlessly seeking clemency from the man who had just shot his two companions.

But Steiner was not in the mood for mercy. Once more the Sten gun stuttered and the body on the ground jumped as the bullets shattered his skull.

The Russian who had unwittingly saved his life was barely alive and Steiner could see from the wounds to his stomach that he would die very soon, the grey pallor of death already beginning to mask his boyish features. Alongside him, the still body of Hannah began to stir. Rising to her knees, she looked directly in front of her, not seeing Steiner standing behind her, focussing instead on the Russian. Raising his head, she used the hem of her blouse to gently brush away the loose dirt clinging to his face. Steiner saw the Russian open his eyes and incredibly, offer the sweetest of smiles to her. As if the effort was too much, his body immediately convulsed in what Steiner recognised as his final death throe. Realising what was happening, Hannah began to sob uncontrollably and drew the Russian's face closer to her own, feeling his last breath expire against her cheek.

Moved by her compassion, Steiner took a step towards her, resting his hand on her shoulder as he knelt down beside her. Feeling his touch, Hannah looked up, blinking through misty eyes, unable to comprehend what she was seeing. 'Kurt... is it really you?'

Instead of replying, Steiner took hold of her hands and together laid the head of the young soldier on the ground. Pulling her gently to her feet, he drew her away from the carnage on the weed strewn gravel and moved into the sheltered area of the barn. Once there, he pulled her close and whispered 'dear God. I thought I would never see you again!'

Shivering with emotion and delayed shock, Hannah tried to speak but the words dried in her throat, unable to believe she was once more in the arms of the man she knew she loved beyond life itself

Holding her in a clinging embrace, it was Steiner who broke the charged silence. 'The noise of that gunfire will attract every Russian within miles so we need to get out of here as soon as we can.' Easing himself back, he looked into her tear-stained face and softly kissed her forehead. 'Those men came in a vehicle and provided it's unguarded, we can use it to reach German lines. But first,' he glanced up at the entrance to the inner room, 'I must find some water... I'm dying of thirst.'

'And food? What about food?'

'I haven't eaten for three days, so find as much as you can while I check out the vehicle.'

Apprehensive and hardly daring to ask, she finally found her voice. 'Can you wait until I come down? I'm desperately frightened of being separated from you again. '

'Is that an admission that you actually need me, Hannah?'

Still in shock and utter disbelief at their reunion, Hannah reached out and savoured the grime on his cracked lips as she kissed him for the first time since leaving Auschwitz. 'More than you will ever know' she whispered.

The Peugeot saloon car had been driven into a small clearing and the still warm engine started easily when Steiner turned the key which the Polish driver had obligingly left in the ignition. Driving it to the barn he replenished the car's fuel from the large tank at the rear of the building before quenching his thirst with water which tasted like nectar to his parched throat.

Whilst Hannah collected an assortment of preserved fruit from the barn, Steiner quickly examined the bodies of the three dead Poles. With his foot, he cautiously pushed the body of the nearest Partisan onto his back and as his arm became exposed, he spotted an impressive Swiss-made watch which he straightaway transferred to his own wrist. The appalling casualties suffered by both sides at Stalingrad had inured Steiner to the sight of dead men but looking at the young Russian soldier who had unknowingly saved his life, he felt a pang of regret. Seeing his youthful countenance locked in the grim rictus of death, he imagined him being someone's son or brother; a youngster who would never see them or his homeland again.

Looking round the narrow clearing, he suddenly remembered the man he had lain out in the undergrowth. He was still where Steiner had left him but was now fully conscious and sitting up. Seeing the German approach, a look of undisguised terror etched itself on his face.

Looking at the defenceless Pole, Steiner felt a sudden revulsion at the thought of more killing. But could he risk letting this man live knowing he would undoubtedly summon other Partisans desperate to seek revenge for the slaughter of their comrades? Without the car to enable them to put some credible distance between himself and a bunch of bloodthirsty Partisans, he would have to either kill or disable him. Reaching down, he pulled the gag from the man's mouth but left his arms still pinioned behind his back.

'I'm giving you the chance to walk away and find your comrades, which is more than you deserve, you murdering bastard.'

'That's rich coming from a German.' Behind him stood Hannah holding a crudely weaved basket containing what he hoped would be food.

'I didn't hear you coming.' A touch of edginess crept into his voice. 'Don't ever creep up on me like that again; you could get yourself shot.'

Looking at her forlorn figure, he saw tears streaming down her face. 'I've just seen that poor Russian boy. Did you kill him?' There was no mistaking the accusation in her voice.

'It was one of those men down there, not me.' Looking at her tearstained face, he knew they had to leave this place without further delay. Taking her arm, Steiner led her towards the waiting car. 'Time to go, we can talk as we drive.'

The interior of the Peugeot was sumptuous by any standard, the type of car that Steiner had admired since his days as a young officer cadet. Sinking into the luxurious Epeda upholstery, he glanced down at the foot well, noting the peculiarly shaped accelerator pedal which the French manufacturer had curiously fashioned in the shape of a mushroom!

Hannah was attempting to control her emotions but barely succeeding. Furtively glancing sideways at her, Steiner wondered why the death of the Russian soldier was causing her such obvious grief.

Not wanting to think too much about this he chose instead to speak about the car. 'This is the car I lusted for as a young man.'

Tearfully, Hannah tried her best to show interest. 'How can you lust after an inanimate object? Surely a car is something which takes you from here to there.' Wanting to soften her admonition, she gently placed her hand over his as he engaged first gear.

'Sorry Kurt.' Taking several deep breaths, her poise began to reassert itself. 'Please take me away from this awful place.'

Responding to her imploration, Steiner pressed his foot down on the accelerator and felt the Peugeot surge forward over the rough farm track.

To avoid the main arterial roads until they crossed what he hoped would be the front line, Steiner drove the Peugeot on secondary farm tracks. His fear of encountering units of the Red Army didn't materialise and soon Hannah spotted the first German troops.

'Remember, you're a Nurse under orders to report to Berlin. You were travelling with me and an injured serviceman when we ran into a Russian unit. They took your Orders and ID and you escaped exactly as it happened. OK?' Steiner looked for a response before his next question. 'Can you remember the name of the nurse?'

Still thinking about the young Russian, it took several moments for her to recall the dead girl's name. 'Becker; Nurse Ingrid Becker. That was the name wasn't it?'

'I'm impressed.' He drove on in silence before asking, 'and the name of your patient?

'Don't!' The manner of Corporal Erlich's brutal execution flooded into her mind. 'I can't think of that dear man without wanting to scream out in anguish.'

'Well get a grip on yourself because the SS won't be so understanding if they stop us and question you.' Taking his eyes off the road, he stared at Hannah. 'It's imperative we corroborate every detail so apart from your identity, stick to the facts and tell it as it happened. You'll find that much easier, believe me.'

'I do believe you but that doesn't stop me from being frightened.'

Reassuringly, Steiner brushed his hand across her cheek. 'You'll be OK, Bergman. Just be your normal haughty self.'

Seeing the half-smile on Steiner's face, she felt herself begin to relax. 'Is that how you see me, Kurt?'

'I did until we...' He paused in mid-sentence, his face reddening... 'until we made love.'

Rising from her seat and leaning towards him, she gave him a gentle nudge on his cheek with her wet nose. 'Was it really love or was it a sexual happening because I just happened to be there on that night?'

Realising he was being drawn into uncharted territory, Steiner's brow furrowed into dark creases. 'Which of the many occasions are you referring to?'

'The night when you realised you were in love with me.' She smiled at Steiner's growing discomfort; 'it's a very simple question requiring a very simple answer. Or are you having difficulty in driving and thinking at the same time?'

Removing his foot from the accelerator Steiner let the car draw to a halt before turning to face her. 'I think I began to fall in love with you almost from the moment I first saw you in the Kapo's room that night. The fact you were naked didn't influence my judgement one small bit!' He smiled sheepishly.

It was her turn to blush. 'That was the worst moment of my entire life. I would be dead if you hadn't rescued me from that animal.'

'You should thank your friend Von Hartman for my being there that night. Without his telephone message to me, I wouldn't have had any idea that you even existed let alone being held in Auschwitz.'

Unable to prevent her emotions rising to the surface again, Hannah squeezed Steiner's hand in silent memory of his cousin.

Sensing her sadness, Steiner made a visible effort to busy himself. Engaging gear, the Peugeot slipped forward once more, every metre bringing the car and its two occupants closer to their ultimate destination... Berlin.

***

After what seemed an eternity but which in reality was just over an hour, the sturdy little Peugeot, its black paintwork coated in grey dust, finally left the rough farm tracks of the forest behind and joined an arterial highway carrying endless streams of military traffic. The road's metalled surface enabled Steiner to increase speed except on those stretches of road torn up by the tracks of tanks and other heavy vehicles. Fortunately, in the bright light of day, Steiner was able to manoeuvre the small saloon around the potentially axle-breaking depressions and pot-holes.

He was acutely aware that the small Peugeot, a civilian vehicle, would inevitably attract attention on an arterial highway carrying so much military transport especially from SS patrols with orders to arrest any military personnel suspected of desertion.

They passed the first of two checkpoints and to his relief the Peugeot was merely waved through by the soldiers manning the barrier recognising his rank. But approaching a small town south of Schwiebus Steiner thought their luck had run out. Ahead of their car, a queue of military vehicles had been halted with the occupants of each vehicle being checked against their travel authorisation documents.

Drawing to a stop behind a truck carrying troops from the front, Steiner watched as two SS guards climbed aboard and began to inspect each individual soldier's Service Book. From her seat alongside Steiner, she watched with growing apprehension as the resentment of the exhausted soldiers turned to growing anger when one of the SS guards roughly ordered a soldier off the truck at gunpoint. Suddenly there was an eruption of bodies as the other soldiers turned on the two SS men with pent up fury. Responding to the shouts of his fellow comrades, the driver edged the truck forward and broke through the wooden barrier before gaining speed. Other SS guards standing outside the small shed-like gatehouse looked on in disarray, reluctant to shoot knowing their two fellow guards were still on board the lorry.

Leaping from the car, Steiner bellowed an incomprehensible order to the guards, pointing towards the fast disappearing vehicle before clambering back into the Peugeot and driving off in apparent pursuit of the truck. It worked. Two minutes later and with no sign of the truck, they spotted two dishevelled SS troopers; one lying down beside the road and the other kneeling on the tarmac nursing his bloody head. Passing by at full throttle, she heard Steiner give a contented chuckle.

Joining convoys of military trucks heading West, the Peugeot was stopped twice more but recognition of Steiner's rank were again sufficient for their car to be waved on.

Approaching the Polish/German border, Steiner thought back to the optimism and excitement that he had experienced when Operation Barbarossa was unleashed on poorly equipped Soviet troops, creating the belief that the war on the Eastern front would be over in a matter of weeks. But that was before the Russian winter intervened, effectively halting the German blitzkrieg in its tracks.

He remembered the hell-hole of Stalingrad where the devastating bombing campaign by the Luftwaffe had unwittingly created the ideal terrain for countless hordes of Red Army troops to not only resist but to begin the fight-back which Steiner knew would inevitably end in Berlin.

Looking at a drowsy Hannah desperately fighting against sleep, Steiner realised they had to stop. After walking all night and having driven for most of the day, he could barely keep his own eyes open. He also needed to re-fuel the car from the cans of petrol in the trunk.

'We will stop as soon as we can find somewhere to eat and rest.'

The prospect of being able to stop and rest had the same effect as a cold douche. 'Both of which would be extremely welcome, my mind-reading man.'

Steiner loved her informality. How very different from the German officer - Jewish prisoner relationship they had shared until that fateful night when status and ethnicity were pushed aside; replaced by the simple desire of a man and a woman to live for the moment. He faintly remembered Erlich once telling him that if mankind were to remove their nationalistic labels then we would all become just men and women thereby ending the need to go to war! A simple belief expressed by a simple man, a friend and comrade without parallel.

'I'm very tired but you must be exhausted.' Looking at him, she pursed her lips together and blew him an imaginary kiss. To her delight, he playfully jolted his head as though it had found its target.

Crossing the border into Germany just before dusk, Steiner managed to locate a small hostelry on the outskirts of Neuzelle. The low beamed building appeared to be deserted and it was some time before an elderly man with a weather-beaten face and a thatch of white hair appeared.

The sight of a German uniform noticeably unnerved him causing him to stutter. 'I'm afraid we can offer very little in the way of food; perhaps a glass of beer maybe but that's about all.'

Looking at the man's portly figure, Steiner gave a short laugh. 'This war has been going on for 6 years, old man, yet you look as though you haven't gone hungry once in that time. So when did you last eat?'

Hearing Steiner's tone of voice, the man's courage visibly faltered. 'We only eat what we grow in our small garden but let me speak with my wife to see what we have in the larder.'

'That sounds much more encouraging.' Steiner's voice softened; 'we will also need a room for the night so we can refresh ourselves while you prepare a meal.'

Anxious to get away before any further demands could be placed on his limited resources, the man made to leave but Steiner beat him to it.

'And bring a couple of beers while we wait for you to discover what food you have in that larder of yours... or would you like me to look for myself?'

In full submission, the man held up both hands in a gesture of polite refusal. 'That won't be necessary, Colonel. I'm sure I can find something to satisfy you on both the food and accommodation.' Pointing towards a small table behind him, the man turned and made a nervous adjustment to the cutlery placing. 'Will this table be suitable for you?'

Standing just behind Steiner, Hannah saw sweat begin to glisten on the old man's brow and felt a touch of sympathy for him. 'Perhaps I can go to the room and freshen up while you have your beer, Colonel, if this gentleman will kindly show me the way?'

Visibly grateful for Hannah's intervention, the man literally dashed into the rear room, returning moments later with a bottle of beer and a polished glass.

'Would you like me to pour or can I leave you to do that whilst I show the lady to her room.'

'I'm sure you meant to say *our* room, didn't you?' Hannah's steely interjection surprised even her. Blushing, she waited for the old man to lead the way. It took him several moments to react. Making her way towards the stairs she heard Steiner give an expressive chuckle.

Taking his time to savour the cold beer Steiner reflected on what might lay ahead on the morrow. Without official orders, he knew their chances of reaching Berlin without being stopped and questioned would be extremely remote. But they had no alternative other than to press on. If subjected to questioning, he knew that Hannah would be seriously at risk. If she gave way under pressure then he too, despite his rank, would be arrested for being a party to her escape. But on the other hand, the haughty manner in which she had spoken to the inn-keeper... that showed yet another aspect of this amazing woman. He recalled the conversation in his quarters shortly after her arrival when he had told her she wouldn't last long in this war. Yet not only had she survived months in Auschwitz before his intervention but back once more on German soil, she was heading towards Berlin and her young child. 'Perhaps I misjudged that woman from day one,' he ruefully admitted to himself.

Arriving at the room on the first floor, he knocked gingerly on the panelled door before entering.

'I'm in here, Kurt.' The voice came from the bathroom.

'May I come in?'

'Of course you may; reticence doesn't become you and it's far too late for misplaced modesty on my part.'

The bath was similar to those fitted in Alpine ski lodges, designed to be sat in rather than lie flat. Coyly holding a flannel across her breasts, she gave him a seductive smile. 'Welcome Colonel... sorry you can't join me but I won't be too long. I'll leave the water for you?'

'Sweetheart, you missed you vocation; you should have been a diplomat.'

Slightly bemused, it took a moment for her to decipher Steiner's remark. Letting the flannel slowly drop into the water, she watched his eyes follow it. 'Ok, I will rephrase that in non-diplomatic language... you smell!'

Rising up before he could react, she stepped out of the bath, attempting to wrap a small towel round her waist but finding it too short she quickly placed it in front of herself.

'Your unstated gratitude is matched only by your insubordination so maybe you deserve some form of punishment.' Stepping towards her, he reached out as though to embrace her naked form but then suddenly drew back. 'But on the other hand, you do have a point.'

'In which case, jump in the tub and then we will go and eat.' Stepping round him, she hurried into the bedroom and quickly dressed. By the time he reappeared, she had dusted down his uniform and boots but his grey shirt, after days spent sleeping rough in the forest, required washing.

'Put this on for the moment and I will wash it later. 'As she spoke, she held up his green service-issue underpants at arm's length; and these too!'

Unabashed by his nakedness, Steiner grinned. 'Why don't we just order room service then neither of us will need to dress?'

Pretending to be un-amused, Hannah gave him a stern look. 'I don't think that would be a good idea.'

'Well I do and that fat little man can also arrange for his wife to wash our clothes ready for tomorrow.'

The prospect of being able to wear a clean blouse and skirt was irresistible. 'Kurt, you have this unfortunate talent of being able to upset even nice people so let me speak to the woman. OK?'

'I don't care which of us speaks to her, so long as I have a clean shirt to wear in the morning.'

Finding her way to the kitchen area, Hannah had difficulty in reconciling the diminutive woman busying herself at the log-fuelled stove with the obese proportions of her inn-keeper husband. Dressed in a simple grey dress which almost touched the floor and a black scarf tied up at the back of her head, she had the appearance of a diminutive dwarf. Hearing Hannah enter, she turned from the stove and clasping both hands together, gave a polite bow from the waist. Straightening up with obvious difficulty, Hannah noticed that she walked with a pronounced limp as she moved towards her. The unhealthy pallor of her complexion almost matched the drab colour of her dress and looking at the frail old woman she oddly felt sorry for her.

Clasping her own hands together, Hannah smiled as she politely asked whether she could enter the kitchen which was somewhat superfluous as she was already standing in the centre of the elderly woman's domain.

Whether the same thought crossed the woman's mind was uncertain but impressed by Hannah's politeness her expression went from shyness to pleasure in a matter of seconds. 'Please' she said waving towards the cooking range, 'you are most welcome.'

Looking over the shoulder of Gerda Hoffmier, Hannah was pleased when she invited her to assist in the cooking process. From the game pantry the old woman produced a skinned rabbit and skilfully dissected the pink meat into small portions while Hannah prepared a mixture of carrots, pearl barley and potatoes to give the meaty stew added flavour. It wasn't too long before the aroma of cooking attracted the old man to the kitchen. Clearly unaware of Hannah's presence, the man's heavily jowelled face expressed a look of bewilderment.

Trying not to laugh she saw his bushy eyebrows lift up, compressing the lines on his forehead into deep creases.

'Is everything in order here' he enquired, trying to sound casual.

Turning to face him, his wife gave him the sweetest of smiles. 'Everything here is under control Herman. Is the dining room laid up as the meal will be ready sooner than we expected thanks to this dear lady helping me.'

Hearing this, Hannah gave a slight squeeze on Gerda Hoffmier's bony shoulder and saw her grey pallor slightly colour, embarrassed by the contact. Busily, she moved to the far end of the cooking range to stir the anaemic-looking rabbit stock bubbling noisily in a small steel saucepan.

Chided, her husband made for the kitchen door, muttering in a voice so low, it was difficult to hear against the noise of the firewood crackling in the range; 'I will attend to that immediately; just give me a few moments.'

Seeing him depart, Hannah broached the subject which had brought her to the kitchen in the first place. 'I need to wash several garments later but you will need to show me where I can do this.'

Looking at Hannah as though she had misheard, the elderly woman stopped stirring. 'You wash clothes? I wouldn't hear of it. There is a woman in the village who will do that and have them ready by the morning so let me have them after dinner.'

'You can have them before dinner; we'll eat in the upstairs room.' Turning round Hannah saw the partly dressed figure of Steiner, stripped to the waist, holding his bedraggled shirt, socks and undergarment at arm's length, enter the kitchen 'Where shall I leave these?'

Anxious to spare the old woman's blushes, Hannah hurriedly took hold of them and discretely tucked them out of sight behind her. Giving Steiner what she hoped was a disapproving look, she quickly excused herself and nodded for him to follow her to the room.

Closing the door, she felt Steiner's hand grip her around the waist and spin her round to face him. Wordlessly, he leaned forward and pressed his lips to hers, suppressing the rebuke which he knew Hannah was about to deliver.

Breaking away, he quickly placed a finger against her full lips. 'I've wanted to do that since we met in the forest. How about you?'

Looking into his grey eyes, she detected a slight twinkle. 'Can this really be the same man who said I was too naïve to survive?

'The very same' he replied. 'By the way, I have some bad news but his eyes showed otherwise. 'I discovered two dressing gowns in that old wardrobe so that puts an end to my hope of a naked supper.'

Dinner that evening was eaten in a sombre mood despite the excellent red wine produced by the begrudging inn-keeper. The timbered beams and dark furnishings added to the solemn ambience which even the prospect of sleeping between clean sheets did little to lift.

Compared to what they had eaten since first being captured by the Red Army patrol, the rabbit stew was almost too rich for each of their digestive systems but neither that nor the first-rate wine could dispel the thought of their imminent separation growing in their minds.

Making an effort to lighten the atmosphere Steiner forced himself to smile. 'With luck and a fair wind, we should make Berlin tomorrow. Remember, our Service books and Travel Orders were taken by the Soviets,' adding as an afterthought, 'and memorise the Service number of Ingrid Becker. It could mean the difference between life and death... for both of us.'

Reaching across the table, Hannah touched Steiner's hand. 'Sweetheart, I won't let you down and if the worst should happen then we will face it together.'

Rising slowly, Steiner came around the table and gently pulled Hannah to her feet. With surprising tenderness, he led her towards the bed and smoothly unfastened her white dressing gown, letting it slip noiselessly to the floor. Opening the heavy feather eiderdown, he placed Hannah's naked body on the cool under-sheet before replacing the top covering.

'Try very hard not to go to sleep before I join you.'

Returning to the table, he recovered his glass of wine before retracing his steps.

'Good evening Nurse Becker; may I join you in bed?'

In reply, Hannah threw back the eiderdown on the opposite side of the bed and watched as Steiner unhurriedly positioned the wine glass on the bedside cabinet, slowly disrobed and moved in beside her. As their bodies came together, Hannah slowly felt the familiar charge of sexual excitement begin to course through her body to a level of arousal she had experienced only with the man now holding her close. She felt his hardness press into her stomach and inching her leg up to his thigh, she expected him to enter her receptive body.

But Steiner did not move. Instead he gave her the lightest of kisses. 'Assuming we get to Berlin in one piece, you realise that will be where we have to part company at least until this damn war comes to an end.' He again found her lips and this time the kiss carried more emotion. 'When it does then who knows when or if we will meet again.'

Hannah felt Steiner's body move as he lowered his head to look more closely at her.

'Are you trying to tell me this could be our last night together, Kurt?'

Steiner gave the slightest of nods. 'That is precisely what I was about to say, my sweet young girl.'

Trying hard to hold her own emotions in check, she had to draw a deep breath before replying. 'So we should make this a night to remember then.'

'We should but before we do that I need to tell you what our plan will be.'

Reaching up, she placed her warm fingers over Steiner's mouth. 'We can speak about that tomorrow as we drive but tonight, let's forget all the bad things we have been through and just relax and enjoy this special moment.' Removing her fingers, she leaned up and kissed him.' Promise?'

'I promise but not yet. There are some things we really have to discuss first.'

'So are these things really that important, Kurt?' Pushing closer to him she poked her tongue in his ear. 'Can't you feel how much I want you?'

Feeling her softness against the hard muscles of his stomach, Steiner edged forward, his hard penis sliding between her soft inner thighs. 'I still have difficulty in believing you're that same sexually repressed, Jewish girl who came to my quarters straight from the camp. But,' he grinned, 'I should have known you were different when you half-killed that Danuta woman within an hour of arriving.'

'Well that straight-laced woman you refer to is now in the past.' Moving her hips to further stimulate his quickening arousal, Hannah was disappointed when he did not respond.

'Do you want me or not, Kurt?

For a moment, there was a brief silence, her question unanswered for a second or two.

'Do I want you? Of course I want you as much as I want us to survive this war but you told me you believed you were pregnant so is that still the case? Can we make love without harming our baby?'

Touched by his unexpected paternalism, Hannah didn't know whether to laugh or cry. 'Now who's being naive?' Taking his hand, she fractionally moved away and placed it on her stomach. 'There's nothing showing but I've missed two periods, had morning sickness and I've experienced no blood loss so I believe I am pregnant. Does that relieve or disappoint you?'

'A mixture of both.' Feeling Hannah attempt to pull away, Steiner pulled her back. 'I'm relieved because in normal circumstances, what man in his right senses wouldn't want a child by you. But these aren't normal times Hannah and being pregnant could be a handicap when you get to Berlin.'

Sensing he wanted to say more, she gave him the gentlest of kisses, barely passing her lips over his. 'Is that the only reason you feel concerned?'

Steiner took a deep breath and she felt his whole body stiffen with pent-up emotion.

'I am very aware I won't be around to see our baby born or grow up. You will need to lose yourself when we get to Berlin and I will go back to the front which means it will be a miracle for our paths to ever cross again in this life.'

'Darling, whatever may happen to us in the future and whatever thoughts I had about you in the past, I will never love you as much as I do at this moment.' Forcing herself away from him, she sat up and slid over his unresisting body. Reaching down, she forcefully guided his hard penis into her before raising herself above him. 'You really think our baby will be a handicap? If this is our last night together then the most precious thing you could ever give me is a son like you.' Feeling him push up, she began to ride his body with a rhythmic motion. 'And will this hurt our baby?' Gasping as she felt her first orgasm begin to form in her loins, she was hardly able to answer her own question, 'No! No! No!'

Later, when smothered by Steiner's rejuvenated body, Hannah felt as though she was drowning in an ocean of physical lovemaking. She felt as though she had known this man for all of her adult life and knew she could never love any other man as much as she now loved him. The sheer intensity of their lovemaking was too distracting to think of what might happen in the days and weeks ahead. Several times she attempted to draw away from his all-consuming passion only to be pulled back into his embrace. Only when the first flecks of dawn began to pierce the dark sky did their exhausted bodies fall into the deepest of sleeps. Seconds before succumbing, Steiner murmured, 'you said our baby would be a boy. I would like that, Hannah... I would like that very much.'

SEVENTY ONE

The following morning the journey to Berlin was less arduous than Steiner had expected. Driving on the main arterial road, their Peugeot attracted some attention but Steiner was hoping this would also lend a sense of immunity to their journey. Overnight he had rationalised that no military person escaping from the Eastern front would openly drive a civilian vehicle along a military route with numerous check-points.

But conversely, he knew these checkpoints would be manned by SS troops with no regard for his Wehrmacht rank.

Approaching a barrier flanked on each side by sandbagged machine gun emplacements, their vehicle was directed into a slip road and ordered to stop by a soldier pointing a Russian-made automatic rifle at Steiner indicating he was to get out of the car.

Easing himself out of the driving seat, Steiner deliberately ignored the threat posed by the rifle-wielding sentry as he opened the rear door to allow Hannah to alight from the vehicle. Seeing Steiner's rank made no impression on the soldier until Steiner walked forward and pushed the muzzle of the gun upwards.

'Take me to your senior Officer or NCO and do it now!'

Encouraged by Heinrich Himmler, SS troops regarded themselves as an elite force and not subject to the orders of Wehrmacht officers no matter how senior they might be. Standing just behind Steiner, Hannah saw a look of doubt cross the soldier's face before he lowered his weapon and motioned them towards a grimy wooden hut several metres behind him. She was thankful that she and Steiner were both wearing their freshly laundered items of uniform which she hoped would add a degree of gravitas to their presence.

The hut was small and Steiner's sudden appearance caught the young SS Lieutenant off-guard. Sitting with his feet on the scarred wooden table, Steiner saw he was reading an outdated information sheet published each week by the Reich's propaganda office informing its military forces how the war was being won despite the reality now prevailing on all fronts.

'Morning Lieutenant.' Steiner's tone was purposely brusque. 'I am Colonel Kurt Steiner and this is Nurse Ingrid Becker travelling from the Upper Silesia region to Berlin HQ. And you are?'

Regaining his composure quickly, the SS officer removed his feet from the table and stood up. Unlike the aggressive truculence of the Sentry, the officer's manner was taciturn but he ignored the request to identify himself. 'And how can I be of assistance, Colonel?'

'I need a temporary Travel Pass for myself and this nurse. Our original documents were seized when we were captured by a forward unit of the Red Army. My NCO and driver were both shot. We were able to escape during a counter-attack by our forces and we have been hiding in a forest until yesterday.' Not wishing to complicate his version of events, Steiner made no mention of the encounter with the Polish partisans.

Glancing out of the window, the Lieutenant saw the dusty Peugeot. 'And where did you acquire that vehicle? His high-pitched voice seemed incongruous to a man of his height and physique.

'We stumbled across a barn complete with tractor, car and fuel. I took the car, fuel, and a few scraps of food but left the tractor.'

The Lieutenant smiled. 'I'm afraid those few scraps of food you refer to are more than you will get here, Colonel. We are living on our iron rations and only enough for each of those men out there.'

Turning to Hannah, the Lieutenant ran an appreciative eye over her. 'And what about her? Aren't the Ruskies supposed to have a penchant for German women or is that just another of the rumours being spread by our desk-bound warriors in Berlin?'

'Together with our glorious 'victory' at Stalingrad?' Steiner smiled, his sarcasm designed to test the Lieutenant's reaction.

But his response was difficult to assess. 'Yes... quite so.'

Moving to get a better view from the window, Steiner was able to see the soldiers manning the machine gun emplacements and was thankful he had chosen to halt at the barrier and not attempt to ram it. As he watched, a convoy of Army trucks, each filled with troops, many no more than teenagers, were slowly being allowed through towards the front.

The Lieutenant joined him by the window. 'Day and night... they never cease. We are now sending boys and old men armed with pitchforks and Panzerfaust that wouldn't stop that old car you're travelling in let alone a T.34.' He stopped abruptly and changed the subject. 'What is the situation in Silesia, Colonel?'

'In a word... grim and getting worse by the day.' Steiner made to look at his watch and saw only his bare wrist. 'The bastards took my watch as well.' In his trouser pocket, he imagined he could hear the ticking of the watch he had taken from the dead partisan.

The action wasn't lost on the Lieutenant. 'I expect you need to be on your way, Colonel. I can certainly issue you with a temporary Travel Pass but whether this will get you to Berlin without too much delay will be a matter of who stops you next and where.'

Inwardly relieved, Steiner showed no emotion. 'That will be most helpful, Lieutenant; I'm grateful.' Moving back towards the desk, he stopped as though remembering something; 'by the way, would you know how many other check-points there are between here and Berlin?'

'Yes and no.' Catching Steiner's look of puzzlement, he smiled. 'There are three standard check points similar to this but a number of tempory road blocks have been set up to catch those who know their way around the permanent check points.' He lowered his voice and glanced nervously at Hannah as though he didn't want to compromise himself in front of her. 'Troops are deserting in their hundreds but when they're caught we usually shoot them. After a court martial, of course.'

Steiner gave a wry smile.

'Whether my authorisation will carry sufficient weight as you approach Berlin remains to be seen but good luck anyway.'

Glancing at Steiner, he reached into the drawer of the desk and drew out an unholstered pistol which Steiner recognised as a standard issue Walther P.38. 'I notice the Ruskies also took your firearm Colonel so you may need this.' Pushing it across the table, he watched as Steiner expertly checked its magazine. 'It's fully loaded but I'm afraid we have no spare ammunition for it.' A sardonic smile crossed his unlined face. 'It's this damn war, you know.'

Leaving the check point behind, Hannah detected a change of mood in Steiner. Reaching over the gear lever, she placed her hand on his thigh. 'Sweetheart there's something on your mind; what is it?'

'It's that young man, the Lieutenant and thousands like him and those teenagers now being sent to the front like lambs to the slaughter. Germany is finished Hannah and all because we allowed a madman to lead our country into this senseless war.' Taking a deep breath, he noisily expelled a lungful of air through pursed lips. 'If I hadn't met you, then I think I would have shot myself rather than be part of what is happening to this country of ours.' Gripping the wheel until his knuckles showed white, he fought to regain his composure as he pulled into a deserted rest area. Stopping the car, he walked round to the passenger side and opened the door. Extending his hand, he drew Hannah from the vehicle and wordlessly led her into the wooded area behind the timber stools and tables which in pre-war times would have been used by passing families.

As they walked Hannah looked at Steiner's face... a face she had explored with her sensitive fingers on so many occasions. Stopping, she gently let go of his hand and turned to face him.

'Kurt, I can guess why you have stopped and there is nothing more I would like than to make love to you right now but I can't do it. If we are to part in Berlin then I want last night to be our last time and to also help me retain the hope that, despite everything, we will meet again.

Also, I want you to leave me for a few moments to let me do something to honour that young Russian soldier who saved my life. Without him I wouldn't be here with you. Will you do that for me, my precious man?'

'He saved my life too, Hanna, so go ahead; I will wait in the car.' Turning, he walked away and for some strange reason, he thought of Ernst Erlich, his friend, comrade and confident killed so needlessly only a few days ago.

Within the wooded area, Hannah knelt down and for the first time since her arrest murmured a Hebrew prayer she had memorised as a young child; a prayer of thankfulness to her God.

With her bare hands, she scraped away the soft earth in front of her and from her pocket produced a metal service disc and chain. Placing it gently in the depression, she covered it with the loose earth and patted the surface flat. Lowering her head, she whispered, 'May your God bless you, Yuri Vasilevski. Let this be my memorial of gratitude to you.'

Standing up, she looked at the small area of disturbed earth and in her mind again visualised that boyish grin which seemed to be a permanent feature on the face of that very special young person.

Once back in the car, Steiner sensed her sombreness and wisely chose not to speak, each locked in their separate thoughts. Armed with the lieutenant's Travel Pass on SS notepaper, they passed through several more check points until as evening loomed they finally entered the suburbs of Berlin.

SEVENTY TWO

The Berlin of late 1943 bore little resemblance to the city Hannah had known before her arrest and transportation to Auschwitz. Cautiously making their way round mountainous piles of rubble and debris, it seemed that every major building had either been damaged or destroyed. Gangs of gaunt-faced women were listlessly passing bricks in seemingly endless chains, many wearing scarves around their mouths to avoid breathing the billowing clouds of brick dust blowing through the skeletal shells and caverns of their once-proud city.

Whilst in Russia Steiner had witnessed the unquestioning loyalty of SS troops personally loyal to the Fuhrer; bound by their personal covenant of allegiance to him as though he were some kind of deity. But this same blind allegiance was also a weakness and today it was to Steiner's good fortune. Any document bearing the signature of an SS officer was rarely challenged. Aware of this Steiner felt sufficiently confident to continue to rely on the Travel Pass provided by the nameless SS lieutenant to openly drive around a city now largely reduced to rubble by the Allies remorseless bombing offensive.

Driving slowly along Bismarckstrasse it seemed as though a giant hand had devastated every major building on this famous avenue. In each district, the picture was the same, with desolate groups of civilians passively queuing at stand-pipes for whatever water was available and everywhere clouds of cloying dust blowing like whirlpools in a storm. Fortunately some of the main avenues were still passable, cleared by gangs of forced labourers whom Steiner guessed, were probably from Eastern Europe. Drawing closer to Charlottenburg, she noticed that the destruction appeared to be less severe which did little to lessen the anxiety growing within her. Approaching the apartment block where Frieda lived and where she had last seen Aaron, she was immensely relieved to see it appeared to be largely undamaged.

Leaving Steiner in the car, she entered the building with acute trepidation. Was she about to regain one precious part of her life whilst at the same moment lose the love of her life? Or would fate decree she lose both?

'Can I help you?'

Startled, Hannah looked round for the source of the voice and in the dank gloom of the unlit vestibule, she dimly made out the figure of a man standing by the stairwell entrance. Stepping closer, she thought there was something vaguely familiar about him. Instead, it was the man who made the connection.

'Hannah! It is you isn't it; Hannah Bergmann?'

Haltingly, she gingerly approached the strange voice.

'Oh dear God, you're Victor... Frieda's brother?'

Impulsively throwing her arms around him, Hannah felt him lurch backwards with the momentum of her embrace. Suddenly off-balance, he clung to her for support.

'It's my leg' he explained; 'I lost it in the Ukraine. I normally walk with a crutch but I heard a car stop outside the window and I thought I recognised you but I couldn't be certain so I came out to investigate after I heard the front door open.'

Appraising Hannah more fully in the light, his lips pursed in open admiration.

'Look at you Hannah Bergmann; you're more beautiful than I ever remember.'

Embarrassed by Victor's unexpected compliment, Hannah felt herself blush.

'There must be something wrong with your memory, Victor. I actually feel like an old hag after the journey I've just had.'

Conscious that their voices were being carried in the emptiness of the entrance hall, she carefully led him towards the open doorway of the apartment she had last visited in...

Her mind went blank. 'God... I can't remember the date I was last here.'

What she did recall from her previous visits to this apartment was the enticing aroma of Frieda's baking which seemed to pervade every square metre of the apartment. But now, entering the gloomy hallway, her nostrils detected an overriding smell of dampness and inwardly, a dark foreboding began to form in her mind.

Entering the lounge, she cautiously helped Victor to a high-backed wooden chair and watched as he gingerly lowered himself on to it.

Knowing he wasn't the reason for her being there, Victor pointed towards another chair and waved her to sit down. The room with its two large windows overlooking the street outside was poorly furnished but even in the late-evening gloom, Hannah could see the concern in Victor's features.

'I guess you must be wondering about Aaron and Frieda?'

'More than just wondering, Victor. Are they both here?'

Shifting uneasily on the polished chair seat, she saw him draw a deep breath before looking at her. 'Look, there's no easy way to tell you this but Frieda was killed in an air raid some two months ago.' She saw his shoulders visibly sag and his face reflected the obvious grief he still felt for his sister.

Dreading what he was about to say next, an ominous feeling of impending fear filled her mind. 'And Aaron... was he with Frieda?' Waiting for Victor to reply seemed an eternity.

'No, thankfully Aaron was here with me at the time.' He glanced towards the bedroom door. 'He's fast asleep in there.'

Torn between wanting to rush in to take hold of the child she thought she would never see again or commiserate with Victor, she chose the latter. Moving to his chair, she knelt down and took hold of his two hands. 'Victor, I am so deeply sorry. Frieda was a dear friend to my family and she was very proud of you.' She saw his eyes moisten as he lowered his head.

'She was a good sister to me too, Hannah. I miss her dreadfully.' Glancing up, he made a futile attempt to brush back the emotional tears rolling down each cheek.. 'Without young Aaron to look after, I think I would have gone mad staying in this apartment day after day.'

Victor's heartfelt admission struck a chord with her. To take Aaron away so soon after losing his sister could present a very lonely and uncertain future for him, a disabled ex-soldier, in war-torn Berlin.

Impulsively, she heard herself say, 'Victor, I could stay here for a while until I'm able to find a safe refuge elsewhere. Would you like me to do that?'

His reaction was slow in coming: 'I would like that very much but I couldn't really expect you to stay in this place.'

'This place..?' She laughed out loud before repeating herself. 'This place?' She swept her hand round in a gesture meant to encompass the entire apartment. 'Compared to most of the places I've been in since my arrest, this is absolute paradise especially with you and Aaron being here.' A serious note entered her voice. 'But before you decide, you do know what happens to anyone caught harbouring Jews?'

'Of course I know that. With all this propaganda shit we are fed each day how could I not know that.' Slowly, his face took on the familiar look of defiance she recalled as being the hallmark of his sister. 'Forgive my language but I will decide who stays in this apartment... not Herr bloody Goebbels.'

Hannah waited, choosing not to speak, wondering whether Victor might change his mind.

'So far as anyone in this building is concerned you can be Frieda's cousin from the North. With all this bombing and people moving from one bombed building to another, no one knows or cares anymore.'

Listening to Victor's calmness, she was struck by the contrast between his quiet manner and that of Frieda, recalling her frequent outbursts venting her disapproval of the Nazi Party and its leaders.

Unable to curb her longing to see Aaron any longer, she stood up and gave Victor a reassuring pat on his shoulder, brushing her hand across his head as she turned impatiently towards the bedroom. Although still a young man, she noticed flecks of grey beginning to show in his naturally dark hair.

Entering the darkened room, the slight figure in the bed barely raised a mound in the quilted eiderdown. Approaching him, Hannah saw his pale face twitch as he fought with dragons and trolls in his sleep. Choked with emotion, she reached down and gently stroked the face of her son, the child she thought she would never see or hold again. She let her thumb follow the outline of his eyebrow, something she often did to encourage sleep and a safe passage into his magic world.

Lost in feelings of deep gratitude, she did her best to stem the tears beginning to run down her face. From the lounge, she heard the sound of men's voices and stiffened in fear. Inexplicably, she remembered the morning when she had heard similar sounds coming from Mr. Glikstein's apartment before she and Ephraim had discovered his dead body.

'My dear God,' she thought… why did I think of that?'

In the next room the conversation had stopped and suddenly the silence became ominously sinister. With her heart pounding in her chest, she turned and saw the silhouette of a burly uniformed figure framed in the doorway of the bedroom. The man advanced towards her and to her relief she saw it was Steiner.

Taking her by the shoulders, he glanced down at the still form of Aaron.

'So this is your son. From where I'm standing he looks a fine boy.'

Still in suspended shock, she clutched at him. 'You can't possibly see whether he's a fine boy or not. But you're right... he is a fine boy.'

Seemingly unable to take his eyes off Aaron, it was impossible to know just what thoughts were going through Kurt Steiner's mind. Time seemed to stand still before he softly kissed Hannah on her forehead as he gently moved her away from the bedside and out of the room.

Re-entering the lounge, she looked for Victor and saw him sitting stiffly upright in the small armchair at the far end of the room as though wanting to put as much distance between himself and Steiner. Sensing the tension, Hannah knew she had to say something quickly. 'Victor, this is Colonel Kurt Steiner who has assisted me in returning to Berlin.'

As a former Wehrmacht soldier, Victor rose awkwardly to his feet and attempt to stand to attention by clutching the back of the chair.

'Colonel... welcome, sir.'

Dropping his arm from around Hannah's shoulders, Steiner focussed his attention on Victor. 'I'm at a disadvantage. You know my name but I don't know who you are?'

'Victor Gleis, Colonel. Former corporal, V111 Corps, 76 Infantry Division.'

Gesturing with his hand for Victor to sit down, Steiner noticed the awkwardness of his movement. 'I see you've been wounded, corporal. Where did that happen?

'On the Eastern Front, Colonel, at a place called Tatsinskaya during another of our glorious victories.'

Choosing not to encourage Victor's sarcasm, Steiner changed tack. 'Hannah tells me that your sister was more than just a friend which was why she felt able to entrust her son with her. Is she here now?'

Cutting in before Victor could reply, Hannah quickly explained the reason for Frieda's absence.

'I'm sorry to hear that, soldier.' He gave Victor a quizzical look. 'Does that mean you have been caring for this lady's child since then?'

Wanting to be on the same level as Steiner, Victor again struggled to a standing position. 'Yes I have because that is what my sister would have wanted. Softening his voice, he added, 'and that little chap is no trouble at all.'

Visibly now more at ease in Steiner's presence, Victor spoke directly to Hannah. 'You haven't mentioned your husband. Is he still alive?'

Sensing that Victor's question really centred on her relationship with the Wehrmacht officer and his obvious affection for her, Hannah decided to be bold. 'I have no way of knowing whether Ephraim is alive or dead, Victor, but,' looking at Steiner, she added, 'what I do know is that this man has not only rescued me from the concentration camp at Auschwitz but has now brought me back to Berlin to be reunited with Aaron. I know that doesn't answer your question concerning Ephraim so we will have to wait until this war is over before we can know.'

Clearly bewildered by her reply, Victor's brow creased in thought. 'But the Colonel is a German officer and you're a Jew. How is it possible for him to do this for you?'

'How was it possible for your sister and yourself to associate with a Jewish family like ours? And why have you looked after a Jewish child since your dear sister died?'

Falling back onto his chair, Victor hung his head in his hands. 'Forgive me, Hannah. I didn't mean to say that.' Inclining his head to meet her gaze, Hannah sensed he wanted to say more. Kneeling down, she took hold of his hands and saw him attempt to control his emotion. Finally, he spoke. 'There's something I must get off my conscience which may explain why you and your husband were arrested in the first place.'

Completely mystified, Hannah felt Victor's hands begin to shake.

'I don't understand. We were arrested and transported with thousands of other families for no other reason than we were Jewish.' It was her turn to take a deep breath. 'Why on earth would you think you were in any way responsible for what happened to us?'

'Because of your position with the orchestra you seemed immune to what was happening to other Jews; that was until,' his voice faltered; 'that was until I murdered that Nazi thug who beat up my sister in your apartment.'

From the corner of her eye, Hannah saw Steiner lean forward, wanting to catch Victor's every word.

Dredging through the recesses of her mind, she vaguely remembered this being mentioned during her interrogation by the two SS officials in the building on Prinz Albrechstrasse.

'Victor, listen to me. Whatever may have happened to that awful brute was in no way related to the arrest of Ephraim and me. We were marked down for arrest before that happened so you can expunge that from your conscience this very instant?'

Turning to Steiner, she knew she had to quickly say something in Victor's defence even if it meant embellishing the facts. 'Three Gestapo thugs nearly killed Victor's sister who we employed as housekeeper and child-minder for Aaron. They came to our apartment to order Ephraim and myself to report to Gestapo Headquarters the following day but in the process gratuitously beat poor Frieda half to death.'

Pulling Hannah to her feet, Steiner stood in front of the hapless Victor. 'Tell me precisely what happened, soldier.'

Gathering himself before answering, Victor leaned back in his chair and Hannah saw his shoulders droop, at last able to shed a long -held burden.

'I was on leave from France en-route to the Eastern Front when my sister came home looking as though she'd been hit by a truck.' She told me what had happened so I went looking for the three men that night. I found out that the SS officials from their HQ used a certain pub and sure enough, there they were, the three of them, drinking and loudly boasting about what they had done to this 'Jew-lover,' meaning my sister.'

So I waited for them to come out and followed the one I knew was responsible for my sister's beating.' He paused to either refresh his mind or to again relive the events of that night.

'Before going out that night, I had armed myself with a British Webley pistol which I'd picked up as a souvenir in France. We came to a quiet part of the residential area where I called out to him to stop. He saw my uniform and told me to piss off so I hit him with the pistol and he fell to the ground. He sat up against the base of one of those large trees and wouldn't get up so I told him I was going to kill him for what he done to my sister. He just laughed and said I was bluffing so I shot him twice; once in the stomach and then in the head. I left the gun in his hand hoping the Gestapo would think he had shot himself but when Hannah and her husband were arrested I thought it was because the Gestapo believed they were responsible.'

Victor's calm analytical description of the cold-blooded execution was chilling and for several seconds, neither he nor Steiner spoke. Inevitably, it was Steiner who broke the awkward silence.

'This man you shot... how certain were you that he was responsible for what happened to your sister?

'He was boasting about it in the pub so yes, I was certain. Nor did he deny it when I told him I was going to kill him.'

'And since then, you've been to the Eastern Front, wounded, lost your leg and now you're back in Berlin. From his chair, Victor affirmed Steiner's brief resume with a nod of his head.

'Have you ever spoken about this to anyone else? Maybe a fellow soldier, comrade, priest or whoever?'

'Not a soul, believe me.'

'What about your sister. Did she know what you had done?'

'I think she may have guessed but I never admitted it to her.'

Listening to Victor, Hannah thought it was uncanny how he reflected so much of Frieda's way of speaking. 'Two peas from the same pod' was how Frieda had once described her brother and herself.

Steiner again took centre stage. 'Listen to what I am about to tell you and regard it as an order. You have committed to what in normal circumstances would amount to murder. So the question is whether the circumstances prevailing at the time would justify such an act. Clearly if you went before a military tribunal you would be found guilty and face a firing squad. You do understand that, don't you?'

Looking at the studious expression on Steiner's face, Hannah could almost believe he was enjoying the role of judge and jury. For his part, Victor looked downcast.

'Having made me, a senior Wehrmacht officer aware of this incident, Corporal, it is now my responsibility as to what action I will take. In short, you have discharged your part in this matter and it is now for me to decide what happens next.' He paused dramatically. 'I will be returning to my command in Silesia in the next day or so where I will become extremely busy with the Red Army knocking at the gates.'

'If I am still around when this damn war ends then your statement will be of no import to the Allied forces. Who knows, they may even give you a medal! So listen to what I'm about to tell you. Keep your own counsel and in return for my amnesia I want you to look after my friend and her child until the Allies reach Berlin. Will you do that?'

Not waiting for a bemused Victor to reply, he reached out and led Hannah back into the room where Aaron was still sleeping soundly. Gazing at the child's innocent countenance, he tried hard to retain his composure. Turning to Hannah, he reached out and embraced her closely.

'Sweetheart, its time I wasn't here.' Gently dabbing yet more tears from Hannah's cheeks, he clasped her hands and gently kissed her fingers. 'Whether we'll ever meet again in this life will be in the lap of the Gods but I want you to know I have never loved any woman as I love you.' He forced himself to smile. 'You are truly the love of my life and I am deeply thankful you are bearing our child.' I know he'll be a boy and maybe one day he and Aaron will grow up as brothers in a world unlike the one that brought us together

Full of emotion, his voice dropped to a whisper. 'Whatever may happen to me, I want you to know that my last thought in this life will always be of you and our son. So shalom my dear sweet girl and may your God preserve you - at least until the Allies arrive!'

Choked with emotion and unable to speak, she could only marvel at his parting humour. Looking up, she kissed Steiner for the last time before breaking away from his embrace. Easing herself on the bed so as not to wake Aaron, she snuggled up to him and closed her eyes

Hearing Steiner's departing footsteps in the hall, Hannah pressed her ear into the soft pillow in a vain attempt to shut out the sound of his leaving but the now familiar noise of the Peugeot's engine bursting into life and the squeal of its tyres on the paving blocks outside heartlessly penetrated the cold darkness of the room.